READER'S DIGEST
SELECT EDITIONS

The condensations in this volume
are published with the consent of the authors
and the publishers © 2009 Reader's Digest.

www.readersdigest.co.uk

The Reader's Digest Association Limited
11 Westferry Circus Canary Wharf London E14 4HE

For information as to ownership of
copyright in the material of this book,
and acknowledgments, see last page.

Printed in Germany
ISBN 978 0 276 44435 7

SELECTED AND CONDENSED
BY READER'S DIGEST

THE READER'S DIGEST ASSOCIATION LIMITED, LONDON

CONTENTS

We are delighted to bring you this spell-binding new blockbuster from Wilbur Smith, who ranks among British readers' favourite storytellers. Epic in content and scope, *Assegai* will transport you to Wilbur's native Africa, where young Leon Courtney is about to begin the adventure of a lifetime with his loyal Masai friend, Manyoro. Hired to work with a renowned East African safari guide, Leon will learn to track and hunt. He will also discover the true value of love and loyalty.

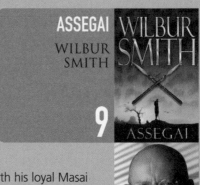

Once again, Alexander McCall Smith, author of *The No.1 Ladies Detective Agency*, delves into the very heart of human life with this touching, Suffolk-based story of wartime courage, hope, and tender love postponed. He describes how a country community adapts to changes brought by the Second World War, helped by 'La', a village newcomer who forms an amateur orchestra. Even as she brings solace to many, she finds her own happiness at last.

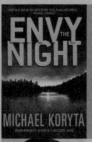

ENVY THE NIGHT
MICHAEL KORYTA

327

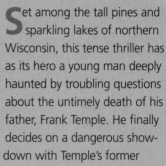

Set among the tall pines and sparkling lakes of northern Wisconsin, this tense thriller has as its hero a young man deeply haunted by troubling questions about the untimely death of his father, Frank Temple. He finally decides on a dangerous show-down with Temple's former underworld partner, and sets off to confront him at an isolated log cabin. Up-and-coming American author Michael Koryta is making his first appearance in UK Select Editions with this exciting crime novel.

In 1989 Ann Ming's 22-year-old daughter, Julie Hogg, went missing. Three months later, it was Ann herself who found Julie's body. Reeling with shock and grief, she heard that a local man, Billy Dunlop, had been arrested, but at trial he was acquitted and walked free. Worse still, an ancient British legal rule of 'double jeopardy' excluded a retrial. For almost two decades, Ann worked heroically to over-turn the law and eventually succeeded. Her story, in her own words, is an inspiration.

FOR THE LOVE OF JULIE
ANN MING

465

ASSEGAI

WILBUR SMITH

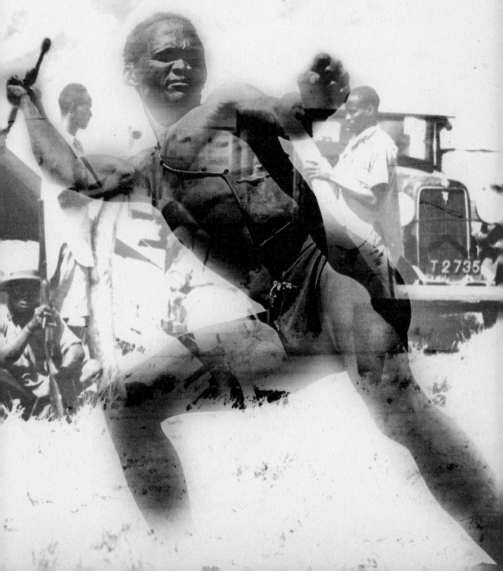

At nineteen, Leon Courtney is hungry for adventure—and there's plenty of that in his battalion of the King's African Rifles. But when his uncle arranges for him to work alongside one of the continent's most legendary big game hunters, his heart soars in anticipation of days filled with the thrill of the chase, in the company of some of Europe's most powerful men . . . He'll require nerves of steel, and the finest tracking skills, as taught by his Masai companion, Manyoro.

As it turns out, however, out-running lions is just the start of it. Before long, Leon is spying for his country, becoming a pilot, and falling in love, perilously, with the mistress of a ruthless, wealthy German industrialist . . .

August 9, 1906, was the fourth anniversary of the coronation of Edward VII, King of the United Kingdom and the British Dominions, and Emperor of India. Coincidentally it was also the nineteenth birthday of one of His Majesty's loyal subjects, Second Lieutenant Leon Courtney of C Company, 3rd Battalion, 1st Regiment, the King's African Rifles, or the KAR, as it was more familiarly known. Leon was spending his birthday hunting Nandi rebels along the escarpment of the Great Rift Valley in the far interior of British East Africa.

The Nandi were a belligerent people much given to insurrection against authority. They had been in sporadic rebellion for the last ten years, ever since their paramount witch doctor had prophesied that a great black snake would wind through their tribal lands belching fire and smoke and bringing death and disaster to the tribe. When the British colonial administration began laying the tracks for the railway, which was planned to reach from Mombasa on the Indian Ocean to the shores of Lake Victoria almost 600 miles inland, the Nandi saw the dread prophecy being fulfilled and the coals of smouldering insurrection flared up again.

When Colonel Penrod Ballantyne, the officer commanding the KAR regiment, received a despatch informing him that the tribe were attacking isolated government outposts along the proposed route of the railway, he remarked, with exasperation, 'Well, I suppose we shall just have to give them another good drubbing.' And he ordered his 3rd Battalion out of their barracks in Nairobi—the colony's fledgling capital—to do just that.

Offered the choice, Leon Courtney would have been otherwise occupied on that day. He knew a young lady whose husband had been killed quite recently by a lion on their coffee *shamba* in the Ngong Hills. Leon had played on her husband's polo team. As a junior subaltern, he could not afford to run a string of ponies, but some of the more affluent club members were pleased to sponsor him since he was a fearless horseman and a prodigious striker of the ball. After a decent interval had passed, Leon rode out to the *shamba* to offer his condolences. Even in her widow's weeds Leon found Verity O'Hearne very fetching. And when she looked up at the strapping lad in his best uniform and burnished riding boots, she saw in his comely features and candid gaze an innocence that roused some feminine instinct in her. On the wide, shady verandah of the homestead she served him tea and sandwiches and drew him out skilfully, speaking in a soft Irish brogue that enchanted him. When he rose to take his leave, she walked with him to the front steps and offered her hand in farewell. 'Please call again, Lieutenant Courtney. At times I find loneliness a heavy burden.'

Leon's duties, as the youngest officer in the battalion, were many and onerous so it was almost two weeks before he could avail himself of her invitation. Once the tea and sandwiches had been despatched she led him into the house to show him her husband's hunting rifles, which she wished to sell. 'My husband has left me short of funds, so I am forced to find a buyer for them. I hoped that you might give me some idea of their value.'

'I would be delighted to assist you in any possible way, Mrs O'Hearne.'

'You are so kind. I feel that I can trust you completely.'

He could find no words to answer her. Instead he gazed abjectly into her large blue eyes for by this time he was deeply in her thrall.

'May I call you Leon?' she asked, and before he could answer she burst into violent sobs. 'Oh, Leon! I am so lonely.' She had fallen into his arms.

Later he tried to re-create exactly what had happened next, but it was all an ecstatic blur. He could not remember how they had reached her bedroom. As they lay together on the feather mattress the young widow gave Leon a glimpse of Paradise.

Now, these many months later, in the shimmering heat of the Rift Valley, as he led his detachment of seven *askaris*, locally recruited tribal troops, in extended order with bayonets fixed, through the lush banana plantation that surrounded the thatched buildings of the district commissioner's headquarters at Niombi, Leon was thinking of Verity O'Hearne's bosom.

Out on his left flank Sergeant Manyoro clicked his tongue. Leon jerked back to the present and froze at the soft warning. He lifted his right hand in the command to halt and the line of *askaris* stopped on either side of him. He glanced from the corner of his eye at his sergeant.

Manyoro was a *morani* of the Masai. A fine member of that tribe, he stood at well over six feet, yet he was as slim and graceful as a bullfighter, wearing his khaki uniform and tasselled fez with panache, every inch the African warrior. When he felt Leon's eyes on him he lifted his chin.

Leon followed the gesture and saw the vultures. There were only two turning wing-tip to wing-tip high above the rooftops of the *boma*.

He had not been expecting trouble: the centre of the Nandi insurrection was reported seventy miles further west. This government outpost was in Masai territory. Leon's orders were to reinforce the government *boma* with his few men against any possibility that the insurrection might boil over the tribal borders. The district commissioner at Niombi was Hugh Turvey. Leon had met him and his wife at the Settlers' Club ball in Nairobi the previous Christmas Eve. Turvey was only four or five years older than Leon but already he had earned a reputation as a solid man.

Leon gave the hand signal to his *askaris* to load their Lee-Enfield rifles. Another hand signal and they went forward cautiously.

From directly ahead Leon heard the loud flapping of heavy wings and another vulture rose from beyond the screen of banana plants. He felt a chill of dread. *If the brutes are settling, that means there's meat lying out there.*

Again he signalled the halt. He stabbed a finger at Manyoro, then went forward alone, Manyoro backing him. Leon stepped past the last banana plant and stopped at the edge of the open parade ground. Ahead, the mud-brick walls of the *boma* glared, with their coating of limewash. The front door of the main building stood wide open. The verandah and the parade ground were littered with broken furniture and government documents.

Hugh Turvey and his wife, Helen, lay spread-eagled in the open. Their five-year-old daughter lay just beyond them. She had been stabbed once through her chest with a broad-bladed Nandi *assegai* spear. Both her parents had been crucified and killed. Sharpened wooden stakes had been driven through their feet and hands into the clay surface.

So the Nandi have learned something at last from the missionaries, Leon thought bitterly. He looked round the border of the parade ground, searching for any sign that the attackers might still be nearby, then went forward, stepping carefully through the litter.

'The Nandi are not men.' Manyoro's contempt and tribal enmity were undisguised. 'I will find those who did this. They will not have gone far.'

Leon looked away from the sickening butchery to the heights of the escarpment that stood a thousand feet above them. With a visible effort he brought his emotions under control.

'First we must bury these people,' he told Manyoro, speaking in Swahili. 'We cannot leave them for the birds.'

Cautiously they searched the buildings and found them deserted—the government staff had fled. Then Leon sent Manyoro and three *askaris* to secure the perimeter of the *boma*.

Meanwhile, he found the Turveys' living quarters. It had also been ransacked but he found a pile of sheets in a cupboard. He gathered up an armful and took them outside. He pulled out the stakes with which the Turveys had been pegged to the ground, wetted his neckerchief with water from his canteen and wiped their faces clean of dried blood. Then he wrapped their bodies in the sheets.

The earth in the banana plantation was soft and damp from recent rain. While he and some of the *askaris* stood guard against another attack, four others started to dig a single grave for the family.

In the heights of the escarpment, screened by a small patch of scrub, three men leaned on their war spears. Before them, the floor of the Rift Valley was a vast plain, brown grassland interspersed with stands of thorn, scrub and acacia trees. The grasses were highly prized by the Masai, who ran their long-horned cattle on them but, since the most recent Nandi rebellion, they had driven their herds to a safer area much further to the south. The Nandi were famous cattle thieves.

This part of the valley had been left to the wild game, whose multitudes swarmed across the plain as far as the eye could see. At a distance the zebra were as grey as the dust clouds they raised as they galloped, the kongoni, the gnu and the buffalo were darker stains on the golden landscape. The giraffe stood tall above the flat tops of the acacia trees, while the antelope were creamy specks that danced and shimmered in the heat. Here and there larger masses moved ponderously through the lesser animals. These were the mighty pachyderms: rhinoceros and elephant. It was a scene both primeval and awe-inspiring, but to the three watchers it was commonplace. Their interest was focused on the cluster of buildings directly below them.

The oldest of the three men wore a kilt of leopard tails and a cap of the same black and gold-speckled fur. This was the regalia of the paramount witch doctor of the Nandi tribe, Arap Samoei, who had led the rebellion against the white invaders for ten years. The faces and bodies of the men with him were painted for war: their eyes were circled with red ochre; a stripe was painted down their noses and across their cheeks. Their kilts were made of gazelle skins and their headdresses of genet and monkey fur.

'The *mzungu* and his bastard Masai dogs are well into the trap,' said Arap Samoei. 'Seven Masai and one *mzungu* will make a good killing.'

'Is it time to carry the spears down to them?' asked the Nandi captain.

'It is time,' answered the witch doctor. 'But keep the *mzungu* for me. I want to cut off his balls with my own blade. From them I will make a powerful medicine.' He touched the hilt of the *panga* on his leopardskin belt. It was a knife with a short, heavy blade. He turned and strode back to the crest of a rugged rock wall, and looked down. His warriors squatted patiently in the short grass, rank upon rank of them.

Samoei raised his clenched fist. 'The fruit is ripe!' he called. 'Let us go down to the harvest!'

The grave was ready. Leon nodded at Manyoro, who gave a quiet order to his men. Two jumped down into the pit and the others passed the wrapped bundles down to them.

Leon removed his slouch hat, went down on one knee at the edge of the grave and began to recite the Lord's Prayer.

'For thine is the kingdom, the power and the glory, for ever and ever, amen!' Leon ended and began to rise, but before he stood upright the oppressive silence of the hot African afternoon was shattered by a deafening hubbub of howls and screams. He dropped his hand to the butt of the Webley pistol holstered on his Sam Browne belt.

Out of the dense foliage of the bananas swarmed a mass of sweat-shining bodies. They came from all sides, the sunlight sparkling on the blades of their spears and *pangas* as they raced towards the tiny group of soldiers.

'On me!' bellowed Leon. 'Form up on me! Load! Load! Load!' The *askaris* reacted with trained precision, forming a tight circle round him, rifles at the ready, bayonets pointing outwards. Leon saw that his party was surrounded except on the side nearest the *boma*'s main building.

'Commence firing!' Leon shouted, and in the crash of the seven rifles he saw only one of the Nandi go down, a chieftain wearing kilts and a headdress of monkey pelts. Leon knew who had fired the shot: Manyoro was an expert marksman, and Leon had seen him single out his victim.

The charge faltered as the chief went down, but at a shriek of rage from a leopard-robed witch doctor in the rear, the attackers rallied. Leon fired two quick shots at him, but the distance was well over fifty paces and neither bullet had any effect.

'On me!' Leon shouted again. 'Close order! Follow me!' He led his men at a run straight into a narrow gap in the Nandi line, making directly for the main building. The tiny band of khaki-clad figures was almost through before the Nandi surged forward again and headed them off. Both sides were instantly embroiled in a hand-to-hand melee.

'Take the bayonet to them!' Leon roared, and fired the Webley into the grimacing face ahead of him. When the man dropped, another appeared immediately behind him. Manyoro plunged his long silver bayonet full length into his chest and jumped over the body, plucking out the blade as he went. Leon followed closely and between them they killed three more Nandi before they reached the verandah steps. By now they were the only members of the detachment still on their feet. All the others had been speared.

Leon took the verandah steps three at a time and charged through the open door into the main room. Manyoro slammed the door behind them. Each ran to a window and blazed away at the Nandi as they came after them. Their fire was so accurate that within seconds the steps were cluttered with bodies. The rest drew back in dismay, then turned tail and scattered into the plantation.

Leon stood at the window reloading his pistol as he watched them go. 'How much ammunition do you have, Sergeant?' he called to Manyoro.

The sleeve of Manyoro's tunic had been slashed by a *panga*, but there was little bleeding and Manyoro ignored the wound. He was loading bullets into the magazine of his rifle. 'These are my last two clips, Bwana,' he answered, 'but there are many more lying out there.' He gestured through the window at the bandoliers of the fallen *askaris* lying on the parade ground.

'We will go out and pick them up before they can regroup,' Leon said.

Manyoro propped the weapon against the windowsill and moved to the doorway. Leon joined him, grinning at him as he did so. It was good to have the tall Masai at his side. They had been together ever since Leon had come out from England to join the regiment a year ago and the rapport they had established was strong. 'Are you ready, Sergeant?' he asked.

'I am, Bwana.'

Leon threw open the door and they burst through it together. Leon hurdled the low retaining wall and landed on his feet, running. He raced to the nearest dead *askaris* and dropped to his knees. Quickly he unbuckled his webbing and slung the heavy bandoliers of ammunition over his shoulder. He jumped up and ran to the next man as a loud, angry hum rose from the edge of the plantation. He slung another set of webbing over his shoulder. Then he leaped up as the Nandi swarmed back onto the parade ground.

'Get back, and be quick about it!' he yelled at Manyoro, who was also draped with bandoliers. Leon snatched up a dead *askaris*'s rifle before he raced for the verandah wall. There he paused to glance back over his shoulder. Manyoro was a few yards behind him, while the leading Nandi warriors were fifty paces away and coming on swiftly.

'Cutting it a little fine,' Leon grunted. Then he saw one of the pursuers unsling the bow from his shoulder. 'Run!' he shouted at Manyoro, as he saw the Nandi release an arrow, which shot upwards and fell in a silent arc. 'Look out!' Leon screamed, but the warning was futile, the arrow too swift.

The strike of the arrow was hidden by Manyoro's body but Leon heard the meaty *whunk* of the iron head piercing flesh, and Manyoro spun round. The head of the arrow was buried deeply in the back of his thigh. He tried to take another pace but the wounded leg anchored him. Leon pulled the bandoliers from round his own neck and hurled them and the rifle over the retaining wall and through the open door. Then he started back. Manyoro was hopping towards him on his unwounded leg, the other dangling, the shaft of the arrow flapping.

Leon reached Manyoro and wrapped his right arm round his sergeant's torso beneath the armpit. He lifted him and ran with him to the wall, surprised that the tall Masai was so light. Leon was heavier by twenty pounds of solid muscle and every ounce of his powerful frame was charged with the strength of fear and desperation. He reached the wall and swung Manyoro over it. Then he cleared the wall in a single bound as more arrows clattered around them. Leon swept Manyoro into his arms and ran through the door as the first of the pursuing Nandi reached the wall behind them.

He dropped Manyoro on the floor and picked up the rifle he had retrieved from the dead *askaris*. As he turned back to the open doorway he levered a fresh cartridge into the breech and shot a Nandi dead as he was clambering over the wall. Swiftly he fired again. When the magazine was empty he put down the rifle and slammed shut the heavy mahogany door. It shook as the Nandi hurled themselves against it.

Manyoro had dragged himself across the floor to the rifle he had left propped beside the other window. Using the sill to steady himself, he had pulled himself onto his good leg. He fired through the window and Leon heard the sound of another body falling on the verandah. '*Morani!* Warrior!' he panted, and Manyoro grinned at the compliment.

'Do not leave all the work to me, Bwana. Take the other window!'

Leon snatched up the empty rifle, cramming cartridges into the magazine. He reached the other window and threw out a sheet of rapid fire. Between them they swept the parade ground with a fusillade that sent the Nandi scampering for the cover of the plantation again. Manyoro sank slowly down the wall and leaned against it, legs thrust out before him, the wounded one cocked so that the arrow shaft did not touch the floor.

With one last glance across the parade ground Leon left his window and went to his sergeant. He squatted in front of him and tentatively grasped the arrow shaft. Manyoro winced, and the sweat poured down his face.

'I can't pull it out so I'm going to break off the shaft and strap it,' Leon said.

Manyoro looked at him, then smiled, his teeth showing large, even and white. His earlobes had been pierced in childhood, the holes stretched to hold ivory discs, which gave his face a mischievous, puckish aspect.

'Up the Rifles!' Manyoro said, and his lisping imitation of the regimental war cry was so startling in the circumstances that Leon guffawed and, at the same instant, snapped off the shaft of the arrow close to where it protruded from the oozing wound. Manyoro closed his eyes, but uttered no sound.

Leon found a field dressing in the webbing pouch he had taken from the *askaris*, and bandaged the stump of the arrow shaft to stop it moving. Then he unhooked the water bottle from his own webbing, unscrewed the stopper and took a long swallow, before handing it to Manyoro. The Masai hesitated: an *askaris* did not drink from an officer's bottle. Frowning, Leon thrust it into his hands. 'Drink,' he said. 'That's an order!'

Manyoro tilted back his head and poured the water directly into his mouth without touching the neck with his lips. Then he screwed on the stopper tightly and handed it back to Leon.

'We will move out as soon as it's dark,' Leon said.

Manyoro considered this for a moment. 'Which way will you go?'

'*We* will go the way we came. We must get back to the railway line.'

Manyoro chuckled. 'It is almost two days' march to the railway line.' He touched his bandaged leg. 'When you go, Bwana, you will go alone.'

'Are you thinking of deserting, Manyoro? You know that's a shooting offence.' He paused, and then said, 'I will carry you.'

Manyoro smiled and asked politely, 'For two days, Bwana, with half the Nandi tribe chasing after us, you will carry me? I should call you "Horse".'

They were silent for a while, and then Leon said, 'Speak, O wise one. Give me counsel.'

Manyoro paused. 'This is not the land of the Nandi. These are the grazing lands of my people. These treacherous curs trespass on Masai lands. If we go towards the railway we will be moving back into Nandi ground. However, if we move down the valley . . .' Manyoro indicated south with his chin '. . . we will be moving into Masai territory. They will not follow us far.'

Leon shook his head dubiously. 'There is nothing to the south but wilderness and I must get you to a doctor before the leg festers.'

'Less than a day's easy march to the south lies the *manyatta* of my mother,' Manyoro told him. 'She is the most famous witch doctor in all the land. She has saved a hundred of our *morani* who have been struck down by spear and arrow or savaged by lions.' Manyoro sank back against the wall. His skin now bore a greyish sheen.

Leon nodded. 'Very well. We will go south down the Rift. We will leave in the dark before the rise of the moon.'

But Manyoro sat up again and sniffed the sultry air, like a hunting dog. 'No, Bwana. We must go at once. Can you not smell it?'

'Smoke! The swines are going to flush us out with fire.' Leon glanced out of the window. The parade ground was empty, but he knew their enemy would not come again from that direction. They would come from the rear where there were no windows. He looked at Manyoro. 'We will leave the rifles and bandoliers and take a bayonet and one water bottle each. That's all.' As he spoke, he reached for the pile of webbing they had salvaged. He buckled three of the waist belts together to form a single loop, slipped it over his head and settled it on his right shoulder. He decanted the contents of the salvaged bottles into his own water bottle, then topped up Manyoro's.

'Come on, Sergeant, get up.' Leon hoisted Manyoro to his feet. At that moment something heavy thumped on the thatch above their heads.

'Torches!' Leon snapped. 'Time to go.' He ripped off the tail of his shirt and handed it to Manyoro. 'Cover your face!' He knotted his neckerchief over his own nose and mouth, then lifted Manyoro over the windowsill and jumped out after him. They heard the distant shouting of the Nandi; then a curtain of smoke poured down so densely that they could see no more than an arm's length in front of them. The crackle of flames had risen to a dull roar, and the smoke was hot and suffocating.

Manyoro leaned on Leon's shoulder and hopped beside him as they crossed quickly to the retaining wall. They dropped over it with sparks from the roof swirling round them and stinging the exposed skin of their arms and legs. They went forward as quickly as Manyoro could move on one leg. They were both choking in the smoke, their eyes burning and streaming tears. Then, suddenly, they were among the first trees of the plantation.

The smoke was still thick and, as they groped their way forward, Leon was aware that Manyoro was flagging.

'We daren't stop before we're well clear,' Leon whispered.

'On one leg I will go as far and fast as you will on two,' Manyoro gasped.

'Come on,' Leon croaked, and they went forward again, Manyoro clinging to him, staggering and lurching.

Suddenly the ground gave way under them and they rolled down a steep mud bank into shallow water. They had reached the stream that ran to the south of the *boma*.

Leon knelt in the water and scooped handfuls into his face, washing his burning eyes. Then he drank greedily, Manyoro too. Leon gargled and spat out the last mouthful, his throat rough and raw from the smoke. He scrambled to the top of the bank to peer into the smoke. He heard voices but they were faint with distance. He waited to reassure himself that no Nandi were close on their tracks, then slid back down the bank to Manyoro.

'Let me look at your leg.' Leon unwrapped the field dressing. The violent activity of the escape had done damage. Manyoro's thigh was massively swollen, the flesh round the wound torn and bruised where the shaft of the arrow had worked back and forth. He felt the wound gently. Manyoro's pupils dilated with pain as Leon touched something buried in his flesh.

Leon whistled softly. 'What do we have here?' In the lean muscle of Manyoro's thigh, just above the knee, a foreign body lay under the skin.

'It's the point of the arrow,' he exclaimed. 'It's worked its way right through your leg from back to front.' It was hard to imagine the agony

Manyoro was enduring, and Leon felt inadequate in the presence of such courage. He looked up at the sky. The dense smoke was dissipating on the evening breeze and through it, he could make out the setting sun. His eyes were still burning with the effects of the smoke. He squeezed the lids shut. But not many minutes passed before he opened them again. He had heard voices coming from the direction of the *boma*.

'They are following our spoor!' Manyoro murmured, and they shrank lower under the bank of the stream. Leon realised that there was nowhere for him and Manyoro to hide in the stream bed so he heaved Manyoro upright, draped the other man's right arm over his shoulder and, half carrying and half dragging him, got him up to the top of the far bank.

The halt in the stream bed had not improved Manyoro's condition. When he tried to put weight on the limb, it buckled under him and he would have collapsed had Leon not caught him.

Leon turned his back to Manyoro, then stooped and pulled him onto his back, adjusting the webbing belts to form a sling seat for him. Straightening, with Manyoro perched on his back, legs sticking out, Leon struck out for the foot of the escarpment. The sun was low, balancing like a fireball on top of the escarpment, and the darkness was thickening around them.

'Fifteen minutes,' he whispered hoarsely. 'That's all we need.' By now he was into the bush along the foot of the escarpment wall. It was thick enough to afford them some cover, and with the instincts and eyes of a hunter and a soldier, Leon used it to screen their labouring progress. As darkness settled over them he felt a lift of optimism. It seemed they were clear of pursuit at last. He sank to the ground on his knees, then rolled gently onto his side to offload Manyoro. Neither spoke or moved for a while; then Leon sat up slowly and unbuckled the sling so that Manyoro could straighten his injured leg. He handed him the water bottle.

Manyoro touched his arm. 'Bwana, you are a man of iron, but it would be a great stupidity for both of us to die here. Leave the pistol with me and go on. I will stay here and kill any Nandi who tries to follow you.'

'We haven't even started and you're ready to give up,' Leon snarled. 'Get on my back again before I spit on you where you lie.' He knew his anger was excessive, but he was afraid.

This time it took longer to get Manyoro settled in the loop of the sling. For the first hundred paces or so Leon thought his legs would let him down entirely, but with all the force of his mind and will he drove back the pain and felt the strength gradually trickle back into his legs. *One step at a time. Just one more. That's it. Now one more.*

He knew that if he stopped to rest he would never start again, and went on until he saw the crescent moon appear on the eastern side of the Rift Valley. On his back Manyoro was as quiescent as a dead man, but Leon knew he was alive for he could feel the fever heat of his body.

As the moon started to sink towards the western escarpment on his right, it threw weird shadows under the trees. Leon's mind began to play tricks on him, phantoms appearing and dissolving before him. The last ounces of his strength slipped away. He reeled and almost went down. He felt Manyoro stir on his back, and then, incredibly, the Masai began to sing in a wispy breath. Leon recognised the words of the Lion Song; despite his sharp ear for language, his grasp of Maa, the complicated language of the Masai, was rudimentary. Manyoro had patiently taught Leon the little he knew.

The Lion Song was taught to every young Masai *morani* at his circumcision class. The initiates accompanied it with a stiff-legged dance, bounding high into the air, as effortlessly as a flock of birds taking flight, their red toga-like *shuka* cloaks spreading like wings around them.

> *We are the young lions.*
> *When we roar the earth shivers.*
> *Our spears are our fangs.*
> *Our spears are our claws.*
> *Fear us, O ye beasts.*
> *Fear us, O ye strangers.*
> *Turn your eyes away from our faces, you women.*
> *You dare not look upon the beauty of our faces.*
> *We are the brothers of the lion pride.*
> *We are the young lions.*
> *We are the Masai.*

It was the song the Masai sang when they went out to prove their valour by hunting the lion with nothing but the stabbing *assegai* in their hands. It was the song that gave them stomach for battle. It was their battle hymn.

Manyoro began the chorus again and this time Leon joined in. Manyoro squeezed his shoulder and whispered in his ear, 'Sing! You are one of us. You have the heart of the lion and the strength of a Masai.'

They staggered on towards the south. Leon's legs kept moving for the song's chorus was mesmerising. On his back he felt Manyoro slump into coma. He stumbled onwards until the rim of the rising sun broke clear of the escarpment. Abruptly his legs went from under him and he collapsed as though he had been shot.

THE HEAT OF THE SUN on the back of his shirt goaded him awake, but when he tried to lift his head he dissolved into vertigo, and could not remember where he was. His senses were tricking him now: he thought he could hear voices—children's—calling shrilly to each other. He rolled away from Manyoro and, with a huge effort, raised himself on one elbow. He gazed round with bleary eyes, squinting in the bright sunlight.

He saw cattle streaming past the spot where he and Manyoro lay. Three naked boys were herding the cattle towards a nearby water hole. They were probably between thirteen and fifteen, and calling to each other in Maa.

With another huge effort, Leon forced his aching frame into a sitting position. The tallest boy saw the movement and stopped. He stared at Leon in consternation, clearly on the point of flight but controlling his fear, as a Masai, who was almost a *morani*, was duty-bound to do.

'Who are you?' he asked, his voice quavering.

Leon understood the simple words. 'I am not an enemy,' he called back hoarsely. He reached down and helped Manyoro to sit up. 'Brother!' he said. 'This man is your brother!'

The boy took a few paces towards them and peered at Manyoro. Then he turned to his companions and let fly a string of instructions that sent them racing across the savannah. The only word Leon understood was 'Manyoro!'

The younger boys were heading towards a cluster of thatched huts half a mile away, which were surrounded by a fence of thorn bushes. It was a Masai *manyatta*, a village. The elder child approached Leon now and squatted in front of him. He pointed and said, in awe, 'Manyoro!'

'Yes, Manyoro,' Leon agreed, and his head spun giddily.

The child exclaimed with delight and made another excited speech. Leon recognised the word for 'uncle'. He closed his eyes and lay back with his arm over them to blot out the blazing sunlight. 'Tired,' he said. 'Very tired.'

He slipped away, and woke again to find himself surrounded by a small crowd of villagers. They were Masai, there was no mistaking that. The men were tall and naked under their long red cloaks, and in their pierced earlobes they wore large ornamental discs. The women were tall. Their skulls were shaven smooth as eggshells and they wore layers of intricately beaded necklaces that hung over their naked breasts above beaded aprons.

Leon struggled to sit up and they watched him with interest, the younger women giggling. 'Manyoro!' He pointed at his companion. 'Mama? Manyoro Mama?' he demanded.

Then one of the youngest girls understood what he was trying to tell them. 'Lusima!' she cried, and pointed to the east. 'Lusima Mama!'

It was clearly Manyoro's mother's name. Leon mimed lifting and carrying Manyoro, then pointed to the east. 'Take Manyoro to Lusima.'

Again the same girl divined his meaning. She stamped her foot and harangued the men. Immediately, two ran back to the village and returned with a *mushila*, a litter. Within a short time they were settling the unconscious Manyoro on it. Four picked it up, and the entire party set off towards the east at a trot, leaving Leon lying on the dusty plain. The singing of the men and the ululations of the women faded.

Leon closed his eyes, trying to summon sufficient reserves of strength to follow them. When he opened them again he found the three naked herd-boys who had discovered him standing in a row, regarding him solemnly. Leon rolled onto his knees, then lurched to his feet. The eldest child came to his side, took his hand and tugged at it. 'Lusima,' he said.

His friend took Leon's other hand. He pulled at it and said, 'Lusima.'

'Very well,' Leon conceded. 'Lusima it shall be.' He tapped the eldest boy on the chest with a finger. 'Name?' he asked, in Maa.

'Loikot!' he answered proudly.

'Loikot, we shall go to Lusima Mama. Show me the way.'

With Leon limping between them, they helped him towards the far blue hills, following Manyoro's litter-bearers.

As they made their way across the valley Leon became aware of a single isolated mountain that rose abruptly from the wide floor of the plain. At first it seemed to be merely a buttress of the eastern escarpment and inconsequential in the immensity of the great valley, but as they came closer he saw that it stood alone.

It was the middle of the afternoon before Leon and his three companions reached the foot of the mountain. Manyoro and his party of litter-bearers were already halfway up the footpath that climbed the steep slope.

Leon only managed the first two hundred feet of the climb before he subsided in the shade of an acacia beside the track. His feet would not carry him another step. As he levered off his boot and gingerly peeled off his woollen sock he groaned in pain. His heel was flayed raw. Burst blisters hung in tatters from the sole, and his toes might have been chewed by jackals. The three Masai boys squatted in a semicircle, studying his wounds.

Leon tore the sleeves of his shirt into strips and wrapped his bleeding feet in them. Then he knotted the laces of his boots together and slung them round his neck. Loikot gave Leon his herding stick and he hobbled up the pathway, which grew steeper with every pace.

It was almost dark when they heard voices on the path above them. Loikot shouted a challenge, which was answered by a party of half a dozen cloaked *morani*, coming down to them at a trot. They had brought with them the *mushila* on which they had carried Manyoro. At their bidding Leon climbed into it and four men lifted the pole onto their shoulders. Then they took off at a run, back up the steep mountain path.

As they came over the edge of the cliff face onto the table top of the mountain, Leon saw the glow of fires. The *mushila*-bearers carried him swiftly towards them and into an open space. Large thatched huts were assembled in a circle round a tall, wide-spreading, wild fig tree.

From the fires a number of men and women crowded forward to look at the stranger. The men's *shukas* were of fine quality, and the women's abundant ornaments were beautifully made of the most expensive trade beads and ivory. There could be no doubt that this was an affluent community. Laughing, they gathered round Leon's *mushila* and many younger women reached out to touch his face and tug at his ragged uniform.

Suddenly a hush fell over the throng. A regal feminine figure was moving towards them from the huts. The villagers drew aside to leave an aisle and she came down it towards the *mushila*. Two servant girls followed her with burning torches, which cast a golden light upon the woman as she glided towards Leon. The villagers bowed like a field of grass in the wind as she passed between their ranks. 'Lusima!' they whispered.

Leon struggled up from the *mushila* and stood to meet her. She stared into his face with a dark, hypnotic gaze.

'I see you, Lusima,' he greeted her, but she gave no sign of having heard him. She stood almost as tall as he did. Her skin was the colour of smoked honey, glossy and unlined. If she was indeed the mother of Manyoro she must have been older than fifty, but she seemed at least twenty years younger. Her finely sculpted features were striking and her dark eyes so penetrating that they seemed to reach into the secret places of his mind.

'*Ndio.*' She nodded. 'Yes. I am Lusima. I have been expecting your coming. I was overlooking you and Manyoro on your night march from Niombi.' Leon was relieved that she spoke in Swahili, rather than Maa: communication between them would be easier. But how could she know that they had come from Niombi? Unless, of course, Manyoro had regained consciousness and told her.

'Manyoro has not spoken since he came to me. He is still deep in the land of shadows,' Lusima assured him.

He started. She had responded to his unspoken question as though she had heard the words.

'I was watching over you,' she repeated, and despite himself he believed her. 'I saw you rescue my son from certain death and bring him back to me. With this deed you have become as another son to me.' She took his hand. 'Come, I must see to your feet.'

'Where is Manyoro?' Leon asked. 'Will he survive?'

'It will be a hard fight, and the outcome is uncertain. Now he is sleeping. He must gather his strength for the trial ahead. I cannot remove the arrow until I have the light of day in which to work. You must rest also, for though you have the strength of M'bogo, the great buffalo bull, you have tried it to its limit with your journey.'

She led him to one of the huts and he stooped through the low entrance into the dim, smoky interior. Lusima indicated to him a pile of monkey-skin karosses against the far wall. He eased himself down onto the soft fur and she knelt in front of him and peeled the rags from his feet. Her servant girls prepared a brew of herbs in an iron pot that stood over the cooking fire in the centre of the hut and when the contents were ready the girls brought it to where Leon sat. Lusima tested the temperature, then took his feet one at a time and immersed them in the mixture. It took all his self-control to prevent himself crying out, for the liquid felt as though it was just off the boil, and it was caustic.

Lusima lifted out his feet one at a time, then wrapped them in strips of cloth. 'Now you must eat and sleep,' she said, and nodded to one of the girls, who offered him a calabash. Leon caught a whiff of the contents. It was a Masai staple, which he dared not refuse: to do so would offend his hostess. He steeled himself and lifted the bowl to his lips.

He took a mouthful and his stomach heaved. It was warm and the fresh ox blood mixed with milk had taken on a slick, jelly-like consistency, but he kept swallowing until the gourd was empty.

Lusima smiled. 'Now you must sleep.' She pushed him down on the kaross and spread another over him. A great weight bore down on his eyelids.

WHEN HE OPENED his eyes again the morning sun was blazing through the doorway of the hut. Loikot was waiting for him at the door, squatting against the lintel, but he sprang to his feet as soon as Leon stirred. He came to him immediately and asked a question, pointing at his feet.

Leon sat up and unwrapped the bandages. He was amazed to see that most of the swelling had subsided.

'Dr Lusima's snake oil.' He grinned, until he remembered Manyoro.

Quickly he rebandaged his feet, and hobbled to the large clay water pot that stood outside the door. He stripped off the remnants of his shirt and washed the dust and dried sweat from his face and hair. When he straightened up he found Lusima standing there. 'Come,' she commanded. She led him to the hut that stood beside his. The interior was dark after the brilliant sunlight and it took his eyes a minute to adjust. The air was rank with woodsmoke from the fire and a more subtle odour, the sweet, nauseating smell of corrupting flesh. Manyoro lay on a kaross beside the fire. His head was twisted to one side, and his eyes had receded into their sockets.

'I have removed the arrow head and shaft and washed out the poisons.' Lusima pointed to the pads of dried herbs that she had placed over the wounds. 'There is nothing more I can do. Now it is a battle between the gods of his ancestors and the dark devils. Within three days we will know the outcome.' She looked up at Leon. 'You and I, M'bogo, must take turns to sit at his side and give him strength for the fight.'

Over the days that followed Manyoro lay in such a deep coma that Leon had to place his ear against his chest to listen for his breathing. At other times he gasped and writhed on his sleeping mat. Lusima and Leon sat on each side of him, restraining him when he seemed in danger of injuring himself. The nights were long and neither slept. They talked quietly through the hours with the low fire between them.

'I sense you were not born on some faraway island over the sea, as most of your compatriots were, but in this very Africa,' Lusima said. Leon was no longer surprised by her uncanny perception. He did not reply at once, and she went on, 'You were born far to the north on the banks of a great river.'

'Yes,' he said. 'You are right. The place is Cairo, and the river is the Nile.'

'You belong to this land and you will never leave it.' She reached across and took his hand. 'I see your mother,' she said. 'The two of you are close in spirit. She did not want you to leave her.'

Leon's eyes filled with the dark shadows of regret.

'I see your father also. It was because of him that you left.'

'My father grubs after money. There is nothing else in his life. He is a hard man, and we do not like each other. I suppose I respect him, but I do not admire him. He wanted me to work with him, doing the things he does. It was a bleak prospect.'

'So you ran away. What was it you sought?' she asked.

He looked thoughtful. 'Truly, I do not know, Lusima Mama.'

'You have not found it?' she asked.

He shook his head uncertainly. Then he thought of Verity O'Hearne. 'Perhaps,' he said. 'Perhaps I have found someone.'

'No. Not the woman you are thinking of. She is just one woman among many others.'

The question was out before he could check himself: 'How do you know about her?' Then he answered himself: 'Of course. You know many things.'

She chuckled, and they were silent for a long while. He felt a strange bond with her, a closeness as though she were his mother.

'I do not like what I am doing with my life now,' he said at last. He had not thought about it until this moment, but as he said it, he knew it was the truth.

'Because you are a soldier you are not able to do what your heart tells you,' she agreed. 'You must do as the old men order.'

'You understand,' he said.

'Do you want me to point the way for you, M'bogo?'

'I have come to trust you. I need your guidance.'

She was silent again for so long that he was about to speak. Then he saw that her eyes were wide open but rolled back in her head so that only the whites were exposed. She was rocking rhythmically on her haunches and after a while she began to speak. 'There are two men. Neither is your father, but both will be more than your father. There is another road. You must follow the road of the great grey men who are not men. Learn the secret ways of the wild creatures, and other men will honour you for that knowledge. You will walk with mighty men of power, and they will count you their equal. There will be many women, but only one woman who will be many women. She will come to you from the clouds. Like them she will show you many faces.' She broke off and made a strangling noise at the back of her throat, and Leon realised she was deep in the throes of divination. At last she shook herself violently and blinked. 'Hearken to what I told you, my son,' she said softly. 'The time for you to choose will soon be upon you.'

'You speak in riddles, Mama,' he said, and she smiled an enigmatic smile.

IN THE MORNING Manyoro regained consciousness but he was very weak and confused. He gazed at them blearily. 'What has happened? What place is this?' Then he recognised his mother. 'Mama, is it truly you? I thought it was a dream.'

'You are safe in my *manyatta* on Lonsonyo Mountain,' she told him. 'We removed the Nandi arrow from your leg.'

'The arrow? Yes, I remember . . . The Nandi?'

The slave girls brought him a bowl of ox blood and milk, which he drank greedily. He lay back gasping. Then, for the first time, he noticed Leon squatting in the gloom of the hut. 'Bwana! You are with me still?'

'I am here.' Leon went to him quietly.

'How long? How many days since we left Niombi?'

'Seven.'

'Headquarters in Nairobi will think you are dead or that you have deserted—you must report to Headquarters, Bwana. You must not neglect your duty for me.'

'We will go back to Nairobi when you are ready to march.'

'No, Bwana, no. You must go at once. You know that the major is not your friend. He will make trouble for you.'

'Manyoro is right,' Lusima said. 'You can do no more here. You must go to your chief in Nairobi.'

Leon realised with a guilty shock that it must be more than three weeks since he had had contact with his battalion headquarters.

'Loikot will guide you to the railway line,' Lusima continued. 'He knows that part of the country well. Go with him,' she urged.

'I will.' He stood up. There were no preparations to make. He had no weapons or baggage, and hardly any clothing other than his ragged khaki.

Lusima provided him with a Masai *shuka*. 'It is the best protection I can give you. The Nandi fear the red *shuka*—even the lions flee from it.'

Leon and Loikot left within an hour of making the decision. Leon's feet had healed just sufficiently for him to lace on his boots. Limping gingerly, he followed Loikot down the mountain towards the plain below. At the foot he looked up to see the unmistakable silhouette of Lusima standing on the lip of the cliff. He lifted one arm in farewell, but she did not acknowledge the gesture. Instead she turned and disappeared from his sight.

LOIKOT COVERED THE GROUND with the long, flowing stride characteristic of his people. As he went he kept up a running commentary on everything. By this time, Leon had picked up enough Maa to follow the boy's chatter with little difficulty.

They had carried no food with them and Leon had been puzzled as to how they would subsist. But Loikot provided a strange variety of sustenance, which included small birds and their eggs, locusts and other insects, wild fruit and roots, and a large monitor lizard. The lizard's flesh tasted like chicken, and there was enough to feed them for three days.

Leon and Loikot slept each night beside a small fire, covered with their *shukas* against the chill, and started again while the morning star remained bright in the dawn sky. On the third morning the sun was still below the horizon when Loikot stopped dead and pointed in the direction of an acacia tree only fifty yards away. 'Ho, you killer of cattle, I greet you,' he cried.

'Who is it?' Leon demanded.

'Do you not see him?' Loikot pointed with his staff. Only then did Leon make out two small black tufts in the brown grass. Leon was staring at an enormous crouching male lion, which was watching them with implacable yellow eyes. The telltale tufts were the black tips of its ears.

'Sweet God!' Leon took a step back.

Loikot laughed. 'He will run if I challenge him.' He brandished his staff. 'Hey, Old One, the day of my testing will soon come. I will meet you then, and we shall see which is the best of us.' He was referring to the Masai ritual trial of courage. Before he could be counted a man, the young *morani* would have to confront his lion and kill him with his broad-bladed *assegai*.

'Fear me, you thief of cattle. Fear me, for I am your death!' Loikot raised his staff and advanced on the lion. Leon was amazed when the lion curled its lip in a threatening growl, then slunk away into the grass.

'Did you see me, M'bogo?' Loikot crowed. 'Did you see how Simba fears me? Did you see him run from me?'

'You crazy tyke!' Leon laughed with relief. 'You'll get us both eaten.'

Loikot leaped in the air, pirouetted in triumph and led Leon northwards. As they went, he continued his instruction, pointing out the spoor of large game as he came upon it, and describing the animal that had made it.

Leon was fascinated when Loikot came to a stop and, with the tip of his staff, traced the faint outline of an enormous round pad mark. The ground was baked hard by the sun, and covered with chips of shale and flint, but Loikot could read every detail and nuance of it.

'I know this one. I have seen him often. His teeth are long. He is a great grey chief of his tribe.'

Lusima had used the same description: 'Follow the great grey men who are not men.' At the time it had puzzled Leon, but now he realised she had been speaking about elephant, and he pondered her advice. The lure of wild sports was one of the most powerful reasons why he had enlisted in the KAR. Leon had heard that the army encouraged their young officers to indulge in such manly pursuits as big-game hunting.

So far his hunting had been restricted to a few small antelope he had shot to feed his *askaris* while they were on patrol, but his heart stirred when he watched the magnificent beasts that flourished all around him. He longed for a chance to go after them. Now, he wondered if by counselling him to 'follow the great grey men', Lusima was suggesting he should take to the life of an ivory hunter. It was an intriguing prospect.

Five days after they had left Lonsonyo Mountain, Loikot turned east and led him up the escarpment of the Great Rift Valley into the rolling forested hills of the uplands. They looked down into the shallow valley beyond. In the distance something glinted in the late-evening sunlight. Leon shaded his eyes. 'Yes, M'bogo,' Loikot told him, 'there is your iron snake.'

Leon saw the smoke of the locomotive spurting in regular puffs above the tops of the trees and heard the mournful blast of its steam whistle.

'I will leave you now. Even you cannot lose your way from here,' Loikot told him loftily. 'I must go back to care for the cattle.'

Leon watched him go regretfully. He had enjoyed the boy's lively company. Then he put it out of his mind and went down the hill.

The locomotive driver spotted the tall figure beside the tracks far ahead, recognising his ochre-red *shuka* as that of Masai. It was only as the engine puffed closer that he realised it was a white man in the ragged remnants of a khaki uniform. He reached for the brake lever and the wheels squealed on the steel rails as they drew to a halt in a cloud of steam.

Major Frederick 'Froggy' Snell, officer commanding the 3rd Battalion, 1st Regiment, the King's African Rifles, did not look up from the document he was perusing when Lieutenant Leon Courtney was marched under armed escort into his office.

Snell was a small man and old for his command. His once bright ginger hair had faded and fallen out until he was left with only a scraggly white fringe around a freckled pate. His lips were thin, his eyes round and protuberant. He frowned as he finished reading the handwritten report, then laid it neatly in front of him and at last raised his head.

'Prisoner! Attention!' barked Sergeant Major M'fefe, who commanded the guard detail. Leon stamped his boots on the cement floor and stood erect.

Snell eyed him with distaste. Leon Courtney had been arrested three days earlier when he had presented himself at the main gates of Battalion Headquarters. Since then he had been held on Snell's orders in detention. He had not been able to shave or change his filthy and tattered uniform. But, despite his present circumstances, he still made Snell feel inadequate. Even in his rags Leon Courtney was tall and powerfully built, and he radiated an air of naive self-confidence.

'Well, Courtney, this time you have outdone yourself.' Snell tapped the papers in front of him. 'I have been reading your report. It defies belief.' He shook his head. 'I wonder what your uncle will make of this extraordinary account when he reads it.'

Leon's uncle was Colonel Penrod Ballantyne, the regimental commander. He was many years younger than Snell but already outranked him by a wide margin. Snell hated the man, and hated his bloody nephew.

'Tell me, Courtney, do you understand why I have had you detained since you arrived back in barracks?'

'Sir!' Leon stared at the wall above his head.

'On July the 16th you were ordered to take under your command a detachment of seven men and to proceed immediately to the district commissioner's headquarters at Niombi and take up guard duties to protect the station against Nandi rebels. That is correct, is it not?'

'Yes, sir!'

'It says in your report that you came across the tracks of a large war party of Nandi rebels and decided in your infinite wisdom to disregard your orders to proceed to Niombi but rather to follow up and engage the rebels. Please explain to me how you knew that these tracks were those of a Nandi war party.'

'Sir, I was advised by my sergeant that they were those of Nandi rebels. Sergeant Manyoro is an expert tracker.'

'So you spent six days following these mythical insurgents?'

'Sir, they were moving directly towards the mission station at Nakuru. It seemed they might be intent on attacking and destroying the settlement. I thought it my duty to prevent them doing so.'

'Your duty was to obey orders. Be that as it may, the fact is that you never managed to catch up.'

'Sir, the Nandi became aware that we were in pursuit and scattered into the bush. I turned back and proceeded to Niombi.'

'And when you reached the *boma* you discovered that while you had been wandering around the countryside, the district commissioner and his family had been massacred. Immediately after this discovery you then realised you had led your detachment negligently into a Nandi ambush. You turned tail and ran, leaving your men to fend for themselves.'

'That is not what happened, sir!' Leon was unable to disguise his outrage.

'And that outburst was insubordination, Lieutenant.' Snell relished the word. 'Have you witnesses to support your version of the events at Niombi?'

'Sergeant Manyoro, sir.'

'Of course, I had forgotten how when you left Niombi you placed the sergeant on your back and, outrunning a rebel army, carried him southwards into Masailand.' Snell sneered. 'It should be remarked at this point that you took him in the opposite direction from Nairobi, then left him with his mother.' Snell chuckled. 'How touching! The relief party that reached the Niombi *boma* many days after the massacre found that all the corpses of your men had been so mutilated by the rebels that it was impossible to identify them.' He paused, then continued, 'I think you left your sergeant among those corpses, then skulked in the wilderness until you were able to recover your nerve sufficiently to return to Nairobi with this cock-and-bull story.'

'No, sir.' Leon was trembling with anger, his fists bunched at his sides.

'Since joining the battalion you have displayed a fine contempt for military discipline and authority. Not only that, you have taken upon yourself the role of a lascivious Lothario, outraging the decent folk of the colony.'

'Major, sir, I don't see how you can substantiate those accusations.'

'Very well, I will substantiate. You are probably unaware that during your prolonged absence the governor of the colony has seen fit to repatriate a young widow to England to protect her from your depredations. The entire community of Nairobi is outraged by your behaviour.'

'Repatriated!' Leon turned ashen. 'They have sent Verity home?'

'Ah, so you acknowledge the poor woman's identity. Yes, Mrs O'Hearne has gone back to England. She left a week ago.' Snell paused to let this sink in, gloating at the knowledge that he himself had brought the affair to the governor's attention. 'Well, Courtney, I do not intend to substantiate my allegations any further. All will be decided at your court-martial. Your dossier has been handed to Captain Roberts; he has agreed to act as prosecuting officer. The charges against you will be desertion, cowardice, dereliction of duty and failing to obey the orders of a superior officer. Second Lieutenant Sampson has agreed to defend you. I have arranged that a colonel and two captains will travel up from Mombasa to Nairobi to make up a full panel of judges. They are due to arrive this evening. They have to return to Mombasa by Friday, so the proceedings must commence tomorrow morning. Until then you are confined to your quarters.'

'I request an interview with Colonel Ballantyne, sir. I need an extension of time to prepare my defence.'

'Unfortunately, Colonel Ballantyne is in the Nandi tribal lands making reprisals for the Niombi massacre. It is unlikely that he will return to Nairobi for several weeks.' Snell smiled coldly. 'That is all. Prisoner, dismiss!'

Leon found himself being marched towards the officers' billets. Everything was moving so swiftly that he had difficulty in ordering his thoughts. His quarters were a rondavel, a single-roomed building with circular mud-daub wall and a thatched roof.

At the door Sergeant Major M'fefe saluted smartly and said awkwardly, in Swahili, 'I am sorry this has happened, Lieutenant. I know you are no coward.' M'fefe went on hurriedly to cover his embarrassment: 'After you left on patrol a lady came to the main gates and left a box for you, Bwana. She told me to make sure you received it. I put it in your room.'

'Thank you, Sergeant Major.' Leon turned away and went into the hut. It contained an iron bedstead with a mosquito net suspended over it and a wardrobe made from an old packing case. His scant possessions were arranged with precision on a shelf above his bed. During his absence, Ishmael, his manservant, had been as meticulous as ever. The only item out of place was a long leather case that was propped against the wall.

Leon sat down on the bed. He felt close to despair. Almost without conscious volition he reached out for the leather case M'fefe had left for him, and laid it across his lap. He lifted the lid and stared in astonishment at the heavy rifle nestled in one of the green baize compartments. On the underside of the lid a large label bore the name of the gunmaker: *HOLLAND & HOLLAND, Manufacturers of Guns, Rifles and Pistols*.

With a sense of reverence Leon reassembled the rifle. He lifted the rifle and aimed it at a small gecko on the far wall. The butt fitted perfectly into his shoulder and the barrels aligned themselves under his eye.

He lowered the weapon and read the engraving on the barrels. *H&H Royal .470 Nitro Express*. Then the pure gold oval inlay let into the walnut of the butt caught his eye. It was engraved with the initials *PO'H*.

'Patrick O'Hearne,' he murmured. The magnificent weapon had belonged to Verity's dead husband. An envelope was pinned to the green baize of the lid. He set down the rifle carefully and pulled out two folded sheets of paper. The first was a receipt dated August 29, 1909:

To whom it may concern: I have this day sold the H&H .470 rifle with serial number 1863 to Lieutenant Leon Courtney and have received from him the sum of twenty-five guineas in full and final payment. Signed: Verity Abigail O'Hearne.

With this document Verity had transferred the rifle legally into his name. He folded the receipt and returned it to the envelope. Then he opened the other sheet of paper. It bore handwriting that was scrawled and uneven.

Dearest, dearest Leon,

By the time you read this I will be on my way back to Ireland. I did not want to go, but deep in my heart I know that the person who is sending me away is right and it is for the best. Next year I will be thirty years old, and you are just nineteen. I am sure that one day you will be a famous general covered with medals and glory, but by then I will be an old maid. This gift I leave you is an earnest of my affection for you. I will always hold you in my memory as I once held you in my arms.

It was signed '*V*'. His vision blurred with tears as he reread the letter.

Before he reached the last line there was a polite knock on the door of his rondavel. 'Who is it?' he called.

'It is me, Effendi.'

'Just a minute, Ishmael.'

Quickly he wiped his eyes on the back of his forearm, placed the letter under his pillow and packed the rifle back into its case. He pushed it under the bed and called, 'Come in, Beloved of the Prophet.'

Ishmael, who was a devout coastal Swahili, came in with a zinc bathtub balanced on his head. 'Welcome back, Effendi. You bring the sun into my heart.' He set the tub in the centre of the floor, then set about filling it with steaming buckets of water. Ishmael whipped a sheet round Leon's neck and began to snip at his dust-caked hair. He then fetched a shaving mug and brush, stropped the long blade of the straight razor and handed it to his master. He held the small hand mirror while Leon scraped his jaw clean.

Leon stripped off, then lowered himself into the steaming bath with a sigh of pleasure. Ishmael gathered up Leon's soiled clothing and carried the bundle away, leaving the door open behind him.

Without knocking, Bobby Sampson ambled in. 'Well, old man, you seem to have got yourself into a bit of a pickle.' Bobby was only a year older than Leon. He was a large, gawky but affable youth, and he and Leon, as the two most junior officers in the regiment, had formed a friendship based on a shared instinct for survival.

Bobby went to the bed, dropped onto it, placed his hands behind his head, and crossed his ankles. 'I'm sure you know by now that Snell is accusing you of all sorts of wrongdoing. Quite by chance, I happen to have with me a copy of the charge sheet.' He reached into his pocket, brought out a crumpled ball of papers, and waved them at Leon. 'I'm impressed with your naughtiness. Trouble is, I've been ordered to defend you. Have you any idea what I'm supposed to be doing?'

'You're supposed to bedazzle the judges with your wit and erudition.' Leon was beginning to feel more cheerful. He enjoyed the way Bobby hid his astute mind behind a bumbling façade. He rose from the bath, splashing soapy water over the floor. Bobby balled up the towel Ishmael had left on the end of the bed and threw it at his head.

'For a start, let's read through the charges together,' Leon suggested.

Bobby brightened. 'Brilliant idea. Always suspected you of being a genius.'

Leon pulled on a pair of khaki trousers. 'Bit short of seating in here,' he said. 'Move your fat arse.'

Bobby sat up, serious now. He made room for his friend on the bed, and Leon settled beside him. Together they pored over the charge sheet.

When the light in the hut faded, Ishmael brought in a lamp and hung it on a hook. They worked in the feeble yellow light until at last Bobby rubbed his eyes and yawned. 'It's well past midnight and you and I have to be in court at nine o'clock. We'll have to call it a day. By the way, would you like to know what I think of your chances of acquittal?'

'Not really,' Leon answered.

'If you offered me odds of a thousand to one, I wouldn't risk twopence ha'penny,' Bobby told him. 'If only we could find this sergeant of yours, the story might have a different ending.'

'Fat chance of that happening before nine o'clock tomorrow. Manyoro's on top of a mountain in Masailand, hundreds of miles away.'

THE OFFICERS' MESS had been converted into a courtroom to house the proceedings. The three judges were seated at the high table on the dais. There were two tables below them, one for the defence and the other for the prosecution. On the outside verandah a small boy heaved on the rope that disappeared into a hole in the ceiling above him, and from there over a series of pulleys to the fan hanging above the judges' table. Its blades whirred monotonously, stirring the hot, languid air into an illusion of cool.

Sitting beside Bobby Sampson at the defence table, Leon studied the faces of his judges. Cowardice, desertion, dereliction of duty and failing to obey the orders of a superior officer: all crimes which carried the maximum penalty of execution by firing squad. His skin prickled. These men held over him the power of life and death.

'Look them in the eye and speak up,' Bobby whispered, holding up his notepad to conceal his lips. 'That's what my old daddy always told me.'

The senior judge, Colonel Wallace, was an Indian Army officer whose expression was sour and dyspeptic. He wore the flamboyant uniform of the 11th Bengal Lancers. There were two rows of decoration ribbons on his chest, his riding boots gleamed, and the tail of his multicoloured silk turban was thrown back over one shoulder.

'He looks a right man-eater,' Bobby whispered, following Leon's gaze. 'He's the one we'll have to convince.'

The adjutant, serving as clerk and court recorder, read the list of charges, then Captain Eddy Roberts came to his feet to open the case for the prosecution. He was Snell's favourite, which was why he had been selected. He spoke clearly and convincingly.

'Damn me, but Eddy's rather good, what?' Bobby fretted.

After his preamble, Roberts called Major Snell, his first witness, to the box. He led him through the charge sheet and had him confirm the details set out in the document. Then he questioned him on the accused's service record and the performance of his duties up to the time when he was sent to guard the *boma* at Niombi. Snell managed to make his lukewarm assessments seem like damning condemnation.

'Lieutenant Courtney is a skilled polo player. He also evinces a passion for big-game hunting. These activities take up much of his time when he might be better employed elsewhere.'

'What about his other behaviour? Have you been made aware of any social scandal surrounding his name?'

Bobby jumped to his feet. 'Objection!' he cried. 'That calls for conjecture and hearsay.'

'I believe that the accused's integrity and moral character have a direct bearing on this case, sir,' said Roberts.

'The objection is denied and the witness may reply to the question,' Colonel Wallace said.

It was what Snell had been waiting for. 'As a matter of fact, the accused recently became involved with a young gentlewoman, a widow. So blatantly scandalous was his behaviour that it brought the honour of the regiment into question. The governor of the colony, Sir Charles Eliot, had little option but to arrange for the lady to be repatriated.'

The heads of the three judges turned to Leon. It was only a few years since the death of the old queen, and the older generation were still influenced by Victoria's strict mores.

After a long pause to let the importance of that testimony register with the judges, Roberts picked up a thick book from the desk in front of him. 'Major Snell, do you recognise this book?'

'Of course I do. It's the battalion order book.'

Roberts opened it and read aloud the extract that covered Leon's orders to take his detachment to Niombi. '*"You are ordered to proceed with utmost despatch . . ."*' He looked up at Snell. 'The accused took eight days to make the journey. Would you consider that he acted "with utmost despatch"?'

'No, I would not.'

'The accused has given as his reason for his tardiness the fact that en route to Niombi he came across the tracks of a rebel war party and felt it his duty to follow them up. Do you think that he would have been able to recognise with any certainty that the tracks had been made by Nandi rebels?'

'I do not. Given Lieutenant Courtney's predilection for hunting it was more likely that the tracks of some animal excited his attention.'

'Objection, Your Honour!' wailed Bobby. 'That is merely conjecture on the part of the witness.'

Before the senior judge could make a ruling Roberts cut in: 'I withdraw the question, sir.' He had placed the thought in the minds of the three judges. He led Snell on through Leon's report. 'The accused states that, with most of his men killed and his sergeant badly wounded, he fought a valiant defence against heavy odds and was only driven out of the *boma* when the rebels set fire to the building.' He tapped the page of the document. 'When that happened he placed the wounded man on his back and, using the smoke from the building as a screen, carried him away. Is this credible?'

Snell smiled knowingly. 'Sergeant Manyoro was a big man. He stood well over six feet. The accused claims that he carried him something like thirty miles without being overtaken by the rebels. I doubt that even such a powerful man as Lieutenant Courtney is capable of such a feat.'

'Then what do you think has happened to the sergeant?'

'I believe that the accused deserted him at Niombi with the rest of his detachment, and made his escape alone.'

'Objection.' Bobby jumped to his feet. 'Conjecture!'

'Objection sustained,' said Colonel Wallace, but he glanced disapprovingly at Leon.

'We have heard evidence that the relief column was unable to find the sergeant's body. How would you account for that?' Roberts asked.

'I must correct you there, Captain Roberts. The evidence is that they were unable to identify the sergeant's body among the dead. They found corpses in the burnt-out building, charred beyond recognition. The other bodies were so badly mauled by vultures and hyena that they also were unrecognisable. Sergeant Manyoro could have been any one of those.'

Bobby cupped his face in his hands and said wearily, 'Objection. Supposition.'

'Sustained. Please stick to factual evidence, Major.' Snell and his favourite exchanged a smug glance.

Roberts went on: 'If Sergeant Manyoro had escaped from Niombi with the assistance of the accused, can you suggest where he is now?'

'No, I cannot.'

'Visiting his mother perhaps, as the accused has stated in his report?'

'In my view that is highly unlikely,' Snell said. 'I doubt that we shall ever see the sergeant again.'

The judges adjourned for a lunch of cold roasted guinea fowl and champagne on the wide verandah of the officers' mess. When they resumed, Roberts continued his examination of Snell until the middle of the afternoon, when he turned to the senior judge. 'No further questions, Your Honour. I have finished with this witness.'

'Do you wish to cross-examine, Lieutenant?' The judge asked Bobby, as he consulted his pocket watch. 'I would like to conclude by tomorrow evening at the latest. We have a ship to catch in Mombasa on Friday evening.' He gave the impression that the verdict was already decided.

Bobby did his best to shake Snell's self-confident mien, but he had so little to work with that the man was able to turn aside his questions in a condescending tone, as though he was speaking to a child.

At last the colonel hauled out his gold watch again and announced, 'Gentlemen, that will do for the day. We will reconvene at nine in the morning.' He led his fellow judges to the bar at the back of the mess.

'I am afraid I didn't do very well,' Bobby said, as he and Leon went out on to the verandah. 'It will all be up to you when you give your evidence.'

ISHMAEL BROUGHT their dinner and two bottles of beer from his lean-to kitchen at the back of Leon's rondavel. There was no chair in the hut, so the two men sprawled on the mud floor as they ate with little appetite and went despondently over their strategy for the morrow.

'I wonder if the Nairobi ladies will think you so dashing and handsome when you're standing against a brick wall wearing a blindfold,' Bobby said.

'Get out of here, you dismal johnny,' Leon ordered. 'I want to get some sleep.' But sleep would not come, and he turned, tossed and sweated until the early hours of the morning.

At last he sat up and lit the lantern. Then, wearing only his underpants, he started for the door and the communal latrine at the end of the row of huts. As he stepped out onto his verandah he almost stumbled over a small group of men squatting at the door. Leon started back in alarm and held the lantern high. 'Who the hell are you?' he demanded loudly. There were five of them, all dressed in the ochre-red Masai *shukas*.

One rose to his feet. 'I see you, M'bogo,' he said.

'Manyoro! What the hell are you doing here?' Leon almost shouted, with rising delight and relief.

'Lusima Mama sent me. She said you needed me. I came as swiftly as I could, with the help of these, my brothers.' He indicated the men behind him. 'We reached Naro Moru siding in two days' march from Lonsonyo Mountain. The driver of the train allowed us to sit on the roof and brought us here at great speed.'

'Mama was right. I have great need of your help, my brother.'

Ishmael had been alerted by their voices and he came staggering with sleep from the shack behind the rondavel. 'Are these Masai infidels causing trouble, Effendi? Shall I send them away?'

'No, Ishmael. Run as fast as you can to Lieutenant Sampson and tell him to come at once. Our prayers have been answered.'

'Allah is great! His beneficence passes all understanding,' Ishmael intoned, then set off for Bobby's hut at a dignified jog.

'Call Sergeant Manyoro to the witness stand!' said Bobby Sampson. A stunned silence fell over the officers' mess as Manyoro limped through the door on a crudely carved crutch, wearing his number-one dress uniform. The regimental badge on the front of his red fez, and his belt buckle, had been lovingly polished until they gleamed like stars. Sergeant Major M'fefe marched behind him, trying unsuccessfully to stop himself grinning. The pair came to a halt in front of the high table, and saluted the judges with a flourish.

'Sergeant Major M'fefe will act as interpreter for those of us with limited Swahili,' Bobby explained. 'Sergeant Major, please ask the witness to state his name and rank.'

'I am Sergeant Manyoro of C Company, 3rd Battalion, 1st Regiment, the King's African Rifles,' Manyoro announced proudly.

Major Snell's face crumpled with dismay. Until that moment he had not recognised Manyoro.

'Your Honour,' Bobby addressed the senior judge, 'may the witness be allowed to give his evidence while seated? He has taken a Nandi arrow through his right leg. As you can see, it has not yet healed properly.'

All eyes in the room went down to Manyoro's thigh, which had been swathed in fresh bandages that morning.

'Of course,' said the senior judge. 'Someone fetch him a chair.'

Everyone was leaning forward with anticipation. Major Snell and Eddy Roberts were exchanging agitated whispers. Roberts kept shaking his head.

'Sergeant, is this man your company officer?' Bobby indicated Leon.

'Bwana Lieutenant, he is my officer.'

'Did you and your troop march with him to Niombi *boma*?'

'We did, Bwana Lieutenant.'

'On the march did you come across any suspicious tracks?'

'Yes. We found where a war party of twenty-six Nandi warriors had come down the Rift Valley wall from the direction of Gelai Lumbwa.'

'How did you know that it was a war party?'

'They had no women or children with them.'

'How did you know they were Nandi and not Masai?'

'Their feet are smaller than ours, and they walk in a different way. They do not step first onto their heel and push off with their toe as a true warrior does. They slap their feet down like pregnant baboons.'

'Where were they headed?'

'Towards the mission station at Nakuru.'

Roberts was looking glum now. 'You told all this to your lieutenant?' Bobby asked. 'He gave you orders to pursue this war party?'

Manyoro nodded. 'We followed them for two days until we came so close that they realised we were after them.'

'Then your officer ordered you to break off the pursuit and go to Niombi. Do you know why he did not decide to engage the enemy?'

'Twenty-six Nandi went off in twenty-six directions. My lieutenant is not a fool. He knew we might catch one if we ran hard. But he also knew that we had frightened them off and they would not continue to Nakuru. He had saved the mission from attack and he would not waste more time.'

'But you had lost almost four days?'

'*Ndio*, Bwana Lieutenant.'

'When you reached Niombi what did you find?'

'Another Nandi war party had raided the *boma*. They had killed the district commissioner, his wife and child.'

The judges leaned forward attentively as Bobby led Manyoro through a description of the desperate fighting that had followed.

'During the fight did you see your lieutenant kill any of the enemy?'

'I saw him kill eight Nandi, but there may have been more.'

'Then you received your wound. Tell us about that.'

'Our ammunition was almost finished. We went out to recover more from our dead *askaris*, lying in the parade ground. Bwana Courtney led the way.'

'What happened then?'

'One of the Nandi dogs shot an arrow at me. It struck me here.' Manyoro showed his bandaged leg.

'Were you able to run with that wound?'

'No. When he saw that I had been struck, Bwana Courtney carried me into the *boma*.'

'You are a big man. He carried you?'

'Bwana Courtney is strong. His Masai name is Buffalo.'

Manyoro described in detail how they had held out until the Nandi set fire to the building, how they had used the cover of the smoke to escape into the banana plantation. 'When we reached the open ground I asked my *bwana* to leave me with his pistol and go on alone.'

'But he refused?'

'He wanted to carry me on his back to the railway line. I told him it was four days' march through Nandi tribal lands. My mother's *manyatta* was only thirty miles distant in Masailand, where Nandi curs would never dare to follow. I told him that if he was determined to take me with him we should go that way.'

'When the two of you reached your mother's village, why did he not leave you and return to Nairobi immediately?'

'His feet were ruined by the march from Niombi. My mother is a famous healer. She treated his feet with her medicine. Bwana Courtney left the *manyatta* as soon as he was able to walk.'

Bobby paused and looked at the three judges. Then he asked, 'Sergeant Manyoro, what are your feelings for Lieutenant Courtney?'

Manyoro answered, with quiet dignity, 'My *bwana* and I are brothers of the warrior blood.'

'Thank you, Sergeant. I have no further questions.'

For a moment there was a hush in the courtroom. Then the colonel roused himself. 'Captain Roberts, do you wish to cross-examine this man?'

Roberts conferred hurriedly with Major Snell, then stood up reluctantly. 'No, sir, I have no questions.'

'Are there any more witnesses? Will you call your client to the stand, Lieutenant Sampson?' Colonel Wallace asked.

'With the court's indulgence, I shall call Lieutenant Courtney. However, I have almost finished and will not detain the court much longer.'

'I am relieved to hear that. You may proceed.'

When Leon took the stand Bobby handed him a sheaf of papers and asked, 'Lieutenant Courtney, this is your official report of the Niombi expedition, which you gave to your commanding officer. Do you affirm under oath that it is correct in every detail?'

'I do.'

'I wish this report to be entered into evidence,' Bobby said.

'It has already been entered,' said Colonel Wallace, testily. 'We have all read it. Ask your questions, Lieutenant, and let's have done with it.'

'I have no further questions, Your Honour. The defence rests.'

'Good.' The colonel was pleasurably surprised. He scowled at Roberts. 'Are you going to cross-examine?'

'No, sir. I have no questions for the accused.'

'Excellent.' Wallace smiled for the first time. 'The witness may stand down, and the prosecution can get on with its summation.'

Roberts stood. 'May it please the court to direct its attention to the written report of the accused, and to Sergeant Manyoro's corroborating evidence. They both confirm that the accused deliberately ignored his written orders to proceed with utmost despatch to Niombi station. I submit that the accused has admitted he was guilty of the charge of deliberately refusing to follow the orders of a superior officer. As for Sergeant Manyoro's slavish endorsement of the accused's actions thereafter, I submit that the witness had been briefed by the defence and that he is in the thrall of the accused. I suggest to you that he would have parroted any words put into his mouth.'

'Captain Roberts, are you suggesting that the witness shot himself in the leg with an arrow to cover up his platoon commander's cowardice?' Colonel Wallace asked.

Roberts sat down as the courtroom exploded with laughter.

'Lieutenant Sampson, do you care to refute the defence's summation?'

Bobby came to his feet. 'Your Honour, we reject not only the entire substance of the summation but we take umbrage at the prosecution's slur on Sergeant Manyoro's honesty. We have full confidence that the court will accept the evidence of a valiant soldier, whose devotion to duty is the very stuff that the British Army is made of.' He looked at each of the three judges in turn. 'Gentlemen, the defence rests.'

'The court will rise to consider its verdict. We will convene again at noon.' Wallace stood up and said to the other two judges, in a clearly audible *sotto voce*, 'Well, chaps, it seems we might yet catch that ship.'

As they filed out of the courtroom Leon whispered to Bobby, ' "The very stuff that the British Army is made of." That was masterly.'

'It was rather, wasn't it?'

'Buy you a beer?'

'Don't mind if you do.'

AN HOUR LATER Colonel Wallace sat at the high table, cleared his throat and began: 'The judgment of this court is as follows. On the charges of cowardice, desertion and dereliction of duty we find the accused not guilty.'

There were murmurs of relief from the defence. Wallace went on sternly, 'Although the court sympathised with the accused's instinct to engage the enemy at every opportunity, we find that when he took up the pursuit of the rebel war party in defiance of his orders to proceed with utmost despatch to Niombi station he transgressed the Articles of War, which require strict obedience to the orders of a superior officer. We therefore find him guilty of disobeying the written orders of his superior officer.'

Bobby and Leon stared at him with dismay and Snell folded his arms across his chest. He leaned back in his chair with a smirk.

'I come now to the sentence. The accused will stand.' Leon came to his feet and snapped to rigid attention. 'The verdict of guilty will be recorded in the service record of the accused. He will be detained until this court rises and immediately thereafter will be returned to duty with the full responsibility and privileges of his rank. God save the King!'

Wallace stood, bowed to the men below him and led his fellow judges to the bar. 'There's time for a peg before our train leaves. I'll have a whisky. What about you chaps?'

As Leon and Bobby headed for the door, they drew level with the table at which Snell was still seated. He stood up and replaced his cap on his head, forcing them to come to attention and salute. After a deliberate pause he returned their salutes. 'I will have fresh orders for you tomorrow morning, Courtney. Be at my office at eight hundred hours sharp.'

'He'll make your life extremely interesting from now onwards,' Bobby muttered, as they went out onto the sunlit parade ground.

M any months later two horsemen rode stirrup to stirrup along the bank of the Athi River. Before them, the wide green expanse of the Athi Plains stretched to the horizon, dotted with herds of zebra, impala and wildebeest. A pair of giraffe stared down at them with great dark eyes as they rode past at a distance of only a hundred paces.

'Sir, I can't stand it much longer,' Leon told his favourite uncle. 'I'll have to put in for a transfer to another regiment.'

'I doubt any would have you, my boy. You have a large black mark on your service record,' said Colonel Penrod Ballantyne, commanding officer of the 1st Regiment, the King's African Rifles. 'What about India? I might put in a word for you with a few friends.'

'Thank you, sir, but I would never dream of leaving Africa,' Leon replied.

Penrod nodded. It was the reply he had expected. He took a silver case from his top pocket and tapped out a Player's Gold Leaf. He put it between his lips and offered one to Leon.

'Thank you, sir, but I don't indulge.' Leon read the engraving on the inside of the lid before his uncle closed it. 'To Twopence, from your adoring wife.' Aunt Saffron's nickname for Penrod had originally been Penny but after all their years of marriage she had decided his value had doubled.

'Well, sir, if no one will have me I'll just have to resign my commission—I've already wasted nearly three years wandering in small circles in the wilderness, at the behest of Major Snell. I can't take any more.'

Penrod smoothed his moustache. 'So, what would you do after you've resigned your commission, if you won't go out to India?'

'I thought I might try my hand at elephant hunting,' Leon said.

'Elephant hunting?' Penrod was incredulous. 'As a profession? As Selous and Bell once did?'

'Well, it's always fascinated me, ever since I read the books about all their adventures.'

'Romantic nonsense! You're thirty years too late. Those old boys had the whole of Africa to themselves. They went where they liked and did as they wanted. Things have changed. Now there are roads and railways all over the place. No country in Africa is still issuing unrestricted elephant licences.'

Leon was crestfallen. 'Well, I don't know what I'm going to do,' he admitted at last.

'Chin up, my boy.' Penrod's tone was kindly now. 'You want to be a hunter? Well, a few men are making a fine living doing just that. They hire themselves out to guide rich men from Europe and America who are willing to pay a fortune for the chance to bag an elephant or two. These days, African big-game hunting is all the rage in high society.'

'White hunters?' Leon's face was bright. 'What a wonderful life that must be.' But then his expression crumpled. 'But how would I get started? I have no money, and I won't ask my father for help.'

'I could take you to see a man I know. He might be willing to help you. He's called Percy Phillips.'

'When can we go?'

'Tomorrow. His base camp is only a short ride out of Nairobi.'

'Major Snell has given me orders to take a patrol up to Lake Turkana. I have to scout out a location to build a fort up there.'

'Turkana!' Penrod snorted. 'Why would we need a fort up there?'

'It's his idea of fun. When I submit the reports he asks for, he sends them back to me with mocking comments scrawled in the margins.'

'I'll have a word, ask him to release you briefly for a special assignment.'

'Thank you, sir. Thank you very much.'

THEY RODE OUT through the barracks gates and down the main street of Nairobi. Although it was early morning the wide, unsurfaced road was crowded and bustling like that of a gold-rush boom town. Sir Charles, the governor of the colony, encouraged settlers to come out from the old country by offering land grants of thousands of acres. The road was almost blocked by their wagons, which were piled high with their possessions and families as they journeyed on to the wilderness.

Penrod and Leon picked their way through the ox wagons and mule teams, leaving the town and riding out along the Ngong Hills until they looked down on a sprawling encampment in the forest. Tents, grass huts and rondavels were spread out under the trees in no particular order.

'This is Percy's base, Tandala Camp.' '*Tandala*' was the Swahili name for the greater kudu. 'He brings his clients up from the coast by railway, and from here he can strike out on foot, on horseback or by ox wagon.'

They rode on down the hill, but before they reached the main camp they came to the skinning sheds where the hunting trophies were prepared and preserved. The stench of drying skins was powerful.

They reined in the horses to watch two men working on the skull of a bull elephant with their axes, chipping away the bone to expose the roots of the tusks. As they watched, one man drew a tusk free of its bony canal. The pair staggered away with it, their skinny legs buckling under the weight. They struggled unsuccessfully to lift the immense ivory shaft into a canvas sling suspended from the hook of a beam scale. Leon slipped out of the saddle, took their burden from them and reached up and placed it in the sling.

'Thanks for your help, young fellow.'

Leon turned. A tall man was standing behind his shoulder. He had the features of a Roman patrician. His short neat beard was silver grey, and his bright blue eyes were steady. There could be no question who this was. Leon knew that Percy Phillips's Swahili name was Bwana Samawati, 'the man with eyes the colour of the sky'.

'Hello, Percy.' Penrod confirmed his identity.

'Penrod, you look fit.' They shook hands.

'So do you, Percy. Hardly a day older than when we last met.'

'You must be wanting a favour. Is this your nephew?' Percy did not wait for the reply. 'What do you think of that tusk, young man?'

'Magnificent, sir. I've never seen anything like it.'

'One hundred and twenty-two pounds.' Percy Phillips read the weight from the scale and smiled. 'The best piece of ivory I've taken in the last many years.' He turned back to Penrod. 'I had my cook bake a batch of ginger snaps for you. I remember your penchant for them.' He took Penrod's arm and, limping slightly, led him towards a large mess tent.

'How did you hurt your leg, sir?' Leon asked, as he fell in with them.

Percy laughed. 'Big old bull buffalo jumped on it thirty years ago when I was still a greenhorn. Taught me a lesson I've never forgotten.'

Percy and Penrod settled in the folding chairs under the flap of the mess tent to bring each other up to date with goings-on in the colony. Meanwhile, Leon looked around the camp with interest. On the periphery of the main camp, on the slope of the hill above it, was a small whitewashed and thatched bungalow which was obviously Percy's home. Not far from it was a Vauxhall truck in terrible condition. Somebody had started to strip the engine down, but seemed to have lost interest.

'Your uncle tells me you want to be a hunter. Is that right?'

Leon turned back to Percy Phillips. 'Yes, sir.'

Percy stroked his silver beard and studied him thoughtfully. Leon did not look away, which Percy liked. Polite and respectful, but sure of himself, he thought. 'Have you ever shot an elephant or a lion?'

'No, sir.'

'Rhino? Buffalo? Leopard?'

'Afraid not, sir.'

'What have you taken, then?'

'Just a few Tommies and Grants for the pot, sir, but I can learn.'

'At least you're honest. What *can* you do? Give me a good reason why I should offer you a job.'

'Well, sir, I could mend that.' Leon pointed to the truck. 'I have one of the same make and model,' he went on. 'It was in similar condition to yours when I got it. I put it back together and now it runs like a Swiss watch.'

Percy showed immediate interest. 'Does it, by God? Damn motors are a complete mystery to me. What else? Can you shoot?'

'Yes, sir.'

'Leon won the Governor's Cup at the regimental rifle competition at the beginning of the year,' Penrod confirmed. 'He can shoot, I'll vouch for that.'

'Paper targets are not live animals. They don't bite you or jump on you if you miss,' Percy pointed out. 'If you want to be a hunter you'll need a rifle. I am not talking about a little service Enfield. Have you got a real rifle?'

'Yes, sir. A Holland & Holland Royal .470 Nitro Express.'

Percy's blue eyes widened. 'They don't come better than that,' he conceded. 'But you'll also need a tracker. Can you find a good one?'

'Yes, sir.' He was thinking of Manyoro, but then he remembered Loikot. 'Actually, I have two.'

Percy gazed at a brilliant gold and green sunbird flitting about in the branches above the tent. Then he seemed to make up his mind. 'You're lucky. It just so happens that I am going to need help. I'm to lead a big safari early next year. The client is an extremely important person.'

'This client of yours, could he be Theodore Roosevelt, the President of the United States?' Penrod asked innocently.

Percy was startled. 'In the name of all that's holy, Penrod, how on earth did you discover that? Nobody's supposed to know.'

'The US State Department sent a cable to the Commander in Chief of the British Army, Lord Kitchener, in London. They wanted to know more about you before the President hired you. I was on Kitchener's staff in South Africa during the war, so he telegraphed me,' Penrod admitted.

Percy burst out laughing. 'You're a sly creature, Ballantyne. Here I was believing that Roosevelt's visit was a state secret! So you put in a good word for me. It seems I'm in your debt.' He turned back to Leon. 'Here's what I'll do. I'm going to make you prove yourself. First, I want you to put that heap of rubbish together and get it running.' He nodded at the truck.

'Yes, sir.'

'When you've done that, you'll take your .470 and your two trackers and go out there and bag an elephant. I could never employ a hunter who's never hunted. When you've done that, I want you to bring back the tusks to prove it.'

'Yes, sir.' Leon grinned.

'Have you ten pounds to buy a game licence?'

'No, sir.'

'I'll lend it to you,' Percy offered, 'but the ivory will be mine.'

'Sir, lend me the money and you can have the pick of one tusk. I'll keep the other.'

Percy chuckled. The lad could fight his own corner. He was no pushover. He was beginning to enjoy him. 'Fair enough, boy.'

'If you take me on, what will you pay me, sir?'

'Pay you? I'm doing your uncle a favour. You should pay me.'

'How about five shillings a day?' Leon suggested.

'How about one shilling?' Percy countered.

'Two?'

'You drive a hard bargain.' Percy shook his head sadly but put out his hand. Leon shook it vigorously. 'You won't regret it, sir, I promise you.'

'YOU'VE CHANGED MY LIFE. I'll never be able to repay you for what you've done for me today.' Leon was elated as they rode back towards Nairobi.

'You needn't worry too much about that. You don't think for one minute that I'm doing this because I'm your doting uncle?'

'I misjudged you, sir.'

'This is how you will repay me. First, I'm not going to accept your resignation from the regiment. Instead I shall transfer you to the reserves, then second you to military intelligence to work under my direct orders.'

Leon's face showed his dismay. 'Sir?' he responded cautiously.

'There are dangerous times ahead. Kaiser Wilhelm of Germany has more than doubled the strength of his standing army in the last ten years. He has huge colonies in Africa, but they are not enough for him. Dar es Salaam is their port. They could have a warship there in very short order. They already have a full regiment of *askaris* led by German officers at Arusha and in ten days' march they could be in Nairobi. I have pointed this out to the War Office in London, but they have concerns elsewhere and don't wish to spend money reinforcing an unimportant backwater of the Empire.'

'This comes as a shock to me, sir. The Germans down there have always been very friendly towards us,' Leon protested. 'And the Kaiser is the grandson of Queen Victoria. Our king is his uncle. I cannot believe we would ever want to go to war with him.'

'Trust the instinct of an old warhorse.' Penrod smiled knowingly. 'I'm going to keep a sharp eye on our lovable southern neighbours.'

'How do I fit in?'

'At this stage our borders with German East Africa are wide open. There is no restriction of movement in either direction. I want you to set up a network of informers, tribesmen who move regularly in and out of German East Africa. You will play a clandestine role. Not even Percy Phillips must know what you're up to. As a hunter you'll have the perfect cover story to move freely. You will report directly to me.'

Leon thought for a moment. His uncle's plans sounded exciting. 'If there are questions, I could let it be known that the informers are my game scouts, that I'm using them to keep an eye on the movements of the game herds, especially the elephant bulls, so that I know their exact position at any time and can take our clients straight to them,' he suggested.

Penrod nodded. 'That should satisfy Percy and anybody else who asks. Just don't mention my involvement or it will be all around the club the next time he has a few drinks. Percy is hardly the soul of discretion.'

A FEW WEEKS LATER Leon was spending almost every waking hour lying under Percy's truck, his arms coated to the elbows with black grease. He had seriously underestimated the enormity of the task. He had been working on the engine for ten days when he woke one morning to find

Sergeant Manyoro squatting outside his tent. He was not dressed in his khaki uniform and fez but in an ochre-red *shuka*, and carried a lion spear. 'I have come,' he announced.

'I see you have.' Leon had difficulty in hiding his delight. 'But why aren't you in barracks? They'll shoot you for desertion.'

'I have paper.' Manyoro brought out a crumpled envelope from under his *shuka*. Leon opened it and read quickly. Manyoro had been honourably discharged from the KAR on medical grounds. Although the leg wound had healed he had been left with a limp that rendered him unfit for duty.

'Why have you come to me?' Leon asked. 'Why did you not return to your *manyatta*?'

'I am your man,' Manyoro said simply.

'I cannot pay you yet.'

'I did not ask you to,' Manyoro replied. 'What do you want me to do?'

'First, we are going to mend this *enchini*, engine.' For a moment they contemplated the sorry spectacle of the vehicle. 'Then we are going to kill an elephant,' Leon added.

'The killing will be easier than the mending,' was Manyoro's opinion.

ALMOST THREE WEEKS later Leon sat behind the steering wheel while, with an air of resignation, Manyoro took up his position in front of the truck. He had lost all faith in the eventual success of the manoeuvres he had performed repeatedly over the last three days.

'Retard the spark! Throttle open. Mixture rich!' Leon rotated the control knob until the indicator pointed straight ahead. 'Choke.' He jumped out, ran to the front of the vehicle and pulled on the choke ring, then returned to the driver's seat. 'Manyoro, prime the carb!'

Manyoro spat on his right palm, gripped the crank handle and swung it.

There was an explosion like a cannon shot and a spurt of blue smoke flew from the exhaust pipe. There was a shouted oath from Percy's bungalow and he stumbled out onto the stoep in his pyjama bottoms. He stared in momentary confusion at Leon, who was beaming with triumph behind the steering wheel. The engine rumbled, shook and backfired, then settled down into a loud, clattering beat.

Percy laughed. 'Let me get my trousers on; then you can drive me to the club. I'm going to buy you as much beer as you can drink. Then you can go and find that elephant.'

L eon stood below the familiar massif of Lonsonyo Mountain. He pushed his slouch hat to the back of his head and moved the heavy rifle from one shoulder to the other. He gazed up at the crest of the mountain and picked out a single lonely figure on the skyline. 'She's waiting for us,' he exclaimed in surprise. 'How did she know we were coming?'

'Lusima Mama knows everything,' Manyoro reminded him, and started up the steep path towards the summit. He carried the water bottles, the canvas haversack, Leon's light .303 Lee-Enfield rifle and four bandoliers of ammunition. Leon followed him, and Ishmael brought up the rear.

When they reached the mountaintop Lusima was waiting for them in the shade of a flowering seringa tree. She rose to her feet, tall and statuesque, and greeted them. 'I see you, my sons, and my eyes are gladdened.'

'Mama, we come for your blessing on our weapons and your guidance in our hunting,' Manyoro told her, as he knelt before her.

THE NEXT MORNING the entire village gathered in a circle round the wild fig tree, the council tree, to witness the blessing of the weapons. Leon and Manyoro squatted with them. Leon's two rifles were laid side by side on a tanned lion skin. Beside them stood calabash gourds filled with fresh cow's blood and milk, and baked-clay bowls of salt, snuff and glittering glass trade beads. Lusima emerged from the low door of her hut. The congregation clapped and began to sing her praises,

Lusima wore her full ceremonial regalia. Her *shuka* was thickly embroidered with a shimmering curtain of beads and cowrie shells. Her skin was oiled with red ochre, shining in the sunlight, and she carried a fly switch made from the tail of a giraffe. She circled the display of rifles and sacrificial offerings. 'Let not the quarry escape the warrior who wields these weapons,' she intoned, as she sprinkled a pinch of snuff over them. 'Let blood flow copiously from the wounds they inflict.' She dipped the switch into the gourds and splashed blood and milk onto the rifles. Then she went to Leon and flicked the mixture over his head and shoulders. 'Give him strength and determination to follow the quarry. Let the mightiest elephant fall to the voice of his *bunduki*, his rifle.'

She began to dance in a tight circle, pirouetting faster and faster. When she threw herself flat on the lion skin in front of Leon, her eyes rolled back and white froth bubbled from the corners of her mouth.

'The spirit has entered her body,' Manyoro whispered. 'She is ready to speak with its voice. Put the question to her.'

'Lusima, favourite of the Great Spirit, your sons seek a chief among the elephants. Where shall we find him? Show us the way to the great bull.'

Lusima's head rolled from side to side and she spoke in a hoarse, unnatural voice: 'Follow the wind and listen for the voice of the sweet singer. He will point the way.'

She gave a deep gasp and sat up. Her eyes refocused and she looked at Leon as though seeing him for the first time.

'I don't understand,' Leon said. 'Who is the sweet singer?'

'That is all the message I have for you,' she said. 'If the gods favour your hunt, then in time the meaning will become clear to you.'

SINCE LEON'S ARRIVAL on the mountain Loikot had followed him round at a discreet distance. Now as Leon sat beside the campfire with a dozen of the villager elders, Loikot was in the shadows behind him, listening attentively.

'I wish to know the movements of men and animals throughout Masailand and down the full length of the Rift Valley, even beyond the great mountains of Kilimanjaro and Meru. I want to know only about strangers, the white men and especially the Bula Matari and their *askaris* soldiers.' They were the Germans. The name meant 'breakers of rock' for the earliest German settlers had been geologists. 'I want to know where the Bula Matari build walls or dig ditches in which they place their *bunduki mkuba*, their great guns. I want this information gathered and sent to me as swiftly as possible.'

The village elders listened to his request, then discussed it animatedly, everyone coming up with a different opinion. Finally the spokesman of the group, a toothless ancient, closed the council with the words 'We will think on all these things.' They rose and filed away to their huts.

When they were gone a small voice piped out of the darkness, 'They will talk and then they will talk some more. All you will hear from them is the sound of their voices. It would be better to listen to the wind in the trees.'

'That is great disrespect to your elders, Loikot,' Manyoro scolded him.

'I am a *morani*, and I choose carefully those to whom I give my respect.'

Leon laughed. 'Come out of the darkness, my fine warrior friend, and let us see your brave face.' Loikot came into the firelight and took his seat between Leon and Manyoro.

'Loikot, when we travelled together to the railway line you showed me the tracks of a big elephant. Have you seen that elephant since then?'

'When the moon was full I saw him as he browsed among the trees close to where I was camped with my brothers, three days' journey from here.'

'It has rained heavily since then,' Manyoro said. 'The tracks will have been washed away. By now the bull might be as far south as Lake Manyara.'

'Where should we begin the hunt if not at the place where Loikot last saw him?' Leon wondered.

'We should follow the wind as Lusima counsels,' said Manyoro.

The next morning, as they descended the pathway down the mountain, the breeze came from the west. It blew soft and warm down the Rift Valley wall and across the Masai savannah. When the party reached the valley floor they turned and went with the wind, moving swiftly through the open forest at a steady jog trot. Manyoro and Loikot were picking over the myriad game tracks that dotted the earth. Ishmael fell back until he was far behind.

They went on until Loikot picked out elephant spoor. 'One very old cow,' he opined. 'So old that the pads of her feet are worn smooth.'

An hour later Manyoro pointed to fresh spoor. 'Here passed five breeding cows. Three have their unweaned calves at heel.'

Just before the sun reached its meridian Loikot, who was in the lead, stopped suddenly and pointed out a mountainous grey shape in a patch of sweet thorn forest far ahead. It was a very large bull, feeding on a low bush, his back turned to them. They came up softly behind him, closing in until Leon could count the wiry hairs in his worn tail. Leon slipped the big double rifle off his shoulder.

This was the closest Leon had ever been to an elephant, and he was awed by its sheer size. It seemed to blot out half the sky. Suddenly the bull swung round and flared his ears wide. He stared directly at Leon from a distance of a dozen paces. Dense lashes surrounded small rheumy eyes, and tears had left dark runnels down his cheeks. Slowly Leon lifted the rifle to his shoulder, but Manyoro squeezed his shoulder, urging him to hold his fire.

One of the bull's tusks was broken off at the lip, while the other was worn down to a blunt stump. Leon realised that Percy Phillips would cover him with scorn if he brought them back to Tandala Camp. Yet the bull seemed poised to charge and Leon might be forced to fire. Night after night over the past weeks, Percy had sat with him in the lamplight and lectured him on the skills required to kill one of these gigantic animals with a single bullet.

'The elephant is a particularly difficult animal to tackle. Remember that its brain is a tiny target. You have to know exactly where it is from any angle. If he turns or lifts his head, your aiming point changes. The mistake that gets the novice killed is that he shoots too high, and his bullet goes over the top of the brain.'

Now Leon realised, with dismay, that he was faced with a creature that could crush every bone in his body with a single blow of its trunk. If the bull came at him, he would be forced to try to kill it.

Suddenly the bull shook his head so violently that his ears clapped thunderously against his shoulders. Leon swung the rifle to his shoulder, but the beast wheeled away and disappeared at a shambling run among the trees.

Leon's legs felt weak and his hands were trembling. Understanding of his own inadequacy had been thrust rudely upon him. He knew now why Percy had sent him out to be blooded. This was not a skill that could be learned from a book or from hours of instruction. This was trial by the gun and failure was death.

Manyoro offered him one of the water bottles. He had gulped down three mouthfuls before he noticed that the two Masai were studying his face. He smiled unconvincingly.

'Even the bravest of men is afraid the first time,' Manyoro said. 'But you did not run.'

THEY HALTED in the blazing noon and found shade under the spreading branches of a giraffe thorn tree while they waited for Ishmael to catch up and prepare the midday meal.

Loikot squatted in front of Leon and frowned, which signalled that he had something of importance to impart. 'M'bogo, this is verily the truth that I will tell you,' he began.

'I am listening, Loikot. Speak and I will hear you.'

'It is of no value to talk to those old men as you did two nights ago. They see nothing beyond the walls of their *manyatta*. If you want to know what is happening in all the world, you must ask us.'

'Tell me, Loikot, who do you mean by "us"?'

'We are the guardians of the cattle, the *chungaji*. We move through the land with the cattle. We see everything. We hear everything.'

'But tell me, Loikot, how do you know what the other *chungaji*, who are many days' march distant, see and hear?'

'It is possible,' Loikot assured him. 'We speak to each other. At sunset this evening I will speak to my brothers and you will hear it.'

They ate kebabs of ostrich liver grilled over coals of camel-thorn acacia. Then, bellies filled, they slept for an hour in the shade. When they awoke, they shouldered rifles and packs and went with the wind until the sun was no more than a hand's spread above the horizon.

'We must go to that hilltop,' Loikot told Leon, pointing to a pimple of volcanic rock that stood out directly in their path. The boy scrambled ahead to the summit and stared down the valley. Shaded blue with distance, three enormous bastions of rock thrust up towards the southern sky. 'Loolmassin, the mountain of the gods.' Loikot pointed out the most westerly peak as Leon came up beside him. Then he turned to the east and the two larger peaks. 'Meru and Kilimanjaro, the home of the clouds. Those mountains are in the land that the Bula Matari call their own but which has belonged to my people since the beginning of time.' The peaks were more than a hundred miles on the far side of the border, deep inside German East Africa.

'I will speak to my brothers of the *chungaji*. Hear me!' Loikot filled his lungs, cupped his hands round his mouth and let out a high-pitched, singsong wail. Three times Loikot called, then sat down beside Leon and wrapped his *shuka* round his shoulders. 'There is a *manyatta* beyond the river.' He pointed out the darker line of trees that marked the riverbed.

Leon calculated that it was several miles away. 'Will they hear you at such a distance?'

'You will see,' Loikot told him. 'The wind has dropped and the air is still. When I call with my special voice it will carry that far and even further.'

They waited. Below them, a small herd of kudu moved through the thorn scrub, their shapes ethereal as drifts of smoke.

'Do you still think they heard you?' Leon asked.

'They have heard me,' Loikot said, 'but they are climbing to a high place from which to reply.'

At the foot of the hillock Ishmael had lit a small fire and was brewing tea in a small, smoke-blackened kettle. Leon watched him, thirstily.

'Listen!' said Loikot, and threw back his cloak as he sprang to his feet.

Leon heard it then, coming from the direction of the river. It sounded like a faint echo of Loikot's original call. Loikot cupped his hands and sent his high, singsong cry ringing back across the plain. He listened again to the reply, and the exchange went on until it was almost dark.

'It is finished. We have spoken,' Loikot declared at last, and led the way down the hill to where Ishmael had set up camp for the night. While they ate their dinner of ostrich steaks, Loikot relayed to Leon the gossip he had learned from the *chungaji*. He began a recitation that went on for several minutes, a catalogue of births, marriages, lost cattle and other such matters.

'Did you ask if any white men are travelling at the moment in Masailand?' Leon asked. 'Any Bula Matari soldiers with *askaris*?'

'The German commissioner from Arusha is on tour with six *askaris*. They are marching towards Monduli. There are no other soldiers in the valley.'

'Any other white men?'

'Two German hunters with their women and wagons are camped in the Meto Hills. They have killed many buffalo and dried their meat.'

The Meto Hills were at least eighty miles away, and Leon was amazed at how much information the boy had gathered from across such a wide area. He had read the old hunters' accounts of the Masai grapevine. This network must cover the entire Masai country. He smiled into his mug: Uncle Penrod now had his eyes along the border. 'What about elephant? Did you ask your brethren if they had seen any big bulls in this area?'

'There are many elephant, but mostly cows and calves. The *chungaji* saw a very large bull near Namanga, but that was many days ago and no one has seen him since. They think he might have gone into the Nyiri Desert where there is no grazing for the cattle so none of my people are there.'

'We must follow the wind,' said Manyoro.

'Or you must learn to sing sweetly for us,' Leon suggested.

BEFORE DAWN, when Leon woke, he saw that Ishmael already had the kettle on the fire and the two Masai were stirring. He squatted close enough to the flames to feel their warmth. There was a chill in the air. 'There is no wind,' he told Manyoro.

'Perhaps it will rise with the sun.'

'Should we go on without it?'

'Which way? We do not know,' Manyoro pointed out. 'We have come this far with my mother's wind. We must wait for it to come again to lead us on.'

Leon felt disgruntled. He had pandered long enough to Lusima's clap-trap. He had a dull ache behind his eyes. Ishmael handed him a mug of coffee but even that did not have its usual therapeutic effect. He was about to say something to Manyoro when he was distracted by a loud, rattling call, which sounded like a box of small pebbles being shaken vigorously. They all looked up with interest. Everyone knew which bird had made the sound. A honeyguide was inviting them to follow it to a wild beehive. When the men raided it they would take the honey, leaving the beeswax and the larvae for the honeyguide. It was a symbiotic arrangement that, down the ages, had been faithfully adhered to by man and bird. It was said that if anybody failed to pay the bird its due, the next time it would lead him to a venomous snake or a man-eating lion.

Leon stood up and the drab brown and yellow bird flashed from the top branches of the tree and began to display. Its wings hummed and resonated as it dived and pulled up, then dived again.

'Honey!' said Manyoro greedily. No African could resist that invitation.

'Honey, sweet honey!' Loikot shouted.

The last vestige of Leon's headache vanished and he grabbed his rifle. 'Hurry! Let's go!'

The honeyguide saw them following and darted away, whirring and rattling excitedly. For the next hour Leon trotted steadily after the bird. He had said nothing of it to the others, but he could not shake off the haunting idea that the bird was Lusima Mama's 'sweet singer'.

A little before noon they reached a dry riverbed. The forest along either bank was thicker and the trees taller, fed by subterranean waters. Before they reached the watercourse the honeyguide flew to the top of one of the tallest trees and waited for them there. As they came up, Manyoro cried out in delight and pointed at the tree trunk. 'There it is!'

Like swift golden dust motes in the sunlight, Leon saw the flight of the bees homing in on the hive where, three-quarters of the way up, the trunk forked into two heavy branches.

Hurriedly, Ishmael started a small fire. When it was ready, Manyoro scooped some coals into a bark tube and gave it Loikot, who proceeded to climb with amazing agility up to the tree fork. He took the bark tube and blew a jet of smoke from it into the hive. The bees swarmed briefly, then dispersed, and he extracted the comb, holding it up for them to see. 'Thanks to the skills of Loikot, you will eat your fill today, my friends.' They laughed.

'Well done!' Leon shouted.

Loikot brought out five more combs, each hexagonal cell filled to the brim with dark brown honey, and sealed with a lid of wax. He packed them gently into the folds of his *shuka*.

'Do not take it all,' Manyoro cautioned him. 'Leave half for our little winged friends or they will die.'

Loikot had been taught that when he was still a child and did not reply. He dropped the smoke tube to the base of the tree and slithered down the trunk, jumping the last six feet to land lightly on his feet.

They sat in a circle and divided the combs. In the branches above, the honeyguide hopped and chirruped to remind them of their debt.

Carefully Manyoro broke off the edges of the combs where the cells were filled with white bee larvae and laid the pieces on a large green leaf. He carried the larvae-filled pieces of honeycomb a short distance away, and placed them carefully in an opening in the scrub. As soon as he turned away, the bird flew down to partake of the feast.

Now the men were free to taste the spoils. Sitting round the pile of golden combs they broke off pieces, and stuffed them into their mouths, murmuring with pleasure as they chewed the honey out of the cells.

Leon had never tasted honey like this dark, smoky variety with such intense sweetness that he gasped at the shock. He swallowed and exhaled as sharply as though he had gulped down a dram of Highland whisky.

Half a comb was enough for him. He rocked back on his heels, stood up and left the others to their gluttony. He picked up his rifle and sauntered idly into the bush, heading for where he thought the riverbed might be. The vegetation became thicker as he went deeper into it until he pushed his way through the last screen of branches and found himself on the bank. It had been cut back by flood water into a sheer wall that dropped six feet to a bed of fine white sand a hundred paces wide, trampled by the paws and hoofs of the animals that had used it as a highway.

On the far bank a massive wild fig tree's twisting roots had been exposed. Beneath its spreading branches the white sand had been heaped into large mounds. Scattered around them were several pyramids of elephant dung. He jumped from the top of the bank and set off across the riverbed. When he reached the mounds he realised that the elephant had been digging for water.

There were eight open seep holes. He went to each in turn to examine the tracks. Having been instructed by three grandmasters of the trade—Percy Phillips, Manyoro and Loikot—he had learned enough bushcraft to read them accurately. The shape and size of the footprints that the elephant had left around the first four seeps proved them to have been cows.

When he came to the fifth there was only one set of tracks. They were so large that his first glimpse of them made him pause in mid-stride. He hurried forward and dropped to his knees beside the prints of the front feet. He laid the twin barrels of his rifle across the pad print to gauge its size, and whistled softly. His barrels were two feet long, and the diameter of the footprint was only two inches less. Applying Percy Phillips's formula, he calculated that this bull must stand more than twelve feet high at the shoulder, a giant among giants.

Leon jumped up and ran back across the riverbed. He scrambled up the cut bank and pushed his way through the undergrowth to where his three companions were huddled over the last scraps of honeycomb. 'Lusima Mama and her sweet singer have shown us the way,' he told them. 'I have found the spoor of a great bull elephant in the riverbed.' The trackers snatched up their kit and ran after him.

'M'bogo, this is the bull that I showed you the first time we travelled together,' Loikot exclaimed, as soon as he saw the spoor. 'I recognise him. This is a paramount chief of all the elephants.'

Manyoro shook his head. 'He is so old he must be ready to die. Surely his ivory is broken and worn away.'

'No! No!' Loikot denied it vehemently. 'His tusks are as long as you are, Manyoro, and thicker even than your head!' He made a circle with his arms.

Manyoro laughed. 'My poor little Loikot, you have been bitten by blow-flies, and they have filled your head with maggots.'

Loikot bridled and glared at him. 'And perhaps it is not the elephant but you who has become old and senile. We should have left you on Lonsonyo Mountain, drinking beer with your decrepit cronies.'

'While you two exchange compliments, the bull is walking away from us,' Leon intervened. 'Take the spoor, and let us settle this debate by looking upon his tusks and not merely on the marks of his feet.'

AS SOON AS THEY HAD followed the spoor out of the riverbed, and into the open savannah, it became obvious that the bull elephant had been thoroughly alarmed by the sound of axe blows and their voices as they had raided the beehive.

'He is in full flight.' Manyoro pointed out the length of the bull's strides. 'If he keeps up this pace, by sunrise tomorrow he will be over the top of the escarpment and deep into the desert.'

Loikot grinned cheekily at Leon. 'Pay him no heed, M'bogo. Follow me, and before sunset I will show you tusks that will amaze your eyes.'

But the spoor ran on straight and unwavering. After another hour even Loikot was beginning to wilt. When they stopped for a few minutes to drink and stretch out in the shade they were all quiet and subdued. They knew how far they had dropped behind the bull elephant. Leon stood up. Without a word the others came to their feet. They went on.

The spoor ran on. The bull was moving so fast that when it crossed areas of loose earth it kicked spurts of dust forward with each long stride. When Leon looked up at the sun his heart sank. There was no more than an hour of daylight left, no possibility of finding the elephant before darkness.

He was still gazing up at the sky so he bumped into Manyoro, who had stopped abruptly in his path. Both Masai were poring over the earth. They looked up at Leon and, with hand signals, urged him to remain silent. They were both grinning and their eyes shone.

Manyoro indicated the altered spoor with an eloquent, graceful gesture.

Leon grasped that a little miracle had taken place. The bull had slowed, his pace had shortened, and he had turned aside from his determined flight towards the eastern escarpment of the valley. Manyoro pointed to a grove of *ngong* nut trees a quarter of a mile to their right. He leaned over to Leon and placed his lips close to his ear. 'At this season the trees are in fruit. He has smelled the ripe nuts and cannot resist them. We will find him in the grove. There is still no wind. We can move straight in towards him.'

With the two Masai still leading, they crept forward, moving from one patch of cover to the next. They reached the nearest *ngong* tree. The ground was littered with fallen nuts. They followed the bull's huge pad marks to the next tree, where he had fed again, then moved on once more. This time he had headed towards a shallow depression, above which only the tops of the nut trees showed. They crept forward until they could look down into it.

At the same instant all three saw the enormous black mass of the bull elephant, three hundred paces away, standing in the shade of one of the largest nut trees. He rocked gently from one forefoot to the other, ears fanning lazily, trunk draped nonchalantly over the curve of the only visible tusk. The other was hidden from view by his massive bulk, but Leon stared at the one he could see, hardly able to believe its length and girth.

Leon broke open the barrels of his rifle and removed the fat brass cartridges from the breeches one by one. He examined them for blemishes, polishing them on his shirt before slipping them back into place. He snapped the barrels shut, then nodded to Manyoro and, as they moved forward, Leon took the lead. He angled towards the bull until the tree trunk covered his approach, then turned straight towards it. He moved in steadily, setting down each footstep with exaggerated care. He knew that to be completely certain of his shot he had to get closer. He wanted to reach the trunk of the nut tree and fire from behind its cover.

Now he was so close that he could see the oxpeckers scrambling round on the elephant's wrinkled grey skin. There were five or six of the little yellow birds foraging in the creases of the skin for ticks and insects. Suddenly, they became aware of Leon and ran up the bull's flanks to stand in a line along his spine, staring with glittering eyes at the intruder.

Manyoro tried to warn Leon of what was about to happen but Leon did not see the desperate hand signals. He was still a dozen paces from the *ngong* tree when the row of oxpeckers on the bull's back exploded into flight, uttered their frenzied alarm call. It was a warning that the beast understood well, for the birds were not only his grooms but also his sentinels.

He plunged forward, reaching his top speed in half a dozen strides and heading at a thirty-degree angle away from Leon. For a second Leon was stunned by the speed and agility of the massive creature. Then he raced forward in pursuit, aiming to get ahead of him. For a short distance he gained ground, closing to just under the critical thirty-yard range. He slammed to a halt and fastened his eyes on the bull's head.

All his attention was concentrated on the long slit of the earhole in the centre of the swaying head. The rifle came up to his shoulder and he looked over the barrels, his vision sharp as a diamond drill. He saw beyond the moving wall of grey skin; he saw the brain. It was an extraordinary sensation—Percy Phillips had called it the hunter's eye.

The rifle crashed, and even in the sunlight he saw the flame spurt from the muzzle. He had not been aware of touching the trigger. He hardly felt the recoil of 5,000 pounds of energy kicking back into his shoulder. He saw the bullet strike two inches behind the earhole, precisely where he knew it should go. The bull threw back his head, long tusks pointing for an instant at the sky. Then his front legs folded under him and he collapsed into a kneeling position. The force of the impact sent up a cloud of dust and made the ground tremble beneath Leon's feet. The elephant lay on his folded front legs, head supported by the curves of the tusks, sightless eyes wide open.

'It's the dead elephant that kills you.' He heard Percy's warning in his memory. 'Always put in the *coup de grâce*.' Leon raised the rifle again and aimed for the crease in the bull's armpit. Again the rifle boomed. The beast never so much as twitched as the second bullet drove through its heart.

Leon walked forward slowly and reached out to touch the staring amber eye with a fingertip. It did not blink. His legs felt soft and limp. He sank down, leaned his back against the elephant's shoulder and closed his eyes. He felt nothing. He was empty inside. He felt no sense of triumph or elation, no remorse or sorrow for the death of such a magnificent creature. All that would come later. Now there was only aching emptiness.

LEON SENT MANYORO and Loikot off to some distant villages outside the boundaries of Masailand. Their task was to recruit porters to carry the ivory to the railway. They had to be from some tribe other than Masai, for the *morani* would not stoop to such menial employment.

Leon and Ishmael camped for five days upwind from the putrefying carcass. They guarded the tusks while they waited for them to loosen with rot in their bone canals. The nights were raucous as the scavengers gathered. Jackals yipped, and packs of hyena shrieked and squabbled among themselves. On the third night the lions arrived and added their imperial roaring to the general cacophony.

On the sixth day Manyoro and Loikot returned, followed by a gang of Luo porters whom Manyoro had hired to carry the tusks to the railway.

Leon led the porters to where the remains of the carcass lay and he helped them extract the tusks. When they laid them side by side on a bed of fresh green leaves Leon was amazed by their length and lovely symmetry. Once again he used the barrels of his rifle as a gauge to measure them. The longest of the two was a hand's breadth over eleven feet, and the lesser was almost exactly eleven feet.

Under Manyoro's direction the Luo cut two long poles of acacia wood and strapped each tusk to one. With a porter at each end they lifted the poles and started towards the railway, the remainder of the team trotting behind them, ready to spell them as they tired.

They waited for the night train from Lake Victoria and under cover of darkness they loaded the tusks onto one of the slow-moving goods trucks as it climbed up the escarpment from the floor of the Rift Valley. They clambered up onto the roof and Leon tossed a canvas purse of shillings down to the headman. The porters shouted thanks and farewells until they were left in the darkness behind the guard's van. The locomotives puffed gamely to the top of the escarpment.

It was still dark when they dropped the tusks and their baggage over the side of the truck and jumped from the rolling train as it slowed before steaming into Nairobi station.

P ercy Phillips was eating his breakfast in the mess tent when they staggered into Tandala Camp, bowed under the weight of the tusks. 'Upon my soul!' he spluttered into his coffee, knocking over his chair as he sprang to his feet. 'Those aren't yours, are they?'

'One is.' Leon kept a straight face. 'Unfortunately, sir, the other is yours.'

'Take them to the scale. Let's see what we have here,' Percy ordered.

The entire staff of the camp trooped after them to the skinning shed and gathered around the scale as Leon lifted the smaller tusk into the sling.

'One hundred and twenty-eight pounds,' said Percy, noncommittally. 'Now let's try the other.'

Leon hoisted the second into the sling and Percy blinked. 'One hundred and thirty-eight.' Percy's voice cracked a little. It was the largest tusk that had ever been brought into Tandala Camp.

Percy said to Manyoro, 'Put both tusks into the truck.' Then he looked at Leon and his eyes twinkled. 'All right, young fella, you can drive me into the club. I'm about to buy you a drink.'

As the vehicle bounced and rattled over the track, Percy had to raise his voice to be heard above the racket of the engine. 'Rightyho! Tell me all about it. How many shots did it take you to put him down?'

'One brain shot. And then I remembered your advice and put in a finisher when he was down.'

Percy nodded his approval. 'Now tell me the rest.'

As he listened, Percy was impressed with Leon's account. One of the most important duties of a white hunter was to entertain his clients. They wanted more than to simply mow down a few animals: they were paying a fortune to take part in an unforgettable adventure. The hunters who were dour and taciturn never had a return client.

This lad was willing and eager. He was modest, charming and tactful. He was articulate. People liked him. Percy smiled inwardly. Hell, even I like him.

When they reached the club Percy made him park the truck directly in front of the main doors. He led Leon into the long bar where a dozen regulars had already taken their seats. 'Gentlemen, I want you to meet my new apprentice, and then I'm going to take you outside and show you a pair of tusks. And I do mean a pair of tusks!'

When they trooped out to the front of the building they found that the news had already flashed through the town, and a small crowd was gathered round the truck. Percy invited them all into the bar.

At the end of the evening Percy was carried feet first into the billiard room and laid on the green baize of the table. Leon reached the front seat of the truck, where he passed what remained of the night.

He woke with an abominable headache.

'Good morning, Effendi.' Ishmael was standing beside the truck with a steaming mug of black coffee in his hand. It revived Leon sufficiently for him to call for Manyoro. Between them they were able to start the truck and drive down the main street to the headquarters of the Greater Lake Victoria Trading Company. Below the name on the board: *Prop. Mr Goolam Vilabjhi Esq.* was written: '*Dealer in gold, diamonds, ivory carvings and curios, and all manner of natural produce.*'

The proprietor hurried to meet Leon as he entered through the front door, carrying the lesser tusk. Mr Vilabjhi was a plump little man with a beaming smile. 'By golly, Lieutenant Courtney, for me this is a great honour.'

'Good morning, Mr Vilabjhi, but I am no longer a lieutenant,' Leon told him, as he laid the tusk on the counter.

'But you are still the greatest polo player in Africa, and I have heard that you have become a mighty *shikari*. What is more, I see you bring proof of that.' He shouted to Mrs Vilabjhi in the back of the store, asking her to bring coffee and sweetmeats, then ushered Leon between rows of heavily laden shelves into his tiny book-lined office. 'Please be seated, kindest sir.'

Mrs Vilabjhi bustled in with the coffee tray. When she had filled the glasses with the thick black liquid, her husband shooed her away and turned to Leon. 'Now, tell me, Sahib, what is your pleasure?'

'I want to sell you that tusk.'

'Alack and alas, revered Sahib, I will not purchase that ivory from you.'

Leon looked startled. 'Why the hell not?'

Mr Vilabjhi laughed. 'Sahib, if I buy that tusk I will send it to England to be made into the keys of a piano or carved into pretty billiard balls. Then one day when you are an old man you will think back on what I did with your trophy and you will say, "Ten thousand curses on the head of that infamous scoundrel Mr Goolam Vilabjhi Esquire!"'

'On the other hand, if you do not buy it I will call down a hundred thousand curses on your head right now,' Leon warned him. 'Mr Vilabjhi, I need the money and I need it badly.'

'Ah! Money, she is like the tide of the ocean. She comes in and she goes out. But a tusk like that you will never see again in all your existence.' He posed a moment longer in thought, then raised one finger and touched his temple. 'Eureka! I have it. You will leave the tusk with me as security, and I will loan you the money you require. You will pay me interest at twenty per cent per annum. Then one day, when you are the most famous *shikari* in Africa you will come back and repay the debt. Then I will return your magnificent tusk to you, and we will be lifelong friends until the day we die!'

'Mr Goolam Vilabjhi Esquire, I call down ten thousand blessings on your head.' Leon laughed. 'How much can you let me have?'

'I hear that the weight of that tusk is one hundred and twenty-eight pounds.'

'My God! How did you know that?'

'Every living human creature in Nairobi knows it already.' Mr Vilabjhi cocked his head to one side. 'At fifteen shillings a pound I am able to advance you ninety-six pounds sterling in gold sovereigns.'

Leon blinked. That was the most money he had ever held at one time.

Manyoro and Ishmael were still waiting outside the front of the store when Leon left. He paid them the wages he owed them. 'What are you going to do with all that money?' he asked Manyoro.

'I shall buy three cows. What else, Bwana?' Manyoro shook his head at such a foolish question. To a Masai, cattle were the only real wealth.

'What about you, Ishmael?'

'I am going to send it to my wives in Mombasa, Effendi.' Ishmael had six, the maximum that the Prophet allowed.

Leon and Manyoro drove out to the stock yards on the town outskirts.

'Manyoro, I wish to send a cow to Lusima Mama to thank her for her help in the matter of the elephant.'

'Such a gift is customary, Bwana,' Manyoro agreed.

'Nobody is a finer judge of cattle than you, Manyoro. When you have chosen your own beasts, pick one out for Lusima Mama.' That cost Leon another fifteen pounds, for Manyoro selected the best animal in the yard.

Before Manyoro set off to return to Lonsonyo Mountain, Leon gave him a canvas bag of silver shillings. 'This is for Loikot. If he keeps talking to his friends and brings the news to us, there will be many more bags of shillings. Soon he will have enough to buy himself a fine cow. Now go, Manyoro, and return swiftly. There is much work for us to do.'

Driving the cows ahead of him, Manyoro took the rutted track that led down into the Rift Valley. He turned and shouted back to Leon, 'Wait for me, my brother, for I shall return in ten days' time.'

Leon drove back to the club to pick up Percy Phillips. He found him slumped in one of the armchairs on the wide stoep overlooking the sun-parched lawns. He was in a foul mood. His eyes were bloodshot, his face as wrinkled as the khaki bush jacket in which he had passed the night. 'Where the hell have you been?' he growled at Leon and, without waiting for an answer, stumped down the steps to the truck. He climbed into the front seat and did not speak again until they were bumping down the final section of the track into Tandala Camp.

'I managed to have a few words with your uncle Penrod last evening. He had received a cable from the American State Department. The now former President of the United States of America and his entire entourage will be arriving in Mombasa in two months' time aboard the luxury German steamship *Admiral* to begin the grand safari. We must be ready for them.'

When they parked in front of the mess tent Percy shouted for tea to be brought. Two mugs of the brew restored his good humour.

'Now, here is a broad picture of what this safari will involve,' he began. 'Apart from the former President there will be his son, and his guests, Sir Alfred Pease, Lord Cranworth and Frederick Selous.'

'Selous!' Leon exclaimed. 'He's a legend. I was weaned on his books.'

Percy nodded and went on: 'Roosevelt has taken on five white hunters other than myself. The ones I know well are Judd, Cunninghame and Tarlton, all fine fellows. I understand from Penrod that there will be more than twenty naturalists and taxidermists from the Smithsonian Institute, the museum that is partially sponsoring the safari. The American Associated Press is sending out a separate safari of journalists that will shadow ours closely all the way, sending back copy to New York.'

'That means our safari will be a party of more than thirty people. There will be a small mountain of baggage, equipment and supplies to deal with.'

'Indeed,' Percy agreed. 'The initial estimate from New York is that they will be shipping out about ninety-six tons. They intend to do much of the hunting on horseback. Roosevelt wants a string of at least thirty horses. That is one of your fields of expertise, so I am putting you in charge of the horse lines. You will have to recruit a team of reliable grooms to take care of them.' He paused. 'Lord Delamere is lending us his chef from the Norfolk Hotel. There will be four or five sous-chefs. I will sign on your man Ishmael to work in the camp kitchens. Oh, and by the way, Cunninghame will be recruiting around a thousand native porters to carry the baggage and provisions for the safari. I told him last night that you were fluent in Swahili and that you would be happy to help him with the job.'

'Did you mention that I would also be pleased to help him with the actual hunting?' Leon asked innocently. He gave Percy his most winning smile.

Percy had difficulty preventing himself smiling back. He liked it more and more that the lad could take what he handed out without whining. 'There will be well over a thousand mouths to feed. Under the game laws of the colony, buffalo are classed as vermin. There is no limit on the numbers that can be shot. One of your jobs will be to keep the safari in meat. You will have all the hunting your heart could desire. That I promise.'

Two months and six days later the German passenger liner SS *Admiral* steamed into the deep-water harbour that served as a port for the coastal town of Mombasa. At her mainmast head she flew Old Glory and at her foremast the black eagles of the Kaiser's Germany. On the foredeck the band blared out 'The Star-Spangled Banner' and 'God Save the King'. The beach was crowded with spectators and government dignitaries, headed by the governor of the territory and the commander of His Britannic Majesty's forces in British East Africa.

Lying out in the deep water, a flotilla of barges waited to ferry the passengers to the beach. Former President Colonel Teddy Roosevelt and his son were first to climb down into one of the waiting boats.

The governor had placed his private train at the disposal of Roosevelt and his entourage. As soon as they were all safely aboard, the large crowd burst into a chorus of 'For He's a Jolly Good Fellow'. Teddy Roosevelt stood plump and beaming on the balcony of the leading carriage and acknowledged the cheers as the driver blew his whistle and the train pulled away at the start of the journey up-country to Nairobi.

One hundred miles inland the train halted at Voi siding, the southernmost extent of the vast plains that lay between the Tsavo and Athi rivers. A wooden bench had been built as a viewing platform over the cowcatcher at the front of the locomotive. Teddy Roosevelt and Frederick Selous climbed up and settled themselves on the bench. Selous was the most revered of all the African hunters, and a naturalist and the author of many books.

While the train puffed across the plains of Tsavo, the two great men huddled together in conversation, discussing the wonders that lay around them. As darkness fell they retired to the comfort of the governor's carriage. When the train pulled into Nairobi station the following morning the entire population was on the platform to catch a glimpse of the former president.

Leon Courtney was not one of this multitude. For the last six weeks he had been setting up supply dumps along the safari's intended route.

RELUCTANTLY, PERCY PHILLIPS had given Leon an assistant. Leon had been horrified by his choice. 'Hennie du Rand?' he protested. 'I know him. He's an Afrikaner Boer from South Africa. The fellow fought against us in the war. He rode with the commando of the notorious Koos de la Rey. God knows how many Englishmen Hennie du Rand has shot.'

'The Boer War ended several years ago,' Percy pointed out. 'Hennie's a true bushman, and he has shot more elephant and buffalo than any other man I know. He's a good motor mechanic too. He can help you with the trucks.'

'But—' said Leon.

'No more ifs or buts. Hennie's your assistant.'

In just the first few weeks, Leon discovered that not only was Hennie an indefatigable worker but he knew a great deal more about motor maintenance and bushcraft than Leon did, and was happy to share this knowledge with him. He was over forty, lean and sinewy. His beard was grizzled, and his face and arms were darkly sunburned. He spoke with a strong Afrikaans accent. '*Ja, my jong Boet,*' he told Leon, after they had run down a herd of buffalo on foot and killed eight fat young heifers with as many shots. 'Yes, my young friend. It seems we're going to make a hunter of you yet.'

With the help of Manyoro and four other men they skinned, gutted and quartered the carcasses, then loaded them into the two trucks and delivered them to within half a mile of the main camp of the safari. This was as close as Percy would allow the vehicles. He did not want his clients to be disturbed by the sound of engines.

Later, when they were alone, Leon and Hennie parked the old Vauxhall under a tree and rigged a block and tackle from the main branch. They hoisted the truck's rear and between them began removing the differential, which had been emitting an alarming grinding sound.

They looked up at the sound of approaching hoofbeats. The rider was a young man in jodhpurs and a wide-brimmed hat. He dismounted and hitched his horse, then sauntered up to where they were working.

'Hello there. What are you up to?' he drawled, with an American twang.

Leon looked him up and down. His riding boots were expensive, and his khakis were freshly washed and ironed. His face was pleasant, and his smile was friendly. It struck Leon that the two of them were almost the same age: twenty-two at most.

'We're having a spot of bother with this old bus,' Leon told him.

The stranger grinned. '"Having a spot of bother with this old bus,"' he repeated. 'God, I love that Limey accent. I could listen to it all day.'

'What accent?' Leon mimicked him. 'I ain't got no accent. Now you, you got a funny accent.' They burst out laughing.

The stranger held out his hand. 'My name's Kermit. I love to tinker with autos. I've got a Cadillac back home.'

Leon took his hand. 'I'm Leon, and this ragamuffin is Hennie.'

'Mind if I sit awhile?'

'If you're a famous mechanic you can lend a hand. How about pulling out that rack and pinion? Grab a spanner.'

They all worked in silent concentration for a few minutes; then Leon asked, 'Are you part of this great Barnum and Bailey circus?'

Kermit laughed delightedly. 'Yeah, I suppose I am.'

'What's your job? Are you from the Smithsonian Institute?'

'In a manner of speaking. Mostly I just sit around and listen to a bunch of old men talking about how things were much better in their day,' he replied.

'Sounds like great fun.'

'Did you guys shoot the buffalo that was brought into camp this morning?'

'It's part of our job to keep the camp in meat.'

'Now that really sounds like fun. Mind if I tag along next time you go out?' Leon and Hennie exchanged a glance. Then Leon asked carefully, 'What calibre of a rifle do you have?'

Kermit went to his horse and drew the weapon from under the saddle flap. He came back and handed it to Leon.

'A .405 Winchester. I hear it's a good buffalo rifle but that it kicks,' Leon said. 'Can you shoot it worth a damn?'

'I reckon.' Kermit took the weapon back. 'I call it Big Medicine.'

'All right. Meet us here at four in the morning the day after tomorrow.'

AT FOUR IN THE MORNING it was still dark. Leon and Hennie drove up to the rendezvous in two of the camp vehicles, with the skinners and trackers, but Kermit was waiting for them. Leon was impressed. He had doubted that he would show up.

They followed a game trail through the remaining hours of darkness and into the next day. By the end of the day, there were nine dead buffalo and Kermit believed he'd shot three of them. 'That was the best fun I ever had.' Kermit was grinning broadly.

Leon was amused by Kermit's childlike jubilation. He could not bring himself to tell him that he and Hennie had worked with machine-like rapidity to finish off any animal Kermit had wounded. Instead he laughed with him. 'Well done, Kermit!' He punched his shoulder. 'That was some shooting. I've never seen anything like it.'

Kermit grinned at him ecstatically. Not for a moment did Leon realise that with a tiny white lie his life had changed for ever.

THE FOLLOWING MORNING, after they had breakfasted, the trackers and skinners loaded the bloody buffalo joints into the trucks and then sat in the back themselves. Kermit cajoled Leon into letting him drive one truck and Hennie followed in the second.

Once again Kermit's mood was carefree and Leon found him a pleasant companion. They were both passionate about horses, motor cars and hunting. Although Kermit did not elaborate, he hinted that he had a father who was rich and powerful and dominated his life.

'My father was just the same,' Leon told him.

'So what did you do?'

'I said, "I respect you, Dad, but I cannot live under your rules." Then I left home and joined the army. That was four years ago. I haven't been back since.'

'Son of a gun! That must have taken some guts. I often wish I could do that, but I know I never will.'

Leon found that the better he came to know Kermit, the more he liked him. During the conversation he discovered that Kermit was a keen naturalist and ornithologist. He told Kermit to stop the truck whenever he spotted some interesting insect, bird or small animal to show him.

Hennie kept going and disappeared into the distance ahead.

They were only a few miles from the camp when, suddenly and unexpectedly, two men stepped out of the bush into the track in front of them. One was armed with a large camera and tripod.

'Damn it to hell! The gentlemen of the fourth estate,' Kermit muttered.

The tallest of the two strangers hurried to the driver's side. 'Excuse me, gentlemen.' He smiled ingratiatingly. 'May I ask you a few questions? Are you connected to the Roosevelt safari, by any chance?'

'Mr Andrew Fagan of the Associated Press, I presume, to paraphrase Dr David Livingstone.' Kermit pushed his hat back and returned the smile.

The journalist recoiled in astonishment, then peered more closely at him. 'Mr Roosevelt Junior!' he exclaimed. 'Please forgive me. I didn't recognise you in that get-up.' He was staring at Kermit's filthy, blood-stained clothing.

'Mr Who Junior?' Leon demanded.

Kermit looked embarrassed, but Fagan hastened to reply. 'Don't you know who you're riding with? This is Mr Kermit Roosevelt, the son of the former President of the United States.'

Leon turned accusingly to his new friend. 'You didn't tell me!'

'You didn't ask.'

'You might have mentioned it,' Leon insisted.

'It would have changed things between us. It always does.'

'Who is this young friend of yours, Mr Roosevelt?' Andrew Fagan asked.

'This is my hunter, Mr Leon Courtney.'

'He looks very young,' Fagan observed dubiously.

'You don't have to grow a long grey beard to be one of the greatest hunters in Africa,' Kermit told him.

'. . . greatest hunters in Africa!' Fagan scribbled shorthand on his pad. 'How do you spell your name, Mr Courtney? With one *e* or two?'

'Just one.' Leon glared at Kermit. 'Now see what you've got me into.'

'I guess you've been out hunting.' Fagan pointed at the head of the bull buffalo in the back of the truck. 'Who shot that creature?'

'Mr Roosevelt did. It's a Cape buffalo, *Syncerus caffer*.'

'It's huge! Can we have some photographs, please, Mr Roosevelt?'

'Only if you give us a couple of copies. One for Leon and one for me.'

'Of course. Bring your guns. Let's have one of you on each side of the horns.' The photographer set up his tripod and arranged the pose. Kermit looked composed and debonair, Leon as though he was facing a firing squad. The flash powder exploded in a cloud of smoke.

'OK! Great! Now can we have that tribesman in the red robe in the picture? Tell him to look fierce.'

'This mad fool thinks you're dressed like a woman,' Leon told Manyoro in Maa, and Manyoro scowled murderously at the photographer.

'Great! God, that's so great!'

It was another half an hour before they were able to drive on.

'Does that happen all the time?' Leon asked.

'You get used to it. You have to be nice to them or they write all sorts of garbage about you.'

'I still think you should have told me who your father is.'

'Can we hunt together again? They've given me an old fellow called Mellow as my hunter. He lectures me as though I'm a schoolboy.'

Leon thought about it. 'In two days' time the main camp is moving on up to the Ewaso Ng'iro River. I have to ferry the tents and heavy equipment up there ahead of it. But I'd like to hunt again with you if my boss gives me a chance. You're not a bad fellow despite your lowly antecedents.'

'Who's your boss?'

'A gentleman called Percy Phillips.'

'I know him. He often dines with my father and Mr Selous. I'll do what I can. I don't think I can take much more of Mr Mellow.'

FATE PLAYED into Kermit's hands. Two nights after the grand safari moved into the camp on the south bank of the Ewaso Ng'iro River, the chef Lord Delamere had loaned to Roosevelt prepared a banquet to celebrate American Thanksgiving Day. There was no turkey so Roosevelt himself shot a giant Kori bustard. The chef roasted the bird and concocted a stuffing that contained spiced buffalo liver.

The next morning half the men in camp were struck down by virulent diarrhoea—the buffalo liver had deteriorated in the heat. Even Roosevelt, he of the iron constitution, was affected. Frank Mellow, Kermit's hunter, was one of the worst stricken, and ordered to the hospital in Nairobi.

Kermit, who had not eaten the stuffing, seized his advantage: he negotiated the appointment of his replacement hunter with his father through the door of the long-drop outhouse to which Roosevelt was confined. He put up only token resistance to his son's proposal.

That evening Leon was called into Percy's tent.

'I don't know what you've been up to, but Kermit Roosevelt wants you to replace Frank Mellow as his hunter and has talked his father into allowing it.' He glared at Leon. 'You aren't yet dry behind the ears. You haven't dealt with lion, leopard or rhino, and I told the President so. But he's sick and didn't want to listen. Kermit Roosevelt is a wild and reckless young rascal, just like you. If you get him hurt, I'll never have another client, and I'll strangle you slowly with my bare hands. Do you understand?'

'Yes, sir, I understand.' Leon began to leave, but Percy stopped him.

'Leon!'

He turned back in surprise. Percy had never before called him by his first name. Then, with even greater surprise, he saw that Percy was smiling. 'This is your big chance. You'll never have another like it. If you're lucky and clever, you'll be on your way to the top. Good luck.'

THE NEXT DAY Leon and Kermit rode out, not seeking any particular quarry but ready to take on whatever the day brought.

Manyoro was trotting ahead of the horses, but suddenly pulled up and leaned on his spear, waiting for the horsemen to come up. He pointed ahead across the open plain at the huge dark shape that stood on the edge of a clump of bush.

'Rhino. From here it looks like a big bull.' Leon fished his binoculars out of his saddlebags. He focused the lenses and studied the distant shape. 'It's a rhino, all right, and the biggest one I've ever seen.'

'Bigger than the one my father shot five days ago?'

'I'd say much, much bigger.'

'I want it,' said Kermit, vehemently.

'So do I,' Leon agreed. 'We'll circle out under the wind and stalk him from those bushes.'

'You sound just like Frank Mellow. You want me crawling round on my hands and knees. I've had enough of that. I'm going to show you how the old frontiersmen used to hunt bison back out west. Follow me, pardner.' With that, he clapped his heels into the flanks of his mare and bounded away across the plain, galloping straight at the distant animal.

'Kermit, wait!' Leon shouted after him. 'Don't be a fool.' But Kermit did not glance back. 'Percy's right. You're a wild and reckless rascal,' Leon lamented, as he urged his own horse in pursuit.

The rhino heard them coming but his eyesight was so weak that he could not place them immediately. He switched his whole massive body from side to side, kicking up dust and snorting ferociously.

'Yee-ha!' Kermit let out a cowboy yell.

Guided by the sound, the rhino focused on the shape of horse and rider and instantly burst into a charge, coming directly at them. Kermit stood high in the stirrups, raised his rifle and fired from the back of the galloping horse. His first bullet flew high over the rhino's back. He reloaded and fired again. Leon heard the meaty thump of the bullet slapping into the beast's body but the rhino did not even flinch as he tore in to meet the horse.

Kermit's next wild shot missed again. He fired once more, and Leon heard this shot tell on the grey hide. The bull bucked in agony and tossed his horn high, then lowered it expectantly to gore the horse as they came together.

But Kermit was too quick for him. With the skill of an expert polo player, Kermit used his knees to turn his horse across the line of the charge. Horse and rhino passed each other in opposite directions, and although the latter hooked at Kermit with his long horn, the point flashed a hand's breadth past his knee. At the same time Kermit leaned out from the saddle and fired with the muzzle almost touching the grey hide between the bull's shoulders. As the rhino received the bullet he bucked again. He swung round to chase after the horse, but now bloody froth dribbled from his open mouth and he slowed to a walk. The great head hung low, and he staggered unevenly from side to side.

Coming up at a gallop, Leon was appalled by the brutal display. It ran contrary to every concept he had of the fair chase and the humane kill. Up to this moment he had been unable to intervene for fear of hitting Kermit or his mount, but now his field of fire was clear. The wounded rhino was less than thirty paces away, and Kermit was well out on the flank reloading his rifle. Leon sprang to the ground, bringing up the Holland as he landed. He aimed for the point where the rhino's spine joined the skull, and his bullet cleaved the vertebrae like the blade of an executioner's axe.

Kermit rode up to the carcass and dismounted. His eyes sparkled. 'Thanks for your help, pardner.' He laughed. 'By God! That was really exciting! How did you like the Wild West style of hunting? Grand, isn't it?' He showed not the least guilt or remorse for what had just happened.

Leon had to take a breath to keep his temper. 'It was wild, I'll give you that. I'm not so sure about the grand bit,' he said, his voice level. 'I dropped my hat.' He swung up into his saddle and rode back for it.

What do I do now? he wondered. Do I tell him to find himself another hunter? He saw the hat on the ground ahead, rode up to it and dismounted. He picked it up and dusted it against his leg. Then he jammed it on his head. Be sensible, Courtney! If you walk away, you're finished.

He mounted and rode slowly back to where Kermit stood beside the dead rhino, stroking the long black horn.

Kermit looked up at Leon as he dismounted, his expression thoughtful. 'Something bothering you?' he asked quietly.

'I was worrying about how your father is going to feel when he sees that horn. It must be damn nigh five feet long. I hope he won't turn bright green.' Leon succeeded in keeping his smile natural.

Kermit relaxed visibly. 'I can't wait to show it to him.'

Leon glanced up at the sun. 'It's late. We won't be able to get back to the main camp this evening. We'll stay here tonight,' he said neutrally.

Ishmael had been following them on one mule and leading another, which carried the cooking pots and other necessities. As soon as he came up he set about putting together a rudimentary fly camp.

Before it was fully dark he brought their dinner to them. They leaned back against their saddles with the enamel plates balanced on their laps and tucked into the yellow rice and Tommy buck stew.

Leon put the last spoonful into his mouth. Still chewing, he looked over at Kermit.

'Let's suppose for the moment that I am your fairy godmother,' Leon suggested, 'and that I can grant you any wish. What would it be?'

Kermit pondered for only a few seconds. 'How big was that elephant my father got a few days ago?'

'Ninety-four and ninety-eight.'

'I want to do better.'

'You worry a lot about doing better than him. Is this a competition?'

'My father has always succeeded in everything. Hell, he was a war hero, a state governor, a hunter and sportsman all before he turned forty, and as if that wasn't enough, he became the youngest President of America ever. He respects winners and despises losers.'

'You think your father despises you?'

'No. He loves me but he doesn't respect me. I want his respect more than anything else in the world.'

'You've just taken a bigger rhino than he has.' They looked across at the enormous carcass.

'That's a start; however, knowing my father, he'd put much more value on an elephant or a lion. Find one of those for me, Fairy Godmother.'

Manyoro was sitting at the other fire with Ishmael, and Leon called across to him, 'Come to me, my brother. There is something of importance we must discuss.' Manyoro got up and came to squat across the fire from him. 'We need to find a big elephant for this *bwana*.'

'We have given him a Swahili name,' Manyoro said. 'We have named him Bwana Popoo Hima.'

Leon laughed.

'What's so funny?' Kermit asked.

'You have been honoured,' Leon told him. 'Manyoro at least respects you. He has given you a Swahili name. Bwana Popoo Hima.'

'That sounds disgusting,' Kermit said, suspicious.

'It means "Sir Quick Bullet".'

'Popoo Hima! Hey! Tell him I like that!' Kermit was pleased. 'Why did they choose that name?'

'They're very impressed by the way you shoot.' Leon turned back to Manyoro. 'Bwana Popoo Hima wants a very big elephant.'

'Every white man wants a very big elephant. But we must go to Lonsonyo Mountain to seek the counsel of our mother.'

'Kermit, the advice I have from Manyoro is that we go to a Masai witch doctor on a mountaintop. She will tell us where to find your elephant.'

It was late in the day when they stood under the towering mass of Lonsonyo Mountain, and dark before they rode into the *munyatta* and dismounted in front of Lusima's hut. She had heard the horses and stood tall in the doorway with the firelight behind her.

Leon walked across to her and went down on one knee. 'Give me your blessing, Mama,' he asked.

'You have it, my son.' She touched his head. 'My motherly love is yours.'

'I have brought another petitioner to you.' Leon stood up and beckoned Kermit forward. 'His Swahili name is Bwana Popoo Hima.'

'So this is the prince, the son of a great white king.' Lusima looked closely into Kermit's face. 'He is a twig of the mighty tree, but he will never grow as tall as the tree from which he sprang. There is always one tree in the forest that grows taller than any other.' She smiled kindly at Kermit. 'These things he knows in his heart, and it makes him feel small and unhappy.'

Even Leon was amazed at her insight. 'He longs desperately to earn his father's respect,' he agreed.

'So he comes to me to find him an elephant.' She nodded. 'In the morning I will bless his *bunduki*, his weapon, and point the way of the hunter for him. But now you will feast with me.'

THEY GATHERED AT NOON the next day under the council tree. Kermit's rifle, Big Medicine, lay on the lion skin. The sacrificial offerings had been set out. Leon and Kermit squatted at the head of the lion skin with Manyoro and Loikot behind them.

Lusima emerged from her hut, magnificent in her finery. She squatted in front of Leon and Kermit and asked the ritual questions: 'Why do you come to my mountain? What is it you seek from me?'

'We beg you to bless our weapons,' Leon replied. 'We beseech you to divine the path that the great grey men take through the wilderness.'

Lusima rose and sprinkled the rifle with blood and milk, snuff and salt. 'Make this weapon as the eye of the hunter that it may slay whatever he looks upon. May his *popoo* fly straight as the bee returning to the hive.'

Then she went to Kermit and, with the giraffe-tail switch, sprinkled the blood and milk on his bowed head. 'He has the heart of the hunter. Let him follow his quarry unerringly. May it never escape his hunter's eye. If he waits on the hilltop the hunter will be thrice blessed.'

Leon whispered the translation to Kermit, and after each sentence she spoke, they clapped and said the refrain to her prayer: 'Even as she speaks, let it be so.'

MAMA LUSIMA'S PREDICTION was fulfilled and Kermit shot three elephant with Big Medicine the next day. Manyoro assembled a gang of porters from the nearby Samburu villages to take the tusks back to the base encampment on the Ewaso Ng'iro River. On the return march they made a detour to pick up the cached rhino head. The long file of porters was carrying an impressive array of big-game trophies as they approached the camp.

They were still several miles short of the river when they saw a group of horsemen riding towards them from the direction of the camp.

'I bet this is my dad coming to find out what I've been doing.' Kermit was grinning in anticipation.

Leon brought up his binoculars and studied them. 'Hold on! That isn't your father. It's that newspaper fellow and his cameraman. How the hell did they know where to find us?'

'I reckon they have an informer in our camp.'

Andrew Fagan rode up and lifted his hat. 'Good afternoon, Mr Roosevelt,' he called. 'Are those elephant tusks that your men are carrying? I had no idea they grew so large. Those are gigantic. I offer you my heartiest congratulations. May I have a closer look at your trophies?'

Leon called to the porters to lay down their burdens. Fagan dismounted and went to inspect them, exclaiming with amazement. 'I'd love to listen to your account of the hunt, Mr Roosevelt,' he said, 'if you could spare me the time. My readers would be fascinated to hear of your adventures.'

An hour later Fagan and his cameraman had finished, and the photographer had exposed several dozen flash plates of the hunters and their trophies. Fagan was eager to get back to his typewriter. He intended to send a galloper to the telegraph office in Nairobi with his copy.

Leon and Kermit rode into the main camp on the river in the late afternoon. Nobody was expecting them. Roosevelt was sitting under a tree outside his tent, reading. With a bemused air he regarded the uproar that his son's arrival had created. The entire personnel of the camp, almost a thousand strong, was hastening from every direction to greet the returning hunters. They crowded round them for a closer look at the tusks and the rhino head.

Teddy Roosevelt laid aside his book, stood up from his chair, tucked in his shirt over the bulge of his belly and came to find the cause of the commotion. The crowd parted deferentially to allow him through.

Kermit jumped from the saddle to greet his father. They shook hands warmly and Roosevelt took his son's arm. 'Well, my boy, I was starting to worry about you. Now you'd better show your old man what you've brought home.' The two went to where the porters had laid out their bundles for inspection. Leon was still mounted and close enough to Roosevelt to have a clear view of his face over the heads of the crowd.

He saw mild, indulgent interest give way to astonishment as Roosevelt counted the tusks lying on the ground. Then astonishment gave way to dismay as he took in the size of the ivory shafts. He dropped Kermit's arm and walked slowly down the line of trophies. Leon saw his dismay harden to envy. He realised that for him to have reached his position of eminence he must be one of the most competitive men on earth. He was accustomed to ranking first in any company. Now, for once, he had been outshone by his son.

At the end of the line Roosevelt stood with his hands clasped behind his back. He frowned heavily. Then he smiled as he turned to Kermit.

Leon was filled with admiration for how swiftly he had controlled his emotions.

'Splendid!' said Roosevelt. 'These tusks beat anything we already have, and almost certainly anything we'll get before the end of the expedition.' He seized Kermit's hand again. 'I'm proud of you, really and truly proud.'

Over Roosevelt's shoulder, Leon could see Kermit's face. It glowed.

Roosevelt held his son at arm's length, beaming into his face. 'I'll be damned if I haven't sired a champion,' he said. 'I want to hear all about it at dinner.' He looked across at Leon. 'I'd be pleased if you'd join us for dinner as well, Mr Courtney. Shall we say seven thirty for eight?'

WHILE LEON USED his straight razor on the dark stubble that covered his jaws, Ishmael filled the bath almost to the brim with hot water. When Leon stepped out of it, his body glowing, a set of crisply ironed khakis lay on Leon's bed and beneath it stood a pair of mosquito boots, polished to a gloss.

A short time later, Leon set off towards the circus-sized mess tent, determined not to be late for the dinner. As he passed Percy Phillips's tent the familiar voice hailed him. 'Leon, come in here for a minute.'

He stooped through the fly to find Percy sitting with a glass in his hand. He waved it to indicate the empty chair across the floor from where he sat. 'Take a pew. The former President keeps a dry table.' He pointed at the bottle on the table beside Leon's chair. 'You'd better fortify yourself.'

Leon poured himself two fingers of single malt. He tasted it. 'Elixir! I could get addicted to this stuff.'

'You can't afford it. Not yet anyway.' Percy raised his glass to Leon. 'Mud in your eye!' he said.

'Up the Rifles!' Leon returned. They savoured the fragrant liquor.

Then Percy said, 'By the way, did I congratulate you on your recent spectacular successes?'

'I cannot recall you doing so, sir.'

'Damn me, I could have sworn I did. I must be getting old.' His eyes twinkled. 'You earned your spurs today. I'm damned proud of you.'

'Thank you, sir.' Leon was deeply moved.

'In future you can drop the "sir", and make it Percy.'

'Thank you, sir.'

'Percy, just plain Percy.'

'Thank you, Plain Percy.'

They drank in companionable silence for a while. Then Percy went on, 'I suppose you know I'll turn sixty-five next month?'

'I'd never have thought it.'

'The hell you wouldn't. You probably thought I was well over ninety. This is probably not the time to bring up the subject, but I feel myself slowing down. Nowadays every mile I walk feels like five. I need some help round here. I was thinking of taking on a partner. A junior partner.'

Leon nodded cautiously, waiting to hear more.

Percy took the silver hunter watch from his pocket and snapped open the engraved lid, studied the dial, closed the lid, drained his glass and stood up. 'It would never do to keep the former President of the United States of America waiting for his dinner.'

There were ten for dinner in the big tent. Freddie Selous and Kermit had the seats of honour on each side of the former President. Leon was placed at the foot of the table, in the chair furthest from his host.

Teddy Roosevelt was a born raconteur, his knowledge encyclopedic, his intellect monumental, his enthusiasm infectious and his charm irresistible. He held the company spellbound as he carried them from one subject to another, from politics and religion to ornithology and philosophy, tropical medicine to African anthropology. Leon let the eland steak on his plate grow cold as he listened with rapt attention to him.

Suddenly the former President singled him out. 'My son likes to hunt with you, Mr Courtney. He tells me that the two of you have made plans to build upon your recent triumphs over elephant and rhinoceros.'

'I am delighted that Kermit wishes to continue hunting with me, sir. I enjoy his company immensely.'

'What is your next quarry to be?'

'Kermit wants to take a good lion.'

'Cheeky young devil!' He punched Kermit's shoulder playfully. 'Not content with beating me at jumbo and rhino, now you want to make it three in a row!' The company laughed with him and Teddy Roosevelt went on, 'OK, buddy, you're on! Shall we have ten dollars on it?' Kermit and his father shook hands to seal the bet.

Leon walked with Percy as they made their way back to their tents. 'I'm impressed, Leon. It seems to me that you've managed to set both feet securely on the ladder to the stars. Just as long as you don't get Teddy Roosevelt's son bitten by a lion. They're devilishly dangerous creatures.'

THEY SPENT the following day hastily assembling the personnel and equipment. They picked out a string of six ponies, and three pack mules. Then, with the high spirits of schoolboys escaping the surveillance of their headmaster, Leon and Kermit rode northwards, camping the first evening beside a small waterhole. They rolled into their blankets as soon as they had eaten, and both men were asleep within minutes.

In the wee hours Leon shook Kermit awake. He sat up groggily. 'What's happening? What time is it?'

'Don't worry about the time, just listen,' Leon told him.

Kermit looked round and saw that the two Masai and Ishmael were sitting by the fire. They had fed it with wood chips and the flames danced brightly. Their faces were intent and rapt. They were listening.

Suddenly the night was filled with sound, a mighty bass booming, rising and falling. It made the skin tingle and the hair rise on the back of the neck. Kermit threw aside his blanket and sprang to his feet.

'What the hell was that?' Kermit gasped.

'A lion. A big dominant male lion proclaiming his kingdom,' Leon said.

They stretched out again beside the fire, prepared to sleep when another thunderous roar echoed through the night.

'Listen to him!' Kermit murmured. 'The son of a gun's inviting me out to play. How can I sleep with that racket going on?' The last sawing grunts died into silence, and then came another sound, almost a distant echo of the first roar, far away and faint. They shot upright, and the Masai exclaimed.

'What the hell was that?' Kermit asked. 'It sounded like another lion.'

'That's exactly what it was,' Leon assured him. 'It's the first lion's rival and enemy to the death.'

Kermit was about to ask another question, but Leon stopped him. 'Let me talk to the Masai.' The discussion was in quick-fire Maa, and at the end Leon turned back to Kermit. 'The first lion is the older and dominant male.

This is his territory and he almost certainly has a large harem of females and their cubs. But he's getting old now. The second male is young and in his prime. He feels ready to challenge for the territory and the harem for the death battle. The old man's trying to frighten him off.'

'Manyoro could tell all that from listening to a few roars?'

'Both Manyoro and Loikot speak lion language fluently,' Leon told him, with a straight face.

'Tonight I'll believe anything you tell me. So we've got two big lions?'

'Yes and they won't be moving far. The old man dare not leave the door open, and the youngster can smell those ladies. He won't be moving either.'

After this, there was no question of anyone sleeping. They sat at the fire, planning the hunt with the Masai until the first rays of the sun gilded the treetops. They ate breakfast; then Ishmael and the Masai broke camp and loaded the mules. The air was still sweet and cool when they rode out to see what the day would bring.

They rode on down the river, and into the area where the lions had been roaring during the night. Every mile or two Leon shot whatever large mammal offered itself: giraffe, rhino or buffalo. By sunset they had laid down, over a stretch of ten miles, a string of highly attractive lion bait.

That night they were again deprived of a full night's sleep by the roaring of the two antagonists. At one time the older lion was so close to where they lay that the ground trembled under their blanket rolls with the imperious power of his voice, but this time there was no answer from his challenger.

'The young lion has found one of our baits,' Manyoro interpreted the silence. 'He is feeding on it.'

Two hours after midnight the old lion had stopped roaring. 'Now he's found a bait for himself,' Manyoro observed. 'We'll have them both tomorrow.'

As soon as it was light enough for the trackers to read the sign, they started back along the chain of bait. Leon and Kermit wore heavy jackets, for the morning was chilly.

The first three baits they visited were untouched. When they came to the fourth, Leon halted a few hundred yards from it and, with the binoculars, glassed the pile of branches that covered it.

'You're wasting time, pal. There ain't nothing there,' Kermit told him.

'On the contrary,' Leon said softly, without lowering the glasses. 'There's a big male lion right there. Here.' Leon handed him the glasses. 'Use these.'

Kermit stared through the lens for a minute. 'I still don't see a lion.'

'Look where the branches have been pulled open. You can see the striped haunches of the zebra . . . Do you see two small dark lumps on the far side? Those are the tops of his ears. He's lying flat behind the zebra watching us.'

'My God! You're right! I saw an ear flick,' Kermit exclaimed. 'Which lion is it? The young or the old one?'

Leon conferred quickly with Manyoro. At last he turned back to Kermit. 'It's the big one. Manyoro calls him the lion of all lions.'

'What do we do now? Do we ride him down?'

'No, we walk him up.' Leon was already swinging down from the saddle and reaching for the big Holland. He opened the action, drew the brass cartridges from the breeches and exchanged them for a fresh pair from his bandolier. Kermit followed his example with the lighter Lee-Enfield.

Leon gave Kermit his instructions. 'You'll take the lead. I'll be three paces behind you so I don't block your field of fire. Walk slowly and steadily, but not directly towards him. Keep your eyes on the ground ahead of you. If you stare at him, you'll spook him into charging prematurely. You must hit him before he starts to move or before you can blink he'll be doing forty miles an hour straight at you. When I call the shot, take him just under the chin in the centre of his chest.'

They moved out in open order, Kermit leading, Leon a few paces back and the two Masai coming up behind him, with their *assegais* presented.

'Excellent,' Leon encouraged Kermit softly. 'Keep up that speed and direction. You're doing fine.' Within another fifty paces Leon saw the lion lift his head a few inches and raise his mane in a threatening gesture. It was dense and black as Hades. Kermit halted in mid-stride.

'Steady, steady. Keep moving!' Leon cautioned. They walked on, and now they could see the lion's eyes. They were cold, yellow and inexorable.

Another ten slow paces and the lion growled. It was a low, deep, infinitely menacing sound. It stopped Kermit in his tracks and he turned to face the beast head on. Kermit's direct stare triggered the lion.

'Look out!' Leon said sharply, but the lion was already in full charge, rushing at Kermit, black mane fully erect with rage.

'Shoot him!' Leon's voice was lost in the sharp crack of the .303.

The bullet, hastily aimed, flew over the lion's back. Kermit was quick on the reload. His next shot was low and struck the ground between the beast's forelegs. The lion kept boring straight in, a yellow blur of speed.

Sweet Christ! Leon thought. It's going to get him down! He swung up the Holland, focusing on the great maned head. His forefinger tightened on the front trigger. The instant before the lion crashed his full 550-pound body weight into Kermit's chest at forty miles an hour, he fired his third shot.

The muzzle of the .303 Lee-Enfield was almost touching the lion's nose. The light bullet lanced into the brain. The tan body turned slack and flabby as a sack of chaff. Kermit hurled himself aside at the last instant and the lion piled up in a heap on the spot where he had been standing. He stared down at it, his hands shaking, breath sobbing in his throat.

'Shoot him again,' Leon shouted, but Kermit's legs gave way under him and he sat down. Leon ran up and stood over the lion. At point-blank range he shot him through the heart. Then he turned back to where Kermit was sitting with his head between his knees. 'Are you OK, chum?' he asked.

Slowly Kermit raised his head and stared at him as though he was a stranger. He shook his head in confusion. Leon sat beside him and put a muscular arm round his shoulders. 'Easy does it, chum. You did a great job. You stood to the charge. You never broke. You stood there and shot him down like a hero. Your daddy would have been proud of you.'

Kermit's eyes cleared. He took a deep breath and then he said huskily, 'Do you think so?'

'I damn well know so,' Leon said, with conviction. 'You killed him yourself, without any help from me.'

Kermit did not speak again but sat staring quietly at the magnificent body of the lion.

'Leave him be,' Manyoro told Leon. 'Popoo Hima is taking the spirit of his lion into his own heart. It is the way of the true warrior.'

The sun had set before Kermit left the lion and came to the small fire where Leon sat alone. Ishmael had placed a log at each side to act as seats and another, up-ended, on which he had set two mugs and a bottle. As Kermit sat down facing Leon he glanced at the bottle. 'Bunnahabhain whisky. Thirty years old,' Leon told him. 'I begged it from Percy in case something like this happened and we were forced to celebrate.'

'I feel different,' Kermit said, and took a sip.

'I understand,' Leon said. 'Today was your baptism by fire.'

'Yes!' Kermit answered vehemently. 'That's it exactly. It was a mystic, almost religious experience. I feel as though I'm somebody else, not the old me, somebody better than I ever was before.' He groped for words. 'I feel as though I've been reborn. The other me was afraid and uncertain. This one is no longer afraid. Now I know I can meet the world on my own terms.'

'I understand,' Leon said. 'Rite of passage.'

'Has it happened to you?' Kermit asked.

Leon remembered the pale naked bodies lying crucified on the baked earth, heard again the flitting of Nandi arrows and remembered the weight of Manyoro on his back. 'Yes . . . but it was nothing like today.'

'Tell me about it.'

Leon shook his head. 'These are things we should not talk about too much. Words can only sully and belittle their significance.'

'Of course. It's something very private.'

'Exactly,' Leon said, and raised his mug. 'The Masai have a description for this shared truth. They say simply, "brothers of the warrior blood".'

They sat for a long time in companionable silence, then Kermit said, 'I don't think I'll be able to sleep tonight.'

'I'll keep vigil with you,' Leon replied.

After a while they began to recall and discuss the tiniest details of the day's hunt, how the first growl had sounded, how big the lion had appeared as he rose to his full height, how swiftly he came. But they skirted the emotional aspects. The whisky level sank slowly in the bottle.

EVENTUALLY THE GREAT safari left the banks of the Ewaso Ng'iro River and trundled on ponderously towards the northeast through the beautiful hinterland.

Kermit and Leon made the most of the dwindling days that remained to them. They rode afar and hunted hard, more often than not with marked success. Was it Lusima's spell, Leon wondered, or simply that he had instilled into Kermit his own code of ethics, understanding and respect for the quarry they pursued together? Kermit had matured into a highly skilled and responsible hunter, a man of poise and self-confidence. Their friendship, tried and tested, took on a steely, durable character.

Four months after leaving the Ewaso Ng'iro the safari came upon the mighty flow of the Victoria Nile at a place called Jinja at the head of Lake Victoria. Here they had reached the parting of their ways.

Percy Phillips's contract ended at the river. On the eastern bank of the Nile they could see another vast encampment: Quentin Grogan was waiting to take over from Percy, and conduct the Roosevelts northwards through

Uganda, the Sudan and Egypt to Alexandria on the Mediterranean. From there he and his party would take ship for New York.

Roosevelt ordered a farewell luncheon on the bank of the Nile. Although he did not partake himself, he allowed champagne to be served to his guests. It was a convivial gathering, which ended with a speech by Roosevelt. One by one he picked out each of his guests and regaled the others with some amusing or touching anecdote regarding the person he was addressing. At last he came to Kermit. 'I almost forgot. Didn't I make a bet with you, Kermit? Something about the biggest lion, wasn't it?' Roosevelt smiled, amid laughter from the guests. There were amused cries of 'Ten it was! Pay up, sir! A bet is a bet!'

He sighed and reached for his wallet, selected a green banknote and passed it down the length of the table to where Kermit sat. 'Paid in full,' he said. 'You are all my witnesses.'

Too soon the luncheon drew to a close. The boats were waiting on the bank to ferry the party across the river. Leon and Kermit walked together down the bank in silence. Neither was able to think of words to say that would not sound maudlin or trite.

'Would you take a gift to Lusima from me, pardner?' Kermit broke the silence as they came to the edge of the water. He handed Leon a roll of green banknotes. 'It's only a hundred dollars. She deserves a lot more.'

'It's a generous gift. It will buy her ten good cows. There is nothing more desirable to a Masai than that,' Leon said.

'So long, pardner. In Limey, it was all jolly good fun,' replied Kermit.

'In Americanese, it was super awesome. Goodbye and Godspeed, chum.' Leon offered his right hand.

Kermit shook it. 'I'll write you.' He went down into the waiting boat. It pulled away from the bank and out across the swift, wide waters of the Nile. Almost beyond earshot Kermit stood up in the stern and shouted something. Leon just made out the words above the roaring of the waters in the falls downstream. 'Brothers of the warrior blood!'

'AND NOW, MY FRIEND, it's time to come back down to earth. For you the fun is over. You've work to do. First, you must make sure the horses are taken back safely to Nairobi. Then you will gather up the trophies we left at the the camps along the way. Make sure they're well dried and salted, pack them up and get them to the railway at Kapiti Plains. They have to be shipped to the Smithsonian in America as soon as possible. You must service all the equipment and the vehicles. Then you must get it back to Tandala Camp so that it can be made ready for Lord Eastmont—it's two years since he arranged his safari with me. Of course, you'll have Hennie to help you, but even so it'll keep you out of mischief for quite a while. Not much time for the Nairobi ladies, I'm afraid.'

Percy winked at him. 'As for me, I'm going to leave you to it. I'm heading back to Nairobi. My old buffalo leg is hurting like blue blazes and Doc Thompson's the only man who can fix it.'

A few months later Leon finally drove into Tandala. Since dawn that day he had come almost 200 miles over rutted and dusty roads. He switched off the engine, which stuttered to a halt. He climbed down stiffly from the driver's seat, took off his hat and slapped it against his leg, then coughed in the resulting cloud of talcum-fine dust.

'Where the hell have you been?' Percy came out of his tent. 'I'd just about given you up for dead. I want to speak to you, sharpish.'

'Where's the fire?' Leon asked. 'I've been driving since three this morning. I need a bath and a shave before I utter another word, and I'm in no mood to take bullshit from anyone, not even you, Percy.'

'Whoa now!' Percy grinned. 'You have your bath. You sure as hell need it. Then I'd like a few minutes of your precious time.'

An hour later Leon came into the mess tent, where Percy was sitting at the long table with his wire-rimmed reading glasses on the end of his nose. On the table in front of him was a pile of unanswered letters, and accounts.

'I'm sorry. I shouldn't have gone for you like that.' Leon was contrite.

'Think nothing of it.' Percy replaced his pen in the inkwell and waved him to the chair on the opposite side of the table. 'Famous man like you has the right to be uppity sometimes.' He pushed a pile of newsprint across the table. 'You'd better read these. Give your sagging morale a boost.'

Mystified at first, Leon began to make his way through the sheaf. He found that the clippings had been taken from dozens of newspapers and magazines from across North America and Europe, publications as diverse as the *Los Angeles Times* to *Deutsche Allgemeine Zeitung* in Berlin. There were more articles in German than there were in English. However, his schoolboy German was sufficient to enable him to follow their gist.

He studied one that read: 'Greatest White Hunter in Africa. So says the son of the former President of America.' Below it was a photograph of Leon, looking heroic and dashing. He laid it aside and picked up the next, which had a photograph of him shaking hands with a beaming Teddy Roosevelt. There were forty-seven articles, byline Andrew Fagan.

When he had skimmed through them, Leon slid them back across the table to Percy, who said, 'I want you to read this other mail. It's much more interesting.' Percy passed a stack of envelopes across the table.

Leon shuffled through them. 'What are they?'

'Enquiries from people who have read Andrew Fagan's articles and want to come hunting with you, poor benighted souls,' Percy explained briefly.

'They're addressed to me but you opened them!' Leon accused him.

'I thought you'd want me to. They might have contained something that needed an urgent reply,' Percy answered, with an apologetic shrug.

They were quiet as Leon skimmed through the last of his correspondence.

'There's one from a German princess, Isabella von Hoherberg something or other.' Percy broke the silence. 'She sent her photograph. Not at all bad.'

'Do shut up, Percy.' At last Leon looked up. 'I'll read the rest later.'

'Do you think this might be the time to talk about a partnership?'

'Percy, I didn't think for one moment you were serious about that.'

'I am. Let's talk.'

It was almost evening before they had thrashed out the framework of their new financial arrangement.

'One last thing, Leon. You must pay for your private use of the motor. I'm not going to sponsor any frivolous forays into Nairobi.'

'That's fair enough, Percy, but if you're going to make such a stipulation, I want to make two of my own.'

Percy looked uneasy. 'Let's hear what they are.'

'The name of the new firm—'

'It's Phillips and Courtney Safaris, of course,' Percy cut in hurriedly.

'That's not alphabetical, Percy. Shouldn't it be Courtney and Phillips, or more simply C and P Safaris?'

'It's my show. It should be P and C Safaris,' Percy protested.

'Not any more is it your show. It's our show now.'

'Cocky little bugger. I'll spin you for it.' He groped in his pocket and brought out a silver shilling. 'Heads or tails?'

'Heads!' said Leon.

Percy spun the coin high and caught it on the back of his left hand. He covered it with the right, then peeped under his hand and sighed. 'This is what happens to the old lion when the young one starts feeling his oats.'

'Lions don't eat oats. Let's have a look at what you're hiding.'

Percy showed him the coin. 'Very well, you win,' he capitulated. 'It's C and P Safaris. What's your second demand?'

'I want the contract backdated to the first day of the Roosevelt safari.'

'Ouch, and shiver my timbers! You really are rubbing my nose in it! You want me to pay you full commission for your hunt with Kermit Roosevelt! That'll amount to almost two hundred pounds!'

'Two hundred and fifteen, to be precise.'

'You're taking advantage of a sick old man.'

'You look hale and hearty to me. Are we in agreement?'

'I suppose I have no other option, you heartless boy.'

Percy smiled and held out his hand. They shook and Percy grinned triumphantly. 'Welcome aboard, partner. I think we're going to get along together rather well. I suppose you want your money right this minute?'

'You suppose right. I want it now. It's almost a year since I had a moment to myself. I'm taking a couple of days off. I have business to attend to in Nairobi, and possibly even further afield.'

LEON'S FIRST STOP in Nairobi was at the headquarters of the Greater Lake Victoria Trading Company. Goolam Vilabjhi Esquire rushed out of his emporium to greet him. He was followed by Mrs Vilabjhi and a horde of small caramel-hued cherubs with raven hair and enormous dark eyes, all clad in brilliant saris and chittering like starlings.

Mr Vilabjhi seized Leon's hand and shook it vigorously. 'You are a thousand and one times welcome, honoured Sahib.'

He led Leon into the store without releasing his grip on his right hand. With the other he swatted at the circling swarm of children. 'Away with you! Be gone!' he cried. 'Please forgive and forget them, Sahib. Enter! I beg of you, Sahib. You are ten thousand times welcome.' Mr Vilabjhi and the smallest cherub led him to the back wall of the store. On the wall was a large gold picture frame with a wooden plaque. It bore the legend: *Respectfully dedicated to Sahib Leon Courtney Esquire. World-renowned polo player and* shikari. *Esteemed friend of Colonel Theodore Roosevelt, President of the United States of America, and of Mr Goolam Vilabjhi Esquire.*

Behind the glass of the frame were pasted a number of English-language newspaper clippings originating from the American Associated Press.

'My family and I are very much hoping that you will sign one of these splendid publications to be the jewel in the crown of my collection of cherished memorabilia of our friendship.'

'Nothing would give me greater pleasure, Mr Vilabjhi.' Despite himself Leon was deeply touched. He signed a photograph of himself and, blowing on the damp ink, Mr Vilabjhi assured him, 'I will treasure this personally handwritten autograph for the rest of my days.' Then he sighed. 'I suppose that now you wish to speak about redeeming your ivory tusk.'

Manyoro and Loikot carried the tusk out to the truck a little while later as Leon followed them. He climbed into the driver's seat, then drove on to the new Muthaiga Country Club where Penrod was waiting for him.

As soon as they had shaken hands Penrod suggested, 'Shall we go to lunch? Today it's steak and kidney pie. We can talk as we eat.'

He led Leon to a table on the terrace under the pergola of purple bougainvillaea, set discreetly out of earshot of other diners, then asked, 'I suppose Percy's shown you the articles written by Andrew Fagan, and the letters from prominent people that they have evoked?'

'Yes, I have them, sir,' Leon replied. 'As a matter of fact, I found them rather embarrassing. I'm certainly not the greatest hunter in Africa. That was Kermit's idea of a joke, which Fagan took seriously. I'm still a greenhorn.'

'Never admit it, Leon. Anyway, from what I hear, you're learning fast.' Penrod smiled. 'To tell the truth, I had a small hand in the whole subterfuge. Rather neat, I thought. A little stroke of genius.'

'How are you involved, Uncle?' Leon was startled.

'I was in London when the first articles appeared. I cabled the military attaché at our embassy in Berlin and asked him to tout the articles to the German press. My plan was to lure the notables to go on safari with you. This will give you the opportunity to gather all kinds of intelligence.'

'Why would they want to confide in me?'

'Leon, my lad, people seem to like you. Safari life has a way of inducing even the most reticent to lower their guard and speak more freely. And why would a senior figure in the Kaiser's Germany suspect a fresh-faced innocent like you of being a nefarious secret agent?'

Penrod waved for the waiter to bring on the steaming platters of steak and kidney pie. Then he fell to with a will, and spoke through a mouthful:

'I took the liberty of going through your mail, especially that from Germany. I just couldn't wait to see what fish we had in our net. Hope you don't mind?'

'Not at all, Uncle. Please feel free.'

'I picked out six letters worthy of our attention. Four are from especially influential persons and confidants of Kaiser Bill.'

Leon nodded and Penrod went on, 'I have discussed this with Percy and told him that you are, over and above all your other responsibilities, a serving officer in British Military Intelligence. He has agreed to cooperate. By the way, how is your German, Leon?'

'It was once fair to middling, but is now more than a little rusty.'

'You'd better brush up. You're going to spend a great deal of time in the company of Germans soon. I've found a language tutor for you. His name is Max Rosenthal. He was an engineer at the Meerbach Motor Works in Wieskirche before he came out to German East Africa. He's a bit of a drunk but when he's sober he's a first-rate worker. I persuaded Percy to employ him to manage your safari camps and to sharpen up your use of the lingo.'

When they parted on the front steps of the club, Penrod told him seriously, 'I know you're new to the business of spying so I offer a word of advice. Write nothing down. Keep no notes of what you observe. Rather, record it all in your head and report it to me when next we meet.'

When Leon met Max Rosenthal at Tandala Camp he proved to be a powerfully built Bavarian, with huge hands and a bluff, jovial manner. Leon liked him on first sight.

'Greetings.' They shook hands. 'We'll be working together. I'm sure we'll get to know each other well,' Leon said.

Max let out a fruity chuckle that shook his belly. 'Ah, so! You speak a little German. That's very good.'

'Not so very good,' Leon corrected him, 'but you can help me improve it.'

Max proved invaluable, a gifted teacher, and a hard, efficient worker, who relieved Leon of much of the mundane work of camp organisation. Leon communicated with Max only in German and, as a consequence, his grip on the language strengthened with surprising rapidity.

Lord Eastmont was only weeks away from arriving for his safari when Leon received a cable from Berlin to the effect that the Princess Isabella Madeleine Hoherberg von Preussen von und zu Hohenzollern had decided to come out to Africa on the next sailing of the SS *Admiral*. Her royal duties were such that she could only afford six weeks in Africa before she must return to Germany. She demanded that all be ready for her on her arrival.

This peremptory communication threw Tandala into turmoil. Percy raged through the camp, hindering rather than helping the frantic efforts of Leon and his staff to change the elaborate arrangements already in place for Eastmont. They now had two major safaris to run simultaneously, which they had never attempted previously. In the end the only circumstance that saved the day was that the princess would stay just six weeks, while Lord Eastmont had arranged a four-month adventure.

THE HOHENZOLLERN SAFARI kept Leon extremely busy for weeks. He devised a series of small game drives, which gave the princess endless pleasure. She was a superb horsewoman. When she bowled over three running Grant's gazelles at a range of 300 yards in three consecutive shots without dismounting, Leon decided she was probably the most deadly shot he had ever met. In the evenings she would regale him with stories about well-known personages from the upper reaches of the German aristocracy and military. What she was relating as amusing titbits of scandal was political cordite. Leon wondered what his uncle Penrod would make of this volatile information.

WHEN PENROD RODE out to Tandala Camp Ishmael had a pot of Lapsang Souchong tea and a plate of ginger snaps ready to welcome him. After Penrod had fortified himself, he and Leon mounted up and set out on the eight-mile return ride to the Muthaiga Country Club.

'I was really looking forward to a bit of a canter,' Penrod said. 'Never seem able to get away from my desk, these days.' He glanced at Leon. 'On the other hand, you look to be in fine fettle, dear boy.'

'The princess kept me hard at it. Did I tell you how many animals she killed?'

'I rely on you to bring me up to date. That's why I came to fetch you. Out here we can talk without fear of eavesdroppers.'

The leisurely ride to Muthaiga took almost an hour and a half, just long enough for Leon to make his report on what the princess had told him. Penrod did not interrupt except to confirm a name or to ask him to enlarge on some detail. They were riding up the driveway to the club before Leon was able to say, 'That's about it, Uncle.'

'More than enough,' Penrod replied. 'You have accomplished more than I could possibly have hoped for.'

Penrod was silent until they reached the end of the driveway and pulled up their horses in front of the clubhouse.

'Come, let's go to lunch. I've something to celebrate—I've just heard I'm to be made brigadier general.'

Once they reached the terrace, they settled into their chairs under the bougainvillaeas. The waiter opened and poured the wine, then served the hors d'oeuvre of marrow bones on toast and withdrew discreetly.

Penrod scooped a large greasy lump of marrow out of the bone onto his toast and then said, 'Now, you have another large accumulation of mail, which includes a dozen or more enquiries for your services as a hunter. I picked them up from the post office and read them to save you the trouble. Most of these communications were from nobodies—I discarded those. However, others show great promise, all from our favourite country, Deutschland. The most attractive from our point of view is the industrialist Graf Otto von Meerbach. The Graf is the head of the Meerbach Motor Works, the single largest contractor to the military.'

'I know of them.' Leon was impressed. 'They developed the Meerbach rotary engine for aeroplanes. They're in competition with Count Zeppelin working on dirigible airships. I'd love to meet the fellow. I'm fascinated by the idea of taking to the skies.'

Penrod smiled at his boyish enthusiasm. 'You might soon have your chance. With Percy's blessing I have replied to von Meerbach in your name. I gave him full details of what you have to offer, including available dates. Oh, and by the way, there's also a letter from your pal Kermit Roosevelt.'

'Which you opened to save me the trouble?'

'Good Lord, no.' Penrod was horrified. 'That's your private mail.'

'As opposed to all my other correspondence, which is public, Uncle?' Leon asked.

Penrod smiled comfortably. 'Line of duty, my dear boy.'

LEON WAS IN PENSIVE MOOD when he got back to Tandala and went to his tent to read his mail. There were three of his mother's marvellously fond and entertaining letters. Although dated a month apart they had arrived at the Nairobi post office together. He laid them aside for reply, then slit open the letter with the New York postmark and Kermit's red wax seal on the flap.

Kermit's letter was breezy and chatty. He described the last months of the great safari with Quentin Grogan up the Nile where Big Medicine had continued to wreak havoc among the game herds. He went on to describe a dinner party at the home of Andrew Carnegie, the steel multi-millionaire. One of the other guests had been a German industrialist from Bavaria. His name was Otto von Meerbach.

Otto is an extraordinary character, straight out of the pages of a lurid novel, complete with duelling scar and all. He is a great mountain of a man, booming with energy and self-assurance. He is the proprietor of the Meerbach Motor Works, one of the biggest and most successful enterprises in all of Europe. He is also an avid hunter. He has huge estates in Bavaria where he hunts stags and wild boar. I told him about our safari, and he was very interested. He asked me for your address and of course I gave it to him.

'So that's how von Meerbach found out where to get hold of me,' Leon said aloud. 'Thank you, Kermit.' The letter continued for a few more pages.

Otto's wife, or maybe she is his mistress, is truly one of the most beautiful ladies I have ever laid eyes upon. Her name is Eva von Wellberg. She is very refined and quiet but, my sweet Lord, when she turned those eyes on me my heart melted like butter in a skillet. I would readily have fought a duel with Otto for her favours.

Leon laughed. The hyperbole was so typical of Kermit. Kermit ended by exhorting Leon to reply soon and concluded, 'Salaams *and* Waidmanns Heil *(Otto taught me this; it means "Hunter's salute")* from your BWB.' It took a moment for Leon to work out what the letters stood for. He smiled again. 'And all the best to you, too, Kermit, my brother of the warrior blood.'

The journey south to Percy's hunting camp on Lake Manyara was over brutally rough tracks for the first 200 miles. The Vauxhall driven by Leon took cruel punishment and they were forced to stop and repair punctured tyres at least a dozen times. Manyoro and Loikot had become past masters at the art of removing the thorns that had pierced them.

The boundary between British and German East Africa was neither marked nor guarded. Navigating chiefly by instinct and the heavens, they at last reached the bush store run by a Hindu trader at Makuyuni River. Percy had left a pair of good horses with the store owner to await their arrival.

Leon parked the truck at the back of the store and saddled up one of the horses. From there it was a ride of at least fifty miles to Percy's current hunting camp, which was set on a promontory above the lake shore. Leon and his Masai reached it an hour after dark on the following day. He found out that neither Percy nor his client, Lord Eastmont, had returned to camp. Percy's cook served Leon a dinner of grilled hippo heart and cassava porridge with pumpkin mash and thick Bisto gravy.

Afterwards Leon sat at the fire and watched the flamingos flying across the moon in dark, wavering lines. A bush fire was burning on the far shore of the lake. It was past ten o'clock when he heard the horses coming and went to the perimeter of the camp to meet them.

As Percy dismounted stiffly from the saddle, he recognised Leon waiting in the shadows. His face creased in a smile of welcome. 'Well met indeed!' he called. 'Your timing's immaculate, Leon. Come to the fire and I'll introduce you to his lordship. I might even pour you a dram of Talisker.'

Eastmont was a tall, gangling figure, with huge hands and feet and a head the size of a watermelon. In the flickering firelight his features were gaunt and bony, his expression dark and morose. He said little but instead left the talking to Percy. Once the glasses were charged he sat staring into the fire while Percy described the day's hunting,

'Well, his lordship wanted a truly monumental buffalo and, by golly, we found one this morning. He was an old solitary and I swear by all that's holy he's fifty-five if he's an inch.'

'Percy, that's incredible! Show me the head,' Leon said. 'Are your people bringing it in tonight, or will the skinners come in with it tomorrow?'

There was an awkward silence, and Percy glanced across the fire at his client. Eastmont seemed not to have heard.

'Well,' said Percy. 'There's a small problem. The buff's head is attached to his body, and the body is still very much alive.'

Leon felt a chill at the back of his neck, but he asked carefully, 'Wounded?'

Percy nodded reluctantly, but admitted, 'Yes, but pretty hard hit, I think.'

'How hard, Percy? In the boiler room or the guts? How much blood?'

'Back leg,' said Percy, then hurried on: 'Broke the gaskin bone, I do believe. He should be stiff and crippled by tomorrow morning.'

'Blood, Percy? How much?'

'There wasn't very much of it.'

'How far did you track him?'

'A couple of miles.'

'Shit!' said Leon, as though he truly meant it.

'The polite version of that word is "*merde*",' Percy tried for humour.

They were silent for a few long minutes. Then Leon asked, 'How thick is the cover he's in, Percy?'

'It's thick,' Percy admitted. 'We'll follow him up tomorrow at first light. He'll be sore. Shouldn't take too long to catch up with him.'

'I have a better plan. The two of you stay here and have a quiet day in camp. I'll follow him up and finish the business,' Leon suggested.

His lordship suddenly let out a bellow. 'You will do no such thing, you impudent whippersnapper. It's my buffalo and I will finish him off.'

'With all due respect, my lord, too many guns could turn a potentially dangerous situation into a fatal one. Let me go. This is what you pay us so much money to do.' Leon smiled in an unconvincing attempt at diplomacy.

'I paid so much money for you to do as you're bloody well told, my lad.'

Leon's mouth hardened. He looked at Percy, who shook his head.

'It'll be all right,' he said. 'We'll probably find him down tomorrow.'

Leon rose to his feet. 'As you wish. I'll be ready to ride at first light. Good night, my lord.' Eastmont did not reply and Leon turned back to Percy. He looked old and sick in the firelight. 'Good night, Percy,' he said gently. 'Don't worry. I have a good feeling about this. We'll find him down, I know it.'

THEY RODE for an hour before they reached the spot where Percy had abandoned the blood spoor the previous evening. It was a bad place. The thorn bush was dense and grew low to the ground. Percy's tracker, who had been with him for thirty years, was named Ko'twa. He pointed out the stale spoor, which had been almost obliterated by the passing of other large animals during the night, and Manyoro and Loikot took it away at a jog trot.

The three hunters followed on horseback. Even though the bush was thick they covered the first two miles quickly. Within another hour the sun was well up and baking hot. There was no breeze and the air was stifling. Even the birds and insects were quiescent. The silence was brooding and ominous, and the thorn grew thicker. Even from horseback the view ahead was severely curtailed.

Leon checked his mount and whispered to Percy, 'We're making too much noise. We must leave the horses.' They unsaddled and hobbled the horses, leaving them nosebags and water, and the small party went on in battle formation, behind the trackers.

Suddenly there was a sound from directly ahead, like two dry twigs tapped together. The trackers froze. Loikot was standing on one leg, the other stretched out to take the next step.

'What was that?' Eastmont asked. His voice sounded like a foghorn.

Percy seized his shoulder and squeezed hard to silence him. Then he whispered in his ear, 'Buff heard us coming. He's close. Keep very quiet.'

Nobody else spoke, and nobody moved. Loikot was still on one leg. They were all listening, standing still as waxwork dummies. It lasted for an eternity. Then Loikot lowered his foot to the ground, and Manyoro turned his head to look back. He made an eloquent gesture with his right hand to Leon. 'The buffalo has moved forward,' said the hand. 'We can follow.'

They went on cautiously but heard nothing and saw nothing. Now the tension was like the twanging of steel wires stretched to breaking point. Leon's thumb was on the safety catch of the Holland, and the butt of the rifle was clamped under his right armpit. He could mount, aim and fire instantaneously. He heard it then, soft as rain in the grass. He glanced left, and the buffalo was coming.

It had doubled back and waited in ambuscade, hidden in an impenetrable thicket of thorn. It had let the trackers pass and now it came out, black as charcoal and big as a granite mountain. The sweep of the great curved horns was polished and gleaming. The points were dagger sharp, and the boss between them was gnarled like the shell of a gigantic walnut, and massive as a monolith of obsidian.

'Percy! On your left! He's coming!' Leon yelled with all the power of his lungs. He stepped out to give himself a clear field of fire, but as he lifted the rifle into his shoulder, the buffalo galloped behind an intervening clump of thorn scrub. He couldn't get a bead on him.

'Your bird, Percy! Get him!' Leon yelled again, and he saw Percy turn left and shuffle to get into position. But his crippled leg dragged and slowed him down. He braced himself and leaned into his rifle, levelling it at the charging bull. Leon knew that Percy would brain him from that range. Percy was an old hand. He wouldn't muck it up, not now, not ever.

But they had forgotten about Lord Eastmont. As Percy tightened his forefinger on the trigger, Eastmont's nerve snapped. He dropped his rifle, spun round and ran for safety. His eyes were wild and his face was ash-white with panic as he lumbered back down the path. He seemed not even to see Percy as he crashed into him with all his weight. Percy went down and the rifle flew from his grip as he hit the ground on his shoulders and the back of his head. Eastmont did not even check his run, but bore straight down on Leon. The path was too narrow for Leon to avoid him. He reversed his rifle and used the butt in an effort to fend off Eastmont's rush.

It was futile. Eastmont was an enormous man and he was mad with terror. Nothing could stop him. Leon hit him in the centre of the chest with the rifle butt. The walnut stock snapped cleanly at the pistol grip, but Eastmont did not even flinch. He came into Leon like an avalanche. Leon was flung aside by the collision. Eastmont kept going. Leon landed on his right shoulder on the side of the path. Desperately he looked along the path to where Percy had gone down.

Percy was struggling to his knees. He had lost his rifle and was dazed by the blow to the back of his head. Behind him Leon saw the buffalo burst out of the thorn scrub into the narrow pathway. Its little eyes were bloodshot and they fixed on Percy. It lowered its massive head and swerved towards him. Leon lifted the shattered rifle. The butt-stock was gone but he was going to fire single-handed. He knew that the recoil might break his wrist.

'Percy, get down!' he screamed. 'Fall flat! Give me a chance.' But Percy stood up to his full height, blocking his shot. He was shaking his head with confusion, staggering drunkenly and looking around vaguely. Leon tried to shout again but his throat seized with horror and he could not utter a sound. He watched the buffalo roll its head to one side, winding up for the hook, as it covered the last few yards to reach Percy.

The point of a horn caught Percy in the small of the back at the level of his kidneys. The buffalo tossed its head high and he was impaled. With disbelief Leon saw that the point of the horn had emerged from his friend's stomach. The buffalo shook its head in an effort to dislodge the limp body. Percy was whipped round and his arms and legs flailed slackly. Leon raced forward, slipping the safety catch off the broken rifle. Before he could reach them, the buffalo lowered its head and wiped Percy off against the ground.

Leon dropped to one knee beside the buffalo's shoulder and pressed the double muzzles of the Holland into its neck at the juncture of spine and body. He had expected the recoil of the rifle to snap his wrist but such was his furious abandon that he barely felt it, and thought that the cartridge had misfired. But the bull reeled away and dropped into a sitting position on its haunches, its forelegs braced in front of it. Its head was lowered, and at last Leon could reach the brain. He jumped up and ran forward again, careful to stay outside the sweep of those lethal horns. He thrust the muzzle of the unfired barrel into the back of the skull behind the horny boss and fired the second barrel. It flopped forward, then rolled onto its side. It let out a long, mournful death bellow, then lay still.

Leon dropped the shattered stock of his rifle and wheeled back to where Percy lay. He fell to his knees beside him. Percy was on his back with his arms thrown wide as a crucifix. His eyes were closed. The wound in his stomach was hideous. The violent movements of the bull had enlarged it so that the torn and tangled intestines bulged through the opening.

'Percy?'

His partner opened his eyes and, with an effort, focused on Leon's face. He smiled regretfully, sadly. 'Well, I didn't get away that time and now they've done for me, good and truly.'

'Don't talk such rot.' Leon's voice was harsh, but his vision was blurring. 'As soon as I've patched you up, I'll get you back to camp. You're going to be all right.' He stripped off his shirt and bundled it into a ball. 'This might be uncomfortable, but we have to plug the leak you've got there.' He stuffed the shirt into the hole in Percy's abdomen.

'I can't feel a thing,' Percy told him. 'This is going to be a lot easier than I ever imagined it would be.'

'Do shut up, old man.' Leon could not look into his eyes where the shadows were gathering. 'Now, I'm going to carry you back to your horse.'

'No,' Percy whispered. 'Let it happen here. I'm ready, if you'll help me.'

'Anything,' Leon told him. 'Anything you want, Percy. You know that.'

'Then give me your hand.' Leon gripped his hand firmly. Percy closed his eyes. 'I never had a son,' he said softly. 'I wanted one, but I never had one. I guess I'll just have to settle for you instead.' The old twinkle was in his eyes.

Leon tried to reply but his throat was choked. He coughed and turned his head away. It took him a moment to find his voice. 'I'm not good enough for that job, Percy.'

'No one ever wept for me before.' There was wonder in Percy's voice.

'Shit!' said Leon.

'*Merde*,' Percy corrected him.

'*Merde*,' Leon enchoed.

'Now, listen.' There was sudden urgency in Percy's tone. 'I knew this was going to happen. I had a dream, a premonition. I left something for you in the old tin cabin trunk under my bed at Tandala.'

'I love you, Percy, you tough old bastard.'

'Nobody ever said that either.' The twinkle in the blue eyes began to fade. 'Get ready. It's going to happen now. Get ready to squeeze my hand to help me across.' He closed his eyes tightly for a long minute, then opened them very wide. 'Squeeze, my son. Squeeze hard!' Leon squeezed and was startled by the power with which the old man squeezed back.

'Oh God, forgive me my sins!' Percy took one last gulp of air. His body stiffened, and then his hand in Leon's went slack. Leon sat beside him for a long while. He was unaware that the trackers were squatting close behind him. Leon gently closed Percy's staring eyes.

Carefully Leon lifted Percy in his arms as if he was a sleeping child. He started back to where they had tethered the horses.

WHEN LEON REACHED the lakeside camp he found that Max Rosenthal had arrived from Tandala in the other truck. Leon told him to make the arrangements for Eastmont's luggage to be packed and loaded. When Lord Eastmont, guided by Manyoro, arrived at the camp, he was hangdog and sullen.

'I'm sending you back to Nairobi,' Leon told him coldly. 'Max will put you on the train to Mombasa, and book you a berth on the next sailing for Europe. I'll send the buffalo head and your other trophies to you as soon as they have been cured. You will be happy and proud to know that your buffalo is well over fifty inches. I owe you some money as a refund for this curtailed safari. I will let you have a banker's order as soon as I have calculated the amount. Now get into the motor, and stay out of my sight. I have to bury the man you killed.'

THEY DUG PERCY'S GRAVE deep, under an ancient baobab tree on the headland above the lake. Leon stood beside the mound of earth while Manyoro led the others in the lion dance.

Leon stayed on after all the others had gone back to the camp. He sat on a dead branch that had fallen from the baobab and gazed out across the lake. He made his last farewell in silence. If Percy was lingering near, he would know what Leon was thinking without having to be told.

Looking out across the lake, Leon was satisfied with the beautiful place he had chosen for Percy to spend eternity. He thought that when his own time came he would not mind being buried in such a spot.

LEON TRAVELLED the rough track to Arusha, the local administrative centre of the government of German East Africa. He went before the district Amtsrichter, and swore an affidavit as to the circumstances of Percy's demise. The judge issued a death certificate.

Some days later when he reached Tandala Camp, Max and Hennie du Rand were anxiously awaiting his return to find out what fate had in store for them now that Percy was gone. Leon told them he would speak to them as soon as he knew the position of the company.

After he had drunk a pot of tea to wash the dust out of his throat, he shaved, bathed and dressed in clothes freshly ironed by Ishmael. He went up the hill to the little thatched bungalow that had been Percy's home for the last forty years and sat for a while on the stoep. He was reluctant to go into Percy's bungalow. At last he stood up and went to the front door. It swung open to his touch. In all those years Percy had never bothered to lock it.

Leon went into the cool, dim interior. The walls of the front room were lined with bookcases, the shelves packed with hundreds of books. He walked into Percy's bedroom and looked around diffidently.

He sat on the edge of the bed. The mattress was as hard as concrete and the blankets were threadbare. He reached under the bed and dragged out a battered steel cabin trunk, then threw back the lid.

The interior was neatly packed with all of Percy's valuables, from his passport to his accounts and his chequebook, from small jewellery boxes of cufflinks and dress studs to old steamliner tickets and faded photographs. There were also several neat wads of documents tied with ribbon. On top of this hoard a folded document, sealed with red wax, was inscribed in block capitals: TO BE OPENED BY LEON COURTNEY ONLY IN THE EVENT OF MY DEATH.

Leon reached for the hunting knife in its sheath on his belt. Carefully he prised open the wax seal and unfolded a single sheet of heavy Manila paper. It was headed 'Last Will and Testament'. Leon glanced at the bottom of the page. It was signed by Percy, and his two witnesses were Brigadier General Penrod Ballantyne and Hugh, the 3rd Baron Delamere.

He read the entire handwritten document. The gist was clear: Percy had left his entire estate to his partner and dear friend Leon Ryder Courtney.

It took Leon some time to come to terms with the magnitude of Percy's last gift to him. He still had not the slightest idea of Percy's total wealth, but the intrinsic value of the estate was of no concern to Leon: it was the gift itself, the earnest of Percy's affection and esteem, that was the real treasure.

He carried the trunk out to the stoep where the light was better and settled into the easy chair that had been Percy's favourite, and began to unpack. Leon opened his cashbook and blinked with astonishment when he saw the balances of the deposits held by the Nairobi branch of Barclays Bank, Dominion, Colonial and Overseas to the credit of Percy Phillips Esq. They totalled more than five thousand pounds sterling. But that was not all. He found title deeds to land and properties not only in Nairobi and Mombasa but in the city of Bristol, the place of Percy's birth, in England.

There was a bundle of Consols, the 5 per cent perpetual bearer bonds issued by the government of Great Britain. Their face value was twelve and a half thousand pounds. The interest on that alone was more than six hundred per annum. It was a princely income.

When it grew dark Leon went into the front room and lit the lamps. He worked on until after midnight, sorting documents and reading accounts. When his eyelids drooped he went through to the austere little bedroom and stretched out under the mosquito net on Percy's bed. The hard mattress welcomed his weary body. It felt good. After all his wanderings he had found a place that felt like home.

HE WOKE to the dawn chorus of a thrush under the window. When he went down the hill he found Max Rosenthal and Hennie du Rand in the mess tent. Ishmael had breakfast ready, but neither had touched it. Leon took a seat.

'You can relax, and stop sitting on the edge of your chairs. Help yourselves to the eggs and bacon before they get cold and Ishmael throws a tantrum,' he told them. 'C and P Safaris is still in business. Nothing changes. You still have your jobs. Just carry on exactly as you were before.'

As soon as he had finished breakfast he went out to the Vauxhall.

After Manyoro had cranked the engine to life, he and Loikot scrambled into the back and Leon headed for town. His first stop was at the little thatched building behind Government House that served as the Deeds Office. The clerk notarised Percy's death certificate and his will, and Leon signed the entries in the huge leatherbound ledger.

Back in the Vauxhall he drove through the front gates of the KAR barracks and parked the truck in front of the headquarters building and went up the steps, acknowledging the salutes of the sentries as he passed. The adjutant was sitting in the duty room.

'I'd like to see the general,' Leon said.

Minutes later Leon was ushered through into his uncle's office.

Penrod stood up and reached across his desk to shake Leon's hand, then indicated the chair facing him. 'This comes as a bit of a surprise, Leon. Didn't expect you back in Nairobi for another month or so.'

'Percy's dead, sir.' Leon's voice caught as he made the bald statement.

Penrod stared at him speechlessly. Then he left his desk and went to the window to stand gazing out across the parade ground, his hands clasped behind his back. 'Tell me what happened.'

Leon did so, and when he had finished, Penrod said, 'Percy knew it was coming. He asked me to witness his will before he left town.' He stood up and placed his cap on his head. 'It's a bit early, sun isn't over the yardarm, but we're duty-bound to give Percy a decent wake. Come on.'

Apart from the barman, the mess was empty. Penrod ordered the drinks and they sat together in a quiet corner. For a while their conversation revolved round Percy and the manner of his dying. Finally Penrod asked, 'What will you do now?'

'Percy left everything to me, sir; so I'm going to keep the company running, if for no other reason than to honour his memory.'

'I'm pleased about that,' Penrod said, in hearty approval. 'However, I suppose you'll change its name.'

'I've already done so, Uncle. I registered the new name at the Deeds Office this morning.'

'Courtney Safaris?'

'No, sir. Phillips and Courtney. P and C Safaris.'

'You've given his name priority over your own!'

'The old name was decided on the spin of a coin. This is just my way of trying to repay a little of all he did for me.'

'Well done, my boy. Now, I have some good news for you. P and C Safaris is off to a flying start. Graf Otto von Meerbach has accepted the quotation from Percy that I sent him and confirmed that he'll be coming with his entourage at the beginning of next year for a six-month safari.'

Leon grimaced and swirled the ice in his glass. 'Somehow it doesn't seem to matter very much, now that Percy has gone.'

'Cheer up, my boy. Von Meerbach is bringing out a couple of prototypes of his flying machines. He wants to test them under tropical conditions and he plans to use them to spot game from the air. That's what he's saying but, given his connections with the German Army, I believe he'll be using them to scout the back country along our border with German East Africa, with an eye to any future military offensives against us. Be that as it may, you might get the opportunity to fulfil your dream of sailing among the clouds while picking up some useful snippets of intelligence for me.'

Leon was waiting on the beach of Kilindini Lagoon when the German tramp steamer SS *Silbervogel* anchored in the roadstead. He went out to her in the first lighter. When he went up the companion ladder, five passengers were waiting to meet him on the afterdeck, the engineer and his mechanics from the Meerbach Motor Works, part of the team that Graf Otto von Meerbach had sent out as his vanguard.

The man in charge introduced himself as Gustav Kilmer. He was a muscular, capable-looking fellow in his early fifties. He and Leon went over the inventory of the cargo that was stowed in the *Silbervogel*'s holds, which comprised fifty-six huge crates weighing twenty-eight tons in total. In addition, three Meerbach motor vehicles were strapped under green tarpaulin covers on the afterdeck.

Gustav explained that two were heavy transport trucks and the third was an open hunting car that had been designed by himself and Graf Otto and built in the Wieskirche factory. It was the only one of its kind in existence.

It took the lighters three days to ferry this vast cargo ashore. Max Rosenthal and Hennie du Rand were waiting at the head of a gang of 200 porters to transfer the drums and crates from the lighters to the goods trucks that were standing in the Kilindini railway siding.

When the three motor vehicles were brought ashore, Gustav checked them for damage. Leon was impressed by the big, robust trucks but it was the open hunting car that filled him with wonder. From the upholstered leather seats, fitted cocktail bar and gun racks to the enormous 6-cylinder 100-horsepower engine, it was a symphony of engineering genius.

By now Gustav had taken to Leon's boyish charisma, and was further flattered by his interest in, and unstinting praise of, his creations. He invited Leon to be his passenger on the long drive up-country to Nairobi.

When at last the main cargo had been loaded onto the railway wagons, Leon ordered Hennie and Max aboard to shepherd it to Nairobi. As the train pulled out of the siding and puffed away through the littoral hills, Gustav and his mechanics mounted the three Meerbach vehicles. With Leon in the passenger seat of the hunting car, Gustav led the trucks out onto the road.

They beat the goods train to Nairobi by almost five hours and were on the platform to welcome it when it chugged in, its steam whistle shrieking. The driver shunted the trucks onto a spur rail to be unloaded the following morning. Leon had hired a contractor who operated a powerful steam traction engine to haul the cargo to its final destination.

Leon had built a large open-sided hangar with a tarpaulin roof to serve as a workshop and storage area on the open plot of land he had inherited from Percy. It adjoined the polo ground, which he planned to use as a landing strip for the aircraft, which were still in their crates awaiting assembly.

These were busy days for Leon. One of Graf Otto's cables gave detailed instructions for the provision of creature comforts for himself and his female companion. At each hunting location, he was to prepare adjoining quarters to accommodate the couple; he had been issued with detailed specifications for these luxurious suites. Furniture was packed in one of the crates, and included beds, wardrobes and linen. Graf Otto had also sent full sets of bone china and silver, with a pair of enormous solid-silver candelabra. There were 220 cases of champagnes, wines and liqueurs, and 50 crates of canned and bottled delicacies: sauces and condiments, rare spices like saffron, foie gras from Lyon, Westphalian ham, smoked oysters, Danish pickled herring and Russian beluga caviar.

Over the weeks that followed, Leon delegated to Max and Hennie most of the petty details, while he spent every hour he could afford in the hangar at the polo field, watching Gustav and his team assemble the two aircraft. Slowly, the jigsaw puzzle of assorted engine parts, rigging wire and struts, wing and fuselage started to take on the recognisable shape of aircraft.

When at last Gustav had completed the assembly, Leon was amazed by their size. Their fuselages were 65 feet long, and the wing spans a prodigious 110 feet. The aircraft were painted in flamboyant patterns and colours. The first was a dazzling chessboard of brilliant scarlet and black squares and the name painted on its nose was *Das Schmetterling*—the *Butterfly*. The second was decorated with black and golden stripes. Graf Otto had christened it *Das Hummel*—the *Bumble Bee*.

Three weeks later, when the assembly of the machines was completed, Gustav told Leon, 'Now it is necessary to test them.'

'Are you going to fly them?' Leon had difficulty containing his excitement.

'*Nein!* I am not a crazy man. Only Graf Otto flies these contraptions. I am only going to ground-taxi them, but you shall ride with me.'

Early the following morning Leon mounted the boarding ladder to the commodious cockpit of the *Butterfly*. Gustav, in a long black leather coat and matching helmet with a pair of goggles, followed him and seated himself on the pilot's bench at the rear of the cockpit. From there Leon watched Gustav's every move as he waggled the elevators and ailerons with the joystick. When he was satisfied that the controls were free he gave the signal to his assistants on the ground and began the complicated starting routine. Finally all four engines were running smoothly, and Gustav gave the thumbs-up sign to his assistants, who dragged away the wheel chocks. The *Butterfly* rolled majestically out of the hangar and made four ponderous circuits of the polo ground.

'Come, take the controls!' Gustav shouted, above the din of the engines. 'Let's see if you can drive her.'

Joyfully Leon took his place on the pilot's bench and swiftly gained the feel of joystick and rudder bars.

'*Ja*, my engines can feel that you respect and cherish them. You will soon learn to get the very best out of them.'

At last they returned to the hangar, and when Leon had climbed back down the ladder to the ground, he reached up on tiptoe to pat the *Butterfly*'s nose. 'One day I'm going to fly you, my big beauty,' he whispered.

Gustav came down behind him, and Leon pointed out the racks of hooks and braces under the wings on each side of the fuselage. 'What are these for, Gustav?'

'They are for the bombs,' Gustav replied guilelessly. Leon kept his manner mildly curious. 'Of course,' he said. 'How many can she carry?'

'Many!' Gustav answered proudly. 'She is very powerful. She can lift two thousand pounds of bombs, plus a crew of five and her full tanks of fuel. She can fly at a hundred and ten miles per hour at an altitude of nine thousand feet for a distance of five hundred miles and after that return to her base. There is no other machine in the world to match her,' he boasted.

By noon the following day Penrod had cabled the precise performance figures of the Meerbach Mark III Experimental to the War Office in London.

A FEW DAYS LATER, Leon bribed his way on board the pilot boat when it went out through the mouth of Kilindini Lagoon to meet the German passenger liner SS *Admiral* from Bremerhaven as she hove up over the horizon. As he ran up the companion ladder he was challenged by the ship's fourth officer. When he mentioned his client's name, the man's manner changed quickly and he led Leon up to the bridge.

From Kermit's description, Leon recognised Graf Otto von Meerbach at first glance. He was standing in the wing of the bridge smoking a Cohiba cigar and chatting to the captain, whose manner towards him was obsequious. Graf Otto was the only passenger allowed on the bridge during the complicated manoeuvre of anchoring the massive liner. Leon studied him for a few moments, then went up to him to introduce himself.

Graf Otto wore an elegant cream tropical suit. He was as big as an oak tree and gave the impression of being all muscle. He carried himself with the poise and overbearing self-assurance of a man of limitless wealth and power. His features were hard and uncompromising. His mouth was wide, and a puckered white duelling scar ran from one corner to just under his right ear so that it seemed frozen in a lopsided sneer. His pale green eyes had an intelligent sparkle, and his short-cropped hair was bright ginger.

This is one tough, formidable bastard! Leon thought as he approached him. 'Do I have the honour of addressing Graf Otto von Meerbach?'

'*Jawohl*, you do indeed. May I ask who you are?'

'I am Leon Courtney, sir, your hunter. Welcome to British East Africa.'

Graf Otto smiled with patronising geniality, and extended his right hand.

'I have been looking forward to meeting you, Courtney, ever since I spoke to Mr Kermit Roosevelt.' Leon could match the power of Graf Otto's big, freckled hand, but it required all his strength to do so. 'He has a high opinion of you. I hope you will be able to show me some good sport?'

'Indeed, sir. I have obtained hunting permits in your name for a full bag of species. But you must inform me which quarry interests you most. Lions? Elephant?' At last Graf Otto released his hand.

'Your German is good. To answer your question, I am interested in hunting both of those species, but especially lions. I have heard that the blacks here hunt the lions with a spear. Is that true?'

'It is, sir. For the Masai and the Samburu it is a test of the young war-rior's courage and manhood.'

'I should like to witness this manner of hunting.'

'I shall arrange for you to do so.'

'Good, and I also wish to obtain several pairs of large elephant tusks.'

'You understand, sir, that although I will do my best to help you procure trophies, these are wild beasts and much will depend on luck?'

'I have always been a lucky man,' Graf Otto replied. It was a statement of fact, not a boast.

'That is abundantly obvious to even the most simple mind, sir.'

'And it is obvious that you do not have a simple mind, Mr Courtney.'

Like two heavyweight boxers at the opening of the first round, they watched each other's eyes as they smiled, keeping up their guard as they checked each other out.

Then, unexpectedly, Leon became aware of a subtle perfume on the warm, tropical air. He saw Graf Otto's eyes flick to look over his shoulder. Leon turned his head to follow his gaze.

She was there. Her loveliness surpassed Kermit's meagre description. He had been correct in one detail only: her eyes. They were an intense blue, a shade darker than violet and softer than dove grey, slanting up at the outer corners. They were wide-spaced and fringed with long, dense lashes. Her forehead was broad and the line of her jaw finely sculpted. Her hair was a lustrous sable. She wore it scraped back from her face but, beneath the brim of a fashionable little hat, soft tendrils had escaped and curled out over her ears. She was tall, almost reaching Leon's shoulder, but he could have circled her waist with his two hands.

'Eva, may I present to you Herr Courtney? He is the hunter who is to take care of us during our little African adventure. Herr Courtney, may I present Fräulein von Wellberg?' Otto said.

'Enchanted, Fräulein,' Leon responded, suddenly stuck for the German words that had until so recently come easily to him. She smiled and proffered her right hand, palm down. When he took it he found it was warm and firm. He bowed, then released her hand and stepped back a pace. She held his eyes for a moment. Looking into their depths, he had the sensation of gazing into a pool whose secrets could never be fully fathomed.

When she turned away to speak to Graf Otto, he felt a pang of elation and regret. In a blink of time it seemed he had discovered something of infinite value that, in almost the same instant, had been snatched away. When Graf Otto placed one large freckled hand on Eva's tiny waist and drew her closer to him, Leon hated him with a bitter relish.

THE TRANSFER ASHORE was soon accomplished, for Graf Otto and his lovely consort had little luggage with them. Everything else had been sent out in the first shipment aboard the SS *Silbervogel*. This luggage was quickly loaded into the Meerbach truck that stood above the beach ready to receive it.

Graf Otto turned to Leon. 'You may introduce your assistants,' he said, and Leon called Hennie and Max forward. Leon watched them fall under the German's spell. He had a way with men, but Leon knew that if anyone ever crossed or disappointed him he would turn on them mercilessly.

'*Sehr gut, meine Kinder.* Very well, children. Now we can go to Nairobi,' Graf Otto proclaimed. With the Meerbach mechanics, Hennie, Max and Ishmael climbed into the back of the waiting truck, Gustav took the wheel, and the huge vehicle roared away along the road to Nairobi.

'Courtney, you will ride with me in the hunting car,' Graf Otto told Leon. 'Fräulein von Wellberg will sit beside me, and you will take the back seat to show me the road and to point out to us the sights along the way.'

He made a fuss of settling her in the front passenger seat, with a mohair rug to cover her lap and a pair of goggles to protect her eyes from the wind. Finally he checked the three rifles in the gun rack behind his seat, then climbed behind the steering wheel, adjusted his goggles, revved the engine and accelerated away in pursuit of the truck.

He drove very fast but with effortless skill. Once the road had climbed away from the coast they entered the game fields and soon they were speeding past herds of gazelle and larger antelope. Eva laughed and clapped with delight at the multitudes as the car roared past.

'Otto!' she cried. 'What are those pretty little animals, the ones that dance and prance in that delightful manner?'

'Courtney, answer the Fräulein's question,' Graf Otto shouted.

'Those are Thomson's gazelle, Fräulein. You will see many thousands more in the days ahead. They are the most common species in this country. The peculiar gait you have noticed is known as stotting. It is a display of alarm that warns all other gazelle in sight that danger threatens.'

'Stop the car, please, Otto. I would like to sketch them.'

'As you wish, my pretty one.' He shrugged indulgently and pulled over.

Eva balanced her sketchbook on her lap. Her charcoal flew over the page and, leaning forward unobtrusively, Leon saw a perfect impression of a stotting animal, its back arched and all four legs held stiffly, appear magically on the paper before his eyes. Eva von Wellberg was a gifted artist.

From then onwards the journey was interrupted repeatedly as Eva picked out subjects she wished to draw. Although he humoured her, it was obvious that Graf Otto was becoming bored with these delays. At the next stop he dismounted and took down a rifle from the gun rack. Standing beside the car he killed five gazelle with as many shots as they bounded across the road in front of the car. It was an incredible display of marksmanship.

Although Leon despised such wanton slaughter he kept a civil tone as he asked, 'What do you wish to do with the dead animals, sir?'

'Leave them,' said Graf Otto, offhandedly, as he replaced the rifle in the rack. 'I was merely checking the sights of my rifle. Let us go on.'

Eva was pale as they drove on, Leon noticed, and her lips were pursed. He took this as evidence of her disapproval, and his opinion of her rose.

A little after midday they came round another bend in the dusty road and found Gustav standing on the verge, waiting for them. He flagged down the car, and when Graf Otto braked to a halt, he ran to the driver's side. 'I beg your pardon, sir, but your luncheon has been prepared.' He pointed to where the big truck was parked in a grove of fever trees off the road.

'Good. I'm ravenous,' Graf Otto replied. 'Jump up on the running board, Gustav, and I'll give you a lift.' With Gustav clinging to the side of the car they bumped across the rough ground towards the truck.

Ishmael had spread a sun awning between four trees and in its shade he had set up a trestle table and camp chairs. The table was covered with a snowy linen cloth, silver cutlery and china. As they climbed stiffly out of the car and stretched their limbs Ishmael came to each in turn with a basin of warm water, a bar of lavender soap and a clean hand towel.

As soon as they had washed, Max showed them to the table. Platters of carved ham and cheese were laid out, with baskets of black bread, crocks of butter and an enormous silver dish filled with Russian beluga caviar.

Eva picked delicately at the food, but Graf Otto fell to like a trencherman. When the meal was over he had polished off two bottles of Gewürztraminer on his own account, and had left the caviar dish, the platters of ham and cheese in sorry disarray.

He showed no ill-effects from the wine when he took his place in the driver's seat once more and they drove on towards Nairobi, but his speed increased substantially, and his sense of humour became less decorous.

When they came upon a party of women walking along the edge of the road with bundles of cut thatching grass balanced on their heads, Graf Otto slowed to a walking pace to study the girls' naked breasts openly. Then, as he pulled away, he laid a hand on Eva's lap in a possessive manner.

She grasped his wrist and replaced his hand on the steering wheel. 'The road is dangerous, Otto,' she remarked evenly, and Leon seethed with outrage at the humiliation he had inflicted on her.

Why did she allow herself to be the butt of such behaviour? She was not a whore. Then, with a shock, he realised that that was precisely what she was. She was a high-class courtesan, Graf Otto's plaything, and had placed her body at his disposal in return for a few tawdry ornaments and fripperies. He tried to despise her but he knew that it was far too late to hate or despise her because he had already fallen hopelessly in love.

THEY DROVE INTO TANDALA Camp as the sun was setting, and Graf Otto disappeared with Eva into their luxurious quarters. Ishmael and his kitchen staff carried their dinner into their private dining room. The couple did not reappear until after breakfast the following morning.

'We will go to the airfield,' Graf Otto announced. 'I will fly my machines.'

During the night the hunting car had been washed. Once again Leon sat in the back, and Graf Otto drove them into town and to the polo ground.

When they arrived Gustav already had the *Butterfly* and the *Bumble Bee* drawn up on the edge of the field. Graf Otto walked round each aircraft, inspecting them carefully. Then he went to the boarding ladder and climbed into the cockpit of the *Bumble Bee*. While he buckled the chinstrap of his flying helmet he signalled to Gustav to start the engines. When they were running sweetly, he taxied down to the far end of the polo field.

The four engines burst into a lion-throated roar and the *Bumble Bee* started to roll towards where Eva and Leon stood in front of the hangar. Swiftly the *Bumble Bee* gathered speed. She lifted her tail wheel from the ground and Leon held his breath as he watched the massive undercarriage bounce lightly over the turf, then rise into the air. With a mere twenty feet to spare, the machine bellowed over their heads. The crowd ducked instinctively—everyone except Eva.

As Leon straightened he saw that she had been watching him covertly. A faintly mocking smile lifted the corners of her mouth. 'Goodness me!' she taunted him lightly. 'Is this the fearless slayer of wild animals?'

It was only the second time that she had looked him full in the face, and the first that she had addressed him directly.

'Fräulein, I hope this is the only time that I fall short of your expectations.' He gave her a small bow.

She turned away, terminating the brief contact, and shaded her eyes to watch the *Bumble Bee* circle the field. Leon followed her gaze and saw that the *Bumble Bee* was already dropping towards the field for a landing.

Graf Otto touched down and taxied back to the hangar. He cut the engines and clambered down. Gustav rushed to meet him, and the two men walked across to the *Butterfly* deep in conversation. Graf Otto left Gustav at the foot of the ladder, climbed up into the cockpit and started the engines. He taxied her to the end of the polo field, turned her and came thundering back towards them, sweeping low over their heads.

This time Leon stood stock still, and when he glanced at Eva she was watching him again. She inclined her head and her violet eyes sparkled with fun. Her voice was drowned by the hubbub of the spectators, but he could read her lips as they formed a single word: 'Bravo!' The aircraft circled the field, then touched down and taxied to where they stood in front of the hangar. Graf Otto leaned over the side of the cockpit and signalled to Eva to come to him. She moved quickly to do his bidding, Gustav and two of his men running ahead of her with the boarding ladder.

Eva reached the bottom of the ladder and climbed up the rungs, then disappeared over the rim of the cockpit. Graf Otto's helmeted head turned towards Leon and he beckoned. Taken by surprise, Leon touched his own chest in an interrogatory gesture. 'Me?' Graf Otto nodded emphatically.

His heart pounding with excitement, Leon scrambled up the ladder. Eva barely turned her head in his direction as he dropped into the cockpit. From somewhere she had found herself a leather flying helmet, which she anchored under her chin. Then she covered her eyes with the goggles.

'Sit here!' Graf Otto indicated the seat beside him. Leon sat in it and fastened the safety strap across his lap. Graf Otto cupped his hands into a trumpet and bellowed into his ear, 'You will navigate for me, *ja*?'

'Where are we going?' Leon shouted back.

'To the closest of your hunting camps.'

'That's more than a hundred miles away,' Leon protested.

'A short hop. *Ja!* We will go there.' He taxied back to the far side of the field, then slowly pushed the four throttle levers forward. The *Butterfly* bounded forward, bumping over every irregularity in the ground.

Leon clung to the rim of the cockpit, peering ahead. Tears started from his eyes as the wind ripped at them, but his heart was singing. Then, suddenly, he looked over the side and saw the earth dropping away below him. 'We're flying!' he shouted into the wind. 'We're really flying!' He saw the town below him but everything looked so different. He had to take his bearings from the snake of the railway line before he could pick out other landmarks: the pink walls of the Muthaiga Country Club; the whitewashed bulk of Government House and the governor's residence.

'Which way?' Graf Otto demanded.

'Follow the railway line.' Leon pointed westwards.

Graf Otto pointed at a cubbyhole in the side of the cockpit. Leon opened it and found another leather flying helmet. He pulled it over his head, then adjusted the goggles over his eyes. Now he could see, and the side flaps of the helmet protected his eardrums from the roar of the rushing wind.

Eva had meanwhile risen from her seat and moved to the front of the cockpit where she was standing, holding the handrail that ran round the rim of the plane's nose, balancing against the motion of the *Butterfly*. Leon noticed the safety belt buckled round her waist and the karabiner snap-link at the other end of the lanyard hooked into a steel eye bolt in the floorboards between her feet.

Graf Otto grinned at Leon and gestured, 'Go forward. Go forward to where you can see ahead to guide me.' Leon edged gingerly to the front of the cockpit. Without a glance in his direction Eva moved aside to make room for him and he took up his position beside her. They braced themselves with both hands on the rail.

They were approaching the rim of the Great Rift Valley. Leon picked out the glint of the steel tracks where the railway began its descent to the valley floor. He gave Graf Otto a hand signal to turn ninety degrees southwards. The German nodded and the *Butterfly* dropped one wing and went into a lazy left-hand turn. Centrifugal force pushed Eva against him, and for a long, exquisite moment Leon felt the outside of her warm thigh press against his. She made no move to pull away. The Graf Otto lifted the port wing and the *Butterfly* came back on to an even keel again. The contact was broken.

The Great Rift Valley opened before them. From this altitude it was a breathtaking vista: the seared and rocky hills, the lion-coloured plains blotched with dark expanses of forest, and the blue palisades of hills and mountains stretching away into infinite distances.

Suddenly the deck canted under their feet as Graf Otto lowered the

Butterfly's nose and she dropped into the airy void. The valley floor loomed up to meet them and Leon saw Eva's fists tighten into balls on the handrail.

Graf Otto pulled the *Butterfly*'s nose up out of her dive and Leon's knees buckled under the force of gravity. Eva was pushed against him once more. She swayed away as the *Butterfly* came back again on to even keel.

Leon saw what appeared to be a swarm of large black scarab beetles crawling along a mile or so ahead. It was only when the *Butterfly* raced down on them that he saw it was a large herd of buffalo charging away in panic. He made another hand signal to Graf Otto, and the *Butterfly* banked steeply towards the fleeing herd. Once again Eva was pressed against him, but this time she gave him a deliberate bump with her hip. With a surge like electricity through his loins, he understood she was letting him know that she was just as aware of these physical contacts as he was.

They flew on until Eva waved excitedly and pointed out on her side of the fuselage. Graf Otto banked in the direction she was pointing. The *Butterfly* lined up on five huge elephant bulls, wading through the dense, thorny undergrowth a short distance ahead. Eva gave him another cheeky little bump with her hip. It was a dangerous game they were playing, right under Graf Otto's nose. Leon laughed and, without moving her head, Eva peeped at him through lowered lashes and smiled.

Graf Otto climbed several hundred feet above the ground and flew on southwards until they could make out Kilimanjaro looming on the southern horizon a hundred miles or more ahead. Graf Otto pointed out a closer mountain. The table top was unmistakable.

'Lonsonyo Mountain!' Leon cried, his voice almost lost in the roar of the engines. 'Go there!' He made vehement hand signals, and Graf Otto opened the throttles wide. The *Butterfly* rose upwards, but the table of Lonsonyo stood almost 10,000 feet above sea level, near the aircraft ceiling. At first she climbed rapidly, but as the altitude increased she became so sluggish that they cleared the top of the cliffs by no more than fifty feet.

Before them, Leon picked out the pattern of the huts and cattle pens that formed the *manyatta*, and signalled to Otto to turn towards the village. Goats, chickens and naked herd-boys scattered at their approach. It was easy to single out Lusima's hut, the largest and grandest.

There was no sign of Lusima until they were almost directly overhead. Then, suddenly, she appeared, ducking out of the low doorway of her hut and staring up with an expression of bewilderment.

'Lusima!' Leon yelled, and ripped off his helmet and goggles. 'Lusima Mama! It is me! M'bogo, your son!' He waved frantically and suddenly she recognised him. He saw her face light up and she waved with both hands, but then they were past and dropping down the far side of the mountain.

When they flew out of the shadow of the mountain, the sun was already low on the horizon. Leon gazed out over the purple plain, searching for the hunting camp. At last, far ahead, he picked out the silver sausage of the windsock that marked the airstrip he had had cleared. He signed to Graf Otto to turn towards it, and soon they could make out the cluster of canvas and newly thatched roofs of what Leon had named Percy's Camp.

As Graf Otto touched down and let the *Butterfly* run out to the far end of the strip, they saw a cloud of dust tearing down the rutted track from the camp. A motor car clattered into view with Hennie du Rand at the wheel, Manyoro and Loikot perched at the back.

'So sorry, boss!' Hennie greeted Leon, when he came down the ladder from the cockpit. 'We were not expecting you to arrive for another few weeks at least. You've taken us by surprise.' He was visibly flustered.

'I'm as surprised to be here as you are to see me. The Graf works to his own timetable. Is there food and liquor in camp?'

'*Ja!*' Hennie nodded. 'Max brought plenty from Tandala.'

'Is there hot water in the shower? Are the beds made up, and is there paper in the thunderbox?'

'There will be before you can ask again,' Hennie promised.

'Then we shall be all right.' Leon turned to Graf Otto as he came down the ladder. 'I'm pleased to be able to tell you that all is in readiness for you, sir,' he lied blithely, and led the couple to their quarters.

SOMEHOW HENNIE and his chef had performed a miracle of improvisation. They had put together a passable meal from the crates of provisions Max had brought from Tandala.

When Eva entered the mess tent, Leon only just took his eyes off her in time before Graf Otto came in behind her.

Hennie had cooled a few cases of lager in canvas wet-bags. The Graf drank nearly half a gallon of it before dinner was served. When he took his seat at the head of the table, he changed his tipple to Burgundy, a notable Romanée Conti 1896. It went perfectly with the hors d'oeuvre of gerenuk liver pâté and the entrée of wild duck breasts on slices of fried foie gras.

Graf Otto rounded off the meal with a few glasses of a fifty-year-old port and a Montecristo cigar from Havana.

He sighed with pleasure as he leaned back in his chair. 'Courtney, you saw those buffalo we flew over while we were coming in to land, *ja*?'

'I did, sir. But not one is worth the price of a cartridge.'

'Ah, so, would they not be dangerous?'

'They would be very dangerous, but—'

Graf Otto cut him off and scowled. ' "But" is a word I do not like very much, Courtney.' His mood had altered dramatically.

Leon had not yet learned that this was a danger sign. He went on regardless: 'I was just going to say that—'

'I have no great interest in what you were going to say, Courtney. I would rather you listened to what *I* have to say.'

Leon flushed at the rebuke, but then he saw Eva, who was sitting out of Graf Otto's direct line of sight, purse her lips and shake her head almost imperceptibly. He drew a deep breath and, with an effort, took heed of her warning. 'You wish to hunt those bulls, sir?'

'Ah, Courtney, you are not such a *Dummkopf* as you often appear to be!' He laughed as he switched back into geniality. 'Yes, indeed, I wish to shoot those bulls. You can show me how dangerous they truly are, *ja*?'

'I did not bring my rifle from Tandala.'

'You do not need it. I am the one who will do the shooting.'

'You wish me to accompany you unarmed?'

'Is the sauce too rich for your stomach, Courtney? If so, you may remain in bed tomorrow or under it. Wherever you feel warmest and safest.'

'When you hunt, I shall be at your side.'

'I am pleased that we understand each other. It makes everything simpler, does it not?' He drew on his cigar until the tip glowed brightly, then blew a perfect smoke ring that rolled across the table towards Leon's face.

Eva intervened smoothly to quench their rising tempers. 'Otto, what was that beautiful flat-topped mountain you flew us over this afternoon?'

'Tell us about it, Courtney,' he commanded.

'It is called Lonsonyo Mountain, a sacred site to the Masai, and the home of one of their most powerful spiritual leaders. She is a seer who is able to divine the future with amazing accuracy.'

'Oh, Otto!' she exclaimed. 'That must have been the woman we saw coming out of the largest hut. What is her name, this prophetess?'

'You are amused by all this magical mumbo jumbo?' Graf Otto asked.

'You know I love to have my fortune told.' She smiled prettily. 'Remember the Gypsy woman in Prague? She told me my heart belonged to a strong, loving man, who would cherish me always. You, of course!'

'Of course. Who else could it have been?' He turned from her and raised a ginger eyebrow at Leon. 'What is her name, this diviner?'

'Her name is Lusima, sir,' Leon answered.

'How well do you know her?' Graf Otto demanded.

'She has adopted me as her son so we are well enough acquainted.'

'Ha, ha! If she has adopted you, it seems she is not a woman of good judgment. However . . .' Graf Otto spread his hands in surrender as he gazed at Eva '. . . I see that I will have no peace until I agree to this whimsy of yours. Very well, I will take you to visit this old woman of the mountain.'

'Thank you so much, Otto.' Eva stroked the back of his hand. Leon felt an acidic flood of jealousy burn the lining of his stomach. 'Now you see that the Prague Gypsy was right. When will you take me there?'

'We shall see,' Graf Otto hedged, and changed the subject. 'Courtney, I will be ready at daybreak. It is no more than a few kilometres to where we last saw that herd. I wish to arrive before the sun is up.'

By the time they returned to camp at the end of the next morning's hunting, Graf Otto had killed three buffalo. He turned breakfast into a celebration of his prowess. He sat at the head of the table wolfing ham and eggs, and swigging the coffee he had laced with cognac while he regaled Eva with a highly coloured description of the hunt.

Outside the tent they could hear Hennie du Rand and the skinners getting into the back of a horse-drawn cart, armed with axes and butcher's knives. 'What are those people doing, Courtney?'

'They are going to bring in your dead buffalos.'

Graf Otto stood up. 'I will go with them to watch.'

This was another of his typically idiosyncratic decisions, but still it took Leon by surprise. 'Of course, I will come with you.'

'No need for that, Courtney. You can stay here and see to the refuelling of the *Butterfly* for the flight back to Nairobi. I will take Fräulein von Wellberg with me. She will be bored sitting in camp.'

I would do my best to entertain her if you gave me half a chance, Leon thought. 'As you wish, Graf,' he acquiesced.

HENNIE WAS OVERAWED to have such illustrious company travelling with him in the truck, even for the short ride to where the carcasses lay. As he climbed into the driver's seat, Graf Otto put him more at ease by offering him a cigar. After the first few puffs Hennie had relaxed to the point at which he was able to answer Otto's questions coherently, rather than in an embarrassed mumble.

'So, du Rand, they tell me you are South African, *ja*?'

'No, sir. I am a Boer.'

'Is that different?'

'*Ja*, it is very different. South Africans have British blood. My blood is pure. I am one of a chosen Volk.'

'To me it sounds as though you do not like the British very much.'

'I like some of them. I like my boss, Leon Courtney.'

'But you fought against the British during the war, didn't you?'

Hennie said in a noncommittal tone, 'The war is finished.'

'*Ja*, it is finished, but it was a bad war. The British burned your farms. They put your women and children in the camps. Many died there.'

'*Ja*. It is true,' Hennie whispered. 'Many died.'

'Now the land is ruined and there is no food for the children, and your Volk are slaves to Britain, *nein*?'

Hennie's eyes were filled with tears. He wiped them away with a callused thumb.

'Which commando did you ride with?'

'I did not say I rode with any commando.'

'Let me guess,' Graf Otto suggested. 'Perhaps you rode with Smuts.'

Hennie shook his head with an expression of bitter distaste. 'Jannie Smuts is a traitor to his people. He and Louis Botha have gone over to the khaki. They are selling our birthright to the British.'

'Ah!' Graf Otto exclaimed. 'You hate Smuts and Botha. I know then who you rode with. It must have been Koos de la Rey.' He did not wait for an answer. 'Tell me, du Rand, what manner of man was General Jacobus Herculaas de la Rey? I have heard tell that he was a great soldier. Is that true?'

'He was no ordinary man. To us he was a god.'

'If there were ever to be another war, would you follow de la Rey again?'

'I would follow him through the gates of hell. We all would.'

'Would you like to meet de la Rey again?'

'That is not possible,' Hennie mumbled.

'With me everything is possible. I can make anything happen. Say nothing to anybody else. Not even to your boss. This is between you and me alone. One day soon I will take you with me to see General de la Rey.'

Eva was crammed in beside him. She was obviously uncomfortable and bored with the conversation in English, a language she did not understand. Graf Otto knew that her only languages were German and French.

Leon refuelled the *Butterfly* from one of the fifty-gallon drums that had been brought from Nairobi by Gustav in the big Meerbach truck. While he was doing this he sent Manyoro and Loikot to the top of the hill above the camp to join the Masai grapevine and gather any news that might be of interest. He was washing his hands in the basin in front of his tent when the two Masai came down from the hill and reported to him the few items of interest they had gathered.

It was said that four lions had come down into the Rift Valley from the direction of Keekorok, all young males. Two nights previously the youngsters had killed six heifers from the *manyatta* directly to the west of Lonsonyo Mountain. The call had gone out to the *morani* to gather at this village, which was named Sonjo. They were going to deal out to these four cattle-killing lions a summary lesson in manners.

Leon was pleased with this news. Graf Otto had expressed a keen desire to watch a ceremonial hunt, and this was a most fortuitous coincidence. He despatched Manyoro to the Sonjo *manyatta*, which was hosting the lion hunters, with a gift of a hundred shillings for the local chieftain and a request that he allow the *wazungu* to be spectators at the hunt.

By the time Graf Otto returned from butchering the buffalo carcasses, Leon had the horses saddled and the pack mules loaded with supplies. As his client disembarked Leon hurriedly told him the good news.

Graf Otto was excited. 'Quickly, Eva! We must go at once. I do not want to miss the show.'

They pushed the horses along at a canter, covering almost twenty miles before it became too dark to see the ground ahead. Then they dismounted and unsaddled. They ate a cold dinner and slept rough. The next morning they were away again before it was fully light.

Some time before noon the next day, as they neared Sonjo, they heard drums and singing. Manyoro had come from the village to await their arrival. 'All is arranged, M'bogo,' he said. 'But you must hurry. The *morani* are becoming restless. They are eager to blood their spears and win honour.'

The *morani* were gathered in the centre of the cattle pen. They were young men, fifty strong, dressed in red leather kilts decorated with ivory beads and cowrie shells. Their naked torsos gleamed with a coating of fat and red ochre. Their hair was dressed in an elaborate style of coiled plaits. They were lean and long-limbed, elegantly muscled, their features handsome and eyes bright and rapacious.

They had formed up in single file, shoulder to shoulder. At their head was a senior *morani*, an experienced warrior. His war-bonnet was the headskin of a black-maned lion which he had taken single-handed with the *assegai*. He had a signal whistle made from the horn of a reed buck hanging on a thong round his neck.

Several hundred older men, with women and children, lined the outer stockade to watch the dance. The women clapped and ululated. As the three whites rode into the *manyatta* the drums took on an ever more savage and frenetic rhythm, working the warriors into a fighting frenzy.

Then the leader blew a shrill command on his whistle and the troop began to sally forth from the cattle pen, single file, down the grassy slope. They carried on their shoulders their long rawhide shields, each painted with a single large eye of black and ochre, the pupil glaring white.

'How do they know where to find the quarry?' Graf Otto asked.

'They have scouts watching over the lions,' Leon answered. 'They have killed, and they will not leave until they have finished the meat.'

Manyoro was running at Leon's stirrup. He said something and Leon stooped in the saddle to listen to him. When he straightened up he told Graf Otto, 'Manyoro says the dead cattle are lying in a shallow basin over the next rise.' He pointed ahead. 'If we circle out to the right, and take up position on the high ground, we will have a grandstand view.'

He led them off the track and they cantered in a wide circle to get ahead of the file of *morani*. Manyoro had given them good advice. When they reined in on the crest, they had a fine view of the rotting carcasses of the cattle.

Now the single file of warriors split into two. The twin lines opened to form a noose that would encircle the grassy hollow. Swiftly the manoeuvre was completed. A wall of shields and spears ringed the basin.

'I cannot see the lions,' Eva said. 'Are you sure they have not escaped?'

But before either man could answer her, a lion stood up in full view.

He had been lying flat against the earth, his coat blending perfectly with the sun-scorched brown grass. Although he was young, he was big and rangy. He snarled at the *morani*, his lips peeling back from his long, bright fangs.

They returned his greeting: 'We see you, evil one! We see you, killer of our cattle.'

The sound of fifty voices alarmed the other lions. They rose from their hiding places in the short grass, crouched low and glared at the ring of shields. Their tails twitched; they snarled and growled with fear and anger.

The *morani* began to chant the chorus of the Lion Song and moved forward in unison, shuffling and stamping. Slowly they closed in on the four lions. One lion made a mock-charge at the wall, and the *morani* shook their shields and called to him, 'Come! We are ready to welcome you!'

The lion broke off his charge, coming up short on stiff front legs. He glared at the men, then spun round and ran back to join his siblings. They milled uneasily, growling, and erected their manes in a threatening display.

'The big one will be the first to charge,' said Graf Otto and, as he spoke, the largest of the four lions launched himself straight at the shields. The senior *morani* blew a blast on his whistle. Then he pointed out a man who was directly in the line of the charge. 'Katchikoi!' he shouted.

The warrior who had been chosen sprang high in the air, then broke out of the line and raced to meet the charging lion with long, bounding strides. The lion saw him coming, and swerved towards him.

As they came together the *morani* altered the angle of his charge, turning into the lion, forcing him to come in from the right, into his spear arm. Then he dropped on one knee behind his shield. The point of his *assegai* was aimed at the centre of the lion's chest, and the beast ran straight onto the steel. Katchikoi released his grip on the haft, leaving the blade buried in the lion's chest. He raised the rawhide shield and the lion crashed headlong into it. He did not try to resist the weight of the great cat's leap; instead he rolled over backwards and curled himself into a ball holding up the shield.

Despite the *assegai*, the lion's strength was undiminished. He tore at the shield with both front paws, raking deep gouges in the leather.

The hunt master blew a short blast on his buckhorn and four of Katchikoi's comrades raced forward until they had the lion surrounded. Their *assegais* rose and fell as they drove the long blades deep into the lion's vital organs. The beast gave a mighty groan, then collapsed and lay still.

Katchikoi sprang to his feet, seized the handle of his *assegai*, placed one foot on the lion's chest and drew the blade clear. Brandishing the bloody steel, he led his four companions back to their places in the ring of warriors. They were greeted with shouts of acclamation, and a salute of raised spears. Then the ring of *morani* moved forward again, tightening inexorably round the remaining three lions, their shields overlapping.

In the centre the three lions rushed back and forth, seeking escape. They charged, then broke off and turned back. At last one screwed up its courage and charged. The *morani* who met him drove the blade of his *assegai* fully home, but as he went over backwards with the lion on top, its claws ripped the shield aside, exposing the man's head and his naked torso. While its claws tore the man's chest open, the mortally wounded lion opened its jaws to their full extent and crushed the human skull like a walnut in a nutcracker. The dead man's comrades speared the lion in a fury of vengeance.

In quick succession the last two lions charged into the front rank of warriors, which broke over them, like an ocean wave upon a rock. They died under the spears, crackling with snarls, lashing out with hooked claws and desperate futility, as the razor steel stabbed deeply into them.

His brothers laid the torn body of the dead *morani* on his shield. Then, they lifted him high in the air and bore him home singing his praise song. As they passed the watchers on the hilltop, Graf Otto lifted a clenched fist in a salute. The *morani* acknowledged it with raised *assegais* and a wild shout.

'There was a man who died a man's death.' Graf Otto spoke with solemn intensity. 'This makes all the ethics of the hunt that I have believed in seem ignoble. How can I count myself a true hunter until I have stood to meet such a magnificent beast with only a spear in my hand?' He swivelled in the saddle and glared at Leon. 'Get me a lion, Courtney, a full-grown black-maned lion. I will take him on foot. No guns. Just the beast and me.'

THEY CAMPED THAT NIGHT at the *manyatta* of Sonjo and lay awake listening to the drums beating a dirge for the dead *morani*. In the darkness before dawn, they rode out again. When the sunrise broke over the Rift Valley it swamped the eastern sky with a blazing grandeur of gold and crimson, dazzling their eyes and warming their bodies so that they shrugged off their overcoats and rode on in shirtsleeves.

Eva pointed with her riding crop and called out gaily, 'Oh, see that small creature snuffling around in the grass? What is it?'

Leon felt that she was sharing the moment with him alone and answered,

'It is a honey badger, Fräulein. He appears gentle but he is one of the most ferocious creatures in Africa. He is without fear and immensely powerful.'

Eva gave him a flash of her violet eyes, then turned to Graf Otto with a purr of sweet laughter. 'In all of that he resembles you. In future I shall think of you as my honey badger.'

To which of them was she speaking? Leon wondered. With this woman a man could never be sure of anything.

Before he could decide, she stood in the stirrups and pointed towards the southern horizon. 'Look at that mountain over there!' The distant shape of the flat-topped summit was dramatically highlighted by the rising sun. 'Surely it must be the mountain on which the Masai prophetess lives.'

'Yes, Fräulein. That is Lonsonyo Mountain,' Leon confirmed.

'Oh, Otto, it is so close!' she cried. 'You promised to take me there.'

'Indeed I did,' he agreed. 'But I did not promise when.'

'Then promise me now. When?' she demanded. 'When, darling Otto?'

'Not now. We must return to Nairobi at once. This delay was an indulgence. I have important business to see to. This African safari was not all for pleasure.'

'Of course not.' She grimaced. 'With you it is always business.'

'How else could I afford you?' Graf Otto asked, with heavy humour, and Leon turned away so as not to reveal his quick anger at the unkind remark.

But Eva seemed neither to hear nor to care. 'And when your business is done, will you take me to Lonsonyo Mountain?' she persisted.

Graf Otto shook his head in mock-despair. 'You do not give up easily. Very well. I will make a bargain with you. After I have killed my lion with the *assegai* I will take you to see this witch.'

They rested the horses at noon, in a grove of stately pod mahogany trees beside a small reed pool. After an hour they saddled up to ride on, but standing beside her mare Eva exclaimed irritably, 'The safety clasp on my right stirrup is locked. If I were to fall I would be dragged.'

'See to it, Courtney,' Graf Otto ordered.

Leon went quickly to Eva's side. She was beside him as he stooped to examine the steel, both hidden from Graf Otto's view by the body of the horse. Leon found she was right: the safety clasp was locked. It had been open when they had left Sonjo that morning—he had checked it himself. Then Eva touched his hand, and his heart tripped. She must have altered the clasp herself as an excuse to have him alone for a moment. She was so close that he could feel her breath on his cheek. For an instant he looked into the violet depths of her eyes and saw the woman behind the lovely mask.

'I must go to the mountain. There is something there for me.' Her whisper was so soft he might have imagined it. 'He will never take me. You must. Please, Badger.' The heartfelt plea and the new pet name with which she had dubbed him made him catch his breath.

'What is the matter, Courtney?' Graf Otto called.

'The clasp was locked.' Leon drew out his knife and used the blade to prise open the clasp. 'It will be all right now,' he assured Eva. He dared to stroke the back of the hand that lay on the saddle. She did not pull it away.

'Mount up! We must ride on,' Graf Otto ordered. 'We have wasted enough time here. I wish to fly back to Nairobi today. We must reach the airstrip while there is still sufficient daylight for the flight.'

LEON BELIEVED that the visit to Percy's Camp and the buffalo hunt signalled the start of the safari in earnest. His assumption was incorrect.

The second morning after their return from the camp, Graf Otto sat at the head of the breakfast table at Tandala Camp with a dozen envelopes stacked in front of him. Every one was an invitation.

Graf Otto translated excerpts from each missive to Eva. It seemed that all of Nairobi society was agog to have in their midst Graf Otto von Meerbach. Like any other frontier town, Nairobi needed little excuse for a party.

The governor of the colony was hosting a special dinner at Government House in the Graf's honour. Lord Delamere was holding a formal ball at his new Norfolk Hotel to welcome him and Fräulein von Wellberg to the territory. The committee of the Muthaiga Country Club, not to be outdone, were throwing a ball to initiate him into club membership.

Graf Otto was delighted by the furore he had stirred up. He accepted every one of the invitations, and in return issued his own to spectacular dinners and balls that he would host at the Norfolk, the Muthaiga or out at Tandala Camp. However, his masterstroke of hospitality, which earned him the instant reputation of being a cracking good fellow, was his open day. He issued a public invitation to a picnic on the polo ground at which selected guests such as the governor, Delamere and Brigadier General Penrod Ballantyne would be given a flight over the town in one of his aeroplanes. Eva exerted her influence and persuaded him to extend the invitation to every boy and girl between six and twelve. The entire colony went into raptures. The ladies were determined to turn the open day into an African equivalent of Ascot. From a simple picnic it snowballed into an almost royal occasion.

Leon was sucked into this feverish activity. Graf Otto needed a second pilot to deal with the hordes of children. He would pilot the senior guests, but he was not enthusiastic about filling his cockpit with their offspring.

'Courtney, today I will teach you to fly,' Graf Otto said.

LEON SAT BESIDE GRAF OTTO in the cockpit of the *Bumble Bee* and listened intently as he described the functions of each dial and instrument. Despite their complexity, he already had a working knowledge of the flight-deck layout, acquired from watching when Graf Otto flew.

Leon was pleasantly surprised by the Graf's patience. They began on engine start-up and shut-down, then moved on quickly to ground taxiing: cross wind, down wind and into the wind. Leon started to feel the controls and the big machine's response to them, like the reins and stirrups of a horse.

Nevertheless he was surprised when Graf Otto tossed him a leather flying helmet. 'Put it on.' They had taxied to the far end of the polo ground, and he shouted above the engine roar, 'Nose to wind!' Leon put on full starboard rudder and gunned the two port engines. The *Bumble Bee* came round and put her nose into the wind.

'So fly!' Graf Otto shouted into his ear.

Leon gave him a horrified, disbelieving look. He wasn't ready yet.

'*Gott in Himmel!*' Graf Otto bellowed. 'Why are you waiting? Fly her!'

Leon took a long, slow breath and reached for the bank of throttles. He opened them gradually and felt the joystick come alive in his hands. His heart began to sing in the rush of the wind and he felt the *Bumble Bee* bounce lightly under him. She wants to fly, he thought. We both want to fly!

Beside him Graf Otto made a small gesture, and Leon pressed the joystick gently forward. Behind him the massive tailplane lifted clear of the grassy surface. Once, twice, the wheels bounced and then she was flying. He lifted the nose and settled it on the horizon ahead. They went up and up. He was flying. He was really flying.

Beside him Graf Otto nodded approvingly, then gave him the signal to level out of the climb, to bank left and bank right. Stick and rudder together, Leon put the *Bumble Bee* over, and she responded docilely.

Graf Otto nodded again and raised his voice so that Leon could catch the words: 'Some are born with the wind in our hair and the starlight in our eyes. I think you may be one of us, Courtney.'

Under his instructions Leon circled wide, then lined up on the runway. He pushed the nose down and dived towards the field, coming in much too fast. The *Bumble Bee* hit the ground with a crash and ballooned up off the grassy strip. He was forced to open the throttles wide and go round again. Beside him Graf Otto laughed. 'Try again.'

On the next approach he did better. She touched down with a jolt but did not bounce. Graf Otto laughed again. 'Good! Much better! Go round again.'

Leon was getting the feel of it quickly. Each of the next three landings was an improvement on the preceding effort, and on the fourth, the main undercarriage and tail wheel kissed the ground in unison.

'Excellent!' Graf Otto shouted. 'Taxi to the hangar!'

When he swung the *Bumble Bee* round in front of the hangar he reached for the fuel cock to shut off the engines, but Graf Otto forestalled him. 'No! I am getting out, but you are not. I promised to teach you how to fly, and I have done so. Now go and fly, Courtney.' Graf Otto von Meerbach scrambled over the side of the cockpit and disappeared, leaving Leon, after the grand total of three hours' tuition, facing his first solo flight.

His mind was in a spin. He had forgotten everything he had just learned. He began his takeoff run with the wind behind his tail. The *Bumble Bee* ran and ran, building up speed so gradually that he was only able to wrench her into the air seconds before she hit the boundary fence. He cleared it with three feet to spare, but at least he was flying. He glanced over his shoulder and saw Graf Otto standing in front of the hangar with his fists on his hips, his head thrown back and his body convulsed with laughter.

'Wonderful sense of humour you have, von Meerbach. Deliberately sending up a complete novice to kill himself. Anything for a laugh!' But his anger was ephemeral and forgotten almost immediately. He was flying solo.

The sky was bright and clear and the wide expanse of the Athi Plains opened ahead. He dropped to thirty feet above the earth and charged across the treeless wilderness. He climbed again and turned towards the line of the Ngong Hills. From two miles out he picked out the thatched roofs of Tandala Camp. He turned back towards the airstrip and saw the horse directly ahead, the grey mare Eva favoured. Then he saw her standing at its head. She wore a yellow blouse and a wide-brimmed straw hat. She looked up with indifference at the approaching aircraft.

Of course, she thinks it's Graf Otto. Leon smiled to himself and dropped towards her. He pushed back his goggles and leaned over the side of the cockpit. The moment she recognised him she threw back her head and he saw the flash of her teeth as she laughed. She snatched off her hat and waved it as he thundered over her.

GRAF OTTO VON MEERBACH'S open day at the airfield seemed to overshadow almost any other event in the history of the colony. By sunrise of the great event a small city of tents surrounded the polo ground. Most housed the settler families who had come in from the surrounding countryside. The others were refreshment booths from which, throughout the day, Lord Delamere dispensed free beer and lemonade, and the Women's Institute handed out chocolate cakes and apple pies. The chef from the Norfolk Hotel was supervising the roasting of the oxen on the spits over live coals. The KAR band was tuning its instruments in readiness for the arrival of the governor. Lines of excited children were queuing for the promised flights, squealing with excitement.

By this time Leon had flown a total of twelve hours in the *Bumble Bee* and Graf Otto assured anxious parents that their offspring would be quite safe with such an experienced pilot.

Eva assumed responsibility for controlling the hordes of children. Her face was radiant and her eyes shone as she passed little ones up into the cockpit of the *Bumble Bee*, where Leon and Hennie du Rand strapped them onto the benches. When the cockpit was filled almost to overflowing Leon started the engines and the children squeaked in delicious terror. Then the *Bumble Bee* taxied out onto the field, following Graf Otto in the *Butterfly* with his more dignified passengers. The two aircraft took off in formation and circled the town twice, then returned to the field for landing.

Leon was fascinated by this new manifestation of Eva's inner warmth. This was a different woman from Graf Otto's beautiful, enigmatic consort. It seemed to Leon that she had become a child herself, totally happy and natural, and as the day wore on she was indefatigable. He glanced round. Graf Otto had taken off in the *Butterfly* for his next circuit. For the moment they were not under surveillance.

'Eva!' he called.

She returned the children to their mothers and came to the side of the aircraft where she pretended to fuss with those who were waiting. She spoke to Leon without looking at him. 'You like to live dangerously, Badger. You know we should not talk in public.'

'Is there no way we can ever be alone together? There is so much I want to say to you. I think you know how I feel about you.'

'Yes, Badger, I know. You're not good at keeping secrets,' she laughed. 'Be patient. Please. No more now.' She pushed Vilabjhi's daughter up the ladder into the cockpit and went to where Mr Vilabjhi was watching anxiously from the gate. When Leon brought the *Bumble Bee* back into the field after the flight she was still standing at the gate in conversation with him.

Every man in the colony is fascinated by her and I am right at the back of the queue. Leon was surprised by the strength of his own jealousy.

LADIES' NIGHT at the KAR regimental mess was another towering success for all but Leon. He stood at the bar and watched Penrod waltzing with Eva. His uncle was a striking figure in his dress uniform and danced gracefully. Eva was light in his arms, her shining dark hair swept up and her shoulders bare. As they whirled past, Leon picked up snatches of their conversation. They were talking French, and Penrod was at his most charming.

The evening dragged on interminably for Leon. The jokes of his brother officers creaked with age, the speeches were dull, the music loud and tuneless, and even the whisky tasted sour. He escaped out into the night.

The air was sweet, the sky clear, and the stars were wondrous. Leon thrust his hands into his pockets and sauntered glumly round the parade ground. As he completed the circuit and came back towards the mess, he saw a small group of men on the verandah. They were smoking cigars, and Leon heard a familiar braying voice holding forth from the centre of the group. Froggy Snell, he thought irritably. Just when I was starting to feel better, the last person in the world I wanted to meet.

Fortunately there was a rear entrance to the dance hall so he made his way quietly along the side wall of the building, which was covered with a dense trumpeter vine.

As he turned the corner a Vesta flared in the darkness close by and he saw a couple standing among the concealing curtain of the vine's leaves and flowers. The woman had her back to him. She had struck the Vesta and was holding it for the man, who stooped over the flame to light his cigar. He straightened up, puffing out streams of smoke. Leon saw that the man was Penrod. Neither he nor the woman was aware of his presence.

'Thank you, my dear,' Penrod said, in English. Then he spotted Leon and his expression changed to one of mild alarm. 'It's Leon!' he exclaimed.

An odd remark, Leon thought. It sounded like a warning rather than a friendly greeting. The woman whirled round to face him, still holding the burning Vesta. She let it drop but he had seen the expression on her face. She and Penrod were behaving like a pair of conspirators.

'Monsieur Courtney, you made me jump. I didn't hear you coming.'

She spoke in French – but why, only seconds before, had Penrod been speaking to her in English? 'Forgive me. I'm intruding.'

'Not at all,' Penrod denied it. 'The air in the hall is oppressive. Fräulein von Wellberg needed a breath of fresh air. And I, on the other hand, needed a smoke.' He switched to French when he addressed Eva: 'I was telling my nephew that you were a little indisposed by the heat and the stale air.'

'I am feeling perfectly well now,' she replied, in the same language.

Something strange is going on here, Leon thought with some bitterness. He bowed to Eva. 'Please excuse me, Fräulein, but I am not as strong as you two are. I shall go home to get some sleep. Will you and the Graf be returning to Tandala Camp after the ball, or will you stay at the hotel?'

'I understand that Gustav will drive us back to the camp,' Eva replied.

'Very well. I have instructed my staff to have everything ready for your return.' He nodded at Penrod and left them. When he reached the door of the hall he glanced back. Just what are the two of you up to? Who are you really, Eva von Wellberg? The closer I get to you, the more elusive you become. The more I learn about you, the less I know.

LEON WAS AWAKENED later that night by the sound of the Meerbach hunting car coming down the track from the town. He heard the car come to a halt, and the slamming of its doors, of Graf Otto's voice shouting good night to Gustav, and Eva's laughter. Leon felt a stab of jealousy and muttered to himself, 'By the sound of it you've taken a skinful, Graf. I hope you have a brutal hangover in the morning.'

He was to be disappointed. Graf Otto appeared in the mess tent a little after eight, looking cheerful and rested. He shouted to Ishmael to bring coffee, and when it arrived he poured a dram of cognac into the steaming mug. 'Drinking makes me extremely thirsty. That mad Englishman Delamere ran out of people to toast, so towards the end of the evening we were hailing his favourite horse and his hunting dog.'

'As I recall, it wasn't Lord Delamere who stood on his head in the middle of the dance floor and drank a glass of cognac while inverted,' Leon said.

'No, that was me,' Graf Otto admitted. 'But I was challenged by Delamere. Did you know that he was bitten by a lion when he was younger? That is why he limps. He was trying to kill it with a knife. Madman!'

'Tell me, is it not just as crazy to try to kill one with an *assegai*?'

'*Nein!* Not at all! A knife is stupid, but a spear is extremely logical.' Graf Otto drained his coffee. 'I am grateful to you for reminding me, Courtney. Summon those two tall heathens of yours and take *Das Hummel* to the hunting grounds. Spread the word to the tribes that I am searching for the biggest lion that ever came out of Masailand. I will pay a reward of twenty cattle to the chief whose people find it for me. Go now, and do not return until you have good news to bring me.'

WHEN EVA ENTERED the mess tent an hour later Graf Otto was alone at the long table, a sheaf of documents stacked in front of him. He was poring over one that bore the black eagle crest of the German Ministry of War and making entries in his notebook. He laid it aside and looked up at her as she stood in the entrance to the tent with the morning light behind her. She wore a light summer dress that made her as winsome as a schoolgirl.

Ishmael had been poised for her arrival. 'Good morning, Memsahib. May your day be filled with the perfume of roses.'

'Away with you, you smirking infidel,' Graf Otto intervened. 'My coffee is cold. Get me a fresh pot.' As soon as Ishmael had gone, his manner changed and he became serious. 'Well, I've got rid of Courtney. I sent him out into the hunting grounds to find my lion. He will be well out of the way for as long as it takes to see to the real business. Despite his guileless manner, he is much too astute for my taste. Last evening he was wearing army uniform. That was the first inkling I had that he is on the British Army reserve list. Also, I learned from Delamere that Brigadier General Ballantyne is his uncle. In future we must be more circumspect with him.'

'Of course, Otto.' She took the chair beside him and turned her attention to the platter of fruit.

'There was a cable from Berlin yesterday. They have arranged my meeting with von Lettow for the seventeenth,' he continued. 'It's a long flight to Arusha, but I cannot be gone long. There are too many people watching us. Pack some of your pretty things, Eva. I want to be proud of you.'

'Do you really need me with you, Otto? It will be all men's talk and so dull. I would rather stay here and do some painting.'

Her attitude of mild disinterest in his affairs of business and state was a pose she had perfected over her long association with him. Once again her patience had paid off handsomely. For the first time since they had left Wieskirche he had mentioned von Lettow Vorbeck. She knew that this was the real purpose of their African expedition.

'Yes, indeed, *Liebling*. You know that I always need you with me.'

'Who else will be there? Will there be any other women?'

'I doubt it. Von Lettow is a bachelor and it will not be a social occasion. The most important person at the meeting will be the South African Boer commando Koos de la Rey. He is the pivot on which it all hinges.'

'Maybe I'm just a silly girl, but would it not have been easier for this Boer to have come to Berlin—or couldn't we have sailed to Cape Town?'

'In South Africa de la Rey is a marked man. He was one of the Boer leaders who fought against the British. Since the armistice he has made no secret of his anti-British feelings. Any contact between him and our government would set off alarm bells in London. The meeting has to be outside his own country. Ten days ago he was picked up off the South African coast by one of our submarines and brought to Dar es Salaam. After our meeting he will return by the same route.'

'The whole business must be very important for you to have spent so much time on it when you might have been hunting.'

'It is.' He nodded seriously. 'Believe me, it is.'

Instinct warned her that she had gone far enough for the moment. She sighed and murmured, 'Very important, and deadly boring. If I come with you, will you buy me a nice present when we get back to Germany?' She fluttered her long dark lashes at him. This was more in line with the character she had built up to please him.

'It will be the prettiest present we can find in all of Berlin,' Graf Otto chuckled, then shouted: 'Ishmael! Send for Bwana Hennie!'

Within minutes Hennie du Rand appeared in the fly of the tent. The frown on his brown, weatherbeaten face was anxious.

'Come in, Hennie. Don't just stand there.' Graf Otto greeted him with a friendly smile, then looked at Eva. 'You must forgive us, *Liebling*. You know that Hennie has no German so we will be speaking English.'

'Please, Graf Otto, do not worry about me. I have my book of birds and my binoculars. I shall be quite happy.' She stooped to kiss him as she passed his chair, then went to sit just outside the tent near the feeding table that Leon had set up for her entertainment. Noisy flocks of songbirds gathered around it: fire finches, weavers and wild canaries.

Although they were within earshot she ignored the conversation of the two men in the mess tent as she concentrated on capturing in her sketchpad the forms and colours of the tiny jewel-like creatures.

Graf Otto gave Hennie his full attention. 'How well do you know Arusha?'

'I worked for a timber company there for two years. They were logging on the lower slopes of Mount Meru. I came to know the area well.'

'There is a military fort on the Usa River, *ja*?'

'*Ja*. It is a local landmark. People thereabouts call it the Icing Sugar Castle. It is painted brilliant white.'

'We are going to fly there. Do you think you can find it from the air?'

'A blind man could pick out that building from fifty miles away.'

'Good. Be ready to leave tomorrow morning at first light. I need you to introduce me to an old friend of yours.'

The sun was still below the horizon when the *Butterfly* took off from the polo ground. It was cold in the rush of pre-dawn air, and everyone in the cockpit was bundled up in greatcoats. Graf Otto headed due south at 3,000 feet, and not long after they crossed the escarpment of the Rift Valley, the sun shot above the horizon with startling rapidity and lit the great mountain bastion of Kilimanjaro.

Eva was alone in the rear seat of the cockpit, out of view of Graf Otto, Gustav and Hennie. She was huddled down behind the windscreen in her heavy loden coat. Her hair was covered with her helmet; her eyes with the smoked lenses of her goggles. For once she did not have to act. For once she was able to allow her emotions to run free. She wept silently and secretly. It was the first time she had shed tears since the cold November day six long years ago when she had stood at the graveside and watched her father's coffin lowered into the earth. She had been alone ever since. It was too long.

In all the years she had been forced to play the game of shadows and mirrors, she had always been strong. She had always known her duty and been steadfast in her resolve. But now something had changed.

Then she felt the aircraft bank steeply under her and saw a mountain appear high above. It was so ethereal that it floated on a silver cloud. Then, with a start, she realised it was Lonsonyo. She felt the despair slough off her soul like an old skin and strength flow back into her. Until now she had believed that strength alone held her on her charted course, but now she knew it was resignation. There had been no other road open to her. But now hope suddenly overwhelmed her.

'The hope that springs from love,' she whispered to herself. She had never been able to love and trust a man before. Now she had found a man who had made her dare to hope.

HENNIE DU RAND gestured to Graf Otto, who banked sharply along the lower slopes of Mount Meru and flew on past the town of Arusha at the foot of the mountain. Hennie pointed ahead and they all saw the white crenellated walls of Fort Usa sitting above the river. As Graf Otto flew low past the white walls, a staff motor car drove out through the main gates and headed towards the open ground along the bank of the Usa River.

A strip of ground had been cleared in preparation for their arrival. Lightly Graf Otto touched down and let the *Butterfly* run to where the staff car was parked. A uniformed German officer stood beside the open front door of the vehicle with one foot on the running board.

As soon as Graf Otto had clambered down the boarding ladder the officer came forward to greet him. He was a tall, spare but broad-shouldered figure in a field grey tunic. He wore red and gold staff officer's tabs on his collar, and the Iron Cross, first class, at his throat.

'Count Otto von Meerbach?' he asked, as he saluted smartly. 'I am Colonel Paul von Lettow Vorbeck.' His voice was brisk and precise.

'Indeed, Colonel. After all our correspondence, I am delighted to meet you.' Graf Otto shook his hand and examined his features keenly. He knew von Lettow Vorbeck's impressive service record.

'Colonel, may I present Fräulein von Wellberg?'

'Enchanted, Fräulein.' Von Lettow Vorbeck clicked his heels and bowed as he held open the door to the staff car for Eva to take her seat. They left Gustav and Hennie to secure the *Butterfly* and drove up towards the fort.

'Has our visitor from the south arrived safely, Colonel?'

'He is waiting for you in the fort.'

'Does he live up to his reputation?'

'Difficult to say. He speaks no German or English, only his native Afrikaans. You will have some difficulty communicating with him, I fear.'

'I have made allowance for that. One of the men I brought with me is an Afrikaner. In fact, he fought under de la Rey against the British in South Africa. He also speaks fluent English, as I know you do, Colonel.'

'Excellent! That will certainly make matters easier.' Von Lettow Vorbeck nodded as they drove through the gates into the courtyard. 'After your journey, you and Fraülein von Wellberg will want to rest for a while. At four o'clock, Captain Reitz will bring you to our meeting with de la Rey.'

As von Lettow Vorbeck had promised, Reitz knocked on the door of the guest suite at precisely four o'clock.

Graf Otto checked his watch. 'He is punctual. Are you ready, Eva?'

'Yes, Graf Otto. I am ready.'

He called to Captain Reitz, who entered and saluted respectfully. Behind him, Hennie du Rand stood in the open doorway. He wore a fresh shirt, had shaved and slicked down his hair with pomade.

'If you are ready, will you please follow me, sir?' Reitz invited him, and they followed him along the stone-flagged passageway to the circular staircase that led up to the battlements. There, on the terrace, Colonel von Lettow Vorbeck waited for them under a canvas awning, at a heavy teak table on which was set out a selection of refreshments.

At the far end of the battlements stood another tall figure in a black frock coat. His back was turned to them and his hands were clasped behind it. He was staring out across the river towards Mount Meru in the distant mist.

Von Lettow Vorbeck stood to welcome them, and once he had enquired politely as to the comfort of their quarters, he eyed Hennie with interest.

'This is Hennie du Rand,' Graf Otto introduced them. 'He rode commando with de la Rey.' At the mention of his name, the black-clad figure standing at the far end of the battlements turned towards them. He was in his sixties, and his silver-shot hair had receded to leave his forehead high and domed. His remaining locks hung to his shoulders. His beard was dense, profuse and untamed. His eyes were as piercing and fanatical as those of a biblical prophet. Indeed, he carried a small Bible in his right hand, which he stuffed into the pocket of his frock coat as he strode towards Graf Otto.

'This is General Jacobus Herculaas de la Rey,' said von Lettow Vorbeck, but before he reached them Hennie ran forward to intercept him.

'General Koos, I am Hennie du Rand. I was with you at Nooitgedacht and Ysterspruit.'

'*Ja*, I remember you. You were the one who guided us to the river crossing after the fight at Langlaagte when the khaki had us surrounded. You saved the commando that night.'

Graf Otto stepped forward. 'Please tell the general that I am deeply honoured to meet such a brave soldier and patriot.' Hennie fell quickly and readily into the role of translator.

'I hope you do not mind Fraülein von Wellberg being present at our deliberations,' Graf Otto said. 'I vouch for her. Nothing that is said here today will go with her when she leaves. The Fraülein is an artist of repute. With your permission, gentlemen, and as a memento of such an historic conclave I have asked her, while we talk, to make portraits of you.' Von Lettow nodded, as did de la Rey once Hennie had translated for him.

Graf Otto turned back to de la Rey. 'You have Hennie du Rand to translate for you, General. Colonel von Lettow Vorbeck and I will use English if that is agreeable to you?' When Hennie translated this, de la Rey inclined his head, and Graf Otto continued, 'First I want to present a letter of introduction from the Minister of Foreign Affairs in Berlin.'

'I would not have come on such a terrible journey under the sea if I had not known who you are, Graf Otto,' de la Rey said. 'Germany was a good friend of my people during the war with the British. I look upon you as a friend and an ally still. Tell me why you have invited me here.'

'Despite the great courage with which they fought, the Afrikaner people have suffered terrible humiliation. The British are a warlike and rapacious nation. They have dominated most of the world, and still their appetite for conquest is unassuaged. Although we Germans are a peaceable people, we are also proud and prepared to defend ourselves against aggression.'

De la Rey listened to the translation. 'We have much in common,' he agreed. 'We were willing to make a stand against tyranny. It cost us dearly, but I and many like me do not regret it.'

'The time is coming on apace when you may be forced to make that stand again. Germany will face the same dreadful choice.'

'It seems that the fates of our two peoples are linked. But Britain is a terrible enemy. Her navy is the most powerful in all the oceans. If Germany were forced to oppose it, would the Kaiser send an army to defend your colonies in Africa?' de la Rey asked.

'There are differing opinions on that. The prevailing view in Germany is that our colonies must be defended in the North Sea, not on their own ground. Germany has two colonies in sub-Saharan Africa south of the equator, one on the southwest coast, the other here on the east coast. At present the forces defending them are tiny. Am I correct, Colonel?'

'I have two hundred and sixty white officers and two and a half thousand *askaris* under my command. In addition there is a police gendarmerie of forty-five white officers and a few more than two thousand police *askaris*.'

'With the British Royal Navy in command of the oceans round the continent, the chance of reinforcing and supplying this tiny force would be negligible,' the Graf pointed out. 'But all that would change most dramatically if South Africa entered the war on the side of Germany.'

De la Rey stroked his beard thoughtfully. 'Smuts and Botha have gone over heart and soul to the British. And a large part of the South African population is of British descent and their loyalties lie with Britain.'

'The war ended almost fourteen years ago,' von Lettow Vorbeck pointed out. 'Since then, all four of the old South African republics have been amalgamated into the Union of South Africa. The Boers have twice the power and influence they had before. Will they be satisfied with this, or will they risk it all by siding with Germany?' Von Lettow waited for the old Boer's response.

'The existing army of South Africa is perhaps sixty thousand strong and well equipped,' De la Rey said at last. 'Whichever government commands it will have control of the sea routes and the harbours around the continent. It will control the resources of the Witwatersrand gold fields, the Kimberley diamond mines and the new steel and armament works in the Transvaal. If South Africa threw in its lot with Germany, Britain would have to divert a large army from Europe to try to recapture the country, and the Royal Navy would be stretched to its limit to defend and supply it. South Africa might well be the pivot on which the outcome of such a war would turn.'

'If you decided to ride against the British again, which way would your old comrades go?' asked Graf Otto. 'We know Botha and Smuts would support Britain, but would the others be with you or with Botha?'

'I know these men,' de la Rey said softly. 'It was a long time ago, but they have not forgotten the terrible things that the British did to them, and to the land we love. In my heart I know they would ride out commando with me against the enemy, and for me the enemy is still Britain.'

'That is what I hoped to hear you say, General. I have been given total authority by the Kaiser and by my government to promise you whatever you require in the way of supplies, arms and money.'

'We will need all of those things,' de la Rey agreed, 'especially in the beginning, before we have been able to wrest control from Botha and seize the army arsenals and vaults of the Reserve Bank.'

'Tell me what you will need, General. I will get it for you from Berlin.'

'For a start, I will need one hundred and fifty heavy machine guns and fifty trench mortars. Then we will need medical supplies . . .' Graf Otto made notes on his pad, as de la Rey enumerated his requirements.

'What else do you need?'

'Money,' de la Rey replied. 'Two million pounds in gold sovereigns.'

'That is a great deal of money,' Graf Otto said.

'That is the price of the richest land in the southern hemisphere. It is the price of victory over the British. Do you really believe it to be too high, Graf?'

'No!' Graf Otto shook his head emphatically. 'When you put it like that, it's a fair price. You shall have the full two million. I will see to it.'

'How could you deliver the goods to us?' de la Rey asked.

Graf Otto glanced at Eva. Obviously she had not followed a single word of the discussion. He reached a decision. 'It can be done. It will be done. I give you my word, General. I will deliver everything that you need to wherever you need it. But our watchword must be secrecy. I shall inform only you and Colonel von Lettow much nearer the time of the method of delivery that we will employ. At this stage I must ask you to trust me.'

De la Rey stared at him with those smouldering fanatical eyes, and Graf Otto returned his gaze calmly. At last de la Rey said, 'You have given me your word, Graf Otto, and now I give you mine. On the day that the scourge of war sweeps across Africa once again, I will be ready for you with an army of sixty thousand fighting men at my back. Give me your hand, Graf. From this day on I am your ally to the death.'

From dawn to dusk over the past four days Leon Courtney had flown the *Bumble Bee* at tree-top height over the wide savannah. Manyoro and Loikot were perched in the front of the cockpit, vigilant as cruising vultures, watching and searching. They had found many lions but they were females and cubs, young males and toothless old solitaries. But Kichwa Muzuru had told them, 'He must be big and his mane must be as black as the hell hound.' Manyoro and Loikot had named Graf Otto 'Fire Head' for the colour of his hair and also for his apparent lack of fear.

On the fourth day Manyoro had wanted to give up the search in Masailand and fly up to the wild area between Lake Turkana and Marsabit. Loikot had strenuously opposed the move. He had told Leon about a pair of legendary lions that held a huge territory between Lake Natron and the west wall of the Rift Valley. 'Many times I have seen these lions over the years that I herded my father's cattle. They are twins, brothers born from the same lioness on the same day. By now they are in their prime. They have killed a hundred head of cattle, maybe more,' Loikot said. 'They have killed eighteen of the *morani* who set out to hunt them down. No man has been able to stand against them.'

That evening, as they sat round the campfire, Loikot tried to keep up their flagging enthusiasm. 'I tell you, M'bogo, these two are the paramount chieftains of all the lions in the valley. There are no others greater, fiercer or more cunning. These are the ones that Kichwa Muzuru has sent us to find.'

While he drained the coffee in his mug Leon considered the choice. They were already low on fuel for the *Bumble Bee* and had enough for only a day or two more. 'One more day, Loikot.' He made the decision. 'Find those beasts of yours tomorrow or we leave them and go elsewhere.'

They took off before sunrise and resumed the search. An hour later and twenty miles out Leon picked out an enormous herd of buffalo streaming back across the savannah from the lake shore where they had drunk. He banked towards them. He knew that lion prides often followed such large herds to pick off the weaklings and stragglers.

Suddenly in the front of the cockpit Loikot was making agitated hand signals, and Leon leaned forward to see what had excited him. A pair of buffalo had become separated from the main herd, and were trailing a quarter of a mile or so behind it. He wondered why Loikot was making such a fuss about them. Then, as he studied them, the pair emerged from the long grass into open pasture, and Leon felt every nerve in his body snap tight. They were not buffalo but lions. Never before had he seen lions of that size or colour. Their manes were deepest Stygian black and shaggy as haystacks, ruffling in the breeze as they stopped to stare up at the approaching aircraft.

Leon turned towards the landing strip. He laughed into the wind. 'Graf Otto, you had better sharpen your *assegai*. You're going to need it.'

As Leon touched down and let the *Bumble Bee* roll out on the airstrip below Percy's Camp, the two Masai were stamping and laughing joyously.

'Loikot,' Leon said, 'you must follow your lions and stay with them until I can bring Kichwa Muzuru for the hunt.'

'I know those lions. They will not elude me,' Loikot vowed. 'I have them in my eye.'

'When I return and you hear the sound of the engines, you must light a smudge fire. The smoke will guide me to you.' Leon turned to Manyoro 'Who is the chief of the area in which we found the lions today?'

'His name is Massana and his *manyatta* is at Tembu Kikuu.'

'You must go to him. Tell him there is a bounty of twenty cattle on each of his lions. But tell him that we will bring him a *mzungu* who will hunt them in the traditional way. Massana must bring together fifty of his *morani* for the hunt, but the killing will be done by Kichwa Muzuru alone.'

'I understand, M'bogo, but I do not think Massana will understand. A *mzungu* hunting a lion with the *assegai*? It has never been heard of before. Massana will think Kichwa Muzuru is mad.'

'Manyoro, you and I know that Kichwa Muzuru is indeed as crazy as the wildebeest with snot worms in his brain. But tell Massana not to worry too much about the condition of Kichwa Muzuru's head. Tell him to consider rather the twenty head of cattle. Is there a place close to his *manyatta* where I can land the aeroplane?' Leon asked.

Manyoro picked his nose thoughtfully before he replied. 'There is a dry salt pan close to the village. It is flat and without trees.'

'Show it to me,' Leon ordered. They took off again and Manyoro guided him towards it. It was a huge expanse, flat and glaring white, clearly visible from many miles out. He put the *Bumble Bee* down gingerly, and taxied to the edge of the pan. 'How far is it to the *manyatta* from here?' he asked Manyoro.

'It is close.'

'And how far to where we left the lions?' Leon demanded of Loikot. With his spear he pointed out a small segment of the sky, indicating two hours' passage of the sun. 'Good. So, here I will leave both of you. Watch for my return. When I come back I will have Kichwa Muzuru with me.'

As LEON MADE THE APPROACH to the Nairobi polo ground he could make out the gaudy scarlet and black shape of the *Butterfly* parked in front of the hangar. Gustav and his assistants were working on her engines. However, there was no sign of the hunting car, so instead of landing he circled out over Tandala Camp and found it parked outside Graf Otto's quarters.

Leon made another pass over the camp and the Graf emerged from his tent, shrugging on a shirt over his naked torso.

Leon felt a sharp pang of jealousy and resentment. Of course he has Eva in there with him, he thought. She has to earn her keep. The idea made him feel sick. Graf Otto gave him a perfunctory wave, then went to the hunting car. Leon turned the *Bumble Bee* back towards the polo ground.

Pull yourself together, Courtney! You know that Eva von Wellberg isn't a vestal virgin. She's been under the same mosquito net as him every night since they arrived, he told himself, as he lined up for the landing. As he side-slipped the *Bumble Bee* in over the boundary fence, his heart bounded as he saw her sitting at her easel in the shade of the *Butterfly*'s chequered wing. It seemed ridiculous, but he was relieved to know that Graf Otto had been alone in the private quarters.

As he set the aircraft down and taxied towards the hangar, Eva jumped up from her easel and started impulsively towards him. Even at this distance he could see the eagerness in her smile. Then she seemed to realise that Gustav was watching and came on at a more demure pace. She hung back as he placed the boarding ladder against the fuselage, and Leon swarmed down it. He saw that she was flustered and nervous. He nodded casually at her. 'Good day, Fräulein,' he said politely, then turned to Gustav.

'The starboard number two engine's running rough and blowing blue exhaust smoke.'

'I'll check it at once,' Gustav said, and shouted to his assistants.

When his head disappeared into the engine cowling, Leon and Eva were alone. 'Something has happened to you—something's changed,' he told her softly. 'You're different, Eva.'

'And you're perceptive. Everything's changed.'

'What is it? Has there been trouble with Graf Otto?'

'Not with him. This is between you and me. I have made a decision.' Her voice was low and husky, but then she smiled.

Her smile was the most beautiful thing he had ever seen. 'I don't understand,' he said.

'Nor do I, Badger.'

Her use of that name was too much for him. He took a step towards her, and she recoiled sharply. 'No, don't touch me. I can't trust myself not to do something stupid.' She indicated the dust thrown up by the hunting car as it drove towards them. 'Otto is coming. We must be careful.'

'I cannot go on like this much longer,' he warned her.

'Neither can I,' she replied. 'But for now we must keep away from each other. Otto is no fool. He will see that something has happened between us.'

As he drove the hunting car in through the gate of the boundary fence, Graf Otto called, 'So you are back, Courtney. You have been gone long enough. Where were you? Cape Town? Cairo?'

The brief exchange with Eva had left Leon in an ebullient and reckless mood. 'No, sir. I was looking for your bloody lion.'

Graf Otto saw Leon's elation and his own face lit up. 'Did you find it?'

'I wouldn't have come back if I hadn't. He's the biggest lion I've ever seen, and the other is even bigger.'

'I don't understand. How many lions are there?'

'Two,' said Leon. 'Two enormous brutes.'

'When can we leave to go after them?'

'As soon as Gustav has checked the engine of the *Bumble Bee*.'

'I can't wait that long. The *Butterfly*'s tanks are full, all our gear is loaded and she is ready to go. We will leave now! At once!'

GRAF OTTO WAS at the controls of the *Butterfly* as they headed southwest towards the *manyatta* of Massana. Eva sat beside him, Ishmael squatted on the deck with his precious kitchen bundle beside him, while Leon, Gustav and Hennie were at the front of the cockpit.

They had been flying for little more than twenty-five minutes when Leon spotted a feather of smoke rising straight into the still, breathless heat of midday. 'Loikot!' On the ground, Loikot pointed with his spear towards the jagged outline of a small kopje, indicating the whereabouts of the quarry.

Swiftly Leon assessed the changed situation. During his absence the lions must have headed in the direction of Massana's *manyatta*. They were now many miles closer to it than they had been when they had first spotted them. He picked out the ghostly shape of the salt pan. It lay almost equidistant between the *manyatta* and the kopje where the lions were now lying up. He moved back in to where he could talk to Graf Otto above the engines.

'Can you see that salt pan?' Leon pointed it out. 'If you put us down there, we'll be close to the quarry and to the village where the *morani* are assembling for the hunt.'

Massana's *manyatta* was large, a hundred or more large huts laid out in a wide circle round the cattle pen. Graf Otto circled the settlement at a low level. A dark mass of humanity had gathered in the central cattle pen. Manyoro had done his job, and prevailed on Massana to assemble his *morani* for the great hunt. Graf Otto turned the *Butterfly* towards the salt pan, landed and taxied to the treeline along its western edge.

'We will be camping here for a while until the *morani* arrive,' Leon told him. All the equipment for a fly camp was packed into the cargo hold of the *Butterfly*. It did not take Leon long to set it up. He sited the tents in the shade beneath the aircraft's wings. Ishmael built a cooking fire at a safe distance from the aircraft and was soon serving coffee.

Leon drained his mug, then looked up at the sky to judge the time. 'Loikot will be here at any minute now,' he told Graf Otto, and had barely finished the sentence when Loikot trotted out from among the trees.

Leon left the shade and walked into the sunlight to greet him.

'So, Loikot, mighty hunter and intrepid tracker, what of your lions? Do you still have them in your eye?'

Loikot shook his head lugubriously.

'You have lost them?' Leon asked angrily. 'You have let them escape?'

'No! It is true that the smallest lion has disappeared but I still have the largest one in my eye. I saw him no more than two hours ago. He is alone, still lying up from the heat on top of the hillock I pointed out to you earlier.'

'We should not bewail the disappearance of the other,' Leon consoled him. 'One lion on his own will be easier to work with.'

'Where is Manyoro?' Loikot asked.

'We flew over the *manyatta* of Massana. The *morani* were gathered there, but they and Manyoro must already be on their way to join us.'

'I will go back to keep watch on my lion,' Loikot volunteered. 'I will return early tomorrow morning.'

It was still two hours from sunset when they heard singing and saw the people coming through the open forest towards them. Manyoro was leading them, and he was followed by the long file of armed *morani* decked out in full hunting regalia, carrying shields and *assegais*.

Behind them came hundreds of men, women and children. They had gathered from every *manyatta* for fifty miles around. By the time the sun had set, this conglomeration of humanity was encamped round the *Butterfly*, and the night air was redolent with the aromas from the cooking fires. Excitement was running at fever pitch and the singing and happy laughter of young people went on throughout the night.

The next morning, before it was light, Loikot returned. He reported that the lion had taken a young kudu cow and was still feeding on the carcass. 'He will not leave his kill,' Loikot said with conviction.

The hunters waited for the sun with mounting anticipation. They sat round the fires sharpening their *assegais*. When the first rays of the sun struck the cliffs of the escarpment, the master of the hunt blew a blast on his whistle to signal the start. They sprang up and formed their ranks on the white salt plain. They began to dance and sing, softly at first but with increasing abandon as the excitement built up.

Suddenly Graf Otto appeared from his tent and marched onto the white pan. A roar went up from the *morani* ranks when they saw him. He was dressed in a red tribal *shuka*. The skirt was belted round his waist and the tail was thrown back over one shoulder. The skin of his upper torso was exposed, white as an egret's wing. The hair on his chest was as bright as copper wire. His shoulders were wide and his limbs were hard and muscled, but his belly was full, beginning to soften with age and good living.

The young girls shrieked with laughter. They had never imagined a white *mzungu* would dress in tribal costume. They gathered round him, still giggling. They touched his milky skin, and stroked his red-gold body hair in wonder. Then Graf Otto began to dance. The girls backed away, and clapped the rhythm for him, urging him on with shrill, excited cries.

Graf Otto danced with extraordinary grace for such a big man.

He leaped high, spun, stamped and stabbed at the air with the *assegai* in his right hand. He flourished the rawhide shield that he carried on his left shoulder. The prettiest and more daring of the girls took it in turns to come forward and dance face to face with him. The air was thick with the dust raised by their flying bare feet, musky with the smell of their sweat, and charged with the prospect of blood, death and carnality.

Leon leaned against the fuselage of the *Butterfly* and seemed to give his full attention to this display of primeval abandon. However, almost within arm's length of where he stood, Eva was perched on the leading edge of the *Butterfly*'s wing, legs dangling. From this angle he was able to study her face without seeming to do so. Eva showed no emotion at the display other than mild amusement.

Almost as though she could feel his eyes on her, she looked down at him from her perch on the wing. Her expression was calm and her eyes betrayed nothing. Then, as their gazes locked, she allowed him to see into the secret, well-guarded places of her soul. Such manifest love for him shone forth from her violet eyes that he caught his breath. All at once he was aware of the depth of the change that had overtaken them. They were now committed to each other. Nothing and nobody else counted.

The moment was shattered by the blast of a whistle and the hunters formed up in column. Loikot took his place in the front rank to guide them to where the quarry was lying up. Singing the Lion Song, the *morani* followed him, winding through the trees, with the gleaming white body of Graf Otto in their midst. The spectators trooped after them.

Leon and Eva were left alone. He went to where she sat on the wing. 'If we are to be in at the death, we must hurry.'

'Help me down,' she replied. She lifted her arms and leaned towards him. He reached up, placed his hands round her narrow waist, and when he set her on her feet she pressed her hand against his cheek, and read his eyes. 'I know, Badger. I know so well how you feel. I feel it too. But we must be patient a little longer. Soon! Soon, I promise.'

She dropped her hand from his face, and he saw that Manyoro had come silently and was standing at his shoulder. He had the Holland rifle in one hand and the ammunition bandolier in the other.

'Thank you, my brother,' Leon said, as he took them.

'Graf Otto said there were to be no guns on this hunt,' Eva reminded him.

'Can you imagine what might happen if he wounds that lion and it gets in among all those people?' Leon asked grimly. 'It's one thing for him to have a pact with the devil but quite another if he intends to include a dozen women and children in the bargain.' He loaded the rifle with two fat brass cartridges. Then he took her arm and they ran after the column of *morani*, which was drawing away rapidly from the rabble of spectators.

They passed the stragglers and caught up with the main body of hunters, and were not far behind the leading warriors when the hunt master blew his whistle again. The *morani* moved into their twin-horned battle formation.

'They have caught up with the lion,' Leon said.

'Where is Otto?' Eva gasped to catch her breath.

'He's right in the thick of it. Where else would we expect him to be?' Leon pointed, and she saw his pale form standing out clearly in the first rank of dark warriors that was closing round the rocky hillock.

'Can you see the lion yet?'

'No. We'll have to get closer.' He took her arm and they began to run again.

The first line of *morani* was no more than 150 paces ahead of them when Leon stopped abruptly. 'Oh sweet God! There he is!'

'Where? I can't see it.'

'There, on the high ground.' He put an arm round her shoulders and turned her to face it. 'That huge black thing on top of the highest rock.'

'I can't see . . .' But then the lion raised his mane, and she gasped. 'I never realised it would be so big. I thought it was a gigantic boulder.'

The lion swung his massive head from side to side, surveying the host of enemies that surrounded him. He snarled and bared his teeth. Even at a distance Leon and Eva could clearly see the ivory flash of his fangs and hear the furious crackling growls. Then he lowered his head and flattened his ears against his skull as he picked out the moon-pale flash of Otto von Meerbach's body in the centre of the ranks. He needed no further provocation. He growled again, then launched his charge, bounding down the side of the kopje straight at Graf Otto.

A challenging shout went up from the *morani* ranks and they drummed on their shields, goading the lion. At the foot of the slope he flattened out with the speed and power of his rush, snaking low to the earth, the dust spurting up from under the massive paws, grunting with every stride.

Without a moment's hesitation Graf Otto lifted his shield and held it high as he charged forward to meet the great beast.

'It's going to kill him!' Eva whispered, but at the last possible instant Graf Otto moved with the coordination of a consummate athlete. He dropped to one knee and covered himself with the rawhide war shield. He brought up the *assegai* in his right hand and presented the point to the charging lion. The beast took it in the centre of his chest, and its heart was spitted cleanly by the razor steel. His jaws gaped wide as he roared, and from his throat shot a fountain of bright blood that sprayed over Graf Otto's head and shoulders. The lion reeled back with the spear still buried in his heart, staggered in a circle and collapsed into the grass. It was a perfect kill.

Graf Otto bounded to his feet, bellowing triumphantly, his face contorted under the glistening coating of the lion's blood. A dozen *morani* rushed forward to stab the blades of their *assegais* into the corpse. The Graf confronted them, bellowing possessively, keeping them away from his kill. He ripped his own spear from the lion's chest and shook it at the warriors as they crowded forward, driving them back. They yelled furiously at him. They were demanding to share the glory, their entitlement to wash their spears in the blood of the lion. Graf Otto hurled the *assegai* at one, and the *morani* raised his shield but the blade cut through the rawhide targe and slashed open the blood vessels in his wrist. His companions roared with fury.

'Dear God! The madness is on him,' Eva panted. 'Someone will be killed, either himself or the Masai. I must stop him.' She started forward.

'No, Eva. You cannot stop them. They're all mad with blood rage.' He seized her arm.

'I've been able to quiet him before. He will listen to me . . .'

'It's too late, Eva,' he hissed into her ear, pointing over the heads of Graf Otto and the *morani*. 'Look up there, on top of the kopje.'

She looked as he directed, and saw the second lion. He was standing on the crest of the hillock, a huge creature. He hunched his back, opened his jaws wide and roared, a full-throated earth-splitting blast. The hubbub of the watchers, the tumult of Graf Otto and the embattled warriors died away into a deathly silence.

The two lions had separated three days previously when the elder had been lured away by an irresistible perfume on the cool pre-dawn breeze. It was the odour of a mature lioness in full oestrus. He found the lioness an hour after sunrise, but another lion was already mating with her, a younger, stronger suitor. The two had fought and the older lion had been injured, driven off with a bite in the shoulder that had cut down to the bone. He had come back to join his twin, limping with pain. The two lions had been reunited a little after moonrise and the wounded one had retreated to a rocky overhang in the side of the hill.

He had been too sore and stiff to take any part in the attack by the *morani* hunters, but the angry roaring and the death throes of his twin had brought him out of his hiding place. Now he looked down on the killing ground where the corpse of his sibling lay and he knew rage, a terrible consuming rage. The pale colour of Graf Otto's body acted as a focal point for the lion's anger. He sprang forward and charged down the slope.

A dreadful wail went up from the women, who scattered like a flock of chickens before the stoop of a peregrine. The *morani* were taken completely off-guard. By the time they had rallied to face this new threat the beast had covered most of the ground to reach Graf Otto. Leon thrust Eva behind him and shouted at her, 'Stay here. Don't come any closer!' Then he raced forward in an attempt to protect his client.

The lion smashed into Graf Otto with all its speed and massive weight.

He was bowled over backwards with the beast on top of him. It enfolded him in the crushing embrace of its forelegs, and drove its claws like butcher's meat-hooks deep into the flesh of his back. At the same time its back legs raked the front of his lower body and thighs, cutting deep gouges into his flesh and slicing open his belly. It crouched on top of him and went for his face and throat, but Graf Otto thrust his forearm into the gaping jaws in an effort to keep it away. The lion bit down, and as Leon ran up he heard the bones splinter.

Leon slipped the safety catch off the rifle and rammed the muzzles into the lion's ear. At the same instant he pulled both triggers. The bullets tore through the skull and blew out through the opposite ear. The lion flopped onto its side and rolled off Graf Otto.

Leon stood over the man and stared in horrified disbelief. Graf Otto was awash with blood, and more spurted from the hideous wounds in his arm and shoulder. It poured, too, from the deep gouges in the front of his thighs and from the slashes in his belly.

'Is he alive or dead?' Eva had ignored his instruction to stay back.

'A little of each, I think,' Leon told her grimly. He dropped to his knees, drew his hunting knife, and started to cut away the blood-soaked *shuka*.

'Sweet God, it's torn him to shreds. You'll have to help me. Do you know anything about first aid?' he asked Eva.

'Yes,' she said, as she knelt beside him. 'I've had training.' Her tone was calm and businesslike. 'First we must stop the bleeding.'

Leon stripped away the last of Graf Otto's tattered *shuka* and cut it into strips as bandages. Between them they placed tourniquets on the shattered arm and the torn thighs. Then they strapped improvised pressure pads to the other deep punctures left by the lion's fangs.

Leon watched Eva's hands as she worked quickly and neatly. 'You know what you're doing. Where did you learn?'

'I could ask you the same question,' she retorted.

'I was taught the basics in the army,' he replied.

'The same with me.'

He stared at her in astonishment. 'The German Army?'

'One day I may tell you my life story, but for the moment we must get on with the job.' She wiped her bloody hands on her skirt while she appraised what they had done, then shook her head. 'He may survive the injuries, but infection and mortification will probably kill him.'

'You're right. The fangs and claws of a lion are a seething hothouse of germs. Dr Joseph Lister's little friends. We must get him to Nairobi right away, so that Doc Thompson can stew him in a hot iodine bath.'

'If we try to lift him now, his bowels will fall out. Can you stitch him?' she asked.

'That's a job for a surgeon,' Leon said. 'We'll just strap him up and hope for the best.' They bound up his stomach with lengths of *shuka*. Leon was watching Eva, waiting for her to express some emotion, but she was working with professional detachment.

At last they were able to lift Graf Otto onto a war shield. Six of the *morani* carried him to where the *Butterfly* stood waiting. Under Manyoro's supervision they lifted the makeshift litter into the cockpit and Leon lashed it to the ring bolts in the deck. Then he looked up at Eva. Pale and dishevelled, she was squatting opposite him, her skirts filthy with blood and dust.

'I don't think he'll make it, Eva. But perhaps Doc Thompson can pull off one of his miracles, if we get him to Nairobi in time.'

'I'm not coming with you,' Eva said softly.

He stared at her in amazement. It was not only the words themselves, but also the language in which she had spoken them. 'You speak English. That's a Geordie accent,' he said. Its lyrical cadence was sweet to his ears.

'Yes.' She smiled sadly. 'I am from Northumberland.'

'I don't understand.'

She pushed the hair back from her eyes and shook her head. 'No, Badger, you cannot understand. Oh God! There's so much you don't know about me, and which I can't tell you . . . yet.'

'Tell me one thing. What do you truly feel for Otto von Meerbach? Do you love him, Eva?'

Her eyes darkened with horror. 'Love him?' She gave a short, bitter laugh. 'No, I don't love him. I hate him with all my heart.'

'Then why are you here with him?'

'You're a soldier, Badger, as I am. You know about duty and patriotism.' She drew a long, deep breath. 'But I've had enough. I cannot go on. I'm not going with you to Nairobi. If I do I'll never be able to escape.'

'Who are you trying to escape from?'

'Those who own my soul.'

'Where will you go?'

'I don't know. Some secret place where they cannot find me.' She took his hand. 'Find me a place to hide. Leave me there. Come back for me as soon as you can. That is my only chance of winning my freedom.'

'Freedom? Aren't you free now?'

'No. I am the captive of circumstances. I have become a whore and an impostor, a liar and a cheat. I am caught in the jaws of a monster. Once I was like you, good, honest and innocent. I want to be like you again. Will you have me? Shop-soiled and dirty as I am, will you take me?'

'Oh God, Eva, there's nothing I want more. I've loved you from the first moment I laid eyes on you.'

'Then no more questions now. I beg you. Hide me here in the wilderness. Take Otto to Nairobi. If anybody there asks about me, and I mean anybody at all, don't tell them where I am. Tell them simply that I've disappeared. Leave Otto at the hospital. If he survives they will send him back to Germany. But as soon as you can, you must return to me. I will explain everything to you then. Will you do it? Will you trust me?'

'You know I will,' he said softly. Then he shouted, 'Manyoro! Loikot!'

They were waiting close at hand. The orders he had for them were to the point. He turned back to Eva. 'Go with them,' he told her. 'You can trust them.'

'I know I can. But where will they take me?'

'To Lonsonyo Mountain. To Lusima,' he answered.

'To our mountain?' she said. 'Oh, Leon, from the first moment I saw it I knew Lonsonyo had a special significance for us.'

While they were speaking Manyoro had found the carpet bag in which Eva carried her personal things. He dragged it out of the stowage hatch at the rear of the cockpit and tossed it down to Loikot, who was standing below the fuselage, then vaulted over the side. For the moment Leon and Eva were alone together. He reached out to touch her, and she came into his arms with swift, lissom grace. Her lips quivered against his cheek as she whispered, 'Kiss me, my darling. I have waited so long. Kiss me now.'

Their lips came together, lightly at first, then stronger, deeper. That first kiss seemed to last an instant yet all of eternity. Then with an effort, they broke apart and stared at each other in awe.

'I knew I loved you, but not until this moment did I realise how much,' he said softly.

'I know, for I feel it also,' she replied. 'Until this moment, I never knew what it would be like to trust and love somebody completely.'

She tore her eyes from his and looked out across the pan to where the *morani* and the villagers were streaming back towards them. Some were carrying the carcasses of the two lions slung on poles, their heads hanging.

'Gustav and Hennie are coming,' she said. 'They must not see me leave.' She kissed him again swiftly, then broke away. 'I shall wait for you to come back to me, and every second that we are apart will be an eternity.' She sprang out of the cockpit and with Manyoro and Loikot on each side of her ran for the trees, screened from Gustav and Hennie by the fuselage of the aircraft. Leon was surprised by the desolation that came over him now that she was gone, and he made a conscious effort to brace himself to meet Gustav, who was scrambling into the cockpit.

He fell on his knees beside Graf Otto's body. 'Oh my God,' he cried. 'He is killed!' Tears streamed down his weathered cheeks. 'Please, God, spare him! He was more than my own father to me.'

'He's not dead,' Leon told him brusquely, 'but he soon will be if you don't get the engines started so I can take him to a doctor.' Gustav and Hennie sprang to work, and within a few minutes all four engines were rumbling. Leon shouted at Gustav and Hennie, 'Hold him steady!'

They crouched beside the makeshift stretcher on which Graf Otto lay and took a firm grasp. Leon pushed the throttles forward to the stops. The aircraft roared and rolled forward. As he lifted her over the trees he looked over the side, searching for Eva. He saw her then. She and the Masai were already a quarter of a mile beyond the perimeter of the pan. She stopped and looked up, swept off her hat and waved. She was laughing, and he knew that her laughter was for his encouragement. He felt his heart squeezed by her courage and fortitude, but he dared not return her wave for it might draw Gustav's attention to the little figure far below. The *Butterfly* roared on, climbing towards the rampart of the Rift Valley wall.

It was late afternoon and the sun was setting when Leon set the *Butterfly* down on the Nairobi polo ground. He taxied to the hangar where the hunting car was parked, shut down the engines and they manhandled the stretcher over the side of the cockpit and lowered Graf Otto to the ground.

The German's skin was deathly pale and he showed no signs of life. But when Leon touched Graf Otto's neck he felt the carotid artery throbbing feebly. Any normal human being would have been dead long ago, but this bastard is as tough as the skin on an elephant's backside, he thought.

'Bring the hunting car,' he told Gustav. They placed the litter across the back seat, where Gustav and Hennie held it securely while he drove carefully to the hospital, avoiding the ruts and bumps in the track.

The hospital was a small building of mud-brick and thatch, across the road from the new Anglican church. The entire building was deserted and Leon hurried to the cottage at the rear.

He found Doc Thompson and his wife sitting down to their dinner, but they left it on the table and rushed with Leon to the hospital. Mrs Thompson was the only trained nursing sister in the entire colony and under her supervision Gustav and Hennie carried Graf Otto into the clinic. While the doctor cut away the makeshift bandages, they dragged in a galvanised iron bath and filled it with hot water into which Mrs Thompson emptied a quart bottle of concentrated potassium of iodine. Then they lifted Graf Otto's broken body off the table and lowered him into the steaming brew.

The pain was so excruciating that he was jerked out of the dark fog of coma, shrieking and struggling as he tried to drag himself out of the caustic antiseptic. They held him down mercilessly so that the iodine could soak into the deep, terrible wounds. Despite his antipathy towards the man, Leon found the spectacle of his agony harrowing. He backed to the door and slipped quietly out of the clinic into the sweet evening air.

By the time he reached the polo ground the sun had set. Paulus and Ludwig, two of the Meerbach mechanics, had got there before him: they had heard the *Butterfly*'s earlier landing and had come to find out what was happening. Leon gave them a brief account of the Graf's mauling, then said, 'I must get back. I don't know what has happened to Fräulein von Wellberg. She is there alone. She may be in danger. The *Butterfly*'s fuel tanks are almost empty. What about the *Bumble Bee*?'

'We filled hers after you brought her in earlier,' Ludwig told him.

'Help me to get the engines started,' Leon said.

'You cannot fly in darkness!' Ludwig protested.

'The moon is only two nights from full and will rise within the next hour. Then it will be as bright as day. Give me a hand to get her started.' He climbed into the cockpit and began the routine.

As soon as he had cleared the trees at the end of the field he turned onto a heading for Percy's Camp. As he gained altitude the moon seemed to rush eagerly over the black horizon to light him on his way. From fifteen miles out, the hill above the camp was gilded by moonlight, guiding him in on the last leg of the journey. To attract Max Rosenthal's attention he circled the camp three times, revving the engines, then throttling back. On the last circuit he saw a motor car's headlights below him, grinding its way over the rough track to the airstrip. Max understood what was required of him and lined up the vehicle to orientate Leon for the landing.

Leon landed the *Bumble Bee* and threw his pack over the side. Scrambling down, he hurried towards the truck.

'Max, I want four of our best horses and one of the grooms to go with me. We'll each ride a horse, and take the spares on lead reins.'

'*Jawohl*, boss. Where are you going? When do you want to leave?'

'Don't worry about where I'm going, and I want to leave at once.'

Leon hurried to his tent and threw a few essential items into his light pack, then went down to the picket lines. There, the horses and the groom were already waiting, but instead of four animals, there were five. Leon's frown cleared, replaced by a grin as he recognised the figure mounted on the black mule. 'May the Prophet shower blessings on you!' he greeted him.

'Effendi, I knew that you would starve without me,' Ishmael said.

They rode hard for the rest of that night, changing horses twice. In the dawn the shadowy blue bulk of Lonsonyo Mountain lay low on the distant horizon ahead. By noon it filled half of the eastern sky, but this aspect was unfamiliar to Leon. He had never before approached the mountain from this direction. Now it was presenting its more rugged northerly slope.

By this time they had been riding for almost thirteen hours since leaving Percy's Camp and he had pushed the horses hard. They unsaddled beside a small waterhole and hobbled the animals, then turned them loose to graze.

Ishmael brewed coffee, then cut slices of cold venison and pickled onions onto a hunk of unleavened bread. When he had eaten Leon slept until nightfall. Then they saddled up and rode on into the darkness. In the cool night the horses went with a will and at dawn the mountain towered above them.

Leon knew from Loikot that there was a pathway, beside a waterfall, that scaled the cliffs to the summit and this was the route by which they had intended to take Eva to Lusima.

Ishmael and the groom were unable to keep pace with him as he urged his mount forward. After an hour he swung down from the saddle and squatted beside one of the numerous game trails that crisscrossed the savannah. Three sets of human footprints were freshly impressed in the fine dust. Manyoro had been in the lead—the slight drag of the toe was unmistakable. Loikot had followed, with his long, lithe paces, Eva behind them.

The tracks were headed directly towards the mountain, and he remounted and followed them at a canter. The path became steeper with each pace. Soon he was forced to dismount and lead his horse. As he strode on, the rest of his party struggled after him but were losing ground rapidly. He reached a step in the mountainside, and as he topped it he stared in wonder. Before him lay a large circular pool, its size dwarfed by the cliff above it and the thunderous white deluge of the waterfall.

Then he heard a voice, faint and almost drowned by the din of cascading waters and his heart surged with excitement. Eagerly he scanned the cliffs. 'Eva!' he shouted, and the diminishing echoes mocked him.

'Leon! Darling!' He saw a flash of movement high above the pool and realised she was standing on a ledge that angled up the cliff face. But as he watched she started back down towards him, running with the speed and agility of a rock hyrax over the treacherous footing.

'Eva!' he yelled. 'I'm coming, my darling!' He dropped his horse's reins and scrambled up the mountainside to meet her. Now he could see the two Masai on the path above her. Even at this distance he could read the astonishment on their faces as they watched this extraordinary display. He and Eva reached the beginning of the ledge at almost the same time, but he was below the lip and she was on top of it, six feet above his head.

'Catch me, Badger!' she called and, trusting in his strength, flung herself over the edge. As she dropped he caught her, but her momentum brought him to his knees. He knelt over her, hugging her to his chest as they laughed.

'I love you, you crazy girl!'

'Never let me go again!' she said, as their lips came together.

'Never!' he promised, speaking into her sweet mouth.

Much later when they drew apart to breathe, they saw that Manyoro and Loikot had followed Eva back down the path, and were squatting on the ledge just above them, watching their performance with grins of delight.

'Take my horse and go down the mountain until you meet Ishmael,' Leon ordered them. 'Tell him to make camp at the foot. Wait for us.'

'*Ndio*, Bwana,' Manyoro answered.

'And stop giggling like that.'

The two Masai staggered down the mountain, racked with paroxysms of laughter.

'That was, no doubt, the funniest incident ever to be recorded in the history of Masailand. You and I will go down in tribal mythology,' Leon told Eva, as the two men disappeared down the path. He picked her up in his arms and carried her to a flat ledge beside the pool. 'You don't know how I've longed to hold you like this,' he whispered.

'All my life,' she replied. 'That's how long I've waited for this to happen.'

He stroked her face, tracing the arches of her eyebrows with his finger-tips, then burrowed his fingers into the tresses of her hair, filling his hands with the thick, glossy locks. She seemed so fragile and delicate that he was afraid he might hurt or alarm her. She was nothing like the other women he had known. She made him feel inadequate, unworthy.

She understood his timidity, but she wanted him desperately and could not wait. She knew she must take the lead.

He felt her unbuttoning his shirt and one of her hands slipped through the opening and began to caress the muscles of his chest.

He shivered with delight. 'You're so hard, so strong,' she murmured.

'And you're so soft and tender,' he countered.

She leaned back a little way so that she could look into his eyes. 'I'm not breakable, my Badger. I'm flesh and blood as you are. I want what you want.' She took the lobe of his ear between her teeth and nibbled it softly. He felt goosebumps rise on the nape of his neck.

Her words roused in him a feverish impatience. He plucked open her blouse and reached inside. She threw back her shoulders so her breasts swelled out to meet his exploring fingers.

'Forgive me, my darling, but I cannot wait any longer,' she cried, her tone almost desperate. She tugged at his belt. He lifted himself just enough to enable her to push his breeches down to his knees. She hoisted her long skirt to her lower ribs—she wore nothing under it—and her waist was fluted, like the neck of a Grecian vase, curving into the swell of her hips.

For both, it happened so swiftly and intensely that they were left unable to speak, barely able to move, clinging together like the survivors of some devastating earthquake or typhoon.

Eva spoke first: 'I never imagined it could be like that.' She laid her head on his chest to listen to his heart. He stroked her hair and she closed her eyes. They slept, and came awake to the barking of a troop of baboons high on the cliff face. She sat up slowly and pushed the hair back from her face. It was still wet with sweat. 'How long were we asleep?' She blinked.

'Is it important?' he asked.

'It's very important. I don't want to waste a single moment of the time we have together in sleeping.'

'We have the rest of our lives.'

'I pray God that is so. But this world is so cruel.' She looked forlorn and bereft. 'Please don't ever leave me.'

'Never,' he said fiercely.

'You're right, Badger. We're going to be happy for ever. I refuse to be sad on this wonderful day. The world can never catch us.' She sprang to her feet and shed her clothing, scattering it over the rock.

'What are you doing, you shameless hussy?'

'I'm going to take you for a swim in our magical pool,' she cried. 'Throw off those dusty old clothes, sir, and come with me.'

He flung aside his breeches and started after her. She squealed with mock-alarm, ran to the end of the ledge and dived into the pool. She struck the water like an arrow, so that there was almost no splash as she slipped beneath the surface. She went deep, then shot up again so swiftly with her hair slicked over her shoulders, like the pelt of an otter.

'It's cold! I bet you're too much of a sissy to chance it,' she shouted.

'You lose your bet, and here I come for my payment.' He dived in and seized her from behind. 'Pay up!' he demanded, and turned her to face him.

She placed both arms round his neck and her lips on his. Kissing, they sank deep below the surface only to come up again, spluttering and laughing. She twisted out of his grip and darted away. She only looked back when she reached the far side of the pool. At first she was laughing, but then, as she saw no sign of Leon, she became anxious. 'Badger! Leon! Where are you?' she cried.

He had followed her across the pool, but then had taken a deep breath and duck-dived. Once he was below the surface he swam on downwards. The bottom appeared below him and, even at this depth, the water was so clear that he could see it was covered with a jumble of rocks that must have fallen from the cliffs. He reached the bottom and found scattered a bizarre collection of Masai artefacts: ancient *assegais* and axes, pottery shards, necklaces and bracelets made from beads, small carvings of hardwood and ivory, all offerings made by the Masai over the ages to their tribal gods.

By now his lungs were heaving for air and he swam for the surface. As the light strengthened he saw above him a pair of long, shapely feminine legs dabbling below the surface. He swam up under them, seized the ankles and jerked their owner into the pool on top of him. They came to the surface again, clinging together and gasping for air.

Eva recovered her voice before he did. 'You heartless swine! I thought you were drowned or swallowed by a crocodile.'

They swam back to where they had left their clothes.

'We don't want you to catch your death of cold,' Leon told her, and made her stand naked on the ledge while he dried her with his shirt.

'What big eyes you have, sir. You're doing a great deal more looking than drying.' She reached out to him and in the divine madness of their passion they were insatiable.

IT WAS almost dark when, hand in hand, they went down the pathway to the campfire burning not far below. When they reached it they found that Ishmael had placed a log in front of the flames as a bench for them.

Eva sniffed the air. 'What is that delicious aroma, Ishmael?'

He showed no surprise that, for the first time, she was speaking English rather than German or French. 'It is green-pigeon casserole, Memsahib.'

'Ishmael's celestial version thereof,' Leon added.

Immediately after they had eaten, they were overwhelmed by a wonderful weariness. Manyoro and Loikot had built a small thatched shelter for them, well away from their own huts, and Ishmael had cut a mattress of fresh grass and covered it with blankets. Over it he had hung Leon's mosquito net. They shed their clothes and Leon blew out the candle stub.

'It's so safe and intimate and cosy in here,' she whispered, and he lay behind her and enfolded her in his embrace.

SHE WOKE in the dawn to find Leon sitting cross-legged next to her. 'You've been watching me!' she accused him.

'Guilty as charged,' he admitted. 'I thought you were never going to wake up. Come on!'

'Where do you want to go at this ridiculous hour?'

'For a swim in your magical pool.'

'Well, why didn't you say so?' she asked, and threw back the blanket.

The waters were cool and slippery as silk over their bodies.

They sat naked in the early sunlight to dry off and when the warmth had soaked into them, they made love yet again. Afterwards she said solemnly,

'I thought nothing could be better than yesterday, but today is.'

'I want to give you something that will always remind you of how happy we were on this day.' Leon stood up and dived from the ledge.

She watched him growing smaller and less distinct as he swam down, until finally he had faded into the depths. He was down for so long that she grew anxious until, with a lift of relief, she saw him coming up. He swam to the bank below her and clambered up onto the ledge. Then he held up a necklace of ivory beads strung on a leather thong.

'It's beautiful!' She clapped her hands.

'Two thousand years ago, when she passed this way, the Queen of Sheba offered it to the gods of the pool. Now I give it to you.' He looped the necklace round her throat and tied it at the nape of her neck.

'Did the Queen of Sheba really pass this way?' she asked.

'Almost certainly not.' He laughed at her. 'But it makes a good story.'

'They're so lovely, so smooth and delicate.' She turned one between her fingers. 'Oh, I wish I had a mirror.'

He led her to the end of the ledge and stood beside her with his arm round her waist. 'Look down,' he told her. Silently they regarded their images in the mirror-like surface of the water. At last Leon asked softly, 'Who is that girl in the water? Her name isn't Eva von Wellberg, is it?' He watched her eyes mist with tears. 'I'm so sorry.'

'No!' She shook her head. 'You did the right thing. It's time to face reality.' She looked up at him. 'You're right, Leon. I'm not Eva von Wellberg—von Wellberg was my mother's maiden name. My name is Eva Barry.' She took his hand. 'Come and I'll tell you all you want to know about Eva Barry.' She led him back to the ledge and after they had dressed they sat crosslegged, facing each other.

She drew a deep breath, then started: 'Twenty-two years ago I was born in a little village in Yorkshire called Kirkby Lonsdale. My father was an Englishman, but my mother was German. I learned the language at her knee. By the time I was twelve my German was almost as good as my English. That was the year my mother died of a terrible new disease, which the doctors called poliomyelitis. The sickness paralysed her lungs and she suffocated. Within days of her death my father was struck by the same disease and his legs withered away. He spent the rest of his life in a wheelchair.'

She began to weep. He took her in his arms and hugged her. She pressed her face to his chest, and her tears were hot on his skin.

He stroked her hair. 'I didn't mean to cause you distress. You don't have to tell me. Hush now. It's all right, Eva, my darling.'

'I do have to tell you, Badger, but please hold me tight while I do it.'

He picked her up and carried her to a place in the shade where he sat with her in his lap. 'If you must, then tell me,' he invited her.

'Daddy's name was Peter, but I called him Curly because he had not a hair on his head. I loved him so very much.' She smiled. 'He was an engineering genius. Sitting in his wheelchair, he dreamed up revolutionary mechanical principles. He formed a small company and hired two mechanics to help him build the models of his designs. But he hardly had enough money to feed us after he had paid his workmen's wages and for the materials. Without money, the patents were worthless.'

She broke off and sniffed back her tears, then took a deep breath. 'One day a man came to Curly's workshop. He said he was a lawyer, and represented a German who owned factories that built steam engines and rolling stock, motor cars and aeroplanes. The client had seen Curly's registered designs in the patents office in London. He had recognised their value. He proposed an equal partnership. Curly would provide his intellectual properties and this man the finances. Curly signed an agreement with him. The contract was in German and Curly understood no more than a few words of it. He was a gentle, gullible genius, not a businessman. I was fifteen, and Curly never mentioned the contract to me before he signed it.' She broke off and sighed, then visibly braced herself to continue.

'The name of Curly's new partner was Graf Otto von Meerbach. Only he wasn't a partner. In a very short time Curly learned that by signing the contract he had sold all the patents he owned to Meerbach Motor Works for a pitifully small sum. One of Curly's patents led directly to the creation of the Meerbach rotary engine, another to a revolutionary differential system for Meerbach heavy vehicles. Curly tried to find a lawyer to help him regain what rightfully belonged to him but the contract was iron clad.

'The money from the sale of the company did not last us long. Although I scrimped and saved, Curly's medical expenses ate it up. Then two days after my sixteenth birthday Curly had one of his attacks. I ran to fetch the doctor. When he and I got back to the room in which we lived, we found that Curly had killed himself with his old shotgun.'

Her body was racked by silent sobs, and he could find no words to console her. 'That's enough, Eva. This is taking too much out of you.'

'No, Badger. It's cathartic. I've kept it bottled up inside me for years.'

'Tell me the rest.'

'There's not much more to tell. I was alone and the funeral took all the money that I had left. I didn't have enough to pay the rent. I took a job in the mill for two shillings a day.

'One day a stranger came to visit me. She was very elegant. She said she was a childhood friend of my mother's who had only heard my tragic story recently and had determined to look after me for the sake of my mother's memory. She was so kind and friendly that I went with her unquestioningly.

'Her name was Mrs Ryan and she had a splendid house in London. She gave me my own room and new clothes. I had a tutor and a dancing teacher. I had a riding instructor, and my own horse. The strangest thing was how assiduously Mrs Ryan made me practise my German. I had a succession of German teachers and worked with them for two hours a day, six days a week. I read all the German newspapers and discussed them with my tutors. Within the first year of this intense study I could have passed readily as an educated native-born German speaker.

'Mrs Ryan was like a mother to me. She knew so much about me. She knew how Curly had been tricked, and told me about Otto von Meerbach. She said he had murdered Curly just as surely as if it had been his finger on the trigger of the shotgun. I began to hate him with a burning passion, and Mrs Ryan fuelled the flames of my loathing. She had an important job in the government. We spoke often about how we should welcome any opportunity to serve King and Empire. I took her words deep into my heart and worked even harder than she demanded.

'One day, soon after my nineteenth birthday, Mrs Ryan took me to an office in Whitehall to meet a man called Mr Brown. He was kind and avuncluar. He told me I was privileged to have been selected for a task that was vital to the security of Britain. I couldn't understand what this had to do with me—until he mentioned the name of Otto von Meerbach. My attention was immediately riveted. He suggested that I was in a position to perform a service for King and Empire, and at the same time find retribution for the terrible wrongs my father and I had suffered at the hands of Graf Otto. All I had to do was induce him to tell me information that would be vital to Britain's military interests.'

She laughed again but this time with genuine amusement. 'Can you imagine, Badger? I was such an innocent little ninny that I hadn't the faintest idea how I was supposed to make him tell me his secrets. I asked Mr Brown outright, and he looked mysterious and exchanged a glance with Mrs Ryan. "If you agree to do as we ask, you will be taught," he said.

'As I recall, my exact words to him were "Of course I will. I just want to know how."' She broke off, sat upright and looked solemnly into Leon's face with the violet eyes he adored. 'Nearly a year after I made that contract with the devil they deemed I was perfect in the role they had chosen for me. I learned everything there was to know about Graf Otto. By then I knew that he was estranged from his wife of ten years, but as both he and she were good Catholics they were unable to divorce. Mr Brown and Mrs Ryan arranged through one of the military attachés at the British Embassy in Berlin that I should be invited to his hunting lodge at Wieskirche. I had been taught my duty and I did it,' she said flatly. 'I was a virgin when I met Otto von Meerbach, and in mind and spirit I still was, until yesterday.' She paused. 'Now that you know about me, do you despise me?'

Her voice was muted, her expression stricken. He reached out and cupped her face, gazing into her eyes so that she could see the truth of what he was about to tell her. 'Nothing you have done, or ever will do, could make me despise you. You have let me into your soul and I have found only goodness and beauty there. You must remember also that when you look at me you are not looking at a saint. It was you who told me we are both soldiers. I have killed men in the name of duty and, like you, I have done many other things of which I'm ashamed. None of that matters. All that matters is that we are together now and we love each other.'

At last she smiled. 'You're right. We love each other and we have each other. That is all that matters.' She reached out for him. 'I want you to take me to Lusima Mama,' she whispered. 'The very first time you spoke of her I felt as though I already knew her. Somehow I know that she holds the key to our happiness.'

MANYORO AND LOIKOT warned Leon that the last section was too steep for the horses so he sent Ishmael and the groom back down to the base of the mountain with orders to circle to the southern side and bring the horses up along the easier familiar route.

Once they had disappeared, Leon, Eva and the two Masai started up the track beside the waterfall. The way became more difficult with every step they climbed. At some places they were forced to traverse the face of the mountain on ledges that only one could pass at a time. The walls and the shelf under their feet were wet and slippery with a coating of slimy algae.

It was noon when they came out on the plateau of the summit. They sought shade under one of the trees and threw themselves down to rest.

'How far to Lusima Mama's *manyatta*?' Leon asked.

'Not far,' replied Loikot. 'We will be there before sunset.'

'A mere stroll of twenty miles or so.' Leon smiled. 'Let's go.' The two Masai picked out the overgrown pathway unerringly and set an easy pace.

At one point they descended into a steep gorge and climbed up the far side to reach an open tableland as flat as a polo ground and devoid of trees. At one end, the cliff fell away abruptly for hundreds of feet. Leon strode down the length of the clearing, counting his paces and examining the ground underfoot.

Eva found a tree stump and sank down on it thankfully. She felt hot and tired. On the far side of the clearing Leon and the two Masai were in deep conversation. After a while Leon came back to her.

'What did you find? Gold or diamonds?' she teased him. 'Why are you so fascinated by this bare ground?'

'Because this is a natural landing strip, Eva. If I side-slipped her between those tall trees at the end of the clearing I could put the *Bumble Bee* down here as sweetly as spreading a spoonful of honey on a slice of toast.'

'Why on earth would you want to do that, my darling man?'

'That's the only thing I don't like about flying,' he answered. 'Every time you take off you have to think about where you're going to land. I've got into the habit of making a note of every possible landing strip I come across.'

'But on top of this mountain? I'll give you a kiss if you give me one good reason why you might ever want to put her down here.'

'A kiss? Now you have my interest.' He lifted his hat and scratched his head thoughtfully. 'Eureka! Got it!' he exclaimed. 'I might want to bring you up here for a champagne picnic on our honeymoon.'

'Come and get your kiss, clever boy!'

As they left the clearing it started to rain. An hour later, with dramatic suddenness, the rain stopped and the sun burst out again. At the same time they heard distant drums.

'Such a stirring sound.' Eva cocked her head to listen. 'It's the very pulse of Africa. But why are the drums beating in the middle of the day?'

Leon spoke to Manyoro, and then he told her, 'They are welcoming us.'

'But how could anyone know we're coming?'

'Lusima knows. She always knows when we're coming, sometimes before we know it ourselves.'

The sun was low and smoky red when they emerged from the forest and smelled woodsmoke. Then they heard voices and the lowing of the herds, and at last they saw a crowd of figures in red *shukas* coming towards them, singing the songs of welcome.

They were swept up and carried along with the laughing, singing throng to the village. As they approached the large central hut the others hung back and left Leon and Eva standing alone before the hut.

'Is this where she lives?' Eva asked, in an awed whisper.

'Yes.' He took her arm possessively. 'She will make her entrance after keeping us in suspense for a while.'

As he spoke Lusima appeared before them through the doorway of the great hut, and Eva started with surprise. 'She's so young and beautiful.'

'I see you, Mama,' Leon greeted her.

'I see you also, M'bogo, my son,' Lusima replied. Then she glided towards Eva with regal grace and stopped in front of her. 'Your eyes are the colour of a flower,' she said. She looked at Leon. 'This is the one of whom I spoke. This is your woman. Now, tell her what I have said.'

Eva's expression lit with joy as she listened to the translation. 'Please, Badger, tell her I've come to ask for her blessing.'

'You shall have it,' Lusima promised her. 'But, child, I see that you have no mother. She was carried away by a terrible disease.'

The smile faded from Eva's face. 'She knew about my mother?' she whispered to Leon. 'Now I believe all that you have told me about her.'

Lusima reached out and cupped Eva's face. 'M'bogo is my son, and you shall be my daughter. I shall take the place of your mother who has gone to be with her ancestors. I give you a mother's blessing. May you find the happiness that for so long has eluded you.'

'You are my mother, Lusima Mama. May I give you a daughter's kiss?'

Lusima smiled. 'Although it is not the custom of our tribe, yes, my daughter, you may kiss me, and I shall kiss you back.' Almost shyly Eva went into her embrace. 'You smell like a flower,' Lusima said.

'And you smell like the good earth after rain,' Eva replied, after a pause to hear Leon's translation.

'Your soul is full of poetry,' Lusima said, 'but you are hurt and tired to the depths of it. You must rest in the hut we have built for you. Perhaps, here on Lonsonyo Mountain, your wounds will be healed.'

The hut to which Lusima's handmaidens led them was newly built. It smelled of the smoke of the herbs that had been burned to purify it. There were bowls of stewed chicken, and roasted vegetables waiting for them, and after they had eaten, the maidens led them to the bed of animal skins. 'You will be the first to sleep here. Let our joy at your coming be your joy also,' they told them as they withdrew and left them alone.

In the morning the girls came to fetch Eva and take her to the pool in the stream that was reserved for the women. When she had bathed they braided her hair with flowers. They brought her a fresh unworn red *shuka* to replace her own torn and dusty clothing. Then they took her to the great council tree under which Lusima and Leon were waiting. The three shared a breakfast of sour milk and sorghum porridge.

After they had eaten they talked together for the rest of the morning. Eva and Lusima sat side by side. They were in such complete accord that Leon's translations were mostly superfluous, for they seemed to understand each other implicitly on a level above that of speech.

'You have been alone for a long time,' Lusima said at one stage.

'Yes, I have been alone for too long,' Eva agreed, then glanced at Leon and reached out to touch his hand. 'But no longer.'

'Loneliness erodes the soul as water wears away rocks.' Lusima nodded.

'Will I ever be alone again, Mama? Your son M'bogo says that you can see what lies ahead for all of us.'

'The future is not simple. When I have looked deeper into your soul, perhaps I will be able to scry your future better.'

'Oh, Mama! That would make me so happy.'

'Do you think so? If I see things that would make you sad, would you want to hear them?'

'All I want is that you tell me M'bogo and I will be together for ever.'

Lusima studied Eva's face, saw the pain and took pity on her. 'This much I can tell you. As long as you are together, you and M'bogo will know true happiness, for your hearts are linked like these two plants.' She laid her hand on an ancient vine that twisted round the trunk of the council tree. 'See how the vine has become part of the tree. See how the one supports the other. You cannot separate them. That is the way it is with the two of you.'

'If you see dangers that lie ahead for us, will you not warn us?'

Lusima shrugged. 'Perhaps, if I think it will be to your advantage to know. Go now, my children. Take what remains of the day and be happy together. We will talk again tomorrow.'

So the days passed, and under Lusima's gentle counsel and guidance, Eva's fears and uncertainties gradually faded and she entered a realm of contentment so complete that she had never suspected its existence.

'I knew we had to come here, but I never knew why until now. These days spent on Lonsonyo Mountain are more precious than diamonds. No matter what happens they will be with us for ever,' she told Leon.

THE DAYS FLEW by in such a dreamlike blur that they lost track of time. Like two children, they wandered hand in hand through the enchanted forests of Lonsonyo Mountain. With each small delight they came across—a tiny sunbird of brilliant plumage or a monstrous horned beetle—the worries of the outside world receded further from their minds.

Even when Ishmael's carefully hoarded store of coffee was exhausted, they laughed when he told them the tragic news. 'It is a sin that shall not be written against your name in the golden book O Beloved of the Prophet,' Leon comforted him, but Ishmael went away muttering dolefully.

Leon realised that almost two moths had passed since they had climbed the pathway beside the waterfall to the summit. When he pointed this out to Eva, she smiled. 'Time means nothing, Badger. Just so long as we are together. What are we going to do today?'

'Loikot knows where there is an eagles' breeding site in the cliffs on the far side of the mountain not far from Sheba's Pool. Would you like to see the young ones?'

'Oh, yes, please, Badger!' She clapped her hands, as excited as a child at the promise of a birthday party. 'Then on our way back we can go to the falls and swim once again in those enchanted waters!'

It took them three days of easy travel to cross the mountain at its widest point, for the gorges were deep and rugged, the forest was dense, and there were delightful distractions at every turn of the path. But at last they sat on the brink of the precipice and watched a pair of eagles sailing in elegant flight far below them, circling their eyrie, calling to each other and their young ones in the nest, bringing in the carcasses of their prey to feed them.

Then Loikot led them along the edge of the cliff to a narrow and precarious open ledge. They moved along it with their backs to the cliff wall until, suddenly, it widened. Loikot stretched out flat on the rock and peered over the edge, then grinned at Eva, beckoning her to join him. She crawled cautiously to his side and looked down. 'There the chicks are!' she exclaimed with delight. 'Oh, Badger, come and see them.'

He lay beside her and placed one arm round her shoulders. The nest was no more than thirty feet directly below, a massive platform of dried sticks wedged into a cleft in the rock. In the centre of the indentation two eaglets crouched on wobbly legs, so young they could barely hold their heads upright. Their huge beaks were out of proportion to their fluffy grey bodies.

It was a fascinating experience to be allowed so close to such magnificent wild creatures and observe them caring for and feeding their young. Leon and Eva spent the rest of the day on the ledge. When at last daylight was fading and it was time to go, they left reluctantly. In the rudimentary overnight shelter that Loikot and Manyoro had built for them they spent the night under a single blanket.

THEIR RETURN to Lusima's village was a happy homecoming. The herd-boys spied them from afar and shouted the news to the villagers, who trooped out to welcome them. Lusima was waiting for them under the council tree. She embraced Eva and made her sit on her right-hand side. Leon took the stool on her other side and helped with translation. Suddenly he broke off in mid-sentence and raised his head to sniff the air. 'What on earth is that wonderful aroma?' he demanded, of no one in particular.

'Coffee!' cried Eva. 'Wonderful, glorious coffee!' Ishmael came towards them with a pair of mugs in one hand and a steaming coffee pot in the other. His grin was triumphant. 'You are a worker of miracles!' Eva greeted him. 'That is the only thing I needed to make my life perfect.'

'I have also brought you many of your beautiful clothes and shoes so that you no longer have to wear the garments of the infidel.' He indicated her *shuka* with a grimace of the deepest disapproval and disgust.

'Ishmael!' Leon's voice was sharp. 'While we were away, did you go down to Percy's Camp to fetch the coffee and the memsahib's clothes?'

'*Ndio*, Bwana.' Ishmael grinned with pride. 'I rode hard on my mule and I was there and back in only four days.'

'Did anybody see you? Who else was at the camp?'

'Only Bwana Hennie.'

'Did you tell him where we are?' Leon demanded.

'Yes, he asked me,' Ishmael answered. Then his face fell as he saw Leon's expression. 'Did I do wrong, Effendi?'

Leon turned away as he struggled to suppress his anger and the dread that had engulfed him. When he turned back his face was blank. 'You did what you thought was right, Ishmael. The coffee is excellent, as good as any you've ever brewed.' But Ishmael knew him too well to be taken in by his words. It was not clear to him how he had erred, but he was stricken with guilt as he backed away to his kitchen hut.

Eva was watching Leon. Her face was pale. 'What is it, Badger?'

'While we were away, Ishmael went down to Percy's Camp to fetch supplies. Hennie du Rand was there. Ishmael told him where we are.'

'Is that so bad? Hennie wouldn't do anything to hurt us?'

'Not deliberately, but he has no idea of our delicate circumstances. We cannot chance it, Eva. If Graf Otto is alive, he will come after you.'

'He must be dead, my darling.'

'We cannot be sure. And if your masters in Whitehall find out where you are, they will not let you go. We must run.'

'Where to?'

'If we can get to one of the aircraft, we can fly across the German border to Dar es Salaam, and from there take a ship to South Africa or Australia. Once we get there we can change our names and disappear. Will you come with me?'

'Of course,' she replied. 'From now on, wherever you go, I go also.'

Leon smiled at her and said simply, 'My heart, my dear heart.' Then he turned back to Lusima. 'Mama, we have to leave.'

'Yes,' she agreed at once. 'This I have foreseen.'

Somehow Eva understood what Lusima had said. 'Will you tell us what you have seen?' she asked eagerly.

'It is not much, and little of it is what you want to hear, my flower.'

'I will hear it nonetheless.'

Lusima sighed. 'As you wish, but I have warned you.' She clapped her hands and her girls came running. Lusima gave them their orders and they scampered away to her hut. By the time they returned, carrying the paraphernalia Lusima used for divination, the sun had set. The girls laid her tools close to Lusima's hand, then built up the small fire. One of the girls brought a clay pot and placed it on the fire in front of her. It was filled to the brim with a liquid that reflected the flames like a mirror.

'Come and sit beside me.' She motioned to Eva and Leon. They formed a circle with her round the pot. Lusima dipped a horn cup into the liquid and offered it to each in turn. They swallowed a mouthful of the bitter brew, and Lusima drank what was left.

'Look into the mirror,' she ordered, and they stared into the pot. The liquid began to bubble and boil as Lusima chanted softly, and her eyes glazed over as she stared into the rising clouds of steam. When at last she spoke her voice was harsh and strained: 'There are two enemies, a man and a woman. They seek to sever the chain of love that binds you to each other.'

Eva gave a small cry of pain, but then was silent.

'I see that the woman has a silver flag on her head.'

'Mrs Ryan in London,' Eva whispered, when Leon translated this to her. 'She has a streak of silver in the front of her hair.'

'The man has only one hand.'

Leon shook his head. 'I don't know who that might be. Tell us, Mama, will these two enemies succeed in their designs?'

Lusima moaned as though in pain. 'I can see no further. The sky is filled with smoke and flame. The whole world is burning. It is obscure, but I see a great silver fish above the flames that brings hope of love and fortune.'

'What fish is this, Mama?' Leon asked, but Lusima's eyes had cleared and focused again.

'There is no more,' she said regretfully. She reached forward and overturned the clay pot, spilling its contents onto the fire, extinguishing it in a cloud of hissing steam. 'Go to your rest now. This may be your last night on Lonsonyo Mountain for a long, long while.'

BEFORE THEY WENT to their hut Leon issued instructions to the two Masai and Ishmael to have the horses saddled and make all preparations for departure at dawn on the morrow.

The night was quiet but they slept only fitfully. When they started awake they reached out for each other instinctively, seized by a formless sense of dread. When the birds in the surrounding forest began their greeting to the dawn, Leon whispered, 'Time to go, my beloved. Get dressed.'

He rose and threw on his clothes before he went to the door and pulled it open. The forest round him was black. The morning star was still aloft, and pricked the dark velvet sky. The light was leaden and dull. Eva came through the doorway behind him and he placed his arm round her. He was about to speak when he saw the men.

They had been waiting in the darkness at the edge of the forest, but now they came towards them and, as they drew closer, Leon saw that there were five *askaris* and two officers. The *askaris* carried rifles slung over their shoulders, the officers only side arms. The senior man stopped in front of them, but he ignored Leon and saluted Eva.

'How did you find us, Uncle Penrod? Did you have somebody watching Percy's Camp who followed Ishmael here?'

Penrod nodded. 'Of course.' He turned back to Eva. 'Good morning, Eva, my dear. I have a message for you from Mrs Ryan and Mr Brown.'

Eva recoiled. 'No!' she said. 'Otto is dead and it's all over.'

'Graf Otto von Meerbach is not dead. The doctor had to amputate his left arm and sew the rest of him together but he is as tough as elephant hide. He is still very weak but he is asking for you, and I had to make up a cock-and-bull story about you being snatched by Nandi tribesmen to explain your absence. I think he truly loves you, and I have come to take you back to him so that you can finish the job you were sent to do.'

Leon stepped between them. 'She is not going back. We love each other and we are going to marry as soon as we can get back to civilisation.'

'Lieutenant Courtney, may I remind you that I am your commanding officer. Now, step aside at once.'

'I can't do that, sir. I can't let you take her back.' Leon hunched his shoulders stubbornly.

'Captain!' Penrod snapped, over his shoulder, and a younger officer stepped forward smartly.

'Sir?' he said. It was Eddy Roberts, Froggy Snell's toady.

'Arrest this man.' Penrod's expression was grim. 'If he resists, shoot him in the kneecap.'

'Yes, sir!' Roberts sang out jubilantly. He drew his Webley revolver from its holster and Leon started towards him. Roberts stepped back, cocked the hammer and raised the weapon, but before he could level it Eva jumped between them and spread her arms. Now the pistol was aimed at her breast.

'Hold your fire, man!' Penrod shouted. 'For God's sake, don't harm the woman.' Roberts lowered the weapon uncertainly.

'What do you want of me, General?' Eva voice was cold and calm.

'Just a few minutes of your time, my dear.' Penrod took her arm, but Leon intervened again. 'Don't go with him, Eva. He'll talk you round.'

She glanced back at him, and he saw that her eyes were veiled and the spark had been extinguished: she had gone back to that place where nobody could follow her, not even the man who loved her. 'Eva!' he pleaded. 'Stay with me, my darling.'

She gave no indication that she had heard, and allowed Penrod to walk her away. He led her to the edge of the cliff so that Leon could not hear a single word of their conversation. Penrod towered over her, head and shoulders. Eva looked like a child beside him as she gazed up solemnly into his face and listened to what he was saying. He placed both hands on her shoulders and shook her gently, his expression grave. Leon could barely restrain himself. He wanted to protect and defend her.

'Yes, Courtney, do it!' Roberts said, in a gloating tone. His finger was on the trigger and the weapon was aimed at Leon's right leg. 'Do it, you bastard! Give me the excuse to blow your bloody leg off.'

Leon knew he meant it. He clenched his hands until his fingernails dug into his palms. Eva was still staring up into Penrod's face as he talked. At last her shoulders slumped in capitulation and she nodded. Penrod placed an arm round her shoulders in an avuncular manner, then led her back to where Leon stood. She did not look at him. Her expression was dead.

'Captain Roberts!' Penrod said. He would not look at Leon either. 'Use your handcuffs to restrain the prisoner.'

Roberts snapped the bracelets onto Leon's wrists.

'Keep him here! Don't harm him, unless he deserves it,' Penrod ordered. 'Don't allow him off this mountain until you receive orders from me. Then take him to Nairobi under guard and bring him directly to me.'

'Yes, sir!'

'Come along, my dear.' He turned back to Eva. 'We have a long ride ahead of us.' They walked to the horses, and Leon called after them, his voice cracked with despair, 'You can't go, Eva. Please, my darling.'

She paused to look back at him with opaque, hopeless eyes. 'We were two silly children playing a game of make-believe. It's over now. I have to go. Goodbye, Leon.'

'Oh God!' he groaned. 'Don't you love me?'

'No, Leon. The only thing I love is my duty.' And he was not to know that her heart was breaking as she walked away, the lie still scalding her lips.

As soon as Penrod and Eva had gone down the mountain, Captain Roberts had his *askaris* drag Leon back into the hut and sit him down with his legs on each side of the central pole that supported the roof. Then he unlocked the cuffs from his wrists and clamped them on to his ankles.

'I'm not taking any chances with you, Courtney. I know just what a slippery brute you are,' Roberts told him, with sadistic relish. He allowed Ishmael to visit him in the hut once a day to feed him and to carry away the night-soil bucket. Leon was forced to sit there for twelve long, degrading days until Penrod's messenger came up the mountain track with a note written on yellow order paper. Then Roberts allowed him out of the hut and the *askaris* lifted him onto his horse. Leon's ankles were so swollen and raw from the manacles that he could barely walk. Nevertheless Roberts ordered his men to rope his ankles together under the horse's belly. With his ankles bound, Leon was unable to pace with the gait of his mount and was bounced around savagely.

Penrod was furious when two *askaris* almost carried his nephew into his office in the KAR headquarters building in Nairobi. He helped him into a chair. 'I did not intend you to be treated in that fashion,' he said, which was as close to an apology as Leon had ever heard him come.

'Where is Eva, Uncle?'

'She's probably somewhere in the Suez Canal by now, on her way back to Berlin.' His expression softened. 'I think I did you a great service by bringing you to your senses and getting rid of her for you, my lad. She's a spy, did you know that? She's totally scheming and unscrupulous.'

'No, sir. She's a British agent. She's a beautiful young woman of great courage who has done more than her patriotic duty for you and Britain.'

'You're an idiot, a lovesick puppy, incapable of rational thought.' Penrod reached for his uniform tunic, which was hooked over the back of his chair.

As he buttoned it up, Leon saw a new insignia on the shoulders. 'If you've finished insulting me, sir, perhaps you might allow me to congratulate you on your meteoric rise to the lofty rank of major general.'

Leon had broken the tension and Penrod accepted the peace offering. 'We all did what we had to do, Leon. Did you know that while you were honeymooning on Lonsonyo Mountain some Serbian madman assassinated the Archduke Franz Ferdinand of Austria-Hungary? The heavy-handed retaliation of that country against the Serbs has set off a chain reaction of violence. Half of Europe is already at war, and Kaiser Wilhelm is spoiling to get into it. It's all happening just as I predicted. Full-scale war within a few months.' He searched his pockets for his cigarette case. 'I was with Allenby in the Boer War, and now he's in charge of the Egyptian Army. He wants me to take command of his cavalry. I sail for Cairo next week.'

'Who's taking over from you here in Nairobi?'

'Your old friend Froggy Snell has been promoted to colonel and given the job.' He saw Leon's face fall. 'Yes, I know what you're thinking. However, I have transferred you to act as liaison and intelligence officer to Hugh Delamere. He's keen to have you fly reconnaissance for his volunteer unit. He knows about your rift with Snell and will protect you from him.'

'Very decent of him. But there's one small problem. I have no aeroplane for these reconnaissance flights.'

'The minute Kaiser Wilhelm declares war you'll have your aeroplane— in fact, you will have two. Both of von Meerbach's aircraft are safely parked in the hangar at the polo ground. He left them with his mechanic, Gustav Kilmer, to take care of them. As soon as war breaks out we'll commandeer them as the property of an enemy alien.'

'That's good news indeed. As soon as you dismiss me, sir, I intend to go out to Tandala Camp to check on what Max Rosenthal and Hennie du Rand have been up to in my absence. After that, I'll go down to the polo ground and make sure the aircraft are safely stowed.'

'Oh, you won't find du Rand at Tandala. He's gone to Germany with von Meerbach.'

'Good Lord.' Leon was genuinely surprised. 'How did that come about?'

'The Graf must have taken a shine to him. Anyway, he's gone. As I will have next Friday.' Penrod stood up. 'You're dismissed.'

'One last question, if I may, sir?'

'Go ahead and ask it, but as I suspect I already know what your enquiry concerns, I don't promise to answer.'

'Do you have an arrangement in place for exchanging messages with Eva Barry while she's in Germany?'

'Ah! So that's the young lady's real name. I knew that "von Wellberg" was a *nom de guerre*. It seems you know a great deal more about her than I do.'

'None of that answers my question, General.'

'It doesn't, does it?' Penrod agreed. 'Shall we leave it at that?'

LEON RODE OUT TO TANDALA CAMP, and when he went into his tent he found Max Rosenthal packing his kitbag. 'Leaving us, Max?' Leon asked.

'The locals are starting a pogrom against us. I don't want to spend this war in a British concentration camp like the ones Kitchener put up in South Africa, so I'm heading for the German border.'

'Wise man,' Leon told him. 'I'm going to the polo ground to talk to Gustav about the two aircraft. If you're there at first light tomorrow morning, I may be able to give you both a lift south to Arusha and safety.'

It was dusk when Leon rode down the main street of Nairobi, but the entire town was bustling. He had to weave his way through the throng of carts and wagons, all crammed with the families of settlers coming in from the remote farms. A rumour was flying that von Lettow Vorbeck had massed his troops on the border ready to march on Nairobi, burning and plundering the farms along the way. The men were headed for the recruitment office in the Barclays Bank building where Lord Delamere was taking on men for his volunteer regiment.

When Leon rode past the front of the bank the volunteers were standing in excited groups on the dusty street, discussing the prospect of war. At that moment a man ran out of the cablegram office across the street, waving a form over his head. 'Message from London!' he yelled. 'Kaiser Bill has declared war on Britain and the Empire! All aboard for glory, lads!'

There was a raucous chorus of cheers and shouts of 'Rot the bastard!'

Leon was about to dismount and join them when a thought occurred to him. How is Gustav going to react to this declaration of war? What orders did Graf Otto leave for him to cover this eventuality? He whipped up his horse and pointed it in the direction of the polo ground.

It was dark when he reached it. He pulled his mount down to a walk as he approached the hangar. The turf muffled the sound of the horse's hoofs, and he saw a flickering light in the hangar through the tarpaulin wall.

He kicked his feet out of the stirrups and dropped to the ground. Silently he ran to the door and paused to assess the situation. The light he had seen was a burning torch, which Gustav was holding aloft. Leon saw that both aircraft were parked tail to tail on their usual stands at opposite ends of the hangar. Each had its own doorway, an arrangement that allowed them to be wheeled in or out without the other machine having to be moved.

Gustav had chopped up most of the heavy packing crates in which the planes had been shipped out from Germany and had piled the wood in a pyramid under the *Butterfly*'s fuselage. He held the burning torch in his right hand, an open schnapps bottle in the left. He was in the middle of a drunken valediction to the two flying machines.

'This is the hardest thing I have ever been asked to do. I built you with my own hands. You are a monument to my skills and genius.' He broke off with a sob and took a long swig of schnapps. 'Now I must destroy you.' He hurled the torch towards the pile of wood, but the schnapps had affected his judgment and it arched up, leaving a trail of sparks. It struck the propeller of the near-side port engine and rebounded, rolling back to Gustav's feet. With an oath he stooped to pick it up.

Leon crashed into Gustav from behind just as his fingers closed on the handle of the burning torch. He knocked the German off his feet but somehow Gustav managed to keep his grip on the torch.

With amazing agility for such a big man he rolled onto his knees and glared at Leon. 'I will kill you if you try to stop me!' He threw the torch again, and this time it lodged on the wood. Leon ran forward, trying to reach it before the fire took hold, but Gustav staggered to his feet and blocked his path. Leon went straight at him and kicked him in the crotch. His spurs ripped into the soft flesh between Gustav's thighs. He screamed and reeled back, clutching his injured genitals with both hands.

Leon shouldered him aside, grabbed the torch and hurled it towards the door. Gustav leaped onto his back and wrapped a muscular arm round his neck in a deadly stranglehold. He had both legs locked round Leon's body. He tightened his grip, and Leon choked.

Through streaming eyes he saw one of the propeller blades of the big Meerbach engine hanging in front of him at head level. It was made of wood, but the leading edge was clad with metal, like a knife blade. He pirouetted quickly, bringing Gustav in line with the blade, then ran backwards. It slashed into the back of the man's skull, cutting to the bone. His grip loosened and Leon tore himself free. Gustav was staggering in a circle, blood spurting from the wound. Leon clenched his right fist and punched the side of his jaw. Gustav went down, sprawling on his back.

Gasping for breath, Leon looked around wildly. The torch was lying in the doorway where he had thrown it. It was still alight and now the flames had rekindled and were burning up brightly. As Leon bent to pick it up he heard a scuffling sound behind him and ducked to one side. He heard something hiss past his right ear. He whirled round.

Gustav had armed himself with an eight-pound sledgehammer from the workbench against the wall. Then he had charged at Leon and had swung it at Leon's head. If Leon had not ducked, it would have shattered his skull.

Leon had just enough time to hurl the torch aside before Gustav began swinging the sledgehammer in great sweeps at Leon's face, and he was forced to give ground before the menace of its heavy steel head.

He came up short with his back against the corner of the hangar wall and he knew that Gustav had him trapped. With both hands Gustav lifted the hammer high, and paused with it aimed at Leon's head. Leon knew that when the blow came there was not enough space for him to dodge. He stared into Gustav's eyes, trying to control him with the force of his gaze, but schnapps and pain had turned the man into an animal.

Then Gustav's expression changed subtly. The mad rage faded from his eyes, replaced by bewilderment. He opened his mouth, but before he could speak a thick gout of bright blood spewed over his lips. The hammer dropped and clattered to the hangar floor. He looked down at his body.

The blade of a Masai *assegai* stood out a hand's breadth from the centre of his chest. He shook his head as though in disbelief. Then his legs buckled. Manyoro was standing close behind him and, as Gustav fell, he plucked out the blade from where he had driven it home.

Leon stared at Manyoro. The last time he had seen him was almost a week ago on Lonsonyo Mountain. How had he arrived so fortuitously? Then he saw that Loikot was with him and, before he could stop him, had plunged his own *assegai* into the inert body.

Leon was assailed by horror and dread. No matter the circumstances in which it had happened, they had killed a white man. There would be retribution in the form of the hangman's noose. The administration of the colony could not afford to condone such a heinous offence in a land where whites were outnumbered fifty to one by tribesmen. 'How did you get here?' Leon demanded of the two Masai.

'When the soldiers took you from Lonsonyo we followed you.'

'I owe my life to you. The Bula Matari would have killed me, but you know what will happen if the police catch you.'

'No matter,' Manyoro said, with dignity. 'They can do with me as they wish. You are my brother. I could not stand by and watch him kill you.'

'Does anybody else know you are in Nairobi?' Leon asked, and they shook their heads. 'Good. We must work quickly.'

Between them they wrapped Gustav's corpse in a tarpaulin from the storeroom with a fifty-pound crank shaft lashed to his feet, then carried it to the *Butterfly* and loaded it into the main bomb bay in the fuselage. Still working fast, they tidied the hangar, getting rid of any trace of the fight and the fire. They spread fresh earth over the bloodstains, trampled it down and sprinkled engine oil over the spot to disguise the nature of the stains. If any questions were asked about Gustav's disappearance, it would be assumed that he had gone on the run to escape incarceration in a concentration camp.

When Leon was satisfied they had covered up as much of the incriminating evidence as they could, they wheeled the *Butterfly* out of the hangar and he climbed into the cockpit to begin his start-up procedures. The two Masai stood ready to swing the propellers. Then they stiffened and stared into the darkness from which came the sound of a horse at full gallop.

'Police?' Leon muttered. 'This could mean trouble.'

He held his breath, then released it as Max Rosenthal rode out of the night and dismounted. He carried a large rucksack slung on his back as he hurried to the side of the *Butterfly*. 'You told me you'd help me,' he said, looking terrified. 'Up at the parade ground they've just shot three Germans they accused of being spies. Mr Courtney, you know I'm no spy.'

'Don't worry, Max, I'll take you out,' Leon said. 'Climb aboard!'

As soon as the engines started, the two Masai scrambled up to join Max in the cockpit and, with the moon lighting the way, Leon turned south and headed for the border with German East Africa. Three hours later the silver expanse of Lake Natron came up ahead, shining like a mirror in the moonlight. Leon let the *Butterfly* sink down until they were skimming its surface. In its centre he pulled the lever that opened the bomb bay, then leaned over the side of the cockpit and watched the tarpaulin-shrouded corpse plummet into the water. He circled back low over the surface to make certain that the metal ballast had pulled it under. There was barely a ripple on the surface.

He turned back for the eastern shore. Lake Natron overlapped the boundary between the German and British territories. At this dry season of the year the beaches were exposed and as the water was rich in soda they were brilliant white, the soda hard-packed. Leon could land the *Butterfly* safely on one of them. He made a pass down a stretch of beach, came round again and touched down gently.

'Where are we, Manyoro?' Leon asked.

The two Masai discussed the question before they replied.

'We are in the land of the Bula Matari. It is half a day's walk to the border.'

'Are there any Germans close by?'

'The nearest post is at Longido.' Manyoro pointed southeast.

'Are there any villages close by?'

'*Ndio*, M'bogo. Less than an hour's walk along the shore from here there is a large village of fisherfolk.'

Leon and the Masai bade Max farewell and watched him set off jauntily on foot for the fishing village from where he could make his way to the German post of Longido. As soon as he had disappeared into the bush, they started the *Butterfly*'s engines and climbed into the cockpit. When they were airborne, Leon turned north on to a heading for Nairobi.

THE FOLLOWING DAYS were feverishly busy as Leon took over his new job as Lord Delamere's intelligence and liaison officer. Despite all this distraction, Eva was never far from his mind.

As Leon was leaving Lord Delamere's office in the Barclays Bank building he felt a small soft hand press into his. Startled, he looked down—into the huge dark eyes of Latika, Mr Vilabjhi's youngest daughter. She placed a folded square of paper in his hand. 'My daddy said I should give this to you.'

Leon unfolded it and read quickly: '*I must speak to you. Come to my emporium as soon as you can. Signed by Mr Goolam Vilabjhi Esq.*'

The child was tugging at his hand, and he allowed her to lead him away to where his horse stood at the hitching rail down the street. He mounted, then reached down from the saddle to lift her behind him. She clasped him round the waist, and they rode the length of the street.

When they entered the shop, Mr Vilabjhi rushed out of the back room to welcome him, and his wife brought in a tray of strong Arabic coffee and sweetmeats. She was followed by all of their daughters, but before they could entrench themselves their father drove them out, with fond cries of 'Be gone, you rowdy female personages!' He turned to Leon. 'I have a most urgent matter on which I plead for your wise counsel.'

Leon sipped the coffee and waited for him to proceed.

'Without any doubt you are aware that before he left last week, your uncle, the eminent sahib Major General Ballantyne, asked me to receive messages from the lovely memsahib von Wellberg on his behalf and forward these to the correct authority.' He looked at Leon quizzically.

Leon was about to deny any knowledge of this arrangement, but then he realised that would be a mistake so he nodded, and Mr Vilabjhi looked relieved. 'The reason that the general chose me is that I have a niece who lives with her husband in Altnau, a small town in Switzerland on the north shore of Lake Bodensee. Across the lake is the town of Wieskirche in Bavaria. This is where the castle of the German count is situated, and also the main factory of the Meerbach Motor Works. It is also where Memsahib von Wellberg lives.' Mr Vilabjhi had phrased it delicately. 'My niece works in the Swiss cablegram company. Her husband has a fishing boat on the lake. The shore is not heavily guarded, so it is easy for them to cross the water at night and pick up any message at Wieskirche, then telegraph it to me. I take it to General Ballantyne. Before the esteemed general left he told me I should deliver any future messages to the man who has taken over his job at KAR Headquarters.'

'Yes. Colonel Snell,' Leon said calmly, although his heart raced. Eva.

'Ah, of course I am telling you nothing that is not already well known to you. However, a terrible thing has happened.' Mr Vilabjhi broke off and rolled his eyes tragically.

Leon's heart was chilled with dread. 'Something has happened to Memsahib von Wellberg?' he asked.

'No, it has happened to me! After the departure of the general I took the first despatch from my niece to the office of Colonel Snell. I learned in no ambivalent terms that the man is an enemy of the general. Now that he has left for Egypt, Colonel Snell will not foster any enterprise initiated by your honourable relative. I think it is because the praise arising from it would be to the general's credit, rather than to Colonel Snell himself. Also it seems he knows that you and I are friends and he looks upon you as an enemy. He drove me away with harsh words.' Mr Vilabjhi paused. 'He told me not to go back to him with my claptrap about secret despatches. I know not what to do so I appeal to you.'

Leon rubbed his chin thoughtfully. He chose his words carefully. 'You and I are loyal subjects of King George the Fifth, are we not?'

'Indeed we are, Sahib.'

'If the beastly man Snell is a traitor, then you and I are not.'

'No! Never! We are true and resolute Englishmen.'

'In the name of our sovereign, we have to take over this enterprise from Snell and steer it to a victorious conclusion.' Leon had picked up Mr Vilabjhi's floral turn of phrase.

'I rejoice to hear such words of wisdom, Sahib!'

'First, you and I must read the message that Snell has rejected. Have you kept it safe?'

Vilabjhi sprang up from his desk and went to the iron safe in the wall. He brought out a large cashbook. Tucked under the rear cover was a Post Office envelope. He handed it to Leon. The flap was sealed.

'You did not open it?'

'Of course not. That is not my business.'

Leon split the envelope with his thumbnail. He drew out the folded buff sheet and spread it on the desk. Then he sagged with dismay. It was covered with rows and columns of numbers, no letters.

'Damn it to hell! It's in code,' he lamented. 'Do you have the key?'

Mr Vilabjhi shook his head.

'But you know how to send a reply?'

'Of course. I arranged the link with the memsahib through my niece.'

E va ran lightly down the magnificent marble staircase of the *Schloss*. As she reached the lowest landing she heard voices coming up the stairwell. She stopped to listen.

Otto was in conversation with at least two other men, and she recognised the voice of Alfred Lutz, the commodore of his fleet of dirigible airships, and that of Hans Ritter, the senior navigator.

Otto's tone was loud and hectoring. Since his mauling by the lion his previously overbearing manner had become ever more authoritarian. 'We will leave from Wieskirche and fly to Mesopotamia where we will land to top up our tanks with fuel, oil and water. From there we go on to Damascus, then across the Red Sea to the Nile Valley, Khartoum and the Sudan.'

He went on, 'From the Sudan we will fly on down the Rift Valley to Arusha, where von Lettow Vorbeck are holding stores of fuel and oil for us. From there, we will observe strict radio silence until we are over the central Kalahari. Only then will we contact Koos de la Rey by radio.'

She felt a deep sense of accomplishment. This was the most vital piece of information, which until now she had been unable to discover. Now she knew exactly how Otto intended to convey his cargo of arms and bullion to the South African rebels. Penrod had suggested that it would be sent by submarine to some uninhabited beach on the west coast of South Africa. No one had thought of a dirigible airship. But now she had the entire plan. With this information she would have given Penrod Ballantyne everything he needed except the date the journey would begin.

She started as she heard the voices becoming louder and clearer. She must not be found eavesdropping. She ran on down the last flight of stairs, making no attempt to cover the sound of her descent. The men were standing in a group in the centre of the hall. The airmen saluted her respectfully, and Otto's face lightened with pleasure.

'You are going out for a ride?' he asked.

'I told Chef I would go into Friedrichshafen and see if the old lady in the market has any black truffles for your dinner. I know how you love them. You don't mind if I leave you for a few hours, Otto? I might stop on my way back to sketch views of the lake.'

'Not at all, my dear. Anyway, I am going to the factory with Lutz and Ritter to check the final assembly of the new airship. Do not make any plans for next week.'

'Are you ready to fly the airship?' She clapped her hands in feigned excitement.

'Perhaps, perhaps not,' he teased, with heavy humour. 'But I would like you to be there when we walk her out from her hangar for her maiden flight.' He lifted his left arm and clicked open the metal thumb and finger of the prosthesis that was fitted to the end of the stump. He placed a Cuban cigar in the jaws of the metal appendage and secured it in place with a lateral twist of his wrist. Then he lifted it, and placed the tip between his lips, and Lutz struck a Vesta and held it for him.

Eva suppressed a shiver of unease. The artificial hand frightened her. It had been made for Otto by the engineers in his factory to his own design. It was an extraordinary creation with which he had already developed an alarming dexterity. Holding a bottle between the steel fingers, he could pour wine for his dinner guests without spilling a drop, button the front of his coat, clean his teeth or tie his shoelaces. The hand also had a formidable spiked battle-mace fitting. With this terrible club replacing his hand, she had seen him put a horse with a broken leg out of its misery with a blow that had shattered its skull.

Otto kissed her, then led his guests down the front steps of the *Schloss* into a black Meerbach touring car. Eva waved him out of sight, then, with a sigh of relief, ran down to the forecourt, where one of the grooms was holding her favourite mare. She kicked her heels into the mare's flanks and urged her into a headlong gallop through the forest to the lake. These solitary rides were her only escape from the gloomy old castle and Otto.

Since she had known Leon it had become almost impossible for her to sustain her carefully rehearsed role as the Graf's dutiful mistress. She could not go on much longer before she made a mistake and he discovered that he had been gulled. When that happened his vengeance would be merciless. She was afraid and longed to be safe in Leon's arms.

'I love him but I know I'll never see him again,' she whispered, and the tears blew back across her cheeks with the speed of the mare's gallop. At last they burst out on her favourite view across Lake Bodensee to the snow-clad heights of the Swiss Alps on the far side. She stopped and gazed out across the blue waters. A tiny fishing boat was running before the wind under a reefed mainsail and jib. A man was slumped lazily over the tiller in the stern, and a dark girl in a brightly coloured dress sat on the foredeck gazing across the water at Eva. Though they knew each other well, they had never spoken. Eva did not know her name. Their relationship had been arranged by Penrod Ballantyne and Mr Goolam Vilabjhi.

The girl turned her head and said something to the man in the stern. He put the tiller over and tacked the fishing boat. As it came across the wind, the blue swallow-tailed pennant at the masthead unfurled and flapped open. It was the signal that there was a message for Eva. The boat came about on the starboard tack and settled on a course for the shore.

Eva was relieved. For the past weeks she had been expecting a response to her last signal to Penrod in Nairobi. His silence had made her feel even more vulnerable. Although she was still bitter that he had separated her and Leon, Penrod was the only ally she had in all her lonely world. She trotted the mare along the shore in the direction of Friedrichshafen.

At one point ahead a copse came to the water's edge, the trees marking the junoturo of tho boundary wall with the lake. She reached the wall and dismounted to open the gate in it. The wall was a substantial construction of dry-packed stone blocks. She hitched the mare to the gate, climbed up onto the stone blocks and, her sketchpad open in her lap, gazed about as though she was admiring the scenery.

When she had satisfied herself that she was not observed, she reached down casually and lifted a mossy stone from its niche. In the recess beneath it lay the folded sheet of thin rice paper that the girl had placed there.

Eva put back the stone carefully before she unfolded the paper. She was alarmed to see that the script was in clear language, not coded. Swiftly she scanned the two lines of text, then gasped with astonishment. 'Uncle gone stop What code are you using query Badger.'

Joy surged through her. 'Badger!' she exclaimed. 'My darling Badger, you've found me.' Although he was half a world away she was no longer completely alone. She put the scrap of rice paper into her mouth, chewed it and swallowed. Satisfied that Otto had not sent any of his men to spy on her, she tore a small strip from the foot of the pad and wrote: *Macmillan English dictionary July 1908 edition stop First numeral group is page stop Second numeral group is column stop Final numeral group is word from top stop*. Finally she wrote: *You are in my heart for ever*. She folded the sheet and placed it carefully in the niche under the stone. The girl from across the lake would come for it after dark. She would transmit it to Mr Vilabjhi, and by tomorrow evening Badger would be reading it in Nairobi. She sat for a while longer, pretending to draw, but her spirits were bubbling like a freshly opened bottle of Dom Pérignon champagne.

'To get back to Africa and the man I love. This is all I desire. Please, dear God, have mercy on me,' she prayed aloud.

Leon spent the morning in conference with Hugh Delamere and his other officers. The little man had thrown himself wholeheartedly into the formation and training of his force of more than two hundred volunteer troopers. Delamere was renowned throughout the colony for his energy and enthusiasm, and it had taken him less than two weeks to bully and cajole the regiment into a state of campaign readiness. Now he wanted an enemy to fight and had turned to Leon to find one.

'You're the only pilot we have, Courtney. Our border with the Hun is long and the best way to keep an eye open for the movements of von Lettow and his *askaris* is from the air. My guess is that he will try to reach up the Rift Valley from the main German base at Arusha. I want you to fly regular reconnaissance patrols from Percy's Camp. I also know you have a network of Masai *chungaji* keeping watch for elephant. You should let them know that, for the time being, we are more interested in the Hun than in ivory.'

By noon Leon's notebook was half filled with his lordship's instructions. Delamere dismissed his officers for lunch with orders to return promptly at

1400 hours. When Leon strode out into the street little Latika Vilabjhi was waiting for him by the hitching rail in front of the bank. She was feeding his horse with sugar cubes, which both of them were enjoying.

'Hello, Lollipop. Did you come to see me or my horse?'

'My daddy sent me to give this to you.' She pulled a sealed buff envelope from her apron pocket and offered it to him. She watched his face as he opened it and read the cablegram.

Then he said, 'Come on, I'll give you a ride back home.'

Mounted up behind him, Latika chattered happily all the way to her father's shop.

Goolam Vilabjhi Esquire came out onto the pavement to welcome them. 'Welcome! Mrs Vilabjhi is serving her world-famous chicken curry and saffron rice for lunch. She will be sad if you do not sample it with us.'

While Mrs Vilabjhi and her daughters put the finishing touches to the luncheon table, Leon went to stand in front of the bookshelf in Vilabjhi's office and ran his eye over the display of books. Then he grunted with satisfaction and took a copy of a Macmillan's English dictionary from the upper shelf. 'May I borrow this for a while?' he asked.

Mr Vilabjhi looked knowing. 'General Ballantyne kept a copy of that book on his desk. It was the first thing he reached for whenever I took him a cable. Maybe Memsahib von Wellberg has sent you the code.' Then he covered both ears with his hands and said, 'But do not tell me about it.'

The curry was exquisite but Leon, eager to compose his response to Eva, hardly tasted it. As soon as the girls were clearing away the empty dishes he sequestered himself in Mr Vilabjhi's office and, within twenty minutes, had encoded a message to be sent to Eva. He began with a fervent protestation of his love, then explained Penrod's absence and went on: *With my uncle transferred to Cairo I am left in the dark stop I need to have all intelligence that you have in your possession stop Eternal love stop Badger*.

Four days later he received Eva's reply. She had briefly outlined the information she had gleaned during a flying visit with Otto and Hennie to German African territory to meet von Lettow Vorbeck and Koos de la Rey. She explained the plot to raise a rebellion in South Africa and listed the materials and stores Graf Otto had promised to deliver.

When he read the inventory Leon whistled softly, then said, 'Airship! Not by ship but by bloody great airship, and my little darling has discovered the exact route they will fly. If only she could tell us when they plan to come.'

When the house party finished breakfast Graf Otto led them down the steps of the *Schloss*, where five black Meerbach limousines were drawn up. There were five high-ranking officers from the War Office in Berlin, all accompanied by their wives. The women had parasols and feathered hats; the men wore dress uniform, with swords hanging on their belts. Eva found herself in the third car with an admiral of the fleet and his large, horsy wife as her companions.

It was a twenty-minute drive to the main Meerbach factory, and as he approached the main gate Graf Otto, at the wheel of the leading limousine, sounded his horn. The gates swung open and the guards presented arms, then stood stiffly to attention as the convoy rolled through.

This was Eva's first visit to the citadel at the centre of the Meerbach engineering empire, which sprawled over an area of almost twelve square kilometres. The three sheds that housed the fleet of dirigibles stood at the furthest corner of the complex. She was unprepared for their sheer size: they seemed as tall and commodious as Gothic cathedrals.

The weather was delightfully sunny and warm as the party made their way to the row of armchairs set out for them under spreading umbrellas. When they were seated, three waiters in white jackets came down the row carrying silver trays laden with crystal glasses of champagne. When everyone had a glass in hand, Graf Otto mounted the dais and gave a short speech of welcome. Then he went on to set out his vision of the role his dirigibles were destined to play during the fateful years ahead. He was too shrewd a salesman to bore his audience with too many technical details. He kept his canvas broad, his brushstrokes heavy and vividly colourful.

'My friends and distinguished guests.' He turned to the shed's gigantic doors and spread his arms like a conductor calling his orchestra to attention. 'I give you the *Assegai*!' The doors trundled open and his guests rose to their feet and burst into spontaneous applause, gazing up at the 110-foot-high monster that filled the shed. Painted across the nose in ten-foot-high scarlet letters was her name, *Assegai*. The airship had been carefully weighed off so the lift of her hydrogen-filled gas containers exactly balanced the 150,000-pound dead weight of the hull. The watchers gasped with surprise as ten men lifted her off the landing bumper and carried her through the tall doors into the sunlight.

Her handlers manoeuvred her to the sturdy mooring tower in the centre of the field and secured her to it by the nose. She lay there like a beached whale. She was 795 linear feet from stem to stern. Her four massive Meerbach rotary engines were housed in boat-shaped gondolas that hung on steel arms beneath her keel. They could be reached from the main cabin along the central companionway, which ran along the length of the airship. The control car was well forward under the nose. From here, the airship was flown by the captain and navigator. The passenger coach and cargo holds hung beneath the centre where their weight was evenly distributed.

After he had given them time to admire his creation, Graf Otto invited them to board her, and they assembled in the luxurious lounge. Glass observation windows ran the length of the outer walls of the long room. The guests were seated in leather-covered easy chairs, and the stewards served more champagne and a lunch of oysters, caviar and smoked salmon.

When they had finished eating, Graf Otto asked jovially, 'Which of you has flown before?'

Eva was the only one who held up her hand.

'Ah, so!' He laughed. 'Today we will change that.' He looked across at Commodore Alfred Lutz. 'Lutz, please take our honoured guests on a little flight over the Bodensee.' They crowded to the observation windows, chattering and laughing like children, as Lutz started the engines. The *Assegai* seemed to come to life and quivered eagerly on her moorings. Then she rose gently aloft and her link to the mooring tower dropped away.

Lutz flew them as far as Friedrichshafen, then back down the centre of the lake. The water was a magical shade of azure, and the snows and glaciers of the Swiss Alps glowed in the sunlight. Then the airship returned to the Wieskirche factory and hovered 3,000 feet above the field. Quite unexpectedly, Graf Otto returned from the control car to the lounge, and his guests stared at him, perplexed: he had a large rucksack on his back held in place by an elaborate arrangement of harness straps.

'Ladies and gentlemen, you must have realised by now that the *Assegai* is an airship of surprises and wonders. I have one more to show you. The contraption on my back was dreamed up by Leonardo da Vinci more than four hundred years ago. I have taken his idea and made it reality by fitting it into a canvas pack.'

'What is it?' a woman asked. 'It looks very heavy and uncomfortable.'

'We call it a *Fallschirm*, but the British know it as a parachute.'

'What does it do?'

'It breaks your fall.' He turned to two crew members and nodded. They slid aside the boarding doors. 'Goodbye, dear friends!' Otto ran across the cabin and launched himself headfirst through the open door. The women shrieked and covered their mouths. There was a rush for the observation windows and they stared down in horror at Graf Otto's body, dwindling rapidly in size as it fell towards the earth. Then, suddenly, a long white pennant streamed from the bulky rucksack strapped to his back, snapped open and assumed the shape of a monstrous mushroom. Graf Otto's death plunge came to an abrupt halt and, miraculously, he was suspended in mid-air. The horror of the watchers was transformed to wonder, cheers and clapping. They watched as the gently sinking figure reached the ground and tumbled in an untidy heap, shrouded in the white sheet. Graf Otto struggled back to his feet and waved to them.

Lutz vented the valves on the airship's main hydrogen tanks and it sank down as softly as a feather from the breast of a high-flying goose. It settled on its bumpers along the keel and the ground crew rushed forward to secure the mooring line to the anchor mast.

When the main doors of the cabin were opened Graf Otto was standing at the threshold to welcome his guests back to earth.

DINNER THAT EVENING was a formal occasion in the main dining room of the *Schloss*, at a long walnut table, with an orchestra playing in the gallery. The men were in full dress uniform, with swords and decorations. The ladies were glorious in silks, satins and a dazzling array of jewels.

Eva von Wellberg far outstripped the others in beauty and elegance, and Otto was unusually attentive to her. When the band struck up a sequence of Strauss waltzes he monopolised her as his dance partner. For such a big man, Otto was remarkably light on his feet and in his arms Eva was as slim and graceful as a reed. He was fully aware of what a striking pair they made, and the stir that followed them round the floor.

As the evening drew to a close, a trumpeter blew a flourish to draw the attention of the company. The senior officer present, Vice Admiral Ernst von Gallwitz, rose to his feet to make a speech of thanks to the host for his hospitality, dwelling on the technological marvels they had been shown at Wieskirche. Then he said, 'The world and our enemies will soon be given a demonstration of the power and potential of Graf Otto's creation. As we are among friends, I can tell you that Kaiser Wilhelm the Second, our revered leader, has given his unconditional sanction for Graf Otto to embark immediately on a daring plan that will stun the enemy with its genius.'

He turned to Graf Otto at the head of the table. 'Ladies and gentlemen, it is not gross overstatement to tell you that the man sitting among us quite literally holds the outcome of this war in his hands. He is about to set off on an epic journey, which, if he accomplishes it successfully, will deliver an entire continent into our hands to the total confusion of our enemy.'

Graf Otto rose to his feet to acknowledge the applause. He glowed with pride, but his short speech of thanks to the admiral was modest and self-deprecating. They admired him all the more for it.

MUCH LATER, when they were upstairs in Otto's private wing of the *Schloss* readying themselves for bed, Eva heard him singing in his bathroom and, at intervals, letting fly a guffaw.

She put on one of her most fetching satin nightdresses. She brushed her hair onto her shoulders, as she knew he liked it, and touched her lashes with mascara, skilfully giving her face a haunted and sorrowful aspect. As she worked she whispered to her image in the mirror, 'You have no inkling of the fact yet, Otto, but I know where you're going, and I'm going back to Africa with you . . . to Africa and to Badger.'

When Otto strode into the room he was still clearly buoyed up by the honour and acclaim showered on him that day. Eva was standing in the centre of the room, drooping tragically. As he held her in his arms he became aware of the coolness of her response and drew back to study her face.

'What is it that troubles you, my love?'

'You're going away again, and this time I know I will lose you for ever. Last time I so nearly lost you to the lion, and then I was taken by those savage Nandi tribesmen. Now something equally horrible is going to happen.' She let tears swamp her violet eyes. 'You can't leave me again,' she sobbed, 'Please! Please! Don't go.'

'I have to go.' He sounded bewildered, uncertain. 'You know I cannot stay. It is my duty and I have given my word.'

'Then you must take me with you. You cannot leave me behind.'

'Take you with me?' He seemed totally at a loss.

'Please, Otto! There is no reason why I should not go with you.'

'You do not understand. It will be dangerous,' he said, 'very dangerous.'

'I have been in danger before with you at my side,' she pointed out.

'I will be safe if I am with you, Otto. I will be in much greater danger here. Soon the British may send their aeroplanes to bomb us.'

'What nonsense!' he scoffed. 'Only an airship can fly so far. The British do not have airships.'

But for once he was uncertain. In all these years he had never dared enquire too deeply into why she had stayed at his side for so long, apart from the material benefits she received. But surely by now there must be some other more compelling incentive. He had never wanted to know those deeper reasons because they might devastate his manhood. Now he gazed deep into her eyes.

'You have never told me, and I have never dared ask, what do you truly feel for me, Eva, in your heart? Why are you still here?'

She had known that, in time, she would be faced with that question. She had rehearsed the reply so often that it resonated with sincerity: 'I am here because I love you, and I want to be with you as long as you will have me.'

For the first time ever, he looked vulnerable. He sighed softly. 'Thank you, Eva. You will never know how much those words mean to me.'

'So you will take me with you?'

'Yes.' He nodded. 'There is no reason why we should ever be apart again. I would marry you if it were in my power to do so. You know that.'

'Yes, Otto. However, we have agreed not to speak of it again,' Eva reminded him. Athala, his wife of almost twenty years, still refused to release him from his vows. He smiled and visibly his usual ebullience and self-confidence flowed back into him. 'Then pack your bag. Take a pretty dress for the victory parade,' he said. 'We are going back to Africa.'

She stood on tiptoe to kiss his mouth. For once not even the taste of his cigar repelled her. 'To Africa? Oh, Otto, when shall we leave?'

'Soon, very soon. As you saw today, the airship is battle-ready, and the crew is fully trained. Now all depends on the moon phase and the forecasts for wind and weather. Ritter will be navigating day and night and he needs the light of the full moon. Our departure must be within three days either side of that.'

FOR MOST OF THAT NIGHT Eva lay awake, listening to Otto's snores. She was thankful for this last opportunity to consider what she had to do. She must get one last message to Leon, confirming that Otto was bringing the *Assegai* to Africa, laden with arms and bullion for the Boer rebels, and that, almost certainly, he would fly down the Nile and through the Rift Valley on his way southwards. When she told him the date on which the *Assegai* would come, Leon's duty would be to prevent the airship getting through by any means. However, her immediate dilemma was whether or not she should warn him that she would be on board. If he knew she was, his concern for her safety might weaken his resolve. She decided not to tell him, and they would both have to take their chances when they met again in the high blue African skies.

The outbreak of the Great War had taken place like a train smash in which coach after coach had run without braking into a huge pile of wreckage. Austria had declared war on Serbia, Germany had declared war on Russia and France, and finally, on 4 August 1914, Britain had declared war on Germany. The fire and smoke that Lusima had foreseen had spread out to envelop the world.

Once more the population of the newly united South Africa was divided. Most of the Boer leaders hated the British and were strongly in favour of joining the conflict on the side of the Kaiser's Germany. It was only by the narrowest margin that Louis Botha, the former commander of the old Boer Army but a British loyalist, carried Parliament with him. He was then able to inform the British Government that they were free to release all the imperial forces in southern Africa, because he and his army would take over the defence of the southern half of the continent against Germany.

Botha was only one of three former Boer leaders and heroes known as the Triumvirate. The other two were Christiaan de Wet and Koos de la Rey. De Wet had already declared for Germany and all his men went with him. They were holed up in their fortified encampment on the edge of the Kalahari Desert.

Although de la Rey had not come out openly against Botha and Britain, nobody doubted that it was only a matter of time before he did so. They did not suspect that he was awaiting news from Germany on the flight of the *Assegai* from Wieskirche coming to his aid.

In Wieskirche the *Assegai* was taking on her final cargo. Graf Otto von Meerbach and Commodore Alfred Lutz struggled all night with the loading manifest. Much of the calculation was a matter of guesswork: no man alive had experienced flight in an airship over the Sahara Desert during the summer months, when air temperatures could range from fifty-five degrees centigrade at noon to zero at midnight.

All the coin had been struck in eighteen-carat gold. There were almost equal amounts of authentic British sovereigns and Deutches Reich ten-mark coins. The money was packed first into small canvas bags, which were then placed in sturdy ammunition cases, the lids securely screwed down. The value of Graf Otto's cargo in round terms was nine million dollars, the equivalent of the agreed two million pounds sterling.

'That should be enough to keep the Boers smiling sweetly for a long time to come!' Graf Otto personally supervised the baggage handlers as they packed the cases in neat rows down the length of the main salon of the *Assegai* and lashed each one to the ring bolts in the deck. On top he laid the cases of ammunition and the crates of Maxim machine guns.

THE LAST DINNER before departure was a banquet held in the *Assegai*'s shed. At the last moment one of the Meerbach limousines brought Eva from the *Schloss*. She was wearing her flying gear, with boots, gloves and a helmet. The chauffeur carried her valise, which was all the luggage she had. The crew had not known she would be travelling with them. Graf Otto introduced her as the expedition's mascot. Her beauty and charm had made her a universal favourite, so they gave her a hearty welcome. Rough and graceless man of the soil that he was, Hennie du Rand bowed and kissed her hand. His companions hooted with glee and he blushed like a schoolboy.

She went to join Graf Otto at the head of the dinner table. The plates were piled high with Bavarian delicacies. Only the liquor was stinted: Graf Otto wanted clear heads and eyes on board when they took to the skies. The toasts were drunk in a light pilsener.

At 2100 hours Graf Otto came to his feet. 'Ah, so! My friends, it is time we were on our way to Africa.' There was a burst of cheering, then the crew hurried aboard and stood to their action stations. Standing in his radio room Graf Otto made final contact with Berlin Central. He received the Kaiser's personal good wishes and was told, 'Godspeed.' He gave the launch orders to Commodore Lutz. The *Assegai* slipped her nose cable, rose gently into the golden summer twilight and turned onto a heading of 155 degrees.

Over the past weeks they had planned the flight in detail, so Lutz knew precisely what Graf Otto required of him. They ascended to their maximum safe cruising altitude of 10,000 feet as they floated over the Bodensee and ran on due south to cross the Mediterranean coastline a little after midnight, a few miles west of Savona. They had a strong following wind as they crossed the island of Sicily, which carried them swiftly to their landfall on a bleak stretch of the Libyan Desert, somewhere west of Benghazi. As the sun rose Eva stood at the forward observation windows of the saloon and watched their gigantic shadow flitting across the ridges and dunes of the rugged brown terrain below. Africa! she exulted silently. Wait for me, my love. I am coming back to you.

The heat came up at them, sunlight reflected by the rock, and powerful eddies swirled round the ship, like the currents of some great ocean. The *Assegai* was lighter now that her engines had burned off 6,000 pounds of fuel and oil and, as the sun heated the hydrogen in its container, their lift increased. Inexorably the airship began to rise, and Lutz was forced to valve off 230,000 cubic feet of gas, but still she continued to climb until, at 15,000 feet, the crew felt the enervating effects of oxygen starvation.

They were now flying light with six degrees of down angle on the controls. The airspeed bled away from 100 knots to fifty-five and the *Assegai* was failing to respond adequately. Then the forward port engine cut out. With this sudden loss of power the airship stalled and dropped from 13,000 to 6,000 feet before she came back on an even keel. It had been an alarming plunge and part of the main cargo had broken loose.

Even Graf Otto was shaken by the *Assegai*'s erratic behaviour in the superheated air and agreed without argument to Lutz's suggestion that they should land and anchor the ship for the remainder of the day, to continue the journey in the cool of evening. Lutz picked out an outcrop of black rock on the desert floor ahead that would afford an anchor point for the mooring cable and eased the ship downwards to the desert floor.

The last cablegram that Goolam Vilabjhi Esquire had received from his niece contained only a single number group. When Leon decoded it he found it was the date that Eva had promised to send him: that on which the *Assegai* would commence its flight from Wieskirche. In her previous cables, she had given him the name that Graf Otto had chosen for his machine, with its design number. The *Assegai* was a Mark ZL71. She had already outlined the course he intended to follow on his flight to South Africa. From this Leon had calculated when the airship might arrive over the Great Rift. Now all he needed was a plan of action that offered even a remote chance of bringing the massive ship to earth. With Penrod gone and Frederick Snell able to block his efforts, Leon was on his own.

He had seen drawings of the type of airship he was up against. When Graf Otto had been evacuated from Nairobi to Germany after his mauling, he had left piles of technical magazines in his quarters at Tandala Camp. One contained a long, illustrated article on the construction of a Mark ZL71 dirigible. Now Leon retrieved it and studied it carefully.

He found the illustrations and descriptions thoroughly discouraging. The airship was so enormous and so well protected, it flew so fast and high, that there seemed no possible way to prevent it getting through. He tried to imagine a comparison for the little *Butterfly* and this behemoth of the skies: a field mouse alongside a black-maned lion, perhaps.

He cast his mind back to the prophecy that Lusima had made for them when first he had taken Eva to Lonsonyo Mountain. She had conjured up the image of a great silver fish obscured by smoke and flame. When he looked at the illustrations, in Graf Otto's book, of the airship with its mighty fish-tailed rudder and generally piscine shape, he had no doubt that this was what she had foreseen.

Leon was isolated and abandoned. He had lost Eva and he knew that there was only a remote chance that he would see her again. Penrod was gone too. He never thought he would miss his uncle, but he felt the loss intensely. He needed help and advice, and there was only one person left in his life who might provide it.

He called for Manyoro, Loikot and Ishmael. 'We're going to Lonsonyo Mountain,' he told them.

Within half an hour they were airborne and winging down the Rift Valley, headed for Percy's Camp.

When they landed he found it in disarray. Leon had been so distracted by Eva that he had left the camp to his untrained and unsupervised staff. He was not seriously concerned by this state of affairs. The future was uncertain, and it was highly unlikely that there would be any hunting guests to entertain until after peace was restored. He lingered in camp just long enough to select horses before they rode out towards the mountain. His spirits lifted with every mile that brought them closer to it.

They made camp that evening at the base of Lonsonyo, and he sat late beside the fading embers of the campfire, studying the dark massif against the starry splendour of the African night sky.

It had worried him that he would have to wait until Loikot's *chungaji* scouts spotted the airship's approach before he could take off to intercept it. He would be at an enormous disadvantage. The *Assegai* would be at her cruising altitude of 10,000 feet so he would have to climb up and over the massif of Lonsonyo Mountain under full power from all his engines to meet her, which meant burning most of her fuel reserves. And, if the winds and air temperature were in the *Assegai*'s favour, she might sweep on over his head and be gone before Leon could coax the *Butterfly* high enough.

He stared up angrily at the mountain. At that moment a ripple of distant sheet lightning far down the Rift Valley backlit the heights boldly. The massif seemed like an enemy castle, a great obstacle he must overcome.

Then the play of lightning changed his perspective. He started to his feet, knocking his coffee mug flying. 'It's been under my nose all along!' he shouted at the sky. 'Lonsonyo is not my obstacle but my springboard!' Now the ideas poured over him, like water from a ruptured dam wall.

That open tableland in the rainforest that Eva and I discovered, he thought to himself. *It's a natural landing strip on the highest point of Lonsonyo. With fifty men I could clear the undergrowth in a couple of days, enough to be able to land the* Butterfly *up there and get her off again. I'll be able to swoop down on the* Assegai *instead of climbing up laboriously to intercept her.* He was so excited that he slept only a few hours, and was on the pathway to the summit long before sunrise the next morning.

LUSIMA MAMA WAS waiting for them under a favourite tree beside the path. She greeted her sons and made them sit one on each side of her. 'Your flower is not with you, M'bogo.' It was a statement, not a question.

'When will she return, Mama?' Leon asked.

She smiled, 'Do not seek to know that which is not for us to know.'

Leon shrugged helplessly. 'I have a favour to ask of you, Mama.'

'I have fifty men waiting for you. It is fortunate that the lightning has already cleared much of the ground for you.' She smiled slyly at him.

Lusima accompanied the expedition to the open tableland above the waterfall. She sat in the shade and watched her men labour. Under Lusima's eye the team worked like a pack of demons and by noon on the second day Leon was able to pace out the extent of the ground they had opened up.

At such high altitude the air was thin and he would have to maintain a high approach speed to avoid stalling his aircraft. It would be a near-run thing to get the *Butterfly* down on such a short runway.

He had not yet considered the nub of the problem. If everything worked out as he hoped, the *Assegai* would come down the Rift Valley from the north. She would not be flying higher than 10,000 feet above sea level: her crew would be in danger of oxygen starvation if she flew higher than that for an extended period. There was no possibility the monster would not be spotted by the network of bright-eyed *chungaji*, so Leon would have ample warning of his approach, certainly enough time to get the *Butterfly* airborne. *But what happens then?* he asked himself. *A gunfight between the two?*

He laughed at that ludicrous notion. From the illustrations he had seen of the airship, the *Assegai* would be armed with at least three or four Maxim machine guns, which would be served by trained German airmen. Taking them on from the *Butterfly*, with his two Masai armed with service rifles, would be a novel means of committing suicide.

He had been able to beg two hand grenades from Hugh Delamere, and had a vague idea of dropping one on *Assegai*'s domed hull. The resulting fireball would be spectacular, but he was worried about timing the six-second delay on the fuses. 'I have to find a plan before I run out of time,' he murmured ruefully. 'According to Eva's last cablegram, there were only five days to go before the *Assegai* was due to leave Wieskirche.'

Leon decided to sleep that night at Lusima's hut and head down the mountain at first light the next day. He and Lusima sat at the fire, sharing a bowl of cassava porridge for dinner. She was in an expansive mood and Leon was encouraged by this to speak of Eva and his love for her.

'The little flower is worthy of that love,' Lusima agreed.

'Yet she has gone from me. And I despair that I will ever see her again.'

'You must never despair, M'bogo. Without hope we are nothing.'

'Mama, you spoke to us once of a great silver fish in the sky that brings fortune and love. It comes to me that soon the fish will take to the sky. I thought that you might be able to tell me how to catch this fish.'

She was silent for a long time and then she shook her head. 'I know nothing about the catching of fish. You should ask a fisherman about that. Perhaps one of the fishermen of Lake Natron might teach you.'

He stared at her in astonishment, then slapped his forehead. 'Of course!' he said. 'Fishing nets!'

LEAVING LOIKOT AND ISHMAEL on the mountain, Leon and Manyoro rode quickly to Percy's Camp. He wanted to keep the load on the plane for landing on the mountain to a minimum.

From Percy's Camp they took off almost immediately for Lake Natron. Leon put the *Butterfly* down on the firm surface of the soda pan. In the nearby fishing village Manyoro bargained with the chieftain and finally bought four lengths of old, damaged netting from him, each roughly 200 paces long. As they had not been used recently they were dust dry, but even so, the weight taxed the power of the *Butterfly*'s engines.

By the afternoon of the second day they had all four nets laid out on the open ground. They sewed them together in pairs so that finally they had two separate nets, each about 400 paces long.

There would be no opportunity for practice in packing and deploying the nets. They would go straight into action against the *Assegai*, and had only one chance of unfurling the nets successfully. Leon hoped that, with the first attack, he might be able to entangle the propeller of the airship's two rear engines and slow her down to the extent that he had time to return to the landing strip and load the second length for another attack.

One of the many critical aspects of the scheme was to pack the net so that it would unfurl from the bomb bay and stream out behind the *Butterfly* in an orderly fashion. Then, once Leon had entangled the airship's propeller in the mesh, he had to be able to release the net from its retaining hooks before the *Butterfly* became snarled up in it. If he failed to break away cleanly his aircraft would be dragged along tail-first behind the stricken airship. Her wings and fuselage would be broken up by the unnatural forces brought to bear upon them. There were so many imponderables that it would all depend on guesswork, teamwork, quick reactions to any unexpected development and an inordinate amount of good old-fashioned luck.

By the evening of the fourth day the *Butterfly* stood at the head of the short strip of cleared ground with her nose pointed down the slope, the cliff face falling away abruptly at the end of the runway. Twenty *morani* waited in readiness to give her a push-start down the slope.

At dawn and dusk each day Loikot had stood on the heights of Lonsonyo and exchanged shouts with his *chungaji* companions across the length and breadth of Masailand. It seemed that the eyes of every *morani* in the territory were fastened on the northern sky: all hoped to be first to spot the approach of the silver fish monster.

Leon and his crew sat under a thatched sun shelter beside the fuselage of the *Butterfly*. When the call came they could be at their stations in the cockpit within seconds. There was nothing they could do now but wait.

It looked like a solid unbroken wall in the sky, stretching across the eastern horizon and reaching from the dun desert floor to the milky blue of the heavens. Eva was alone in the control gondola of the *Assegai*. The airship was on the ground, moored for the day, and she was standing her watch like any of the officers. Graf Otto was in the nacelle that housed the forward port engine. Despite four hours of determined effort he and his men were still unable to restart it, and they were stripping the crank case to get to the root of the problem.

Eva knew that sounding the alarm was not a decision that could be taken lightly. She hesitated a few moments longer, but in the short time that the eastern horizon had been blotted out by the approaching yellow wall, the speed of its advance was startling. She could see that it was no longer solid but swirled and rolled upon itself, like a dense cloud of yellow smoke. Suddenly she knew what it was. She had read about it in books written by desert travellers. She breathed the single word 'Khamsin!' and darted across the bridge to the ship's main telegraph. She yanked down the handle and the jangling of the emergency bells drowned every other sound.

From the main cabin, crew members stumbled from their mattresses, still more than half asleep, and stared out at the approaching sandstorm, stunned into silence by its size and ferocity.

Graf Otto came racing up the companion ladder from the gondola of the damaged engine. He stared at the storm for only a second before he took control. Within minutes, two of the three serviceable engines were running, and he signalled the docking team to release the mooring cable.

The third engine in the forward port gondola was still silent. The engineer was having difficulty starting her. 'Take command, Lutz!' Graf Otto shouted. 'I have to get that engine running.' He ran out onto the open cat-walk and disappeared down the ladder to the engine nacelle.

Lutz ran to his control panel and opened all eight gas valves. Hydrogen rushed into the *Assegai*'s gas containers and she flung up her nose so violently that Eva and those men who had no handholds were thrown to the deck as she went into a nose-high climb.

The atmospheric pressure dropped so rapidly that the needle of the barometer spun giddily round the dial. Lutz, who was suffering from an infected sinus, squealed with pain and clutched at his ears. A thin trickle of blood ran down his cheek as an eardrum ruptured. He doubled over and fell to his knees. Eva dragged herself to her feet and, pulling herself along the handrail, reached Lutz. 'What must I do?' she screamed.

'Vent!' he moaned. 'Blow the gas from all the containers. Red handles!' She reached up and forced them down with all her strength. She heard the escaping gas howling from the main vents above. The airship shuddered and bucked, but her uncontrolled climb steadied.

Graf Otto had come up from the forward engine gondola. Now he was pinned on the open catwalk, clinging to the siderail while the *Assegai*'s violent manoeuvres threatened to hurl him into space. He was fifty feet from Eva and yelled at her urgently, 'Both starboard throttles, full ahead.'

She obeyed him instinctively and the engines thundered, driving the airship's nose round in a counter-turn. For a few moments the airship steadied sufficiently for Graf Otto to release his death grip on the rail and run lightly along the catwalk. He burst in through the main doors and grabbed the controls. He gentled the great airship like a runaway horse, but before he had her steady she had climbed to 14,000 feet and was taking a terrible buffeting from the khamsin winds. However, the full force of the storm passed under the hull and left her at 9,000 feet on an even keel. She had been battered by the winds: the forward port engine was damaged beyond hope of repair, and a number of struts in the framework of the gas containers had been broken. But she was still making eighty knots and her cargo had been secured and lashed down.

Ahead of them they could just make out the shape of the Nile winding through the desert. Suddenly the radio squawked.

'It's the naval radio at Walvis Bay on the southwest coast.' The operator looked up from his set, 'They're asking for a secure contact with Graf von Meerbach. They have an urgent top-secret message for you.'

Graf Otto handed the helm to Thomas Bueler, the first officer, and put on the earphones. He listened intently, his expression darkening. At last he ended the contact and went to stand at the forward window, staring down at the mighty river passing below.

At last he seemed to reach a difficult decision and growled brusquely at Bueler, 'In ten minutes, assemble the entire ship's company in the control room. I want them seated in two ranks down the centre of the deck, facing forward. I am going to make an important announcement.' He stumped out and went to the tiny cubbyhole cabin that he and Eva shared.

When he emerged, Eva was filled with dread: he had changed his artificial hand. In place of the steel finger and thumb, he now wore the spike-headed mace. The crew, too, were staring at the strange weapon as he took up a position facing the two rows of seated men. He glared at them in silence, then said in a cold, hard tone, 'Gentlemen, we have a traitor on board.' He let them think about that for a while. Then he went on, 'The enemy has been alerted to our mission. They have been alerted to our course and movements. Berlin is ordering us to abort the operation.'

Suddenly he lifted his armoured fist and slammed it into the chart table. The panel shattered into splinters. 'I am not turning back,' he snarled. 'I know who this traitor is.' He prowled down the front rank of seated figures, and stopped behind Eva. She felt herself cringe inwardly and steeled herself. 'I am a man who does not readily forgive treachery. The traitor is about to learn that.' He touched the top of her head gently. 'Who is it? you are wondering,' he whispered.

She opened her mouth to shout defiance at him. Then she felt him lift his hand from her head, and he walked on down the line. She felt hot, bitter bile rise in her throat.

At the end of the line of men Graf Otto turned, and then he was coming back towards her. His footsteps stopped and she drew a quivering breath. It sounded as though he was directly behind her again.

She heard the blow and almost screamed. It was a muffled thump and she clearly heard bone break. She whipped round as Hennie du Rand fell forward on his face. Graf Otto stood over him and swung the iron fist again and again, lifting the mace high, then putting all his strength behind the blows. When he straightened up he was breathing hard and his face was speckled with droplets of blood.

'Throw the filthy dog overboard,' he ordered, in a milder tone, and he was smiling. 'It's always those you trust most who betray you. I repeat, gentlemen, there is no turning back. But we cannot allow our cargo to fall into the hands of the British. If we maintain our speed, by noon tomorrow we will have reached Arusha in German territory.'

He walked slowly from the cabin and Eva covered her eyes with both hands as two crewmen laid hold of Hennie's ankles and dragged his corpse out onto the catwalk. Between them they lifted him over the rail and let him drop into the Nile Valley, far below. Eva found herself weeping silently, each teardrop seeming to burn her eyes like the sting of a bee.

Leon was still asleep, buried in his blankets. He heard distant voices through the last shreds of sleep, the calling of the *chungaji* in the stillness of the dawn. Something in their tone had alerted him. He forced himself awake as Loikot shook him with a hand on his shoulder. 'M'bogo!' His voice rang with excitement. 'The silver fish is coming! The *chungaji* have seen it. It will be here before the sun is over the horizon.'

Leon leaped to his feet and was, in the instant, fully awake. 'Start up!' he shouted at Manyoro. 'Number-one port side.' He scrambled up onto the *Butterfly*'s lower wing, then swung himself over the cockpit coaming.

The machine seemed as eager for the hunt as he was. The engines caught and fired on the first swing of the propeller. While he waited for them to run up to full operating temperature he peered up at the sky. From the clouds he saw that a stiff breeze was coming in from the ocean, blowing straight down the short, narrow runway. It was perfect for takeoff.

Loikot and Ishmael climbed into the cockpit, and Manyoro scrambled up behind them. Leon eased open the throttles and the *Butterfly* rolled forward. The Masai *morani* at the wing-tips swung her round to line up on the runway and then, as he opened the throttles wide, they shoved with all their strength on the trailing edges of the wings. The *Butterfly* accelerated away swiftly, but she was still under her flying speed as they came to the end of the runway and the cliff face dropped away. Leon's instinct for survival warned him to stand hard on the wheel brakes, but he went against it and kept all the throttles pressed hard up against the stops. The engines were howling at full power and, at that moment, he felt a stronger blast of air his face. It was a freak, a stray unlooked-for gust. He felt it get under the *Butterfly*'s wings and give her a gentle lift. For a moment he thought even that was not enough. He felt one wing drop as she staggered on the edge of stalling, and forced her nose down mercilessly. She bit into the wind and suddenly they were flying. His airspeed rocketed to 100 knots. She climbed away gamely, but he was panting with fear. For a moment they had been on the verge of death.

He put the fear behind him and looked ahead. They all saw it at the same time: the enormous silver fish gleaming in the early sunlight. Her sheer size astonished Leon. She was several hundred feet below the *Butterfly* and a few minutes more, they would have lost her for ever. But she was in a perfect position, above and behind her, sitting perfectly in her blind spot. He pushed the nose down and as he closed with her swiftly, the *Assegai* filled his entire field of vision. He saw that one of the forward motors was out of commission, the propeller standing rigidly upright. He was so intrigued that he almost forgot to give his crew the order to deploy the entangling net.

He knew that this was one of the most critical moments of the plan. It would be so easy to entangle his own tail skid or landing gear as the net spread out behind him. But the easterly monsoon wind pushed its heavy folds gently to one side so that they streamed out perfectly 400 feet behind the *Butterfly*. He let her slide down the side of the airship overtaking slowly until he was flying level with the observation cabin.

It came as a shock to see people behind the glass windows. Somehow the airship had seemed to have a monstrous life of its own. There was Graf Otto von Meerbach only fifty feet away, glaring at him with an expression of outrage, his mouth working silently as he shouted obscenities. Then he spun round and ran to man the machine gun mounted in the bridge.

Leon froze with shock when he saw Eva standing behind the German. For an instant he was looking into her deep violet eyes as she stared back at him. Graf Otto was working the loading bolt and traversing the gun towards him. Leon roused himself and put the wing of the *Butterfly* hard over just as Graf Otto fired the first burst. The tracer bullets flew high and behind him.

The *Assegai*'s two rear engines were hanging down vulnerably below the keel. Leon glanced back at the long line of netting trailing behind the *Butterfly*, and then, judging the relative angles and speed of the two aircraft finely, he dragged the net across the spinning propeller blades of the airship's engines. They snatched up the folds and wound them almost instantly into tight balls that smothered them. It had happened so quickly that he was almost taken off guard.

'Let fly!' Leon screamed at Manyoro, who reacted swiftly, heaving with both hands on the release handle. The retaining hooks opened, allowing the heavy rope to drop away cleanly, an instant before it could pluck the *Butterfly* from the sky. The airship's huge fishtail rudder brushed their upper wing as it passed over them. And then the *Butterfly* was free and clear. Leon brought her round and climbed back into position above and behind the *Assegai*, keeping in her blind spot.

He watched smoke billow from the airship's rear engines. The netting was so deeply tangled in the propellers that both had seized up. The *Assegai* was no longer responding to her helm. The single forward engine did not have the power to hold her against the crosswind of the monsoon and she began to drift straight for the rocky cliff face of Lonsonyo Mountain. The helmsman was running her with the throttle wide open and the strain was too much. Now the surviving engine started to blow blue smoke as it overheated.

Graf Otto ran across the control room, flung the helmsman aside, and seized the wheel. The cliffs were only half a mile away, and the only way to avoid colliding with them was to inflate the gas containers to their utmost and take her up and over the top as fast as she would climb. He reached for the valve control and pulled it wide open. Instead of a rush of hydrogen squealing through the inlet pipes, there was a weak hiss and, although the airship shuddered, she rose only sluggishly.

'Hydrogen tanks are flat!' he screamed with frustration. 'We blew off all the gas, fighting against the khamsin. We're going to run into the cliff. We'll have to jump! Ritter, get out the parachutes. There are enough for all of us.'

Ritter led a rush for the storeroom behind the bridge and they started to fling the parachute packs into a pile on the deck. There was a panic-driven scramble as the men fought over them. Graf Otto grabbed one in each hand. He ran back to Eva. 'Put this on.'

'I don't know how to do it,' she protested.

'Well, you have about two minutes to learn,' he told her grimly, and slipped the harness over her shoulders. 'As soon as you're clear of the airship, count to seven, then pull this cord.' He pulled the straps of the harness tightly across her chest. 'As soon as you hit the ground, open these buckles and get rid of the chute.' He buckled on his own parachute and day pack, then dragged her towards the doorway, which was already blocked with men fighting to get out.

'Otto, I can't do this,' Eva cried, but he seized her round the waist and carried her bodily, struggling, to the doorway. With powerful kicks he booted the two men ahead of him out of the way, then threw Eva out. As she dropped away he shouted after her, 'Count to seven, then pull the cord.'

He watched her fall towards the top gallery of the forest below. Just when it seemed she must crash into the branches her parachute burst open and jerked her so violently that her body swung on the shrouds like a puppet's. He stepped out into space and plunged towards the trees.

LEON HELD THE *BUTTERFLY* in a tight turn above the cliffs and peered down at the human bodies spilling out of the hatchway in the airship's control cabin. He saw at least three parachutes fail to open and the men drop, arms and legs flailing, until they hit the treetops. Others were carried away on the monsoon wind like thistledown and scattered across the mountainside. Then Eva was falling free, smaller and slimmer than any of the men. He bit his lip hard as he waited for her parachute to open, then shouted with relief as the white silk blossomed above her. She was already so low that, within seconds, she had been sucked into the dense green mass of the jungle.

The *Assegai* floated on, nose high and yawing aimlessly across the wind. She was rising slowly but he knew at a glance that she would never clear the top of the cliff. Her tail touched the trees and she came round abruptly. Like a stranded jellyfish she rolled onto her side and her cavernous gas containers snagged in the upper branches of the trees. They collapsed and the airship deflated like a punctured balloon. Leon braced himself for the explosion of hydrogen that he was sure must follow—it needed but a spark from the damaged generators—but nothing happened. As the hydrogen gushed out and was dispersed by the wind, the *Assegai* settled in a shapeless mass of canvas and wreckage on the jungle treetops, breaking down even the largest branches under her massive weight.

Leon turned and flew back only a few feet over the wreck. He tried to see down into the forest, hoping desperately for a glimpse of Eva, but there was nothing of her.

He turned again and put the *Butterfly* into a climb for the landing strip, keeping low along the cliff face so that he did not waste a moment. He wanted to get back and find Eva. He was only a few minutes' flight from the wreck of the *Assegai*, but he knew it would be heavy going to cover the same ground on foot.

The moment he landed and cut the engines he reached under the seat to pull out his gun case. With three quick movements he reassembled the stock and barrels and loaded the chambers of his big Holland. Then he swung his legs over the side of the cockpit and jumped down, shouting orders to the *morani* who ran forward to meet him.

'Hurry! Get your spears. The memsahib is out there alone in the forest. She may be hurt. We have to find her fast.' He raced down the slope, hurdling low bushes. The warriors following him were hard put to keep him in sight through the trees.

SWINGING WILDLY on her parachute shrouds, Eva stared down as the forest tops rushed up to meet her. She crashed through the uppermost branches, twigs breaking and crackling round her head. Each time she collided with another branch it slowed her a little more, until she hit the ground in a small clearing on the mountainside.

The slope was steep so she let herself roll head over heels until she came to rest in a patch of swamp. She remembered Graf Otto's advice and tugged frantically at the buckles of her harness until she could shrug herself free. Then she got gingerly to her feet and checked herself for injuries. There were only a few scratches on her arms and legs.

She squared her shoulders and said aloud, 'Now, where will I find Badger? If only I had some idea of where he came from, but he popped up out of the blue.' She thought for a few seconds before she answered her own question. 'Sheba's Pool, of course. It's the first place he will look for me.'

She knew the ground well because she and Leon had wandered over it on their forays about the slopes during the enchanted months they had spent at Lusima's *manyatta*. Now a glimpse of the cliff face through the jungle helped her to orientate her present position with the waterfalls. 'It can't be more than a few miles to the south.'

She started off, using the direction of the slope to guide her and keeping the line of the cliff on her right hand. But then she pulled up sharply. There was a commotion in the bushes ahead and a hideous spotted hyena bolted out of the thicket, a strip of tattered raw flesh dangling from its jaws.

She went forward cautiously and found the corpse of the first officer, lying crumpled in the shrubbery. Bueler was one of those whose parachute had failed to open. She saw that he had a small rucksack fastened to the front of his harness—that was why the parachute had failed to open: it had snagged the shrouds of his chute.

She knelt beside the corpse and opened the rucksack. She found a small first-aid kit, several packets of dried fruit, a tin of Vestas for fire-making and a 9mm Mauser pistol with two spare clips of ammunition.

She disentangled the rucksack from the parachute harness and slung it over her shoulder, then jumped up and hurried along the game path. Half a mile further on she heard Otto's voice, calling plaintively from a little higher up the slope: 'Can anybody hear me? Ritter! Bueler! Come! I need your help.' She moved cautiously towards the sound. When he called again, she looked up and found him. His shrouds had wrapped round a large branch, and he was dangling seventy feet above the ground, swinging himself back and forth, trying to get a grip on the branch from which he was suspended, but he could not muster sufficient momentum to reach it.

Eva looked around her carefully. None of the *Assegai* crew was in sight. They were alone in the forest. She was about to sneak away when he spotted her. 'Eva! Thank God you have come.' She stopped. 'Come, Eva, you must help me to get down. If I open my harness, I will fall to my death. But I have a light rope in my pack.' He reached under its flap and pulled out a hank of jute twine. 'I am going to drop the end of it to you. You must pull me towards the branch so I can get a hold on it.' She stood perfectly still, staring up at him. Now that he knew she had survived the crash she could not leave him. He would never let her escape.

'Hurry, woman. Don't just stand there,' he shouted impatiently.

For the first time in their long relationship he was totally in her power. This was the man who had murdered her father, the one who had humiliated and tortured her mentally and physically. This was the moment for retribution. Moving as slowly as a sleepwalker, she came towards him, at the same time reaching into Bueler's pack.

'Yes, Eva, that's good. Take the rope.' There was a wheedling tone in his voice that she had never heard before. She felt resolution flowing through her body. The hilt of the Mauser fitted perfectly into her hand. She drew the pistol, and pulled back the slide.

'What are you doing?' Graf Otto shouted in consternation. 'Put that gun down. Somebody will get hurt!' Slowly she lifted it and aimed up at him.

'Stop, Eva! In the name of God, what are you doing?'

'I am going to kill you,' she said softly.

'Are you mad? Have you lost your mind?'

'I have lost more than my mind. You have taken everything from me. Now I am taking it back.'

She fired. She had not expected the report to be so loud and the recoil to be so vicious. She had aimed at his black heart, but the bullet had nicked his left arm above the elbow. Blood trickled down his forearm.

'Don't do this, Eva. Please! I will do anything you say.' She fired again and this shot flew wider than the first. It did not touch him. Graf Otto was wriggling in the harness, jerking from side to side. She fired again and again. He was screaming with terror. 'Stop! Stop, my darling! I will make it up to you, I promise.' She drew a deep breath and levelled the pistol for the last time—but before she could fire a strong arm whipped round her from behind and a hand fastened on her wrist, pushing the gun down.

'Good man, Ritter!' Graf Otto bellowed. 'Hold her fast! Wait until I can get my hands on the treacherous bitch.'

Ritter twisted the pistol out of Eva's hands, then bore her to the ground. He held her hands behind her back while one of his crew secured them with half a dozen workmanlike knots. Ritter ran to bring Graf Otto down from the tree. He grabbed the end of the dangling line and pulled it across. Graf Otto took a firm hold on a branch, then swung himself up until he was lying across it. There, he unbuckled his harness and let it fall. As agile as a huge ginger ape, he swarmed down the main trunk to the ground. He paused to catch his breath, then walked slowly to where Eva lay. 'Pick her up,' he ordered the crewman, 'and hold her firm.' He smiled at her and showed her the metal fist. 'This is for you, my darling!' He hit her. He had judged the strength of his blow carefully: he did not want her to die too quickly.

'Treacherous bitch!' he said, and took a handful of her hair, twisting it until she fell to her knees. 'Now I understand that it was you all along, not that pathetic Boer creature.' He pushed her face into the rain-soaked earth and put his boot on the back of her head. 'I don't know what is the best way for you to die. Should I drown you in mud? Should I strangle you slowly? Or should I pound your beautiful head to jelly?' He lifted her face and stared into her eyes. The blood oozing from her nose mingled with the mud, and dripped off her chin. 'Not so beautiful any more. More like the dirty little whore you truly are.'

Eva threw back her head and spat at him.

He wiped his face on his sleeve and laughed at her. 'This will be great sport. I shall enjoy every moment.'

Ritter stepped forward and tried to intervene. 'No, sir. You cannot do this to her. She is a woman.'

'I will prove to you that I can. Watch this.' He lifted the armoured hand again, but as he leaned towards Eva, a deafening thunderbolt numbed their eardrums. It was the distinctive report of a .470 Nitro Express rifle. Graf Otto was hurled backwards, arms flailing, as the heavy bullet tore into the centre of his chest.

'There is another bullet for anyone who wishes to dispute the issue further. Hands high, please, gentlemen!' Leon said in German, as he stepped from the bushes with Manyoro, Loikot and twenty Masai *morani*.

'Manyoro, tie these people like chickens going to market. Have the *morani* take them to the army fort at Lake Magadi and hand them over to the soldiers,' he said, then ran to where Eva knelt in the mud. He jerked his hunting knife from its sheath and cut the rope. Then he cupped her face in his hands and lifted it to his.

'My nose,' she whispered. He brushed a kiss across her lips.

'It's broken, and you will have a lovely pair of black eyes, but it's nothing that Doc Thompson can't deal with as soon as I can get you back to Nairobi.' He lifted her and held her tightly to his chest as he started back up the mountainside to where the *Butterfly* waited on the landing strip. There, he laid her tenderly on the deck and covered her with a sheet of tarpaulin for she was shivering with shock.

When he stood up he saw that Lusima was standing by the fuselage. 'I'm taking her to Nairobi,' he told Lusima, 'but there's a great service you can do for us.'

'I will do it, my son,' she said.

'The silver monster lies broken upon the mountainside. Manyoro will take you and your *morani* to it. This is what I want you to you to do for me . . .'

'I am listening to you, M'bogo.' He spoke urgently. When he had finished she nodded. 'All these things I will do. Now take your lovely broken flower to safety and cherish her until she is healed.'

It was four years almost to the day before they returned to Sheba's Pool. They left Lusima, Manyoro, Ishmael and Loikot at the old campsite and rode up alone to it. Leon came to lift Eva down from the saddle and kissed her before he set her on her feet. 'How is it that you grow younger and more beautiful every day?' he asked.

She laughed and touched the side of her nose. 'Except for a little kink and a bump here and there.' Even the medical magic of Dr Thompson had not been up to the challenge of straightening her nose completely.

'You call that a little bump?' he asked, as he laid his hand on her belly. 'What about this one?'

She looked down at it proudly. 'Just watch it grow.'

'I'm agog with anticipation, Mrs Courtney.' He took her hand and led her to her seat on the rocky ledge. They sat side by side and gazed down into the dark waters.

'I bet you've never heard of the missing Meerbach millions,' Eva said.

'Of course I have.' His face was straight and serious. 'It's one of the great mysteries of Africa. On a par with the lost mines of King Solomon.'

'Do you think somebody will solve the mystery soon?'

'Perhaps today,' he replied. He stood up and began to unbutton his shirt.

'It's been lying here for almost four years. What if somebody has found it already?' she asked, and her light mood began to fade.

'That could never have happened,' he reassured her. 'Lusima Mama put a curse on the pool. Nobody would dare go in there.'

'But aren't you afraid?' she asked.

He smiled and touched the little carved ivory charm that hung on a thong round his neck. 'Lusima gave me this. It will ward off the curse.' He hopped on one leg as he shed his trousers, then dived into the water.

She jumped to her feet and shouted after him, 'Come back! I'm afraid to know the answer. What if it's all gone, Badger?'

He trod water and grinned at her from the middle of the pool. 'You're a determined pessimist, my love. In a few moments from now we'll know the worst or the very best.' He drew four deep breaths and ducked. She knew it would be some time before he surfaced and let her mind travel back over the last four years. They had been filled with excitement and danger, but also with love and laughter. She had been with him most of the time he was on campaign with Delamere's Light Horse Cavalry in the bush against von Lettow Vorbeck. Leon had taught her to fly the *Bumble Bee* and to act as his observer and navigator. The two of them had made a famous team. Once, when Leon was not with her, she had landed the aircraft under heavy fire from the Germans to rescue four wounded *askaris*. Lord Delamare had pulled every trick in the book to see to it that she was awarded the Military Medal.

She jumped up as Leon burst out of the water with a mighty splash. 'Tell me the bad news!' she yelled.

He did not reply but swam to the ledge below her and lifted his right hand out of the water. He was holding something and threw it at her feet. It was a small canvas bag and it was heavy, for the mouth burst open as it hit the ledge. Golden coins poured from it and sparkled in the sunlight, and she squealed with excitement and fell to her knees.

'Some of the cases have burst open, probably when Lusima's *morani* dropped them into the pool from the top of the waterfall, but it looks as though none or very little is missing.' He slithered out of the water like an otter and she reached out to hug his cold, wet body.

'Don't we have to give it all back?' she whispered into his ear.

'Give it back to Kaiser Bill? I think he went out of business recently.'

'I feel so guilty. It doesn't belong to us.'

'Why don't you look upon it as full and final payment from Otto von Meerbach for the copyright he stole from your father?' he suggested.

She rocked back, held him at arm's length and stared at him bemusedly. She started to smile. 'Of course! When you look at it like that, it's really quite different.' Then she laughed. 'I can find no fault with your reasoning, my darling Badger!'

WILBUR SMITH

Born: Northern Rhodesia, January 9, 1933
Former profession: chartered accountant
First major book deal: 1964

At seventy-six, Wilbur Smith looks at least ten years younger than his age, tall, fit, with a warm smile and bright sparkle in his eye. He looks as though he might actually be one of the heroes of his books, in fact, and hearing him refer to each new story as a 'voyage of exploration', reinforces the impression that he lives and breathes his tales of adventure, enjoying every moment of the journey. His own life and career have been as colourful and epic as any of his sagas—a thrilling *Boy's Own* adventure, no less.

Firstly, there was his idyllic childhood in Northern Rhodesia (now part of Zambia), where his stern, disciplinarian father (pictured below, seated on a chair, and opposite) presided over the family ranch, but allowed the young Wilbur and his friends to roam free in what must have been boy heaven. Africa was a romantic place back then, and he remembers his grandfather, Courtney James Smith, a commander in the Zulu Wars, telling stories that made his grandson's young eyes start out of their sockets. Wilbur was hooked. At just eight years old, he had his first Remington rifle in his hands, the smell of lions and other animals in his nostrils, and the spirit of Africa in his blood.

Nurtured and inspired by his gentle, artistic mother (seated right, with her son perched on the table), Wilbur buried himself in books. 'She was often a buffer between me and my father,' he remembers, and goes on to relate how she not only introduced him to boys' books, like *Just William* and *Biggles*, but made him an ominivorous reader—a habit

that has served him well. 'One thing I remember is the discovery of the tomb of Tutankhamun. Mum was fascinated by it and read everything about it that she could get her hands on. Of course that came out later, in my books about Ancient Egypt.' Four of them, in fact, full of the atmosphere of that distant but fascinating era.

Modern-day Egypt, when Wilbur visited in the Fifties and Sixties, was far more magical, one senses, than it is now. 'I'd stop off there on my way to and from Europe, and I used to spend a lot of time in Karnak, and going right up to the Aswan Dam, as well as taking trips into oases by camel. There weren't so many tourists on the Nile then. Now it's a penance to go there, with the teeming multitudes.'

Wilbur had begun writing three decades before the appearance of his first Egyptian novel, *River God*, in 1993. Not with any deliberate plan to become an author, but more because of what he describes as 'an itch that demanded to be scratched'. Like his growing wanderlust, it was impossible to resist. Picture the tall, handsome, young man reduced to work in the 'Deceased Estates' department of his local tax office, his father having told him that journalism would be far too risky and that he must get a 'real job' . . . Picture him stealing 'a hundred and fifty pages of Her Majesty's stationery to take home each night', on which he would furiously scribble his many ideas. It is as romantic a beginning to a writing career as anyone could create.

Wilbur's story grows still more exciting. He posted his second manuscript, a story called *When the Lion Feeds*, to London. In those days, communications travelled slowly, and when, several weeks later, he received a brief message of acceptance from his future publisher at William Heinemann, he was taken aback. 'There wasn't a direct dialling system then. Calls had to be pasted through Cairo or Nairobi or wherever. So we sent telegrams, on those special buff forms. They were delivered by a gentleman on a bicycle with a little leather satchel hanging from the crossbar, and a cap with a brass badge. I was so delighted, I tipped him half a crown!'

Further, larger tips exchanged hands as more deals, one for an appearance in Condensed Books (as Select Editions was known), and another for film rights, came through, and the postman would wave excitedly each time he cycled up to the house.

The African continent, Wilbur's birthplace and home, furnished him with the ideas, characters and inspiration for the bulk of his *oeuvre*, the much-loved Courtney and Ballantyne stories, as well as many stand-alone novels such as *Elephant Song*. When he talks of it, the light in his eyes burns most intensely. 'Africa is just such an incredible treasure house of stories, of strange and wonderful characters. So much has happened there; the slave trade, the wars of colonisation, the discovery of gold and diamonds. The Olduvai Gorge was where our ancestors first stood on their hind legs and became humanoid. It was the cradle of mankind. Later, there was the proliferation of tribes through Africa. And of course there's the huge diversity of animal and bird life. The array of species there is greater than anywhere else on earth.'

Africa may be in Wilbur's blood, and the place he thinks of as home, but it's clear that he also thrives on an adventurer's rootlessness, and prefers a nomadic life to one that would tie him, and his ideas, to one place. 'Home is wherever my pc is,' he says vehemently. 'From very early in my writing career, I taught myself not to look on any place as totally essential. So this'—he gestures at the light, clutter-free lounge of his Knightsbridge town house—'is a camping ground. And so is a place I have in Switzerland. Home in Cape Town is a little more elaborate,' he adds with a grin. 'I keep my nice cars, and paintings, and my collection of rifles there.'

Ten years ago, Wilbur embarked on another new and exciting chapter in his life with Mokhiniso, who is from Tajikistan and who he met, very romantically, through a chance encounter in a London bookshop. They married in 2000. Before that he had spent twenty-eight long and very happy years with Danielle, who died from  a brain tumour in 1999. He and Mokhiniso, who's almost forty years his junior, are clearly very much in love, and bound on a series of exciting new adventures together. At the time of writing, they had just arrived in London from Rome, and were soon to be flying off again to other far-flung places.

Yet the glamour and trappings of life as a literary superstar don't seem to have in any way dented the focus and integrity with which Wilbur goes about his craft. He has very definite advice for would-be authors. 'Write for yourself, not for a perceived audience. If you do, you'll mostly fall flat on your face, because it's impossible to judge what people want. And you have to read. That's how you learn what is good writing and what is bad. And then the main thing is application. So many people who have a good book in them don't know how to go about writing it. You have to realise, first of all, it's hard work. And it's very lonely work. There's no one to tell you what to do, or to discuss it with. Those are the challenges to overcome—the distractions and the loneliness.'

Despite the glossy, outward veneer that surrounds any international best-selling author, there is something about Wilbur which goes right back to the small boy standing before a father 'who would not hesitate to pull his belt out of the loops of his trousers and give me taste of the buckle end'. Smith Senior seems to have been a key influence— both good and bad, perhaps— imbuing the boy with the discipline that would take him to the top, and imposing a fiercely Victorian code of 'spare the rod and spoil the child', for which Wilbur now expresses a certain respect. He says he and his father were friends to the end, and tells a touching story about the first time he ever kissed his dad. 'He was lying in a hospital bed and I went over and planted a kiss on the top of his bald head. His breath stopped, you know? He was very shocked. But after that, whenever he saw me he'd offer the top of his head in a very formal way, to be kissed.'

In closing, can he name three things he particularly loves or admires? 'I enjoy success. I enjoy encouragement from readers of my books. And I love being with a woman I love—the closeness and intimacy of an extended love affair.' And the flip side to that: things he can't abide? 'Cruelty. Of man to man, man to animals, a ruler to his subjects . . . Cruelty to children I particularly detest. And inconsideration, which is really a form of cruelty. Bad behaviour, indiscipline . . . Most other things I'm prepared to avoid, ignore or pass over. I'm quite easy to please.'

What remains is that image of the eight-year-old English boy, standing with that shiny Remington in his hands, looking out across the vast African plains . . . A small boy who has prospered mightily, and found lasting happiness and success, from the discipline of sitting down and transferring to paper the many riveting adventures that take shape in his head.

LA'S ORCHESTRA SAVES THE WORLD

ALEXANDER McCALL SMITH

Can any of us make a difference to the great events that determine our fate?
Is it ever too late to find love?
La, surviving a failed marriage and facing a future alone, will find out the answers to these and other important questions when, shortly before the Second World War, she moves from London to the Suffolk countryside to make a brand-new life for herself . . .

PART ONE

ONE

Two men, who were brothers, went to Suffolk. One drove the car, an old Bristol drop-head coupé in British racing green, while the other navigated, using an out-of-date linen-backed map. That the map was an old one did not matter: the roads they were following had been there for a long time and were clearly marked—narrow lanes flanked by hedgerows following no logic other than ancient farm boundaries. The road signs— promising short distances of four miles, two miles, even half a mile—were made of heavy cast iron, forged to last for generations of travellers. The black lettering, sharp and clear against chalk-white backgrounds, pointed to villages with names of long-forgotten yeoman families, of the crops they grew, of the wild flora of those parts—comfortable names, reminders of a gentle country that once existed in these parts.

They almost missed the turning to the village. There were oak trees at the edge of a field and immediately beyond these, meandering off to the left, was the road leading to the place they wanted. It was narrow, barely wide enough for two vehicles. Here and there, informal passing places had been established by local use—places where wheels had flattened the grass. But you only needed these if there were other road-users, and there were none that Saturday afternoon.

'It's very quiet, isn't it?' remarked the driver when they stopped to check their bearings at the road end.

'That's what I like about it,' said the other man. 'This quietness. Do you remember that?'

'We would never have noticed it. We would have been too young.'

They drove on slowly to the edge of the village. The tower of a Norman church rose above a stand of alders. Behind the church, the main street, a winding affair, was lined mostly by terraced houses. Some of these were built of stone, flinted here and there in patterns—triangles, wavy lines; others, of wattle and daub, painted either in cream or in that soft pink that gives to parts of Suffolk its gentle glow. There were a couple of shops and an old pub where a blackboard proclaimed the weekend's fare.

'Just beyond the end of the village,' said the driver. 'It's on the right. Just before . . .'

His brother looked at him. 'Just before Ingoldsby's Farm. Remember?'

The other man thought. A name came back to him, dredged up from his memory. 'The Aggs,' he said. 'Mrs Agg.'

THE CURRENT INHABITANT of La's house had been waiting for them, they thought, because she opened the door immediately after they rang the bell. She smiled when they introduced themselves and gestured for them to come in.

'I remember this house,' the driver said, looking about him, 'because when we were boys'—and he looked at his brother—'when we were boys we lived here with Dad and La. Until I was twelve. But you forget.'

His brother nodded in agreement. 'Yes. You know how things look different when you're young. They look much bigger.'

The woman laughed. 'Because at that age one is looking at things from down there. Looking up.'

She ushered them into a drawing room into which French windows let copious amounts of light. Beyond these windows, an expanse of grass stretched out, lined with herbaceous beds.

'That was hers,' said the woman, pointing to a lavender hedge. 'It needs cutting back, but I love it so much I can't bring myself to do it.'

She left them and went to prepare tea. The brothers stood in front of the window.

'What I said about things looking bigger,' one said. 'You might say the same about a person's life, don't you think? A life may look bigger when you're a child, and then later on . . .'

'Narrower? Less impressive?'

'I think so.'

'And La's life?'

'I suspect that it was a very big one. A very big life led here, in this sleepy little village.' He paused. 'I suspect that our La was a real heroine.'

Their hostess had come back into the room, carrying a tray. She put it down on a table and gestured to the circle of chintzy sofa and chairs. She had heard the last remark, and agreed, 'Yes. La was a heroine. Definitely.' She poured the tea. 'Then she became ill, didn't she, not so long after you all left this place. You can't have been all that old when La died.'

One of the men stared out of the window. The other replied, 'I was seventeen and my brother was nineteen. She was a big part of our lives. We remember her with . . .'

The older man supplied, 'Love. We remember her with love. And pride. But you know how people fade. We wanted to hear what people here thought. That's why we've come.'

'Of course.' She looked at them over the rim of her teacup. 'By the time I came to this part of the world you had all gone,' she said. 'The person who bought this house from La—it was a Mrs Dart—welcomed me to the village when I first moved to Suffolk. Of course La's orchestra was already a thing of the past then, but people still talked about it.' She paused. 'I still think of this as La's house, you know. And that's what some people in the village call it—even people who never met La. It's still La's house.'

When they had finished their tea, she suggested that they walk the short distance to the church hall.

'It's a tin hall,' she said, as they approached it. 'Made entirely of corrugated tin.'

They stood still for a few minutes and admired the modest building from the end of its path. The walls of tin had been painted in a colour somewhere between ochre and cream, and the roof was rust-red. At one end of the building was a small verandah, dominated by a green door.

'I have a key,' she said, reaching into a pocket. 'It's a privilege of being on the parish council. We can look inside—not that there's much to see.'

They walked down the path. The lock, an old-fashioned one, was stiff, and had to be coaxed into opening, but at last the door was pushed open and they found themselves standing in a vestibule. She pushed open the inner door, which was unlocked. The air inside was cool with a musty smell.

'Nowadays,' she said, 'the place is used for the school play and the occasional village dance.'

'And the orchestra?'

She gestured about her. 'Under this very roof. Right here. This is where the orchestra played—so I'm told.' She pointed at the windows, through which sunlight filtered. 'They were covered, of course. Black-out curtains. I met somebody who had played here,' she continued. 'Apparently, the orchestra sat over there, at the far end of the hall, and when they gave a concert the audience sat at this end.'

The brothers looked around them, then up at the ceiling, which was made of large expanses of white board nailed onto the roof beams. The board was discoloured here and there from leaks.

'If you've seen enough,' she said, 'perhaps we should go back.'

She locked the door behind them, and they walked back in silence, until they had almost reached the house.

'Could you tell us more?' the driver asked. 'About the orchestra?' He paused. 'If you have the time.'

She turned to him and smiled. 'In this village there's not a great deal to do. But remembering is something we're rather good at. Go to any small village anywhere in the world and see what they remember. Everything. It's all there—passed on like a precious piece of information, some secret imparted from one who knew to one who yearns to know.'

TWO

La's childhood was spent in the shadow of Death. He was an uninvited guest at their table, sitting patiently, watching La's mother, his target, bemused, perhaps, that such courage and determination could keep an illness at bay for so long. But he was in no hurry and would make his move when every one of the expensive treatments had been tried, and failed. The last of these involved a trip to Switzerland, where optimistic doctors prescribed Alpine air and light. When, shortly after her return to England, the end came, La was just fifteen and at boarding school.

La's father did his best to fill the gap, but he was not a demonstrative man and he simply could not express the love and concern he felt for the child who was the living reminder of his wife in all her gestures and looks. A female child, he felt, needed a woman to look after her. For this reason, he hired a housekeeper who doubled up as mother and, as La realised with shock, as wife. She heard conversation from behind the closed door of her father's bedroom, lowered voices. He could not marry her—no, it was impossible. Why was it impossible? Silence. Was he ashamed of her, of her very ordinary origins? More silence. That's it, isn't it? Ashamed.

The house they lived in was in Surrey, on the brow of a hill. If conditions were right, London could be seen as a distant smudge against the horizon. La liked the fact that they lived on a hill, and would introduce herself as one who came from the top of a hill in Surrey.

'I am going to university in a very flat place,' she said to her father. 'You're sending me down from my hill to a very flat place.'

'Cambridge is indeed flat,' he said. 'And . . .' She waited for him to say more, but he often failed to complete these utterances.

Cambridge had been La's choice, even if one that had been heavily backed by her English teacher, a graduate of Girton. She knew the admissions tutor, she said; they had gone walking in France together as students and she would make sure that any application would be sympathetically viewed. La did not want to be accepted because of some remote bond of friendship, the outcome of a walking tour.

'I'm not saying that,' said the teacher. 'But you'll learn as you go through life that friendships and contacts lie behind so many of the decisions that people make. It's just the way the world is.'

Girton accepted her, and in 1929 she began the study of English literature. Everybody in Cambridge seemed to be talking about Mr Leavis, who was on the verge of publishing a great work of criticism, it was said. She met Leavis, and his new wife, Queenie Roth, who talked to her at a party about Jane Austen. It was just one of the heady experiences that Cambridge had in store for La, and it made the hilltop in Surrey seem irredeemably dull.

Her tutor, Dr Price, was ambitious for her. 'You could do a further degree. There's so much to choose from.'

That was not how La saw it. In her view there was so little choice—if one was a woman. 'It's men who have all the opportunities,' she said. 'Look at what they can do. At the most, we have their leavings, the crumbs from their table. It's 1931 and that's all we have. Still.'

'That's because women haven't learned to live their lives as if men did not exist,' said the tutor.

That was easily said by a tutor in a women's college. But La did not point this out.

'It breaks my heart,' the tutor went on, 'to see all these intelligent girls come to us and then leave, more or less promised to some man. And they go off and marry him and that's the end. What a criminal waste.'

Seeing La's reaction, the tutor offered a list of names. 'Andrews last year; Paterson too, such a brilliant person. Married. Buried away in some dim town somewhere, playing bridge and practising domestic economy. Is that what Cambridge is for?'

La agreed with Dr Price, on that, at least, if not on other matters. She had not come to Cambridge to find a husband; she found it astonishing that there were girls who did just that—she had met some of them. Our best chance, one said. You'd have to be a fool not to take it. La said nothing; she had come, she believed, to be taught how to think. At school she had been subjected to rote-learning intended to enable her to recite the opinions of others; now she wanted to form her own views, but was finding it difficult.

'Don't you think it exciting, La, to be alive at a time of crisis?'

The speaker was Janey Turner, a young woman who had befriended her at a poetry reading and invited her afterwards to a tearoom.

La wondered about the crisis. Everybody said there was a cultural crisis—that the old certainties had been so destabilised that they were no longer capable of providing any answers. But if that was so, then how were we to know what to believe in? Janey knew the answer: the common man, she said. He's the future. We must believe in what he believes in.

'Which is what?'

'The ending of oppression. Freedom from hunger. Freedom from the deception of the Church and the tricks of the ruling class: flags, national glory, militarism.'

La pondered this. She agreed that freedom from hunger was an admirable goal. And oppression was bad, too; of course it was. But the Church? She thought of the college chaplain, a mild man with a strong interest in Jane Austen and in Tennyson, who was distantly related to Beatrix Potter and who would never have engaged in deception, surely?

'Is there a crisis in literature?' La asked Dr Price.

The tutor looked at her. 'Of course. We all know there's a crisis.'

Except me, thought La. I'm prepared to accept that there's a crisis—if only somebody would explain how the crisis had come about and just how it manifested itself.

'Why?' she persisted. 'Why is there a crisis?'

Dr Price waved a hand in the air. 'Because of lies and rottenness.

Simplicity and sincerity have been replaced by obfuscation and pretence. Men, of course. They love to create mystery where none exists.'

'So simplicity is a literary virtue?'

Dr Price looked at her severely. 'Yes, of course it is. And it is a virtue that is more assiduously practised by members of our own sex, if I may say so.'

La found that this conversation, as was the case with many of her discussions with Dr Price, left her dissatisfied. If it was a teacher's role to bring enlightenment, then Dr Price failed in her calling. She behaved as if she were the custodian of a body of knowledge to which her students might aspire, but she did not impart that knowledge willingly.

La was happy enough at Girton, even if she found that the enlightenment she had hoped for was slow to arrive. When she returned after her first long summer vacation, she decided that there would be no sudden moment of insight; at the most she would start to see things slightly differently. She did not worry about that. She joined a music society, and played the flute in a quartet. She had learned the instrument at school, where it had been something of a chore. Now she took it up without the pressure of practice and examinations, and found that she enjoyed it. They struggled through Haydn and Mozart, and gave a concert at the end of the term. A young man, Richard Stone, came to that, wearing a blue cravat that caught La's eye. He was tall, with the confident bearing of an athlete. She looked up from her music at the end of the first piece and noticed him. He caught her eye and smiled. Then at the end of the concert, when they went into a room where tea had been prepared, he came up to her and introduced himself.

After a few minutes he invited her to come with him and a group of his friends to a picnic at Grantchester. She hesitated for a moment, but only for a moment, before accepting.

She learned more about Richard from a friend whose brother knew him. He did not have a reputation as a scholar but was effortlessly popular, she was told; he could row, although he would never make the college eight.

'Are you keen on him?' asked the friend who had imparted the information about Richard. 'He's good-looking, isn't he?'

La felt flustered. 'He's nice enough. But that's about it.'

'Pity. Because he likes you. It's obvious.'

'Is it?'

The friend laughed. 'Have you seen the way he looks at you?'

La had seen. At the picnic in Grantchester, he had stared at her with a quiet solemnity. But it had not occurred to her that anybody could admire her in that way. She did not consider herself attractive; I am too tall, she thought. At school a spiteful girl had said to her: 'Boys won't look at you, La. Never. They don't look at tall girls.'

She had grown up with the assumption that this was true and had decided that if a boy came along, one she liked, she would have to do the pursuing. But that was not yet. That would be at some unspecified time in the future, when she was twenty-eight, thirty perhaps. I have not come here to find a husband, she told herself.

They went to another picnic, then Richard took her to tea and started cycling out to see her every afternoon. Soon she came to expect him, just after four o'clock, even in the rain, to which he seemed indifferent. 'It's just water,' he said.

They talked to each other easily, as if they were old friends. In the cinema he took her hand and then kissed her. He tasted of tobacco, and she imagined, absurdly, that she might reveal this to Dr Price. 'Do you know, Dr Price, that men taste of *tobacco*? Did you know that?'

Six weeks after their first meeting, he had told her that he hoped she would marry him; he would be honoured, he said. 'I've never proposed to anybody before. I really haven't.'

She almost laughed. There was a seriousness about the way he spoke which made her think he was reciting lines that somebody had taught him. 'It's very sudden.' That was all she could think of to say, trite as it was.

'Which means yes? Please tell me that this means yes. If you had wanted to say no, then you would have said it. Anything else must mean yes.'

She wanted to be firm, but it was difficult. He was like an eager schoolboy. 'You can't expect somebody to make up her mind just like that. It's been five weeks.'

'Six. Almost seven. And I knew immediately. I really did, you know. I was quite certain that you were the one. You have to marry me.'

Now she laughed, and he had taken that as her answer. In her first private moment thereafter, she looked into a mirror, staring at herself, wide-eyed. You are a person to whom another person has proposed. It seemed absurd, risible. She had laughed earlier on, immediately after he had declared himself, but her laughter had been taken as some sort of assent. She would have to clear it up. She would brush aside Richard's persuasive banter and get to the essential point: she was not ready to get married. They could get to know one another better and there was always the possibility that at some point their friendship might become something more, but not now.

She tried that, but he seemed not to take her seriously. 'Fine,' he said. 'We can think about things. But you and I know how we feel, don't we?'

'Well, frankly, Richard, I'm not sure that you know how I feel . . .'

But as the months went past, she found that her feelings were changing. She looked forward to their meetings now, counted the hours and minutes before they would be together. Was this what it meant to *fall* for somebody? She believed it was. And if she had to marry *someone*—and she mostly assumed that she did—then would she ever find anybody quite as charming as Richard? He would be kind to her. They would have fun together. Could one ever really expect anything more than that out of marriage?

Her father approved of Richard, approved of his prospects. Richard was going into the family firm of wine merchants, substantial ones, with a warehouse in Bordeaux and a share in another one on the Douro. And Richard charmed him, as he could charm anybody, simply by smiling.

'I'm so happy for you, my dear,' her father said. 'After all that sadness, the business with your mother, and all that . . .'

'I'm glad that you like him. He's a nice boy, isn't he?'

His father waved a hand in the air. 'Of course. But you never would . . .' She waited. What would she never do? Choose the wrong sort of man? Richard was not that; she was sure of it. He was gentle, and amusing, and so she said yes, she would marry him. Later.

He looked at her earnestly. 'After we leave Cambridge?'

'Of course.'

'June, then.'

She had not meant it to be that soon, but he was impossible to argue with. She acquiesced.

Her friend Janey, the one who had taken her to the poetry reading, quizzed her. 'Are you completely sure?' she asked.

'Yes. I suppose I am.'

Janey frowned. 'Not suppose. You shouldn't say "suppose". People who are madly in love with another person never say "I suppose I love him".'

La thought out loud. 'I do love him. We laugh at the same things. He's kind. What more could one ask for?'

'Romance,' said Janey. 'Passion. An aching for the other person. An emptiness in his absence. That sort of thing.'

'Maybe,' said La. 'Anyway, we're getting married.'

The marriage took place in the chapel of St John's, his college. La's small family, her father, uncle, aunt and a few distant cousins, filled a couple of pews; Richard's list was much longer and included numerous school friends, who gave him a party the night before and threw him in the river.

La felt a strange, unaccustomed tenderness for him at the altar, noticing the nervous trembling of his hands as he slipped the ring onto her finger.

'I'm so happy,' he whispered.

After the honeymoon, they went to London, where they rented a flat. Then, a few months later, Richard paid a deposit for the purchase of a house in Maida Vale that was too large for them, but which had a long strip of garden that La started to cultivate. He was now working in the family firm, a job that allowed him to leave the office at four in the afternoon. La wanted to work, but received little encouragement from Richard.

'Why?' he asked. 'Why work when you don't have to?'

She looked at him. 'I don't want to spend my life sitting about. I want to do something with it.'

He seemed genuinely puzzled. 'But you are doing something. You're my wife. That's something, isn't it?'

She did not think that was enough, but did not say anything.

'And there'll be children,' he added, reaching out to touch her. 'Soon.'

They had not discussed this. It would be something that just happened, and she was not sure how she felt about it. One part of her wanted to be a mother; another understood that that really would be the end of her hopes to do something more with her life. But as the months wore on and nothing happened, she began to wonder whether anything would happen. Nothing was said.

They went to the theatre, to concerts, to the opera; Richard indulged her in all of these, although his tastes were not musical. 'That part's missing in my brain,' he said 'I hear the notes, but they don't mean very much to me.'

'Are you happy?' her father asked her on an occasion when they met for lunch in town.

'Of course I am,' said La.

'And Richard too?'

'Very. He doesn't talk about happiness, of course. Men tend not to. Men don't talk about their feelings.'

Her father nodded. 'So true. And yet men have feelings, I think, in much the same way as . . .' He looked out of the restaurant, at the passers-by in the street outside. Some of them looked worn out, ground down by what he called 'general conditions'. 'General conditions are so . . .' he said.

La knew what he meant. She felt guilty that she should be comfortable when others were suffering.

'What can one do?' she asked her father.

'Not much. If you gave your money away it would be gone in a puff of smoke and not make much difference to anybody. So just concentrate on small, immediate things. They make a difference to the world.'

'But look what's happening in Spain and Germany.'

He did not think that there was too much cause to worry. 'Spain's Spain, and always has been. They're cruel. They've always been cruel—and not just to those unfortunate bulls. Germany is full of militaristic bravado,' he added. 'But they're weak. Our Empire is much more solid.'

La had never taken a close interest in politics, but she read the newspapers and it was impossible to be indifferent to what was happening. She took to attending lectures on economics and unemployment, and felt the outrage that gripped the audience. It was intolerable that people should be deprived of the fundamental dignity of being able to work for a living. Everybody was suffering, she read, but she did not think this was true. She and Richard were still well off; it was to do with not having too much invested in the stock exchange, Richard said, and in the continued demand for good wine.

She volunteered to teach a course in literature for the Workers' Educational Association. Richard did not like her going off to the East End alone, but she did so nonetheless, and became involved in a soup kitchen.

Richard said, 'I'm not happy about all this, La. You have everything you need. I know that things are bad for some, but there's not much we can do, is there? You don't have to spend so much time trying to change things.'

They disagreed on this, but La's view prevailed. Her feelings for Richard had changed over the first year of their marriage; she was used to him now and the fondness she felt for him had deepened. She took his hand at odd moments and held it to her breast. 'I do love you, you know,' she said. 'So much. You know that, don't you?'

He smiled. 'Strange woman.'

'Strange that I should love you?'

He winked. 'Maybe.'

She went to a doctor, discreetly, without telling Richard that she had made the appointment. The doctor said, 'It's difficult to tell. People can wait for years, you know, and then suddenly a child comes along. We can do some investigation, of course. But it may not reveal anything.'

But it did. The doctor, who understood these things, who knew that the wife might not want the husband to know, did not write her a letter, but waited for her to telephone back for an appointment.

'It's not good news, I'm afraid, Mrs Stone.'

She left his surgery and walked back along the street, past the underground station where she should have caught her train. She walked on, along unfamiliar pavements in the hinterland of Harley Street. One future had closed to her with the doctor's few words.

She told Richard. He seemed surprised that she had consulted the doctor without telling him. 'You should have spoken to me about it, La,' he said.

'We never spoke,' she said. 'I always felt it was a subject you didn't want to address. I'm sorry if I was wrong about that.'

He spoke angrily. 'You were.'

'I'm very sorry. And it's my fault that we can't have children.'

He softened. 'It's not your fault. It's not.'

'Well, put it this way—I'm the reason.'

'It doesn't matter. Come here.' He put his arms round her. 'I have you and you have me. That's enough, isn't it?'

She wept, and he comforted her. This whole experience, painful though it was, brought them closer together and she thought, I am truly in love with him. Truly. I know it now.

Now it seemed that Richard provoked a far more profound need within her. She wanted all his attention; she wanted him to feel about her what she found herself feeling about him. He had suddenly become so important to her that even his possessions seemed to have gathered an aura about them; his handkerchiefs—*his*—his leather key wallet, his jacket. She asked herself how other people—people who came into contact with him at the office, for instance—could not feel the same way about him, could not understand how completely special he was.

She marvelled at her discovery. It was the most universal of human emotions—love—but now, for the first time, she knew what it meant. It imbued everything with value; made each day into something precious, a gift.

She could not tell him how she felt; she had no words for it. She could say, 'I love you so much,' but what would that convey? People said that all the time—she herself had said it—but they could not possibly be feeling what she felt. And so she used simple words, the formality of which somehow seemed more fitting. 'Thank you for marrying me,' she said.

And he replied, 'I should thank you. I am the fortunate one.'

She smiled. 'Can you imagine what it must be like to live with somebody you can't stand any more? Can you imagine that?'

He closed his eyes for a moment as he thought of this; then opened them and smiled his disarming smile. 'Difficult,' he said quietly.

RICHARD EXPLAINED TO HER what he did at the office. 'It's not very complicated,' he said. 'It's exactly what my father did and my grandfather too, when they were my age. We have agents in Bordeaux who buy the wine for us. We arrange to ship it and put it in our cellars here in London. Then we sell it to smaller merchants and hotels, and to people who buy for their own cellars. My job is to see that it's looked after once it's landed here. I also check the inventories and arrange the tastings.'

'It must be interesting,' she said. 'You must have to keep a lot of figures in your head.'

He looked at her. 'Hardly. But, yes, it has its moments, like any job.'

He showed her an album of photographs that his father had built up. She saw a photograph of their office in Bordeaux itself—a building with the family name painted on the front and a staff of six or seven men standing outside, smiling dutifully. At the edge of the picture, under the shade of a tree, two small boys were playing what looked like a game of marbles, unconcerned by the world of adults. Her eye took in the small details.

Then there were the photographs of the chateaux, with the name of each, or of their location, written in ink beneath them. Richard had spent the last few summers in Bordeaux, working with the agents.

'Could we go there?' she asked.

He seemed hesitant, almost as if the world they were looking at was just for him. But then he said, 'Of course we can. One of these days.'

THEY HAD BEEN MARRIED two years when Richard's father, Gerald, came to the house one afternoon. The moment La answered the door and saw him standing there, his expression grave, she knew immediately that Richard was dead—there could be no other explanation for such a call. She felt her legs give way underneath her, and she cried out. Gerald, who had been carrying his umbrella, dropped it and reached out, managing to catch her under the arms as she sagged forward.

'My dear,' he said. 'My dear.'

'He's dead.'

'No, my dear. No. No.' He helped her to a chair in the hall, then knelt beside her so that his face was at her level. He was always impeccably groomed, his thick, dark hair swept neatly to each side of a railroad-straight parting. 'I'm afraid that something has indeed happened,' he said. 'But there has not been an accident. Richard is not dead.'

He looked down at the floor, then rose back to his feet.

'What has happened, my dear, is that my son . . .' He paused. There was pain in his voice. 'My son, I'm sorry to say, has let us all down. He has left the country and gone to France. On the boat train. This morning.'

She tried to make sense of what he was saying. 'He's gone to the office over there? Is that it?'

Gerald sighed. 'I'm afraid that it's not that innocent. He has gone to France, but I'm sorry to say that he has gone because there is a woman there. He informed me this morning, presented me with a fait accompli. He did not have the courage to tell you and left me to do it. My son did that.'

Richard's mother appeared half an hour later. She had been weeping and her eyes were red. She insisted that La should go home with them; they could not countenance her staying by herself. La said nothing, but packed a bag mutely. She felt completely numb, as if she had been disembodied.

She did not want to talk, but the following day, tired to the point of exhaustion through lack of sleep, she started to ask them questions. Where had he gone? They believed that it was Margaux. And the woman? She was somebody he had met when he had worked in the office in Bordeaux. She was the daughter of a business acquaintance, the owner of a vineyard there.

'You had no idea that there was somebody else?' This was from his mother.

'Of course not? How could I?'

'She had been coming to London on and off. He confessed that to me,' said Gerald.

That silenced her. There had been nights when he had had late meetings—or so he said—and had stayed in his club. And she recalled that weekend when he had gone to watch a rugby game in Cardiff . . .

'He took long lunch breaks,' Gerald began. 'Perhaps . . .' But he was silenced by a look from his wife, who glanced anxiously at La.

'I'm going to France,' announced Gerald. 'I'm going to bring him back.'

La shook her head. 'If he doesn't want to be with me, then I wouldn't want him brought back.'

Gerald looked awkward. 'Do you want to divorce him?'

'I suppose I'll have to,' La replied.

'We'll support you in every way,' said Gerald. 'His share in the business will be made over to you. I've already informed our solicitors.'

'All in good time,' said Richard's mother. 'He might change his mind. We can hope.'

'No,' said Gerald. 'We can't.'

La watched them. Of the two, she thought, I feel sorrier for her. A man can divorce his son if pushed to that extreme; a mother could never do that.

She went back to the house in Maida Vale. A friend from school days, Valerie, a woman who had married a banker and who lived in a flat in Chelsea, came and stayed for a few days. It was a help to have somebody with her, especially an old friend. Valerie talked when she wanted to talk and was silent when she wanted to be silent. She was direct and pragmatic. 'Bad choice,' she said. 'Bad luck. It could happen to anybody. It's not your fault at all. It's men. That's what they do. All the time. He's not going to come back—not after doing this. So you'll have to forget him, I'm afraid.'

'I suppose you're right.'

'Of course I'm right.' Valerie lit a cigarette. 'And now?'

'I want to get out of this place. I don't want to live here.'

Valerie looked thoughtful. 'You could stay with us if you like,' she said. 'For a while. Eventually we'd get on one another's nerves, I suppose.'

La laughed. It was the first time that she had laughed since it happened, ten days ago. She put a hand on her friend's arm. 'I'm very grateful. But no, I don't think it would be a good idea. Richard's parents have a house they never use. They said that I could have it if I wished.'

Valerie blew smoke into the air. 'Here in London?'

'No. It's in the country. In Suffolk. In a village there.'

Valerie frowned. 'You can't go and live in the country. You can't go and bury yourself out there. Suffolk. It's miles away. What will you do, La?'

'I'll go for walks. Listen to music. Talk to people.'

'But everybody will be ancient.'

La smiled. 'There are people our age in the country. Bags of them. You forget that I come from a hilltop in Surrey.'

THREE

Standing before her new front door, with its peeling paint—it looked as if it had been olive green once, but had declined to grey—La thought, as might anybody who had made a precipitate move, What have I done?

The answer was simple, of course: she had left London behind her, city and friends, without thinking of the implications. In a sense that was what she wanted: even if she still thought of Richard, and, curiously, still missed him, she did not wish to live in the physical space that her ruined marriage had occupied, and had turned her back on that. Suffolk was not the end of the world, nor was London the world's centre, no matter that a good number of its inhabitants thought just that. The village, in fact, was only eighty miles from London—a couple of hours on the train and then not much more than twenty minutes in a car along these winding lanes. In three hours she could be back in town meeting her friends for lunch; it was not as if she had gone to Australia. But it might have been, as she stood there at the doorway, the taxi driver helpfully bringing her suitcases down the path.

'The Stones never came here very much,' he said, huffing from the exertion of carrying La's heavy luggage. 'Only once or twice, I think, after the old lady died. So how long are you going to be staying?'

How long was she going to be staying? For ever? Until she was seventy, or even beyond? She would be seventy in 1981, but she could imagine neither being that age nor what the world would be like in 1981. 'I'm going to live here,' she said quietly. 'Permanently.'

The driver put down a case and extracted a handkerchief from his pocket. 'You'll be needing my services then,' he said. 'Getting you to the station. Into Bury. That sort of thing. I'm always available.'

'Thank you. But I think I shall buy a car.' She had not thought about it before this, but it was obvious now that this was what she would have to do. She would buy a small car—one of those open-topped ones that looked such fun in the summer, but that could be battened down for the winter.

'A car? I can sell you a car,' said the driver. 'I have the local garage, you see. I have reliable cars for sale. What sort do you want?'

'An open-topped one.'

LA'S ORCHESTRA SAVES THE WORLD | 231

The driver smiled. 'I have just the one for you. I'll bring her round.'

She wondered whether this was the way things were done in the country. She had not asked about the colour, which was more important to her than any mechanical detail. But it seemed reasonable; she was going to live here, among these people, and she should give them such custom as she could. It was very quiet and there would not be much doing by way of commerce.

The driver went off for the last of her suitcases and brought them back. She reached for her purse to pay him, but he laid a hand on her forearm. 'That won't be necessary. Not if we're going to be doing business together.'

'That would never happen in London,' she said, laughing. She was touched by his gesture.

'Never been there,' said the driver. 'No need for me to put up with their unfriendly ways.'

La, momentarily taken aback, glanced at him and then looked away. Of course there were people in the country who had never been to London; she should not be surprised by that. But where, she wondered, did his world end? At Newmarket? Or Cambridge, perhaps?

'I've been to Ipswich,' he said, as if he had guessed the question that had taken shape in her mind. 'And Norwich, once.'

'You don't need to go to London,' she said quickly. 'I'm pleased to be away from it, as you can see.'

If he had taken offence, it did not show. 'London's all right for them that wants to live on top of one another,' he said. 'But if you like a bit of sky'—he pointed up—'then Suffolk's your place.'

She fumbled with the key that her father-in-law had given her.

'Rain,' said the driver, taking the key from her, 'gets into a lock and brings on rust. She'll ease up once you're using her. A spot of oil, that helps.'

He pulled the door towards him and twisted the key in the lock. The door opened and, in headlong flight towards the light, a bird flew past them, out into the air. La screamed; the driver turned round and looked at the disappearing bird. 'A magpie,' he said. 'They get down the chimney. That one can't have been trapped for long—still plenty of energy in him.'

They entered the hall. There were bird droppings on the floorboards. La looked about her. 'Poor bird. What a nightmare to be imprisoned.'

'Put a cowl on the chimney,' said the driver. He thought of further perils. 'And you could get bats, you know. They like to get in under the eaves; swoop around at night. Dive-bomb you.'

La wondered whether he was trying to scare her, as country people might do with somebody from the city. She thought she would tell him. 'I grew up in the country,' she said. 'In Surrey. I know about bats.'

He put a suitcase down and went out to collect another from just outside the door. Once he had brought them all in, he took a step back and smiled at her. 'People will help you,' he said. 'Mrs Agg at the farm. She'll be round soon enough.'

He left, promising to bring the car a few days later—after he had attended to one or two little problems. 'Nothing big, mind. Spark plugs and the like.'

Alone, La closed the front door. It was summer, and yet the air inside had that coldness and dankness that one finds in a house that has been shut up too long and not lived in. But these would be dispelled once the windows were open. The air outside had been warm and scented with grass, a sweet scent that would quickly pervade the house once it was admitted.

She moved through the hall, a square room on each side of which were closed doors, panelled and painted in the same stark white that had been used on the walls. At the far end of the hall a corridor led off to the back of the house where light, a bright square of it, flooded through a window, yellow as butter. A pane was missing—she could see that from where she stood; that was what had provided ingress for the magpie, and could be more easily remedied than the lack of a cowl on the chimney.

La opened the door to her left. Richard's mother had told her about the sitting room: that it enjoyed the sun in the mornings and that they had taken breakfast in there as the kitchen, on the other side of the house, was cold until the late afternoon. Now, at midday, the sitting room seemed warm.

'It's not a grand place,' she had been warned by her mother-in-law. 'It's a farmhouse, really, nothing more. There's some panelling—of a sort—in the sitting room. That's its sole distinction, I'm afraid.'

She saw the panelling, wainscot high, left unpainted; it had been faded by the sun, which, through the unusually large windows, must reach into every corner of the room. There was an attempt at a cornice at the top of the walls, a strip of plaster relief running round the room and, in the centre, a halfhearted plaster rose from which the ceiling light descended. The floor was made of broad oak boards, faded and uneven, and a large russet-coloured, square carpet dominated the centre of the room. Armchairs, shrouded with dust sheets, had been moved against the walls, watched over by paintings of country subjects: a still-life of a hare and pheasant shot for the pot; a watercolour of a flat landscape; a hunting print.

La moved to a window and looked out. This was her first glimpse of the garden, as it was concealed from the front and one could only guess at what lay behind the house. Somebody had cut the lawn—quite recently, it seemed, which would explain the smell of grass on the air outside. At the end of the lawn, a line of plane trees interspersed with chestnuts marched several hundred yards to a low stone wall, and beyond the trees were fields. It was a warm day, and there was a slight haze hanging above the horizon.

She turned away from the window and continued her exploration of the house. Halfway down the corridor a steep wooden staircase, painted light grey, ascended to the floor above. La climbed this, the boards of the stairs creaking beneath her. She looked into the bedrooms; there was a well-stocked linen cupboard, she had been told, but the beds were bare. There was a bathroom with a claw-foot iron tub and a generous shell-shaped porcelain basin. She turned a tap and water flowed, brown for the first few seconds, and then clear. A large cake of soap, cracked and ancient, had been left in a small china soap dish by the side of the bath.

She went out onto the landing, and that was where she was standing when she heard the sound of somebody downstairs.

MRS AGG EXPLAINED that she had come into the house because she had seen the front door open.

'I didn't mean to give you a fright,' she said. 'I saw you coming, see. And I thought, That'll be the woman from London. Mrs S wrote to tell me.'

Mrs S, thought La. Mrs S and her husband, Mr S, and their son, R . . .

'I didn't realise that I'd left the door open.'

'It was closed. But not locked. We don't lock our doors in the country.'

La wondered whether there was reproach in the tone of voice and felt a momentary resentment; she was not going to be condescended to because she came from London.

'Actually, I was brought up in the country myself,' said La. 'Surrey.'

They looked at one another in appraising silence. La saw a woman in her fifties, with a thin face under greying hair pulled back into a bun, dark eyes. And Mrs Agg, for her part, saw a woman in her late twenties—much younger than she had expected—dressed in a London way, or what she thought they must be wearing in London. She glanced down at La's shoes: they would not last long in the mud.

'I didn't tell you my name,' the older woman said. 'Glenys Agg.'

'And I'm La Stone.'

Mrs Agg frowned. 'La—is that Lah, with an h? Or Lar, with an r?'

'La, with nothing. As in do-ray-me-fa-so.'

Mrs Agg looked puzzled. 'It's short for something, is it?'

La sighed. 'Lavender, I'm afraid.'

'No reason to be afraid of that,' said Mrs Agg. 'Plenty of lavender round here. And they could call you Lav, couldn't they, which would never do, would it?'

La wanted to talk about something other than names. She asked about the farm.

'It's on the other side of your place,' said Mrs Agg. 'Ingoldsby Farm. Ingoldsby was my husband's great uncle on his mother's side. His son died in the war, and so when old Ingoldsby himself passed on five years back we got the farm.'

La nodded towards the kitchen. She assumed there were chairs there and she could invite Mrs Agg to sit down.

'I can't stop,' said Mrs Agg. 'Not now. But I've brought you some things to tide you over. It's not easy moving into a new place. You never have any food in the house.'

La saw that there was a basket at Mrs Agg's feet. Her eye took in the contents: a few eggs, a handful of green beans, a loaf of bread wrapped in a cloth; a jar of butter; some tea. 'That's very thoughtful of you,' she said.

They went through to the kitchen and unpacked the basket. There was a meat-safe in the wall, a wooden cupboard that vented out through gauze into the open air outside. She put the bread and eggs in there and placed the rest of the foodstuffs on the kitchen table.

Mrs Agg pointed to the range on the far side of the room. 'There's coal outside,' she said. 'I had them drop some by when they brought our load the other day. Two shillings' worth. You'll need to get the range going if you're going to have tea today. Do you know how to do it?'

La thought that her visitor knew the answer. It was not the sort of thing one learned in London, nor in Surrey for that matter. But she did not want to admit, to Mrs Agg at least, that she had never fired up a range. 'I'll cope.'

Mrs Agg looked doubtful. 'If there's anything else you need, I'm at the farm. All the time.'

La thanked her, and the other woman left. By herself again, she completed her exploration of the house, finding the linen cupboard and making a bed for herself in the airiest bedroom at the back of the house. The linen was clean and smelled fresh, with small sachets of lavender laid upon it. Mrs Agg kept an eye on the house, she had been told, and cleaned it thoroughly every month. La thought of the broken pane and the magpie; the pane must have been recently broken or Mrs Agg would have noticed it. How did a pane of glass break like that? Perhaps a bird had flown into it.

She investigated the garden. In the summer afternoon the plane trees cast long shadows across the lawn and against one side of the house. An unruly hedge of elder bushes, twelve feet high or so, shielded the garden from the lane. The bushes were in flower, and she picked a head from one as she walked past. She could make elderflower wine, perhaps, or cook the flowers with sugar to make an old-fashioned sweet. Or weave elder branches about the kitchen door to ward off flies; her mother had sworn by that remedy.

She stood still for a moment and looked at her garden. Cutting the grass had given it a not altogether deserted look, but at all the edges it was unkempt. The lavender that Mrs Agg had mentioned was there, but had grown woody. What had been a vegetable patch was almost entirely over-grown by weeds, although La spotted a ridge of potato plants that had loyally persisted. She bent down and, scrabbling in the earth beneath the foliage, retrieved a handful of small potatoes. She took these into the kitchen; they would do for supper tonight, with the eggs that Mrs Agg had brought. My first night in my new home, she thought; my first night. And then, sitting down on one of the kitchen chairs, she looked at the ceiling and thought, Have I made a terrible mistake?

THERE WAS A WIRELESS in the sitting room, which she switched on after supper. There was still light in the evening sky, although it was now after nine o'clock. She turned on a table light, a single bulb under a cream-coloured shade. It provided a small pool of light, enough for comfort, but barely enough to read by. The wireless was comforting too, another presence in the house, and a familiar presence as well: the national service of the BBC. There was a literary discussion: Mr Isherwood and Mr Auden had returned from China the previous month. Mr Auden had written a number of poems and Mr Isherwood had kept a diary.

La wondered how she would do if she went off somewhere, as Auden and Isherwood had done. She had known somebody who had gone to Spain, to drive an ambulance with the International Brigade, where he had witnessed a massacre by the Nationalists. Almost every adult male in a particular village had been shot. He had returned to England silent and withdrawn.

People were talking of another war, but La thought that was unlikely, if not impossible. Rational men, meeting round a table, could surely never sanction something like that again. They all knew—they had seen the newsreel footage—of the sheer hell of the trenches; the pitiless carnage. How could anybody envisage doing something like that again? It was inconceivable, and Mr Chamberlain obviously understood that very well. But did Mr Hitler, with all his strutting and ridiculous bombast? thought La.

If war came, then what would she do? There would be no point in going back to London, as she would have nowhere to stay and she would just be another mouth to feed. It would be better to remain in the country, to grow vegetables and contribute to the war effort in whatever other way she could. But it would not come. At the last moment people would surely pull back from something that brought with it a risk of their destruction.

The voice on the radio caught her attention. 'War seems inevitable to me,' he was saying, 'because the monster of fascism can survive only if it has people to devour. The best hope for us is to become strong; for trades unionists and workers to assert themselves and to make sure that the country allies itself with the great progressive force of our modern world—and by that I mean the Soviet Union. Sooner or later the working people of Germany and Spain will rise up and defeat their oppressors. That's the way to avoid war. The dictators will fall at the hands of their own people.'

La went to bed. The sheets smelled strongly of lavender, a soporific smell; sleep overtook her quickly. It was so quiet; she was used to the constant background noise of London, the distant rumble of trains, the sound of traffic. Here there was nothing, just the occasional creaking of the house and a scurrying sound of mice or some other small creatures across the roof or in the attic above her head.

She woke in the night, disorientated, and it took her a few seconds to remember where she was. She switched on her bedside lamp and looked about her; her door was open—had she left it like that? She got out of bed and pushed it shut. She had locked the front door before she had turned in. Would Mrs Agg censure her for that, she wondered? Was one meant to leave one's front door open at night as well?

The following morning, La walked down to Mrs Agg's farm. Agg himself was not there, but she saw a man in the distance, in a field where sheep were kept, and that was Agg. Mrs Agg was happy enough to sell La a large packet of seed potatoes—'Late-growing,' she said. 'You will still have time to plant these and to harvest them in the late autumn, before the ground becomes hard.' She paused. 'Why is a young person like you shutting herself away in that house? Sorry to ask.'

La thought for a moment before replying. 'My husband ran away with another woman, Mrs Agg. I was very unhappy. I wanted to get away.'

Mrs Agg nodded. 'I thought it was something like that. Any woman who's unhappy—look for the cause and it'll be a man.'

La cleared a patch of vegetable garden. The long roots of the weeds yielded only under protest, clinging to the soil, and it was hard work. But by late afternoon she had two freshly turned mounds of earth in which the potatoes could be planted. It was good soil, clay loam. I shall not starve, she thought. Whatever happens in the world, I shall not starve here in this quiet corner of England.

A FEW DAYS LATER, La drove to Bury in the car that she had bought for sixty-five pounds from the garage man, Mr Granger. It was an Austin Seven, a small car painted in dark green with a hood that could be taken down in fine weather. La kept the hood on that day, as she was not sure how to operate the mechanism that released it. Mr Granger had shown her, but she had forgotten; there were levers that had to be pushed a particular way.

La had some experience of driving, even if not a great deal. Richard had owned a car, which she had taken out from time to time when she went to play tennis in Richmond. She realised now that she had no idea what had happened to that car. Perhaps he had taken it on the boat with him to France; perhaps the Frenchwoman would be sitting in her seat—La's seat—and driving with Richard along the winding roads of Aquitaine; in her seat; with her husband. She put the thought out of her mind; if she allowed it to stay, then for the rest of the day it would be like a nagging pain, refusing to budge. She would not let that happen now that she had started this new life.

You can forget his car, she told herself. You have your own car now. And you have your own life, here in Suffolk, with your own friends . . . But that is where the attempt at reassurance stumbled. There were no new friends; not yet. The only person she had spoken to so far, apart from Mrs Agg and Mr Granger, was Ethel, the woman who ran the village post office. Mrs Agg was solicitous, yet she could hardly imagine herself developing a friendship with the farmer's wife. La was no snob, but they had no interests in common, other than the cultivation of vegetables, on which subject Mrs Agg had revealed her misgivings about the extent of La's knowledge.

I can grow potatoes, La thought, through the mental equivalent of clenched teeth. But she had never grown potatoes in Surrey, she had to admit. There may have been potatoes in the walled kitchen garden, but there had been a gardener who came three days a week; her involvement with potatoes had extended at this point merely to the eating of them.

There was always Bury, thought La, which was not too far away and which had the sort of population that one might expect to find in a prosperous market town: professional people, business people, teachers and so on. These were people with whom she would be able to discuss things, who read books and had views. And people of her own age, with a social life.

She drove into Bury and parked a short distance away from the Cornhill. It was market day and stalls stood in a colourful row along the side of the street. On impulse she bought a large ball of string—it was something one always needed. Soap, a roll of white bandage for domestic injuries, two large boxes of cook's matches; these were all cheaper here, and she would need them too. She found a stall selling books, and could not resist a book on the growing of roses. She noticed that the author's name was Thorn and pointed this out to the stallholder, who nodded and said, 'Terry Thorn. Big rose man over in Ipswich.'

'I suppose he had to write books about roses,' said La. 'It was inevitable.'

Then she found a grocery store and went through the list of supplies she had written out the day before.

'We haven't seen you before, madam; would you like to establish an account?'

'Of course. Thank you.' An account gave her a feeling of belonging.

The grocer's boy carried her purchases to the car. He whistled as he walked behind her, but stopped when La turned round to smile at him.

'Don't stop. Whistling's nice. Cheerful. You must be happy.'

'I can't complain.'

Suddenly she felt that she had to ask him something. 'How old are you?'

He looked away. 'Sixteen. Seventeen in December.'

She was walking beside him now, not ahead. 'And do you think there's going to be a war?'

He was surprised by her question. He's just a boy, she thought.

'Maybe,' he said. 'Mr Evans in the shop says that there's going to be a war very soon. He says that old Hitler has wanted it for years to make up for the fact that they lost last time. He says that if there is one, then he'll have to get a girl to do my job as I'll have to go off and fight.'

She looked at him and saw him, in her mind, in a uniform. It would be too big for him; too big round the shoulders.

'And what do you think about that? Going off to fight?'

He shrugged and shifted the weight of the box of groceries in his arms. 'If the other lads go, I'll go. I don't mind. Might meet some girls.'

She wanted to say to him that one did not join the army to meet girls, but instead, she said, 'Have you ever read any poetry?'

The boy shook his head. 'No. I can't say I have.'

She had been thinking of Dr Price, her tutor, who had introduced her to the work of Wilfred Owen. She wanted to talk about Owen now, rather urgently, but could not, of course, to this boy, even if he was exactly like one of the gentle, rather passive boys that Owen wrote about; innocents who had been tossed so heartlessly into veils of gunfire. *The shrill demented choirs of wailing shells; And bugles calling for them from sad shires.*

The boy muttered, 'What did you say?'

She had not been aware of saying anything; but she had. 'I was thinking about how horrible war is.'

'Is it?'

'I'm afraid it is. That's why I hope that there isn't going to be one.'

IT WAS WHEN La returned to the house after this trip to Bury that she noticed it. She was unpacking her purchases in the kitchen when she saw that the tea caddy had been moved. It was not something that she would normally have paid much attention to, but she remembered very clearly placing it back on the lowest of the kitchen shelves, just above the hook on which the largest of her saucepans was hung. She remembered that because she had spotted a patch of grease on the saucepan and had dabbed at it with a towel. Then she had given the tea caddy a quick wipe. She had replaced it on the lowest shelf and now it was on the topmost one.

She crossed the room, stepped onto the stool and took down the caddy. Reaching for it gave her another reason to be sure: she could not reach the higher shelf unless she stood on a stool. Suddenly she was frightened. She stepped down off the stool and spun round; she did not want her back turned to the open kitchen door and the corridor beyond. Somebody had been in her kitchen and that person could still be in the house.

She left the kitchen and made her way slowly down the corridor towards the front of the house. Once in the hall, she pushed the sitting-room door open and peered in. There was nobody. Nor was there anybody in any of the other rooms. She returned to the kitchen, where she riddled the cooking range before feeding in fresh coal. Then she put on the kettle and sat down at the kitchen table. She could not remember whether she had locked the back door on leaving for Bury; and if she had locked it, then had she locked the front door as well? She thought that she had, but she could not be sure.

She rehearsed the possibilities in her mind. If she had locked up, the only other person who could have been in the house was Mrs Agg. She still had the key that she had used when she had been looking after the house, and La had suggested that she keep it. 'I'll need somebody to have a key in case I lock myself out,' she had said. 'Will you hold onto it?'

Mrs Agg had agreed, but had not used it, as far as La knew. After their first encounter, when Mrs Agg had come into the house unannounced, she had only visited a couple of times, and on each occasion had made a point of knocking. It was possible, she concluded, that the farmer's wife had come into the house, but it seemed unlikely.

La decided to speak to her. She left the house, locking the back door carefully this time, and walked down the lane to Ingoldsby Farm. Mrs Agg was in the yard, gathering washing from the line, and waved to La as she saw her approaching.

'I saw your new car,' she called as La crossed the yard towards her. 'It's a very nice little one.'

'Thank you. Mr Granger—'

'He knows his cars,' said Mrs Agg. 'If Agg bought a car it would be from Mr Granger. But he hasn't '

'I'll run you anywhere in mine,' said La. 'Just let me know.'

She was standing before Mrs Agg now, watching the other woman putting wooden clothespegs into the pocket of her apron.

'Mrs Agg,' she began. 'Thank you for keeping an eye on the house.'

The farmer's wife looked up in surprise. 'Don't do much,' she said. 'When I walk past, I cast an eye to make sure you're not on fire, or something awful like that. Apart from that, don't do anything as I can see.'

La caught her breath. 'But I thought that you dropped in today.'

Mrs Agg shook her head. 'No. I've been busy here all the time.'

La could tell that she was telling the truth. 'Oh, well . . .'

Mrs Agg looked at her expectantly, and then changed the subject. Would La fancy a couple of duck eggs? She went to fetch the eggs from the kitchen and handed them over to La: pale blue things, larger than hen's eggs, fragile, warm to the touch. La carried them back to the house, one in each hand, gingerly. But her mind was on other things. When she got back, she laid the duck eggs down on a clump of grass outside the kitchen and reached into her pocket for the key to the door.

She would not need it. The door had been forced, from the inside, the split wood of the frame sticking up in splinters, like small pieces of straw.

FOUR

The policeman lived in a neighbouring village, in a house behind a sign saying POLICE HOUSE. He heard La out on the doorstep, raising an eyebrow when she explained that it looked as if the door had been forced from within.

'Very unlikely,' he said. 'Don't you think? People break in to houses, not out of them, at least in my experience.'

La looked at the man standing in front of her: a tall, well-built man with sandy-coloured hair and a bemused expression. She wondered whether she had misinterpreted the evidence. 'But the wood had been splintered on the outside; if you pushed on the door from the outside, it would have broken on the inner part of the jamb.'

The policeman frowned. 'Which way does the door swing? Out or in?'

La thought for a moment. She could not answer, and the policeman's frown became a tolerant smile. 'You see? Sometimes things look black and they're really white. And the other way round.' He paused, watching the effect of his remark on her.

He was one of those men who treated women with well-meaning condescension, thought La. She had encountered them first in Cambridge, among the undergraduates who were the products of all-boys schools, whose only contact with women had been with their mothers, or domestic staff.

There was a silence. It made more sense for the door to have been forced from outside; otherwise . . . the thought appalled her. If it had been forced from inside that would have been because she had locked somebody up in the house when she had gone to see Mrs Agg.

'I shall come and take a look,' said the policeman. 'I'd be obliged if you would drive me in your car.'

'Of course.'

In the car, La asked him whether there had been burglaries in the district. 'I can count on the fingers of this hand,' he said, raising his right hand, 'the number of burglaries we've had in the last eight years, since I came to this job. And most of those were carried out by Ed Stanton over at Stradishall.'

He was relaxed now in her company and La was warming to him.

'Ed left the district after the last one,' the policeman went on. 'He was roughed up by the victim's son, who happened to be a boxer. That sorted him out. That, and his missus giving him his marching orders. Burglars are usually cowards, in my experience. Say "boo" to them and they turn and run. That's where women go wrong, in my view.'

La was puzzled. 'How do women go wrong?'

The policeman looked straight ahead. They were almost there and perhaps, thought La, it was the wrong time to get involved in a debate about what women did or did not do. He continued, 'Burglars are scared of people who aren't scared of them. That's human nature, isn't it? If women stood up to burglars, then they'd back down. Scarper. Burglars have mothers, you see. No burglar likes getting a tongue-lashing from his mum.'

She had to laugh, and he laughed too. They were on the edge of her village now, and she slowed the Austin down. Soon they arrived at the cottage and La pulled the car into the drive. The gravel was vocal underneath the tyres of the car; a crunching sound, like waves breaking, thought La.

'So this is where you live,' said the policeman. 'Some people by the name of Stone own this place, I understand.'

'My husband's parents,' La began. She could tell, as she spoke, what he was thinking. 'He lives in France now, my husband. It's just me here. I'm Mrs Stone too.'

'Ah,' said the policeman. Then, as the car stopped, 'By the way, I never even told you my name. It's Brown, but everybody around here calls me by my Christian name and my surname together, Percy Brown.'

'Everybody calls me La,' said La, although nobody in the village, she realised, called her anything. Mrs Agg knew her name, but had not used it, as far as she could recall. If anybody else referred to her—and they must have said something among themselves, even if only to note her arrival— then they must have called her 'that woman', perhaps, or 'that woman who lives by herself'. That, she thought, was what she was to them.

La showed Percy Brown the door, which she had shut and locked before fetching him. He opened it, and as he did so more splinters came away.

'You see,' she said. 'It looks as if it's been pushed from the inside.'

Percy Brown made a noncommittal noise and bent down to examine the door. He was in his shirtsleeves and La noticed sweat-stained patches under his arms; it had been a hot afternoon and these were now damp. There was something very masculine about him, she thought.

He straightened up and ran his finger down the inside of the jamb. 'Yes,' he said. 'Here, and . . . and here.'

La peered at the place where his fingers had stopped.

'You see?' he said.'Can you see the marks? That's where they've prised at the door. A screwdriver, maybe. Something of the sort.'

'From the inside?'

Percy Brown sniffed. 'Looks like it.'

She made him a cup of tea and they sat together at the kitchen table. He drummed his fingers lightly on the surface, which irritated her. He noticed the direction of her gaze and checked himself.

'Sorry,' he said. 'Mrs Brown says that's my worst habit. But it helps me to think.'

'I don't mind,' said La. She did. 'And I don't want to stop you thinking.' She did not.

He leaned back in his chair and folded his hands across his stomach. 'Let's go over this again. You went to Bury and may or may not have left one of your doors unlocked. Correct?'

'Yes. I think I locked up, but maybe I didn't. I don't know. My neighbour says that nobody locks their doors round here.'

Percy Brown nodded. 'No, they don't. And most of the time that's fine. But let's assume that you didn't lock up. If somebody came in, then he would have had to do so while you was . . . you were in Bury. Then you came back and noticed that somebody had interfered with things in the kitchen. The business with the tea caddy.'

La, who was sitting facing the window, looked beyond Percy Brown's shoulder into the garden outside. She had left a long-sleeved blouse on the line and its arms were flapping in the breeze.

'So,' the policeman continued. 'That means that the intruder was probably in the house when you searched. You must have walked right past him. Not a nice thought, Mrs Stone, is it? That worries me, you know.'

La was silent. She had wanted reassurance; she had even hoped that he might come up with some explanation, but instead she was receiving what amounted to a warning. She waited for him to say something.

He looked at her and unfolded his hands. 'Sometimes we get Gypsies,' he said. 'They camp down by Foster's Fields, a few miles away. They can be trouble. Stealing. Theft of livestock. Sheep aren't safe when they're around.' He paused. 'But they don't go in for housebreaking. That's not their style.'

She felt that she had to say something. 'Not Gypsies?'

'I don't think so. I think I'll just have to report this as an unknown intruder. We get cases like that. Somebody sees a door left open and goes into a house to take a look round, to see if there's anything that can be easily taken. We call them opportunistic thieves. But what I don't like about this is the fact that he was fiddling. Fiddling with the tea, of all things. That tells me something.'

She waited. He was looking at her now, with an eyebrow slightly raised. 'What does it tell you, Mr Brown?'

He examined his nails for a moment, then folded his hands again. 'It tells me that he might be interested in you. If people are snooping round a house and nothing's stolen, then it sometimes means that somebody has too close an interest in another person. Watching them, so to speak.'

THAT NIGHT, or at least the earlier part of that night, was difficult. La left it as late as possible before she went upstairs to bed. She switched on all the lights downstairs and turned the wireless up. She chose Radio Normandie, which was playing dance music. When she went from the sitting room into the kitchen, the sound of the radio followed her. In the kitchen it sounded as if somebody was having a party at the other end of the house; all that was missing was the hum of voices. Perhaps she would have a party some time; but where, she thought, would the guests come from?

There was no curtain in the kitchen, and so when she stood by the sink, filling the kettle, she was looking out upon darkness. Suddenly she noticed a shape a few feet into the dark, at the limits of the light that came from the window. She gave a start, putting the kettle down quickly, spilling water from the spout. But then she realised what it was. The long-sleeved blouse she had seen earlier in the day was still hanging on the line.

She leaned forward towards the glass pane of the window and looked out again. There was the shape of the elder hedge and the trees black against the night sky. There was very little moon—just a sliver—and no other illumination. The Aggs' farmhouse could not be seen from this vantage point so there was not even a light from that.

La took a deep breath. If I am to live here, she thought, then I cannot let myself be frightened by emptiness and isolation. She moved towards the door and opened it, trying not to look at the signs of its earlier forcing. She did not wish to be reminded of her conversation earlier that day with Percy Brown—a conversation that had ended with his concluding that there was very little that he could do about her break-in. Now she took a few steps into the dark and began to remove the wooden pegs that kept the blouse on the line. The garment was dry and had the smell of cotton that has been left out in the fresh air, something that her clothing never had in London.

She held the blouse against her cheeks and breathed in. She looked about her, her eyes gradually becoming accustomed to the dark. The shapes became more defined now: the woody lavender emerged, a line of box. She took a few steps deeper into the darkness, looking up as she did so, up at the stars, fields of them, it seemed, stretching across the sky above. As a girl she had known the names and position of the constellations. She would renew her acquaintance with them now that she was here in a place where the sky was not spoiled by light.

Suddenly she thought of Richard. She still thought of him every day. He was a stubborn presence, like a scar. Now, at this moment, she would give anything to have him here beside her; to be with him right now, under this sky, in this place. Without him, the experience was half what it could be.

She put the thought out of her mind. Shortly after Richard had left, a friend in London, to whom the same thing had happened—at the hands of a charming womaniser—had said to her that the trick was to forget the man. 'If they're not there, then we feel much better, you know. So banish him.'

'But how? How do you stop thinking of somebody when that person is the only person you want to think about?'

'You do what monks do when they think about women. You train yourself to think of something else. In their case, the Holy Ghost, I suppose.

Or the Devil, if they wish to frighten themselves.' She made a face.

She had decided to do that. Every time he came to mind, she would think of something else, of something very far from Richard. Dr Price, perhaps, her Cambridge tutor, about whose person there was not the faintest whiff of sulphur, but who could stand in for the Devil. And now, out in the garden at night, Richard was gone.

The lawn stretched before her, a dark sward, beyond which the plane trees were a black expanse reaching up to the rather lighter sky. She decided to walk in the direction of the trees. The conquering of her fear made her feel almost giddy and for a few moments she felt as if she might break into song. Once on the lawn, she slipped off her shoes and felt the grass soft beneath her feet. Somewhere in the distance an owl cried, a sharp sound that she remembered from her childhood; there had been owls in the barn beside the house in Surrey.

She reached the plane trees and stood beneath them, relishing the sound of their leaves in the slight breeze that had blown up. Within moments the breeze dropped and the trees were silent again. A leaf dropped, and touched her gently on the cheek as it fell.

Then she saw the movement. A dark shape on the other side of the lawn detached itself from a shadow and moved, to become another dark shape closer to the house. La caught her breath and stared into the darkness.

The man moved suddenly; just a few yards, but enough to make himself distinct against the light that was coming from a corner of the large window in the sitting room; the curtains did not meet exactly and light escaped, enough to silhouette the figure of a man.

'Boo!'

It came to her spontaneously; so quickly, in fact, that she was unaware of any decision to shout out. She saw the man jerk, like a cut-out in a shadow play, as if invisible strings holding him up had been jerked. Then she heard the thudding of his feet as he tore along the path beside the house to make good his escape.

She stayed where she was for a few moments. She was shaking, but felt strangely elated. She had done exactly what Percy Brown had implied one should do to a burglar. You should say boo, and then, exactly as he had predicted, they would run, or 'scarper', as he put it. He had been talking of a metaphorical boo, but she had taken him at his word and done as advised.

La crossed the lawn, back towards the house. Then, following the path round, she found herself on the drive. She felt no fear now as she walked down to the point where the drive joined the lane. The intruder would be well down the road now, heading back to wherever he came from; which must be, she thought, her village, or possibly the neighbouring village two miles away. That thought unnerved her: the idea that this sleepy little place could conceal somebody given to creeping round—and into—the houses of others was not a comfortable one. And yet criminals had to live somewhere; burglars had their neighbours, as indeed did murderers. Such people also had jobs, in many cases; worked alongside workmates, stood or sat beside them in the pub; passed the time of day with others at the bus-stop. In spite of all this, of course, such people still did the things that they did: looked through windows, forced doors, and worse. But in the city crime was anonymous; here it was personal.

From the edge of the drive, La noticed a light at Ingoldsby's farmhouse in the distance, in spite of the lateness of the hour. Agg was up, or Mrs Agg, perhaps, baking bread in the kitchen. She toyed with the idea of going over there right away, to tell her that there was a prowler on the loose. But she decided she would go tomorrow.

She made her way to the kitchen door and pushed it open—or was it already open? She stopped. Had she left it ajar when she had gone into the garden, or had she closed it behind her? She closed her eyes. She had been at the kitchen window when she had seen the flapping of her blouse on the line; she had opened the door—she remembered the light from the door falling across the stone paving outside—and then . . . then she had closed it because she remembered how dark it became when she did so.

And now the door was slightly ajar and she did not have to turn the handle. This meant that the intruder, rather than running down the drive, as she had imagined he would do, had gone into the house. She opened her eyes. She had forgotten that she had left a full kettle on the range and it was boiling vigorously now. In the air there was the smell of onions; she had fried some onions earlier on to have with a piece of liver. The thought occurred to her: he would have smelled that smell when he came in; he would have become party to that bit of her domestic life—her choice of dinner.

She hesitated. She wondered whether she should telephone Percy Brown and tell him that she suspected that the intruder was in the house again. But the policeman would probably be asleep by now and, anyway, she could not end up running off to Percy Brown every time she felt nervous. Besides, what had happened outside had shown her that the nervousness was on the other side. Would a nervous man have run into the house? Hardly. Doors can be blown open by the wind; doors could swing open entirely by themselves if not hung true.

La closed the door behind her, slammed it for the noise, and then locked it. Radio Normandie was still playing dance music at the other end of the house. She walked down the corridor and went into the sitting room to turn off the radio. Now there was silence, and she heard her own breathing, and her heart, too, she imagined; you could hear such things in a quiet house, if you listened hard. She switched off the lamps in the sitting room but left the light in the corridor burning, both for reassurance and in order to light her way up the first part of the stairs.

Upstairs, she again went from room to room and found nothing. She opened the door of a large wardrobe in the spare room and looked inside; she peered into the bathroom cupboard and behind curtains in her room. She said to herself, There is nobody in this house but me. I am not afraid.

THE BIRDS HAD BEEN in full throat from five o'clock, asserting their territory to anybody who cared to listen, announcing the beginning of the rural day. Such a bright light penetrated La's bedroom curtain; it was midsummer and the sun was already above the horizon. She was not a late riser, but five was too early, even for her. She lay under her blankets for another forty minutes or so, drifting in and out of sleep, before eventually she slipped out of bed and walked barefoot into the upstairs bathroom.

Through the bathroom window—a rectangle of old glass with a vertical fault line of trapped bubbles—La looked out over the fields on the other side of the lane. The field nearest the house had Agg's sheep in it and a couple of his Jersey cows. The cows had been milked already, she could see; Mrs Agg had told her that Agg got up at four to do this, every day, month in, month out, and had been doing that since he was twelve. That was not uncommon in the country, where everybody seemed to have been in the same place, doing the same thing, for most of their lives. Percy Brown had told her that his father had been a policeman in a small town nearby, and the vicar, whom she had met briefly, had been born in a vicarage in Bury.

After breakfast La walked over to Ingoldsby Farm. Mrs Agg was shelling peas in the kitchen and called her in from outside.

'I could help you,' said La.

'You don't have to,' said Mrs Agg.

'I want to. Please let me.' La sat down at the table alongside her neighbour. 'I had an intruder last night,' she said. 'In the garden. A man.'

Mrs Agg continued with her peas. She did not look up. 'A Gypsy, I'd say. Foster's Fields. There's a gaggle of them down there.'

La remembered what Percy Brown had said. Gypsies were thieves. But surely not all of them; how could everybody be a thief?

'Yes,' Mrs Agg continued. 'They come round here on the lookout for anything not nailed to the ground. Like ducks. They slink away pretty quickly if you shine a light at them. They're like foxes.' She looked up. 'You weren't worried, were you? You can come over here if you're worried.'

They lapsed into silence. La felt relieved; if what Mrs Agg said was true, and the man had been a Gypsy, then at least she could stop worrying about being watched. Gypsies stole, she had been told; they did not watch.

They worked for a further ten minutes. Mrs Agg was not one for unnecessary conversation and La assumed that there was nothing to be said. When they reached the end of the peas, the farmer's wife stood up and brushed at her apron. As she did so, a door behind her opened and a young man entered the room. He was about to say something, and had opened his mouth to do so, when he spotted La and stopped himself in surprise.

'This is my Lennie,' said Mrs Agg.

La looked up at the young man. He was tall—considerably taller than his father—and well built. He had a shock of dark hair and one of those broad, country faces that could so easily become, as it did in this case, slightly bovine. It was not an intelligent face, La thought, nor a comfortable one; there was resentment in it. Things were not quite right for Lennie.

Lennie stared at La for a few moments before his gaze slipped away to the side. As this happened, though, Mrs Agg's eyes moved up and met La's briefly, as if in enquiry.

La forced a smile. 'Hello, Lennie.'

'Yes,' he said. 'Yes.'

Mrs Agg brushed at her apron again. 'Those ewes, Lennie,' she said. 'Dad says he wants them moved over to the big pasture.'

Lennie nodded and moved off towards the back door. La saw that his thick grey trousers had patches of mud upon them, caked dry. On the sleeves of his shirt, which were rolled halfway up the forearm, there were dark stains that looked like treacle: they basted something dark on the hoofs of the sheep—she had seen it—to protect them from foot-rot. Some of this was on Lennie's shirt now. She noticed that the skin on the back of his neck, just above the collar, was tanned by the sun, red-brown, leathery.

With Lennie out of the room, Mrs Agg glanced at her watch. 'I have to let the ducks out,' she said. 'We keep them in at night or the fox would get them.' She paused. 'Lennie is a worry to me, you know. I sometimes wish that there was more for him to do round here, but there isn't. He's twenty-three. They have a dance in the village hall from time to time, but Lennie's not very good with girls.'

La felt a surge of sympathy for Mrs Agg. 'I'm sure he'll find somebody.'

La saw the appreciation in the look she received from Mrs Agg. She lived in a world of taciturn men, of hard work, thought La.

'I hope so. But not every girl is going to want to marry a farmer, these days. Girls have ideas about living in town. The comforts. Our life here . . .' She looked about her, at the kitchen, the stack of wood by the range; at the blackened griddle; at the rush mats on the floor with their frayed edges.

'Farmers' daughters?' asked La.

'Yes, that would be good. But Lennie, you see . . .' The sentence was not completed.

It then occurred to La that it was Lennie she had seen in the garden the previous evening. And it further occurred to her that Mrs Agg knew that, but could not bring herself to say as much. She was his mother, after all, and few mothers accept the truth about their sons.

OVER THE WEEKS that followed, the second half of July, La saw no more of the intruder. She was now convinced that it had been Lennie, and that Mrs Agg might by now have spoken to him. It was also possible that he had merely been curious, and that having met her in the farmhouse kitchen had somehow taken the mystery out of her presence. Whatever it was, she was not frightened of him; rather, she felt sorry for him, for this farm boy whose world began and ended with Ingoldsby Farm. She wondered what went on in his head. Did he listen to the news? Did he know where Germany was; who Hitler and Mussolini were? For such a young man, the arrival of a new neighbour must have been an event of tremendous import—enough to lure him into trying to find out more about her. Viewed in that way, Lennie was nothing to worry about. Indeed, when she saw him next she would try to reach out to him, to engage him in conversation.

FIVE

On a Thursday morning, a young man rode a bicycle up La's drive. La spotted him from the kitchen. She saw him dismount, prop his bicycle against the sycamore sapling at the edge of the drive, and then take off his post-office cap, wiping the sweat from his brow. She dried her hands and went out to meet him.

'Mrs Stone?'

She nodded. He had extracted a telegram from his pocket and she was going over in her mind which of her elderly relatives could have died. Her father, now in a nursing home in Brighton, was frail. There was an aunt in York who had been ill . . .

She took the telegram and signed the small notebook that the young man produced. She searched his face for a sign; they knew what was in these telegrams, these men, but affected ignorance. They avoided smiling, she had been told, when the news was bad. His face was expressionless.

'Hot day, isn't it?' he remarked, looking away.

'Yes.' She thanked him and gave the notebook back. He nodded, and went back to his bicycle.

She had not expected it to be Richard, and the bearer of this news to be his father.

REGRET RICHARD VERY ILL IN FRANCE STOP SHALL COME TO SEE YOU
LATE AFTERNOON STOP CAR FROM BURY STOP WILL LEAVE AGAIN
FOLLOWING MORNING STOP GERALD

She went back into the house and sat down on one of the kitchen chairs. Rereading the telegram, she tried to extract further meaning from the sparse words. But she could not read anything more into the terse message: Richard was ill, his father was coming to see her and then leaving the next day.

La thought: Richard is dying. She closed her eyes and saw him standing before her, smiling as she remembered him smiling, the palms of his hands facing outwards in an ambiguous gesture somewhere between greeting and apology.

She went outside, intending to busy herself with some task that would take her mind off the wait for Gerald's arrival. She had planted several rows of spinach in her newly cleared vegetable patch and now she bent down and began to pluck the weeds from either side of the spinach plants. She felt the moisture of the soil against her knees; she was ruining a good skirt, which was not made for such tasks, but she did not want to go back into the house to change. She plucked at the weeds and flung them to the side; she wept, and she saw a tear fall on the dry soil. Why should she cry for a man who had let her down so badly? Who loved another woman rather than her? Because women did; they wept for the men who misused them and betrayed them; and because La had wanted him and still did; she wanted him with her, and because not an hour of her day went by but that she thought of him.

When Gerald arrived she was still in the garden.

'I'm a mess,' she said. 'Just look at me.'

He seemed surprised, almost irritated, at her small talk. 'There has been an accident,' he said. 'He was in one of the wine cellars and a structure holding a barrel collapsed. A large piece of wood . . .'

She could not imagine the scene. How high was this structure? Was it a shelf? And where did the wood come from? It all seemed unlikely: wine cellars, barrels; these things did not *injure* people.

He looked down, and as he did so she reached forward and took his hand.

He swallowed. It was an effort to speak. 'A large piece of wood struck him on the head . . . apparently. Had he been standing a few inches to the side nobody would have been hurt.'

She pressed his hand. This was a father talking about a son, his only son. 'Oh, Gerald . . .'

He looked up again and she saw the redness about his eyes. 'They took him off to hospital, but apparently the injury to the head is terribly serious and he . . . he's unconscious. The brain, you see.'

She moved forward and embraced him, feeling the large frame heave as he began to sob. 'They don't think there's much hope of his pulling through. That's what they said to me. My son. He was my boy. Just my boy.'

She hugged him. 'Yes. Yes.'

'I'm going to go first thing tomorrow. A boat to La Rochelle, I think. Winifred is with her sisters. They don't want her to make the trip, her heart being what it is. I don't know.'

She hesitated, but only for a moment. 'I'll come. I'll come with you.'

He said nothing, but she knew this was what he wanted, why he had come. He pulled away from her, gently, and took a handkerchief out of the top pocket of his jacket. He wiped at his eyes. 'I shouldn't,' he said. 'It doesn't make things any easier. I'm sorry.'

'But tears do make things easier,' she said, taking his hand again. 'They do.'

GERALD AND LA were dropped by the taxi driver at the door of the hospital in Bordeaux. Immediately within was a reception hall, at the side of which was a glass booth. A man sat behind a desk in this booth, a telephone beside him, a newspaper spread out before him.

Yes, he was expecting them. He gestured to a row of seats against the wall; if they would care to sit there for a few minutes, a doctor would be with them shortly. They waited ten minutes or so before the doctor arrived. He walked towards them, holding out a hand, initially towards Gerald and then, as if noticing her for the first time, to La.

'I am the daughter-in-law,' said La. 'I am married to Monsieur Stone.' Her French was rusty, but good enough for the present task.

The doctor appeared confused. 'But, Madame . . .'

'We are in the process of divorcing one another,' said La.

He understood. 'My apologies. I was not aware.'

'There is no reason why you should have known,' said La. She paused. 'Is . . . is Madame here?'

The doctor shook his head. 'She said that she would return later. I think she knew that you were coming.'

La looked at him. 'Can you tell us what the position is?'

'What does he say?' Gerald interjected.

'I'm asking him now. I'll tell you.'

The doctor invited them to sit down again. He drew up a chair and sat facing them. 'I'm afraid that the situation is grave,' he began. 'The coma is profound and his breathing is becoming very laboured. I do not think that he will recover consciousness. I am very sorry to have to tell you this.'

Gerald leaned forward. 'No hope?' he said.

La looked down; Gerald knew.

'I can escort you to his room,' said the doctor. 'In these cases there are things that one might wish to say. Sometimes the patient hears, you know.'

They followed the doctor along a corridor, then up a staircase that turned back upon itself.

'Here,' said the doctor, gesturing to a half-open door. 'I will return later. There is no hurry.'

They stood in uncertainty until La pushed the door open and led the way in. Gerald moved past her to the top of the bed. He reached for Richard's hand and held it. La felt the tears brim in her eyes and wiped them away. She looked at Richard's face. He was simply sleeping; it was that deceptive. The antechamber of death, she thought; the sleep that will become death.

Gerald muttered something and she looked away, wondering whether she should leave him there alone with his son in this final farewell.

'I'll wait outside,' she said. But Gerald shook his head and then bent down, awkwardly, to kiss his son. He replaced the hand on the counterpane.

'I shall be in the corridor,' he whispered, turning away.

La stood beside the bed. She looked at the bandage that was wound round the top part of Richard's head. There was a dressing underneath, to the side, and blood had seeped through, had turned black. She looked at his eyelids; if there was consciousness within, if he was merely sleeping, there would be movement; the skin was taut and still.

What should she say? What did one say to the dying in their beds? *It's a fine day outside; we saw people on the benches, under the trees, enjoying the autumn sun. The trip from England was smooth; just a little rough in the early morning. I am enjoying living in Suffolk. I am lonely without you.*

Instead, she moved closer and sat on the edge of the bed, in silence. She took his hand. It was warm to the touch, but it was as though there were no muscles controlling it, just passive flesh and bone. That hand had caressed her; that hand had placed a ring upon her finger. She remembered that now.

'I'm so sorry, Richard. I'm so sorry.'

A sound came from his lips. She looked up sharply, but it was just breathing; faint breathing, an almost imperceptible movement of air.

'I have come to tell you that I forgive you, my darling.'

She waited for a response, but what did she expect? Some sign, perhaps, that he had heard, that he had understood. But there was nothing.

She stood up. She felt as she had on the day, shortly after her thirteenth birthday, when she had been taken to the bishop for confirmation. She thought that the experience of that oiled finger making the sign of the cross on her brow would change her, that she would feel herself transformed, filled with the inrush of some sort of spirit. But she had not. There had been no rush of the Holy Spirit, no roaring as of a waterfall, nothing; just the face of the bishop, who had cut himself shaving that morning, a nick on the chin. Her words were unheard. But she had bestowed her forgiveness upon him and, as she left the room, she thought, You can be forgiven without knowing it, and for the forgiver it does not matter that the recipient is unaware; just as one may be loved by another without ever knowing it.

A different taxi driver drove them back from the hospital. The one who had taken them there had been taciturn; this one was conversational.

'So you are going back to England? That is very wise. We are in greater danger here in France, as you no doubt know. You see that road over there, that one? That leads to the cavalry stables. They have turned the horses out of their stalls to accommodate the animals from the Paris Zoo. They have evacuated the animals from the zoo up in Paris because they know that the Germans will be coming. Or German aeroplanes, rather. Paris will be destroyed. They are trying to save the animals, even if they cannot save the people.

'Your king is still there in London, I believe. Well, you tell *monsieur le roi* that if he had any sense he would be out of London. And get the animals out of London Zoo until the fighting is over.'

At the harbour Gerald seemed strangely composed. La looked at him anxiously as they boarded the ship. 'Are you sure you are all right?' she enquired. 'Are you sure you want to travel?'

He was adamant. He had accompanied her to France and he would see her back safely. He went to his cabin, but only after he had seen La to hers. Then, each alone in their different forms of sorrow, they began the crossing.

THE FOLLOWING MORNING, shortly before twelve, the ship's engines stopped. They were four hours' steaming from Southampton and the skies had clouded over. The colour of the sea had changed, silver darkening into a grey-green, but it was calm and there was no other shipping to be seen. Some of the passengers had come up on deck, and an off-duty member of the crew leaned over the railing, watching the wavelets below lap against the ship; there was clearly no emergency.

The captain's voice came over the loudspeakers. 'This is the captain speaking. I am very sorry to tell you that the radio room earlier today received a message from shore telling us the Prime Minister has addressed the nation. War has been declared on Germany. That is all we have heard.'

After he had spoken, there was a short pause before the engines were started and they got under way again. La was standing near the starboard lifeboats. She put her hand against one of them; the stanchions holding it were rusted. She wondered whether these ill-kept lifeboats could be released, if someone attacked them now. War. It was what people had feared for so long, like a brewing thunderstorm. Why had those who remembered the last time, and all its horrors, not risen up and shouted at the politicians, made them listen: *Never again?* War.

She felt a cloying, leaden dread. Whether the war was businesslike and swift, or hopelessly drawn out, young men would lose their lives in their tens of thousands, their millions, perhaps. It was happening; in a dreadful form of slow motion, it was happening. And this time, she feared, it would not be possible to hide away from it.

For the rest of the voyage and on the train from Southampton, La did her best to comfort Gerald. He moved between silence and talkativeness, bringing up memories of Richard, sobbing occasionally, covering his face.

She travelled with him as far as London, where they said their farewells on a station platform within earshot of a newspaper man calling out, 'News from the war.'

'There can't be anything,' said Gerald. 'Not yet.'

'It won't last long,' said La. 'There'll be peace.' He was grieving already for his son. She did not want him to have to worry about the war.

'No, there won't,' Gerald said.

LA RETURNED to Suffolk. From the train window she saw that everything was normal: the crops were being brought in; boys leaned over bridges to watch the train go by. In a taxi from the station, Mr Granger gave her his views on the situation.

'They'll sort Hitler out quickly enough,' he said. 'The War Office. The generals. They've never let us down.'

La was silent. 'They're very strong,' she said. 'The other side. They've been pouring money into armaments.'

'We'll be all right,' said Mr Granger. 'Look at the Spanish. Look at Napoleon. Look at the Kaiser. We dealt with them all. Sent them packing.'

He helped her with her luggage and then left. As she opened the front door, La saw the telegram that must have been sent shortly after she had left Gerald in London. He must have heard within minutes of his arrival home. She knew what it would say and so she did not open it, but placed it on the kitchen table, from where it stared at her, daring her to open it. She went into the dining room and wound up her gramophone. She chose Bach's Mass in B Minor, but only played one side of the first record. She moved to Mozart, because he had the greatest healing power. The music reminded her: love and loss were inextricably linked. This world was a world of suffering; music helped to make that suffering bearable. She listened intently, and then, as the record came to its end and the needle scraped against the last swirling grooves, she rose to her feet and lifted the arm of the gramophone and let the turntable spin round until its spring unwound completely.

PART TWO

SIX

Now they had a war to fight, La wondered whether she should get back to London and volunteer. There were plenty of things for women to do: she had friends who were in the Wrens and the Women's Auxiliary Air Force; another drove an ambulance in Liverpool. Everybody, it seemed, could find war work—*should* find war work.

In the February after the outbreak of war La visited a recruiting office in Cambridge, where she was interviewed by a carefully groomed major. His hands, she noticed, were small. 'You are a widow, I see.'

She was not used to being called that and hesitated before nodding. Did the army and the air force have anything against widows? La studied the major. He was a man in his forties, spruce and handsome in an asexual sort of way. Men in uniform may have interested some women, but they had never meant anything to La. Uniforms destroyed individuality, she thought. Their characterless maleness was of no interest to her.

'I'm sorry,' the major said. 'You have lost your husband very young.'

'Thank you. And, of course, being by myself now means that I can be flexible in the work I undertake.'

'Yes. Naturally.' He paused, then spoke; but not to La, more to himself, as if reviewing possibilities. 'We shall need more nurses. You would have to train . . . and, well, they're taking single girls first. Young women. Eighteen or so.'

'I see.'

'I suppose that it's something to do with being able to train an eighteen-year-old more easily. Nurse training is very strict. Very demanding.'

La folded her hands. 'I have a degree,' she said. 'I am a graduate of the university.' She said this because she felt that she was every bit as trainable, surely, as an eighteen-year-old fresh out of school.

The major lowered his eyes and she realised that an unpromoted major in this unglamorous work, at the tail end of a career, would not have a degree. 'Which university?' he asked. He spoke in an offhand manner—as if he did not really expect, or want, an answer.

La looked out of the window. She could see the spires of King's College from where she sat; if he turned, he could too.

'The one behind you,' she said, and smiled.

He did not seem to hear her answer. 'I note from your address that you live in the country, Mrs Stone.' He articulated his words carefully. 'We shall need people to work on farms. You will have noticed the introduction of rationing of bacon and butter. Sooner or later the authorities will have no alternative but to ration everything. We have to import so much.'

La was silent. War was not just the movement of troops, of tanks; it was the cutting of coal, the tilling of fields, the boxing of munitions . . .

'You think I should work on the land?'

The major nodded. 'Suffolk is a richer county than people imagine. I've always said that. Reasonable soil. Rich clay.' He reached into a drawer and took out a blue folder. 'I have a form here which I shall pass on to the Women's Land Army. They know where the need is. When spring comes, they will be crying out for people—especially if more young men join up.'

He gave her the form and she filled it in, there and then, leaning on the uneven surface of his metal desk. He watched her as she wrote, but his eyes moved away when she looked up.

She finished filling in the form and gave it to the major. The section on experience was thin: she had written *gardening*, and left it at that. As she handed the form back to him, she asked, 'Do you think we'll win this?'

She could see the effect of her question on him. He stiffened. 'Of course. There is no question about it.'

'I am not defeatist,' said La. 'But I'm concerned. The ease with which the Germans have overtaken Poland—'

'Aided by their Russian allies,' interjected the major.

'Germany seems so strong. They have so many more tanks and planes than we do.'

The major looked at La pityingly. 'I wouldn't worry unduly about these things, Mrs Stone. We have the General Staff to do our worrying for us.' He paused. 'And as Voltaire said, "*Il faut cultiver son jardin*". One must cultivate one's garden.' He held her gaze.

IT WAS NOT until April that La was contacted by an official of the Women's Land Army. They had heard she was available for work, and that she had offered to work without pay. They could arrange something, they said: an elderly farmer in her area was having difficulty coping with his chickens after the young man who had been helping him had joined up. The farmer's arthritis was getting worse. It would be a few hours a day of feeding the birds and cleaning out the coops, and the farm could be reached by bicycle from her home. Would she do it?

La telephoned the official and accepted. She went to tell Mrs Agg. She was curious to find out if her neighbour knew the farmer for whom she would be working. Madder's Farm was only about four miles away.

Mrs Agg smiled. 'Henry Madder,' she said. 'He's a kind man. And all his difficulties.'

La raised an eyebrow. 'I heard that he had arthritis. Is there something else?' She was talking to Mrs Agg outside the farmhouse kitchen. A basket of damp laundry was at Mrs Agg's feet and she reached into this to extract a pair of trousers to hang out on the washing line. They were Agg's trousers; La had seen him in them; grey trousers with large outside pockets.

'I wasn't talking about his health,' said Mrs Agg. 'Though it's true he has arthritis. I was talking about the business with his son, and with his wife after that. It was all because of the son that Helen Madder went, I think.'

La waited for her to explain. From the trousers, only half wrung, fell a few small drops of water.

'It all started when Henry Madder ran over his young son,' said Mrs Agg. 'In his cart. He still has a cart and an old Percheron to pull it. The boy was about five or six, as I recall. He was doing something or other in the farmyard and Henry just did not see him. The wheel crushed his skull.

'Helen Madder would not forgive him. She turned quiet on him, staying inside, keeping him out of her room, locking herself away. Then, about six months after the tragedy, she put on her fanciest dress and went off to Bury to get herself a man. She found one soon enough, and people talked. Henry knew, but put up with it because he thought that the boy's death had been his fault. It wasn't, but nobody could persuade him otherwise. He thought that he deserved the punishment that she was doling out to him.

'Then she went off altogether and never came back. They say that she moved to Ipswich, but there were those who saw her in Newmarket—with the new man, who was some sort of market trader. Henry pretty much stopped talking to people after that. Stopped going to church. Stopped going to the pub. So that's Henry Madder—a good man ruined by one little bit of carelessness. If he had moved his head just a few inches, just for a moment, he would have seen his boy and the accident wouldn't have taken place. But that's the same for everything, isn't it? If things were just a little bit different, then life would have worked out differently.

'Take that Mr Hitler. Just think what would have happened had his mother dropped him when she picked him up for his feed. And he had hit his head on the floor. Or had he been strangled by the cord when he was born. What a difference. We wouldn't be at war as we are right now. Wouldn't be in this pickle. Have you thought of that?'

La had not, and shook her head. 'There could have been somebody else.'

'Other than Hitler? Somebody other than Hitler?'

'Yes. There could have been somebody else who would have had the same idea of whipping people up; who had the same madness within them. People are the products of their time, Mrs Agg.'

Mrs Agg glanced at her.

'What I mean, Mrs Agg, is that the times throw up their man. If there hadn't been a Nelson, there would have been another sailor like him. There would have been plenty of small, nasty people like Hitler, even if he had never existed.'

She let Mrs Agg think about this as the farmer's wife attached several pairs of socks to the line with large wooden clothespegs. She returned, though, to the subject of Madder's Farm. 'Who was he, this boy who was helping him, the boy whose job I'm taking on?'

Mrs Agg, who had been holding a clothespeg in her mouth while she attended to the socks, took the peg out of her mouth to answer. 'A really nice boy called Neil. The son of Mrs Howarth who used to work in the post office. He went off and volunteered. That's what all young men want to do.'

La thought for a moment. All young men? What about Lennie?

Mrs Agg glanced at her. It seemed she had guessed what La was thinking. 'Lennie can't,' she said. 'Or, rather, I don't think he should. Lennie's a loner. He doesn't . . .' She left the sentence unfinished, reaching for the last of her washing. Then, quietly, she said, 'Lennie doesn't trouble you, I hope.'

La looked up at the sky. After the incident in the garden, Lennie had not troubled her. In fact, she could barely remember when she'd last seen him.

'Lennie doesn't trouble me, Mrs Agg. You needn't worry.'

Mrs Agg finished hanging up the rest of the washing and dried her hands on her apron. 'Good. You see, Mrs Stone . . . You see, Lennie is not all that easy. A lot of men aren't. But we get by.' She turned and smiled at La. 'Which is all that we can hope for in this life, don't you think? To get by?'

That was quite true, thought La. In a way, all our human systems, our culture, music, literature, painting—all of that—was effectively an attempt to make life more bearable, to enable us to get by. She got by. She had got by, in this quiet corner of England, for two years now, and was happy enough. She had stopped thinking of Richard every day, and she found it harder to bring up a mental image of him. There was a face, certainly, but it was fading, as an old photograph will fade. She was getting by quite well without him. And the country was trying to get by in the face of a terrifying nightmare that was about to get much more vivid and more frightening.

'They're coming,' said the butcher in the village. 'They're coming over, Mrs Stone. God help us, so He must.'

'There's the RAF,' said La. 'They'll have to get past them.'

'Have you seen the boys they're using?' asked the butcher. There was a base nearby, at Stradishall, used for bombers. 'Some of them are not shaving yet.'

'Boys have quick reactions,' said La. It was a glib remark, of the sort that came from inner conviction; but La felt despair. The strutting demagogue, with his insane shouting, had fixed his eyes on them, and he was coming.

POOR HENRY MADDER, she thought; look at him. His hands were twisted, as if they had been placed in a vice and wrenched out of true. And he could not flex his knees, which seemed to have been locked at an angle, giving him a curious, deliberate-looking gait, as if he were walking through a bed of treacle. But he brushed off La's concern impatiently.

'Don't worry about me,' he said. 'As long as I can hook Tommy up to the plough, I'm all right. I'm not an old man yet.'

He was somewhere in his forties, La thought, but the crippling disease had aged him prematurely.

'I could do more here,' she said. 'It's much easier than I thought, looking after your chickens. There must be other things.'

He shook his head. 'I have to do something and they've promised me a man, full-time.' He smiled. 'Heaven knows when that will be or what I'll get. A chap let out of prison on condition that he works on the land maybe. Billy Stevens got somebody like that. A thief from London.'

La's work was light. The chickens were kept on the edge of a field in two large coops. These were elongated, flimsily built structures with tin roofs. Inside there were rows of nesting boxes and high perches on which the hens could take refuge at night from predators. There was also a fence that had been designed to protect the birds from the fox, but he could burrow his way under that, as the wire did not always reach far enough down. One of La's jobs was to pick up the feathers where the fox had made a kill; feathers that told the story of the sharp and one-sided little conflict. For La it was like attending the scene of a crime—the feathers on the ground, the hens clucking away in disapproval of what had happened, the place where the fox had pushed up the fence wire. There was always only one suspect.

La made her way up to Madder's Farm shortly after breakfast every day. She had to cycle there; fuel was in short supply and she wanted to husband the small amount she could get. Cycling kept her fit, and it was pleasant enough, too, in the mild April weather; of course, it would be different in winter, with those dark mornings and the cold wind, which, in that part of England, swept straight across the North Sea from Siberia. I shall be tougher then, she told herself, and if the war was over, then she would no longer have to work on Madder's Farm and could lie in bed on winter's mornings. War did not last for ever; one hundred years at the most.

On arrival at the farm she reported to Henry, if he was in the farmyard, or went directly about her duties, if he was not. She collected the eggs first, making her way along the nesting boxes, taking out the eggs and placing them carefully in baskets. If a hen was still in the box, she would feel under her for eggs, among the soft belly feathers, warm and downy, and the hens would occasionally peck at her, quite hard. She started to use an old pair of gardening gloves that she had found in the house; the hens ineffectively pecked at the leather and La would blow in their faces to distract them.

She cleaned the floor and changed the straw in the nesting boxes. Then she filled a wheelbarrow with feed and distributed that among the brood.

Henry Madder said, 'You've taken to this like a duck to water.'

'Chicken,' she said.

He smiled. 'They said you didn't want any pay. Is that correct?'

'I have enough to live on,' La said. 'I have more than enough. If they don't pay me, then the money can go to other Land Army workers.'

'You're the type who'll win this war for us,' he said. He looked up at the sky, and La followed his gaze. It was broad, limitless, unclouded now; the wide sky of East Anglia.

She took her leave and began the cycle back. She reached home at about half past eleven every morning, her labours done. Then she read, and worked in the garden. She had started to sew, thinking it might be useful; she could make things for people when clothing became scarce. Everything would become scarce, she thought: soap, clothing, shoes. Hitler wanted to starve them into submission, and they would have to grub around, turning to every little bit of earth to coax food from it. She looked at her lawn. She would dig it up and plant potatoes. It could yield sacks of potatoes that would see her through the winter, if supplies of everything dried up.

Henry Madder gave her eggs, which she turned into omelettes. There were chives in the garden and these were chopped up to add flavour. She ate the omelettes at her kitchen table, a glass of cider beside her plate. She would have liked to talk to somebody, but the house was empty.

Occasionally, after one of her lonely suppers, La would retrieve the flute that she kept in a drawer in her bureau. She had rarely played the instrument since leaving Cambridge, and her technique had suffered. But she could still manage most of the pieces in a large book of flute music she had found in a secondhand bookshop near the British Museum: Byrd, Morley, Tallis.

Music was her refuge. There was madness abroad, an insanity of killing and cruelty that defied understanding—unless one took the view that this violence had always been there and had merely been masked by a veneer of civilisation. La thought that music disproved this. Reason, beauty, harmony: these were ultimately more real and powerful than any of the demons unleashed by dictators. But she feared that here in the country she was losing touch with these values—that she would forget if she did not go back.

One evening she reached a decision. She would return to London where the house in Maida Vale could be reclaimed from its tenant. She would take up with her old friends and bring an end to this unnatural life of seclusion.

She wanted company; she wanted to talk to somebody about books, about music. There were people in Bury, of course, with whom she had interests in common, but that was Bury, and there was no petrol to go there for purely social purposes. Cambridge would have been even better, but was further away, and people who went back there ended up like Dr Price.

She telephoned Valerie. 'I want to come back to London,' she said.

There was silence at the other end of the line. Then, 'Are you mad, La? Anybody with any sense is trying to get *out* of London. Have you heard of the Luftwaffe down there in Suffolk?'

La said nothing.

'The point is,' Valerie continued, 'the point is that this is a very different city from the one you left.'

La understood that places changed. 'I know that. I don't expect it to be the same. I've changed.'

Valerie laughed dismissively. 'I don't think you're grasping what I want to say. People are frightened, La. Anybody who is in a position to leave is thinking about it. They deny it, of course, but then everybody's trying to look brave. We have to, because if we start to show what we really feel the whole place will come to a grinding halt. London is not the place to be.'

It was hard to argue against such a warning, and La did not. Their conversation continued briefly and without much understanding; it seemed to La that they now lived in different worlds.

SEVEN

At frequent intervals, La heard the drone of engines as a flight of bombers from the nearby base at Stradishall crossed the sky. Like everyone else, she had studied the outlines printed in the newspapers so that she could distinguish plane from plane, but it was hard to tell when they were little more than black dots against the white of the clouds. Spitfires, of course, were easily recognised, and over that summer and into the autumn she looked out for them. The battle that would determine the course of the war had begun, everyone knew that. And the Spitfire, with its stubby wings and its long nose, would, along with the Hurricane, determine the fate of the country—and the rest of the world. They had to win this part of the struggle; if Britain fell, then Europe was lost to a devouring evil that would not stop.

One day, she saw a Spitfire coming in from the coast. The main battle was being fought further to the south, but planes would sometimes chase raiders up over the North Sea until they reached the limit of their range and had to make for home. This one was flying low and was trailing smoke, limping across the sky to refuge at Stradishall. She watched it getting lower and lower, and she thought of the pilot within. He would be twenty, perhaps even younger, a young man struggling to keep his wounded aircraft airborne, gasping for breath against the fumes from his burning plane. And then the Spitfire was gone, vanished behind distant trees, and she did not know what had happened.

An air-force officer drove up to the house one Saturday afternoon and parked his small green open-topped car in the driveway.

'I'm very sorry turning up out of the blue,' he said when La opened the door to him. 'I'm Tim Honey. I'm a friend of your cousin Lilly. She said that I should call on you if I was in the area.'

La remembered that Lilly was working in Whitehall and met officers in the course of her work. She looked at the man standing on her doorstep. He was a few years older than she was, in his mid-thirties and slightly plump. She invited him in. 'I don't have any coffee,' she said. 'But I have some tea.'

Tim smiled, and fished in one of the pockets of his jacket. 'I anticipated that,' he said, drawing out a small packet. 'This is Jamaican, believe it or not. I don't know how we got it at the base.' He laughed. 'It's amazing what you find in the back of a bomber once you begin to unpack it.'

She took the packet and led the way into the kitchen. 'Lilly,' she said.

'Yes, dear Lilly. She says she hasn't seen you for ages.'

'No. I moved down here a few years ago, before the war started.' She did not want him to think that she had fled from London.

He nodded. He was looking about the kitchen, appraisingly.

'I've got everything I need in this house,' said La. 'It's quite comfortable.'

'Yes. It looks it.' He turned towards the window. 'They look after us pretty well at the base. We have a very good mess—all the papers and magazines and jolly good Suffolk beers. Everything we need, really.'

There was a silence. Except company, thought La. Except women. Home cooking. Love.

'I'm married,' Tim went on. 'Four years ago. And I never thought that this would blow up and I'd find myself at one end of the country and Joyce at the other end. She's in Cardiff, staying with an aunt for the duration. It's safer there, I think, than where we lived in Kent. In Maidstone.'

'You must miss her.'

'Yes, I do. Awfully. But think of all those chaps who have been sent overseas. At least I can go down for the occasional weekend.'

The smell of coffee began to pervade. 'We can drink our coffee in here,' said La. 'There's a drawing room of sorts, but it's more comfortable in here.'

They talked. Tim told her about what he had done before the war and what he did now, approximately. 'I shouldn't say exactly,' he said. 'Not that I imagine you're a German spy, but you know the rules. Suffice it to say that I sit behind a desk all day and talk on the telephone, telling other people what we want. I'm in charge of supplies. Not that I should probably tell you that. Do you know anywhere where I could get some supplies of aviation fuel?'

La laughed. 'Or Jamaican coffee?'

'We're all right for that. Fuel is the big thing. I live in fear of what might happen if they really get going on despatching our tankers to the bottom of the ocean with their U-boats. What then? You can't fight a battle for control of the skies if your planes can't take off.'

They talked about what La was doing. She told him about the chickens, and her battle against the fox.

'Jerry's a fox,' said Tim. 'Trying to get in under the chicken wire. And Goering's the biggest fox of all.'

Her own war was so small by comparison with his: a few eggs added to the national supply, that was all. She told him about Henry Madder and of his determination to continue farming, in spite of his arthritis.

'They've been promising him somebody,' she said, 'but he must be at the bottom of the list. A smallish farm, tucked away out of sight. The bigger places will be getting whoever becomes available.'

Tim frowned. 'I know how he must feel. I have to ask for all sorts of things and often they just ignore your requests. They tell you that you'll get things shortly, but it's never like that.' He paused. 'The man'd be paid?'

'I assume so,' said La. 'I'm not, but I said that I didn't need to be. Henry paid the boy who helped him. And he's got a cottage on the farm that's empty. The boy stayed there.'

Tim looked up at the ceiling. 'I might know somebody.'

'To work?'

He nodded. 'Yes. We've got a Polish chap. Feliks Dabrowski. We call him Dab for short. He's had a pretty frustrating war. He got out to Romania and then to France. They set up something called the Groupe de Chasse Polonaise there and gave them worse than useless planes. The Jerries shot them out of the sky. Dab was badly hurt—lost the use of an eye, in fact, although it looks almost normal to me. But he's blind as a bat on that side.'

La sighed. 'Poor man. But he's alive. Which is something these days.'

'Indeed. You know how many we've lost in just one of our squadrons . . .' He stopped himself. 'Sorry, I shouldn't talk about that.'

She was not sure what to say. 'Your men are so brave.'

Tim shook his head. 'No, they aren't. Well, maybe some are, but most of us are just very ordinary and scared stiff half the time. When I was on active flying duty I remember shaking when I got out of the cockpit at the end of a sortie. I knew that I had defied the odds and that they would catch up with me sooner or later. And I was not at all brave about it. Nightmares. Sweating. Stomach turning to water. I had all of that.'

He reached for his coffee cup and drained it. 'But this chap Dab I was talking about. He pitched up when the Poles started to get out of France. One of our medical officers looked after him—tried to do something about his eye, but couldn't. So there was no chance of any more flying for him. He had nowhere to go, so we gave him maintenance duties on the base. But you can't let a chap with one eye tinker with the planes . . .'

'You think that he might work for Henry Madder?'

'Well, it would suit both of them, don't you think? Dab would get a bit of money, and presumably his rations, and a roof over his head.'

La shrugged. 'I could ask Henry.'

Tim stood up and reached for his cap. 'Let me do that,' he said. 'Tell me how to get there and I'll go and have a word with him.' He started to leave, but stopped when he saw La's flute on the kitchen dresser. 'You play?'

'A bit. I played in a quartet when I was in Cambridge. And you?'

'As a matter of fact,' said Tim, 'I was a very indifferent trumpet player in my day.'

La smiled. 'We could hardly play together. The flute, I'm afraid, is a rather quiet instrument.'

'We have chaps at the base who would love to play in a band,' said Tim. 'One of them came to see me the other day and asked whether I could get hold of instruments. I ask you! I've got my hands full enough as it is.'

La said nothing. It had occurred to her that she might be able to do something. The idea came suddenly, as perfectly formed ideas sometimes do. She would start an orchestra. She would get instruments for the men at the base who wanted them. She would find people in Bury who would join in. People needed something to keep their spirits up.

'What if I got hold of some instruments?' she asked Tim. 'Would your men be able to come and play music with some locals? People from Bury, people from round here—if I found any who could play?'

Tim hesitated. 'It would depend. Most of them can't get away very much. And transport is always a problem.'

'Once every two weeks?' said La. 'Or even once a month?'

'Once a month would be more likely.' Tim scratched the back of his neck. 'I'll ask the CO.'

'Call it morale-boosting,' said La. 'That works, doesn't it?'

Again he hesitated before replying. 'Yes. It does. And this seems like a good idea. La's Orchestra. How about that?'

'And you'll be in the trumpet section?' asked La.

'I thought you would never ask,' Tim said. 'Yes. You can sign me up.'

IT WAS RAINING when La cycled over to the farm the next morning. She had not expected the rain and was unprepared for it. By the time she cycled into the farmyard, she was soaked, her hair across her forehead in thin, wet ropes, her blouse clinging uncomfortably to her skin.

Henry Madder, standing in the yard in his heavy waterproof jacket, was amused. 'You look a sight. Like a mouse washed down the drainpipe.'

La leaned her bicycle against the side of the house. 'Thank you,' she said. 'It's nice to start the day with a compliment.'

'No compliments on a farm.'

'So I'm discovering.'

He smiled. 'Come inside and dry off. I'll get you a towel, and you can have a hot bath if you like. I'll stoke up the fire.'

She went with him into the kitchen. A kettle stood on the range, steam emerging from the spout in wisps. While he fetched her a towel, La warmed her hands against the range; the rain had been warm, and there had been no wind with it; so she did not feel too cold.

'Don't bother,' she shouted after Henry. 'I'm sure I'll dry quickly enough.'

But he was back in the kitchen bearing a towel. He handed it to her. 'I had a visitor yesterday,' he said. 'Your friend, Squadron Leader Honey.'

'I only met him yesterday,' said La. 'I can hardly call him a friend yet.'

'He said he knew your cousin,' Henry went on. 'Not that it matters. The point is: he's got somebody to help us. He's coming tomorrow.'

La smiled. 'The man they call Dab?'

'Feliks something or other,' said Henry. 'Dab comes into it. A Polish airman. Aged thirty-four. He told me that these Poles are real characters. Our boys are always a bit afraid that they'll do something silly.'

'I'm sure that he'll do nothing silly on the farm,' said La. 'Tractors and Spitfires are rather different, don't you think?'

Henry Madder sat down at the other side of the table. He watched La drying herself on the towel. 'Will you be going?' he asked suddenly.

La did not understand. 'Going where?'

'Leaving the farm? Stopping work.'

La laid aside the towel. 'Why would I want to stop doing the chickens? Because of this Pole? I want to carry on, if it's all right with you.'

It was clear that Henry was relieved. 'Yes. Yes. There are plenty of other things for him to do,' he said. 'And the hens are used to you, aren't they?'

La greeted this with laughter. 'Can they tell us one from another?'

'Hens know,' said Henry. 'Hens feel comfortable with a woman. They were upset when Helen . . .' He broke off. La looked up, and saw him turn his face away. It was the first time she'd heard him mention his wife.

'When she left you?'

'Yes. When she left, the hens went off their lay. They missed her.'

La reached for the towel again. 'You mustn't blame yourself,' she said quietly. 'Accidents happen, and then people look around for somebody to blame. It's human nature, I suppose, but it's not very helpful.'

He was watching her intently. 'Do you think so?'

'Of course I do. You shouldn't let yourself be tormented by it.'

He thought about this for a moment, then said, 'You can't undo what's done. But I still feel bad. How could I not feel bad?'

'By understanding that it was not your fault.'

He looked away. 'She didn't think that. She thought it was my fault.'

'Perhaps she felt guilty herself. And if she did, then one of the ways in which she might deal with that would be to blame you.'

He stood up from the table. 'Maybe,' he said. 'Maybe not. But I have to go out and look at a fence. And the hens will be waiting for you.'

La followed his example and rose from the table. She decided to change the subject. 'Will the new man live in the cottage?'

'Yes. I'm getting it ready today.'

'I'll do that,' La offered. 'After I've done the chickens.'

IT WAS DARK inside the cottage. The curtains in the sitting room—the room one entered directly from the front door—had been drawn closed and there was no light from any source other than the door. La moved across the room and drew the curtains back. The cottage was very small: the sitting room, furnished with two easy chairs over which stained, threadbare rugs had been thrown; the kitchen, where there was a small dining table; and a tiny single bedroom. There was no bath, just a tin tub that had been stacked against the wall of the bedroom. A large china ewer stood beside the tub.

La looked about her for a switch to turn on a light; there was little natural sunlight in any of the rooms. But there were no switches anywhere, and then she noticed the oil lamp on the kitchen table, and the saucer in which a half-used candle still stood, a pool of hardened melted wax at its base.

For the rest of that morning she swept, scrubbed and polished. She cleaned out the tub, swept the ashes out of the fireplace in the sitting room and washed the black stains the soot had created from the lino. She lifted the coir mattress in the bedroom and shook it vigorously; fine dust flew up in small clouds, making her cough. Henry had followed her in with sheets and blankets, which she now put on the bed. A patchwork counterpane, which had been draped over a chair, fitted the bed exactly. With that in place, and with the floor swept, the bedroom looked inhabitable.

Henry returned later, bringing La a mug of tea. 'You've made it very nice for him, La,' he said.

'He's far from home,' said La. 'We need to make it look homely.'

Henry was silent. 'It could happen to us, I suppose. We could be uprooted. Chucked out of our homes—if they invade.'

'Yes,' said La.

'I wish I could get out there and take a pot shot at them,' said Henry. 'I feel useless.'

'You're doing more than enough as it is,' said La. 'Our boys have to eat.'

'Oh, I know,' said Henry. 'But it's not the same.'

LA DID NOT SLEEP well that night. Somewhere in the small hours she was woken by the sound of aircraft overhead. She lay in bed thinking, This is what people hear when bombers come. And it could be that this plane was a German plane, laden with bombs that it could drop at any moment; bomber crews did that—if they could not find their target, they would drop the bombs anywhere—but the plane headed off.

She imagined the men in the plane, sitting there in their darkened cabins, going about their business of destruction. They would have no qualms, of course, because they would know the justice of their cause—whichever side they were on. She tried to picture German fliers. What sort of faces would they have? The same as ours, of course.

But these men were ruthless; they were the men who flew the wailing Stukas that strafed the columns of refugees—they were not men like Tim Honey. She had read an account of a British airman who witnessed German pilots shooting men who were floating down by parachute: they shot them in cold blood, riddling their bodies with the very ammunition they used to down aircraft; nobody could stand a chance against that. They shot prisoners, too, and civilians in reprisal for attacks on occupying forces. She could bring herself to hate these strutting scions of the Master Race.

She lay in bed thinking of what the war was doing to people. By six o'clock she realised that she had not slept since half past two, and now it would be too late. If she went back to sleep now—and she was feeling drowsy enough for that—then she might sleep in late, and she could not keep the chickens waiting. Anyway, this was the day on which the Pole arrived.

After breakfast, La set out for the farm. Yesterday's clouds had been blown away by a change in the wind, and the morning sky was high and open. This was good weather for bombers in search of targets, but it would also be good news for the RAF, who liked a sun out of which to swoop. Things were getting worse now. The battle was intense. Every day, almost without letup, flights of marauders came in, wave upon wave of them. Every day the RAF committed virtually all its men and machines to the air in desperate sorties, one after the other, mercilessly.

And here, in spite of all that was happening, was a summer morning, with ripening ears of wheat, of barley, swaying in the wind, with a man walking a dog alongside a hedgerow . . .

She did not see the car until it was upon her. She had plenty of time to stop, though, to dismount and pull her bicycle over to the side; the road was too narrow there for both of them and cycles gave way to motor vehicles.

The driver wound down his window and inched the car forward until it was level with her.

'Early to work, I see.'

She smiled. It was Tim Honey, driving a different car. This was an official one, a dark blue Austin with a military number plate.

'I didn't recognise you. Your nice little sports car . . .'

He tapped his hand on the wheel. 'This goes with the job. I use my own for social purposes—when I can lay my hands on any petrol for it.' He jerked his head in the direction of the farm. 'I've just dropped Dab—Feliks, rather—up there. I saw the billet you'd prepared for him. Madder said it was all your work. Dab can't believe his luck.' Tim glanced at his watch. 'I mustn't linger, I'm afraid. We're very busy right now, and I'm due back on duty in half an hour. By the way . . .'

La knew what he was going to ask. 'My orchestra?'

'Yes. I spoke to those chaps I mentioned, and to a couple of others. They're very keen.'

'So you might be able to fix something up?'

'Yes. And Dab plays the flute too. He hasn't got one, but when I told him about our conversation he let slip that he used to play. He's an educated man, you know. A lot of those Poles are. You think you know them, and then you discover something extraordinary about them—that they had a big factory somewhere, or were trained as doctors, or were becoming priests when this business all started. All that sort of thing.' He sighed. 'It makes it even tougher for them, I think. To lose your country and your family and everything—position, respect and all the rest . . . Well, that can't be easy.'

'We'll try to look after him.'

Tim smiled and stretched a hand out of the window. She shook it.

LA LEANED HER BICYCLE against the wall and bent down to remove the cycle clips that she placed round her trouser legs. She wore trousers for her work on the farm; not the most glamorous of outfits, she said, but very practical: strong gaberdine trousers of worsted that she had brought with her from London. Straightening up, she saw a light in Henry Madder's kitchen, a dark room that received little sun. Even so, Henry was not one to waste electricity. The light, then, was in honour of Feliks.

She approached the back door and knocked.

'We're in here,' Henry called out. 'Come right in, La.'

When La entered the room, she saw Henry standing near the range, holding the kettle, which he was about to put on the plate. At the table, half turned round to face her, sat a man wearing a leather jacket of the sort favoured by pilots. La's first thought was that it was too warm to be wearing that, but then she saw that he had a thin, collarless shirt underneath. And below that, dark trousers, of what looked to her like thin linen. When she entered, he sprang to his feet and stood facing her.

'Dabrowski,' he said, inclining his head. 'Feliks Dabrowski.'

La moved forward. He had extended his hand towards her.

'This is my other assistant,' said Henry. 'La Stone. Saviour of the hens.'

La glanced at Feliks. He looked younger than thirty-four. Twenty-eight, perhaps. And he was definitely Slav; she could tell from the smooth cheeks and high cheekbones; it was a quite different look, an almost feminine beauty. His eyes . . . she wondered which one had been ruined.

'The left eye,' said Henry, pushing the kettle onto the plate with his twisted hand. 'Feliks was telling me he lost the sight in his left eye.'

La dropped her gaze guiltily. 'I'm sorry to hear that.'

Feliks sat down now. 'Thank you. I have become used to it. You can get by with one of most things. There are men at the base with one leg or one arm. They get by too.'

His accent was foreign, yet it was clear enough and had a soft lilt to it.

'La will show you the henhouses,' said Henry. 'Just so that you know everything that's going on. But she does all the work down there.'

Feliks looked at La and smiled. 'That will be good.'

There was a silence. La looked at the kettle. Henry's range was always slow; it would take ten minutes for the water to boil. She would have liked to stay, but had no idea what she would say.

'I'll get on with things,' she said.

Henry Madder nodded and Feliks rose to his feet again as La turned to the door. She thought, This is not a man who will be used to working on a farm. She wondered what he had been before the war. That was the extraordinary thing about what the war achieved: it transformed lives, made heroes out of the mildest of people, showed the bravery that must always have been there but merely lacked the occasion to manifest itself.

She made her way to the henhouses, where she worked for the next two hours. The fox had been active the previous night, having dug up a small section of chicken wire at the end of the run. There were feathers on the ground and, at the end of one of the henhouses, obscured by shadows, the limp body of a hen. La deduced that the fox had killed more than he needed and had been unable to carry away his second victim.

When she had finished the repairs and had fed the chickens, she picked up the dead hen and carried it back to the house. Seeing her approach, Henry came out and examined the dead fowl.

'The devil!' he said. 'He kills out of spite. What animal does that, La?'

'Cats,' said La. And then added, 'Men.'

Henry took the hen from her and shook his head. 'A fine layer, no doubt. What a waste!' He handed it back to her. 'See if he wants it. Him.' He jerked his head in the direction of the cottage. 'He looks as if he could do with feeding up. A nice chicken casserole will go down well, I suspect.'

'You take it.'

Henry shook his head. 'No, you. I need to sit down. Take it to him. He's getting himself sorted out and will be starting work after lunch. Take it.'

She left him, got on her bicycle and cycled to the cottage. Feliks must have seen her coming from the window, as he appeared at the door.

'This is for you. A fox killed it.'

He frowned. 'They are a nuisance.'

'Round here they are.'

He reached for the chicken. 'Thank you.' He looked at it, then put it down on a shelf to the side of the door. 'What do you say? Waste not . . .'

'Want not.'

'Yes. That's it.'

She turned to go.

'You are kind. People have been so kind. Everyone. The English.'

She stopped. 'Really?'

'Yes. Very kind.'

'I thought that maybe you met with . . . well, the opposite. Suspicion. Selfishness. What are you doing here? That sort of thing.'

He shook his head. 'There might be a little of that. But not usually. Usually it's kindness. The English are a kind people.'

La waited for him to say something else, but that was the end of his observations on the English national character.

'Oh well. Maybe.' She turned away again and he closed the door.

She walked back to her bicycle, which she had left by the fence, and set off on the ride home. The day had become warmer, the sun floating up the sky, painting the top of Henry Madder's wheat crop with streaks of gold. She cycled slowly, thinking. Something had happened, something within her. It was an unsettling feeling, something she had not imagined she would feel again. A mile or two down the lane, she stopped and dismounted from her bicycle by a gap in the unruly hedgerow that bordered the road. She crawled through and flopped down on a bank of grass. She looked up. The sky was quite cloudless, a singing, echoing emptiness.

This good place, this kind country, so gentle, so threatened. She lay back and closed her eyes. The strange, unsettling feeling was still with her; curiously, it made her aware of just how much she loved the piece of earth upon which she lay, that particular grass, that particular tiny patch of Suffolk.

OVER THE WEEKS that followed, La saw very little of Feliks. There was no sign of him when she arrived for work, nor when she left.

'How's he settling in?' she asked Henry Madder when he came down to the henhouses to inspect the place where La had fixed the fence.

'Just fine. He's a hard worker. Your squadron-leader friend was right.'

'He said that he was a good worker?'

Henry kicked at the fence repair to test its strength.

'Nice job, La. No, he said that he was a good man. Amounts to the same thing.' Henry kicked at the fence again. The repair held. 'Damn fox.'

La sighed. 'Poor hens. They have no idea there's a war on.' She brought the conversation back to Feliks. 'Where is he? I haven't seen him.'

Henry pointed towards the far end of the farm. 'Down there. Pott's Field. He's digging drainage. I've been meaning to do that for years.'

She saw him a few days later. Henry had asked him to cut grass for fodder; he was using a scythe and had taken his shirt off for the heat. La watched him for a few moments, and then, fastening the hen-run door, she made her way up to Henry's kitchen.

Henry was sitting at the table with an open account book before him. He looked up when La entered.

'If I had to pay you and Feliks proper wages,' he said, 'I'd be bankrupt.'

'You don't expect me to believe that, Henry,' said La. 'I think that you're one of these farmers who keeps a lot of money under his bed.'

Henry shifted in his seat. Just slightly. 'What makes you say that?'

'Oh, just a suspicion.' La moved to the sink. 'Anyway, I'd like to take Dab some water,' she said. 'It must be hot work, out there in the sun.'

'There's lemonade in the cupboard,' said Henry. 'Take a look.'

She found the large bottle and poured a glass. Then she put it on a small tray and made her way down to the field. Feliks saw her coming before she arrived, and he stopped working, leaning on his scythe, waiting for her. She gave him the lemonade and he took it and drank it in one draught. He smiled at her, as if in triumph at the short work he had made of the drink, handing her back the empty glass.

The feeling that she had experienced came back. She felt her heart thumping. Ridiculous, she thought. Ridiculous. She looked down at the ground. 'Would you like to come and have a meal at my house? Tonight?' She surprised herself. This had not been planned.

He moved his hands on the handle of the scythe. 'Yes, I would like that. You must show me how to get there. Henry says there is a bicycle . . .'

La explained and he listened. She gave him the directions and left him. Up at the house, Henry took the glass from her wordlessly and returned to the scrutiny of his account book. But then, a few moments later, he looked up and said, 'Don't go and get any silly ideas about that Pole.'

La caught her breath. 'What I do or don't do is none of your business, Henry. Thank you.'

He assumed a pained expression. 'Sorry! I was only thinking of you. Men could take advantage of you, you see.'

La's answer was cold. 'Thank you for worrying about me.'

I am not in love, she said to herself. I am finished with love.

WHEN SHE RETURNED to the house that morning, the postman had delivered a letter from Tim, written on RAF stationery.

I have spoken to the CO about your orchestra. He was sceptical at first, pointing out that there were so many comings and goings it would be difficult to have any continuity. So I persisted, because that's the way you get anything done with him. If you ask two or three times the answer is usually no, four times and he begins to think of it, and then five times and you get a yes.

He said that we could use transport to get people to your village, and that we could collect people from Bury St Edmunds and drive down to you, as long as they don't mind travelling in a truck! Once a month, though; no more, I'm afraid.

I put a sign up in the mess and on station notice boards. We've had

seven people say that they're interested and that makes eight, with me.
So all you need to do is to get the word out in Bury and then we're
ready. I'm calling it La's Orchestra, by the way. Nice name! Have you
found a conductor? Or will you do it yourself?

She smiled as she read the letter. The orchestra had been an impulsive idea on her part, and she had not imagined that it would get this far. But, well, why not? A little orchestra would entertain the players even if it never entertained anybody else. And an orchestra would certainly help morale. Orchestras played in the face of everything, as the orchestra on the *Titanic* did when it was sinking. It played. Well, we shall play while the country is fighting for its life. We shall play no matter what the enemy throws at us. They would prefer silence—so we shall answer them with music, or cacophony—it did not matter a great deal. As long as it was not silence.

She put the letter aside but brought it out that evening when she was waiting for Feliks. He had said that he would be there at seven, but it was now almost a quarter to eight. La thought it unlikely that he had forgotten, and he seemed too well-mannered to stand her up. He had lost his way, perhaps . . .

She felt uneasy, on tenterhooks, and went out into the garden to look at the rows of potatoes she had planted in a dug-up section of the lawn. The garden was almost entirely given over to vegetables now—a wartime garden in which flowers and shrubs took second place. But she could not concentrate and found herself looking anxiously down the lane for Feliks. When he eventually arrived, she felt only relief.

'I'm very sorry,' he said. 'Henry cut his finger. I had to make a bandage.'

She winced. She had seen Henry fumbling with a vegetable knife. 'I have told him that I can cut things for him,' said Feliks. 'But he is proud.'

'Yes. He does not want to be an invalid.'

He had ridden over on Henry's old bicycle and La showed him where he might stow it, then took him into the house. 'It is very beautiful,' he said, looking about him. 'These houses in England are so peaceful.'

She led him into the sitting room. When she had first come to the house, she had found a bottle of Gerald's expensive sherry, which she now opened. She poured a small glass for each of them and passed one to him. He raised it politely, bowing slightly in her direction. The gesture seemed to her to be very formal, almost Prussian. This was an educated man, a member of a landed family, for all she knew. Many of the Poles in their air force were from that sector of society, she had heard.

While they drank the sherry, she asked him about his English. He had studied it at university level, he said. English and Polish literature. He told her that when the war was over, if Poland was still there, he would return to the university and complete the doctorate he had embarked upon.

She read him the letter from Tim. 'He said that you play the flute. He thought you would be able to play in our little orchestra.'

Feliks was self-deprecating. 'Me? I am not good enough for an orchestra.'

'Nobody in this orchestra will be very good,' she assured him.

'Even so, I have no flute. I'm sorry. I cannot.'

He moved the conversation on to another subject and then they went through to the kitchen, where she had laid a gingham tablecloth on the table. She had made a salad using lettuce and radishes grown in her garden, and a sausage and sultana casserole.

After the meal he looked at his watch. 'I will have to go now.'

'Yes, of course.'

There was still some light left in the sky, and she went into the garden with him and watched him cycle off, waving as he turned out of her drive and onto the lane. She stood for a moment, but he did not look back.

In the kitchen, the gingham tablecloth brought a touch of colour, a splash of red, that cheered the place up, but the house seemed empty now that Feliks had gone, and for her part La felt ill-at-ease. She locked the back door and went into the sitting room, where she listened to a late news bulletin on the wireless in a halfhearted way, before switching off.

She wondered what he thought of her. It was difficult to read him, and she feared that his politeness was just that and no more. He had shown no desire to stay and chat after dinner, and it was difficult to see why he should want to get back to his cottage. He did not want to spend more time in her company; that was the only conclusion she could reach.

She turned out the lights and went into her bedroom to get ready for bed. There was a mirror beside her wardrobe, and she looked at herself in this. I am not attractive, she said to herself. I am just the woman who looks after the hens. If he wants anybody, then it will be somebody younger, somebody more appealing than I am. There are plenty of girls, and with most young men away Feliks could have any of them; he would not be interested in me.

She sat on the bed and glanced again at her reflection in the mirror. There are ways of looking into mirrors, she thought, one of which is to open your eyes and see the person who is looking back at you.

EIGHT

After he had written the letter to La, it was Tim Honey who got in touch with the vicar in Bury. The vicar proved enthusiastic. 'Can't play a note myself. Can't sing either—if you came to evensong here you'd know all about that. But there are plenty of people who would like to join.'

The 'plenty of people' of the vicar's imaginings turned out to be seven, but four of them played strings—three violinists and a cellist—and one of them was a reasonably strong player. The violinists were all women—two sisters, retired teachers, who lived together, and the hospital almoner. The cellist was a youngish bank manager whose asthma prevented him from joining anything more demanding than the Home Guard. They were all enthusiastic, had time on their hands, and had no objection to making the short journey from Bury in the back of an RAF truck.

With the eight volunteers from the base, most of whom were wind players, the orchestra had a core. To this there were added two players whom La had discovered—the village postman, Mr North, who had an ancient set of drums in his attic, and his sister-in-law, who was prepared to assist him in the percussion section 'as long as North keeps me right on the rhythm'.

'I shall do that,' said La. 'I am the conductor. You watch me.'

It was Tim, too, who managed to get together the music to start them off. The Air Force, he explained, had a music department—bands and the like—and they were sympathetic. A crate of sheet music was dispatched and triumphantly delivered to La's doorstep by Tim.

'Everything we need, La,' he said enthusiastically as he dug into the music. 'Look. W. A. Mozart, no less. And this stuff here. "An Evening in a Viennese Café" arranged for school orchestra. More than we need.'

La said, 'Tim, you may call this La's Orchestra, but it's really you who's done all the work.'

He was modest. 'Nonsense. It's La's Orchestra because it was your idea and you're the conductor. Enough said.'

They sorted out the music as best they could and chose a piece for the first meeting. La looked at the conductor's score and wondered how she would cope with the reading of so many parts simultaneously.

THEY MET FOR THE FIRST time in mid-August on a Saturday afternoon. La was waiting for the truck to arrive, standing in the village hall with the postman and his sister-in-law. They had arranged the hall chairs in a semicircle around a portable pulpit that they had borrowed from the church.

The truck arrived and disgorged the players. Three of the men from the base were in uniform, the others were wearing civilian clothes. A couple were officers, both navigators; the other men were ground crew, including the station barber, who had with him a battered silver trombone.

They played for an hour. It was ragged and discordant. Two of the violins, La was sure, were out of tune, and she stopped halfway through.

'We sound a bit flat,' she said.

'It's not me,' said the postman, and everybody smiled.

At the end of the session there was a cup of tea. The village hall had an urn, which had been switched on at the beginning of the practice and was now just at boiling point. Their instruments packed away, the members of the orchestra stood and drank tea together.

'Are we going to give a concert?' asked one of the men from the base.

'Of course,' said Tim. 'We are, aren't we, La?'

She hesitated. Tim looked at her expectantly. 'At Christmas,' she said. 'We shall give a concert at Christmas. Here in the hall. And then . . . and then, at the end of the war, we'll give a victory concert. That's what we'll start practising for. A victory concert.'

There was silence for a moment. The postman looked down at the floor. Then Tim cleared his throat. 'A good idea. Look out suitable pieces, La.'

There were murmurs of agreement.

As they prepared to leave, Tim turned to her and whispered, 'Do you think it worked?'

La smiled. 'Of course it did. You heard it, didn't you? You could tell?'

The engine of the truck was running and the driver was waiting for him. 'Yes, I think it's fine. And that business about being flat . . .'

'It's not our fault,' said La. 'We're in the middle of a war, aren't we?'

Tim chuckled. 'Of course. It's the war.'

'Well, there you are,' said La. She helped the postman and his sister-in-law clear up. They stacked the chairs to the side of the hall and the pulpit was left for the verger to collect. The postman emptied the urn.

'That's it,' said La. 'That's it until next month.'

As she walked back to her cottage, Mrs Agg passed on her bicycle, heading back from the village. 'I heard you,' she called out. 'They all heard you down in the village. Came across lovely. Lovely sound.'

'We're not very good,' said La.

'Sounded fine to me. Tra-la-la!'

The farmer's wife disappeared down the lane, and La continued her walk. I have an orchestra, she thought. It was every bit as sobering as if one awoke one day to find oneself in charge of Covent Garden or La Scala. There were shoulders that bore those very responsibilities, of course, but they did not belong to a woman in her early thirties, who lived at the edge of a small village in Suffolk, and who each morning looked after hens.

THE FOLLOWING SATURDAY, after attending early to the hens, La made the journey into Cambridge by bus. As she began her journey the sky was clear, and the ripening fields made swathes of golden brown, crisscrossed by the dark green lines of the hedgerows.

In Cambridge she alighted on Trinity Street. A couple of women, not much older than La, came out of Heffers. One was holding a book that she had just bought and was discussing it with her friend. La watched this wistfully. She might be in such company, talking about the latest novel, instead of tending hens and digging potatoes in what had once been a lawn.

Paulson's Music Shop was next door to a high-class butcher on the one side and an outfitter's on the other. La paused to look in the window, which boasted a small display of violins and violas, alongside a couple of ornate wooden music stands. The crate of printed music from the RAF had its limitations and La had discussed with Tim what scores they might obtain.

Mr Paulson, who appeared from a back room in response to the bell triggered by the front door, greeted La. 'Such a promising day earlier on,' he said. 'But now, look at that.' He pointed at a bank of heavy cloud, purple with rain, through the window.

'Yes. It looks very threatening.'

'But,' Mr Paulson went on, 'we are not to be dispirited by such small things as the weather. Especially when there is so much else happening.'

La produced the list she had written out and passed it over to him. Mr Paulson took a pair of unframed reading glasses out of his jacket pocket.

'Rossini. Yes. Mozart. Yes, and yes. Yes. That, alas, that piece there, no. That is out of print as far as I know and these days it is more difficult to get things. People often don't answer letters . . .'

'If you can get just half of my list,' said La, 'I shall be very happy.'

Mr Paulson nodded. 'That will be no problem.' He slipped the piece of paper into a drawer. 'This is a school orchestra, I take it?'

La shook her head. 'I suppose that you would call it a village orchestra.'

Mr Paulson was impressed. 'Admirable! There used to be village bands, but now people seem to have lost the habit of making music together. Sad.'

La agreed that it was. Then, 'And I wondered if you had any secondhand flutes in stock.'

Mr Paulson turned and opened a large drawer to his side. He reached in and took out a box covered in black leather. 'This is a very nice instrument,' he said. 'It belonged to a young man who took a commission in the Royal Artillery and sold this to me before he left.' He slipped open the catch on the side of the box and extracted the disjointed pieces of the flute. These he quickly fitted together and handed the instrument over to La.

She raised the flute to her lips and blew across the mouth-hole.

'A very true note,' said Mr Paulson. 'Try it across the range.'

La lowered the flute and handed it back to him. 'It's not for me,' she said. 'It's for a man who would like to play in our orchestra, but who doesn't have a flute.' She paused. 'He's one of those Polish airmen.'

Mr Paulson nodded. 'I see. Well, I'm sure that the young man who owned this would like to see it going to a fellow combatant.'

La saw the price ticket on the box, but Mr Paulson quickly reduced it. 'For our Polish friend,' he said. 'They have suffered so.'

She wrote out a cheque. Her account was flush with funds since there was nothing to spend money on in the village. Gerald had given her Richard's share of the family company in cash and had been generous; she could live on the interest alone.

The flute, and such sheet music from the list as had been in stock, were neatly tied in a brown-paper parcel and handed to La. Then, with an anxious eye at the storm clouds, and with Mr Paulson's assurances that the other sets of music would be found if humanly possible, she left the shop and headed back towards Trinity Street and the bus-stop.

LA WATCHED FELIKS at work on the drainage scheme, a tiny figure, bent over the land. Pott's Field stretched over several acres and it would take some time for the channels to be dug all along the edges. There were root systems to contend with—over the centuries the hedgerows and trees had consolidated their grip on the soil, creating a subsoil through which the spade could cut only with difficulty.

She kept about her business with the hens and then, when she had finished and had washed up, she took a glass of lemonade to Feliks.

'You're spoiling him,' said Henry, half joking, half seriously. La suspected that he resented the attention she was giving Feliks.

'It's hard work. Really hard. Have you been down there? He gets thirsty.'

'There's water,' muttered Henry.

'But there's also lemonade.'

She found a recipe for lemonade that could be made without lemons, which had never been sold in the village store. She made a quantity of this in the kitchen and tested it: it tasted good enough to her, and Feliks liked it. 'You're so kind to me,' he said. He was always telling her that she was kind to him and she wanted to stop him, to say this is what she wanted to do.

Which was what? What was it that she wanted to do? She asked herself the question and could not think of any answer other than that she wanted to look after a man; it was as simple as that. Some deep instinct within her had asserted itself: an instinct to cherish another person, a man in particular.

She found herself thinking of Feliks a great deal. She thought of him as she cycled to the farm in the morning, wondering whether he would already be out in Pott's Field when she arrived. She thought of him in the evenings, when she sat alone in her house and listened to the news and the musical programmes. She tried to stop herself, but could not.

She asked herself whether he would have done this to her had he not had about him that unsettling male beauty, that glowing smoothness and harmony of feature. At first she thought yes, and then she thought no. And it was the no, she imagined, that was more realistic.

He was polite to her, but that was all. He was a shy man, she decided. That would pass, she thought, when they got to know one another better, but she was not sure how to achieve that. There was the flute, of course, sitting there in her house, in its leather-covered box, and she wanted to give it to him. But it was a large present, and she did not want to smother him.

It took a week. Then he came into the kitchen when she was stacking eggs in the box that Henry used to transport them in to Bury. He used straw to prevent them from being broken; the dust from this would tickle her nose, make her eyes run.

She heard his voice behind her. 'You do not like that work. I could do it.'

She turned round, wiping at her eyes with the back of her hand.

He moved past her and began to place the eggs in the box.

La sat down on one of Henry's kitchen chairs. She looked up at him, noticing for the first time that there was a scar under his chin. He fumbled with an egg.

'Careful. Henry gets very upset if I drop one. He shouted at me once. He said, "The Germans want you to drop those eggs."'

Feliks smiled. 'You could tell him it was me.' He paused. 'I'm not sure that he likes me anyway. It would be one more thing for him, maybe.'

La frowned. 'I don't think he dislikes you,' she said. 'It's the way he is. Maybe it's something to do with his illness. He has a lot of pain, you know.'

Feliks nodded. 'Maybe. It can't be easy to be like that. His hands . . . but even so, I think that he does not like me because I am a foreigner.'

La was about to reassure him that this was not true, but she realised that it might be exactly the reason; that, or he was jealous of the attention that she gave to Feliks. But she could not mention that.

'I have something for you. I've bought you a present.'

He placed an egg on the straw and turned to her. He looked puzzled. 'But why? Why have you bought me a present?'

La shrugged. 'You're far from home. Who else is there to buy you one?'

'But just because I'm far from home does not mean that you need to—'

La interrupted him. 'No. Of course I don't need to. But I have. It's at the house. My house. Perhaps you will come and fetch it.'

He came the next day. She was in her garden when he arrived, riding the old bicycle from the farm. She saw him from her bedroom window upstairs and she watched him as he walked across the gravel to knock at her door.

She had put tea in the pot and there was a plate of freshly baked scones.

He gestured to the scones. 'You should not have bothered . . .'

'I had some flour.'

She went out of the room to get the flute. When she came back in, he sprang to his feet and she handed him the box. 'Open it. Please.'

He eased back the catch and pushed open the lid. She noticed that his hands were trembling slightly.

'Oh. Oh.'

He looked up at her again. She found it hard to read his expression.

She smiled. 'You did say that you played the flute, didn't you? Well, there you are. A flute. Try it. I believe it's a good one.'

He shook his head while he eased the flute joints into place. Then he raised the flute to his lips. La saw the concentration and she knew, even before he drew breath, that he would play it well.

After a few notes, a scale, he lowered the flute and shook his head. 'It is so kind of you,' he said. 'But I cannot pay for this. I do not have the money.'

He began to disassemble the flute.

'No,' La protested. 'Don't do that. It's a present. I told you.'

'But I can't accept a big present like this. A small present, perhaps . . . but this is a very big thing. It's a good flute. And I can't pay.'

It was not going well. She had anticipated some awkwardness over her gift, but not this. She had not thought he would insist on paying for it.

'Listen, Feliks. I'm giving it to you because you are far from home. I want you to have this because we are in the same war together.' She sighed. 'All right. When the war is over, pay me then.'

He stopped disassembling the flute. 'At the end?'

'Yes. Whatever will make you happy.'

He thought. 'All right. But you must let me do something for you.' He gestured out of the window. 'I could help you with your garden.'

She felt the release of tension and laughed. 'My garden? Yes, that would be very useful. Such as it is, now that I have all those potatoes.'

'You can make a garden around the potatoes. I could make it beautiful for you. Next spring you would see the difference.'

She accepted. She felt gratitude at the thought that he would be there, in her garden. 'And you can play in my orchestra. We don't have a flautist.'

He made a gesture of modesty, of reluctance. 'I will not improve it. My reading of music is rusty.'

'Anybody would improve us,' said La. 'Even a rusty player. You must.'

He picked up the flute and slipped the joints together again. He held it with love and that convinced her that she had done the right thing.

'Go on. Why not play it? Play something Polish, perhaps.'

'I had an uncle who played beautifully. My uncle in Frank—'

He broke off, his comment left hanging in the air. La looked down at her shoes. One of them, the left one, had a small crust of mud on the tip. She moved her other foot to dislodge it. Perhaps she had misheard.

He did not play the flute, but twisted its sections apart, put them away quickly and then rose to his feet, suddenly formal again.

'I'm very grateful for this gift,' Feliks said.

She forced herself to smile. 'Good.'

'I must go now,' he said.

She watched him from the window, her thoughts in confusion. She saw him walk down the gravel drive towards the bicycle. Then he turned round and looked back at the house. La took a hurried step back so that he should not see her at the window. But he had spotted her, she thought, because his eyes had gone to the window at which she had been standing.

She crossed to the back of the room and pushed the door shut. She noticed that he had left a small canvas shopping bag on the floor. She hesitated for a moment, then picked it up and looked inside. There was a small onion at the bottom of the bag, that was all. What did I expect? she asked herself. Something more than this? She replaced the onion and put the bag on the dresser. She would take it back to him tomorrow, at the farm.

She moved back to the window and gazed out at the field on the other side of the road. What had he said? That he had an uncle in somewhere that sounded like Frankfurt. It was a perfectly innocuous comment: anybody might have an uncle in Frankfurt—if that is what he had said; the husband of his aunt, for instance—a Polish woman married to a German; there must be many such marriages. Poles and Germans spilled across one another's borders, and where exactly these borders should be was one of the issues behind the war anyway. Having an uncle in Frankfurt did not make one a German.

She persuaded herself. It was nonsense. The problem with war was that it made us all so suspicious. We imagined an enemy behind every innocent bush or tree; saw clouds as veils for bombers, and death; saw the world as a place of dread and distrust; saw an honourable Polish airman as a fifth columnist, or even something worse. Feliks was far from home, friendless, and dependent on the charity of others; she would not be the one to challenge him, to make him feel that he was the subject of narrow mistrust.

The decision made, she did not allow herself to think about the matter again. And the next day, when she saw Feliks again, it was as if nothing untoward had occurred. That proves it, thought La. That proves that whatever it was that I heard was nothing of any significance. She made him his lemonade and took it down to Pott's Field. He thanked her and told her that he had tried the flute out when he had got home the previous evening. He would never be able to repay her, he said. It was far too good an instrument for him. She said, 'But you're going to do my garden for me, remember?'

He nodded. 'I'll start tomorrow. After work.'

'Bring the flute. And you will play in my orchestra?'

He hesitated for a moment. 'You really want me to?'

'Of course I do.'

'Then I shall do what you want.'

He arrived at her house the next day, in the late afternoon, as he had promised. They should grow more vegetables, she said, as they walked round the garden. That was what everybody was being urged to do.

'So there should be no flowers in wartime?' he asked.

'There should always be room for some flowers. Even in wartime.'

He reached down and picked a weed that had intruded on a flowerbed. 'Just as there should always be room for God, even in wartime. Some people in Poland, you know, said that he had gone away. Some of them were Jews who felt that they had been abandoned by God.'

'One might understand their feelings. Everybody else seems to have abandoned them. Looking the other way.'

'Not in this country,' said Feliks. 'You have never allowed that. Some people, maybe, have said cruel things. You had your fascists too. But not in the same numbers as back there.'

Cruel things. She liked his turn of phrase. This war was about hatred, she thought; hatred and cruelty on a massive scale.

'We can't afford to be without God,' Feliks continued. 'Even if He doesn't exist, we have to hold onto Him. Because if we don't then how are we to convince ourselves that we have to go on with this fight? If you take God out of it, then right and justice become small, human things.'

La thought about this. He was right, perhaps, even if she did not feel that she needed God in the same way Feliks seemed to need Him. She would do whatever she had to do, even if it was for the sake of simple decency. You did not wipe a child's tears because God told you to do so. You did it because the tears were there.

Feliks worked in the garden for two hours before La called him in for a cup of tea. Then she suggested that they play a duet together; she had looked out some music. He was better than she was; far better. But he was a considerate partner, and they reached the end of the piece together.

He laid down his flute. 'You are very good.'

She laughed. 'I'm not.'

'No, your playing has expression. It is very good.'

They played another piece, then he looked at his watch. 'It's getting late.'

She did not want him to go. She almost said, 'Stay with me and have supper. I have enough food here.' But she did not. She should not allow herself to become involved with this man; she would only make a fool of herself, as he would not reciprocate. If you are going to love him, she said to herself, it is going to have to be from a distance. Secretly.

NINE

It was autumn. Feliks had finished Pott's Field and had brought in Henry's harvest. With the summer crops in, there was not much for Feliks to do on Madder's Farm, and after a call from an official from the Ministry of Agriculture he was allocated to help over the winter on a pig farm several miles away.

On a Sunday afternoon in late November, La drove Feliks to his new cottage with his possessions packed into the back of her car. A cold fog had drifted in from the east that morning and had lingered, a white shroud over the landscape, dusting the hedgerows and the trees with rime.

La found it difficult to accept that the two trunks and a battered cardboard box in the back contained all that a man might own. She asked Feliks about it as they drove. 'What did you leave behind?' she asked. 'You've never told me much about your life. Did you lose a lot?'

His did not answer for a few moments. But then he said, 'Leave behind? Nothing very much. A car. An elderly mother. A sister who is a nun.'

She reflected on his answer. It was a life condensed into telegraphese. And her own life in such terms—what would it be? An unfaithful husband who died. A house in Suffolk. A ragbag orchestra. A vegetable garden.

'You lived in a city?'

He stared out of the car window; wiped at the condensation with his sleeve. 'Yes. Although my mother lived in the country. A small estate with quite a few debts. My father was never very good at such things.'

La felt satisfaction that she had guessed correctly. A gentleman. 'I could tell that you came from a certain background.' She paused. 'Well, to put it very directly, I could tell that you were a gentleman. Not . . .'

He laughed. 'Not a peasant?'

'That's not a word we use in this country.'

He seemed intrigued. 'You have no peasants? What about Henry?'

It was La's turn to laugh. 'Henry, a peasant? That's very amusing, Feliks. No, Henry would not describe himself as a peasant. To call somebody a peasant would be insulting. People are sensitive about that sort of thing.'

'In Poland it's not shameful to be a peasant. It's an honest thing to be.'

La thought that was right. But be that as it may, Henry Madder was certainly not a peasant. 'Henry's quite well off, actually,' she said. 'I think that he's got money tucked away in that house of his.'

'That's what peasants do with money,' said Feliks. 'They tuck it under the mattress. Everybody knows that—and that includes thieves!'

'In Warsaw, were you . . .'

He held up a hand. 'Krakow. Not Warsaw.'

She corrected herself. 'Were you at the university in Krakow? Tim said that you were studying.'

'I was. And then I went off to join the air force with some friends. It was just the thing to be in the air force. Lots of parties and aerobatics.'

Parties and aerobatics: La smiled at this. And then, she assumed, everything had suddenly become very serious.

'And now this.' She took a hand off the wheel and waved it at the fields. 'A pig farm. A funny little orchestra with people who can't play very well.'

'Maybe,' said Feliks. 'But in wartime, the important thing is to be alive, don't you think?'

La thought of Richard. Yes, what Feliks said was right, even if . . . but there was no time to discuss it. They were near the pig farm; they could smell it on the wind. She glanced at Feliks and then looked back at the road ahead. She felt confused: she wanted to be with him, she wanted to be close to him, but if he did not reciprocate her feelings, and she thought that he did not, then she would make sure that she did not have those feelings.

The cottage that he had been allocated by the farmer turned out to be no more than two rooms added on to the end of a tack room. La could smell the leather of the harnesses through the thin walls; the mixture of horse sweat and oil. Everything was run down: the grubby windows let in very little light and there was a pervasive feel of damp in the air.

La was indignant. 'They can't expect you to stay here. Look at the damp patches on the wall. I'm going to talk to the farmer.'

Feliks took hold of her arm. 'Please don't. It's a roof over my head. I'll heat it and the damp will go away.'

She was reluctant, but he insisted. He would not let her stay to help him clean and tidy the place, and so she left him there in her anger and drove home. She had wanted to say that he should come and stay with her; she had more than enough room in the house, but she suspected that it would sound like an invitation to be something more than a lodger.

She asked herself whether that was what she wanted, whether she would like Feliks to be her lover. She was not sure; the war made everything different. He came from a different country, he was a stranger, and sooner or later he would want to go back. She belonged in England and her sense of that belonging was all the stronger now that England was under threat. I love this country, she thought; I love its lived-in shabbiness, its old-fashioned gentleness.

The thought came back to her as she drove along the winding lanes: what if the stranger was not what he claimed to be? She shook her head, as if to rid it of the unwelcome thought. She had set those doubts to rest and she did not want them to recur.

FELIKS JOINED the orchestra. On the first occasion he played he was shy and did not stay for the cup of tea that everybody else took at the back of the hall once they were finished. La looked for him, but he was gone.

'Who is that flautist?' asked one of the violinists from Bury. 'That good-looking man?'

'A Polish airman,' La replied.

'He can certainly play, can't he?'

In December the orchestra performed their first concert. The village was abuzz and turned out in force, even Agg and Mrs Agg, who sat in the front row and clapped loudly even after the applause from the rest of the audience had died down. Their second concert was at the air base, where their final piece was interrupted by the sound of aeroplanes taking off.

Tim asked her about Feliks, and whether he had settled in at the pig farm. 'I think so,' she said, 'but the farmer's a tyrant and there's not much difference between Feliks's accommodation and the sties the pigs live in.'

Tim laughed. 'He's resilient. All these Poles are.' He paused. 'You found a flute for him?'

La wondered whether there was something else behind the question, but decided there was not. She told Tim about the trip to Cambridge and the discount the man in the music shop had given her.

'I'm glad,' said Tim. 'And I'm glad you're keeping an eye on Feliks. He wasn't very popular with a couple of other Poles we had at the base. They seemed to be a bit . . .'

La waited. Tim made a face, as if to portray stand-offishness. La relaxed. 'Keeps himself to himself?'

She wondered how she could put it to Tim that it was probably a social matter. The problem about being direct, was this: Tim himself was not a gentleman. That did not matter to La, who was largely indifferent to such distinctions. But it was difficult, she thought, to explain to one who was not a gentleman that others might dislike another because he was.

'Not so much that,' said Tim. 'It's as if they were a bit suspicious of him.'

La lifted her teacup to her lips and took a sip. She felt cold inside.

'But you never know with these types,' Tim continued. 'The French are always bickering with one another. Maybe it's the same with the Poles.'

La hesitated. Perhaps now was the time to say something to Tim. She could tell him about the Frankfurt incident, but what exactly would she say? That she thought that Feliks had let slip that he had an uncle in Frankfurt? Did she really have to bring up something as slender as that?

She swallowed hard. She had her duty. 'How well do you know him?'

'Dab?' Tim shrugged. 'Quite well, I think. I ended up looking after him, as you know, arranging things. He was a bit of a lost soul. I suppose I got to know him better than the others because he speaks such good English.'

La said that this was not what she had meant. 'About his background? About where he comes from?'

Tim looked at his watch. 'I'm going to have to dash. We've got rather a lot on.' He drained his cup. 'Dab's past? Polish Air Force. Wormed his way in with our boys after he was picked up in Romania. That's where their air force fled after the Jerries and the Russians gobbled their country up. Didn't I tell you about that? Poor chaps. Most of them went to France first, of course. Dab was shot down on his first sortie. He came here to carry on the fight. That, as you know, was not possible.'

La nodded. 'So he would have been checked up on?'

'Of course. Everyone is.' He paused. 'You've got doubts about him?'

'I just wondered . . .'

Tim smiled. 'I really don't think that Dab's anybody to worry about. He's very much a gentleman, you know.'

La broke into a smile.

'Have I said something funny?'

'No. No. Not at all.' She did her best to hide her relief. It was just as she thought: she had been imaginative because she was living in times when the imagination could so easily be overfired. War made heroes of some, she thought, but for most of us it made us frightened—and suspicious of our fellow man. She would not be like that. She would not.

OVER THE NEXT few months, La's orchestra strengthened. Word got round, and new players from the base and from Bury asked to join. In the spring they gave another concert, this time in a church in Bury, and the local newspaper reported it in glowing terms. 'They may be amateurs,' the press report read, 'but they are determined. And what spirit they have! This is what Hitler hasn't taken into account: the determination of the ordinary people of these islands to get on with their lives in spite of everything he throws at them. Watch out for La's Orchestra, Herr Hitler!'

As he had promised, Feliks came to work in La's garden once a week. It was spring now—they were on the cusp of summer—and the herbaceous border Feliks had planted was beginning to get some colour. La now grew carrots, kale, lettuce and beans as well as her large crop of potatoes. Feliks announced that he would try to get hold of Jerusalem artichokes and rhubarb. 'Soup and pudding will be taken care of,' said La. 'Thank you.'

'But what about the course in between?' he asked.

'Henry's hens provide me with eggs,' said La. 'If an egg is cracked, we can't sell it, but it never goes to waste.'

Food: people now thought about it all the time, with a dull, nagging obsessiveness. La knew that she was lucky to have her vegetable garden, and the eggs made a big difference. But what people wanted, as always, was what they could not get: meat, butter, sugar, coffee. The forces did better, of course, and pilots never went without. One of them, who played in her orchestra, brought her chocolate from time to time and slipped it to her after the rehearsal. She made it last, breaking off half a square after dinner each night. In wartime, people took pleasure where they could find it, and with gratitude—chocolate, love, anything that used to be in plentiful supply but which was now hard to find, or rationed.

IT WAS A SATURDAY in August. Feliks had been working in the garden and La had fallen asleep in a deck chair under the willow near what remained of her lawn. She woke suddenly and found that he was sprawled out on the grass beside her, his feet resting against the first hummock of the potatoes that had replaced the lawn. At first she thought that he had become ill from exertion in the heat, but then she noticed that his eyes were open, staring up at the sky, and that he was sucking a blade of grass. She noticed the profile of his nose; it was perfect, she thought. It was what made him so handsome.

'You know,' she said, 'if somebody came and took away your nose, you'd look very different.'

He took the blade of grass out of his mouth. 'What an odd thing to say. Anybody would look different.'

She laughed. 'Yes. Sorry, I was just thinking aloud. But it's more true with some people than with others, don't you think? Mrs Agg, for example. Her nose . . . well, her nose is neither here nor there, if you ask me.'

He continued to stare at the sky. 'They say that the English are peculiar, but you must be very peculiar to say things like that.'

It was rare for them to talk in this relaxed way; it meant nothing, she knew. He would soon get to his feet and carry on with his work, or suddenly pack up and leave. But for now she was enjoying the moment.

'Don't Polish people say silly things from time to time?' La glanced at him. 'Or are they too sad?'

He reached out to pluck another blade of grass. 'We are not always sad. We were very happy when we got our freedom back in 1918.'

'And that was the last time anybody was happy?'

He seemed to think for a moment. Then, 'When we showed the Russians that we would fight for our freedom and when we beat them. We were happy then. That was 1920.'

'And now?' La shifted slightly in her chair and looked up through the leaves of the willow to the clear sky above.

'Now we're too busy to think much about whether we are happy or sad. We've got one thing on our mind. To get the Germans out.'

La nodded. 'Why are they there in the first place?'

'Because they are. They've invaded.'

'But why?' La pressed. 'How would a German explain it? What would a German say?'

'We would say that everything was chaos and that the German invasion was the best thing that had happened to Poland. That is what they would say.'

La lay quite still. She had been staring up through the leaves as he spoke. There was a bird in the branches, almost directly above her, as if unaware of her. She watched his tiny, jerky movements.

Feliks said something else—something about Russia—but she did not hear it. I cannot let this pass, she said to herself. I cannot ignore it now. She sat up. 'Feliks,' she said. 'Do you know what you just said?'

'About Russia?' he said. 'About Stalin wanting his revenge?'

She felt her heart hammering within her. 'No. Before that. I asked you what a German would say about Poland, and you said, "We would say . . ."'

He remained still. 'No, I didn't say that. I said something else.'

'But you did. You said it.'

He sat up, quite abruptly, and turned to her. 'I said that the Germans would say something about chaos and bad government, if they told us what they think. They do not think that the Poles can run a country, or deserve to do so.' He rose to his feet. 'I'm going to tie those beans,' he said. 'Then I'm going to have to go.'

'I must pay you,' she said. After the first few months, when he insisted that he was paying for the flute, La had taken to giving him money for his work in the garden. He had been reluctant to accept it, but she had insisted. Now she got up out of her deck chair and went into the house to fetch the coins from her purse. Inside, she stopped in the corridor. Perhaps it really was a slip of the tongue; he's speaking a foreign language, after all, even if he speaks it very well. That must be it. 'We' and 'they' are easily confused.

She took the coins out to him. He seemed to have forgotten the incident and talked to her about the four rows of beans. 'You will have a very good crop,' he said. 'You wait and see.'

La went indoors and switched on the wireless. Someone was reading a story about a woman who lived in a small town in Kent who took a lodger, a commercial traveller. He was a good tenant; he paid the landlady his rent and was always neat and tidy. On Sundays he went by bus to the Catholic church. The traveller had a leather suitcase in which he kept his samples and the landlady found one evening that her lodger had left his sample case on the landing. She picked it up and took it to his room. She knocked, but he did not reply, and so she opened the door. He was sitting at the table near the window, writing something in a book. When he saw her come into the room, he closed the notebook and stood up. He seemed very uncomfortable that she was holding the sample case, and he took it from her roughly . . .

La turned off the wireless. It was a trite story and she knew where it was leading. People were always being told to be on the lookout, to be careful of what they said and to whom they said it. The landlady would discover a transmitter or a codebook, perhaps. It was all too obvious.

And it was uncomfortable.

She went to stand by the window. It was afternoon and the shadows were lengthening. That evening there was an orchestra rehearsal and she should have been copying out a part for one of the trumpeters rather than listening to the radio. Ridiculous story—like a morality play for the unsophisticated. Did they really want to have everybody looking into everybody's business?

After a few minutes she went back to the wireless and turned it on again.

'. . . at his trial,' said the voice, 'the judge said very little. The case had been one of the worst he had seen; the information sent back to Germany could have cost the lives of many innocent people. There was a sentence provided for by law and that was the sentence that he must now impose.

'He showed no emotion when they took him away. In prison he refused food, right up to the time that they took him from his cell. His legs failed him at the end, though, and they had to carry him to his death; he died a coward. Afterwards he was buried in an unmarked grave. They never knew his real name, but they were sure he was an Englishman.'

That was the end of the story. La turned away from the wireless in her irritation. Why had they called him a coward? She thought that he must have been brave, not a coward at all, taking all those risks and then saying nothing. That was brave, even if he was on the wrong side. And anybody's legs would fail them if they were made to walk to their death.

She sat down. She felt an emptiness, a rawness within her. She loved Feliks; she admitted that to herself now. It was an unreciprocated love, yes, but it was love nonetheless. She did not want him to die, to be carried to his death like the man in the story. Yet just as she admitted to herself that what she felt for him was love, so too she had to admit to herself that her duty was clear: misguided people no doubt believed in Hitler and his cause, might even think they were doing the right thing. Feliks could be one of those; or he might be a patriot, for whom it was not a question of loyalty to Hitler and the Nazis, but to Germany itself. People said that there were offi-cers in the German army who were in that position, men with a sense of personal honour, torn between loyalty and disgust. Oh, Feliks . . .

She had to speak to Tim. She telephoned the base, but he was not at his desk. The flight sergeant who answered said that he would pass on the message to call her back. Fifteen minutes later, La received the call.

'I suppose you've heard,' Tim said to her before she could say anything.

'Heard what?'

'They've arrested Feliks.'

TEN

She did not care that it would make her late for the orchestra. It was not an afternoon for cycling, the strong wind in her face making progress slow, but she had pedalled that route to Madder's Farm so often that she could do it virtually without looking where she was going.

She found him in the kitchen, sitting at the table, a half-drunk cup of tea in front of him. He looked up at her, eyes narrowed. 'So, you've heard.'

She took off her scarf and tossed it down on the table. 'What happened?'

'He stole my money,' he said. 'He stole all of it.'

'When?'

He took the cup in his right hand. 'This afternoon. Lunchtime. I was down at Pott's, and when I came back up I saw somebody cycling away from the house. It was him. I called after him, but he paid no attention.' He paused. 'Then I went in and something made me check the . . . the place where I keep some money I have. It had been taken. All of it. Near on eight hundred pounds, if a penny. Eight hundred.'

La did not like the way he was looking at her. It was as if he felt triumphant, having suspected all along that Feliks was a thief.

'But were you sure it was him?' she asked.

'Yes. Of course I was. I know that man as well as you do.' He looked at her. 'Well, maybe not quite as well as you do . . .'

La ignored this. 'Maybe he came to see you. Maybe the money was already gone.'

Henry eyed her. 'Wasn't gone yesterday.'

'Well, it could have happened any time from when you last checked up on it. Where did you keep it?'

'Cupboard in the sitting room. Round the front.'

La thought for a moment. 'That's a room you hardly ever go into, Henry. The door's always closed there. You know that.'

He stared at her sullenly. 'So? Money's gone. He was here.'

In the past La had noticed that when Henry decided that something was the case, then it was not easy to shift him. He was doing it again. Feliks had been on the farm and the money was gone. The two facts seemed to him to be inextricably linked.

She tried again. 'All that I'm saying is this, Henry. You don't know when the money went missing. It could have been last night.'

He shook his head. 'If somebody came in last night I would have heard him. I'm a light sleeper. I would have heard somebody downstairs.'

'No, you wouldn't necessarily. People can be very quiet. You sleep upstairs, don't you? You do.'

He contemplated this for a moment before he spoke again. 'Anyway,' he said. 'Percy Brown's been down here. He said he was going over to arrest him. So that's it. And all I want to know is—when will I get my money back? They'll find it in his room, likely enough.'

La sighed. 'You could be wrong, Henry. Have you thought of that? And if you are, then you've accused an innocent man of being a thief. How would you feel if you were accused of stealing something and you hadn't?'

'Haven't stolen anything,' he said. 'Not me. So your question makes no sense, La. And here's another thing. Four eggs broken this morning. You've got to be more careful. Four eggs wasted.'

THE TRIP TO Madder's Farm made her arrive ten minutes late at the village hall. They were working on an arrangement of 'Brigg Fair' that had been sent from Cambridge with a recommendation by Mr Paulson. It was on the outer edge of their abilities and they were struggling.

La looked down at the music on the stand in front of her. She tried to keep time, but she lost the place and had to turn a sheet quickly. The orchestra continued, although one or two of the violins faltered. Tim looked up at her sharply. She concentrated on the music, but the words of 'Brigg Fair' returned to her mind. 'And now we're met together, I hope we ne'er shall part.' La put down her baton. She could not continue, for the tears she had fought to suppress now overcame her. She turned away, so that people might not see her cry. She put her hands up over her face.

One of the sisters from Bury was beside her. 'La, dear. La.' There was an arm about her, and she was led to a chair at the side of the hall.

'I'm sorry. I'm just all over the place tonight. I'm sorry.'

'Hush. Hush. You don't have to say sorry. There, La. There.' She leaned forward and whispered, 'It's Feliks, isn't it, La? It's Feliks?'

Tim was standing behind the woman from Bury. 'Is there anything . . .'

'She'll be all right.'

La looked up at Tim. She saw that the orchestra had broken up and people were packing their instruments away. 'Tim, I'm so sorry.'

He nodded to the woman, who moved away to let him forward. She threw an anxious glance at La.

La looked up at Tim, who had reached out to take her hand.

She had a handkerchief and wiped at her eyes. The tears had stopped, but her cheeks were still moist. 'Can I talk to you in private?'

He nodded. 'Of course. The truck can take everybody home. I've got my car this evening. I'll drive you back to your place.'

They did not wait until the hall had been closed off, but went out to Tim's car and drove back down the lane. Tim was quiet, although he said, 'It's been a difficult day for you. I can tell that. I was pretty taken aback myself.'

In the house, she put on the kettle and they sat down at the kitchen table.

'So,' said Tim. 'Dab has been arrested. A nasty business.'

She took a deep breath. 'It's not that. Not the theft. I want to talk about something else. I think that Feliks may be German.'

For a few moments Tim said nothing. Then he reached into a pocket and took out a packet of cigarettes. 'I see.' He extracted a cigarette and tapped it against the table. La watched him. 'And why do you think that?'

She told him about the slips—the uncle in Frankfurt and the 'we' rather than 'they'. He listened carefully, and raised an eyebrow over the 'we'.

'Does that sound fanciful to you?' La asked. 'I was listening to a story on the wireless the other day about a landlady . . .'

He smiled. 'Oh, yes, I heard that. I was in the mess when it came on.'

'It was silly,' said La. 'Very melodramatic. But it made me think.'

'So you think that you and I are in the same position as that landlady? And Dab is our commercial traveller?'

It sounded ridiculous, put that way, but that, she supposed, is what she thought. She nodded. 'Something like that.'

Tim lit his cigarette. 'All right,' he said. 'We can look into it. My first reaction, though, is that there's nothing to it. Lots of Poles are German-speaking. Of course Hitler has grabbed many of those and made them join his army. But there must be some who are not too keen on the Nazis.' He looked at her quizzically. 'I take it that there's nothing else?'

She shook her head. 'Nothing.' She felt there was nothing more to say. She had decided it was her duty to betray Feliks, and now she had done it.

'Well, then, there's a chap at the station who handles this sort of thing. He can get somebody down from London.'

It seemed so bleak. Somebody down from London would interrogate Feliks. If they found out that he was an enemy agent, they would execute him. War was like a game: one side did this and the other side did that. The rules stipulated that those who played without uniforms would be shot.

Tim blew smoke into the air. 'I wouldn't worry, La. It's highly unlikely that Dab is anything other than what he says he is. I like him. I don't think I would ever feel like that about a spy. I like to think I could tell.'

She thought about this for a moment. What he said was reassuring, but there was still the question of the theft. They had not talked about that. La raised it now and Tim shook his head vehemently.

'I just can't imagine him taking anything. He's not a thief, he's . . .'

'A gentleman?' La supplied.

Tim laughed. 'Exactly. I told your policeman Percy Brown it was highly unlikely. He telephoned because Dab had given my name when he was arrested. He said I would speak for him. I said that I didn't think it likely that Dab would steal anything.'

La remembered what Henry had said about the possibility that the money would be found in Feliks's room. She asked Tim about this.

'Brown said he took a look and there was nothing there. He implied that they didn't have much proof, and that it was just the farmer's word.' He paused. 'I think they'll release him, although the intelligence people might want to hold on to him for a little while before they do that. They might take him down to London for a couple of days, but I suspect that he'll be back. He'll be playing the flute again in your little band, La. Don't you worry.'

THE FOLLOWING DAY, when she had finished with the hens, La cycled over to the pig farm. She had seen Henry briefly that morning, but they had not spoken very much. He had made some remark about the weather and she had given a vague reply.

The pig farmer was grooming his horse when she arrived. He did not seem surprised to see her. 'You're the woman who looked after him?' he asked. 'The woman with the garden?'

She nodded. 'Yes. He helped me in the garden.'

The farmer continued with his grooming, running the brush down the animal's flank. 'A nasty business. Percy Brown was round here this morning, with him.'

'With Feliks?'

'Yes. They were in a car. There was somebody from Bury at the wheel, I think. They came to let Feliks get his things. He's cleared out now.' The farmer looked at La and saw the effect of his words. 'Sorry. I can see you're a bit upset. Nice fellow, Feliks. And not a thief, I'm pleased to say.'

La caught her breath. 'No? Percy Brown said that?'

The farmer took a small metal comb out of his jacket pocket and began to scrape the impacted horse hair from the brush. 'Yes. Percy Brown took me aside and said there was no real proof that he had pinched Henry Madder's money. Miser that Henry is. Eight hundred quid! Did you hear that? It'll be one of the Gypsies down at Foster's. Light-fingered lot.'

'So why didn't they let Feliks go?' She knew, but she had to ask.

The farmer started to brush the horse again. 'Who knows? Something to do with being Polish, perhaps?'

SHE WAITED TO HEAR from Tim, thinking that he might telephone her. But no word came. Feliks had been arrested on a Monday and had been driven away on the Tuesday. It was now Friday, and La thought that if Tim had not phoned her by midafternoon, then she would get in touch with him. She did not like to disturb him at the base; they needed to keep their lines open and private calls were discouraged, but she had to ask.

La attended to the hens. Henry was nowhere to be seen. She decided that he must have been told that Feliks had been cleared of the theft and imagined he would be sulking.

Back at the house, she tried to busy herself with domestic tasks. She thought of Feliks in London, facing his accusers. She wondered whether they would present him with the evidence against him—such as it was; if they did, then he would know who had betrayed him.

At noon she decided to go over to Mrs Agg's. She had harvested carrots and had too many.

Mrs Agg was in her kitchen. She took the carrots gratefully. 'Carrot cake,' she said. 'Agg loves it.'

La smiled. 'There'll be more. I've got lots.' She watched as Mrs Agg put the kettle on the range. Then, out of the corner of her eye, she saw a gramophone standing on a table at the other end of the room. It had a small stack of records at its side. 'That's new.'

Mrs Agg glanced in the direction of La's gaze. 'That? Oh yes, that's Lennie's. He loves music—always has. Bands. That sort of thing.'

La rose and crossed the room to stand beside the gramophone. The turntable was covered with a rich red baize; the head of the arm was shining silver. 'His Master's Voice,' she said. 'This is very nice.'

She picked up the record on the top of the pile. *Billy Cotton and his Orchestra* and underneath *Ellis Jackson Plays*. 'Lennie's?'

Mrs Agg nodded. 'He plays them again and again. Drives Agg up the wall.'

La turned round. The door that led from the kitchen into the yard had opened and Lennie had entered. He looked at her quickly and then looked away again. La smiled at him and greeted him, but got only a curt nod in return. She noticed that Lennie was carrying a large parcel wrapped up in brown paper and tied with white string. She did not want to stare, but her eyes were drawn to the parcel and then to the leather jacket that he was wearing—the sort of jacket that pilots wore.

Mrs Agg intercepted La's glance. 'Lennie, Mrs Stone has brought us some carrots for carrot cake. Isn't that kind of her?'

Lennie said something that La did not quite catch and then hurried through the door that led into the rest of the house.

'It looks as if Lennie has been shopping,' said La. 'His new gramophone. And that was a very nice jacket he was wearing.'

Mrs Agg's eyes narrowed. 'Lennie's not a great one for shopping,' she said. 'But he saves up his money and every so often he has a little spree.'

La did not say what she was thinking. The coincidence was just too great. Henry Madder loses £800 and Lennie Agg goes on a shopping spree.

After her cup of tea with Mrs Agg, La walked back down the lane sunk in thought. It was just before one in the afternoon on a still day. Although it was late autumn, the sky was filled with clear blue light and was cloudless, apart from several faint lines and whirls of vapour, fast dispersing, high above her—where aeroplanes had briefly danced, one with another in anger, or so she assumed. Part of a battle that now seemed set to continue for years, as the last one had, until one side bled the other to exhaustion. There could only be one outcome, of course, and everybody, it seemed, knew what that would be; nobody doubted that Hitler would be crushed, but it was taking so long and was such a dispiriting business.

She felt somehow dirtied by what she had seen in the Aggs' kitchen. Lennie had taken advantage of Henry Madder, a virtual cripple, and stolen his £800. Mrs Agg must have known that Lennie had suddenly got his hands on money, with his new gramophone and his leather jacket, and that large parcel, whatever it had contained. She must have wondered where he'd got it; there would be no secrets in a family like that, all living cheek by jowl in that small farmhouse.

La could have mentioned the theft, but had not, because it would have amounted to an accusation and one could not fall out with neighbours in the country. She and the Aggs had to live together and if she denounced Lennie as a thief that would be impossible. Besides, he was, she thought, dangerous. He had broken into her house before, and he would do so again if he thought that she had informed on him. But she knew that this was how evil prospered; this was how appeasement made tyrants confident. One turned a blind eye; it was the same with countries as it was with people.

She made herself a cup of tea and took it out into the garden to drink it there. The ground was hard with the cold. She suddenly felt defeated and lonely. She had not realised how important were the visits that Feliks had paid to her garden. She had watched him working; they had talked. He knew what she was saying; he thought the same way. It was a question of simple *understanding* of the world. He understood. He was a friend—that was all—a friend whom she had come to love, but who would never love her back. She could accept all that, but she would miss him so acutely.

She did not think that she would see him again. They had taken him to London and he would be swallowed up by the city, carried away somewhere on the shifting tides of war, just one more displaced person in an ocean of human flotsam. And it was now, as she walked slowly about her garden, that she decided that she would give up her orchestra. She wanted simply to withdraw to her house, to read, to listen to the wireless, to struggle with her vegetables. She would look after the hens, but she would keep to herself.

But she knew that there was something she must do. The whole point about this war was that it involved doing the right thing. She had to speak to Percy Brown.

She found him in the police house, in his stockinged feet. He looked down. 'I must put on my shoes.'

She held up a hand. 'Don't bother on my account. I won't keep you long.'

He gestured to a chair and then sat down himself. 'Well, I assume it's about that man. That Pole. I've had no news of him, I'm afraid. They took him to London for questioning and they haven't let me know what happened. They never do, these hush-hush types. They don't trust anybody.'

'It's the times we live in,' said La. 'It makes us all suspicious. The powers that be encourage it, don't they?'

Percy Brown agreed with this. 'Quite right, Mrs Stone. Quite right.' He raised an eyebrow. 'So there we are. We'll just have to wait until he comes back—if he comes back.'

'It's nothing to do with his being questioned,' said La. 'It's about the theft of Henry Madder's money. I understand that you decided there was nothing to link Feliks to that.'

'That's right. Henry Madder just caught a glimpse of a man on a bike. I pressed him on this and he had to admit he couldn't say for definite it was the Pole. And if you get a witness like that in court the case usually collapses. Magistrates don't like that sort of thing. It wastes everybody's time.'

'Of course. But what about information that somebody's suddenly begun spending money very freely? If that sort of information comes in just after a theft, what then?'

The policeman frowned. 'It can do. Thieves often give themselves away like that.' He leaned forward. 'You've seen somebody spending money?'

La swallowed. 'Yes.'

'Who?'

La held the policeman's gaze. 'Lennie Agg,' she said quietly.

She had not expected her words to have quite the effect they had. Percy Brown sat back in his chair, as if he had been pushed by an unseen hand. It was a few moments before he spoke. 'What did you see?' he asked.

'A new gramophone. And a leather jacket. And he had something else in a parcel. All wrapped up.'

He considered this. 'I see.'

La felt that she had to explain. 'Lennie never gave any sign of having much money. He dressed simply, mostly in working clothes, even on Sundays. Then suddenly this very expensive leather jacket appeared. Where would you get something like that these days? And the gramophone—it's an HMV—must have been very expensive. There were records too . . .'

Percy Brown was looking away. She could tell that what she had said was not welcome. Again, it must be a question of her having an unfounded suspicion. He must think that she was one of those ridiculous people who imagine all sorts of crimes: first, the man breaking into her house; then Feliks; now Lennie.

'The only reason I mention this,' she said, 'is because I feel sorry for Henry. If Lennie has stolen his money, then you might be able to get it back before it's all spent. It's not easy for me, you know, to come to you and accuse my neighbour's son. You do realise that, don't you?'

He turned to her again. His expression was closed. 'Yes, I realise it, Mrs Stone. And I'm not criticising you for coming to me. It's just that I know that Lennie Agg, whatever else people may say he is, is not a thief.'

'But how can you be so sure?'

'Because he's my nephew,' said Percy Brown. 'And I've known him since he was *that* high.'

ELEVEN

It was two days before Tim came to see her. He came unannounced, at a time convenient for afternoon tea, which they drank in the sitting room, where La had treated herself to a small coal fire. It was the warmest room in the house, anyway, at that time of day, when the afternoon sun, if it shone, painted light on the floor and walls near the French windows.

Tim looked tired. 'We've had a beastly time of it,' he said. 'We've lost more crews than we can afford. Far more. And I'm having difficulty getting supplies. There's some chap in the Air Ministry who seems determined to thwart me. I think it's personal.'

La looked sympathetic. 'Wish for his promotion. Then he can go and make somebody else's life difficult.'

Tim smiled. 'A nice tactic, La. One wishes for the promotion of one's enemies and feels good about one's charitable thoughts.'

'Exactly. I've often noticed how there are people who always talk about doing the right thing. But when you look closely at what the right thing is, it happens to be what's in their best interests anyway.'

'Human nature.'

La nodded. 'That's what they say.'

She looked at Tim. His face was drawn, and there was a pallor about him that she had not seen before. 'You're really tired, aren't you?'

He rubbed his forehead. 'Yes. But I'm alive. When I look at the list of names—the list of chaps we've lost—that brings it home to me.'

She reached across and poured him a cup of tea. 'You need a break. Can't you get some leave? Even a few days.'

He shook his head. He told her that he had applied for a long weekend to visit his wife in Cardiff, but his request had been turned down. He had even arranged the transport—a plane was going over there and they could take him—but it had made no difference. 'So I'm stuck. But . . . I suppose I can take a few hours to practise for the Christmas concert.'

La hesitated. It hardly seemed the time to mention her decision to stop the orchestra, but she feared there would never be a right time.

'I've been thinking,' she began, 'and . . . well, I feel that I've done everything I can with the orchestra. I thought I might stop.'

He stared at her. He was aghast. 'Stop the orchestra?'

I have the right to do this, she thought. 'Yes. We've been going for quite some time now. Struggling through our somewhat limited repertoire. Not playing all that well. It's been fun, but . . . I don't know. You can't carry on indefinitely doing the same old thing, can you?'

He picked up his teacup and drank from it, watching her over the rim. Then, putting down the cup, he leaned forward. 'That's where you're wrong, La. We have to do the same old thing. We have to.'

'Why?'

He leaned forward even further and took her hand. The gesture surprised her and she wanted to withdraw it. But she could not; he gripped her.

'Why? You ask why? Because your orchestra, La, stands for everything that we're doing. We meet once a month and play because that's what we do. It shows anybody who cares to look that we are not giving up. And none of us can give up, can we? If we give up what we're doing, everything's lost.'

She looked down at the floor. He was still holding her.

'Believe me, La,' he went on, 'your little orchestra means a lot to every one of those people playing in it. It means a lot to the chaps from the base. You are one of the things that are keeping us all going. Don't you see that?'

He let go of her hand and sat back. Their eyes were upon one another. She looked at him and she saw a tired man who sent other men to their deaths in lumbering planes; he saw a woman who was lonely and upset and dispirited.

He transferred his gaze out of the window. There was sunlight on the few lavender bushes that had survived the vegetable campaign. The grey-green foliage was briefly touched with gold.

'Oh my God, La,' he said. 'It's so damned hard. It really is. I know I shouldn't be defeatist, but we're on our absolute uppers.'

'The Americans might come.'

He shook his head. 'Do you really think so?'

It was a while before she responded. She closed her eyes and the thought came to her: defeat. She had heard about the *exode* in France over that terrible June. A Frenchwoman whom she had met in Bury had told her about the families aimlessly wandering along the roads of rural France, fleeing the Germans; of the young women who covered themselves in Dijon mustard so that the Germans who raped them might be stung; of the young men being rounded up and taken off in trains; of the abandoned harvests and the empty towns. 'You're right,' she said. 'We have no alternative but to carry on. We—you and I—can sit here and have our doubts about everything, but we can't let people see that. If the orchestra grinds to a halt, then people will know that we're giving up. They could think that, couldn't they?'

He smiled. 'It could get back to Churchill. Somebody could whisper to him, "Bad news, sir. We've lost La's Orchestra."'

They both laughed.

'More tea, then?'

He accepted the offer and she poured the tea into his cup.

'You'll have been thinking about Dab,' he said.

She looked up sharply. She had not wanted to press him, in case he did not want to talk about it.

'I managed to get through the impenetrable barriers of counterespionage. I happen to know somebody in London who does something in that department. He made an enquiry and let me know—off the record.'

She held up a hand. 'You don't have to tell me if you'd rather not.'

He shook his head. 'It's all right. Dab is in the clear. A bona fide Polish airman who had an unequal brush with the Luftwaffe in France and ended up here. As I always thought. Nothing untoward at all.'

She put down her cup. Her relief made her feel shaky.

'So he's coming back?'

Tim sighed. 'Sorry, La. But, no. They've found some work for him in Cambridge. They needed somebody with languages—which Feliks has got. You know he's fluent in German and French as well as English? That sort of chap is very useful and so at long last they'll be using his talents. Listening to radio traffic or something like that. No more pigs.'

La's voice was quiet. 'No. No more pigs.' She waited a moment or two. Then she asked, 'Have you got an address for him?'

'No,' said Tim. 'It was enough of a breach of security for him to tell me even that much. He couldn't say more.'

'Of course not.'

'You're going to miss him, aren't you?'

She closed her eyes. 'Yes, I'll miss him. I'll miss him an awful lot.'

'I'm sorry, La. I'm sorry about all of this. This wretched war. Everything. Maybe at the end of it all, he'll . . . he'll come back here.'

She did not think that likely. 'I doubt it.'

They sat in silence. Then Tim looked at his watch and frowned. 'I'd better go. I'm on duty again in an hour.'

La rose to her feet. 'One last thing. Do you think he knows that I was the one who mentioned his . . . his slips of the tongue?'

Tim was not sure. 'Maybe. It depends on the interrogators. I imagine that they usually protect their informants, but then they may ask things that make it pretty obvious who's said what.' He stopped, and put a hand on her shoulder. He was like a brother, she thought. 'Are you worried? I don't think he's the sort to hold a grudge, if that's any help.'

THE NEXT DAY, when she had finished with the hens, she found Henry struggling to fix the latch on a gate. With his arthritic hands it was difficult to use a screwdriver, and La gently took the implement from him and quickly effected the repair.

'I could do it,' he muttered. 'But my hands are bad today. Thank you, La.'

She looked at him sympathetically. 'You're doing well in the circumstances. Lots of people would have given up.'

'We don't give up,' said Henry. 'My dad didn't. He had the same thing. He never gave up.'

'Good. That's the spirit.'

One of Henry's geese waddled past them and inspected them casually before continuing her journey.

'She's going to make somebody's Christmas,' said Henry. 'Look at her. Fattening up nicely. Getting ready for the big day.'

They began to walk back to the farmhouse, where the eggs were to be stacked before La left. 'I've had news of Feliks,' she said, once they were in the kitchen and Henry was putting on the kettle.

He was about to place the kettle on the range, and his hand stopped in midair before he lowered it. 'Yes?'

'Yes. Are you interested?'

He shrugged. 'Don't think much about him.'

La had not expected this. 'But you think he stole your money. Surely—'

'No. Not any more.'

She stared at him. 'You do know that Percy Brown let him go?'

He stood with his back to her, watching the kettle. 'Knew that. He told me himself. Cycled out here and told me. No evidence, he said. Never liked him, that Percy Brown.'

'But he cleared Feliks. So that's that, isn't it?' She paused. She felt anger rising in her. Henry clearly felt no guilt about Feliks, and this appalled her. Now she said—although he did not deserve it, 'And I have an idea who took your money, if you're interested.'

He turned round to face her. He was smiling. 'Nobody,' he said. 'Nobody took it. It was in the other cupboard. Got a bit mixed up. It's all there.'

She did not drink tea with him, but attended to the stacking of the eggs in silence. He watched her from the other side of the room, and although she tried to ignore him, she was conscious of his gaze.

'You're not cross with me?' he asked.

She did not reply.

'La? You're not cross, are you? I really thought it had gone. I looked and looked. But I had forgotten, you see, that I had moved it. It's easy to make a mistake, La.'

She sighed. 'All right, Henry. All right. I'm not cross with you.'

'Good. Careful with those eggs now. The shells get very brittle, you know, round about this time of year, when the hens are hungry.'

LA REMEMBERED HOW at the beginning, before the war really got going, they had spoken, half in jest but half seriously, about a victory concert. Superstition had taken over and there had been no such hubristic talk after that, until April 1945, when one of the sisters from Bury whispered to La: 'La, it's getting close, I think. Maybe the orchestra should be ready.'

She agreed, but said that they would not talk about it just yet. 'I'll look out some pieces. I'll find something.'

They would avoid triumphalism, she thought. Their victory concert would be one that would give people the chance to think about what they had been through. There would be something reflective, something peaceful, and perhaps, at one point, just silence for a few minutes. Music on either side of a silence made that silence all the more powerful.

The moment itself was really a series of moments. She happened to hear the newsflash: the brief sound of bells and then the words, 'The German Radio has just announced that Hitler is dead.' She sat down and folded her hands on her lap. She stood up and then sat down again. She did not know what to do. It seemed to her that everything would now stop; everything had been geared to this moment, for year after year, and now it had arrived. What would there be to do?

She barely slept and was bone-tired when she went to deal with the hens. Henry produced a bottle of brandy and poured her half a glass. He had been drinking already, and his words were slurred. He kissed her on the cheek, and she smelled the alcohol on his breath.

'You won't leave the hens now, will you?' he asked.

'I haven't thought about it,' she said. 'I don't want to look after them for ever.'

'I understand. But please . . . please not just yet.'

She sipped cautiously at her brandy; it was not a drink that she liked. They listened to the Prime Minister together. La closed her eyes as the familiar voice spoke to them; she heard the words, but her mind wandered. She felt only gratitude that he was there, that he had lived to see this moment. Comfortable, slightly eccentric, kind; it was Mr Churchill she saw, but it was also England.

'We may allow ourselves a brief period of rejoicing,' said Mr Churchill.

She called on the Aggs. Mrs Agg said, 'I can't believe it, Mrs Stone. I just can't.'

'Well, it's true.'

Lennie came into the room. 'Good, isn't it?' he muttered. 'Old Hitler's dead now.'

La rose to her feet and embraced him, planting a kiss on his cheek. She spoke on impulse. 'Our orchestra is going to have a victory concert, Lennie. Would you like to play?'

He looked at her in astonishment. 'Me? I can't play.'

'But you like Billy Cotton, don't you? You must be musical. You could play the drums. We need somebody for that. Our percussionist would like some help.'

Mrs Agg watched anxiously. 'Go on, Lennie.'

He looked at his mother, and she nodded.

'All right. I'll play.'

La's orchestra performed its concert for victory a few days after V-E Day. Word got out in the area and more people came than there were seats. The concert was on a Saturday afternoon, a warm day for that time of year. There were spring flowers on the banks and at the edges of the fields; the trees were coming into leaf. The Bury paper had mentioned the event—SMALL ORCHESTRA PLANS BIG CONCERT—and there had been a brief piece in the *Cambridge Daily News*. It was this report that Feliks had seen, and that had brought him to the concert, arriving slightly later than the other players. He slipped in unnoticed by La, and shared a music stand and music with another flautist. La, who had been busy handing out sheet music, noticed him just before they began the first piece. For a few moments she stood quite still. Then Feliks looked up and their eyes met. He mouthed the word 'Hello'. She nodded and smiled. She did not show her feelings.

Tim stood up and made a short speech. He said, 'I am one of those who are grateful to La for keeping our little orchestra going through thick and thin. I knew one day that we would have this victory concert, but obviously I did not know when, I thought it might be two years; then I thought three. It's been almost five. Now we are here to celebrate what has happened over the last few days and to think about some of the members of this orchestra who cannot be here because they have given their lives for their country—for their countries—and for peace.'

The hall was quiet as he read out the names of a young airman from Lancaster, a mechanic from Nova Scotia and a man from Des Moines who had been shot down over Holland.

Tim sat down. La did not want to be thanked, but the audience was clapping her now, including those who were outside, listening through the door because there were not enough seats to be had. They all applauded. She looked over the heads of the players. She saw Feliks, who had laid his flute on his lap and was clapping too.

It was not easy for her to get through the programme. At the end, when the orchestra played 'Jerusalem' and people started to sing, La cried. She continued to conduct, though, and made it to the end, when she turned and faced the audience and bowed.

Afterwards, there was tea and cake served from tables at the side of the hall. The village had baked for days, and every sultana and cherry for miles around had been committed to the purpose. She found herself talking to Tim, and could tell from his eyes that he had cried too.

She looked through the milling crowd. The whole village, together with everyone from the surrounding farms, was there. And there were at least thirty people from the air base, many in uniform. Where was Feliks?

She saw him near the door, talking to an airman, and slipped through the crowd until she was standing behind him.

'Feliks?'

He turned round slowly. She moved forward and put her arms round him.

'Thank you for coming,' she said. 'I wish I had known.'

'I read about it in the paper,' he said. 'I had to come.'

'Of course.'

She disengaged from the embrace and they stood facing one another.

'You don't blame me, do you?' she asked.

He hesitated, but she knew from his expression that he knew what she was talking about. 'I did. But not now.'

'I didn't know what to do,' she said. 'I was very confused.'

'It was a confusing time,' he said. 'But all that's over now.'

She saw him glance at his watch and she searched desperately for something to keep him. But she could not think of anything.

'Will you come and see me again?' she asked.

He pulled at the sleeves of his shirt. 'One day, maybe. I don't know where I'm going to be, though.'

'Of course you don't. But you know how to get in touch with me.'

Tim had come over and was shaking hands with Feliks. La moved away. There was nothing more she could say.

PART THREE

TWELVE

Tim left the base two months later, when he was given early demobilisation to take up a job with a civilian aircraft manufacturer in Bristol. Nothing had been said about disbanding the orchestra, but somehow everybody had assumed that this was what would happen. With Tim's departure it was inevitable, and La wrote a short letter to everybody telling them that her orchestra had served its purpose.

Tim came to see her the day before he left. 'We had a good innings,' he said. 'But I suppose it's time now, isn't it? What are you going to do, La?'

She had not thought about that. The euphoria and the air of unreality of the previous weeks had kept her from planning a future. Now, without thinking, she replied, 'Oh, I shall probably go and live in London for a while.'

'Lucky you. Theatre, and all that. Proper orchestras.'

'I imagine that it'll take a bit of time to get used to it again.'

She had not entertained the idea of moving back to London—not since Valerie had put her off at the beginning of the war—but the idea must have been there, subconsciously, as it had popped up so readily. She could do it. Richard's parents had died during the war, within a year of one another, and their house in Chiswick, along with a substantial part of their estate, had come to her. She had already been comfortably off financially and the money made no real difference. But the house was empty, looked after by their housekeeper, and she could move in whenever she wished. She could keep the Suffolk house, of course, as a weekend place. And she could get a job—a real job this time—something that would allow her to use her mind.

The plan grew. She visited the house in Chiswick, passing through a London landscape that shocked her in its drabness and destruction. After Suffolk, where at least there was the high sky and the air, London seemed pinched and run-down, battered by what had happened to it.

She was shown round the house by the housekeeper. It had been kept clean, but there was in it that coldness that comes when the inhabiting spirit leaves a building.

'I could be out of my rooms in a week or two. I could go up north . . .' the housekeeper offered.

'You don't have to leave, Mrs Eaton. There's so much room here.'

Two months later La moved from Suffolk to Chiswick. For a couple of weeks she organised the house, making it more habitable. Mrs Eaton kept the kitchen, and proved to be a competent cook.

Next, La found a job. A small music publisher wanted a person to assist its manager. They specialised in the publication of collections of traditional songs, and they needed somebody who could turn a hand to any of the tasks associated with that. At her interview, La was shown a collection of folk songs from the British Isles. The page proofs fell open at 'Brigg Fair'.

'We played that,' she remarked. 'I had a little orchestra in Suffolk. Very amateurish. We played that during the war.' She turned the page. 'And here's "Scarborough Fair"'.

The manager was looking at her across his desk. 'Cambridge,' he said.

'You too?'

'Yes. Do you remember Paulson's Music Shop? We deal with him.'

She said that she did. And she remembered the buying of the flute, and the way that Feliks held it when she first gave it to him.

The manager closed the file in front of him. 'It seems to me that you would be just the person for this position, Mrs Stone,' he said.

The job was perfect. The office, which was near the British Museum, was small and chaotic, filled with scores and proofs of scores and letters to arrangers and composers. La succeeded in bringing some order to it, and was promoted. She was given a new room, with a carpet and a two-bar fire. From her window she looked out onto a small square of garden. At weekends, she went to the house in Suffolk; Mrs Agg would air it for her just before she arrived and make a fire in the range. Lennie cut the hedges and mowed the grass in summer. He talked to her now, and told her that he had somebody he called his 'sweetheart', a young woman from a neighbouring village. He would marry her one day, he said.

'You should marry again, Mrs Stone,' said Mrs Agg. 'I hope you don't mind my saying that. But you're an attractive woman and there must be men enough in London.'

La laughed. 'I'm forty-one now, Mrs Agg. Who would want a woman of forty-one?'

'A man of forty-two, I'd say. Are there any of them in London?'

From time to time, she heard from Tim, and even saw him on occasion, when he came to London on business, and they would go for lunch in a Soho restaurant. They talked about the war, and the orchestra, and he told her the news from the aviation world, which meant little to her. Then, on one of these occasions, he suddenly said to her, 'You know, La, looking back . . . I feel really bad about the Poles.'

She looked surprised. 'But I always thought that you went out of your way to help them. Look what you did for Feliks.'

'It's not me personally. It's what we as a people did. We betrayed them.'

'Yalta.'

'Yes. Of course, there was that. I remember after the news got out, the Poles looked as if they'd been winded. Quite a few of us felt that we just couldn't look them in the eye. We had just given their country to the very enemy who had joined in with the Germans in dismembering it. We gave it to those who had been allies of Nazi Germany.'

La agreed. But she pointed out that it had not been easy to deal with Stalin. Roosevelt had wanted them to join in the war against Japan; he had to give them something. She sighed; the world was rotten. 'Yalta was a disaster, yes, I know. But what else could they do? How could they . . .' She searched for words, but none came. At the heart of the machinations of statesmen were greed and fear and a seeking of advantage. But could one say that without sounding completely cynical?

Tim was watching her. 'Yalta,' he said, 'was the big sellout. But there were other things too. Did you see the Victory parade in London?'

La did. She had watched it alone, in the rain, and had thought about how it must seem to those who had lost their husband, their father, their son or daughter. She replied simply, 'I did.'

Tim looked at her enquiringly. 'And who wasn't there?'

La knew. 'The Poles.'

'Exactly. We didn't let them let those brave men—march alongside everybody else because Stalin had said they were not to be in the parade. Our parade, not his. And do you know something, La? I had a letter from one of them who said that he'd watched the parade in tears.'

He watched the effect of his words. La looked down at the tablecloth.

'And do you know something else?' Tim continued. 'Some of our politicians called the Poles fascists. They were so much in love with their hero Stalin and his beloved Soviet Union that they took their cue from the very Russians who had murdered all those Polish officers. Or had carted people off to die in the labour camps.' He shook his head. 'No wonder, La. No wonder the Poles felt betrayed. They fought for a country that they would never be able to return to. They lost everything. No pensions. Nothing.

'But what makes me sick at heart, La, is the thought of those men watching the parade in tears. They had fought in the Battle of Britain, with us, right beside us, and they were forbidden to take part. That's what sickens me more than anything else. How could Churchill have allowed that?'

La thought, Doesn't he remember? 'He had no power.'

'Or the King?'

La shrugged. 'Even less power.' She reached out to lay her hand on his forearm. 'I'm sure that Feliks would have understood.'

'Would he?' Tim asked. 'Do you really think so?'

They talked about Feliks. 'I've often thought,' Tim said, 'that you and Feliks might have been . . . suited. You were very friendly, weren't you?' He smiled encouragingly. 'Was there ever anything between you?'

La held his gaze. 'Nothing. Not really.'

IN THE LATE SUMMER of 1960, La went to Edinburgh, to the Festival. On the evening before she was due to return to London, she went to an orchestral concert at the Usher Hall. At the end of the concert, there was still some light in the northern sky and the evening was warm. The audience spilled out onto the pavement in front of the hall, talking about the programme, exchanging the welled-up small talk that concert audiences release at the end of a performance. La stood for a moment on the steps, enjoying the festival feel of the occasion, and it was then that she saw Feliks.

He had come out of a side door and was about to walk up Lothian Road when he stopped and turned to face her. It seemed that he was hesitant to approach her, but she made the first move and took a few steps towards him.

They shook hands. It was very formal.

She smiled at him, hoping that he could not hear her wildly beating heart. 'I thought it was you.'

'And it is. Fifteen years later? Yes, fifteen.'

He seemed pleased to see her, in spite of the formality.

'Where . . .' she began to ask. But he cut her short.

'I live in Glasgow now. I have lived there since the end of the war. I was offered a job there by a Pole who had set up a business.'

'Oh.'

She did not look for it, but she saw the ring. He noticed.

'Yes. I married a Scottish lady. Twelve years ago. We have two small boys. One is five and the other is seven.'

La tried to smile. Again he noticed. He could see the effort.

'My marriage is not a success,' he said. 'She calls herself a Catholic, but she is a rather bad Catholic, I'm afraid. I see her every few weeks—she comes to visit the boys—but she is living with a man who has a bar.'

'I'm very sorry to hear that.'

He nodded. 'Not good. But you—where are you?'

'I am in London. But I still go out to Suffolk. I still have the house.'

His eyes lit up. 'With the lavender bushes?'

'Yes. They need cutting back, I think.'

They both laughed. Then La said, 'Feliks, I have to ask you. If I don't ask you now, then I may never know. Do you know why I had to speak to Tim as I did? Do you understand?'

Behind them a woman said something to a man in a dinner jacket and the man chuckled. Feliks glanced at the couple and then back at La. 'Yes, I do understand. You knew that I was German.'

It took her a moment to grasp what he said. 'So I was right?'

'Yes. But you were kind to me and you did nothing about it. You see . . .' He looked over his shoulder. 'You see, my parents were Germans who went to live in Poland. My father was a businessman. I was eight when they went and I went to school there. I learned Polish and spoke it all the time. When I went to university I decided that I would be Polish altogether. The Nazis had come to power then in Germany. I had no desire to go back. Then I joined the air force. I took the identity of a man who had worked for my father and who had died. I joined the air force under his name.'

She reached out and took his hand. He did not resist; they held hands.

'It seemed clear to me,' he continued. 'If I had tried to explain to people who I really was, they would have been suspicious. When I ended up in England, they would probably have interned me.'

He was right. 'Yes, that could have happened.'

'It was simpler to be Polish, which is what I felt. What I feel now.'

She wanted to hug him. 'I understand,' she said.

'They found all this out in London, but the man who interrogated me was sympathetic. He had a German grandfather and he knew that we were not all monsters. He gave me clearance and they found work for me.'

'So,' she said.

'Yes. So.'

He looked at his watch. 'I have to get back to Glasgow. The boys are being looked after tonight by the wife of a friend. But I have to get the last train back.' He reached for a pen from his jacket pocket and started to write on the back of his programme. 'Here is my address in Glasgow. Perhaps one day we shall be able to meet again.'

She took the programme from him and put it in her bag. He pressed her hand briefly, and was gone.

THE FOLLOWING YEAR, in 1961, the year of La's fiftieth birthday, the music publishers were acquired by a larger firm and La resigned. She decided to go back to Suffolk, keeping the London house for when she wanted to spend time in town.

Agg had retired, and sat in the kitchen all day, complaining to Mrs Agg about the weather and the government. Lennie ran the farm, and had married the woman he called his sweetheart. She got on well with her mother-in-law and they seemed happy enough. 'You can't make a farmer's wife,' said Mrs Agg. 'You're born to it or you're not. Lennie's sweetheart was born to it.'

Henry Madder was in a wheelchair, but had stayed where he was; no Madder had ever gone anywhere, he claimed. A nephew on his wife's side had taken over the running of his farm and had got rid of the hens, using the wood from the henhouses to patch up fences and gates. The pig farmer had died in a fall from his horse. Percy Brown had become a sergeant and then had left the force to drive a taxi in Bury in his retirement.

La hoped that Feliks would get in touch with her, but he did not. She sent him a Christmas card that December and told him that she had moved back to Suffolk.

La thought about peace. She had been born just before the first war, and had been seven when it ended. She remembered the Armistice as a time of bells and strange, adult rejoicing. Then there had been her own war, the one which she knew had involved such a narrow escape. She had seen the estimates of the number killed: the mind could hardly contemplate those tens of millions, all those wasted, curtailed lives; all that misery. And then, after all that, an arms race that threatened to obscure the losses of the first fifty years of the century; this could destroy all human life, darken the skies for centuries. It cannot happen, she told herself. Humanity could not be so stupid.

But it almost did happen. The world had become divided into two hostile camps, each bristling with arms, each marking out territory with barbed wire and towers. In one of these camps, people lived under the thumb of a tsar in modern clothing, serfs to an ideology that sought to bend human nature to its particular vision; in the other, human nature could be itself, but that brought injustice and exploitation, not always held in check by the values proclaimed by the rhetoric of freedom. La saw the world change before her eyes: people relaxed, dressed less formally, spoke about the end of the old oppressive structures that had held people down in ways subtle and unsubtle. But for her, life seemed unchanged, barely touched by the movements and shifts of the times.

Again I have missed it, she thought; heady things are happening and I am not there. That is what my life has been. Even in my marriage, Richard's heart was elsewhere. I have been a handmaiden; one who waits and watches; assists, perhaps, but only in a small way.

Standing in her kitchen one afternoon, she looked out of her window, over the fields on the other side of the road and to the sky beyond. Heavy, purple clouds had built up; rain would reach her soon—it was already falling on the fields to the east, a veil of it drifting down, caught in the slanting afternoon light, white against the inky bulk of the clouds behind. She stood transfixed by the moment, as happens sometimes, when we are not expecting it. We stop and think about the beauty of the world, and its majesty, and the insignificance of our concerns and cares. And yet we know that they are not insignificant—at least not to us; even in our ultimate insignificance, pain and loss loom large, are wounding, are sore. So each of us, thought La, each one of us should do something to make life better for somebody, to change the course of events, even if only in the most local sense. Even a handmaiden can do something about that.

The moment passed. La had become accustomed to an uneventful life; a life of reading, of listening to music, of occasional entertaining of friends from London. She travelled to Italy, taking guided art tours in groups of like-minded people. Friendships developed on these trips, but even when promises were made to keep in touch, this rarely happened. La did not mind; she had accepted loneliness as her lot.

A friend passed her literature on the Campaign for Nuclear Disarmament. She read the leaflets and thought: everything they say here is true. We cannot use these weapons; nobody can. But she knew that there were those who did not think this way, and joined a march from Aldermaston, where these weapons were developed, to London. She stood in Trafalgar Square in a crowd of almost 100,000 people and listened to the call for the rejection of these ways of killing us all.

And then, that autumn, it all almost came true. The Russians were placing missiles in Cuba that would enable them to strike the United States at short range. Demands were made and positions taken. Two deadly enemies, each capable of destroying the other, and everyone else with them, faced one another over a chessboard of bristling missiles. When the news sank in, and what it could mean, La went out into her garden. The leaves had fallen and the garden was braced for winter; somewhere, high above her head, there was an aeroplane; the droning of its engine seemed ominous now, just as that same sound had been ominous twenty years previously.

La thought: last time, when evil incarnate threatened us, we each did something, even if it was only looking after hens. The world was smaller, more personal then; now this is being decided by machines with blinking lights, by radar screens, by the switches and levers of a world that has ceased to have anything to do with a person standing in her garden.

On the day after President Kennedy addressed the American people and the full gravity of the Cuban situation came to be understood, La sat down and drew up a list of those members of her orchestra with whom she was still in touch. It came to twelve names, including Tim, Feliks and the two sisters from Bury. She telephoned them all that afternoon and evening.

'I want to hold a concert for peace,' she said. 'In five days' time. I know that it's not much notice, but there isn't much time, I'm afraid.'

She asked people to contact other members of the orchestra and pass on the message. Everyone she spoke to said they would participate.

On the morning of the concert, La woke early and walked in her garden, nursing a cup of tea. She looked up at the sky. If the end were to come, it would be the end of everything—the end of music, the end of her house, of Suffolk, of the birds, of lavender bushes, of England.

They gathered in the tin hall. Many people came—so many that, as at the victory concert, there were people standing outside. The atmosphere was grave. They were silent; nobody talked or smiled as they had done in 1945.

La stood at the podium. She had chosen the music carefully, and although they had not had time to rehearse, they played to the best of their ability and the audience listened with solemnity. Nobody clapped between the pieces. It had hit them abruptly, and with shocking force, that this could so easily be goodbye; that a rash decision could bring the world to an end.

But that was not really why La had called the concert. She had called it because she believed in the power of music. Absurdly, irrationally, she believed that music could make a difference to the temper of the world. She did not investigate this belief, she simply believed it, and so she chose music that expressed order and healing: Bach for order, Mozart for healing. This was the antithesis of the anger and fear that could unleash the missiles.

And then, near the end, somebody outside shouted, and the shout came through the door and into the hall. Mr Khrushchev had made a speech on Moscow Radio. They were not going to die.

They stopped. People dropped their instruments. They embraced one another. They cried. Lennie hit his drums enthusiastically in one long, powerful roll that threatened to burst the instruments' skins. Nobody worried. The loss of drums was nothing to the loss of the world.

La walked back to her house. She would return to the hall, where a party had broken out, but she wanted to fetch a coat for it had turned cold. She was in her kitchen when the car came into the drive. It was Feliks.

He got out of the car and his two small boys were with him. She had seen him in the hall, and they had exchanged a few words, but she had not seen the boys. They looked so like Feliks, she thought.

'I wanted to see you,' he said.

'And you've brought your boys.'

'Yes, these are my boys.'

They sat in the kitchen, where they had sat together so many times all those years ago. The boys played outside, some game that involved one chasing the other. 'They can play like that for hours,' he said. 'So much energy.'

'I don't suppose they have any idea of the danger we've been through,' said La. 'Fortunately for them.'

Feliks nodded. 'Sometimes we don't have an idea of the danger we're in. Did we? During the war? Did we really know how close it came?'

'Perhaps we did. But we couldn't really lead our lives thinking about it. We had to believe that we were going to be all right.' She fell silent.

'And now, here we are again.' He looked at her. 'Happy or unhappy, as the case may be. Which is it, La? Which is it for you?'

'Happy enough,' she said. 'Some parts of my life have been unhappy. I might have been happier if I had had children.'

He looked away. 'Yes, I understand.'

'And if I had been a better musician.' She laughed, and he did too.

'You have time to improve,' he said. 'You could start your orchestra again.'

'There was a special time for that,' she said. 'Not now.'

'Maybe not.'

The kitchen door had been pushed open by a small hand, and the boys had returned. The smaller one had fallen and there was mud on the knees of his trousers. La got up and fetched a damp cloth from the sink. 'I'll do that for you,' she said to the boy. 'Come over here.'

Felix watched. When she had finished wiping off the mud, the boy took a step backwards. He was shy.

Felix spoke. 'La, your orchestra has saved the world—again.'

She made a self-deprecatory gesture. 'I don't know about that,' she said.

'I do,' he said.

She reached out to ruffle the hair of the smaller boy, who had been staring at her. 'What are you going to do now?' she asked Feliks. 'Go back to Glasgow?'

'Yes. I suppose I should.'

She drew breath. In the face of the end of everything, even if the threat had suddenly passed, one might say what one had always wanted to say. 'Stay with me,' she said. 'You could stay here. I think we would be happy.'

Feliks held her gaze, and she looked into his eyes. Then he glanced at the boys. 'But . . .'

'All of you,' she said.

And she picked up the boys, one after the other, and kissed them.

ALEXANDER McCALL SMITH

Born: 1948, Rhodesia (now Zimbabwe)
First book: *The White Hippo* (1980)
Honour: CBE in 2007 for services to literature

The No. 1 Ladies' Detective Agency (2004), a warm and gentle story about a 'traditionally built' lady detective living in Botswana, was the book that launched Alexander McCall Smith, an avuncular Edinburgh professor of medical law in Edinburgh, into the world of global publishing. After seven more books in the series, Mma Ramotswe, the central character, has become a household name in thirty-eight languages and has been portrayed by the actress Jill Scott in a television series airing in the UK in 2009.

Now aged sixty, Alexander McCall Smith is a prolific author. He has written more than sixty books, as well as short stories, radio plays, and a second popular series, about a Scottish-American editor and amateur sleuth, Isabel Dalhousie. Then, setting both series aside, he turned to write a stand-alone novel, *La's Orchestra Saves the World*, focusing on life in Suffolk during a thirty- year period of global turbulence. 'I thought the nineteen thirties was an interesting period because of the growing crisis in Europe,' McCall Smith explains. 'I decided to trace the history of somebody involved in that time up until the early nineteen sixties—the time of the Cuban missile crisis.'

La (short for Lavender) first appeared in a series for Radio 3. McCall Smith says that at that time he had the character, the orchestra and the bones for the story but needed a location. 'Then I thought of Suffolk. I had an aunt who lived there and when I was a child I would go and stay with her, so I got to know the countryside a little.'

McCall Smith returned to Suffolk to reacquaint himself, hoping to add texture to La's surroundings. An old friend played host and drove him round the villages of West Suffolk. 'There are some wonderful villages that seem to have survived the modern age, and I love those little lanes with their old metal road signs. I think there were fewer hedgerows than I remembered . . . In the past I've been to the coast and there's some gorgeous countryside around Aldeburgh. And of course those lovely, huge open skies. I wanted to get across a sense of place in the book, so I was also looking at what was growing at the edge of the roads and in the gardens, things like that.

'I had a very strong sense of La moving from London to Suffolk after her marriage failed. As she gets to know people in the community, there's a gradual build up of tension with the international situation getting worse and worse until along comes the Second World War. It was a period of tremendous heroism. I really admire what so many people did then and how they rose to the occasion. In particular, if you look at the history of the RAF, you cannot but be immensely impressed at the courage of those men and women. The whole idea of the book is that even those who weren't on the front line, so to speak, were nonetheless able to contribute something. In La's case she got an amateur orchestra going with some of the airmen from the RAF base, as well as some locals, playing the instruments. It's a story about how music really can make a big difference to people.'

THE REALLY TERRIBLE ORCHESTRA

In 1995, Alexander McCall Smith founded the Really Terrible Orchestra, comprising 'the cream of Edinburgh's musically disadvantaged', with just ten players. He and his wife, Elizabeth, who plays the horn, and some friends had felt envious when they saw the pleasure that their children felt when making music together. Realising that no professional orchestra would have them, they decided to form their own. McCall Smith, who plays the contrabassoon and sousaphone, said at the time, 'It won't be a good orchestra. In fact, it will be a really terrible one'. The musicians meet fortnightly in Edinburgh and are directed by Richard Neville-Towle, a professional musician. In the beginning, concerts were held in private, but then the RTO were persuaded to perform one concert at the Edinburgh Fringe in 2007. It was a sell-out. Since then, they have performed in London, New York, and at the book launch of *La's Orchestra Saved the World*, when proceeds went to Big Noise, a children's orchestra. See *www.thereallyterrible orchestra.com* for more information.

ENVY THE NIGHT

MICHAEL KORYTA

It's been seven years since Frank Temple learned that his father, a US marshal, maintained a covert career as a contract killer, leading a double life that he ended by suicide, rather than face prosecution. This shocking revelation has triggered years of drifting for Frank, and he has struggled to accept the so-called facts. So when he hears that Devin Matteson, the man who lured his father into the killing game, is returning to an old haunt—a deserted lakeside cabin—Frank is determined to settle the score.

1

Frank Temple III walked out of the county jail at ten in the morning with a headache, a citation for public intox, and a notion that it was time to leave town.

It wasn't the arrest that convinced him. That had been merely a nightcap to an evening of farewells—Frank hanging from the street lamp outside Nick's on Kirkwood Avenue, looking down into the face of a bored cop who'd seen too many drunks and saying, 'Officer, I'd like to report a missing pair of pants.'

It hadn't been the hours in the detox cell, either. Frank was one of six in the cell. Sitting with his back against the cold concrete wall listening to some poor guy retch in the corner, Frank considered the jail, the people who checked in and wouldn't check out the next morning the way he would. He considered the harsh fluorescent lights, the dead air, the hard looks developed to hide the hopelessness, and knew that if he could understand only one thing about his father, it was the decision he'd made to avoid this place.

This was the second time Frank had been in a jail. The first time was for a drunk-driving charge in a small North Carolina town two years earlier. And even if his father hadn't found a coward's way to avoid a life sentence, the number would be the same. Frank wouldn't have visited. But he couldn't hide the thought that maybe the reason he put himself in situations like this was because he wanted a taste, just a taste, something he could walk back into the free world with and think—*that's what it would've been like for him.*

He'd been chased into the night of drinking by one disturbing phone message and one pretentious professor. The message had come first, left by a voice he hadn't heard in years:

'Frank, it's Ezra Ballard. Been a long time, hasn't it? You sound older on your message. Anyhow, I'm calling because, well . . . he's coming back, Frank. I just got a call from Florida telling me to open up the cabin. Now, I'm not telling you to do anything, don't even care if you call me back. I'm just keeping my word, right? Just keeping my word, son. He's coming back, and now I've told you.'

Frank hadn't returned the call. He intended to let it go. Knew that he should, at least. By the end of the day, though, he was done in Bloomington. A single semester of school—his fifth college in seven years—and Frank was done again. He'd come here to work with a writer named Walter Thorp, whose work Frank had admired for years. Bloomington was closer to home than Frank had allowed himself to come in a long time, but Thorp was a visiting professor there, and he couldn't pass up that chance. It had gone well, too. Thorp was good, better even than Frank had expected, and Frank had worked his ass off for a few months. Read like crazy, wrote like crazy, saw good things happening on the page. The last week of the semester brought an email from Thorp, requesting a meeting, and Frank used that to push Ballard's call out of his mind. *Focus on the future. Don't drown in the past.*

That was his mantra when he went to the cramped office on the second floor of Sycamore Hall, sat there and listened as Thorp complimented Frank's writing, told him that he'd seen 'great strides' during the semester, that Frank clearly had 'powerful stories to tell'. Frank nodded and thanked his way through it, feeling good.

'I've never done this for a student before,' Thorp said, arching an eyebrow, 'but I'd like to introduce you to my agent.'

Frank just looked back at Thorp and didn't speak, waiting to see what else would be said.

'In fact,' Thorp added, 'I've already mentioned you to him a few times. He's interested. Very interested. But he was wondering—we both were, really—have you ever given thought to writing nonfiction? Maybe a memoir?'

Frank got it then. He felt his jaw tighten and his eyes go flat, and he stared at the old-fashioned window behind Thorp's head and wondered what the great writer would look like flying through it, landing on the terrace two floors below.

'I only ask because your story, and the way it intersects with your father's story, well, it could be quite compelling. Nate—he's my agent—he thinks the market would be fantastic. You might even be able to get a deal on just a synop and a few sample chapters. Nate thinks an auction would be possible, and that's the sort of circumstance where the dollar figures can go through the—'

He had the good sense not to follow Frank out of the door. Ten hours later, Frank was in the jail, all the amusement left in his drunken mind vanishing when the booking officer looked up from the paperwork and said, 'No middle name?'

Nope. Just that Roman numeral tacked on the end, Frank Temple III, the next step in the legacy, a follow-up act to two war heroes: one a murderer.

They'd left him in the detox cell then, left him with swirling thoughts of his father and Thorp and the message. Oh, yes, the message. He'd deleted it, but there would be no need to play it again. It was trapped in his brain, cycled through a dozen times as he sat awake waiting for morning.

He's coming back.

He was not allowed to come back. Frank and Ezra had promised one another that, agreed that they'd let him live out his days down there in Miami so long as he never tried to return, but now there was this phone call from Ezra saying that, after seven years, the son of a bitch had decided to test their will, call that old bluff.

All right, then. If he would return, then so would Frank.

HE WAS NORTHBOUND by noon, the Jeep loaded with his possessions. Except loaded wasn't the right word, because Frank always travelled light so he could pack fast. The quicker he packed, the easier it was to ignore his father's guns. He didn't want them, never had. Through nineteen states and who knew how many towns in the last seven years, though, they'd travelled with him. Other than the guns, he had a laptop computer, two suitcases full of clothes, and a pile of books and CDs thrown into a cardboard box. Twenty-five years of life, it seemed like he should have more than that, but Frank had stopped accumulating things a long time ago. It was better to be able to move on without being burdened by a lot of objects that reminded you only of where you'd just been.

West through Illinois before heading north, then across the state line and into Wisconsin as the sun disappeared, the destination still hours ahead. Tomahawk, a name Frank would've dismissed as cliché if he'd written it. The town was real enough, though, and so were his memories of it.

His father wouldn't be there. Devin Matteson would be. If Ezra's call was legitimate, then Devin was returning for the first time in seven years. And if Frank had an ounce of sense, he'd be driving in the opposite direction. What lay ahead, a confrontation with Devin, was the sort of possibility that Grady Morgan had warned him he had to avoid. Grady was one of the FBI agents who'd brought down Frank's father. Grady was also a damn good man. Frank had been close to him for a while, but then Frank left Chicago and Grady behind. They hadn't talked much since.

He drove past Madison in the dark and pushed on. He hadn't eaten all day, just drank Gatorade and drove, hoping to do it all in one stretch, with just a few stops for gas. Before he reached Stevens Point, though, he knew he wasn't going to make it. The fatigue was beginning to overpower him. There was a rest stop ahead, maybe the last one he'd see for a while, and he pulled off and parked. He lowered the driver's seat as far as it would go, enough to let his legs stretch a bit, and then he slept.

IT WAS a Big Brother kind of thing, no doubt about it, but Grady Morgan had kept an active monitor on Frank Temple III for seven years. It wasn't proper, or even really legal, because Frank had no role whatsoever in anything that could still be considered an active investigation. But Grady owed the kid at least this much.

The computers that ran checks on Frank's fingerprints and Social Security number had been quiet for a long time. As had the phone lines and the emails. No word from Frank in a while, and there were times when Grady ached to speak to him, but he didn't. He just went to work every day and eyed the calendar that showed retirement was not far away and hoped Frank would continue to stay off the radar screen. Grady didn't want to see a blip.

Now here was one, an arrest in Indiana, and when it first came through to his computer, Grady felt a sick swirl go through his stomach. Then he sighed and read the details. When he'd finished, he let out a breath of relief. Public intoxication. The second arrest in seven years and the second he could chalk up as No Big Deal, Kids Being Kids. He hoped. As he pushed back from his desk and walked to the window and looked out at the Chicago skyline, he sent a silent request across the miles: *Tell me it was just fun. Tell me, Frank, that you were out with some buddies having beers and laughing like happy idiots. Tell me that there was no fight, no violence. You've made it a long way.*

A long, *long* way.

Frank III had been eighteen years old when Grady met him. A slender, good-looking kid with dark features contrasted by bright blue eyes, and a maturity that Grady hadn't seen in a boy of that age before, so utterly cool that Grady actually asked a psychologist for advice on talking to him. 'He's showing nothing,' Grady had said. 'Every report we've got says he was closer to his father than anyone, and he is showing nothing.'

He showed something in the third interview. It had been just him and Grady sitting in the Temple living room, and Grady, desperate for some way to get the kid talking, had pointed at a framed photograph of father and son on a basketball court and said, 'Did he teach you how to play?'

The kid had sat there and looked at him and seemed almost amused. Then he'd said, 'You want to know what he taught me? Stand up.'

So Grady stood up. When the kid said, 'Take that pen and try to touch it to my heart. Hell, try to touch it anywhere. Pretend it's a knife,' Grady hadn't wanted to, but the kid's eyes were intense, and so Grady made one quick thrust, thinking he'd lay the pen against the kid's chest and be done with it.

The speed. Oh, man, the speed. The kid's hands moved faster than any-body's he had ever seen, trapped his wrist and rolled it back, and the pen was pointing at Grady's throat in a heartbeat.

'Half-assed effort,' the kid had said. 'Try again. For real this time.'

So he'd tried again. And again. And by the end he was working into a sweat and no longer fooling around. He was beginning to feel a flush of shame because this was a child—and Grady had done eight years in the army and another fifteen in the Bureau, and he ran twenty miles a week—and he couldn't beat this kid.

When he finally gave up, the kid had smiled at him and said, 'Want to see me shoot?'

'Yes,' Grady said.

What he saw at the range later that afternoon—a tight and perfect cluster of bullets—no longer surprised him. Seven years later, he was thinking about that day while he stared out of the window and told himself that it was nothing but a public intox charge, a silly misdemeanour, and that there was nothing to worry about. Frank was a good kid, always had been, and he'd be absolutely fine as long as he stayed away from a certain kind of trouble.

That was all he needed to do. Stay away from that kind of trouble.

FRANK WOKE to the grinding of a big diesel motor pulling away. He sat up and saw grey light filling the sky. When he tried to get out of the Jeep, his cramped muscles protested. He ate a Snickers bar from the vending machine while he studied the big map on the wall. Tomahawk was only 100 miles ahead.

The closer he got, the more his resolve wavered. Maybe it would be best to pretend he'd never got that message from Ezra, didn't even know Devin was on his way back. Maybe he'd just spend a little time in the cabin, stay for a weekend, catch some fish. It would be fine as long as he didn't see Devin Matteson. If he stayed away from Devin, if it was just Frank and Ezra and the woods and the lake, this could end up being a good trip, the sort of trip he'd needed to take for a while now. But if he did see Devin . . .

He drove with the windows down as the grey light turned golden and the cold morning air began to warm on his right side. Past Wausau the smell of the place began to change—pine needles and wood smoke and, even though there wasn't a lake in sight, water. There would be a half-dozen lakes within a mile of the highway by now. The deeper he got into the tall pines, the faster the memories flooded towards him, and he was struck by just how much he'd loved this place. Maybe he'd stay for a while. The summer stretched ahead, and the money wouldn't run out. Blood money, sure, and hating the methods that had earned it made him a hypocrite at best, but it was there.

He blew right past the Tomahawk exits before remembering that he had nothing in the way of food or supplies. He'd have to come back down after he'd unpacked, grab some lunch and buy groceries, and then head back to the lake.

He exited at an intersection with County Y, a narrow road slashing through the pines, and had gone down it about a mile when someone in a silver Lexus SUV appeared behind him, doing seventy at least. It shifted into the oncoming lane to pass. Had to be a tourist, driving like that. He looked at the licence plate.

Florida.

The car was gone in a silver flash, swerving in ahead of him and pulling away. The muscles at the base of his neck had gone cold and tight, and his breath seemed trapped.

Florida.

It didn't mean anything. A strange little touch of déjà vu. There were several million cars with Florida licence plates. There wasn't even a *chance* that Devin Matteson was driving that car.

'Not a chance,' Frank said aloud, but he pressed hard on the gas pedal and closed the gap on the silver Lexus. A closer look was all he needed. Just that minor reassurance. He kept accelerating until he was only a car length behind, peering into the tinted rear window as if he'd actually be able to tell who the driver was.

There was only one person in the car and it was a male. He pulled a little closer, almost on top of the Lexus now, staring hard.

'It's him,' he said softly. Somehow he was positive—

Brake lights. A flash of red that he saw too late, and then he hammered the brake pedal and slammed the wheel left and hit the back corner of the Lexus at fifty miles an hour. 'Hell!'

The back of the Jeep swung right with the impact, then came back and sent the front end sliding. Even as the skid started, Frank could hear his father's voice—*instinct will tell you to turn away, but you've got to turn into it.* He heard it, recalled those old lessons in the half-second that it took him to lose control of the car, and still he turned away from it. It had happened too fast and the instinct was too strong. The Jeep slid on worn tyres, then spun off the shoulder and into the pines. He heard a crunch and shatter just as the air bags blew out.

His air bag deflated and fell away, leaving his face tingling, and for a few seconds he sat where he was, blood hammering through his veins. He beat the air bags aside and saw spiderwebbed glass on the passenger window, the bent door panel, but nothing terrible. What about the Lexus? Devin Matteson's Lexus. Without any pause for thought, he reached behind his seat, found the metal case, flicked the latch and opened it and then he was sitting behind the wheel with a gun in his hand.

Reality caught up to him then: 'What are you doing?' he said, staring at the gun. 'What the hell are you doing?'

He slid the gun back into the case, got out of the car and walked round to the front. His right front tyre was blown out and the wheel crunched down beneath the mangled front quarter panel. The Lexus was a good hundred feet behind him, facing the wrong direction, in a ditch, and angled against the trees that lined the road. The door opened, and the driver stepped out onto the road.

It was not Devin Matteson. Not by a long shot. Frank walked towards the Lexus as the driver began to survey the damage to his vehicle. Frank's first thought, watching him—*the dude's on speed*.

The guy, tall and thin with a shock of grey hair that stuck out in every direction, was dancing round the Lexus. Literally dancing. He was talking to himself, too, a chattering whisper that Frank couldn't make out.

'Hey.' Frank got no response. 'Hey! You OK?'

The guy stopped moving and stared at Frank in total confusion. Then he looked at the Jeep and nodded once, figuring it out. Up close, Frank saw that he wasn't too old, maybe forty, the grey hair premature. He had a long, hooked nose and small, nervous eyes set above purple rings that suggested it had been a while since he'd had a full night's sleep. 'Yes,' he said. 'Yes, everything's fine. Don't worry about me. I'll just call Triple-A. You can go on now.'

Frank raised his eyebrows. 'Just call Triple-A? I hit *you*, man. You're going to want to hang around and get this worked out for insurance.'

'No, no, I slammed on my brakes, not your fault at all.'

What the hell was he talking about? Frank had been tailgating. 'What I'm saying is, we need to call the police,' Frank said. 'Get an accident report made, so we can make this square with the insurance company, right?'

The grey-haired guy winced. He probably had a high insurance rate.

'Tell you what,' the guy said. 'It'd be a big help to me if we didn't get an accident report. I'll pay for your damage. I know you're thinking I'll take off and stiff you on the bill. But that won't happen. We can find a repair shop and I'll take care of the bill beforehand.'

'I hit *you*,' Frank said again.

'Don't worry about that. It was my fault, my responsibility, and I don't want an accident report, OK?'

Frank shook his head, looking at the Lexus. The front end was crumpled, there was a gash three feet long across the passenger side and steam was leaking out of the hood.

'Please,' the man said, a desperate quality to his voice.

Frank stood there on the shoulder. It was only fair to let him handle it whatever way he wanted. 'All right,' he said.

'Thank you. Oh, man, *thank* you. The car's got a navigation system, you can find anything with it; we can pick any repair shop you want. I'll show you the choices . . .'

2

Jerry was staring at Nora's ass again, nothing subtle about it, but she wondered if she was allowed to care today—she'd done the same thing that morning as she got dressed, looking her butt over in the mirror like some sort of sorority girl instead of a woman with wrench calluses on her palms. Maybe she'd earned the leer. Karma.

The glance in the mirror was important, though, a morning reminder that Nora was still very much a woman. This before putting on the jeans and the heavy work shirt, tucking her hair into a baseball cap. Stafford Collision and Custom was open by seven thirty, and from then until six or six thirty it was a man's business, always had been. The customers probably kept returning more out of loyalty—and pity—for Bud Stafford than for his daughter, though she did have an eye for detail. Too bad an eye for detail wasn't enough to keep the bills paid.

The phone rang out in the office, and Nora straightened up and looked back at Jerry, who promptly averted his eyes. 'I'd like you to take another pass over that front quarter panel,' she said.

'Huh?'

'Nice orange-peel finish in the paint, Jerry. I know you can see that. Doesn't matter if it disappears in the shadows; the first sunny Saturday morning people wash and wax the car they see that orange peel. And then they don't come back.'

She got to the office just in time to grab the phone. She was always forgetting to take the cordless handset out into the shop with her, and when a body shop doesn't answer, people just call the next one. She'd been one ring away from losing this call. 'Stafford Collision and Custom, this is Nora Stafford.'

She sat on the edge of the desk and took notes on one of the old pads that had Bud Stafford's name across the top. The caller wanted a tow truck for two cars that had wrecked up on County Y. She'd have to handle this one herself. Her last tow driver, who'd also been a prep man and part-time painter, had picked up a drunk-driving charge, and she couldn't afford to hire a replacement. Jerry could drive the tow truck, but he wasn't covered by the insurance policy, and she needed him to finish repainting that Mazda.

She promised to be out in twenty minutes, then told Jerry. He just grunted. 'What's the problem, Jerry?'

'Problem?' He dropped his rag. 'You got me wasting my time *re*painting work I shouldn't have had to *paint* in the first place.'

She waved a hand at him, tired already, the argument too familiar. 'Jerry, if you'd done it right the first time, I wouldn't have asked. Instead you half-assed the job and tried to make up for it with the buffer, like usual.'

'Damn it, Nora, last time I painted cars it was with—'

'Single-stage lacquer, spray it on, buff it pretty, don't have to mess with no damn clear coat . . .' Nora captured his drawl so dead-on that Jerry pulled back in anger and grabbed his rag again. He was a small man, strong in the wiry way that comes from years of physical labour. What was left of his hair was thin and brown and damp with sweat.

'OK,' he said. 'Think you're clever. But if you was clever, you'd understand I'm not a combination man. I do bodywork. Been doing it since you was playing with dolls and learning to paint your nails.'

Same old stuff. He'd start bitching about his workload, then slight her gender. 'Tell you something, Jerry? When I was learning to paint my nails, I was also learning how to paint a *car.*' She walked away, heard the *bitch* muttered under his breath, and kept on going, out to the tow truck. She sat behind the wheel and thought, Six months ago, I would've cried about this. Not any more. No way.

IT FELT LONGER than twenty minutes. The grey-haired guy kept up a constant stream of chatter, the words sounding more nervous each time there was a pause, as if he were scared of silence. Frank was relieved when the tow truck pulled up. The door opened, and a woman—a good-looking one—hopped onto the road. She couldn't go an inch more than five-three. 'Sorry about the wait, guys. I got moving as fast as I could.'

'No problem,' Frank said, and he was going to shake her hand when the grey-haired man interrupted: 'Can we do the Lexus first?'

The woman wore jeans and boots and a denim work shirt, sleeves rolled to expose thin forearms. She didn't wear any make-up, but her eyebrows had been carefully shaped. Cool green eyes fastened on the Lexus driver. 'There a reason one needs to go first?'

He forced a smile. 'Well, I was just hoping . . . I've got a meeting to get to, and I was sort of—'

'In a hurry,' the woman finished. 'Right, well, I can give you the first tow unless this gentleman has an objection.'

Frank shook his head.

'Great,' the woman said. 'I'll get the Lexus rigged up and you guys can ride with me, unless you've got someone coming.'

This time Frank and the man shook their heads in unison.

The woman walked over to the Lexus and knelt beside it, studying the front end. She climbed back in the truck, put it in reverse and had it centred in front of the Lexus in half the time it would've taken Frank.

'I have to winch you out of that ditch before I can get it ready to tow,' she told the grey-haired guy. 'Looks like the Jeep is sitting clear enough already.' She hooked the winch beneath the bumper of the Lexus, went back to the truck and turned it on. The Lexus slid away from the trees and up the ditch, shedding branches and broken glass. When she had shut the winch off, she went back and fussed with the chains, then turned to the car's owner.

'This thing's all-wheel drive. We should use the dolly on the rear wheels to keep from hurting your axles or transmission. The thing about that is, we also charge an extra thirty dollars to use it.'

The man stared at her. 'Whatever. Faster the better. I want to get moving.'

Once she had the wheel-lift under the front end of the Lexus, she strapped the tyres to it for added security and disappeared behind the car. Eventually, she walked back round to the front, gave the wheel-lift one last look, and then made a small nod of satisfaction and turned back to them. 'Go on and get in.'

Frank got to the passenger door of the truck first and slid across to the middle seat as the grey-haired man climbed up beside him. The woman got behind the wheel. 'What's your name?' Frank asked her.

'Nora Stafford.' She extended one hand, and they shook.

'I'm Frank.'

'Good to meet you, Frank.' She put the truck in gear and checked the mirror. 'Who's your buddy?'

'I didn't make his acquaintance, just his car's,' Frank said.

'My name's Dave O'Connor. Sorry. Should've introduced myself earlier. I'll be paying for this, which brings up, uh, a question. I was wondering . . . see, I'm from out of town and, well, I don't have my credit cards on me.'

'Credit cards? Sir, I think you're going to want to make an insurance claim. This job is going to be several thousand dollars.'

'What I was wondering was, well, could I give you cash? I've got some on me. If I gave you that, I could come back with a credit card or call and give you the number . . .'

Nora's face hardened just a touch. 'Two cars with substantial damage, parts and paint alone are going to run up a decent bill, Dave. That's without labour figured in.'

'I'll give you two thousand dollars now. Surely that's enough to get started?'

Nora kept her eyes ahead, and so did Frank, but in the few seconds of silence that followed he felt a shared curiosity with her—*no credit cards on you, but two grand in cash?*

'Well . . .' Nora nodded her head as if in discussion with herself. 'Two thousand dollars is a sizable down payment.'

They were on the highway now. Nora's thigh was warm against Frank's. He looked at her hands on the steering wheel, saw no wedding ring. So it wasn't her husband's body shop. This was what she did, drive a tow truck in Tomahawk? A young girl, intelligent, with perfect eyebrows?

'You guys have someone to come get you?' Nora asked.

'Nope,' Frank said, and Dave O'Connor shook his head.

'I've got to get something figured out,' O'Connor said. 'Got a meeting that won't wait all day, like I told you.'

'A meeting at the Willow?' Frank asked.

'No. I, uh, I've got to get to . . . Rhinelander. Little bit of a drive left to make, so, you know, got to figure something out.'

Rhinelander. He'd been westbound on County Y, headed for Rhinelander? That was an interesting route, considering County Y took you out to the Willow, across the dam, and then looped back down to the old highway and into Tomahawk. O'Connor had been driving the exact opposite direction from Rhinelander.

'Any chance you'd have a car you could rent me?' O'Connor asked Nora.

She shot him a glance. 'I don't rent cars. I fix them.'

'You don't have anything around the shop? It'd be one day, and I'll give a couple hundred cash for it.'

'Only drivable vehicle I could give you is a beat-up old Mitsubishi that probably can't do more than fifty.'

'That's fine. I'll take it. I'll pay you—'

'You won't pay me anything. Sounds like you need something to get you to Rhinelander, and the Mitsu will do it. Slowly.'

'I appreciate that,' O'Connor said. 'It'll be a huge help. Save the time of renting a car.'

Save the *process* of renting a car, Frank thought. You couldn't do that with cash—and Dave O'Connor seemed damn concerned with sticking to cash.

DAVE O'CONNOR had the cash out before Nora was even in the door of the body shop, and he put it in her hand and waved away her offer of a receipt, said he knew she was trustworthy. Feeling there was something *off* about this guy—the mannerisms, the tension—she let him take her rusted blue box of a car and drive off, didn't fill out any paperwork, just accepted his money and his promise to return Monday. Even a few months ago she'd never have agreed to something as crazy as this, but a few months ago the shop's debt wasn't suffocating her.

She stood in the parking lot, two grand in cash in her pocket, and watched him load his stuff, then leave. She was in a dream world when she walked back into the shop and pulled up in surprise when she saw the young guy standing there, Frank. How old was he, anyhow? Appearance said he'd be a few years her junior, maybe twenty-six, twenty-seven. Acted older, though. Carried himself all steady and sharp-eyed.

'Hey,' she said, and for some reason she tugged off the baseball cap, shook her light brown hair out.

'Hey. You get things settled with that guy?' He stepped closer to her, a smile on his face but the eyes too thoughtful. A nice-looking guy, runner's body. Needed to grow the dark hair out, though, lose that military cut.

'A pocketful of money to prove it,' she said.

'Feel safe about getting that Mitsubishi back?'

She laughed. 'If I never see it again, that'll only save me money.'

'Different sort of guy, wasn't he?'

'Seemed a little on edge.'

'Uh-huh. Got a gun out of the glove compartment when he was moving his things into your car, too.'

That stopped her. Not just because of the gun, but the way he said it. Relaxed. Casual. And how had he even seen that?

'Handgun,' he said. 'Lots of people carry them.'

She stared at him. 'You were all the way—'

'Good eyes. I've got good eyes.'

'I guess so.' Nora liked blue eyes on a guy with a dark complexion.

Something about the contrast. She pulled open the office door, stepped inside with Frank behind her.

'I'll go back and tow your car in just a minute,' she said. 'You know what you're going to do for a ride?'

'I'll figure something out.'

'Where were you headed?'

'The Willow. Staying at a cabin up there. I've got some errands in town, though, groceries and the like, so I'll deal with them first.'

'You aren't going to rent a car?'

'No need. Once I get up there, I don't plan on leaving for a while.'

She pushed her hair back over her ears. 'Tell you what—if you can kill the afternoon in town, I'll drive you up to your cabin tonight. Come by around six?'

'You don't need to—'

'It's not a problem.'

'All right.' He nodded. 'Six o'clock.'

THING WAS, Jerry didn't dislike women. Was rather fond of them, in their place. And their place was not in a damn *body shop*. Standing in the paint booth as Nora set off on her second trip, he wondered just what he'd done to earn this fate. Working for a woman, him, best body man in the damn town. Could he find work somewhere else? Sure. But even if Nora was a righteous bitch four days out of five, she was also Bud Stafford's daughter. And if Bud ever got better, Jerry wouldn't want to make eye contact with him knowing he'd left the girl on her own.

She'd told him to redo the clear coat on the Mazda. Like he'd painted the thing the wrong colour or something. Hell with that, somebody needed to look at the Lexus. Car all beat up like that, there was some work just to figure out what was wrong. If she wanted the Mazda fooled with again, she could wait till Monday, or do it her damn self.

Jerry found the keys to the Lexus and pulled it into the shop. What a car. More bells and whistles than anything he'd seen.

He got to work inspecting the damage. Hood would need to be replaced, plus the front quarter panel, and the front passenger door. Problem with these fancy new machines was all the stuff you couldn't see. Sensors and computer chips and whatnot. Some of them would be up under the bumper, so he'd have to figure out what the hell they all did when he took that off.

He dropped onto his back and slid beneath the front of the car, wrench in hand. He got the splash shield off, and—wait a second, what the hell was this?

A thin black box, about the size of a remote control, was mounted on the bumper reinforcement. One of those sensors he'd been worrying about? Those were usually wired in, though, and this thing just sat there by itself. Jerry tapped at it gently with the wrench, and the thing slid around a bit. He reached out and got his fingers round it and pulled. Popped right off. It was held on with a magnet. Two wires trailed out of it and he followed them with his fingers, found another box, this one larger, and popped it free, too.

Pushing back out from under the car, Jerry sat up and studied his find. The smaller device was plain black plastic with a small red LED light in the centre. The bigger one looked like some sort of battery pack. The Lexus had a navigation system, but wasn't its GPS unit inside the computer?

That's when he got it. The magnets were there so you could attach the thing to the underside of the car, on the frame. Attach it without the owner knowing. He bounced the black box in his hand and stared at the Lexus. Nora said the guy gave her cash, didn't show a driver's licence or credit card. Drug dealer, maybe? Bank robber? Could there be cops on the way, following him with this gadget?

Jerry walked into the office with the device, opened the mini-fridge and pulled out a can of Dr Pepper. He dropped into the chair behind the desk and cracked the top on the can, took a long swallow and considered his find. No matter the explanation for the black box's presence, Nora was going to be damn interested in it, and, possibly, so would the cops. Should they call the cops, though? Did they have any reason to? Maybe not. That would be Nora's call to make, not his.

He should have heard the tow truck, but the black box had taken his mind other places. When Nora entered the office, he was still in her chair, boots propped up on her desk and soda can in hand.

Her face twisted at the sight. 'Tell me the Mazda is done, Jerry.'

'Listen, Nora—'

'No.' She leaned over and slapped at his boot. 'I will not *listen*. I've heard every excuse and complaint already.'

'Wait a sec—'

'My father would be absolutely disgusted. I wanted you to finish that Mazda, and instead you sit at *my* desk, drink a soda?'

'Reason I sat down was, I started taking that Lexus apart—'

'Lexus? Jerry, I said the Mazda needed to come first. Would you *please* get some work done?'

Jerry kept his hand below the desk, closed his fingers round the black box and felt his jaw clamp tight. He slipped his hand into the pocket of his coveralls, dropped the plastic device inside and swung his boots off the desk. 'Yes, sir, boss.'

On his way through the shop, he stopped at his locker, placed the tracking device inside and locked the door.

3

E zra Ballard, a few hundred yards out on the lake, spotted the blue car shortly after noon and knew that the couple on the island were no longer alone. The car, some sort of beat-up blue Jeep, was parked in the woods across from the island cabin—a cabin that had, for almost two days, been home to a grey-haired man and a blonde woman. Technically, that was Ezra's business. He didn't own the cabin or the island, but for many years he'd been entrusted with their care. Same with the cabin down on the point, less than two miles away. Two cabins that, at least in Ezra's mind, still belonged to men who'd been buried long ago.

Twice a year the Temple boy mailed Ezra a short note with five $100 bills. The note always read: *Thanks for keeping an eye on the place* and included a phone number. The envelope was always void of a return address. For seven years, young Frank had kept that up, and though Ezra wondered when he'd return to the place, he never wondered *if.* Young Frank would be back, but not until he was ready. Maybe Ezra would still be around, maybe not.

The Matteson cabin, here on the island, was a different matter. After Dan Matteson died, Ezra sent the family a few letters, made a few phone calls, and finally received a curt order to ready the place for sale—this from the son, Devin. When Ezra explained that the island couldn't be sold—it was part of a legacy trust that would either remain with the family or revert to the state— Devin swore at him and hung up. Never called again. This was before Frank Temple had taken his own life and Devin's role in that situation became clear, before a few conversations with Frank's son that Ezra probably never should have allowed to take place, before a final call that Ezra had made to Devin.

In the years that followed that last call, Ezra had never heard from Devin or anyone else about the island. He hadn't expected to, though. His message had been succinct enough: if Devin came back, Ezra would kill him. For seven years it seemed that Devin had believed the promise, and he damn well should have. Ezra was not a man given to idle threats and he certainly was not a man with light regard for killing. Not any more.

Though the cabin had sat empty for years, Ezra kept the place in shape, paying all expenses out of his own pocket. Nobody other than Ezra had been inside until this week. Just two days ago a bizarre phone message had been left on his phone, someone claiming to be Devin telling Ezra the cabin needed to be 'opened up for guests'.

The call had sucked the breath from Ezra's lungs. He'd never expected to see Devin again and, even in the corner of his mind that recognised there was at least a chance that Devin might show up, he never imagined a call like that. So casual, so flip. A taunt, as if after all these years he'd decided Ezra was a harmless old man.

Ezra had called Frank's son—probably a poor choice but, again, there was a promise to be kept—and then the visitors had arrived at the island, but Devin was not among them. Not yet.

Now there was this second vehicle. With the fishing season opening on the first Saturday of May, a mere week away, Ezra had decided to run some of the bays and islands, getting depth readings and trying to find new spots to catch walleye. It was on his first run across the lake that he'd noticed the car, and now he'd spent most of the afternoon anchored off the opposite shore, using binoculars to watch the island. Around midafternoon, the grey-haired man moved the car.

He and the woman had arrived in a Lexus SUV that had disappeared this morning. Now the man took his boat back across the inlet, got into the blue car, and drove it out of the mud and back up the hill and then off the road into the pines. Drove it as far into the trees as he could, till the boughs swept over the roof. Only reason you parked a car like that was to hide it. He'd gone too far, though; the car was hidden from the logging road, but he'd driven it right up to the edge of the tree line, so the sun reflected the glare of glass and metal across the lake. Hard to see unless you were on the water. Hard to see unless you were Ezra.

Ezra had been on the Willow for almost forty years now, taking fish out of the lake's waters and deer and bear out of its surrounding woods. Best guide in Oneida County, that was what people said. The people were right, too. At least when it came to hunting.

IT BEING FRIDAY, and a full workload arriving out of the blue like that, Nora was in a good mood as the afternoon wore down. After she'd towed the Jeep in, she picked up lunch for Jerry, one of those Angus burgers he favoured. An obvious peace offering.

She spent the afternoon on her laptop, going over finances. Jerry had given her his damage assessment on the Lexus. From that she managed to cull an actual estimate and printed it out. She was reviewing it when someone pulled into the front parking lot, got out without shutting the engine off, and opened the office door. Four o'clock on Friday afternoon was an unusual time for business.

The visitor came through the door and stopped. Big guy, with a fancy T-shirt stretched over his chest and shoulders, and a loose jacket. He had a bizarre silver belt buckle, with a sort of rippled pattern, like latticework. 'I hope I'm in the right place,' the guy said. 'Friend of mine called and asked me to grab some things out of his car. I think he left it here.'

'What's his name?'

The guy just smiled at her. Patient, as if he was willing to ignore a worthless question. 'The car's a Lexus SUV.'

'I didn't ask for the car. I asked for the guy's name.'

'Vaughn,' the guy said. The longer he stood in the office, the more space he seemed to fill. She had trouble meeting his eyes.

'I'm sorry. Nobody named Vaughn has a car in here.'

'Perhaps there's been some confusion over the name.'

'Then the car's owner will need to come in. I'm not allowed to release personal effects from a vehicle, sir.'

'How about we give him a call? You can ask . . .'

Dave O'Connor had left no number, but even if he had, Nora wouldn't have called. O'Connor had been weird, but this guy was almost threatening.

'No. If the owner—whose name is not Vaughn—calls, we'll see how we can proceed. Until then, I'm afraid not.'

The guy's eyes darkened, and he seemed ready to object when the office door opened and Jerry ambled in. He gave the guy a casual glance, then knelt in front of the little refrigerator, pulled out a Dr Pepper, and walked back into the shop. The visitor watched him go.

'It sounds to me like you might have the wrong body shop,' Nora said.

For a long moment he didn't answer. Then he gave a mock bow. 'Of course. That must be it. Apologies.'

He opened the door and walked back into the parking lot. She went to the window in time to see him climb in the passenger side of a black sedan. That was why he'd left the engine running—he wasn't alone, wasn't driving. She got a clear look at the car as it pulled out to the street, a black Dodge Charger, one of the newer models. She couldn't read the licence plate, but the colours told her it was from out of state. Wait, those colours were familiar. A smear of orange in the middle of a white plate with some green mixed in. She'd just seen that on the Lexus. Florida.

It wasn't five yet, but she turned the lock on the door as she stood there gazing out of the window. The odd feeling that had convinced her to get Dave O'Connor out of her shop and back on the road without any of the normal procedures had just returned, only this guy with the belt buckle made it swell to the edge of fear. He'd called him Vaughn. All that cash, the hurry he was in, the gun Frank had seen—add a fake name to the mix, and she was beginning to feel stupid she'd gone for the money. It wasn't easy to imagine her father handling this in the same way.

Nora walked back into the shop and watched Jerry working on the Lexus. The car was empty. Dave O'Connor had cleared out all his things. 'Jerry,' she said, 'can you give me a minute?' She wanted to explain the situation, ask if he'd found anything. He turned round, an irritated sneer on his face.

'You got another problem needs me to fix it?'

'No, Jerry. I was just thinking . . .'

'Hope you didn't hurt yourself.'

'I was thinking you can go home early, that's all. It's Friday, and we got some nice work in today. Go enjoy the weekend.'

JERRY DROVE DIRECTLY to Kleindorfer's Taproom and had himself a bar stool and a Budweiser before the clock hit five. Carl, the bartender, took one look at him and asked if the Stafford girl had finally fired him. Jerry didn't dignify that with a verbal response.

The room was almost empty, a couple of out-of-towners drinking Leinenkugel in a booth, nobody at the bar except Jerry, nothing on the TV except poker. Jerry sipped his beer and simmered. Jokes about working for Nora were constant. She'd been there almost a year now. Showed up from Madison dressed to the nines, walked into the body shop wearing jewellery and perfume and with her long fingernails polished and told Jerry she was the new boss.

The afternoon Bud Stafford had his stroke, it had been Jerry who found him slumped under a Honda, his shirt smeared with primer. Jerry's hands shook while he dialled for the ambulance. He'd seen two possible outcomes—Bud would die, or he wouldn't. Not this half-death. Nora had called after the stroke to ask him to keep the shop going while Bud was in the hospital. A week after that, she was in charge. Jerry had tolerated it, because he figured Bud would be back and she'd be gone, back down to Madison to finish up graduate school in *art history*, of all things.

Bud had been cutting that girl cheques for years, putting her through school so the kid would accomplish something useful. Well, she wasn't doing squat that Jerry could see except bitching a blue streak about things she didn't understand and losing them business. End of every month, Nora would tell him that they'd kept the bill collectors at bay again, like it was something to be proud of. Didn't realise those bills were paid only through a sort of pie-in-the-sky expectation that Bud would be back eventually. It kept a meagre supply of work coming in.

Jerry had brooded long enough to order a fresh Budweiser when the door opened behind him. Regulars finally showing up, he thought, until the new arrival sat down beside him. Lean guy with a shaved head and a weird tattoo on the back of his left hand. Camouflage jacket over jeans and a T-shirt. Seventy degrees today, and both this guy and the one who'd come into the shop office to talk to Nora were wearing jackets.

Jerry turned to the TV, and the new guy didn't say anything till Carl brought his drink—vodka tonic—and returned to the other end of the bar. 'You work at that body shop, don't you? Stafford?'

Jerry turned and said, 'I don't think I know you, pal.'

'My apologies,' the guy said. 'Name's AJ.'

Jerry didn't answer, just drank his beer and turned back to the TV.

'So you work at the body shop, correct?'

'Uh-huh. And I don't give free advice on cars, so you got one that needs fixing, bring it in Monday, and we'll—'

'The car I'm interested in is already there,' AJ said.

Jerry paused with the bottle to his lips. 'The Lexus?'

AJ smiled. 'Either you guys don't have much business, or you're a smart son of a bitch, Mr . . .?'

'Dolson. Jerry Dolson.' He turned to face AJ again. 'You want to tell me what the deal is with that car? Who the hell you are, and who's the fella you're looking for?'

AJ reached into the front pocket of his jacket and came out with cigarettes, shook one out, and offered the pack to Jerry, who accepted. They lit up and smoked for a minute. 'You work for that girl? She really run the place?'

Jerry scowled. 'Hell, her daddy had himself a stroke. You want to know who *runs* that place, you're looking at him.'

AJ sucked at his cigarette. 'She doesn't seem like the car-fixing type. Problem is, she also doesn't seem like the question-answering type. Friend of mine stopped by today, had a few enquiries about that Lexus you mention. She put on a bit of an attitude.'

'That's Nora, all right,' Jerry said. He finished his beer.

Before he could wave for another, AJ did. 'I got this one.'

Jerry didn't thank him, just accepted the drink and consumed a few swallows of it, feeling a nice buzz beginning. Beer in his right hand, cigarette in his left, a fine start to the weekend. 'Now, you come in here and tell me, how'd you put it? That she wasn't the question-answering type. Seems to me I asked you a question of my own. Don't recall getting it answered.' He felt a smug smile growing as he lifted the cigarette back to his lips.

'Fair enough,' AJ said. He was using his thumb to clear a streak of condensation off his vodka glass.

'You want me to talk to you, you're damn well gonna need to talk to me first. I don't know you, I don't know the son of a bitch drove that Lexus, and I don't have an interest in either of you. Yet.'

'Man who drove that Lexus is of interest to me, Mr Dolson.'

'What did he do, steal something? Drugs, or money?'

AJ shook his head.

'What, then? What are you talking about?'

Silence.

'Your problem,' Jerry said, 'is that you put that cute little box on the underside of the car instead of sticking it to the fella himself. You found the car, but your boy isn't with it.' He laughed, and AJ locked his eyes on Jerry's.

'You're an observant man, Mr Dolson.'

'Wouldn't have seen it 'cept I had to take the car apart.'

'What did the girl say when you told her?'

'Haven't told her. Threw it in my locker and figured I'd think on it for a day or two.'

'You told me you aren't interested in me, or the guy who drove the Lexus,' AJ said. 'And I say that's just right. You shouldn't be interested in us. We're about to move right out of your life. But you can make some money before that happens. Easy money.'

'You want the car? I ain't gonna let you steal that car, man.'

'I don't give a damn about the car. I want to know where its owner went. His name is Vaughn. How about I give you a thousand dollars cash the minute you tell me where he went?'

Jerry sipped his beer and squinted. Had that flushed, dizzy sensation like he'd get about seven beers from now. He stared at the floor, trying to steady himself, saw that AJ wore a pair of shiny black boots, one of them tapping off the bottom rung of the bar stool. Tapping, tapping, tapping.

'Not interested? OK. We'll go on and get out of your life.'

'He didn't tell Nora where he was going,' Jerry said.

'He's not going to abandon that car. He doesn't want you guys to call the police, run his licence plate. You'll hear from him again. When you do, I want to know about it in exchange for the thousand.'

Jerry drank the rest of his Budweiser fast. 'How do I get in touch with you? *If* I decide to.'

AJ wrote a number on a bar napkin and passed it to him.

'All right. I'll see what I can do'

'Excellent decision,' AJ said. 'How do you feel about five hundred bucks up front?'

'Feel fine about that.'

'Give me the device you took off the car, and I'll give you the five hundred'

'Can't do that. Shop's closed and I don't have keys.'

'You can't get in all weekend?'

'Not without Nora, and it sounded like you didn't—'

'No.' AJ shook his head. 'I don't want her involved.'

'Well, Monday, then.'

AJ nodded, resigned, and got to his feet. 'All right, get in touch Monday. Now I'll leave you to the rest of your evening.'

'Not till you buy me another beer, you won't,' Jerry said. He felt good about saying that. Like he was in control.

AJ settled his tab, left a fresh beer in front of Jerry, and walked out of the bar, his boots loud on the floor.

NORA HUNG THE CLOSED sign on the front door as soon as Jerry left, turned off the lights in the office and locked it, with every intention of leaving early herself. The weekend stretched ahead, a chance to relax, get some much-needed Nora time. She'd spend an hour or two with her father and then be free of all responsibilities. There was a pang of guilt at lumping the visit with her father into the responsibilities category, but they were difficult visits.

She was locking the back door of the shop when she remembered Frank. *Damn it.* She'd told him six. She turned the lock back with a sigh and stepped into the shop. There was nothing to do but wait.

It was dark inside, lit by just one emergency lamp above the door. Nora made her way through the room, navigating round the chain fall in the corner, frame rack beside it, paint booth behind that, and toolboxes lining the walls. When she got to the locked office door, she took her keys out of her pocket but didn't use them. There was a stool beside the door, and rather than enter the office, she just sank onto the stool, pulled her feet up, and sat there smelling the paint and the dust and staring at the shadow-covered room. Though she'd told Jerry she'd been learning about the work here since she was a girl, she really remembered being inside only a handful of times, usually accompanied by her mother.

Her parents had divorced when Nora was six. It had been a marriage of whim and romance: her mother was from old money in Minneapolis, and her father was third-generation Lincoln County, Wisconsin, son of a body-shop owner. If there'd been good times when she was a child, Nora couldn't remember them, just a vague sense of tension. After the divorce her mother moved back to Minneapolis with Nora in tow. Nora's father would come about once a year, usually around Christmas. Her mother had only permit-ted a few visits to Tomahawk until high school, when Nora began to make a weeklong trip by herself in the summer. From the time she was a little girl, Bud promised to put her through college, though her mother had remarried to plenty of money . . .

Someone was at the door. Nora put her feet back on the ground and stood up as the door opened. Not the front door of the office but the back door of the shop. Frank, she thought as the door swung inwards. Then the visitor stepped inside and, as his silhouette filled the space, she saw it was too tall, too broad. It was the man who'd come to ask about the Lexus. She kept silent in the dark and watched him.

He stood just inside the door and swung it shut very slowly. Then he walked towards the Lexus, moving in a way that unnerved her.

She flicked the light switch and said, 'You want to tell me what you're doing?'

He whirled and came towards her, fast and aggressive, closing the gap between them to about five feet, and Nora stepped back, stumbling over the stool. He'd frightened her. 'I said—'

'I heard what you said.' His eyes took in the room around them. It was obvious that she was alone.

'You have no right to be in here,' she said. 'Can't you read the sign out front? We're—'

'Closed,' he said, and took another step towards her, that belt buckle glinting under the fluorescent lights. 'Yeah, I saw the sign. You usually sit here in the dark after you close up?'

'Maybe I should start to more often, if people keep breaking into my shop. Now get out. You want to talk to me, I'll be back in on Monday.'

He was one pace away now. 'Door was unlocked.'

'I want you out. Right now. I told you before, if this car's owner wants to call me, he can. Otherwise, stay the hell away, unless you'd like me to call the police.'

'No, I don't think I'd like that. And neither would you.'

The phone was in the office. Her cellphone was in the truck. 'Get out,' she said again. He was in her space, almost chest to chest, and she'd backed up against the office door, which was still locked.

'You're going to listen to me, and listen good,' he said. 'You got no problem here, OK? Just tell me where the guy who drove this car went, and I'm gone.'

'I'll ask you one more time to leave. Then I'm calling the police.'

He didn't say anything. She went for the office door. Had the key raised when his hand closed around her wrist.

She twisted and kicked him on the side of his knee, so his leg buckled, and for a moment he was off balance. Then he jerked her forwards and spun her round. She felt a wrenching pain in her shoulder and her face hit the door, and she knew it was going to get bad, fast.

4

The sign said CLOSED and there were no lights on in the office. So had she forgotten, or was she planning to come back? It was only five twenty. Frank stood on the sidewalk with two grocery bags and wondered what he should do.

She didn't seem like the type to forget. She'd said six. He set the bags down by the front door. Maybe she'd gone out on another tow. He'd check to see if the truck was behind the shop. If not, he'd wait.

He walked round the building. There was a wire security fence round the back parking lot, but the gate was open. He saw the tow truck parked there, his battered Jeep behind it. Where had she gone?

At first, he thought he'd imagined the cry. Short and muffled. He listened and heard nothing but silence. Took a few steps towards the back door. Still no sounds. Then something fell inside, a clang of metal on concrete.

He saw them as soon as he opened the door. A tall man with his back to Frank, shoving Nora Stafford against a toolbox on the far wall. He had her arm twisted behind her back, and his other hand covered her mouth. Frank crossed the concrete floor, fast and quiet, keeping himself positioned behind the tall man's back.

It was maybe fifty feet to where they stood, and Frank made about forty of it before the guy heard him. He twisted his head, saw Frank coming, and shoved Nora Stafford away. She hit the floor as the tall man reached under his jacket and brought a gun up.

For his thirteenth birthday, Frank Temple's father gave him a musty hardbound book, *Kill or Get Killed*, a close-quarters combat text. His grandfather's book. Two weeks later, his father challenged him to try to take a gun out of his hand. The first of many lessons.

The gun facing him now was a 9mm automatic. Frank's first strike, delivered a quarter of a second before the next, was with the edge of his left hand on the wrist that held the gun. The second strike was really two at the same time—he hit the tall man's chin with the heel of his right hand while he brought his right knee up and into the groin. The guy's head snapped back and hit the same toolbox that he'd pinned Nora Stafford against, and now

Frank slammed the man's wrist into the metal edge of the toolbox. The gun bounced away. Frank got his hand behind the man's neck and slammed him forward, using his leg to upend him onto the floor.

The guy took the fall well, rolled back onto his feet and lunged upwards, just in time to be greeted with a socket wrench Frank laced down across the back of his skull, dropping him back to the floor.

It should have been done, but Frank was caught by the tide now, wanting to put that gun to the bastard's knee and blow a cloud of blood and bone onto the concrete. He went for the gun, saw it wasn't on the floor, and looked up to see Nora Stafford standing with the weapon in her hand. She held the gun out. 'Here.'

It was a Glock. By the time it touched Frank's palm, the flush of rage was gone. 'It would seem you should probably call the police.'

FRANK WAS WORRIED about her until she came back out of the office and into the shop. Was she going to fall apart, get hysterical, give him another problem to deal with before the cops showed? But when she stepped into the room and stared at the man stretched out on the concrete, he knew she was fine. The look was laden with anger and disgust, not fear. 'You're early,' she told Frank. 'Thanks for the help. He just walked right in here—'

'You don't know him?'

'No. He came in this afternoon and asked about the Lexus.'

'Car that I hit?'

'You got it.'

He blew out a long sigh as a siren began to close on the body shop. He looked to where the partially disassembled Lexus stood. 'I'm sorry. I should have said something earlier about that guy. Had a bad sense about him, but I was trying to ignore it.'

'I had the same sense, but I didn't count on this.'

She was holding her right wrist in her left hand, rubbing it gently, and he saw the dark red streaks on her skin. 'You OK?'

'Fine.' She dropped her arm as if embarrassed.

'What did he want?' Frank gestured at the unconscious man with his toe.

'To know where your buddy in the Lexus went.'

'No kidding?' Frank looked at the guy on the floor. He'd arrived pretty damn fast after the car was left at Stafford Collision and Custom. And if he didn't know where O'Connor had gone, then how had he found the Lexus?

'He told me the person driving the Lexus was named Vaughn.'

'Dave O'Connor? You see a driver's licence, any sort of ID?'

She shook her head. The sirens were in the parking lot outside and Nora walked to the door. The guy on the floor was starting to come back, rolling his right foot a little.

The cop came in with Nora. Just one guy, about forty, ruddy-faced, thick fingers. He was speaking into the microphone near his collarbone, reporting his position and situation. When he was done, he withdrew a plastic bag from his hip pocket and reached out to Frank. 'Gimme the gun.' His badge said MOWERY.

Frank dropped the gun in the bag and Mowery sealed the plastic lock and jammed the bag into his belt. He nodded at the man at his feet. 'You took it from him.'

'Uh-huh.'

'After he pulled it.'

'Yeah.'

Mowery studied Frank as if he wasn't sure he believed it. 'What'd you hit him with?'

'Hands, at first. Then a wrench.'

'Hmm.' Mowery squatted beside the tall man, whose eyes had fluttered open. 'Looks like he's 'bout ready to rejoin the world.' He got the cuffs off his belt and fastened the man's hands behind his back. The prisoner was fully conscious by the time the second cuff snapped shut, twisting his head to try to look back at Mowery. The man made a soft grunt and laid his cheek back on the concrete.

'I hit him pretty well,' Frank said. 'Might have a concussion. Maybe need an ambulance.'

'He isn't gonna die in my car before he gets to a hospital.' Mowery leaned over and flicked the man's cheek. 'You with us, you son of a bitch? Want to get that headache checked?'

The guy grunted again and Mowery hauled him up with a jerk. 'You can stand,' he said, as the man's legs started to buckle. 'Stand up, damn it!'

When his prisoner held his own footing, Mowery said, 'Let me get him in the car, get him down to the hospital. I finish with him, the three of us are gonna talk.'

The tall man's movements seemed steady enough heading across the room to the door. Frank and Nora stood just inside as Mowery guided him out to the police cruiser, a Lincoln County Sheriff logo on the side. Mowery opened the back door and started to shove him into the seat, so when a man rose from behind the trunk, Mowery never saw him. Nora shouted, and as Frank started towards them, the new man, wearing a camouflage jacket and black boots, hit Mowery on the head with a handgun. Mowery fell, tumbling with his prisoner into the back seat, and then the gun swung down again, and Mowery's nose shattered and blood sprayed the window.

The new man then whirled and lifted his gun. Frank lifted his hands and back-pedalled, and for a moment he was sure the crazy bastard was going to fire anyhow. Then Mowery, sliding to the ground, reached out and got his fingers in his attacker's shirt, and that drew another whip of the gun. It was two seconds of distraction, but it got Frank back inside.

He grabbed Nora and swung the door shut behind them. Her feet tangled with his, and as she hit the floor hard, he reached for the dead bolt, banged the light switch and dropped to the concrete. Then it was just the two of them inside the dark room and Mowery outside with his prisoner and a man with a gun.

'GET THE PHONE,' Frank said. 'Call 911.'

He disappeared then, slithering off into the darkness towards the tool-boxes, and Nora started for the office on her hands and knees, went about ten feet before the gunshots began. Four in succession, muffled by the walls. Pressed down into the dust and grime, she said, 'They killed him.'

'They shot the tyres on the police car.'

She chanced a look back at the door, expecting to see him surveying the scene. There were only shadows, and she finally found him across the room. 'How do you know?'

'You could hear them pop.'

Frank crossed the room, a long ratchet dangling in his right hand, his walk unconcerned. He reached for the dead bolt and she hissed at him in shock. '*What are you doing?*'

'They're gone,' he said, and opened the door. Nora braced for more gun-shots. From the floor she could see the police car, which now rested on its rims, its back door open, Mowery's body slumped behind it. 'Make that call,' Frank said, then stepped outside.

She'd left the phone on the stool by the office door when Mowery arrived, and when she reached for it, she saw the ugly red marks on her wrist.

The pain in her arm and shoulder seemed to pulse. When the 911 operator answered, Nora explained what had happened to Mowery, then disconnected. She went towards Frank, the open back door looming like the most treacherous of gateways.

Frank was kneeling beside Mowery, and there was blood on his jeans. He'd stretched Mowery out on the gravel and the cop made neither motion nor sound. Frank turned to her.

'Ambulance on the way?'

'And the police.' She took a step outside. 'They're gone?'

'Yeah.' He checked Mowery's pulse and loosened his shirt collar.

'Is he OK?' Nora asked.

'He's not going to feel or look right for a while.'

She rocked up on her toes to look past Frank's shoulder at the cop, and when she saw him, her eyes seemed to swim out of focus. His nose was almost unrecognisable, turned into a bloody smear, and shredded lips revealed broken teeth.

Frank pulled his own shirt off and used it to wipe gently at Mowery's face. Then he tilted him onto his side and tucked the shirt under his head.

Nora looked away and reached for the door frame, squeezed it tight. 'I almost missed that phone call,' she said. The Lexus had been one ring from being bound for someone else's body shop, someone else's life.

REPORT A ROUTINE ASSAULT and it takes a while before the cops finish sorting it out. Report an assault on a cop and watch that time frame expand. Frank told the story six times to three different cops—everybody wanted to hear it twice—after Mowery had been taken to the hospital. He and Nora went to the police station to explain it on tape. By the time they were done, the sun was gone and the small town was quiet, moving on towards nine in the evening. One of the officers dropped them off at the body shop. The groceries were still on the sidewalk out front.

Nora stared at them. 'If I hadn't promised you a ride, I wouldn't have been here when that bastard showed up.'

'Sorry.'

She shook her head. 'No, if I hadn't promised you the ride, *you* wouldn't have been here, either. And if you didn't show up . . .' Neither of them said anything for a minute. 'You *still* need a ride, don't you? It's the least I can do.' She managed a smile.

They walked back into the rear lot and out to a little Chevy pick-up with the Stafford Collision and Custom logo emblazoned on the side. Frank opened his Jeep and got to work transferring his belongings into the bed of the truck. Nora helped silently. When everything had been moved, Frank paused to get a fresh shirt out of a suitcase, the blood-soaked one having departed with Mowery. Then he was in the passenger seat, with Nora behind the wheel, and they were northbound, headed out to the Willow.

'Frank Temple the Third,' Nora said as they pulled away from town. 'The name you gave the cops. Sounds fancy.'

He looked out of the window. 'Not really.'

'If you had a son, would you name him Frank Temple the Fourth?'

'No, I certainly would not.' He wished she hadn't overheard him. He'd gone through the internal bracing that he always did, watching the cop's eyes when he gave his name. There wasn't any recognition, though. It had been a few years since his father made headlines.

'You up here by yourself?' she asked.

'Yeah.'

'From?'

'All over. Chicago, originally. I've moved around.'

'But you've been here before.'

'You say that like you're sure about it.'

She accelerated onto the highway. 'You call it the Willow. Not Willow Flowage. First-timers don't say that. But I don't see any fishing tackle in your stuff. Everybody goes to the Willow in May to fish.'

'I may do some fishing. The gear's already up at the cabin.'

'Really? You own the place? Nice.'

'It's my father's.'

'Is he joining you? A little father–son bonding?'

'He's dead,' Frank said, and she winced.

'I'm sorry.'

'That would make you one of the few.' Then, to fill the awkward pause, he said, 'What'll you do with that car? The Lexus?'

'I'm not going to fix it, that's for sure. Minute I hear from him, he'll hear from the cops.'

'They ran the vehicle identity number and the plate, right? Did they tell you who owned it?'

'If they know, they didn't tell me.'

'His buddies knew the car was at your shop, but didn't know where he was, or what name he was using. How?' Frank was thinking about tracking devices, which, when mixed with men who carried Glocks and attacked women, did not present an appealing scenario.

'All I know is I want that damn car out of my body shop.'

'Aren't the cops going to impound it?'

'Yes, but I need to get it put back together first. Can't tow a car that's in a dozen pieces. I'll call Jerry in the morning, ask him to come in and put the parts back on so I can get it out of my sight.'

'Where do you live?' Frank asked, looking for a more relaxed conversation.

'Almost up to Minocqua. You're not far out of the way for me at all.'

'You always lived here?'

'Nope. I've been here for about a year.' It was a disclosure that presented all sorts of questions, but Frank didn't ask them. She was quiet for a bit, then offered another of her own. 'When was the last time you were up here?'

'Seven years ago.'

'How do you know the place is still standing?'

'Guy named Ezra Ballard checks in on it, keeps it in shape.'

'Well, no wonder you're so relaxed about it. Nobody in the world's more reliable than Ezra.'

'You know him?'

'Everyone does. He's one of a kind. Best guide in the area, too. At least, that's what I've been told.'

Frank nodded without comment. A hunter without peer, that was Ezra's reputation. The stories Frank knew were probably far from those Nora Stafford had heard, though. A different sort of prey.

They were on Willow Dam Road now, the Chevy's headlights painting the pines with pale light. Once they were past the Willow's End Lodge, Frank instructed her to take a right turn onto a gravel road. This felt stranger than he'd expected, and he'd expected it to be damn strange. They rumbled left at the three-way fork; then they were facing the cabin.

'Home sweet home?' Nora said.

'Yeah. This is it.' He opened the door and stepped out into a cool breeze that came at him like a kiss. In front of him the dark lawn ran out to a hand-laid log wall that stood above the beach. Stars and a half-moon hung above the lake, everything pristine until Frank turned his head a touch to the right and saw the blinking red lights of a cellular tower, miles away.

He remembered when the cell tower went up. His father hated it. Loathed it. One night, sitting with the Coleman lantern crackling beside them, he'd taken out a gun and emptied a clip in the direction of the tower, the bullets dropping harmlessly into the water of the lake. They'd had a hell of a laugh over that.

'Beautiful,' Nora said softly, and only then was Frank aware of her standing beside him.

'Yeah, it's all right.'

He turned back to the truck and she went with him, grabbed one of his bags out of the bed and started for the cabin.

'Just set it down outside the door. Thanks. I'll get the rest.'

'I'll help you get everything inside. It's not a problem.'

'*No.* Thank you, but no. Just set it outside the door.'

She stood with the bag in her hand and cocked her head, puzzled. Then she raised her eyebrows and dropped the bag to the ground in front of the door. Frank felt a surge of irritation and embarrassment at his snapped words, but he couldn't help wanting her gone. He didn't want anybody walking into that cabin with him when he stepped inside for the first time in seven years.

He pulled a few more bags out of the truck. 'Really, this was a huge help. Thanks for the ride.'

'Hey, least I could do.'

They stood there awkwardly for a few seconds, facing each other in the dark. Then she moved to the truck. 'I'll give you a call, let you know what sort of time frame to expect on your car.'

'Thanks. Let me know what you hear from the police, too, OK?'

'Sure.'

She got in the truck then and started the engine, and Frank reached in his pocket, closed his fingers round an old and well-remembered key, and went to the door.

GRADY LIVED ALONE NOW, in an apartment about the same size as the kitchen in the house he'd shared with Julie, and though it still felt relatively new and certainly nothing like home, it had been nine years since he moved in. Nine years.

Looking back, Grady knew that Frank Temple's kid had wanted to beat his dangerous legacy, wanted to leave that bloody coat of arms behind. But Grady surely hadn't helped him. What he'd done in his time with seventeen-year-old Frank Temple III was his greatest professional shame. With the exception of Jim Saul, an agent down in Miami, nobody knew the way he'd manipulated that kid. And that was what kept Grady checking the computers, showing more devotion out of guilt than he ever had out of love.

The case against Frank's father had been a huge story—nothing attracted attention like a federal agent turned contract killer—and when it broke, the media was loving the Bureau, loving Grady. What they didn't understand was that when Frank's father killed himself he had effectively aborted the future of the investigation. He'd known so much, could have provided information that would have taken down Manuel DeCaster, destroyed one of the deadliest and most powerful crime entities in Florida. It had been shaping up to be one of the most significant organised crime prosecutions in years and then Frank Temple II lifted his gun to his lips, squeezed the trigger and killed the case along with himself.

So even as the story was arriving, it was dying, and all Grady and Jim Saul had left was Frank Temple III. The boy was supposedly closer to his father than anyone else had been, and the stories of his unusual education, the moulding process that had been going on, were legion. He'd even made a trip down to Miami with his father, and there had been at least a short visit to Devin Matteson.

It was for Devin that Jim Saul most hungered. Devin was a phantom, involved in every level of DeCaster's operation, investigated by the DEA and FBI and Miami PD for years without a single conviction. Temple was supposed to be the first domino, Matteson the second, but Temple went down without touching the others. They could start the chain over with Matteson, Saul was sure. And there was a strong chance that Temple's son knew more than they dared imagine. It would take a little bit of a sales pitch, that was all. A few talks about betrayed legacies, a few reminders of just how much Devin deserved his share of the punishment, what a shame it would be to see Frank's father alone bear that load.

He'd walked into that kid's house knowing the truth, but with a professional oath not to share it. Nothing evil in that, right? Except he'd passed off as truth a story that filled a grieving child with white-hot hate and a vendetta.

Grady had spent some time on it. He and the boy had a good many conversations before Frank's mother grew concerned and a newspaper reporter learned of the unusual bond and began to ask for interviews, and the whole thing fell apart, leaving Frank with his hate and Grady and Saul with nothing to show for the ploy.

It had been worth the effort, though. That's what they'd told each other early on, that if it had paid off and the kid actually knew something and shared it, well, then it absolutely would have been worth it. You had to prioritise, after all. Without the boy, they had no case, and they needed a case.

Except they already had one. While Grady was showing Frank pictures of his father with Matteson and talking of loyalty and betrayal, trying to build enough hatred to coax a reaction, a group of rookie agents in Miami were chasing bank records, and two ugly trials later DeCaster was in prison.

No help needed from Frank Temple III, no lies to a grieving son required. It was the sort of thing that was hard to put out of your mind.

Grady kept his eye on the kid, though, and found a measure of relief in each year that passed without incident. Frank was making his own place in the world and it looked like a peaceful one.

Had looked that way, at least, until the day after his arrest for public intoxication down in Indiana, when Jim Saul called Grady at home on a Friday night and asked if he'd heard about Devin Matteson.

Grady took his feet down off the ottoman and set his beer aside. 'Heard what about him, Jimmy?'

'He's in the hospital in Miami, with three gunshot wounds. Looked like he was going to die, but he's making a furious recovery. You know the kind of shape that guy was in. Iron man, right?'

'They have the shooter?'

'Nope. And if Matteson knows, he's not saying. But somebody plugged him three in the back, and you know how he'll handle that. If they've got good leads, I'm not aware of them.'

'Temple's son was arrested in Indiana night before last. Public intoxication. When was Matteson shot?'

'The day before that. How do you know about the Temple kid?'

'Word travels,' Grady said. They hung up, and he dropped the phone onto the cushion beside him and stared at the wall.

Devin Matteson shot, Frank Temple III arrested for drinking a day later. Celebration, maybe?

No, Matteson's list of enemies probably grew by the day.

Frank had wanted him, though. Frank had wanted Matteson badly, and by the end, when Grady was trying to make amends, he'd urged the boy to put that away. Frank had accepted it, too, but Grady remembered going back to the range with him, remembered the look on Frank's face and the perfect cluster of bullets in the target. The kid was seeing Devin Matteson.

And whose fault was that, Grady? Whose fault?

EZRA BALLARD ran an electric fillet knife down the perch in a smooth, quick stroke. Turned the fish and repeated the motion. Moved the fillets to the side and lobbed the fish head over the fence into the dog kennel. Two of his hounds hit the carcass together.

Ezra had selected all four of his hounds when they were just weeks old, trained them himself, spent long summer hours in the woods with them. Though the hunting season wasn't till October, you could run bear in the summers in Wisconsin for dog-training purposes. The dogs were Ezra's family.

He cleaned a final fish, then gathered up the fillets and his knife, turned off the floodlight above the cleaning station and went into the house. He cooked the fish and ate it with potatoes and carrots that he'd seasoned and wrapped in foil and cooked outside on the propane grill, sitting at the kitchen table, facing the mounted head of a ten-point buck taken five years earlier. Everything from the décor of his room to his clothing to his daily activity told him he was a fishing and hunting guide, a woodsman, a local. His clients knew it; his friends knew it; his neighbours knew it. After nearly forty years, he was starting to know it, too. Mission accomplished.

If you tried hard enough, you could take what you really were and force-feed yourself a new life until a better self emerged.

He'd spent twenty years in Detroit and another four in the jungle trying to decide what he'd be if he could choose. He'd been twenty-five when he arrived here, a young man with an old warrior's body count behind him, had no idea where to find a walleye, no idea how to track a deer or run a bear. Now there were moments when it seemed that he'd always been here.

He washed his dishes, gathered his car keys and went out to the truck. Took Cedar Falls Road to the logging road. The uneven track went on a good half-mile past the point, where Ezra brought his truck to a halt, but he didn't want to drive all the way down to the water, have his headlights visible from the island. He took the rest of it on foot, the wet earth sucking at his boots. Here the soil was almost boglike, holding moisture long after the last rain had passed. The lake was surrounded by more than 16,000 acres of forest that were protected by the state, home to bear and deer and three wolf packs.

Ezra knew people who used this logging road as a put-in area for canoes, saved some paddling time if they were headed north. You'd put your canoe in the water and take off across the lake, splitting either north or south round an overgrown island with a few NO TRESPASSING signs posted. The only privately owned island in the entire flowage. It should never have been privately owned, either. Dan Matteson's grandfather had won it in a bizarre legal case.

Matteson's grandfather, a Rhinelander native, had owned forty acres of good timberland several miles east of the Willow. When the adjacent owner, a major paper mill, accidentally clear-cut his property, he sued. The case had gone to arbitration and Matteson had been awarded property on the flowage of comparable value instead of cash: a small tract on a point of land on the eastern shore and one of the only islands in the whole lake that was high enough to avoid regular flooding. Just under five acres in total, a fraction of what he'd lost, but waterfront property.

Dan had grown up around here and, on long days and longer nights in Vietnam, he'd talked of the place to Frank and Ezra. To Ezra, who'd never been more than forty miles from Detroit until he shipped out, the flowage had sounded like a dreamworld. Miles of towering dark forests, pristine lakes, islands. The longer they stayed overseas, the more attached he grew to the idea of the place.

Just before he'd enlisted, Ezra had gone out with his older brother to settle up a debt. The sum owed was $400. Ezra had held the arms of an alcoholic factory worker while his brother swung on the guy with a bottle. When the bottle fractured, the jagged glass bit deep into the unconscious man's chin. The next day, Ezra went to talk to a recruiter.

As his tour wound to a close, Ezra made an official request to Dan: could he head up to this Willow Flowage for a few months, until he figured something else out? Dan had agreed to it and had then headed south for Miami and the sun, while Ezra went north into snow. Frank Temple took his job with the marshals and landed in St Louis, Miami, at the same time as Dan.

Miami ruined Dan. The Willow saved Ezra. Absolutely *saved* Ezra. He'd been on the island five months when he learned that his brother's body had been found in the trunk of a Caprice off Lafayette in Detroit. That summer, Dan and Frank came up for a visit and Ezra made his pitch. He and Frank should pool resources and buy the additional parcel Dan owned on the point, build a cabin there and create a camp that they could share and pass down to their families. The sort of grand plan you can only have when you're young.

Dan had laughed. 'I'll sell you the land, man. But I'm not spending much time on that damn island, middle of nowhere.'

'Then sell the island to me,' Ezra suggested.

Dan shook his head. 'Nah,' he said. 'I can't sell the island. It's a legacy for my family, you know that. I've got a son and the island will be his someday. I want it to be his.'

So he'd kept his island but rarely appeared there, and Ezra and Frank built a cabin on the point and shared some summers and memories.

Ezra had lived in the lake cabin for a time, but as soon as he could afford to, he bought land up the road and built his own house. Frank Temple bought the lake property in full, put it in a legacy trust for *his* son. Now it had been years since anyone spent a night in either the lake cabin or the one on the island.

As he reached the top of the hill, Ezra entered the trees and found the car easily. Flicked his lighter and held the flame close to the bumper. The licence plate was local. Lincoln County. That was a surprise. He memorised the numbers. The Lexus had carried a Florida plate, but now this old heap had taken its place. Why?

He returned the way he'd come through the silent woods. When he reached his truck he decided to go to the Willow Wood Lodge, have a drink and do some thinking before calling it a night.

Upon arrival at the lodge, he walked in, found an empty stool at the far end of the bar, and had hardly settled onto it before a glass of Wild Turkey and an iced water were placed in front of him.

'Glad you came in,' Carolyn, the bartender, said. 'Dwight Simonton said somebody's down at the Temple place. Said there was a fire going outside, somebody sitting there.'

'Right idea, wrong owner. Somebody showed up at the island cabin.'

Carolyn shook her head. 'Dwight said it was the Temple place.'

Ezra frowned. 'I was out there today, had a look at it from the water. Nobody's staying there. He was probably confused.'

Carolyn raised her eyebrows. 'Come on. Not a soul who lives on this lake doesn't know the Temple place, after the way that crazy guy went out.

Dwight told me the fire was right down on the point. You think Dwight can't tell a fire on the island from one on the shore two miles away?'

She was right. Simonton wouldn't have made that mistake.

'You don't think,' she said, lowering her voice, leaning closer, 'it's his kid?'

Of course it was his kid, responding to the message Ezra himself had left, but rather than confirm it, Ezra simply shrugged.

He finished his bourbon, tossed some money on the bar and went to the door. He stepped out into a night that now seemed electric. First there'd been the beautiful woman and her companion in the Lexus. Then the new car in the trees. Now someone, probably Frank's son, was back at the Temple cabin. Ezra didn't like the feel of it, the way this group was gathering on his lake.

5

The letter was right where it belonged, framed on the wall beside the Silver Star. Frank read it while he drank his first beer, right down to President Harry S. Truman's signature:

In grateful memory of Major Frank Temple, who died in the service of his country in the military operations of Korea, on August 22, 1950. He stands in the unbroken line of patriots who have dared to die, that freedom might live, and grow, and increase its blessings. Freedom lives, and through it he lives, in a way that humbles the undertakings of most men.

The letter had hung above his father's childhood bed, the only tie Frank Temple II ever had to the soldier who'd died in Korea, leaving a wife six months pregnant with the son who would bear his name. Frank Temple II grew up without knowing a father but knowing plenty about his legacy—his name was a hero's name. During D-Day, on beaches filled with heroic acts, the first Frank Temple and his fellow Army Rangers had stood out, scaling the protected cliffs at Point du Hoc into a rain of German bullets.

A tough act to follow, but Frank Temple II had done it. He had his war, Vietnam, where he served as a member of a specialised group so covert and so celebrated that it was still the subject of speculation decades later, a special operations group of elite soldiers whose chain of command seemed to end with the CIA. Temple II had matched his father's Silver Star and Purple Heart, then come home to a career as a US marshal.

'You've got a lot to live up to.' That was his mantra for Frank, shared with the same casual frequency most people used for 'Good morning', a constant reminder that Frank's was a line of brave men and heroic deeds.

The hell of it was, Frank had always believed him. Believed *in* him. All the hero talk of honour and courage, it seemed to come from his father's core. It was sacred. Right up until he killed himself and a team of FBI agents arrived at the house, three months before Frank's high-school graduation.

Now, sitting beside a fire, a luke-warm beer in his hands, he wondered how long that would have continued. If his father had never been caught, would they sit here together, sharing a laugh and a beer, Frank steadfast in his faith in the man across the fire from him? Or, wiser with age, would he have smelled the lie in his father's words, seen evil in eyes that had always looked on him with love?

He would've been proud today, Frank thought. The way I brought the socket wrench down, yeah, that's Daddy's boy. He laughed at that; then he lifted his beer to the cabin, a toast to his return. This was their place, a spot of memories shared only with his father, no interlopers here. He wanted to spill some tears, weep for his father. There'd be no tears tonight, though. If this place, with all its good memories, didn't affect him in that way, then maybe no place ever would.

He wouldn't cry for his father here at the Willow, but he might kill for him, if Devin was really coming back . . .

There'd been a day, when he was fourteen, that his dad first broached the subject of justified killing. They'd been downstairs in the mat room, working out, Frank attacking and his father blocking. When, every now and then, Frank would sneak a blow in, his father would smile, almost glow.

They'd finished and were sitting, backs against the wall, breathing hard, and his father had said, 'There's a lot of bull to what I do, son. With the marshals now and the army before.'

Frank had thought he meant red tape. That wasn't it, though.

'We chase down guys who are evil bastards. Guys who steal and kill and rape and commit any other manner of crime. Some go to prison. A lot get off on some technicality, go back on the street, and hurt somebody else. There are guys the system can't touch who aren't worth the air they're breathing. And there's a natural way to settle it.'

A natural way. That's what his father thought of killing. An inherent solution to human conflict, ageless and unsurpassed.

Frank had asked what all of that had to do with the army.

'It's the same thing. There's this system, governments and generals and all the rest, and they're supposed to keep the peace without firing a shot. But they can't. Because there are evil people in the world, son, and they're going to keep doing evil things. And that keeps people who know how to use a gun in demand. People like me and your grandfather, and you.'

Official inclusion in the list had made Frank's head go a little light, the honour hitting deep in his fourteen-year-old boy's heart.

A few years later, his father's body in the ground and face on the front page of the newspaper, the sad truth of moments like that one began to show itself to Frank. He understood what his father has been doing, understood that he'd been rationalising with himself as much as he'd been offering a philosophy to Frank. But he believed what he said, too, and Frank saw the horror in that, saw the fallacy and savageness and the justification. Yes, the justification. Because his father, evil man or not, was dead, and Devin Matteson—evil man for sure—was alive and free. Cut a deal, hung Frank's father out to dry, and then walked away. No punishment, no penance, no pain.

There'd been another conversation down in the basement that stood out in Frank's memory. They'd been working on elbow strikes—Frank's dad always demanding greater speed, greater power. That day had been, Frank would later learn, exactly one week after his father came back from Florida having killed two men to avenge Dan Matteson's death. He'd studied his son with a critical eye.

'Frank, suppose somebody takes me out one of these days.'

It had seemed like a game, and Frank had answered, 'That can't be done, there's nobody out there good enough.'

'It can be done. Probably will be done, someday. Suppose it happens, and suppose you know who's responsible. What would you do?'

Frank didn't answer.

'Frank? What would you do?'

'Kill him. I'd find him and I'd kill him.'

Pleasure in his father's eyes. Respect. He'd nodded and said, 'Damn right you would.' Then he'd laid a hand on Frank's shoulder and said, 'You're a good boy, Frank. Check that—you're a good *man*.'

Frank had endured a lot of pity over the years, some genuine, some false. Sometimes it just showed in people's eyes. *Poor kid. Imagine having such a monster for a father.* The problem was that he'd been a good father. Was a murderer, sure; got paid for it, yes; but that didn't replace seventeen years of love. Frank wished at times he'd come home drugged out and violent, knocked Frank and his mother around, threatened the neighbours—but he hadn't. He'd been quick with a joke and a kind word, supportive.

'Welcome back.'

The voice came from just over his shoulder. He whirled to face the speaker. 'Uncle Ezra?'

The man stepped closer, out of the darkness, and offered his hand. 'Good to see you, Frank.'

Frank got to his feet and accepted the handshake. He was taller than Ezra by several inches. 'You given up on motorised travel?' Frank waved a hand at the dark woods.

'Nice night for a walk.' Ezra settled onto a stump. 'Cabin was in good shape.' A statement of fact, but one he wanted Frank to acknowledge.

'Of course,' Frank said, and he sat, too.

'You intending to let this fire go out?'

It was close to going out, though Frank hadn't noticed that as he'd sat alone with his beer and his memories. 'Uh, no. I just—'

Ezra knelt beside the fire pit and adjusted the wood, fed a few fresh logs into the pile, then returned to his stump. Frank was staring into the fire, but Ezra sat sideways. 'He wants to keep his night vision,' his dad had once said. 'It's an old habit that lingers.'

'Boat's in the shed,' Ezra said, 'but I took the motor off and put it in the cabin.'

'I saw. Yeah, I appreciate that.'

It got quiet after that, just the fire popping and hissing and the trees creaking. There'd been loons when Frank was a kid, lots of them, but tonight he had yet to hear one of those haunting calls.

'I got your message,' Frank said. A fast tremor was working in his chest; just the thought of Devin out there on the island enough to build the anger.

'That seems to have been a mistake. He's not here.'

'Devin?'

'Yes, Devin. He's not up here, Frank.'

'But somebody is?'

'Yes.'

'Who?'

Ezra hesitated. 'I don't know. It's a man and a woman. Might be Devin's renting the place.'

It was crazy to be disappointed. If he'd *wanted* Devin up here, then what, exactly, had he been hoping for? There was an answer to that one, and he didn't want to dwell on it, not even for a minute.

'It's good to see you,' Frank said, and though he'd spoken mostly to fill the silence and take his mind away from Devin, the words were true.

'You ain't kidding, son. Been a long time.'

'Going to be tough,' Frank said. 'Being up here.'

Ezra didn't look at him. 'I would imagine so.'

'Good memories, up here,' Frank offered. 'Less so in other places. But up here, mostly good.'

'He wasn't a bad man, son. Wasn't a perfect one, either, but he damn sure wasn't the way they made him out to be.'

'Tell that to the families of the people he killed,' Frank said, and was surprised by the weariness in his voice. He finally heard a loon then. It cut loose from somewhere across the lake, a sound unlike anything else. 'Like I said, I'm glad to see you, Ezra. Don't want to make you have conversations like that. I'm sorry.'

'No need to be,' Ezra said. 'And I think you do want to. Be surprised if you didn't, at least.'

Frank didn't respond to that.

'I thought it was a bad idea, calling, but I'd promised to do it. Why'd you come up, Frank? We agreed to let it go.'

'That's really what you want to do?' Frank said. 'Let him sit in the cabin, have a nice little vacation? He brought my dad into it, Ezra, used a lot of bull about loyalty to set the hook, then gave him up to buy himself immunity.'

'Think I've forgotten? I'm just wondering about your intentions.'

'I'd like to ask him some questions,' Frank said.

'That's all?'

'That's all,' Frank said, but he was thinking of the guns inside the cabin, beautiful, well-engineered pieces of equipment that had not been built to ask questions.

'Where'd you come from, anyhow?' Ezra asked. 'Postmarks on those letters bounced around over the years.'

'I was in Indiana. Taking writing classes. Had ideas about a book, maybe a screenplay.'

'You were a storyteller even as a kid. I remember that.'

Frank laughed, eliciting a smile from Ezra.

'Good trip from Indiana, I take it?' Ezra said.

'Ten hours of driving, then a few hours of fun because I had a car wreck with someone I thought was Devin. He wasn't Devin, but based on the guys who came after him, he's not exactly peaceful, either.'

Ezra turned to face him. 'You want to provide more detail on that?'

Frank provided the detail. Ezra listened quietly, shaking his head from time to time. 'Hell of a welcome back.'

'No kidding.'

'Nora Stafford's a good girl. You sure she's all right?'

'Other than the scare. I'd be surprised if the car she loaned out is ever returned to her, though.'

Ezra turned away. 'What kind of car you say that was?'

'It was a Mitsubishi. Little box of a thing. Blue paint.'

'Plate number six-five-three-E-four-two,' Ezra said.

Frank stared at the older man. 'Want to explain that?'

Ezra sat quietly for a time, as if there were a decision to be made. At last he got to his feet. 'Let's you and I take a drive.'

IT WAS LONG PAST visiting hours, but they let her in anyhow. Nora was well known at Northwoods Nursing Center.

'Dad?' She spoke as she opened her father's door, and Bud Stafford twisted his head to see her, a smile crossing his face. It was this moment that broke her heart—he was always so damn glad to see her. He couldn't follow conversation, couldn't process simple details, but he absolutely recognised his daughter.

'How you doing?' She kissed his forehead. He struggled with the covers, and she helped him sit upright. Nora had heard the phrase *wasting away* a million times in her life, never stopped to give it thought until her father's stroke. That was exactly what was happening, though. He just . . . faded. The strength had gone first, then the size, leaving a frail man where a powerful one had existed.

'Hello.' The single word came a full minute after she sat beside the bed. It took his brain that long to catch up. When you kept the conversation slow and simple, he could develop a bit of a rhythm, and the sense of truly communicating was better. Get too much going, though, and he became helplessly lost.

'Hello,' she said. 'What was dinner?'

'Yes.' He smiled at her again.

She waited for a few seconds, then said, 'Good day?'

'Good day. We had the birds.' That meant they'd taken him out to a patio with bird feeders. Now a highlight of his existence. 'Do you have cars?'

This joined the smile as the two constants of every visit. He didn't remember that he'd owned a body shop, or was incapable of expressing that he did, but somewhere in his fog-shrouded brain he knew that without cars there would be serious problems.

'I have cars,' she said. 'We have cars.'

He nodded. Hearing that answer always reassured him. She felt his love even through the veil of confusion. There was a notepad on the table, filled with scrawled attempts at his name. That meant it had been a therapist day. Three times a week, an occupational therapist came to work with him. She'd made progress, too.

'You want to try your name for me, Dad?' She passed him the pad and the pen, which he took carefully, his face set in a frown of concentration. Carefully he laid pen to paper. The first three letters of his first name— Ronald—came easily; then he hung up on the *a*. She watched him hesitate, write it again and again. *R . . . o . . . n . . . a . . . a . . . a . . . a . . .* 'You're stuck, Dad. Try the *l*.'

He cocked his head, then wrote the *a* again.

'Let me help.' Nora took her father's rough hand in her own, guiding him. It was a regular part of her visits, but on this night it cut through her with a sort of agony she hadn't felt since the early hospital days. He was her father, supposed to care for *her*. Today she'd been attacked and she was helping him write his own name.

The realisation brought a stinging to her eyes and for a moment she just sat there, fighting tears.

'Done?' he said.

She sniffed and got a laugh out. 'No, Dad. Let's try again.' They went back to the writing, naming each letter as they wrote it.

Later she drove home in the dark. At the house, the effort of preparing dinner seemed too much, so she settled for a glass of wine and sank into an overstuffed couch, feet up on the coffee table. It took thirty minutes of bad TV before she called it a night. She was exhausted and needed to get up early and track Jerry down, coerce him into getting the Lexus back in one piece for the police.

Halfway to the bedroom, she remembered that the police might have used the shop number instead of the house if they'd learned anything or had more questions. It was worth checking. She dialled the shop and got voicemail. One message waiting.

'Hello, I'm calling for Nora. This is Frank Temple. Listen, if you want that Mitsubishi back, I know where it is. But we're going to need to talk some things over first. I think I might . . . there's a chance I might know a little bit about that guy. Vaughn. I've got some things that I should probably explain to you before anybody deals with him. I'd like to talk to you, then probably the police.'

He left his cellphone number, which she already had. Nora stood in the dark living room with the phone to her ear for a minute, then replayed the message, felt a twist of fear counteract the sleepiness of wine and fatigue. Where, in the time since she'd dropped him off, had Frank Temple stumbled across *that* sort of information, alone in his cabin on the lake?

6

He woke to the sounds of birds, but it was anything but pleasant. Harsh, angry caws. Frank rolled onto his side and lifted his body on his elbow, searching for his watch. He found it—ten to eight. He shoved the covers back and, wearing nothing but his boxers, stepped outside into a cloudless morning, the lake glittering beneath sky so bright that he didn't see the osprey until it completed its dive.

The bird came tearing down towards its nest, then at the last second shot skywards again with a shrill scream. There were osprey nests all over the lake. What made this one so angry?

He figured it out when the osprey made its second dive. Just as it neared the nest, another bird bobbed up on the thick pile of sticks, matching the osprey's shriek. This bird was larger, its head pure white. A bald eagle. He was watching the osprey circle when an engine came into hearing range down the gravel drive. A pick-up truck rumbled into view. Nora Stafford.

No real surprise. He'd expected her to call, but cellphone reception was sporadic out here, even with that tower. As he watched, she pulled in beside the cabin, shut off the engine, and walked towards him. At least his under-wear was clean.

Nora looked away. 'Your message was awfully cryptic.'

'I'll explain. Do you mind if I put on some clothes first?'

'I was going to suggest that.'

They stepped inside and he went to the bedroom, pulled on jeans and a sweatshirt while she waited at the kitchen table. Not yet eight on a Saturday. Either she was an early riser or his message had scared her.

When he came out, she had left the table and was in the living room, looking at the Silver Star and the letter. She turned. 'Your grandfather's?'

'Uh-huh.'

'So they gave him the medal after he was dead? That's so sad. I can't imagine what your grandmother thought about that. Proud among other things, I suppose.'

'I suppose.' There were a couple of ways to approach this conversation, and ordinarily Frank would have favoured the less-is-more variation. While Nora was due a warning, a sense of what sort of trouble had arrived with the Lexus, she didn't need to know any information about Frank or his father. But something in the way she was studying the medal twisted him away from that instinct, made him want to tell her whole damn story.

'I'm surprised you got the message so early,' he said, and walked into the kitchen, got the coffeemaker running, just so he could have a task to do.

'I checked it last night.' She returned to her seat at the table. Today she'd traded in the heavy denim shirt for a blue tank top worn over loose white linen trousers, clothes that showed much more of a very nice body. 'I'm going to be honest. I thought about turning up here with the police. In the end, I decided I'd give you the chance to talk, but I didn't like that message. You made it sound as if you knew more than you told me yesterday.'

'I might know more than I told you yesterday,' Frank said, pouring water into the coffeemaker, 'but I didn't at the time. Everything you—and the police—heard from me was accurate. I'd never seen that guy before, Nora.'

'You said you knew where my car was.'

'That's right. Ezra Ballard found it hidden in the woods about two miles up the shoreline.'

She pulled her head back. 'On the Willow?'

'Yes.' He leaned against the counter. 'That guy, Vaughn, he drove it there yesterday. Ezra took me to see it last night.'

'So Vaughn dumped it.'

'No. He's staying here. Ezra saw him go out to an island. There's a cabin on it, has been for years. Apparently, he's with a woman out there.'

She nodded. 'OK. That's good news, isn't it? I can get my car back, and we can tell the police where to find this guy.'

Frank didn't answer.

'What else do you know?' she said, watching his face.

'About him? Nothing. I know something about the cabin he's staying in, that's all. About the man who owns it.'

'And what's that?'

'That he's a killer.'

She looked at him while the coffee burbled on the counter. 'You mean he's a murderer? Some sort of psychotic?'

'A professional.' The coffeepot was full now, and Frank turned and lifted it free. He poured coffee and held out the cup to her. When she shook her head, he took a drink from it himself.

'You're serious,' she said. 'I can see that you're serious. That the guy who drove that Lexus is some sort of assassin.'

'No. After seeing him, I'd have to say he's far from that. What I'm telling you is that the man who owns that cabin is. So if this guy with the Lexus works with him or whatever . . .'

'It's not good for me,' she finished.

'*Maybe* it's not. Like I said, Nora, I don't *know* anything here except what I've told you.'

'How do you know about the owner, though? He just came over to make some neighbourly conversation and told you that he kills people for a living?'

He looked at her and remembered what she'd said about his grandfather's medal—*proud among other things, I suppose.* 'He worked with my father.'

Those cool eyes were beginning to falter. 'Your father.'

'Frank Temple. He made the national news a while back.'

'For?'

'For killing people for money,' he said, and then he held her eyes and drank more coffee, and neither of them spoke.

'I'm sorry,' she said eventually.

'You don't need to be. I'm just telling you so you'll understand how I know these things.'

'So your father and the guy on the island, they *both* kill people for money? This is some sort of retreat for assassins?'

He kept his eyes on the floor. 'My dad served in Vietnam, part of a pretty elite group. He made some friends there. Ezra Ballard was one; a man named Dan Matteson was another. They were from three different parts of the country, but after the war they wanted to stay close. Dan had property up here and Ezra moved up and convinced my dad to build a cabin with him. Dan kept the island and my dad and Ezra bought this place.'

'Is Ezra . . .'

'No. Don't worry about that, Nora. He's a good man.'

'But your father and the other guy?'

'After the war Dan Matteson went into corrupt, beaten-down countries and took a lot of money to fight for one side or the other. He got into something in Central America, I'm not sure what, but he made some contacts out there and got involved in drug smuggling. Became a very big deal with some very dangerous people in Miami. When I was a kid, I got to know Ezra pretty well, but Dan was never around. I never actually met him.'

'Your father was working with him the whole time?'

'No. My father was a US marshal. An honest one for most of his career, I've heard. When I was in high school, Dan Matteson's body washed up on the beach in Miami. They identified him through dental records. Matteson had a son named Devin, working in the same world as his father. I think he's about fifteen years older than me. After the body was found, Devin called my father, asked him to help him avenge Dan's murder.'

'And he did it,' Nora said softly. 'That doesn't sound so evil. I mean, the people he killed, they were the ones who'd murdered his friend?'

'Some of them were,' Frank said, 'but he didn't stop there. By the time they sorted that out, Devin's boss made him another offer. And another. Last count I heard, he killed five people on contract while keeping his marshal's badge.' He paused. 'Eventually, the FBI got Devin into a jam, and to get out of it, he offered to trade some information. He gave them my father. But Dad got wind of it, He killed himself before there was an arrest.'

'I'm sorry, Frank. The way you reacted last night when I asked about your father, it should have told me—'

'That he was a killer?' He laughed. 'No, I don't think so. You've got nothing to apologise for. The only reason I'm telling you this is that I don't like Vaughn's connection to Devin.'

'And I'm to believe this connection between you and Vaughn is an honest coincidence.'

'Well, you can imagine I'm not real pleased by that little twist myself. The people Devin runs with, they're obviously dangerous.'

She forced a laugh. 'OK, I'll let him keep the car. How about that? Just pretend I don't know any of this.'

'That's a good idea. It's not the only problem, though. There are the two guys from last night.'

He could see understanding begin to grow on her face. 'You mean they might come back.'

'Professionals don't leave loose ends. We both saw that guy attack you yesterday and saw his buddy attack that cop, and our testimony could put them in jail for a long time. You and I have just become loose ends. If these guys really are involved with Devin Matteson, then that's a very serious concern.'

WHEN JERRY'S CELLPHONE RANG, he was standing outside the library. He looked at the screen and saw it was Bud Stafford's home number. Nora's number, now. She had no right to bother him on a Saturday.

'You never heard of a day off?' he said when he answered.

'Just rumours,' Nora said.

'That ain't funny. It's Saturday and that's a day off.'

'How'd you like another day off, Jerry?'

'What do you mean?'

'You come in today, for just a few hours, and I'll let you take Monday off. Time and a half, that's what I'll pay.'

'What the hell do you need me there for?'

'I want that Lexus put back together, fast.'

'That car is not a one-day fix. Hell, just to get parts—'

'You're not fixing it. You're just putting it back into one piece so I can get it out of my shop.'

'Guy wants to take it somewhere else?' This was not good. Jerry had a thousand bucks riding on that car.

'The police want to take it elsewhere.'

'*What?*'

'I don't want to get into it on the phone, Jerry.'

Damn. If the cops were onto this car, he might have lost his chance at the grand already. Of course, that AJ character had offered him half of that for the tracking device and Jerry had turned him down because he didn't have weekend access to the shop. Well, he did now.

'All right, Nora. Time and a half and Monday off. I'll come down.' He disconnected the phone, reached into his pocket and extracted the bar napkin he'd put there when he left the house that morning.

AJ answered on the second ring and Jerry told him the situation while he walked away from the library towards the river. 'Deal still stands—you get the tracking box, I get the five hundred?'

'You want to take me up on that deal.' AJ's voice was different today. Kind of uneasy, wary. 'She didn't tell you why she's paying time and a half?' he said.

'I assume the boy you're so interested in is coming back for the car.' Jerry didn't want to repeat Nora's reference to the cops.

'That seems unlikely.'

'Well, I don't know. I'm just saying, if you want your gadget back, now's the time.'

AJ went quiet for so long Jerry thought he'd hung up.

'You there?'

'Yes. All right. You get that tracking device and return to the bar where we talked yesterday. Go there at seven o'clock.'

'And you'll bring the money?'

'Yes, Mr Dolson. I will bring the money.'

BELIEVE IT OR NOT, Nora was anxious for Jerry's arrival. Being alone in the shop again wasn't a good feeling. Frank Temple had offered to come into town with her, but she'd declined, disliking having to rely on some strange male for protection. Besides, she was still reeling from what he'd told her. A *hit man*? At Willow Flowage? She might have considered it a joke, were it not for the sorrow in Frank's eyes.

She looked at the Lexus, sitting alone under the glare of the fluorescent lights. Just standing in its presence and seeing at those crumpled and twisted quarter panels on the floor was creepy.

A sudden, powerful rattling at the side door made her jump. 'Nora! Let me in.'

Jerry. She took one long breath, then moved to the door.

'Can't even unlock the door when you know I'm coming?' He entered the shop with customary good cheer, griping and scowling.

'After last night, I'm never leaving a door in this shop unlocked again,' she said. 'Not when I'm alone, at least.'

That made him lift one wild eyebrow. 'What do you mean?'

She told him what had happened. He looked concerned in a way she wouldn't have imagined he could be, concerned and almost guilty.

'Shoot, Nora. I can't believe that. This fella walking in here and putting hands on you . . . shoot.' He looked around the shop as if hoping to find the culprit on the property. 'You say they hit Mowery, hurt him bad?'

'He looked *real* bad, Jerry. I want to go down to the hospital, see if he's all right and thank him.'

'Yeah.' Jerry's eyes weren't on her, didn't seem to be on anything in the shop. 'I wish I'd been here.'

'I'm not your responsibility, Jerry. Don't worry about that. And I really do appreciate you coming in to get that stupid car put back together and out the door. I'll be glad to see it go.'

'No problem.' Then, banging his fist on the hood of the Lexus. 'You think the guy who drove this thing is going to come back for it?'

'I don't know, but I don't want it here if he does. I've heard some things I don't like, things that scare me.'

'What do you mean?'

'Last night was bad enough, but this morning I talked to the other driver. He's staying at the Willow.' She hesitated. 'He saw a gun in the Lexus. The guy took it with him.'

'You tell the police that?'

'Yes.'

'They say anything? Have any, uh, ideas about this car?'

'Not last night. I don't know if they do today.'

He wouldn't look at her. 'Get on out of here. I'll have this done fast.'

'I'll wait on you.'

He shook his head emphatically. 'No, you don't need to do that. You go on down to the hospital, check on Mowery.'

'Two people should be in this shop, Jerry. Until the car's gone.'

He lifted a hand to his forehead, rubbed above his eyes like an exhausted man with many miles ahead. 'I got something to tell you, Nora.' He looked anguished. 'And I want you to understand this first—I didn't know nothing about this car or what had happened to you at the time, OK? If I'd known what happened . . .'

'Jerry, what are you talking about?'

He lowered his hand and walked past her, pulled open his locker and withdrew a small plastic box. Even when he passed it to her, she had no idea what it was.

'It's a tracking device, Nora. Sends out a signal, and if you got the receiver, you can follow it.' He ran his tongue over his lips. 'It was on that car. I pulled it off the bumper reinforcement yesterday.'

This was the source of the chaos. It had brought those bastards into her life. 'You found this on the Lexus and didn't tell me?'

'I'm sorry, Nora. I wasn't thinking, that's all.'

All she felt was confusion. 'It's all right. You're telling me now. That's what counts.'

'Hang on,' Jerry said. 'There's more.'

WHEN FRANK got the boat in the water and the motor fastened onto the transom, his only thought was of taking a ride, seeing the lake again. But five minutes out of the little bay, just after he hit the main body of the lake, he opened up the throttle. He had to see the Matteson place. Just a look.

It was twenty minutes before the island came into view. Towards the northern reaches of the Willow the lake became more desolate, and tucked into the eastern shore was an area called Slaughterhouse Bay, so named because of the liberal collection of stumps and dead trees that protruded out of the water and could easily ruin a boat. Navigating among the stumps was treacherous.

Skirting the bay and its stumps by several hundred yards, Frank crossed Slaughterhouse Point, approaching the headwaters where the Tomahawk River fed the flowage.

He passed the island on the west side, saw the roof of the cabin and two NO TRESPASSING signs, then circled and was ready to head back when he saw the woman.

She was walking out into the lake, waist-deep now, testing the footing and moving slowly. What in the world was she thinking, going for a swim in

April? Even though the air temperature was unseasonably warm, the water would be freezing. Frank didn't slow or cut the motor or do anything else that would make a clear show of his interest. Instead he gave the throttle an extra twist, picking up speed and angling into the lake away from the island.

She was a beautiful woman. Even from fifty yards out, he'd seen that. Dave O'Connor, or Vaughn, or whoever the hell the grey-haired man was, did not seem a match for her. He was such a strange-looking man, so nervous and awkward. On the other hand, he drove a Lexus and had thousands in cash on him, along with a gun. Maybe she was attracted to money or danger.

But Vaughn didn't seem like a dangerous guy. He didn't fit the mould. There he was, though, staying in Devin Matteson's cabin with a woman who could turn heads from across the lake, two gun-toting badasses in pursuit. Nothing about that scenario felt right to Frank. He brought the boat round and ran back, a little farther out this time. She was leaving the water, and he could see another figure on shore. He assumed it was Vaughn.

Down some 300 yards, then back round for another pass. This time he couldn't see anyone on the beach. They'd gone inside, maybe. Or he'd spooked them. Better to continue on.

He cut the motor in North Bay, no other boat in sight. The sun was unhindered by cloud and he had just pulled his shirt off so he could feel it on his skin, when a harsh ringing sounded.

He couldn't believe he got cellphone reception out here. He took the phone out, saw the number he'd dialled the previous night to leave his message for Nora. She was back at her body shop. 'Hello?'

Static and garbled words. 'Nora? I can't hear you. Nora?'

More garbled words. Something about a tracking device. Fighting a surge of frustration, he asked her to repeat herself. Then the call was disconnected. Perfect.

He sighed and turned to the motor, adjusted the choke and pulled the cord. The motor thundered to life. He'd go back to the cabin, call Nora, and see what the hell was going on.

'DAMN IT.' Nora smacked the phone with her palm, turned it back on, tried again. This time it just rolled over to a message saying the mobile user was unavailable. OK, what now? It was a long drive out to his cabin, but she didn't know what else to do.

'Jerry.' She walked out of the office and into the shop. He was standing over his toolbox. 'I'm going to get Frank. I want him here when we talk to the police. He's got ideas they need to hear.'

Jerry spun a ratchet in his hand. 'What sort of ideas?'

'He thinks he might know something about who these guys are, and who they work with. He also claims to know where the guy who drove that Lexus is staying.'

Jerry frowned. 'All right. I'll get this car put back together.'

'I'd rather you didn't.'

'Huh?'

'I mean, I don't want anyone left alone in the shop.'

'You don't think you can trust me.' He straightened and looked at her, defiant. 'That's what's going on, isn't it? Before I told you about the deal that guy cut me at the bar, you needed this Lexus back in one piece fast. Now why has that changed?'

They looked at each other for a long moment and then his shoulders sagged. 'I'm sorry, Nora. I can see where you wouldn't think real well of me right now. You and I, we've had our problems. But I'll tell you this— ain't a man in this world I respect more than your daddy. The reason I'm still here is I know it's what he'd want me to do, and it's not just about the shop; it's about you. So when you tell me about these bastards walking in here and treating you like that, maybe you don't see how personal that is to me. And all I can say is, I'm sorry.'

'I appreciate everything you just said, Jerry. And I know I haven't been a real easy transition for you. Let's not worry about it, OK? You get the Lexus put back together, I'll bring Frank Temple down, and then the three of us will talk things out and call the police.'

He tipped two fingers off his forehead in a little salute, and she stepped out of the side door and pulled it shut behind her, making sure that it locked.

WHEN SHE WAS GONE, Jerry got to work. He started with the banged-up hood, which he'd removed completely. What had happened wasn't his fault, he understood that, but the fact was, while he was drinking beers and cutting a deal to sell equipment that wasn't his, Nora was back here with some bastard shoving her into a wall. If the kid hadn't showed up when he did . . .

He wrestled the hood back into place on the car, fastened it as tight as it would go. The damage kept it from closing, but it would stay on. By the time he was done, a good sweat was working its way across his scalp. 'Too damn hot,' he said aloud. He crossed to the garage door opener and hit the button, let the big door rise about two feet off the floor and felt the breeze shove through.

It was a pain in the ass putting a car back together without assistance. To fasten the bumper onto the front of the car, he got one side lined up and bolted loosely, then walked into the paint booth and retrieved a rack they used for drying parts, brought it out, and set it up under the bumper in a way that kept the thing level and positioned so that he could get the bolts lined up and tightened. He dragged the creeper over, hitched up his trousers and settled down, face pointed up at the ceiling. Using his heels, he shoved backwards, and the creeper slid under the car so he could get at the bumper bolts, leaving only his lower body exposed.

It was dark under the car, and he had to feel with his fingers to get the wrench in place. He got the bolts on the driver's side fastened and was working the creeper over to the passenger side when he heard the garage door rattle. When he turned his head, he saw two feet. Someone in polished black boots was walking the length of the door. Jerry knew those boots. He'd seen them tapping a soft beat off a bar stool not twenty-four hours earlier.

The son of a bitch was back. This time he didn't have a friend in Jerry, either. What he was *going* to have was a wrench upside his head. Jerry had extended his feet, ready to use his heels to pull himself forwards and out from under the car, when he saw a hand appear next to the boots. AJ was coming inside. Crawling under the door and coming inside.

He was a coward for doing it, but Jerry pushed with his heels instead of pulling and slid all the way under the Lexus. There was something about this that took him from angry to scared in one blink. What was the guy thinking, crawling into the shop? They'd agreed to meet at Kleindorfer's hours from now.

AJ crawled under the door, and then all Jerry could see was his feet as he walked into the shop. Then the feet passed out of his field of vision and he was listening to the slow claps of boot heels on concrete.

He held his breath as the boots came and went. AJ seemed to have made a full circle of the shop, was now probably standing in front of the Lexus. Peering into the office, maybe, seeing that the place was empty. Now, if he'd just crawl back under that door, Jerry could lock the place up tight, give the cops a call.

There was the metallic bang of a gear engaging, and then a loud hum as the garage door lowered and thumped to a stop against the floor, closed tight. 'You going to stay under that car all day, Mr Dolson?'

Jerry was caught. Damn it. He should've met this bastard on his feet, wrench in hand. Jerry slammed his heels down and pulled himself out from under the car and right into the barrel of a gun.

7

Frank tried calling the body shop as soon as he got back to the cabin. Voicemail. A second try found the same result. He didn't have a cell number for her. When his phone rang again and he heard Nora say his name, he was surprised by the relief he felt.

'I just left the shop,' she said. 'Are you at your cabin?'

'Yes.'

'Good. I'm on my way. I'd like you to come into town, and of course you can't do that because you have nothing to drive.'

'Tell me what happened,' he said.

The story she told wasn't a surprising one, but even before they hung up, he was unsettled by her enthusiasm for bringing in the police. If her body man was honest about the situation, and there really was a meeting scheduled at Kleindorfer's Taproom tonight, he could see the appeal of setting a trap. So would the men who'd set the meeting, though. It went back to what he'd already told her: these guys were pros.

And now these two guys, if there were only two, understood that their situation had changed. Tomahawk was a small town, where strangers stood out, and now everyone would be talking about them, the police looking for them. It added an element of pressure. Would they wait patiently for a meeting with Nora's employee? He knew his answer to that and it wasn't comforting.

He pulled a metal case onto the bed, flipped the latches, opened the lid, and withdrew the two holstered and well-oiled handguns beneath. His father's guns: a 10mm Smith & Wesson and a .45-calibre Glock. He had the Smith & Wesson in its shoulder holster and concealed under a thin jacket by the time Nora arrived.

SPEND ENOUGH TIME around firearms and they'll fail to inspire the same sense of terror that might catch a novice, even when the weapon in question is pointed at your heart. Jerry wasn't thrilled to see it, no, but guns were guns. And the man hadn't shot him yet.

'You don't look happy to see me, Mr Dolson,' AJ said.

'I'm not. We had an agreement. Why don't you go on down to Kleindorfer's and wait for me, like we planned?'

'Your boss,' AJ said. 'She have anything to tell you?'

'Nope.'

'You're a bad liar, Mr Dolson.'

Jerry steeled his eyes against the other man's empty gaze. 'And you're a Grade A piece of crap, buddy. Coming in here and beating up a woman.'

'I didn't lay hands on anyone.'

'Then your buddy did. Now you get the damn gun out of my face and get on your way.'

'We had an agreement. I need that tracking device.'

'Don't have it.'

'Who does?'

He started to say Nora's name, then stopped. The thing was still sitting in his locker, waiting to go to the police.

'Put that gun down,' Jerry said.

'Maybe then we can talk this through?'

Jerry stared into that tiny muzzle. 'Maybe we can.'

AJ pistol-whipped him in the face. Jerry had time to lean backwards maybe six inches and half lift the wrench in his hand before the gun knocked him into the Lexus. His ribs slammed against the grille, the wrench fell from his hands, and then he took another blow from the gun across his head. The third swing left him stretched on his back, looking at the corrugated metal ceiling that now bloomed with a dozen colours.

When he felt someone moving his hands, he could make only the slightest resistance. AJ was tying his wrists together.

'Is the girl coming back?'

Jerry didn't say anything. He was tied to something. Maybe the Lexus. He heard AJ walking away, strained to lift his head. AJ was at Jerry's toolbox, was lifting a ten-pound maul out. *No, no, no. Put that thing down. Please put that thing down.*

'Is the girl coming back?' AJ repeated. He took a practice swing.

'Yeah.' Jerry's head was clearing fast, the pain no longer a presence in his mind. 'Maybe an hour.'

'She go to the cops?' AJ was standing over Jerry, the maul held casually against his shoulder.

Instinct said to tell him no, but if the guy thought cops were on the way, maybe he'd cut this short. Was that a good thing?

'Mr Dolson? Jerry, buddy? You want to give me an answer?'

'She went to pick up that kid. Could be they'll go to the cops. You hit a woman, knock a cop around, you've got to expect—'

'What kid?'

'One who jacked up your friend last night.'

'Why's he involved?'

The pain was coming back now, but so was his guilt. He shouldn't be giving so much information. 'Don't know.'

The maul came down and caught Jerry square in the hip. A hellfire shot of pain cut through his leg and into his stomach, filled his chest. He arched his back and hissed through clenched teeth.

'Want to answer that one again?' AJ said.

'He thinks he knows something about you.'

'About *me*? How does he know something about me?'

'I'm not sure.' He had his eyes squeezed shut against the pain but sensed the maul being lifted again. 'I *don't* know, OK? She just told me she needed to talk to him. He thinks he knows where your boy went, the one drove this car.'

'Where?'

'I don't know.'

'You're lying. *Where?*'

'She didn't tell me.'

'Where was she going to pick the kid up?'

'I don't know.'

'You're lying again. Where did she go?'

Jerry knew he had to shut up. The guy was going to chase after Nora. Jerry wasn't about to do that to her.

'Where did she go?' AJ repeated.

'Tell you where *you* can go. Straight to—'

This time the maul was swung straight into Jerry's thigh. He heard the bone snap and he couldn't have screamed if he wanted to. The pain slid into his brain like a fast-moving storm cloud and he faded beneath it.

'One more chance, Mr Dolson. Where did she go?'

Where did she go? Don't tell him, Jerry. Don't tell him. The pain's going to come back soon, going to make you forget some things, but don't forget this.

'Does she have the tracking device? You said yesterday it was in your locker. I bet you still have it. You wanted that money.'

AJ moved away and Jerry took in a long breath and choked on it. There was so much spit in his throat. Or was it blood?

'Thatta boy,' AJ said, and a locker slammed shut.

'You got it,' Jerry said. Tried to say, at least. The words were tough to form. AJ had the tracking device, so maybe he would leave now, and let Jerry alone.

'I got it. But that's not the only thing I need. Where did *he* go, Jerry? Where is the guy who goes with the car?'

Jerry didn't know. He couldn't remember any more. Wait—where *had* Nora gone? The Willow, that was it.

'What's that?' AJ was standing above him now.

He'd been talking. Not good. *Keep your damn mouth shut, Jerry.*

'Willow?' AJ said. 'Is that what you said? Keep going.'

Don't keep talking Don't say anything, Jerry.

'OK,' AJ said. 'You're running out of usefulness. Good news is, you're not going to feel that leg any more.'

The maul was gone, discarded in favour of a knife with a small blade. Good. Jerry didn't know if he could take another swing from the maul. But the knife wasn't good, either, was it? He should ask AJ to stop. Just stop and go away. Couldn't he see that Jerry was hurt?

'I'T'S NOT GOING to be quite that easy,' Frank Temple said as Nora drove down Business 51 into Tomahawk. She was beginning to feel uncomfortable with him. Even if everything he'd told her was the truth, it seemed odd to be *so* leery of telling the police. Any normal person would be *ordering* her to call them. Was he somehow connected to these guys?

'These guys think Jerry's working *with* them, Frank.'

'I don't know if they believe that. Going for some sort of trap with a handful of small-town cops seems like a poor plan to me.'

'You spent this morning convincing me that I should be terrified of these men. Then I tell you that there's a good opportunity to have them arrested, and you're trying to discourage it.'

He was quiet, looking out of the window.

'I'll let you talk to Jerry,' she said, 'but then I'm calling the police. OK? This is *not* your decision. I was the one they attacked, and that damn car is in my shop.'

He just nodded.

Fine, Nora thought. In an hour or so the police will be dealing with all of your strange moods, not me. She drove into town, into the shop lot, and parked just behind the building. Frank beside her, she went to the side door, which was locked. She rapped on the door and they waited. Jerry must have reverted to typical Jerry form and chosen to ignore her knock. She got out her keys and unlocked the door, held it open for Frank. She'd made it maybe two steps inside the shop when he whirled back and put his hand on her shoulder. 'Outside.'

'What?'

He didn't answer, just reached for the door handle. She twisted free from his grasp. 'Let go of me. What are you doing?' He had the door open and was reaching for her again as she saw the blood.

There was a drain in the centre of the concrete floor, and a thin trail of blood was leaking into it. Then she saw Jerry.

He was hanging in an awkward half-lean from the front of the Lexus, his hands bound to the grille with wire, his head flopped sideways onto his left shoulder. There was a thick dark line across his throat, and beneath it was the pool of blood that had spawned the rivulet running into the drain. His left leg was bent unnaturally.

'No, Jerry.' She started towards him.

'Don't.' Frank had her arm again, his grip rough.

'Look at him! He's—'

'Dead. Don't touch him. We need to leave now.'

She started to fight him, but then her eyes focused on Jerry's leg again. They'd broken his leg. Nausea came on in a wave and she started to sink to her knees. Frank caught her and moved her back towards the door. Her jaw went slack and she was sure she'd be ill, but then he had her outside in the fresh air.

'Oh, no, Jerry.' She was on her knees on the pavement now. 'No, Jerry, what happened to him? What did they do to him?'

She tried to get to her feet, but Frank gently shoved her back. 'Stay down. I'm calling the police.'

She put her hands flat on the gravel and squeezed them into fists. 'Did you see his leg?' she said.

Frank was talking in a low voice into his phone. She asked the question a second time as he put the phone back into his pocket and knelt beside her, wrapped his arm round her back.

'Did you see his leg?'

'Yes.' His voice was soft.

'They hurt him,' she said. 'They did that to his leg.'

'I know.'

THEY SEPARATED Frank from Nora almost immediately, and for six hours he didn't see her. None of the cops bothered to search him, but he was conscious of the gun in his shoulder holster and eventually told the officer in charge. The guy took the gun, then searched Frank with rough hands, as if he might have given up the pistol only to attack with a knife.

At first it was nothing but local cops, who all seemed to achieve a certain level of shock that someone had been tortured and murdered at noon on a Saturday in the middle of town. They ran through the motions, asked Frank the basic questions, but nobody seemed focused. He was left alone in an interrogation room at the little police station for more than an hour.

When the door finally opened, the cop who entered wasn't one he'd seen before. Even before the guy settled into a chair across the table, Frank knew he was an outsider. He was about fifty, with a receding hairline and weathered skin, bony shoulders poking at his shirt. One eye drifted just a touch. 'Mr Temple, my name is Ron Atkins. Feel free to call me Ron.'

'Fine,' Frank said. 'Who are you with?'

Atkins raised an eyebrow. 'You imply I'm from a different agency than the one that brought you here?'

'I do. You don't look excited.'

Atkins considered Frank for a long moment. 'I'm with the FBI, Mr Temple.'

'Milwaukee?'

Atkins's eyebrow went up again. 'No, Wausau. We maintain a small field office there.'

Frank nodded.

'First you had this trouble yesterday in which, according to what I've been told, you performed quite admirably. Then, not twenty-four hours later, you found a murder victim in the same building.' Atkins cocked his head. 'No way to start a vacation, right?'

'Nope.'

'So you are here on vacation?'

'Yes.'

'That's what brings most people here. Most, though, don't have a string of bad luck like you're experiencing.'

'I wouldn't think so.' Even this early in the conversation, Frank had reached two conclusions: first, Atkins was smart, and deserving of respect. Second, Frank didn't like him.

'You rent a cabin up here, is that it?'

'Own one.'

'Really? Very nice. Out there on Willow Flowage, is it?'

'Yes.'

'How'd you come into possession of the cabin, might I ask?'

Here was the reason Frank didn't like him, drifting out in these casual questions. The man had come here to ask about Frank's father.

'It was in the family,' Frank said. 'But I don't see what relevance that has to the poor bastard with his throat cut, Mr Atkins. Ron.'

'I understand that. But, see, I may find relevance in places you don't.'

'Tell you what, let's go ahead and talk about my dad. He's been dead for seven years. Tough to blame him for this one.'

'I understand how frustrating this has to be for you, trust me, but when a cop ends up beaten half to death outside a body shop on a Friday and another man ends up killed in the same shop on a Saturday, and the key witness to both events is the son of a hit man—'

'This is what brings the FBI up from Wausau,' Frank said.

Atkins nodded with a theatrical sense of apology. 'Like I said, Mr Temple, I understand this may not be fair to you, but I've still got to ask the questions. Right off the bat, I'm curious about this: I was told you were wearing a gun when the police got to the body shop. A gun with your father's initials stamped into the stock. FT II. You always carry the gun?'

'No.'

'OK. You come up here on vacation, and you think this seems the time and place to pack a pistol?'

'It had started to seem like a dangerous town.'

Atkins nodded. 'Almost from the moment you arrived.'

NORA WAITED FOR FRANK outside the police station as evening descended, the sky tinged with wispy purple clouds.

Jerry was dead. He'd been a cantankerous, combative employee from day one, but he'd also been the only person she was close to in the entire town. That he was gone filled her with the chill of loss. She was feeling the threatening rise of tears when the station door opened and Frank Temple came down the steps to join her, holding his jacket. For the first time, she saw that he was wearing a gun in a holster on the side of his chest.

'Where'd you get that?'

He didn't look at her. 'Had it on when we left the cabin. Cops seemed to want to keep it, but I made a compelling case against that by pointing out that nobody was killed with a gun today. Is your car still around?'

'At the shop.'

'Let's walk down there, then.'

They started down the sidewalk, falling silently in step.

'I was surprised the FBI was here,' she said.

'I'm the only reason they're involved; it's somewhat discouraging. Having the FBI investigate me is not going to help with this mess.'

'Atkins seemed pretty interested in you.'

'Yeah, he did.' He turned to face her. 'Did Atkins say a word to you about Vaughn?'

She thought about it. 'Not until I brought him up. Then he just wanted to know whether you seemed familiar with him.'

'OK, that's basically the same response I got, like he was completely uninterested in Vaughn. Since he should be *very* interested in him, I'm going to guess that my name is not the only draw that attracted our VIP from Wausau. They've got something on Vaughn already. That Lexus rang some bells somewhere; then my name was an extra wild card in the deck. They don't know what to make of it yet.'

'And they don't know where he is.'

The look he gave her then was both knowing and intrigued. 'You didn't mention Ezra's find?'

'No. Did you?'

He shook his head. 'Figured it was your play.'

'There was a lot going through my mind,' she said. 'I was thinking about everything you said about the guy who owns the cabin, and how everyone around him is so . . .'

'Deadly.'

'I guess that's the word.'

She stopped walking and he went a couple of paces ahead before turning back to her.

'I didn't tell them,' she said, 'because I'm scared.'

'You should be.'

'So what do we do?'

'There are only two things I'm certain of right now. First, we should talk to Ezra.'

'We should talk to a *fishing guide*?'

'He's a bit more than that, Nora.'

'OK. And the other thing you're certain of?'

He started to walk again, the gun bouncing a little with each step. 'That if you go home tonight, you probably die.'

8

Grady hadn't dated much since Julie left. The occasional set-up, or maybe somebody he'd meet at a party and see once or twice again, but nothing serious. He had a date for Saturday night, though, a woman who worked computers at one of the major Chicago banks. He was with a team that was trying to trace terrorism dollars and Helen was the liaison the bank had offered up to the Bureau. They'd spent the better part of two weeks together, going over numbers that led nowhere. He wouldn't have asked her out; he'd never been good at that. Two days after he'd broken off from the project, though, she called him at work and asked him to dinner.

He was in a good mood as Saturday afternoon wore down and went for a long run along the lake, feeeling the week's tension leave his muscles. When he got back to the apartment, he showered and decided on a black button-down shirt with a dark green pair of trousers. He was just threading the belt round his waist when his cellphone rang.

'Agent Morgan? Ron Atkins calling from Wausau.'

Wausau? There was a field office up there, but what in the hell could Wausau have cooking on a Saturday evening?

'What can I do for you?' Grady said, standing before the mirror and taking inventory, trying to ignore the grey hair.

'I'm sorry to bother you on a Saturday night like this, but I've been doing a little research, and it looks like you're the foremost expert we've got on Frank Temple.'

Grady's face clouded with alarm. 'Which one?'

'The son,' Atkins said. 'Frank the Third.'

Grady walked out to the living room, the sick taste of defeat in his mouth. Wausau. Hell, that town was maybe fifty miles from the infamous family cabin Frank had spoken of with such warmth, the one his father had purchased with the other soldier, Ballard. 'What's happening?' he said.

'I'm trying to figure that out. Here's what I know: the Temple kid blew into Tomahawk yesterday, a couple of real bad boys from Miami on his heels, and we've already got one body in the morgue and a cop in the hospital.'

Real bad boys from Miami. The words spun through Grady's brain like whirring blades. He sank down on the couch. The kid had done it. He'd gone down to Miami to settle up, put three bullets into Devin Matteson's body, and Grady had sent him there.

'I've been told,' Atkins said, 'you spent some time with the kid. And you brought his father down.'

'He brought himself down.'

'What? Oh, sure. Sure. The thing is, you know, it seems the apple didn't fall far from the tree.'

'I wouldn't rush to that judgment.'

'What rush? He's been adrift for damn near a decade, without a job but with a seemingly inexhaustible supply of cash.'

The supply was exhaustible—probably getting close to exhausted by now, actually. Frank's father had been clever with his banking, setting up hidden trusts and offshore accounts. By the time the kid had disclosed this, Grady was beginning to feel overwhelmed by his guilt, so instead of shutting the money down, Grady merely warned Frank that he ought to separate himself from a bloody slush fund like that.

'I spent some time with him. He had his head on right.'

'Did you not hear me say I've got one dead already? Yeah, when a contract killer's son floats into town, wearing a gun and leaving bodies in his wake, I suppose he really could just be on a fishing trip.'

'He was wearing a gun?'

'Smith & Wesson with his father's initials engraved on the stock.'

Grady pressed his eyes shut. That was the suicide gun. 'Tell me what you know, Atkins.'

'These guys from Miami, they showed up yesterday and attacked a woman who owns a body shop here. The same shop where Temple's car ended up after an accident a few miles north of town. Temple interceded. By the end of the day the cops somehow lost both of these guys, who today killed one of the woman's employees. Nasty scene. The way it looks is that they've lost track of Temple and figured the people at the body shop were the last who'd seen him. There's a guy named Vaughn Duncan, too, these guys are supposedly interested in.'

'Who is Duncan?'

'A prison guard from Florida. Duncan's car had a tracking device. Allegedly. Evidently he called in and quit a few days ago, no warning. Seems he came into some serious cash about a year ago, too, source unknown. Guy's working as a prison guard and driving a Lexus, you know something's wrong.'

'What prison?'

'Coleman.'

'Which part of Coleman? It's a big complex.'

There was a rustle of papers. 'Phase One,' Atkins said.

Manuel DeCaster was in Coleman Phase One. The big boss, the ruthless bastard who'd employed Frank's father, probably still employed Devin Matteson. This was not good news.

'Well,' Atkins said. 'You got any ideas? Anything I should be checking out?'

As an FBI agent, Grady had to tell him. Had to drop that Matteson name and news of the recent shooting, fill in the backstory, draw connections. But he couldn't do it. Not without talking to Frank. So for the second time in his Bureau career, Grady ignored his professional oath. 'I'm not sure,' he told Atkins. 'Let me call around a bit and get back to you.'

Atkins seemed satisfied with that.

Grady still had Frank's number, but when he called, all he got was a message saying it had been disconnected. One perk of working for the FBI, though—if the kid had a number, Grady could find it. He cancelled his date with a sincere apology and headed for the office.

He thought about Devin Matteson as he drove, about that blood debt he'd chosen not to mention to Atkins. About how he'd told himself Devin Matteson was an evil bastard of the first order, a killer and drug-runner and thief, so who cared if the kid thought Devin was the one who'd given up his father?

So long as Frank knew better than to take action, to seek retribution.

EZRA HAD LEFT the note on Frank's door at two that afternoon, after stopping by the cabin to find that Frank was missing, which wasn't a surprise until Ezra noticed the boat was on the beach. If he wasn't fishing and he had no car, where'd he gone? Ezra scrawled a note and fastened it to the door, then left expecting to hear from his friend's son within a few hours.

It was dark now and the phone hadn't rung. He wished the kid would call. There was something riding the air today that Ezra didn't like. That attractive woman had been in the water again this morning. No sign of the grey-haired companion, no movement of the car in the trees. Maybe that was good. Maybe they were nobodies, nothing to worry about.

He couldn't believe that any more, though. Not after hearing Frank's story about the attack on Nora Stafford, two men with guns arriving in pursuit of this grey-haired son of a bitch. So what to do about it? Maybe just wait it out. That was one option.

An option he favoured until the headlights of a truck washed over his driveway and Frank Temple III arrived with young Nora and, right then, even before they got out of the truck, Ezra understood that this thing was not going to be one he could wait out.

They came onto the porch and sat with him and told him what had happened. He listened, and what he heard of a man with bound hands and a cut throat took him back to a place he'd left long ago. Not Vietnam. Detroit. He'd seen men die in both places, but the death in Detroit was a different sort of killing.

'I didn't think Nora should go home,' Frank concluded. 'Am I wrong? Are these guys already trying to disappear?'

'No. You weren't wrong and they aren't gone yet.' Two professionals had come all the way up here to do a job that didn't involve beating up Mowery or killing Jerry Dolson, and because these things were happening, it was clear that the job was not done.

'So what's your advice? Should we go to the cops?'

'I don't think we'll be able to decide that until we find out who the visitors are and what they're running from. I'd imagine asking them directly would be a good start.'

Frank and Nora stared at him.

'We're going there?' Frank said. 'To the island?'

'I think we should. But I'd wait till daylight.'

Frank nodded slowly. 'All right. So you and I go out there in the morning and try to get them to talk.'

'No,' Nora said. 'You're not going to leave me sitting in some cabin while you go out there. I won't do it. They came into my shop and they killed my employee, my friend. If anyone here deserves some answers, it's me.'

Tough to argue with that.

'Fine,' Ezra said. 'We'll all go, then. First thing in the morning.'

'What if they leave?' Nora asked.

'Be tough to leave that island,' Ezra said, 'without a boat.'

Frank's eyebrows rose. 'You're going to steal it?'

'Not steal it. Might disrupt it a touch, is all.'

'What if they see you?' Nora said.

Ezra smiled, and Frank answered, 'They won't see him, Nora.'

It was quiet for a few minutes, then Ezra said, 'You feel safe at your cabin?'

'I do,' Frank said.

Ezra nodded. 'You'll be safe there tonight.' Ezra had a boat and a rifle with a nightscope. Yes, they'd be safe tonight.

'All right,' he said. 'I think I ought to go address that boat on the island. You all go back home. Rest. Any trouble does come up, I'll be around, and I see you got your dad's gun in case you need it.'

Frank looked down. 'How the hell can you tell it's his gun when it's holstered and I'm wearing a jacket?'

Ezra just walked to his truck.

GRADY FOUND an active cell number easily enough. But he called five times over two hours and got nothing but voicemail. He left his numbers and an urgent request to call.

What to do now? He owed Atkins information. Every hour that ticked by made him feel guiltier about that. Finally he picked up the phone again and called Jimmy Saul in Miami.

Saul answered on the first ring, his voice tinged with irritation. 'Hell, Grady,

I was gonna call tomorrow. Should have known you couldn't wait on it till morning like a normal person.'

'Wait on what, Jimmy?'

'What the hell do you think? Matteson.'

Grady stood up. 'Did Matteson die in the hospital?' If he had, then it became murder. Not just attempted, but the real deal.

'Die? Uh, no, Grady. The boy is loose. Matteson bailed out of the hospital under his own power sometime this afternoon.'

'I thought he was in a critical condition.'

'He had been initially. Like I told you yesterday, he was recovering unusually well, but not well enough to be out of the hospital. Doctors seem to think he just signed his own death sentence and nobody has a clue what motivated him to go. He wasn't facing charges for anything.'

He's coming for Frank, Grady thought. *Oh God, he is coming to Wisconsin and he is going to kill Frank.*

Then Saul said, 'Best bet is he's looking for the wife,' and everything changed.

'The wife?'

'Yeah, of course. Oh, wait, I hadn't heard about her the last time we talked, had I? That news came in a little later. Remember when I said there weren't any suspects? Well, that's been blown out of the water. Nobody can find Matteson's wife. Originally the cops thought she was just missing in action, but now their idea is that she took off. Ran. Which makes her—'

'The suspect,' Grady finished.

'You got it,' Saul said. 'Problem with that is there were no signs of a rift with Matteson, no indications of an affair. But, still, until she turns up, that's what'll occupy the focus. Could be she's dead, too. Could be—'

'Devin left the hospital today,' Grady said, no longer interested in hearing the theories.

'That's right. Nobody knows where he's headed, either.'

'I do,' Grady said. 'I could be wrong, but I doubt it.'

'What's going on, Grady?'

'I don't know yet, but here's my advice: check every flight yesterday out of Miami to Wisconsin. Run the name Vaughn Duncan. He's a prison guard from Coleman and he's up in Wisconsin, tangling with Frank Temple and a couple of others. Check him out and get back to me,' Grady said, and hung up.

THE CABIN WAS DARK when they entered and Nora was nervous until Frank got all the lights on. He was still wearing the gun and she was troubled that it comforted her.

'I thought about taking you back so you could get some things together,' he said, 'but it wasn't worth the risk. If they're watching any place, it would probably be your house.'

'Right.'

'Look, you can take whatever bedroom you want. Ezra keeps the place stocked, so there's an extra toothbrush in the bathroom, soap and shampoo.' He looked tense, ill at ease.

'What's wrong?'

He frowned. 'Nothing.' It was quiet for a moment and then he added, 'I'm not like them. I need you to understand that.'

'The guys who killed Jerry? Of course you're not.'

He leaned against the wall, looked down to the gun, back up at her. 'I'm not like him, either.'

'Your father. I don't think otherwise.'

His eyes were so damn sad. 'You would have liked him.'

She had no idea how to answer that.

'Everybody did,' he said. 'You would have, too.'

'Is that what scares you the most?'

'What?'

'That you loved him. That you thought he was good.'

He looked at her for a while without speaking, then he walked to the door and went outside.

She went after him. He was sitting on the log wall that held the soil back from the beach. He pointed at the lake. 'I can see why Ezra never left.'

'It's a gorgeous place.' The air was warm tonight, but the sky was overcast, only a handful of stars showing. 'You don't need to worry,' she said. 'Nothing the cops told me was different from what you'd told me this morning. I don't think you're dangerous.'

'The old man spent a lot of time trying to make me dangerous. It would break his heart to hear you say that.'

She thought of the way he'd come across the body shop, unarmed, the day before. How long had it taken him to knock that guy out with the wrench? Two seconds, tops. Maybe he could be dangerous, but she wasn't scared of him.

He leaned back on the grass.

'Where's your mother?' She surprised herself, asking the question.

'Baltimore.'

'That's where you grew up?'

'No. That's where she is now.'

'Were they divorced?'

'Not officially. They were together until I was fifteen. Anyhow, he moved out. He was always saying they'd get back together.'

'Are you close to her?'

'Not by happy-family standards, I guess, but we talk on the phone; I see her every now and again. She got remarried a few years ago.'

Nora was sitting with her knees pulled up, arms round them, facing the water. The way Frank was leaning back put him behind her, so she couldn't see his face. He seemed more comfortable that way.

'My father killed people, and he took money for it, and that seems so obviously evil to most people . . . but I wish they'd met him,' he said. 'Now he's a monster, you know? There is no more one-dimensional a character than a monster. If Dad was anything he was multidimensional.'

'I'm sorry,' she said. What a horribly hollow phrase.

The silence was interrupted by the soft sound of a motor somewhere out on the lake. Nora sat up straighter to stare out at the water.

'It's Ezra, in his boat,' Frank said.

'How do you know? There are no lights. What if it's—'

'It's not them. Whoever's in that boat took it round the sandbar, and you don't do that by dumb luck. I knew he'd spend the night out there. He takes his responsibilities seriously, and tonight we're on that list.'

The motor disappeared; now she could hear only the gentle thumping of water on the beach.

'So what's your story?' Frank said.

'What do you mean?' She turned back to him.

'You're from Minneapolis. Your dad lived up here, ran that body shop, and then he had a stroke.'

'Yes.'

'So what else is keeping you here?'

'That's not enough?'

He leaned forward, so that she could see his face again. 'Could be. I'm asking you if that's all there is.'

'I came for Dad,' she said carefully. 'But there might have been things going on in my life that made staying here more appealing.'

'OK.'

There was a long pause. 'I was engaged . . . for three years.'

'Long time to wait.'

'That's what he said.'

Frank's laugh, low and genuine, caught her by surprise and relaxed her. She twisted a little, facing him. 'The wedding date was set for a month ago, in fact. I had his full support when I came out here after Dad's stroke. The longer I stayed, though, the pushier he became about me coming back to Madison. And I realised a couple of things. One was that I didn't want my father to be alone in a nursing home, nobody coming to see him, his shop going out of business.'

'And the other?' Frank said.

'The other was that I didn't want to get married. I'd been living with him for two years and yet I kept coming up with delays.'

'Just reluctant, then? No specific reason, no epiphany?'

There had been an epiphany of sorts. A party not long after their engagement, when he had turned to a group of people to introduce Nora and said, 'This is my fiancée.' She'd waited for the *Nora* to follow, but it never came. A simple thing, maybe, a minuscule issue of semantics, but in that moment it had felt chilling. Because she knew that he hadn't misspoken. The name was irrelevant; she was his fiancée. His possession. She flashed forwards twenty years and saw herself introduced as: 'This is my wife.'

'When I had to come up here, it was the first time I'd been on my own in a long while,' she said. 'It felt good. He'd wanted me to forget about a day job, concentrate on my art.'

'Generally considered a positive thing.'

'That's what I thought. But when I came up here and started going through my dad's things, really looking at his life, at how hard he and my grandfather had worked to make a living off that crappy little shop . . .'

'Made you feel soft?'

'Made me realise I *am* soft. My dad got up at three in the morning when it snowed, ran the plough till eight, then opened his shop up and worked all day, all winter. There was *never* a time when that shop did more than struggle to keep bills paid, but they kept them paid. For sixty-eight years.' The wind blew hair into her face and she pushed it back. 'I've never worked for anything that counted. I worked for good grades, worked on my art, but that's not the same. I've never had my back to the wall. I suppose it's awfully childish to say it's a bad thing. I suppose I should just be grateful.'

'Is that what the fiancé told you?'

'Among other things. He gave me an ultimatum.'

'Poor bastard. A name, I require a name.'

'Seth.'

'Horrible.'

'Someone named Frank is criticising another guy's name?'

'Frank was half of the first names of the Hardy Boys. It doesn't get any more solid than that.'

She was laughing, and he seemed to have drawn closer without ever moving, and there was a sudden intimacy to the evening that absolutely did not belong. Even so, she didn't want it to go away. There was a pause that went on a few beats too long, his face close to hers.

'This is where you tell me what a lousy kisser Seth was,' Frank said. 'To inspire me.'

'Inspire you to what?'

He didn't respond.

'Can't do it,' she said. 'He was actually a very good kisser.'

'She sets the bar high,' Frank said, and then his hand was sliding across the back of her neck, pulling her forwards, and his lips were on hers.

IT WAS THE FIRST TIME he'd watched anyone kiss through a rifle scope. When Ezra realised what they were doing, he dropped the gun and looked skywards, despondent. Just what this mess needed. What the hell was the kid thinking?

He lifted the gun again, watched them for a few seconds, Nora Stafford beautiful even bathed in the wavering green light of the scope. OK, *that* was what the kid was thinking. On second look, even through the scope, it made a hell of a lot of sense. Well, good for Frank.

Very good, really. Ezra hadn't liked the boy's look this evening. Reminded him too much of other men he'd known, in other places. Once they got those sons of bitches from Florida sent on their way, the girl could be a wonderful thing for Frank. Ezra hadn't seen her many times, but enough to know that she was a different cut than others her age. As was Frank.

Ezra went into the water 200 feet from the island, swam naked through the cold lake, spent all of thirty seconds on the motor, and then swam off into the darkness again, leaving the outboard disabled. Whole thing had taken maybe five minutes, but they were minutes that took him back to those other places, those other times.

Damn, but the lake had healed Ezra. This place had *healed* him. He liked to believe the violence had drained away slowly, that the lake and forests had soaked it up, taken it from him. What he feared, from time to time, was that it hadn't drained away at all. That it was just a little better hidden.

THEY'D BEEN KISSING for a while when Nora put her palm on his chest and pushed him back.

'What?' he said, breaking away. 'I shouldn't have done that?'

'No, it's just'—she smiled—'not really the night for it, you know?'

He was looking at her, trying to read her, but she got to her feet, dusted off her trousers. He stood up, too. 'Look,' he said, 'I'm sorry. If I did anything—'

'It's fine. You didn't do anything wrong. I just don't want to let that moment turn into something it shouldn't.' Now the awkwardness between them was evident. 'I'm getting cold,' she said. 'Maybe we can go inside?'

She rubbed her upper arms in a false gesture, and he just nodded and walked to the door and held it for her, thinking that he was still concerned about whether she was afraid of him, and it came from a place of guilt. He was asking her to believe in a complete fraud—the idea that his connection to all of this was an extraordinary coincidence. It had been easier to ask her to believe that than to tell her he'd come here to kill someone. She sat on the couch and he took the chair beside it. They spoke in soft voices for about an hour, and then the conversation slowed and vanished, and after a while he realised she was asleep. He repositioned her on the couch, got a pillow under her head and a blanket over her body; then he sat beside her. Wasn't fair to make Ezra do all the watching.

At some point, he got quietly to his feet and went to find his cellphone. He'd turned it off in the police station and now he turned it back on and played the message that was waiting.

GRADY TURNED onto his elbow and grabbed the phone, mumbled a hello that was thick with sleep.

'It's Frank.'

Grady said, 'What the hell kind of trouble did you get into?'

'Atkins didn't tell you?'

'I've heard what he said. Now I'm asking *you.*'

'Can't tell you anything different except that these guys are involved with Devin. That much seems clear.'

'Frank . . . damn it, tell me the truth. Were you down in Miami when it got started?'

'Grady, I haven't been to Miami since my dad took me eight years ago.'

Grady exhaled pure relief. 'So you're telling me—'

'What happened in Miami? You seem to know a lot more than I do.'

'Devin Matteson was shot.'

Silence filled the line. 'Just shot,' Frank said at last, 'or killed?'

'Shot three times in the back. But he didn't die. Listen . . . why are you up there?'

'You want the truth? I heard he was headed this way.'

Grady sighed and rubbed his eyes. 'Who told you that?'

'Ezra Ballard.'

'Well, you should have called me. Now look at what it's turning into. Stay away from Ballard and stay away from whatever ideas he's got.'

'Who said he's got any? But I don't want to argue with you. Tell me what you know about Devin. Who took him out?'

Grady sighed and rubbed his eyes. 'Nobody knows. But his wife went missing the same night he got popped.'

'You mean she might have done it?'

'That, or she bolted with whoever did.'

'His wife disappeared. You know anything about her?'

Grady paused. 'Why are you asking?'

'You surprised to hear I'm interested in who shot Devin?'

Grady didn't like the answer. He'd spent enough time talking to Frank to recognise when he was being evasive.

'Atkins was telling me about the guy you got tangled up with. Vaughn. People in Miami are looking into him. He works at Coleman, as a guard.'

'Coleman,' Frank echoed, and Grady knew he remembered, knew he was thinking of Manuel DeCaster.

'Atkins seems to think the guy is still in your area, though,' he said. 'Thinks that's what today's killing was about. Do you know where he is?'

Silence.

'Frank, if you know, tell me.'

'I hadn't seen the guy before yesterday and I haven't seen him since.'

Again the evasiveness. 'Frank, listen to me—I want you to leave. First thing in the morning. Will you do that?'

'Atkins might not like it. Devin's going to make it? Three bullets weren't enough?'

'He was recovering.'

'Was? So what changed?'

Grady hesitated. 'Frank, he left hospital against doctor's orders. Now, I don't know what the hell is going on up there, but I think he wants a part of it. And you need to be gone when he gets there. All right? You need to be *gone*.'

'I don't have a car,' Frank said, and there was something in his tone that made Grady get out of bed and onto his feet.

'Look, I'll drive up there myself, talk to Atkins, and you can ride back down with me. Leave them to figure it out, Frank—'

'No, Grady. You stay down there. OK? Stay there. Thanks for the insight, though. This is important to know.'

'If you know where Vaughn is, you've got to tell—'

'I'll talk to you soon, Grady. Thanks again.'

He hung up and Grady swore loudly into the dead phone.

THE FLASHLIGHT BLINKED three times, then stopped. Ezra waited for the pause, then tapped the lights on his boat.

It was almost two in the morning, and Frank wanted Ezra to come in? This couldn't be good. Ezra ignored the outboard—too noisy—and turned the trolling motor on, brought the boat in to the beach. Frank waded out, took the bow line and threaded it through the U-bolt Ezra and Frank's father had bored into the log wall long ago.

'You all right?' Ezra stepped off the boat onto firm ground.

'We're fine. Devin's on his way.'

The wind was blowing warm and steady out of the southwest and Ezra breathed it in. 'How do you know?'

'Just talked to Grady Morgan. FBI. Remember him?'

'Didn't seem to be my biggest fan. What did he have to say?'

What Frank told him then made some sense; Ezra had never been able to get his head round why Devin would possibly have called him and told him to open the cabin up. The only reason he could have understood was if it had been a taunt—Devin deciding he'd mess with an old man's head, make it damn clear that Ezra no longer intimidated him or never had. Problem with that was the tone of the call. The message had been simple, businesslike, as if he'd never had a problem with Ezra. The answer, Ezra understood now, was that it hadn't been Devin who made the call. The other guy, Vaughn, had apparently understood Ezra's role as caretaker, but it didn't seem he knew the back story.

'He's out of hospital,' Ezra said when Frank was done, 'with three bullets in him?'

'That's what I've been told.'

'Sounds like Devin's hurt bad, then,' Ezra said. 'Hell, he might not make it up here, son.'

'But you know he's coming. That's his wife out there on that island, and either she shot him or Vaughn did. Could he be headed anywhere else?'

Ezra didn't answer, and after a few beats of silence Frank said, 'He gave my father up to save his own ass.'

'I know the story, son.'

Frank pointed out across the dark water. 'He's coming for them, Ezra. The people out there on that island. Why? Because they tried to take him down, and that's something I sure as hell respect. They did our work for us. I'm not going to let that son of a bitch come out here, to the place my father and his father and you and me all shared, and kill those two, Ezra. I'm not.'

'At least one of those two is headed for jail, Frank.'

'For shooting Devin? Don't you remember—'

'I remember it all,' Ezra said. 'Don't stand there and ask me if I remember. It goes back a hell of a lot farther than you, to places you'll never see and can't imagine. Understand *that*, son?'

There was fury in his words, but the boy held Ezra's eyes for a long time.

'Yeah,' Frank said at last. 'Now you listen to yourself, hear what you just said, and explain to me how you're going to let Devin go out to that island.'

Ezra looked away. 'What do you want to do, then?'

'Get them out of here,' Frank said. 'Is that so much to ask? He's not going to settle up here. Not on this lake.'

'And when you get in the middle of it? What then? Devin comes at you, or comes at the girl inside your cabin, the same way his boys already have?'

'If that happens,' Frank said, 'we deal with it.'

Ezra gave a low, ugly laugh. 'That's what you're hoping for. You want to hang that son of a bitch from one of these pines, but you want it to be justified.'

'It's already justified.'

'Not in a way you can accept, it's not, and you know that.'

Frank didn't answer. The wind picked up and the water splashed into the logs below them. 'It's going into action in the morning,' he said eventually. 'Whether it's cops or Devin or those two bastards he sent up here, somebody is going out to that island. Are we going to let them do it? Step aside and pretend we don't know anything?'

'No,' Ezra said. 'No, we're not going to step aside.'

9

Grady woke sometime before dawn with the knowledge that he had to play it straight with Atkins. There was no way round it. Not at this point. The kid was waiting for Devin and the smart money said he was going to get him, too. It wasn't yet six and Grady lay in the bed wondering how much of this was his fault.

It had been an anonymous tip, damn it. That's what he told people from the beginning, and there were only a few people within the Bureau who knew the truth. On one level, he'd almost been showing *kindness* to Frank by telling him the tip about his father had come from Matteson. It had seemed, back then, a lesser punishment to a boy who was already reeling. Matteson was a low-down, worthless son of a bitch, so what did Grady care if he'd added another layer of tarnish to the man's name?

At ten to seven he called Atkins and said, 'I spoke with Frank Temple last night. I think he knows where all the excitement is headed.'

'Pardon?'

'He didn't kill anyone, and I'm almost certain he's more a bystander than anything else, but I think he might know where Vaughn Duncan is.' A long pause. 'You there?' Grady said.

'I'm here.' The other agent's voice was tight with anger. 'I'm just wondering who to call in Chicago to make a formal complaint.'

'Because I talked to Frank? Listen, Atkins, you don't—'

'No, I'm not going to listen. What you just did is such a flagrant breach of conduct . . . What the hell were you thinking? I tell you this kid is a *suspect,*

I ask you for input, not to get on the damn phone and—'

'I knew I could get you some answers.'

'Bull. And even if you did think that, you don't make a call like that without informing me first.'

'Atkins, Vaughn Duncan may be up there with another man's wife. You want to know who the man is, or not?'

Silence.

'A guy named Devin Matteson was shot in Florida a few days ago. Matteson is a key player for Manuel DeCaster, one of the worst they've got in Florida. He's in prison in Coleman and seven years ago Frank Temple's father was making hits for him.'

Atkins didn't make a sound.

'Matteson won't tell the police who shot him. But his wife is missing. So it's not much of a puzzle, is it? And now this guard from Coleman, Vaughn Duncan, he's up at that lake, and there's a woman with him. You want to take odds on who the woman is?'

Atkins started to speak, but Grady rushed ahead. 'And Matteson's out of the hospital. He's gone. I would bet every dime I have that he is coming up to that lake.'

'And I'm still supposed to believe the coincidence.' Atkins's voice was clipped. 'You out of your mind, Morgan? You expect me to believe this kid just happened to smack his Jeep into his own father's filthy history? That's an *accident*?'

'Look,' Grady said, 'I'm not going to waste my time or yours discussing what I think about that kid. I'm telling—'

'You called a *suspect* and warned him—'

'He knows where Vaughn is and that Devin is coming for him!' Grady shouted. 'Would you shut up long enough to understand that, Atkins? You want to complain about me, call Quantico on Monday. Right now, you've got a dangerous son of a bitch headed your way to settle up with his wife and this other guy, and Frank Temple knows that.'

'How does he know that?'

'Because I told him. If you want to get me fired over that, knock yourself out. But you've got something up there waiting to explode and you need to deal with it.'

'Temple is at his cabin?' Atkins said, his voice still angry.

'Yeah. It's out on some lake—'

'I know where it is.'

'OK. Or he might be with a man named Ezra Ballard.'

'Who is he?'

'He was in special forces with his father. They were tight.'

'Special forces with Frank's father? Morgan, this is unbelievable. I needed to know all of this yesterday!'

'You know it now,' Grady said.

'If you call that kid again, I'll see charges are brought.'

'I won't call him, if you get out there. I'm headed that way now, Atkins, but I don't know how long the drive is.'

'Keep your car in the garage. I don't want you within a hundred miles of this.'

'I'm coming up.'

'Yeah? Well, if I see you, I'm putting you in handcuffs.'

FRANK HAD COFFEE going by the time Nora woke up. Her hair was fuzzed out an extra six inches from static, and she looked at him with one eye squinted almost shut. 'What time is it?'

'Ten past seven.'

'Have you heard from Ezra?'

'I expect he's on his way.' Ezra's boat had been missing when the sun rose.

'Then we'll go to the island,' she said.

'Yes.' He took the coffeepot and poured a cup, then brought it to Nora. Seeing her this way, bleary-eyed and sleepy, made him want to lean down and kiss her forehead, but he wasn't sure how she'd react.

He returned to the kitchen and poured his own coffee, waited for her to wonder aloud whether they should call the cops. She didn't say anything, though, just drank the coffee and smoothed her hair, then rose and went into the bathroom, re-emerging five minutes later looking more awake, fresher. 'Did you sleep?' she said.

'No.'

'Aren't you tired?'

'No,' he said. Anticipation of Devin's arrival provided more fuel than sleep would have. He was ready for him, but Nora was a problem. He would not deceive her. He wished she weren't a part of this, but she was, and he needed to decide how to tell her what he was going to do.

He left her in the cabin and walked out into the day, found the air to be uncommonly still. He stood with his coffee in hand and turned in a full circle, took in the lake and the trees.

Which direction would Devin come from? He knew the pair were on the island. Surely by now his advance team of gunslingers had reported that back to Miami. After Jerry Dolson's murder, the pursuit had effectively ended. The men from Miami knew about the island, had to know by now, and yet they had not moved on it. That meant one thing: they were waiting on Devin.

'ALL RIGHT,' Ezra said as Nora and Frank walked down to his boat. 'We're going out to hear their story; that's all we're doing. Whatever happens next will depend on what we hear.'

He offered Nora a hand as she stepped onto the boat. There was a mammoth outboard at the stern, and Ezra positioned Nora on the rear seat with her back to it, Frank taking the seat in front of her. Ezra settled in without a word and turned the key, and the motor came to life.

He spun the wheel and shoved the throttle forward. The motor roared and the front end of the boat rose several feet out of the water. Frank sat staring straight ahead, his clothes rippling as they tore across the lake. Behind the wheel, Ezra was impassive, his face shaded by a baseball cap with a Ranger Boats logo and his eyes hidden by Oakley sunglasses. They both wore light jackets that Nora knew concealed guns. As she sat there clutching the boat seat, she felt a surge of doubt. They were essentially strangers, and no one—*no one*—had any idea where she was.

The sun was sparkling off the water. They went through a cluster of islands and came out in a large bay, only two boats in sight. Ezra slowed and worked his way round a sandbar, then brought the motor back to a roar, tearing past a bay filled with stumps and half-trees that seemed like menacing guards to the empty shoreline.

A few minutes later Ezra slowed the boat again and the motor quieted. Nora shifted in her seat. Out here there was nothing to look at but trees and water, no sign of another boat. Then she saw an island ahead, over Frank's shoulder.

'There's somebody down there, Ezra,' Frank said. 'Somebody on shore.'

Ezra leaned to the side for a clearer look. 'Sure is. And it looks like the fella's having a bit of trouble with his boat motor. Might be we should stop by and offer a bit of assistance.'

'He'll recognise Nora and me.'

'Bound to happen sooner or later.' Ezra eased in closer and Nora saw the boat and the grey-haired Lexus driver, Vaughn, looking up from the motor. She slid down into the seat and tilted her head a bit, trying to put herself behind Frank, out of Vaughn's sight.

'Little trouble?' Ezra shouted over the sound of the motor.

Vaughn waved them away. 'Nothing I can't handle.'

'Sure about that? Doesn't look like it's going well.'

'It's not a problem.'

'How about I give it a look, then you and me and your girlfriend have a chat? I'm the caretaker of this cabin. Feeling guilty about the way I been neglecting you all.'

Though Ezra's voice had been friendly, Vaughn's body went rigid. He took a step back and let his hands fall away from the motor. 'The caretaker?' he asked.

'Uh-huh. That place has been my responsibility for a long time.'

'We're doing fine,' Vaughn said. His eyes locked on Nora's face and she felt the recognition across the water a split second before he reached behind his back.

'Don't.' It was a single word, spoken and not shouted, but somehow Ezra's voice still seemed to boom out across the water. Nora saw that his arm was extended, his gun pointing at Vaughn. How in the world had he got that out so fast?

Vaughn stood with his arm behind his back and didn't say a word. Ezra kept his gun pointed while he adjusted the wheel with his left hand, bringing the boat in close to shore, the water now shallow enough that Nora could see the bottom. Frank had been keeping his back to Vaughn, but when he heard Ezra's one-word command, he finally turned and Vaughn's eyes flicked to him.

'How you doing?' Frank said. 'You owe the lady here a car and both of us some answers.'

'Don't hurt her,' Vaughn said. His voice was high, and it cracked on the last word. Nora felt a moment's confusion before she realised that he was talking about the woman on the island.

'Nobody here intends to do any hurting,' Ezra said. 'But your buddies have. And we need to talk about that. Now put that gun of yours on the bottom of your boat and then catch the bow line when Frank tosses it to you.'

VAUGHN WAS BACK to that damn chattering even before they were all ashore, the same routine he'd gone through while waiting with Frank for the tow truck two days earlier. '. . . and I don't know what you've been told, but I was going to come back on Monday and give you the money. You know, there's no reason to be pulling guns on me, your car is fine, and—'

'Stop,' Ezra said.

Vaughn stopped and snapped his jaw shut.

Ezra gestured up at the cabin. 'She in there?'

Vaughn nodded.

'Then let's go have us a seat and bit of conversation.'

They walked across the beach to a trail that led up the bluff. Vaughn went first, slipping a few times. Frank was last, following Nora. He didn't know what she was thinking. Probably hadn't been real encouraged by the way Vaughn had reached for that gun.

The cabin was in remarkable shape for a building that had sat empty for so long, but Frank expected no less from Ezra. Vaughn took the steps up to the porch with a quickened stride.

'Renee? We got company. Man here says he's the caretaker—' Vaughn pushed the door open and stepped into the house just as the blonde woman stepped out. Frank saw the gun in her hand, then saw it in Ezra's eye socket. She just stepped onto the porch and stuck the gun in his eye, no hesitation.

'You reach under your jacket any farther,' the woman said to Frank without taking her eyes off Ezra, 'and I'll kill him.'

'Hell, Renee, what are you doing?' Vaughn said.

Renee Matteson. She was something to watch. Even in this moment, when the only ready-to-shoot gun was the one in her hand, Frank was taken with her. So poised, so strong. He let his hand fall from his jacket.

Ezra cleared his throat. 'This isn't a good way to start.'

'He's the caretaker—' Vaughn began, but she cut him off.

'Caretaker my ass. I saw his gun, Vaughn.'

'We're not the ones you should be scared of,' Frank said. 'Though you should know that they are not far away.'

'He makes a good point,' Ezra said. Renee was staring at him, their faces separated only by the length of her arm and the gun.

'Maybe if I took out my gun and set it down,' Frank said, making the slightest motion with his arm. It was enough. She looked at him instead of squeezing the trigger; when she did, Ezra snapped his head sideways and his arm moved with the speed of a whip, laced up and then down, and then Renee's hand was in his own and her gun was pointed at the ground. Frank had the Smith & Wesson out by the time that was done.

Ezra worked the gun out of Renee's fingers. 'Now, we got way too many guns around. It'd be nice to put 'em all away, every one, and do some talking. This porch is nice. Let's have us a seat out here, enjoy the day.'

He put her gun into his waistband and motioned at the porch. Renee hadn't moved, just held his eyes with a cold stare. 'I could have killed you,' she said. 'Now let's see if that was a mistake.'

She turned from him, walked to an old wooden bench and sat down. Vaughn sat beside her and reached for her arm, but she shrugged away from his touch. 'All right,' she said. 'Talk.'

'I think that's *your* job,' Nora said. She'd been so quiet it was as if they'd forgotten her presence. When they all turned to look at her, she met the stares with a shrug. 'We're not responsible for getting good people killed. I want to hear *their* story.' She jabbed a finger at Renee and Vaughn.

Renee looked at Nora as if she were intrigued. Frank tried to guess her age and couldn't. She had the body of a young woman, but her face carried some lines and her eyes were those of someone older. Or were they just tired?

'Where are the police?' she said. 'You found us, so why not tell them to come out here and ask the questions?'

'It wasn't my idea,' Nora answered, 'but I listened to it.'

Renee nodded as if that made sense, then turned to Ezra. 'You're really the caretaker? I've heard about you.'

'From Devin,' Ezra said. 'Where is he?'

'Dead,' she answered.

Frank and Ezra had agreed the previous night not to share information at first, just hear the story as these two were prepared to tell it. Now Ezra merely nodded in Frank's direction. 'You don't know young Frank, I take it?'

Renee turned her cool gaze to Frank and searched his face. He was standing about five feet from her. She shook her head.

'Last name of Temple,' Frank said. 'That help you any?'

Vaughn looked confused, but Renee said, 'Your father. Devin and your father—'

'Killed people together. Allow me to congratulate you on his demise. You're better off with him gone. Everybody is.'

She came up off the bench in a smooth, fast motion and slapped him in the face. Frank took the slap and looked down at Renee with his cheek stinging, didn't say a word.

'Now that we got the greetings out of the way,' Ezra said, 'maybe we ought to talk about people who are still alive. Seems you two led some unfriendly types into the area. Innocent people suffered as a result. Time to hear what it's about.'

The woman stood where she was, eyes challenging Frank to say another harsh word about her husband. He had none. He was too occupied by what that slap meant, by the way she'd risen so fast to defend Devin. It was not the action of a woman who'd wanted him dead. The idea he'd had, then, that these two people had put the bullets into Devin's back, no longer seemed to be the case.

'I'll tell you what it's all about,' Vaughn said, as Renee stalked back to the bench, 'it's about *these* two innocent people'—he waved his hand between Renee and himself—'suffering for Devin's mistakes. You know what he does.'

'Right,' Ezra said, 'but what do *you* do?'

'I work—worked—at a prison in Florida. I'd been at it for about twelve years when Devin approached me. I'd done the job right until then.'

'What did he pay you for?' Ezra said. 'Smuggling to people on the inside?'

'Right idea,' Vaughn said, 'wrong direction.'

'You were taking something *out* of the prison?'

'Instructions,' Frank said. This had made sense since Grady's call. 'He was a postman, Ezra. For Manuel DeCaster.'

'That was the idea,' Vaughn said.

'I understand how that could have brought some trouble down around you,' Ezra said, 'but these boys that followed you to Tomahawk aren't the police sort of trouble. So who are they?'

'They work for DeCaster. I don't know how they found us.'

'There was a tracking device in your car,' Frank said. 'I wonder when they had a chance to put it on your vehicle.'

Renee Matteson's eyes went wide, then squeezed shut. 'Damn it,' she said. 'I should have remembered.'

'You knew about the device?' Ezra said.

She shook her head. 'Not specifically, but I knew at first, a year ago,

Devin was following Vaughn to be sure he could trust him. I didn't think about there being a device . . . and it was *Devin*, not the bastards who shot him.'

'But they would have known about it,' Frank said. It made sense. DeCaster's team would have wanted to make sure there were no meetings with cops, no betrayals.

'How many of them are there?' Renee asked.

'Two that we know of,' Frank said.

'Two? Well, there will be more than that if they call for help,' Vaughn said.

'All right,' Ezra said. 'So we got bad boys and big troubles. You're dancing, though. I asked what you did to attract this.'

'I didn't do squat. Devin, he got his eyes on the throne. The longer Manuel sat in a cell, the cockier Devin got. He started talking about what he could do on his own, talking about eliminating people closest to Manuel, starting with his cousins, guys who are so damn mean that when you look at them—' Vaughn took a deep breath. 'Devin was going to kill DeCaster's cousins and two Cubans involved with him. He wanted a housecleaning.'

'And this had what to do with you?'

'He needed someone to lie to DeCaster, tell him one thing was happening while something else really was, and work it the other way, too, get the information he needed.'

'You agreed.'

'It was a lot of dollars.'

'Someone smelled it out?' Frank said. 'Killed Devin before he made his play?'

'Yes. Then they came for me and Renee. Still are coming for us, I guess.'

Frank felt a hard ache of disappointment in the pit of his stomach. He'd come out here hoping to align himself with these two against Devin, see the type of finale he'd wanted for so long. And that wasn't going to happen.

'Devin's dead. What's the point of killing Renee?' Nora said.

'Renee was around a lot,' Vaughn said. 'She knows things that could hurt DeCaster. So do I. Now that they know Devin violated their trust, they'll try to clean up the mess that surrounded him. Besides, they killed her husband. If anyone in the world is motivated to try to hurt these guys by going to the police, it's Renee.'

Nora turned to Renee. 'Then why *don't* you go to the police?'

Renee smiled at her, and there was genuine warmth in it, something that Frank hadn't been able to imagine on her face until then.

'I lived with Devin for nine years. You have any idea the things I know that the police would *love* to hear?' The explanation didn't seem to satisfy Nora, but Frank understood what she did not: Renee's world was one in which cops were the enemy.

'We'd been here one day,' Vaughn said, 'when I left to get supplies. I was coming back when Frank here hit my car.'

'Why did you come here?' Ezra said.

'It's what Devin told Vaughn to do,' Renee said.

Vaughn nodded. 'Right before he got killed, he told me that if anything happened I needed to get Renee out fast. He told me to bring her here, because nobody else knew it existed. Nobody down there, at least.'

'Well,' Ezra said, 'they sure as hell know about it now.'

TRAFFIC IN CHICAGO was always a headache, but Grady was helped by it being a Sunday morning and he made his way out of the city and into Wisconsin by eight, doing eighty-five up I-90. If anyone stopped him, he'd flash the badge. He had a map on the seat beside him, and Willow Flowage was way up there, just south of Michigan's Upper Peninsula. A five-hour drive at best.

He should have left last night. As soon as Frank had hung up the phone, Grady should have been in the car. Hopefully Atkins was already out there. He'd be giving Frank hell, of course, but that didn't matter so long as he was getting him off the lake. With any luck, they'd have Matteson's wife and her boyfriend in custody by noon.

His phone rang just before nine. 'Good news,' Jim Saul said, 'you won't have to worry about speeding tickets in Miami. Police down here love you dearly.'

'Why do they love me? You turn something up?'

'Turned a murder warrant up. The Miami police guys had one complete fingerprint and one partial on a casing they found in the parking lot where Matteson was shot. Shooter got two of the casings but left one behind, lost it in the gravel. The Miami PD ran the print through their fingerprint identification system and didn't get a match. Which means no record, indicating whoever popped Matteson wasn't a pro and that seems wrong. Then you throw this guy Vaughn Duncan at me and I think, hmm, the good folks at Coleman probably have his prints on file.'

'They matched?'

'Bet your ass they did.'

'Duncan shot Matteson, then left with the wife?'

'That's the flavour of the month. The print's enough for the warrant. Now, care to tell me where you're getting this information?'

'Wisconsin,' Grady said. 'I'll talk to you soon, Jimmy—'

'Hang on, hang on. I also had the flights checked. Guy matching Devin's description got a private charter to some place called Rhinelander, flew out late yesterday, real late.'

'Rhinelander.' Grady felt numb, even though this was what he'd been expecting. The map beside him showed Rhinelander clear enough. 'I gotta go, Jimmy.'

Grady hung up and dialled Atkins, who answered immediately.

'He's not here, Morgan. He's not at his cabin, and I'm getting pretty damn pissed off because I think when he talked to you he heard something that made him bolt.'

'He's not gone,' Grady said. 'Listen, Atkins, I'm on my way north—'

'I told you to stay the hell away from here.'

'I know that, but thought maybe you'd want help serving the murder warrant. You got a pen handy? You're going to want to write some of this down.'

THE CONVERSATION might have gone on all morning if nothing had interrupted them. Ezra and Frank were digging for more information, sorting through the mess of memories Vaughn and Renee offered, when Nora's cellphone began to ring. Checking the display, she saw the call was from her father's nursing home. She answered, and Barbara, one of the receptionists, burst into a tirade of worry.

'I don't know how he got the newspaper, Nora, but your father saw this article and he is *beside himself* because he doesn't understand it, but he knows it's bad. He's so worried. I really think you need to come down and show him you're OK. They've got a photograph of all the police cars outside your shop, and he keeps looking at that and won't let us take it away.'

Nora squeezed her eyes shut. Wonderful. She promised to be in as soon as possible. When she hung up, everyone on the porch was staring at her. 'It's my father,' she said. 'He's in a nursing home and somehow he got his hands on a newspaper. He doesn't understand what happened, but he's worried about me.' She looked at Frank. 'I need to go see him.'

He looked irritated, but said, 'OK. We'll take you. Ezra?'

'There are two boats. Why don't you take her back in mine, and I'll stay here,' Ezra said.

'Don't trust us enough to leave?' Renee said.

'You want to be left alone if your buddies show up?'

'No,' she said.

'So, Frank, stay with her, then come back out. Keep your eyes sharp.'

'You got a phone?' Frank said to Ezra. 'A way we can get you?'

'Most times it doesn't work on the water, but I'll give you the number. It'll ring, if nothing else.'

HE RAN EZRA'S BOAT hard all the way back across the lake. When the motor was roaring, conversation was impossible, and right now Frank didn't want to talk. Everything he'd hoped for last night when he'd stood on the dark beach with Ezra was gone. The situation wasn't what he'd desired, and it was also, he knew, his fault. He'd come up here after Devin, come up with blood in his eyes and caused the accident with Vaughn and set all of this in motion. Seven years he'd dodged the legacy of bullets and bodies—then one phone call from Ezra had pulled him north and they were right in the cross hairs of a bloody feud that should never have involved any of them. Particularly Nora. It was time to get out. Time to hand the whole mess over to Atkins and the FBI and hope he and Nora and Ezra could get the hell away before the fallout.

In a short time they were back at the cabin. He wanted to drive, but it was Nora's truck and she had the keys. She got in the driver's seat and he opened the passenger door and sat down. The motor was started, but she hadn't put the truck in gear before she spoke. 'Do you think we can help them?'

Trying to help Vaughn and Renee would be nothing but an exercise in futility. Either DeCaster would get them or the police would.

'Well?' Nora said, her face beautiful in the half-light of the shade in which she'd parked.

'Her husband isn't dead,' Frank said.

'What?'

'He's alive. Somebody shot him, but he didn't die. He was in the hospital until yesterday and then took off.'

She stared out of the windshield. 'How do you know this?'

He inhaled, looked away. 'I talked to a guy last night.'

'Last night?'

'Around two in the morning. You were asleep. He's with the FBI, was part of the group that investigated my dad.'

Her face was incredulous and then the anger began to show. 'You knew this last night and didn't tell me?'

'I wanted to see what the situation was. The way it was told to me, Renee and Vaughn tried to kill Devin and ran off together.'

She frowned. 'How do you know that's not true?'

'The way she slapped me. That was sincere. She wouldn't have had that reaction if she wanted her husband dead.'

Nora started to nod, then stopped. 'Wait a second, you knew that her husband is alive and you didn't tell *her*?'

'Let the FBI tell her. It was damn nice I got to keep him from existing for a little while. Next best thing to killing him.'

'*What?*'

'I told you what happened to my father. Devin's the piece of garbage who recruited him, then turned him in to the police.'

When she didn't respond, he plunged forward. 'My dad earned his fate, Nora, and I understand that better than anyone. But Devin earned his, too, and he walked away from it. Three bullets in the back and he's still walking away.'

She was shaking her head, not wanting to hear any more. 'What are you really doing here? It's not an accident. None of this could *possibly* be an accident.'

His fingers had curled into his palms and now he flattened them on the seat, breathed, looked at her. 'Ezra called, told me Devin was coming back . . .'

'And you came to kill him,' she finished.

'I'd like to pretend that's not the truth,' he said. 'I'd like to think, to hope, that if he'd been out on that island, I would have been able to stop myself. To walk right to the brink and then turn round and leave. But I doubt I could have done. Think what you want of me, but I've told you the truth. And I'm sorry you're involved. You have no idea how sorry I am.'

'What do we do?' she said, voice soft.

'I think you ought to call Atkins. Tell him where they can be found.' He felt guilty leaving Ezra on the island with no warning that they were turning the whole business over to the police, but ultimately it was the thing to do.

Nora's eyes narrowed, lines showing on her forehead. 'What? Now you *do* want me to talk to the police?'

'I think you should.'

'You want to go to the police?' She repeated the idea again, as if it were incomprehensible.

'No, I want *you* to. I'd actually love it if you could drop me off someplace where I could rent a car. That would be a big favour.'

'What are you talking about?'

'I need a car, Nora. I've got nothing to drive.'

'Where are you going?'

'I'll work that out. If the cops want to find me, they can track me down. I've committed no crimes.'

'You're leaving?' She leaned towards him, eyes aflame.

'I'm not going to die for Devin's wife, Nora. I'm not going to kill for her, either. If I try to help, it's going down one way or the other. Grady, the FBI agent I talked to, this was his advice, to just get the hell away.'

'You're going to leave the rest of us behind?'

Before he could respond, she lifted her hand. 'You know what, I can't think about this right now. I've got to go see my dad, show him that I'm not *dead*, and then I can take you to get a rental car so you can run away, and then I will decide what in the world I tell the police.'

She put the truck into gear, backed up, and started down the gravel drive.

10

It was as if the lake were angry with him. As if it knew what Ezra was doing out here, had listened to Frank plan for violence the night before, and heard Ezra relent. The day that had dawned so beautifully was turning ugly, dark clouds massing in the west, the lake's surface choppy beneath a temperamental wind, waves slapping at the beach. A storm was on the way.

He stood on the porch with his gun in his hand and watched the weather turn, listened to the soft voices from inside. Now and then they rose a bit, usually Renee's first and then Vaughn's. Some sort of a dispute. He didn't trust either of them.

Oh, the story they'd told had made sense enough, but something still felt off, starting with the fact that they were together at all. It was an odd pairing. Vaughn had been nothing more than a courier for Devin and DeCaster. He wasn't . . . competent. He had drawn his gun clumsily, had talked too much and seen too little. No, he wasn't competent in the way that Devin would be, or in the way that you'd expect from one of Devin's hired guns.

But here he was with Renee Matteson, supposedly charged with her protection. If you really feared for your wife, wouldn't you want her with another type of bodyguard?

Vaughn must have earned the trust—but Ezra couldn't see how.

NEITHER OF THEM had spoken during the drive. When Nora pulled into the nursing home parking lot, there were visitors' spaces right by the front doors, but she avoided them today, drove all the way to the employee lot at the back of the building. If anyone was watching for her, they wouldn't expect her to park there and walk in through the employee entrance.

When she turned off the engine, Frank reached for his door handle.

'No,' she said. 'I'll go in alone. You can wait here.'

'It would be safer—'

'*No*. I don't want to frighten my dad or get the nurses talking. It'll be fifteen minutes. You can wait.'

He sat there looking at her. For an instant she felt bad about her tone. Those damn sad eyes of his, working on her once again. Always confident, always strong, but always sad. She'd never seen anything like them. Then she remembered why he'd come here—to kill—and the guilt evaporated. 'I'll make it quick,' she said.

'Take your time. Your father loves you and he's worried.'

The employee entrance door was open and she stepped through and found herself in a hallway that led round to the front desk. Barbara gave her a startled look when she emerged from the back, but didn't question it. 'Hello. He wants to see you. Go on down.'

'Thank you.'

The door to her dad's room creaked when she pushed it open. He was sitting up in bed and turned to face her when he heard the sound. His face split into that smile and she felt her own do the same.

'Hi, Dad.'

'You were *worried*,' he said, meaning he was worried about her.

'I know. I'm sorry.' She kissed his cheek and gave him a hug.

She saw the newspaper on his bed, the word *murder* in huge bold type across the top. What an awful thing for him to see, to struggle to understand. Didn't people here have more sense than to let him get a copy of the damn thing? She tucked the paper into the wastebasket.

Her father watched her. 'It sounds like a problem,' he said, speaking carefully. 'You have a real problem.'

'Everything's all right,' she said. 'We had a bad day, but it's going to be fine.'

She sat on the bed and some of the confusion and fear drained from his face. She was here now, he could reach out and touch her, and even if he didn't understand the rest of it, that was enough.

YOU'VE GOT acres of trees on the north side of the building, offering protection for a watcher as well as a clear view of the entrance to the nursing home. In the back corner of the lot, you can't see a damn thing, but if someone's in those trees, they saw you come in and they're making plans for action. You can't make a counterplan, because you have no idea what the hell's going on.

It was like a chorus that caught in your brain. Frank could almost see his father leaning against the side of the truck, gesturing with one of the cigarettes he was always promising to stop smoking.

You're already beaten, son. How the hell are you supposed to help her if something goes down inside?

Frank drummed his fingers on the armrest, tried to think of a song to hum. Ten minutes had passed. How long would she take? She wanted to get rid of him, was disgusted by his cowardice. Hell with her if that was what she thought. She was nothing but a stranger anyhow.

You don't even know what room she's in, don't know the layout, haven't bothered to get out of the truck and into a protected position, or even clear your gun—my gun—from the holster.

He kept drumming his fingers awkwardly, the rhythm uneven. Why couldn't he think of any songs?

NORA SPENT TWENTY MINUTES with her father before she stood. 'I'll come back tomorrow, Dad. First thing in the morning.'

His face dropped into a frown. She kissed his cheek.

It was always hard to leave. She walked to the door without looking back. As soon as she stepped into the hallway, she closed the door behind her.

The hallway was empty and she turned to the left and started back towards the entrance, made about three steps before the door to a vacant room across from her father's swung open and a hand encircled her mouth and pulled her into the room. She saw a gun in her face, and even though she couldn't see the man who held it yet, she knew it was the one whose hand had left bruises on her arm two days earlier.

'There's a nurse in the room next to your dad's,' he said, his lips close to her ear. 'Anybody causes a problem, I'm going to begin shooting. A lot of people are going to get hurt, including the old man you just left.'

Frank had wanted to come with her. She'd left him in the parking lot instead. But how could she have known . . . *the newspaper.* She'd wondered who would possibly have given that paper to her father. The answer: someone who wanted to make sure Nora came by to see him. This guy had probably been waiting here all morning. It wouldn't have taken much to learn that the only personal connection Nora had to Tomahawk was in this nursing home.

The hand on her mouth released slowly. 'Good girl,' he said. 'It would have been very bad if you'd screamed.'

He reached out and twisted the lock on the door. 'We're going to leave through a window. First thing you need to do is call your friend in the truck.'

She didn't respond. He smiled at her. His face and clothes were as she'd remembered, but the ornate belt buckle was gone.

'If you don't have Frank's cellphone number,' he said, 'I can provide it. Now, do you want to call, or should I?'

She called.

HIS FINGERS FROZE on the armrest when the phone rang. He took it out, saw it was Nora's number.

'There's a problem,' she said when he answered. 'One of them is inside with me, and the other is watching you through a gun scope. I've been asked to tell you to take your gun out, hold it in the air, then put it in the glove compartment. If you don't listen, they will shoot you.'

Told you! It's over now, son, because you got lazy and told yourself it wouldn't matter.

'This guy was waiting in your father's room?'

'No, I—' There was a rustle, a whisper. 'Frank, put the gun in the glove compartment and do it fast.'

Hell. He had no proof the guy with the scope wasn't a bluff, but he had to listen. Moving slowly, he reached inside his jacket and withdrew the Smith & Wesson, held it in the air, then squeezed the phone between his ear and shoulder while he put the weapon in the glove compartment. 'I put the gun away.'

More whispering, then, 'We're coming out. He wants you to get behind the wheel and keep your hands above the dash.'

The call was disconnected, but he kept the phone at his ear as he slid across the seat. Without looking, he punched the CALL button with his thumb, bringing up Ezra's number, entered just before leaving the island.

One ring, then two, no answer, and right then he saw them—Nora and the man he'd knocked out in the body shop, rounding the corner of the building. Either there was another door, or they'd left through a window. He closed the phone without getting an answer, dropped it into his lap and thought, Figure it out, Ezra, figure it out. There's trouble on the way.

Nora walked quickly to the truck. Then the door was open and she was inside and sitting beside him, the tall guy piling in behind her.

'Keys,' the guy said, and Nora fished her keys out and passed them to Frank.

'Start it up and drive out of here. Take a right out of the parking lot and go straight until I say something else. Keep both hands on the wheel, keep the speed down, and keep your mouth shut.'

EZRA ROTATED THE CELLPHONE in his palm and stared out across the water. The wind was coming at the island in uneven gusts, pushing tendrils of grey clouds ahead of it.

The phone had been silent since two rings had come in from Frank Temple's son. Ezra didn't like the two rings. Liked it even less that there had been no second attempt.

He didn't call, though. Because if it hadn't been a mistake, either Frank had been interrupted or he'd made the call as a warning.

Ezra was alone on the porch. Vaughn and Renee were still inside. Ezra went to the door. 'You two got any rain gear?'

They were sitting together in the living room, Vaughn speaking in a whisper, and both looked at him as if they didn't understand the language.

'What?' Renee said.

'Rain gear? If not, I got emergency ponchos in the boat. Those clouds don't look like kidders to me.'

Vaughn stood up. 'What are you talking about? If it rains, we've got a roof over our heads.'

'Not any more. We're going on a boat ride, kids. And we're going on it in a hurry.'

Now Renee was on her feet, too. 'What's wrong?'

'Nothing's wrong,' Vaughn said. 'This guy's crazy. What the hell are you talking about, boat rides?'

'Shut up,' Ezra said, and Vaughn quit talking.

'They're coming, aren't they,' Renee said, without question or alarm.

'They could be,' Ezra said.

'Where are we going?'

'Not quite sure yet, but we need to move fast.'

'I want my gun back,' Vaughn said. 'If they're coming for us, I want my damn gun.'

Ezra gave him a cool, even gaze. 'When it comes time for shooting, I'll see that you got something to do it with.'

THREE TIMES the man with the gun instructed a turn. They'd gone maybe five miles before he told Frank to drive behind a ramshackle bar with CLOSED and FOR SALE signs in the windows. Frank parked and cut the motor. Nothing around them but the deserted building, the trees, and wind-tossed cattails indicating a marsh. It would take a long time before a body dumped in that marsh was found.

'Now we sit and wait, and nobody says a word,' the guy with the gun said. His weapon was a Beretta, resting against his knee and angled towards Frank.

They sat for five minutes, maybe ten, and then gravel crunched under tyres as someone drove into the parking lot. A van, light blue with darkly tinted windows, pulled in beside the truck and the driver climbed out. He was shorter than the guy inside the truck, but quicker. Frank remembered that from the way the guy had whipped his gun into Mowery's face beside the police car.

'Out,' the guy beside Nora said, and Frank opened the door and stepped out onto the dusty parking circle. It was his first opportunity to see the second man face to face, and he didn't like the way the guy stared at him. The guy held that look for a long moment, then turned away from Frank and slid the van's side door open, and Frank found himself staring at Devin Matteson.

The last time Frank had seen him—the only time—it had been eight years earlier, in Miami. He hadn't been round him long, maybe an hour, just enough for dislike to grow, but what he remembered from that meeting were two qualities: arrogance and strength. The strength was no longer present.

Devin was leaning sideways against the seat so that he could face out, a gun resting in his lap, but it looked like just keeping his head up was a real effort. His deep tan and strong jawline had turned into a junkie's face. Bulges from bandages showed under his shirt.

Vaughn was lying. Had to be. The two men pursuing him and Renee were here, but Devin was with them.

'This is a crazy damn world.' Devin's voice came from some tight, trapped place in his chest. 'I send two guys up here to do a job, and who gets in the way but Frank Temple Junior.'

'The Third,' Frank said. 'No junior here.'

Devin looked at Frank for a long moment and then gave a low laugh as his eyes went to his shorter partner. 'You believe that? It's his son, no question. *No junior here.*'

He laughed again, and his laughter swept through Frank as pure white rage. He willed himself still. Let him laugh. Let him enjoy this. Let him think that Frank didn't know what had happened years earlier, and then, when the time was right, let him pay.

Devin stopped laughing. 'Want to tell me, Temple *the Third*, what the hell you're doing here?'

Frank said, 'I came to send you home.'

'What?'

'Ezra Ballard told me that you were coming back. We didn't think that should happen.'

Devin gave him a look caught between anger and wonder. 'Ballard's a crazy old bastard. I don't know what he told you, kid, but it was all nonsense. Me giving your old man up? That's a lie.'

This time Frank didn't think he'd be able to will the anger down. But he fought it down again.

'Whatever,' Devin said. 'I don't give a damn what you think. I'll tell you what I told Ballard—whoever tipped the FBI, it wasn't me. Supposed to be someone close to your dad, though. Hell, could have been you.'

Frank was halfway to the van when the tall man stepped in and swung his gun sideways, going for his throat. Frank blocked it, was still moving forwards when the second man placed the barrel of a gun against his cheek.

He stopped and the tall guy pressed his gun into Frank's ribs, two guns against him now. Devin hadn't moved.

'Your old man never shut up about you,' he said. 'How fast you were, how good with a pistol. And you know what I finally figured out? He had to keep talking about it, because he knew you were yellow. He knew that, and it shamed him.' He got out of the van slowly, almost went down once. When the tall man moved to help him, he put up his hand and shook his head. He steadied himself, took a couple of steps towards Frank. The tall man had moved back to Nora, but the other one kept his gun on Frank's cheek.

'How did you hook up with Vaughn Duncan?' Devin said. 'Did that piece of slime find you, or did you find him?'

'I drove him off the road,' Frank said, each word coming slow, the pressure of the gun working against his jaw, 'because I thought he was you and I was going to kill him.'

'You're serious,' Devin said. 'You're *serious*. Well, hell, kid, sorry to disappoint, but you and him got something to share. You wanted to kill me; he tried.'

It took a second for Frank to process. Then the truth that had felt so close when Renee slapped him finally arrived. Vaughn was after Renee. You didn't take a woman like Renee away from a man like Devin when he was alive. 'Vaughn shot you?'

'Three times,' Devin said.

'That's not what your wife thinks,' Nora said, and everyone but Frank turned to look at her.

'My wife,' Devin said guardedly. 'You've seen her?'

Nora nodded. 'Yes. But she thinks you're dead.'

Devin said, 'AJ,' and waved his hand at the man who held the gun to Frank's face. The man stepped back so Devin could see Nora clearly. 'Tell me,' Devin said, 'what they told you.'

Nora told him. Frank focused on Devin, trying to smell out the lie. He *had* to be lying, didn't he? Vaughn had shot him? But Frank could see that now. Vaughn had told the story, provided all the details, details that were clearly lies. Everything Renee knew about the reason they'd fled came from Vaughn.

'I cannot believe he had the guts,' Devin said when Nora was done. 'That son of a bitch planned it for a while. Had a story ready for her. And I'm lying in the hospital and he's up here with my *wife*.' He banged the butt of his gun against the van, then again and again, until the effort took his strength, and he had to wait a minute to get it back, hanging against the door.

'You thought she left you for him?' Frank said, and Devin's eyes slid unpleasantly back to him. 'That's why you didn't name the shooter for the police? You thought she was involved?'

'I wanted to conduct my own investigation. That's all.'

'Then how did these two get here before you?'

'I sent them. When they told me he'd come here, I left so I could see it to the end in person.'

'If this is the truth,' Nora said, 'then why did you have to kill Jerry? You knew Vaughn was going to that island!'

'Unfortunately, I was out of communication for a while, so these two had to keep following the trail.' That justified it to him. Frank looked at Nora and saw the shock and horror in her face.

'They're on that island?' Devin asked. 'They're on *my* island? Vaughn and my wife?'

Frank nodded.

'Who's with them?'

He didn't say anything. Neither did Nora. But Devin stared into Frank's eyes and said, 'Ballard. He's with them, isn't he?'

Frank still didn't respond, but Devin nodded his head, already convinced. 'OK,' he said. 'AJ, King, get them in the van. We're close, boys. We're close.'

PAST MADISON AND GAINING, maybe two hours away, Grady was driving hard and staring at the clock, willing it to tick a little slower.

He wanted to call Frank, damn it, but Atkins hadn't been kidding when he said he'd press charges over another phone call. He couldn't wait for news any more, grabbed the phone and called Atkins again.

'He's still gone,' Atkins said. 'I've tried to find Ballard, but he's missing as well. Thing is, there's a boat down here now.'

'Where?'

'At Temple's cabin. There was a little aluminium thing the first time I came out, but now there's a fancy bass boat on the beach. I called in to check the numbers and it comes back to Ballard.'

'But they're not inside.'

'No, they're not inside,' Atkins snapped. 'There was a truck here this morning, too, registered to that girl at the body shop, and now that's gone, and none of them are where I can find them. This is fantastic, Morgan. I've got a murder warrant ready to go.'

'You got anybody else involved?'

'Couple of the locals are trying to turn the girl up. Said she was just in at some nursing home visiting her father.'

'Wait there,' Grady said. 'If Ballard's boat is there, they'll probably be coming back to it.'

DEVIN MATTESON made them all ride in the van, first instructing Nora to write a note for her truck that said: *Out of gas, back soon, please don't tow.*

AJ was driving and sat alone in the front, Nora in the middle row beside Devin, Frank all the way in back with the man called King. Devin and King and AJ were all wearing guns. AJ had two, actually; he'd taken Frank's gun out of the truck before they left. It lay on the floor in front of the passenger seat now. Nora could hear it slide around when they took sharp curves.

Devin's true condition began to show itself. He seemed to struggle with every turn, wincing, patting his chest lightly. By the time they'd gone five miles, Nora saw that his face was bathed in sweat.

There was nothing between her and the end of this but twenty minutes in the van, another twenty in a boat. They were going to die. These men weren't going to head home after finding Vaughn, trusting that she and Frank would pretend none of this had happened. All this over a murder, she thought. It wasn't even a murder—Vaughn didn't kill Devin; he just tried. And now how many others would die to atone for one man's attempted killing?

They drove north, the sun pushed beneath clouds that looked ominous to the west. She tried to think of a way to stop this, and Ezra was all she had to hold her hope.

The van rumbled over a stretch of rough road and she saw with surprise that they were already close to Frank's cabin. Minutes later the van came to a stop and she saw the lake through the windshield. There was a car parked beside the cabin. A white Buick sedan.

Devin swore softly. 'Whose car?' he said, leaning close to Nora, his face shiny with sweat.

'I don't know,' she said. Frank didn't speak.

Atkins, the FBI agent, walked round the corner of the cabin. He had a sheaf of papers in his hand and, when he saw the van, he folded the papers and tucked them into his back pocket, cocking his head and studying the van and AJ behind the wheel.

'Who is that?' AJ said.

Nora didn't answer, just stared at Atkins. At the moment Atkins reached into his suit jacket, AJ tensed, but then Atkins's hand was back out with a badge in it. Nora's muscles went soft. What was he doing? Don't pull a badge; pull a *gun*.

'Handle it,' Devin said, and then he pressed a gun into Nora's stomach as AJ opened the door.

Devin said, 'King? Don't let either of them make a sound.'

AJ stepped out into the wind, said, 'Is there a problem, sir?' and then slammed the door.

'No,' Nora said softly to herself. She couldn't let this happen. Couldn't let him talk his way out of this.

AJ was walking towards Atkins, one hand in his jacket pocket. Atkins walked forward to meet him, still holding the badge in the air.

AJ closed the gap to a few feet and Nora realised what was about to happen—AJ's goal had never been to fool Atkins with talk. She screamed then and Atkins looked towards the van as AJ's hand came up out of his jacket and into the FBI agent's stomach.

Atkins hunched and then rocked back onto his heels and kept going, landing on his back with the handle of the knife rising out of his sternum. It was the last thing Nora saw before King slammed his hand across her mouth and pulled her backwards, dragging her head behind the seat, telling her to shut up or she'd die, too.

11

'We didn't need this. Damn it, we didn't *need this*!'

Devin was standing above Atkins's body, his face stricken by pain and anger, staring at AJ.

'You said handle it, man.'

'Handle it—hell, you think that means you *gut* the guy? An *FBI agent*? This is something we needed?'

AJ showed a ghost of a smile, spread his hands. 'Dev . . . what can I say? It's done. I'll deal with it.'

Frank, watching him, thought, He did it because he likes it. Devin was dangerous, but Devin had a brain. This wild son of a bitch, AJ, he was bloodthirsty.

'I mean, I saw a badge, you know? I saw a badge, Dev, I just reacted.'

'You'll deal with it.' Devin shook his head, disgusted, and stared at the corpse at their feet for a long time. When he finally looked up, his eyes found Frank, lingered there, and then he nodded.

'All right,' he said. 'We'll make it work.'

He made Frank drag the body down to the boat, a crimson smear marking their path over the grass, the trail of blood leading right to the cabin door. That's what the cops would see, Frank knew, and what the newspaper and TV people would use for drama. When they were all dead and the cops came up here to sort out the mess, what they'd see was that trail of blood leading to the door of a dead murderer, and the Temple name would be infamous again, Frank accepting the baton from his father. He understood that perfectly as he followed Devin's instructions, leaving fingerprints all over the corpse of an FBI agent who'd surely voiced his suspicions of Frank to colleagues already.

'Take that anchor line,' he said, 'and loop it round his neck. Make it tight.'

Frank was standing in the shallows, knee-deep in the lake, the body slumped face down in the water as he wrapped the line round Atkins's neck. Devin stood above him on dry land, using a tree for support and studying the lake with the gun held down against his leg, checking for other boats. There weren't any, though. The weather was on Devin's side, rain starting to fall now. A Sunday before fishing season, with a storm coming in, guaranteed an empty lake. Empty except for them and those on the island.

Frank finished tying Atkins to the line and set the anchor back into the stern, the body now tied in the middle of the line. Then AJ waved at Frank with the gun. 'Get in.'

Frank climbed into the boat, and Nora and King followed suit. Devin pushed off from the tree, took a wavering step.

'Dev . . .' AJ started towards him, but he was already in motion, trying to walk towards them. He made it four steps before his legs buckled and he went down. AJ caught him, helped him up.

'You got to get out of here, man,' he said as Devin struggled for breath. 'Got to get to a—'

'Shut up.' Devin's hands were on his knees. 'You know what I'm here to do.'

'I'm telling you, we can do it for you.'

'No.'

'Dev, you aren't going to make it in that boat. You aren't. And it's starting to rain, man. Gonna turn ugly soon.'

Devin didn't respond, just took in fast, panting breaths.

'We'll go get him,' AJ said. 'We'll bring him back to you. All right? Him and Renee. We'll bring Renee back, Dev. You got to stay here, though. Out in that boat, man . . .'

Devin rose slowly, stared at the group already waiting in the boat, his eyes lingering on Frank the longest. 'All right,' he said. 'You go out there and bring them back, and do it *fast*, damn it. And be careful—the crazy old guy that's out there, he's good.'

'He's nothing, Dev, don't worry about—'

'No,' Devin shook his head. 'He's good, OK? That's why you need to take them.' He indicated Frank and Nora. 'You make sure he knows you've got the girl. Make that good and clear.'

'We got it, Dev. Now let me get you inside.' AJ walked back to the boat and asked Frank for the cabin's key. Frank took it out of his pocket and passed it over. AJ took the key and went back to Devin, helped him across the yard and into the cabin, Frank watching them go, thinking, I'll be back for you.

The door reopened and AJ stepped out and went to the van, opened the door and leaned inside to grab the extra gun, Frank's father's gun.

'Start the motor,' AJ said, stepping on board and coming back to sit behind Frank.

The big outboard fired at once, smooth and powerful. Frank kept the throttle low until the prop had pulled them into deeper water, then spun the wheel and slammed the throttle forwards.

The rain was driving hard now, blowing into their faces. Water ran down Frank's neck and dripped into his eyes. After they were round the sandbar, into the middle of the lake, AJ leaned over the side of the boat. There was a flash of silver from his knife and then the anchor line parted and slipped overboard, and Atkins's body drifted away as the anchor tugged it slowly beneath the lake.

'Go on!' AJ yelled, and Frank increased the speed, hardly aware that he'd slowed to watch the body.

Devin wanted AJ to have hostages, had made that clear. Hostages gave AJ a bargaining chip for use with Ezra, leverage to force the situation into his favour. One thing was certain though: AJ had never had a hostage like Frank Temple III. Frank held tight to that idea as he squinted against the wind and the spray. All those violent skills he'd spent seven years suppressing were about to have a purpose. Contract killer or not, Frank Temple II was at heart a teacher—and his son had excelled at the lessons.

THERE WASN'T a real road within two miles of where Ezra sat. A couple of trails led up to the Nekoosa Kennedy Fire Lane, but even if Ezra got them out of the boat and to the fire lane, what would he have accomplished? They'd still be a long walk from safety, with the boat marking their entrance point into the woods. Find the boat and it wouldn't be hard to understand where they were headed, if you had a map. He had a feeling these boys would have a map.

'We're just going to *sit* here?' Vaughn said. 'We left the cabin to come up here and sit in a boat?'

The rain was falling now and the dark thunderheads were on top of them. Lightning was a concern and they needed to get on land, even though that wasn't what Ezra wanted. He wondered if he'd made a mistake by coming north. You planned for the worst-case scenario, though, and the worst-case scenario put these bastards close and coming closer. You had to run away from them, not into them.

'If they're out here to find us, they'll search the whole lake,' Renee said. She was sitting in the middle seat of the little aluminium boat, wearing one of the ponchos.

Ezra's mind was unsettled in a way it had never been before in a situation like this. He had some doubts and he wasn't used to doubts. He needed his old mind back, the old instincts, the old moves. He'd spent decades trying to become someone different and now he was afraid he'd succeeded at the task.

THE ISLAND showed itself as a dark silhouette against the grey sky. 'This is it?' AJ said, leaning down to make his words heard over the wind, his face close to Frank's, the gun within reaching distance. Frank wondered if he could get his hands on it.

'Well?' AJ raised the gun a few inches. 'Is it?'

Frank nodded, the cabin now visible between the trees.

'All right, bring it in slow. Everybody look happy. We're all friends, remember.' AJ pressed the gun to Frank's chest.

Thunder hammered through the sky and the darkness was such that the trees across the bay seemed to disappear into night. It couldn't be later than one in the afternoon. Frank was staring up at the house: Ezra would be watching them approach, Frank was certain of that. He throttled down, then cut the engine. The boat scraped into the gravelly bank.

'Get her out,' AJ said to King. 'Keep that gun in her back! Come on!'

King rose awkwardly, then pulled Nora up, his gun in her back. He stepped out into the water. Nora was submerged nearly up to his knees.

AJ gave Frank's stomach a twist with the gun barrel. 'Move.'

Frank cleared the front of the boat with a jump, soaking only his shoes before joining King and Nora on the beach. Then AJ was out. Surely Ezra saw the guns.

Take them, Ezra, Frank thought. Damn it, take them!

No shots came. No sound at all except for more thunder and AJ ordering everyone up to the house. Frank climbed the trail with cold fear squeezing his chest. What if Ezra hadn't got the call?

They came up over the hill, and the cabin came into view. AJ wrapped one hand in Frank's shirt to keep them together. 'If the door's locked, you call out for Ballard.'

Up the steps of the porch as the rain began to fall faster, then to the door, Frank's hand closing round the knob. Locked.

'Call his name,' AJ hissed, and Frank opened his mouth and a laugh came out instead of a name.

'The boat.' He laughed again. 'It's gone. *They're* gone.' How in the hell had he missed that? Staring at the island so intently as he'd brought them in, he'd forgotten the damn boat. They were gone, all right, gone in the boat and out into the storm, and that meant Ezra had understood the warning.

AJ shoved him aside and slammed his foot into the centre of the door, tore the hasp out of the frame and burst into the dark house. He returned with a snarl, his hand so tight on his gun that the muscles and veins in his forearm stood out. 'Where did they go?'

'They left in the boat,' Frank said again.

'I know that!' AJ grabbed Frank's throat and drove him backwards into the cabin wall and pressed the gun into his mouth. Nora screamed.

'You know where they are,' AJ said. 'You know, and do *not* lie again.'

Frank shook his head ever so slightly.

'He doesn't know!' Nora shouted. 'They were here when we left!'

'Shut up.' AJ's eyes never left Frank's. 'He's got one chance to tell me.'

The voice was back then, Frank's father's voice, whispering again. *Trust Ezra. Now you know he got the warning. He's ready for them.*

'He doesn't know.' Nora's voice was tight with tears.

But you do know. You learned from me, listened to all the old stories and remember every one, and who did I learn from? Ezra.

AJ pulled the gun back slowly, the spit-covered barrel sliding out of Frank's mouth. 'Where are they?' he said.

'On the lake.'

AJ's head canted to the right. 'Where on the lake?'

Frank worked his tongue around, still tasting the metal. The last taste his father had in this life. 'The north end. That's as much as I can tell you. They didn't tell me where they were going. He knew you were coming, somehow.'

'Then why would they still be on the lake?'

'He wasn't sure how much time he had. Couldn't know for sure that Nora and I had ever got away from my cabin. So couldn't risk going south to get back to the cabin. Too much of a chance he'd run straight into you.'

'What's north?'

'Nothing,' Frank said. 'Nothing but water and woods.'

NINE TIMES Grady had called; nine times Atkins had failed to answer. Past Wausau in a rainstorm, cruise control set at ninety, all Grady could hope for as Tomahawk neared was that Atkins was busy, interviewing Frank or maybe preparing paperwork, with Matteson and Duncan in handcuffs.

As many optimistic options as Grady could produce, he couldn't believe any of them. Because it was a karmic world, he believed that in his heart, and he'd spent too many days and too many years telling himself that he could always make up for his lie, that there would always be time to set Frank Temple straight, explain that they'd wanted so badly to take Devin down that a little misdirection had seemed insignificant.

Grady had let seven years roll by. Frank had swallowed the lie, and now, after all this time, it was going to hurt him. And all Grady could do was streak up the interstate, destined to be too late.

As THEY HAD so many times in the past, Ezra's ears warned of disaster before his eyes. There was a boat on the water. He could hear the faint growl of a Merc two-twenty-five pounding hard.

'What?' Renee said, seeing his face.

'There's a boat coming.'

'Could be anybody,' Vaughn said, that jerky panic returning to his voice. 'Faster we get back to the car, faster we're out of here.'

'No. It's them,' Ezra said. 'I know the sound of my own boat.'

'It could be that kid and the girl,' Vaughn said. 'Just them.'

'Could be. We'll know soon. Right now, we got to get ready.'

The best scenario would be to take to the trees and get ready to do some shooting. He should never have left his rifle in his own boat. Damn. Combat was a thinking man's game, always had been.

Renee and Vaughn were waiting with anxious faces. Step one, separate these two. It seemed like a bad idea at first blush, but that was almost a good thing, because it meant the boys in Ezra's boat wouldn't expect it. Generally you'd want to keep everyone together, seek safety in numbers. The second layer of this move was that the men from Florida wanted Renee and Vaughn together. So if things played out poorly and these men caught them, better to make it happen one at a time. That would slow things down.

'Is there any way we can get help?' Renee said.

Ezra took his cellphone out to humour her. 'No signal. We got to get moving. First thing we do is split up.'

Vaughn's voice was wary. 'Split up how?'

'You and me are going to be on the shore,' Ezra said, gesturing north of where they sat, 'and she's going to stay on this island. Temporarily.'

Vaughn shook his head. 'No chance I'm leaving her alone.'

'We're splitting up to protect her,' Ezra said. 'She stays here while we go across to the main shore, and we'll make certain they know that we're there. We'll beach the boat in the open, make it obvious.' He looked at Renee. 'You're a swimmer, right?'

'Yes.'

He pointed west across the water as lightning lit up the bay. 'Can you make that shore?'

It was a hell of a swim, but she nodded.

'All right. Anything happens and you're on your own, that's the one to shoot for. Walk far enough, you'll hit a fire lane.'

'I'm *not* leaving her!' Vaughn spun towards Ezra. 'You want to lead them into the woods, go ahead. But I came to take care of her and I'm going to do it.'

'You want to take care of her, help me occupy these boys.'

'I'm not—'

'Please, Vaughn,' Renee said, and her voice was gentler than Ezra had heard before. 'Please.'

That stopped him. 'I can take care of you,' he said. 'We don't need to listen to him, Renee. We don't need him.'

'Yes, we do,' she said.

Ezra couldn't hear his boat's engine any more. That indicated they were stopped, which probably meant they were at the island, checking the empty cabin. 'We got to go, and you're coming with me.'

Vaughn sat in a furious silence while Renee climbed off the boat and into the puddles and mud onshore.

Ezra reached for the gun she'd stuck in his eye. 'Here.'

She took it, and he gave her a good-luck nod and pushed offshore as she walked towards the trees. Before he fired up the motor, he reached behind his back and withdrew the gun he'd taken from Vaughn on the beach earlier that day. 'You ever actually used this?'

Vaughn's eyes were dark and small, his face wet with rain. 'Yes,' he said. 'Probably in ways you wouldn't guess.'

'Fantastic. Maybe you'll tell me the story sometime.'

THEY WERE BACK in the boat as the rain billowed down at them, each gust a solid wall of water. Nora's hair clung to her neck in tangles. She sat in the back with King's hand locked onto her arm, his gun close, as Frank started the engine and took them out into the lake.

AJ's mood was wilder than it had been before the island, his self-control held together by a few overstretched threads—it was now clear that Ezra knew they were coming.

The engine roared behind her and the boat lifted again. They hammered across the lake, the bow banging against wind-blown waves. This far north, there was nothing to see except wilderness. AJ was pointing, sending Frank along first one shore and then the other, searching for Ezra and the others, a random, worthless method, even Nora knew that. Ezra probably had the boat onshore by now, dragged into the woods and covered with underbrush.

So what would AJ and his near-the-breaking-point temper do when he realised they'd never find the boat?

She hadn't formulated an answer to that question when Frank abruptly dropped the throttle and the boat sloshed to a stop, rocking on its own wake. Nora felt her stomach dip with horror. The boat was dead ahead, not hidden at all, in fact, just sitting on the main shore, tied among the trees.

EZRA SAT in the wet leaves with Vaughn at his side, thinking about the line he'd uttered as Ezra passed him the pistol and asked if he knew how to use it. *Probably in ways you wouldn't guess.*

Ezra thought about that and about the desperate way Vaughn had reacted to being separated from Renee. He then put those two moments together with the notion that Vaughn was not the sort of man Devin seemed likely to turn to in a crisis. He considered all of those things and turned to Vaughn and said, 'Devin's alive.'

Vaughn had been staring out at the lake. Now everything in him seemed to shut down, not a breath coming, not a blink.

'He left the hospital yesterday. Hasn't been seen since. Frank heard from the FBI that he might be headed this way.'

Vaughn cocked his head and turned to face Ezra. 'I don't know if I believe you, but if you're serious, then that's good news.'

Ezra said, 'No. It is not good news for you.'

Vaughn's tongue ran across his lips.

'Now,' Ezra said, 'it being just the two of us, I'd like to ask you a question and receive an honest answer. Did you shoot him?'

'What? Man, we sat on that porch, and I *told you*—'

'I know what you told me, and this time I'm asking for the truth,' Ezra said. 'I'm the only chance you've got today. You better know that, friend. And I need the truth.'

There was a long pause. 'She's scared of him. She doesn't love him. How could you, guy like that? But how do you leave him, too? I'd be scared, if I was her.'

'You think she's in love with you? I didn't see that.'

Vaughn tensed. 'She could be. You don't know what you're talking about. So many times she was telling me how much she liked all the ways I was different from him . . .'

His voice trailed off, but Ezra understood what Vaughn never would, that Renee had been part of the game, packaged with the cash to keep this guy happy and playing for Devin's team. Someone in law enforcement—buying him off might not be enough protection. Devin would have wanted to bring

Vaughn in close, lure him as near as possible so he could be watched. You looked for something that kept a guy like Vaughn on the hook: Renee.

'Were you sleeping together?' Ezra asked.

'No. It wasn't there yet. But she was scared of him and she wanted to leave him. *I know that for a fact*,' Vaughn hissed.

'All right,' Ezra said slowly. Then, 'Why'd you run here? Of all the places you could have gone, you came here?' Vaughn didn't offer an answer. 'You needed someplace that would seem like Devin's idea? To convince her?'

That got a nod. 'He'd talked about it once. Offered me the place if I wanted to stay there, you know, a vacation or whatever. He wrote your name down and said I should just call you and say when I was coming. He acted real entertained by it.'

'He would have been,' Ezra said. 'I promised him if he ever came back here, I'd kill him. He probably thought it would be funny if you called me and said he'd sent you. If you thought you'd killed the guy, though, why did you need to run at all?'

'To be with her,' Vaughn said. 'To be with her, away from the rest of it. To show her what I could be. That I could take care of her. That I could be like him, only better. If she knew that he'd trusted me, if she knew . . .' He looked up at Ezra, hope filling his eyes. 'You won't tell her. Will you? You hate him, too.'

'I am a damn fool,' Ezra said. 'An old fool.' Ezra stared down at him, felt contempt for Vaughn. 'People are dead and more are going to die. For you. And I'm out here protecting you.'

'You won't tell her, right?'

'I'll tell her that her husband is alive. She deserves to know that. You didn't kill him and now whatever you were hoping to pull off with her, it's over.'

'It's not over,' Vaughn said carefully, 'if Devin is dead.'

It was quiet for a minute, his suggestion hanging in the air. 'No,' Ezra said. 'I'm not being a part of that.'

'You said you wanted to kill him.' Vaughn was pushing off the ground, his body rising with his voice. 'You just *told* me that. So what do you care?'

Ezra began to speak but stopped. He heard a motor. He leaned to one side to look out of the trees and across the water, saw his boat stop just off shore.

'Is Devin out there?' Vaughn said. 'If he's out there, man, just kill him and let me take Renee and go.'

'Shut up.' The motor came back to life and the boat was headed into shore. Four figures: Ezra recognised Nora and saw Frank behind the motor, and wished again for his rifle.

They landed the boat and Ezra rolled back against the base of a tree. 'They're coming onshore. These guns don't have the range we need, so we've got to sit and wait, wait *quietly*.'

Vaughn didn't answer, just looked at Ezra with blank eyes.

'When they come onshore,' Ezra began, but he was interrupted by the sound of another motor. What the hell? He could only see his boat and the big Merc was shut down. He shifted to the side. Yes, there was someone on board the little aluminium boat he and Vaughn had arrived in, starting the engine. Frank was on the beach, pushing it into the water.

Frank climbed in and then both boats pulled away, into open water. Two hundred yards offshore, the anchor went out from the little boat, which was pitching hard in the wind. 'Damn,' Ezra said.

'What are they doing?' Vaughn said.

'They're moving one of the boats far enough offshore that we can't get to it. Then they'll come back.'

They would come back in his boat, which was bigger and faster and also required a key to start. Ezra had no second key. Far out on the water, men were stepping off one boat into the other.

They'd anchored across from the island where he'd left Renee.

KING BOUND NORA'S HANDS behind her back with duct tape, then wrapped her ankles together. She'd given up on fighting him by then, but when he advanced with the piece for her mouth, she spoke. 'No. Please don't cover my mouth.'

He snapped the tape over her face, wrapped it round her jaw until it tangled in her hair, and then added another, shorter strip. They had stretched her out in the small boat they had taken, which was rolling in the windblown chop.

AJ kept his gun on Frank. The panic that showed in Nora's eyes was tough to take, but Frank knew it would be easier if he was alone with these two. Nora was a liability, an extra concern anytime he decided to take action. With that eliminated, he was a little freer.

'You're staying with her,' AJ told King, and quickly all of Frank's hope for this situation began to disappear. 'The minute we hit shore, you start watching the clock.'

No, Frank thought. No clocks, no countdowns, don't say that.

'Ten minutes go by, you put a bullet in her head. No hesitation.'

'Won't be a problem,' King leaned down close to Nora's horrified eyes, stroked her cheek. 'Will it, hon?'

The lake and the land seemed to tilt and spin, every possible scenario— *ten minutes, ten minutes, ten minutes*—scorching through Frank's brain. It was too little time. 'You can't—'

AJ hit him backhanded, flush in the face, with the gun, and knocked him down, back into the boat. Blood ran down his chin and onto his shirt.

'Get up,' AJ said.

Frank stayed down, looking at his own blood.

'*Get up!*' AJ screamed, then almost lost his balance in a wild kick aimed at Frank's chest that instead hit the seat above him. Frank got to his feet, fat red drops of blood speckling his jeans.

'Start the engine,' AJ said, shoving him into the seat behind the wheel. 'And take us back. We're almost done.'

The motor growled, and they pulled away from the aluminium boat where Nora waited bound and gagged and alone with King.

A sharp ache cut into Frank's ribs as AJ pressed the gun against him and shouted, 'Faster!' into his ear. Frank leaned over the wheel, holding his shirt to his bloody nose, and slammed the boat through the lashing water. He tried to coax some of the old lessons from that voice in his head. None came.

'Slow down and land it,' AJ shouted. There was no real beach on this part of the shore, just trees giving way to rocks. The water was high this early in the year, and some of the smaller trees near the shore were almost submerged, only the tops showing. Frank brought the boat in among them, felt the stern shudder as the prop chewed through some branches. It was going to be a slippery climb to the top of the slope.

'Tie it up!' AJ shouted. 'Cut the motor and tie it up!' Frank tied the stern line to a protruding limb. 'All right,' AJ said, tearing the key out of the ignition. 'You lead the way and stay close.'

Frank stepped out of the boat and sank up to his waist. AJ splashed over the side behind him, and then they were both stumbling through the water, pushing branches aside. Frank slipped and splashed until his foot touched the gravel bank, and it felt like it was coming down on a land mine, that clock— *ten minutes, ten minutes, ten minutes*—starting to tick back on the boat.

'Start climbing,' AJ said, his breath warm on Frank's neck.

Frank fought his way up the slope, using saplings for handholds, his feet sinking into the muck. They got to the top of the hill and stood gasping for breath and staring into dark trees that were shaking with wind and rain.

'Ballard!' AJ shoved Frank forward. 'Ezra Ballard, if you hear this, you listen sharp. Out on the boat is the girl from the body shop. You know Nora, don't you?'

They were into the woods now, and AJ paused when thunder drowned out his words. After a flash of lightning, he shouted, 'That girl's got ten minutes of life left, and then she takes a bullet right in her beautiful face.'

Frank realised AJ was banking completely on the assumption that Ezra was close enough to hear him. What if he wasn't?

'You can stop this!' AJ yelled. 'What I want is Vaughn and Renee! Renee, babe, you hear me? Devin is alive!'

Eight minutes, not ten. That's what Frank expected they had left. Maybe seven? Either way, it was time to act.

'Come on! Let me know you hear me!' AJ screamed, then went quiet, and they both listened. There was no sound.

They walked deep into the woods. The rain was falling harder, slapping through the trees. AJ grabbed Frank's shirt. 'You start talking now,' he said, the gun pressed against Frank's spine. 'Only a couple minutes left.'

'Ezra!' Frank called. 'Nora's back on that boat. Answer us!' His eyes went towards a spot fifty feet ahead, where the ground dipped down a short, steep hill and then rose again on the other side—a sort of sinkhole. He shifted slightly, walking towards it.

'Keep talking,' AJ hissed. He jerked his head round constantly, peering into every shadow. These dark woods were not home to him. His sort of killing was done in different places.

'Ezra, damn it, *answer us*!' Frank shouted.

AJ was using him for a shield, keeping him close, and close was where Frank needed him to be. The drop-off was in full view now, maybe ten feet from top to bottom. A simple step sideways, a fast sweep of his right arm and leg. Almost there, but now AJ was pulling him away from it. Frank stopped, bringing AJ up with him, and pointed into the trees.

'What?' AJ said.

'Somebody moving, I think.' Frank started walking towards the imaginary source of noise, alongside the drop-off. His pulse was drilling away. Four more steps, now two, now one . . .

In the second that he moved, instinct took over. Instead of sidestepping, he simply spun, a full, fast pivot that took his back away from the gun as he lifted his left arm and held it out straight and kept on turning, caught AJ across the shoulder and drove him forwards.

AJ's gun went off a half-second after Frank had spun away from it; then Frank's arm knocked AJ towards the drop-off. They were a step too far away, but Frank had got a foot against the back of AJ's knee. AJ stumbled and fell, and there was the gun in his belt—all Frank had to do was reach out and . . .

He got it. His fingers closed on the stock, and then AJ was gone and tumbling through the wet leaves to the bottom, and the Smith & Wesson was out of Frank's left hand and into his right and lifted and aimed. For one fleeting second, he waited. Just long enough for AJ to land at the bottom of the drop-off and turn back and start to lift his own weapon. Then Frank killed him with a single round below his right eye.

THEY'D BEEN ALONE maybe five minutes before King began to talk. 'Uh-oh,' he said, turning to Nora in the pitching boat. 'Know where they are now, baby? Onshore. You know what that means.' He looked at his wrist and frowned. 'Damn. Look who forgot his watch. How am I going to know when ten minutes go by?'

He leaned close, and she tried to slide away but found it impossible with both hands and feet bound. His face, long and angular and covered with rough stubble, was against hers, his breath on her cheek. 'I'll have to, you know, estimate? I was always bad at that.'

The wind rose again in a hard gust and the boat rolled. He put out his hand to catch himself, falling almost on top of her.

'Look at that.' King ran his fingertips along her forearm, over the bruises he'd left two days earlier. 'Little love marks. They from me? I bet they are.' She was stretched out on the seat, and he was on his knees now in the bottom of the boat, rain dripping down his face onto hers. He took her hair in his hand, squeezed hard enough to make her eyes sting.

'It was dumb-ass luck that kid showed up when he did. We were going to have some fun, you and I. Still might.' He rocked his hand left to right, jerking her head sideways. 'I take that tape off your mouth, we could have some serious fun. But you might be a biter. You're the type. Angry little bitch. So maybe that tape stays.'

He lifted her by her hair, and she'd have screamed if the tape hadn't prevented it. Her eyes were streaming now, pain demanding a physical response. He pushed her against the side of the boat and pressed his body down on hers. The sudden change was almost too much for the boat; they rocked hard.

'Tape on the hands can stay, too. You won't need those.'

He moved suddenly, slammed her head back against the boat hard enough to make her vision blur, and then he got to his feet, moved to the bow, leaned against it and stared into the woods. She tilted her head, tried to see what he was looking at. The angle wasn't right, though. She could hardly see the main shore. There was an island that she could see, but that wasn't where AJ had taken Frank. She let her eyes pass over that shore and then she saw motion.

There was someone on the island. No, couldn't be. She was seeing things, some weird reflection. Where had it gone? Wait, there it was again. Someone was moving through the trees.

King turned and Nora moved her head, but it was a second too slow. He'd seen her staring out across the water.

'Son of a bitch,' he said, lifting the gun, and Nora knew she'd just ruined someone's chance to escape.

EZRA CRAWLED to the top of the rise and looked out at the angry grey lake. There was the aluminium boat, a few hundred yards out, small but visible. He couldn't hear the shouting any more, which could be good or bad. Maybe the idiot was out of shouting range now; maybe he was quietly working his way back to Ezra's boat. They'd tied it up right in the middle of the partially submerged trees that surrounded this part of the shore.

Maybe twenty feet of fairly open ground to cover before he had to plunge into that mess of branches and water, fight his way out to his boat. It would take about thirty seconds to get on board.

He got his breathing steadied. He pushed off, upright for the first time since he'd left Vaughn, and ran down the hill.

It was a slippery, dangerous mess in the rain, and twice he almost went down on his face. He hit the water knee-deep and sloshed through it, hunching. No shots came; no motor roared to life. He waded out to the stern, the water up almost to his armpits, and then braced his hands on the side of the boat and heaved. Damn, his body wasn't what it used to be.

He got over, though, flopped across the side and slid down to the floor, lay there, breathing hard.

Still silence. He pushed himself into a sitting position and cast one glance at the console, saw the empty ignition. They'd taken the key, as he'd feared. That could be dealt with later. Right now, he needed the rifle.

He'd left it in the storage compartment under the floor. He flipped the latch, lifted the cover and peered inside, felt a moment's horror when he saw nothing but fishing rods. But there it was, tucked against the side, a gun that had never seemed as beautiful as it did now. It was a custom-built bolt-action rifle, the best long-range firearm he'd ever held. He pulled the rifle free and slipped the cover off the Yukon night-vision scope. His own enemy had delivered him his sword. Mercy be on their souls now.

Crawling back towards the outboard, he pressed himself in against the bench seat and rested the gun barrel on the stern. Then he lowered his cheek to his shoulder, closed one eye, put the other to the scope. He tweaked the scope to clarify the scene. There were two people in the boat, Nora Stafford, with tape over her mouth, and a big son of a bitch lifting a gun.

The shot rang out loud and clear, and for a second Ezra was absolutely baffled, because the guy was turned away from Ezra and firing across the lake. What the hell? Ezra thought, and then he got it: Renee.

He brought the cross hairs down quick, sighted along the big man's chest. It was a hell of a long shot, even with the scope, at least 160 yards. Tougher still because the guy was standing sideways. Then the son of a bitch fired again and Ezra clenched his teeth, steadied his breathing, and pulled the trigger.

It was maybe the best shot he'd ever made so quickly. The bullet hit the guy in the neck, blew a cloud of blood into the air, and then he was collapsing against the side of the boat. God, he'd fallen right on Nora. As the boat tipped dangerously to the left, the heavy body hung up on the side. The boat rocked back to the right, but then Nora struggled beneath the body, and her motion made it roll left again and, as she kept thrashing, the little boat overbalanced and tipped, spilling them both into the water.

'Damn!' Ezra hadn't meant to send them into the water like that. But Nora could swim, surely, or at least hang on to the upside-down boat until he could get out there.

He kept the scope to his eye and watched and saw nothing.

Then he remembered the tape.

12

Nora had a fraction of a second to suck air in through her nose, and then she was sinking. She fell fast and soundlessly, dropped through the freezing water with a sense of terror she couldn't have imagined. She sank all the way to the bottom. Seeing the shimmer of light that was the surface, she knew she would die staring up at it. Then she bounced. She'd landed on her ass, but a violent twist got her feet under her, and she realised that she could bend her knees.

She pushed off as hard as she could, shot upwards. The lake wasn't deep here, maybe ten feet, and that one massive push was enough to get her to the surface. Enough for one inhalation. Then she sank again.

This time she was sure she'd die on the bottom. The little bit of air she'd got didn't feel like nearly enough. One more bend and push, but she knew it was futile even as she headed to the surface. Her adrenaline-fuelled strength was fading fast. She got a little more air, then sank again. Her feet hit the bottom and she managed to go through the routine one more time, bend and push. This time she came up under the boat.

Panic saved her life. She instinctively jerked her head backwards, as if to clear herself out from under the boat. Instead she wedged the back of her skull between a seat bracket and the side of the aluminium frame. She stuck. Only for a few seconds, but it was enough so that she could get a breath and realise what had happened. Then she felt herself sliding away from the bracket and arched her back. The motion forced her head against the bracket, lifting her body into an awkward floating position.

Breathe. That was all she had to do, just get as much oxygen through her nose into her lungs as possible. She hauled the air in, got in at least five breaths before she began to slide again.

She tried to repeat the motion that had worked before, arching her back, but her head kept sliding.

No, no, no. Come back. I can stay alive here. I can stay alive . . .

The water was over her face and she was sinking again when she realised that it hadn't been her head sliding away from the bracket, but the other way round. The boat was moving. She watched it move as she dropped, was three feet deep and still going when legs bumped against her back, and then an arm encircled her, wrapped round her neck, hooked under her chin and lifted.

A second later she broke the surface, blinked water out of her eyes, and stared at Renee, unable to utter a single word of thanks.

EZRA DROPPED THE RIFLE, got to his feet and looked around his boat for some way to help. The electric trolling motor was the only chance he had. Ezra couldn't make a swim like that, not any more.

Something moved onshore behind him and he whirled back to face it, reaching for the rifle.

'Damn,' he said, and picked up the rifle but left it pointed down. The movement onshore was from Vaughn, who had just stepped out of the trees, holding his gun ahead of him with a wavering grip.

'Come on!' Ezra yelled. 'Get out here.'

Get Vaughn and go after Nora. That's what Ezra was thinking as he stepped up into the bow, the rifle held loosely at his side, his eyes scanning the woods to see if anyone else was approaching.

Vaughn fired from the shoreline and for a second Ezra was stunned, but then he got both hands round the rifle and lifted it as Vaughn took a second shot, missing again, and a third.

The third round caught Ezra in his right side. He tried to keep lifting the rifle, to get it aimed at Vaughn, but the bullet had spun him and now he was stumbling. His knees banged off the side of the boat and he flipped over the side and fell into the tangled branches of a partially submerged tree. The branches snapped under him and he dropped into the water as Vaughn fired, missing again. Ezra tried to lift the rifle, but it was too heavy now. Or was it even in his hand?

Another branch snapped and he dropped again, and then the grey sky was fading into an odd red mist and Ezra couldn't see to fire. The red mist spun into black and then shattered into jagged points of light, and Ezra Ballard closed his eyes and welcomed the water.

RENEE GOT THE TAPE off Nora's hands first, which allowed her to hang on to the boat while Renee freed her feet. The feeling of life that came back as Nora moved her legs and arms was intense. She tore the tape off her mouth.

'Thank you,' she said. 'Thank you.'

The rain was hammering the overturned boat like a drum corps, but even so they both stopped talking and listened as another sound, a series of cracks, echoed over the water. 'Guns,' Renee said. 'Somebody's shooting.'

Nora didn't say anything. Her strength was already fading. Renee was treading water easily.

'All right. Let's roll the boat,' Renee said.

It took them two tries, but they flipped it. They hung off the side until they had the strength to climb into it. The water had been freezing, but Nora felt even colder as the wind fanned over them.

'Where are the others?' Renee's eyes were on the lake.

'On the shore. Well, the guy they left on the boat with me is dead. Someone shot him. That's why we tipped over.' Nora took a deep breath. 'And Devin is waiting at Frank's cabin.'

Renee stared at Nora. 'What did you say?'

'Your husband is waiting at Frank's cabin. He's not in good shape, but he's alive. Vaughn shot him.'

'*Vaughn* shot him?'

'That's what Devin said while he put me and Frank into a van at gunpoint and came out here and had an FBI agent murdered at the cabin. The one named AJ killed him with a knife.'

The words slid by Renee without any apparent effect. She said, 'Vaughn shot Devin? I've been up here with him, and he's the one who shot Devin? He tried to kill Devin?'

'Yes,' Nora said. She was shivering violently.

'Can we start the motor?' Renee said.

Nora turned and looked at it. The thing had been upside down for a while, but it still looked in place, everything as it should be.

'Probably. Where are we going?' Nora asked.

'To my husband. But first we're going to stop at that island. I left a gun there.'

WHEN HE HEARD the first shot, Frank was down in the hole, relieving AJ of his gun and the boat key. The sound overwhelmed him with a sense of defeat. He was too late. Ten minutes had gone by and Nora Stafford was dead. He'd let her die.

Then there was another shot, and a third. This last one hadn't come from a handgun and King didn't have a rifle.

He ran towards the shots but angled too far to the left and ran into a tangle of undergrowth. He fought his way back and moved parallel to the lake, looking for a gap in the brush that would let him down to the boat.

He heard voices, and then there was another volley of shots. Who was shooting? He slapped branches aside and found himself at the top of a muddy bluff. Ezra's boat was screened from sight. The smaller boat was floating upside down in the lake. He could see people in the water.

The bluff was steep and slick with wet mud, but he fought his way down it, his shoes ploughing furrows in the soggy earth, and then he was in the water up to his knees, splashing down the shore towards the collection of stumps and trees where he'd left Ezra's boat.

When he came round the bluff, Ezra's boat appeared and he saw Vaughn in the stern, using the trolling motor to pull away from the island. 'Hey!' Frank shouted. '*Hey!*'

Vaughn turned, lifted a gun and fired two wild shots that hit the water twenty feet to Frank's right.

'Stop shooting, you idiot! It's Frank! Bring it over here! I've got the key!'

Vaughn got the boat pointed in the right direction and, when it reached him, Frank caught the side, took one deep breath, and heaved up, got his knee on the side and used that leverage to force his way onto the boat.

He was collapsed on the starboard seat when Vaughn let go of the trolling motor and held the gun out in a shaking hand. 'Give me the key.'

Frank stared at him. 'What? Get that gun out of my face!'

'Give me the key!'

Out on the lake a motor coughed and caught, and Frank looked towards the sound and saw the aluminium boat was upright again and in motion, headed towards another island, away from them. Vaughn stared after it, and Frank planted his feet on the floor, then rose and swept Vaughn's arm down and away, hit him once in the chest with a closed fist. It knocked Vaughn back against the steering console, and Frank locked his left hand round Vaughn's wrist and twisted until the fingers opened up and the gun fell to the bottom of the boat.

'What the hell's the matter with you?' he said, his face close to Vaughn's, whose entire body seemed to be shaking.

Frank knelt and picked up the gun, wedged it beneath the seat, out of the way and then put the key in the ignition and turned it. As the motor came to life, Vaughn moved away and Frank straightened and stared out at the departing aluminium boat. It looked like Nora was at the motor. He lifted his arm and waved. Finally she saw him and lifted her own hand, but kept taking the boat away towards the island.

'What's she doing?' Frank said, dropping to the seat and moving his hand to the throttle.

'Renee was on that island,' Vaughn said.

'I think she's on the boat now. What happened to the one who was with Nora on the boat, though?'

Vaughn didn't answer.

'What about Ezra?' Frank twisted the wheel and turned the boat to go in pursuit of Nora and Renee.

'They shot him,' Vaughn said.

Frank spun to face him. 'What?'

Vaughn nodded. 'Somebody shot him. He's dead.'

'Who shot him?'

'I don't know.'

'Well, where is he?'

Vaughn lifted an unsteady hand and pointed at the water.

A SICKNESS that had come and gone during those first few shots returned to Frank as he drove Ezra's boat away from the island where his father's old friend had been killed, was somewhere in the water now, joining Atkins, their blood spilling into the lake.

It was on Devin Matteson, all that blood in the water, two more lives taken, adding to the total that included everyone Frank's father had killed, and included Frank's father, and even the two thugs Devin had brought with him, the body count rising. *All* of this was on Devin.

That would end today. Frank was going back to that cabin, and he was going to kill Devin Matteson. Then let the others call the police. Nothing mattered any more but getting back across this damn lake to put a bullet into Matteson's heart.

'I'm sorry, Ezra,' he whispered.

Nora had taken the other boat into the beach of the island and, as they approached, Frank could see that she was still in the stern while Renee was onshore.

'What are you going to do?' Vaughn said. He was in the seat beside Frank, hands trembling on his thighs.

'We're going to get them and get out of here,' Frank said. He'd brought Ezra's boat in alongside the other, was staring at Nora, who looked back at him without saying a word. There were red streaks across her face from the tape that had covered her mouth.

'You OK?' he said, dropping the motor to idle, speaking as his boat thumped against hers.

'I'm here,' she said.

'Ezra's dead.'

She stared at him.

'Vaughn says they shot him. He's dead. Get in this boat, and we'll leave that one behind.'

She nodded and got to her feet, and he reached out a hand to help her step over. As he did it, he turned to Renee, who was walking down from the island. She was moving at a fast pace, stepped right into the lake, moving towards his boat, a gun in her hand.

'Hey,' he said. 'Get in. We're leaving.'

She kept walking, the water up to her knees now. She hadn't even glanced at Frank; her eyes were locked on Vaughn.

'Put that gun down,' Frank said.

She didn't say a word. Just walked along the boat towards Vaughn. Frank's own weapon was on the seat. He turned and reached for it, thinking Vaughn might do the same, but instead Vaughn rose, climbed over the side of the boat and splashed into waist-deep water, moving towards Renee.

'Renee,' he said. He had his hands outstretched, reaching for her. 'Forgive me. It was for you. I love you so much and you could never understand that. I did it because I love you so—'

He was a few feet away when she lifted the gun and fired. The bullet hit him in the temple, snapped his head back and turned his eyes to the sky before he dropped into the water.

Frank had just got his hand on his own gun and Nora was still standing in the rear of her boat, waiting to step across.

'Let go of that,' Renee said.

Frank saw that she was pointing the gun at him now.

'Let go of it and step back,' Renee said. 'We're leaving now. Just like you said.'

Frank dropped the gun back onto the seat and stepped away.

'Turn off that engine and go over there and help her in,' Renee said.

'I'm not going to hurt either of you. OK? But you're taking me back to my husband now.'

Frank cut the engine and Nora took his hand and stepped out of one boat and into the next.

'OK,' Renee said. 'Now help me in. And, please, don't try to take this gun. I don't want to hurt anyone.'

He walked into the bow and she slogged through the water to get closer. He reached for her and she extended her free hand and grasped his. When he had a firm hold, he leaned back to give her an awkward lift. She hesitated and then she put the gun, still in her hand, down on the bow as she tried to get over the side.

Frank slid his foot over and trapped the fine bones of her wrist. 'Let go,' he said.

'Stop. I told you I wasn't going to hurt—'

He shifted his weight, her words cut off in a gasp and her fingers loosened. He leaned down and took the gun.

'Fine,' she said. 'You want the damn gun, keep it. I just want to get back to my husband. Let's get the hell out of here.'

Frank turned and faced Nora, who was standing in the back of the boat watching this all unfold with a horrified expression.

'Nora,' Frank said, 'I'm going to have to ask you to get back in the other boat.'

'What?'

'Please,' he said, his voice gentle. 'If you'd get back into the other boat, I'd like you to take Renee and go to the dam. You know how to get there? There's a bait shop right there, just down the road. Go there and call the police.'

'Frank . . .'

'Take the other boat and go get help. Please.'

'Where are *you* going?'

He didn't answer.

'No, don't go back for him. Let the police—'

'*Nora.*' The strong emphasis made him move his gun hand, almost involuntarily. Her eyes went to the gun, and when she looked at him again, he felt sickened. 'It's safer for you this way,' he said, but she was already moving, had stepped over the side and back into the smaller boat, moving out of fear.

'Where's he going?' Renee said, her voice sharp with alarm. 'What's he talking about? *Where are you going?*'

He didn't answer, just brought the motor to life and pulled away, turning his mind to things that needed remembering, like Ezra's body under the water and Devin waiting at the cabin.

EZRA LOVED THE TREES. They belonged on land, high above the water, but instead they were in it, supporting him, holding him to the surface. The trees didn't want to let him sink. He imagined the bottom was way down there, forty or fifty feet at least. The trees that held him were massive. Oaks probably? He hadn't realised how high the lake had risen this spring. He'd tried to use the branches to pull himself towards shore, but pulling set off wild bells of pain, so he just hung on, waiting.

Vaughn was gone. Ezra had seen him take the boat away, and there had been more gunfire.

For a while he was waiting to die and not afraid of it at all, patient as could be. He wanted to bleed his life out into this beautiful lake that had given that very life to him. It was fine to end out here. It was right.

Rain started again, much lighter now, and it felt good on Ezra's face, helped to push the fog back. He thought he'd been floating but, after a hard blink to focus, he realised that the water only rose to his shoulders. It really wasn't that deep. Maybe if he reached with his foot . . .

Son of a bitch, he could touch the bottom. The bottom should be way down at the base of the tree trunks.

He tilted his head, studied the tree that held him. The branches weren't so thick, in fact little more than twigs. He wasn't in a tree at all. It was a bush, one of the wild tangles that grew along the shore. He was very close to shore.

Ezra was not going to die out here. Not today.

A GENTLE RAIN faded to nothing as Frank crossed the lake, the clouds still heavy and dark but quiet now, the wind settling. He ran the big boat at full throttle, knowing he'd make it to the cabin maybe fifteen minutes before Nora and Renee got to the dam, and that would be more than sufficient.

He discarded the Ruger he'd taken from Renee and took the Smith & Wesson back. *Here's a bullet from the old man, Devin.*

He was completely alone on the lake, even when he came out into the southern portion, where the most boat traffic could usually be found. He dropped the speed as he neared the cabin. He then came in close to shore with the engine as quiet as possible. Finally he saw the cabin. One main window looked out on the water, so Devin could be watching the lake right now. Frank cut the engine and let the boat drift into the weeds several hundred yards away.

He got out of the boat in the shallows, wrapped the bow line round a downed tree, then climbed up the bank and into the woods. He walked quietly but quickly, the gun held down against his leg, finger hooked in the trigger guard.

Through the trees and into the yard. Across the yard and to the door. Hand on the knob. He threw the door open and stepped into the cabin in a shooter's stance, gun raised, ready to kill.

Devin was on the floor. Stretched out on his side, one cheek on the linoleum, his body slightly curled. His gun lay on a table beside the couch, and Frank could see that he'd fallen. There was a small puddle near his mouth, bile maybe, mixed with traces of blood. For a second, Frank thought he was dead. Then he lifted his head, his hazy eyes taking Frank in before flicking to the gun on the table several feet away, no chance of reaching it. He rolled into a sitting position, his back against the wall.

'Where's my wife?'

Frank swung the door shut, never taking his eyes off Devin. 'She's fine, but you're never going to see her again.'

'No?' Devin brought his head off the wall.

'No.' Frank came closer. 'The rest of them are dead. Your boy AJ? I took his gun, and I shot him with it. Watched him die, and then I came back for you.'

Devin sucked air through his mouth in slow, audible breaths.

'He had a chance,' Frank said. 'Hell, he was holding both guns. Wasn't enough. But I'll give you the same.'

'Yeah?'

'Go for the gun.' Frank said, nodding at the table. 'I'll let you get your hand on it.'

Devin just stared at him.

'Going to kill me?' Devin said.

'Yes. Unless you get that gun first. Better move for it.'

'You have to wait until I've got the gun, is that it? Your dad wouldn't have needed to wait.'

'I'm not my dad,' Frank said.

Devin smiled. It was a dying man's smile, a look not of hopelessness but of indifference, and Frank hated him for being so weak. Hated him for being in this condition. He wanted him at full strength, and then Frank would still be better than him, and he'd kill him. 'Get up! Go for the gun, you bastard!'

Again the smile. Devin shook his head. 'Can't reach it.'

Frank moved to the table and kicked its legs, upending it and spilling Devin's gun to the floor. It hit a few feet away from him, slid to a stop almost within reach. '*Pick it up!*'

Devin shook his head again, and this time Frank went for him. He hit him backhanded with the Smith & Wesson, caught the side of his skull, knocked him back to the floor. Devin let out a soft moan of pain but didn't move, didn't reach for the gun. Frank reached down with his free hand and caught Devin's neck, dragged him upright and then slammed his head into the wall, still screaming at him to pick up the gun. Banged his head again, and a third time; then he dropped to one knee and jammed the barrel of his father's gun into Devin's mouth.

It was then that he saw Devin was unconscious. He let go of Devin's neck and pulled the gun out of his mouth. Devin's head fell onto his right shoulder and the torso bent awkwardly, to the floor.

Frank laid his fingers against Devin's neck, felt the pulse there. Devin's eyes fluttered but stayed closed. Frank laid the gun against the back of Devin's skull, feeling the trigger under his finger.

I'd find him and I'd kill him.

It's justified, he'd told Ezra. It is already justified. And Ezra's response? *Not in a way you can accept, it's not.*

Devin made a muffled grunt and stirred. Frank thought of Nora, of the fear in her eyes as she'd looked at him, and he pulled the gun back and walked away. He picked up the table and set it back where it belonged, beneath his grandfather's Silver Star. He looked at the medal for a moment, then he dropped his eyes to the gun in his hand and ejected the clip into his palm. He took Devin's gun from the floor and emptied that clip as well, and then he set both guns on the kitchen counter and ran cold water onto a towel.

When he turned off the water, he could hear a boat motor. Something small and heading this way. He went to the window and saw the aluminium boat. Not surprising that Renee had refused to go to the dam.

He slapped at Devin's neck with the wet towel, then held it over his face and squeezed a trickle of cold water onto his forehead and cheeks. The eyes opened, swam, then focused on Frank.

'Get up,' Frank said. 'Your wife's coming.'

When they arrived, Devin was sitting against the wall, Frank standing in the kitchen with his back against the counter. Renee came through the door and ran to her husband. 'Baby,' he said, reaching for her with one arm as she fell to her knees.

Nora stood in the doorway. Her eyes searched Frank's, then flicked to the guns on the counter.

'They're empty,' he said, and walked into the living room. Renee turned at the sound of his approach, a protective motion, covering Devin with her body.

'Get him up,' Frank said. 'And get out of here. The keys to the van are inside it.'

Renee just nodded.

Frank turned and walked outside. Nora followed, and a few minutes later Renee appeared with Devin on his feet but leaning heavily against her. Frank and Nora stood beside the cabin and watched as she got the van door open and heaved him inside.

Renee slammed the door shut and walked to the driver's door. 'Thank you,' she said. 'And I'm sorry. I'm so sorry.'

Frank looked away from her, out at the lake. He didn't turn when the engine started, didn't turn when they drove up the gravel drive.

When the sound of the van had faded and they were alone, Nora said, 'Is there a phone inside?'

'No.'

'Mine's ruined. The water.'

'Yeah. Mine, too.'

'Where can we go to call the police?'

He waved towards the drive and they started up it together, not speaking. They were halfway to the main road when they heard the hum of an engine and the crunch of tyres.

It was a car. When it slid to a stop and the door opened and Grady Morgan stood up and stared at them, all Frank could say was, 'You're too late, Grady. Too late.'

Grady looked over his shoulder. 'Who was that? In that van?'

'Devin Matteson and his wife,' Frank said.

'I can't let them drive away from here.'

'Sure you can. You never saw them. Didn't know who it was.'

Grady looked at Frank for a long time, then said, 'I've lied about him before. I guess I can do it again. Now what the hell happened out here?'

SIX HOURS LATER, Frank and Nora long departed in police custody and Ezra Ballard evacuated to some hospital, first by boat and then by helicopter, Grady stood alone at the shore and stared out into the dark lake where several bodies waited to be found.

Atkins was dead. Another agent, one who'd been trying to do the job right, was dead, and Grady would see that blood on his hands for the rest of his days, understood that it was the end of his career long before anyone back in Chicago would.

Too late. That was the first thing Frank had said to him. Grady had been too late. Frank had no idea.

Seven years of watching that kid, and it had never been about protecting Frank from anything. It had always been about protecting Grady, about covering his own ass. He'd never had the courage to tell him the truth, and now they were bringing body after body out of this damn lake.

Too late. Yes, Frank, I was too late.

Grady Morgan and the Seven-Year Lie. If Frank had known Devin wasn't responsible for his father's demise, he never would have headed north, never would have seen Vaughn Duncan or had anything to do with it. Those two from Miami would have quietly killed Duncan and taken Renee home.

It was a sick world, Grady thought, when you could stand on the shore of a beautiful lake like this and long for one murder. One murder that would have saved the others.

He was done with the Bureau. Wouldn't have to be—all of this was indirect involvement, he was close to retirement, and the Bureau loved to handle such things quietly and in-house—but he knew he'd resign now. He felt he owed Atkins that much. Atkins wouldn't have wanted a guy like Grady left in his Bureau.

The truth would start with Frank, though. The hell with the people in Chicago who would hear it next; Frank was the one that mattered.

Grady didn't see him until the next morning, and while there were still cops moving around the lake—and divers looking for Atkins—they were sitting in the cabin with their backs to the window that looked out on the grisly activity.

Ezra Ballard was alive and recovering from a single gunshot that had blown through his ribs. 'He'll make it,' Frank said after filling Grady in on all the medical details Grady had already heard. 'One of the few, though, and you don't need to tell me how much of that is my responsibility, Grady. I understand it.'

'That's not the way anyone else is telling it,' Grady said. 'You see the papers? You're on the front page.'

'So was my dad.'

'They're saying different things about you, though. You let Devin go. I saw the reports.'

A nod.

'It was the right thing to do,' Grady said.

'Anybody heard about him?' Frank said. 'Has he turned up somewhere?'

Grady shook his head.

'I was sure that he would. He'll need a hospital. Nobody's blaming me for letting him walk, though. Wasn't my job, they keep saying.'

Grady shook his head. 'It was the right thing to do,' he said again. 'And I need to explain that to you.'

'I get it, Grady.'

'No, Frank. No, you do not.'

And Grady finally opened his mouth and let the truth out.

'I WAS SEVENTEEN YEARS OLD,' Frank said when he was done. It was the first thing he'd said in a long time, Grady talking fast, trying to rush out as much as he could before Frank blew up.

He never blew up. Just listened and didn't show a thing.

'I know,' Grady said. 'You were a child, and we—'

'You loaded me up and pointed me at Devin.' Frank stood and walked to the window. There was a flat-bottomed boat within sight, divers adjusting their masks. 'You are a bastard,' he said, without any venom or energy.

'I'm going to resign.'

'I don't care about that. Kudos on a job well done, Grady. You set out to convince me that Devin deserved retribution, get me fired up about it, *consumed* by it. Well, you got the job done.'

'I want you to know—'

'I came up here to kill the guy for no reason, is what you tell me now. But he's still a piece of garbage. You know that. Maybe I should have gone ahead and done it.'

Grady shook his head. 'No. We didn't want *you* to go after him. We thought that you might know something and we needed to push the right buttons to see if—'

'I had my reasons. Now I don't. But other people have still got theirs, right? So maybe I should have done it for their reasons. Why are theirs any less valid than mine?'

Grady was quiet. Frank said, 'How many sorts of crimes has Devin been involved with, you think?'

'I don't know, Frank. What, dozens?'

'Dozens,' Frank said, nodding. 'And how many deaths?'

'The same. There's a reason we wanted him so bad, Frank.'

'Yeah. There were plenty of reasons.' Frank looked around the cabin. 'I had him here with a gun in his mouth and my finger on the trigger. And if the son of a bitch hadn't looked like he was dying, I'd probably have pulled it.'

'It's good that you didn't.'

'Is it? I don't want to be the one who has to decide.'

They stayed in the living room for a long time without speaking and, eventually, Grady stood and said he was leaving.

'If Devin didn't give my father up,' Frank said, 'somebody did.'

Grady was silent.

'It was an anonymous tip, says the legend. From someone close to him.' Grady had given his word never to reveal that source. But surely Frank was entitled to it by now. 'I'll tell you, and this time it'll be the truth.'

Frank was shaking his head. 'No, I would like . . . not to know.'

Grady nodded, and he left, and he did not tell him. Would never tell him, or anyone, about that day when an attractive woman whose dark hair and skin were contrasted by striking blue eyes came into his office and said, 'I would like to talk with you about my husband. I love him, but he's going to ruin my son, Mr Morgan. And I cannot let that happen.'

THEY LET EZRA OUT of the hospital seven days after he went in, and Frank picked him up in his own truck, drove south from Minocqua, the highway filled with cars towing boats, the first weekend of fishing season under way.

'How've the dogs been?' Ezra asked.

'Disgruntled.'

'Good. Nice to see some concern on the home front.'

'The doctors say when you can get back to work?'

'They might have, but I don't recall listening. I think it'll be soon.'

Frank had already tried offering apologies to Ezra, tried to explain how he'd have handled things differently if he'd understood the situation, how he should never have believed Vaughn. Ezra cut him off every time. 'What about Devin? Any word?'

Frank just shook his head.

'He's got the right sort of friends for this,' Ezra said. 'People who can help him disappear. You talked to Nora?'

'Called a few times. Haven't heard back from her.'

'She still in town? Or has she gone home, after all this?'

'I'm not sure.'

'How about you? Headed home soon?'

'Headed where?' Frank answered, and Ezra nodded, and they drove on in silence.

Nora didn't get back to the shop for five days. The cops had taken Vaughn's Lexus, and now she had no cars but the Mazda Jerry had refused to repaint. She tried to finish it herself, spent three days creating runs and streaks and sanding them back down, then starting over and making it worse. She finally called another shop and towed it over to them.

And then it was just her and an empty shop. No business, no employees. More bills on the way.

Frank Temple called a few times, left messages. Why did he want to see her before he took off again? Did he think there was some sort of closure for this, some neat wrap-up to such awful events? She didn't call back.

Her mother called daily, first to urge her to return home, then to demand it. Nora said she was considering her options, and then she called the local newspaper and put out an ad for a new body man and painter.

The ad ran for a week, and she interviewed two guys. Told them she'd be in touch, but the truth was they couldn't handle the job and she couldn't pay them even if they could. That Friday, she told her father honestly for the first time, No, we don't have any cars. His face fell, and she responded with a lie, promising some were on the way in.

The shop was lost and she supposed she should have felt relief. She could go home now. So why did she feel so damn sad? Her father was part of it, of course—the idea of leaving him in this town without any family still haunted her—but today she was more aware than ever of what had always helped her linger: she didn't know what came next. It was that simple, that sad. While her peers were caught up with families or careers, she still waited for the road sign that told her which way to turn. Tomahawk, and Stafford Collision and Custom, had provided a welcome delay. Now the delay was past and the uncertainty remained, and worst of all, she'd failed. The family shop was closing, and not on Stafford terms.

The next Monday found her alone in the empty shop. The phone rang several times, but it was always a long-distance number. Reporters, not customers. She was getting ready to leave for lunch when Frank Temple came through the door.

'Hey,' he said, letting it close softly behind him.

'Hi,' she said. 'I know, I owe you a call. It's been hectic, though. I figured you might have left town already.'

'No.' He looked around, taking in the quiet place, her sitting alone in the little office. She felt pathetic, didn't want him to see it.

'How are things?' he said, and she meant to tell him they were fine, she really did, but somehow the truth came out instead. She was going to have to close the shop, head back to Madison or maybe, much as she hated to think of it, to her stepfather's house in Minneapolis.

'I saw your ad,' he said. 'If you hired somebody new, couldn't you get it going again?'

'The truth is, I couldn't afford to pay anyone until we'd made some money, and really, I need two people to do what Jerry did.'

'How much would you need to make it till then?'

What was this about? She didn't like the question. 'I don't know,' she said, 'but it's more money than a bank will loan a company that's already overextended and has no employees and no customers.'

He nodded, just taking all this in as if it were minor stuff. 'I was thinking I'd like to invest in something,' he said. 'I've got some money left, and rather than burn through it, I thought it would be a good idea to put it into something promising. An up-and-coming business, maybe, or one with some history. Some tradition. You know, a proven entity.'

She was shaking her head before he was done. 'I don't take handouts. It's generous, a very sweet offer, but no.'

'I don't give handouts,' he said. 'Maybe you missed the investment part of what I said? I'm thinking of something different entirely. More like being a partner.'

'I don't want a partner. If I can't do it alone, I'll just get out.'

'You know,' Frank said, 'being strong doesn't necessarily mean being alone.'

She looked at him for a long time, then pulled her chair closer to the desk. 'Dad told me the only partner worth having was one who'd get his hands dirty, share the job side by side.'

'Then I'll share the job.'

'You don't know anything about fixing cars.'

'No,' he said, 'but we can find some people who do. And I'm pretty sure I could drive a plough in the winter.'

'In the winter.' She said it carefully, a verification.

'Made more sense to me that way. But if you want me to drive the damn plough in the summer, Nora, I'll do it.'

He stopped talking and looked her in the eye, and she saw something surprising there, a deep and powerful quality of need.

'You could think about it,' he said. 'You could do that much, couldn't you? I don't want to go. I'd like to stay here. It's the best chance I've got.'

They sealed the deal on a handshake. It was a start.

MICHAEL KORYTA

Date of birth: September 20, 1982
Favourite crime movie: *The Maltese Falcon*
Hobby: hiking (that's when I get my ideas)

The spare prose and sombre stoicism of Michael Koryta's mysteries are the very essence of a style of crime writing called 'noir'. This popular tough-guy genre had its origins in the United States during the Depression-hit 1930s when it was epitomised by writers such as Raymond Chandler and Dashiell Hammett. When Hollywood later translated classic detective stories by these authors into film, French critics termed the genre 'film noir', or black film, and the name stuck.

Perhaps the most surprising thing about the award-winning Michael Koryta is that he is so young. At only twenty-six, he is the author of four novels, and his first, *Tonight I Said Goodbye*, appeared when he was just twenty-one. Hailed in the US as 'one of the best mystery debuts' of 2004 by *Library Journal*, it was nominated for a prestigious Edgar Award and won the Great Lakes Book Award for best mystery.

That dazzling debut launched the Lincoln Perry private-eye series, which is set in Cleveland, Ohio, Koryta's father's hometown, and which now also includes *Sorrow's Anthem* (2006) and *A Welcome Grave* (2007). His most recent book, *Envy the Night* (2008), is a stand-alone mystery, and the product of a writing class Koryta took from famous American fiction writer Dennis Lehane, author of *Mystic Lake* and *Shutter Island*, among others.

Another feature of Koryta's career, and one that raises eyebrows, is that the author himself is a licensed private investigator, working part-time for the Trace Agency of Bloomington, Indiana, where he began his training in the field as soon as he left high school. What better training for a crime writer? Together with Koryta's degree in criminal justice, his experience as a crime reporter and his other current role as a teacher at Indiana University's School of Journalism, it looks like a perfect portfolio.

How did it all start? Again, with Dennis Lehane: 'When I was sixteen,' says Koryta, 'I read Lehane's novel *Gone, Baby, Gone*, and it was the book that blew me away to the point that I put it down and said, "I have to try to do something like this; I have to write in this genre". Raymond Chandler and Dashiell Hammet hooked me on it, too, and then I moved on to modern writers like Lehane, Crais, Pelecanos, James Lee Burke, Michael Connelly, Robert B. Parker and Elmore Leonard. Lehane's books have been particularly inspiring to me as a writer, and Leonard's essay on fiction writing, with his Ten Rules, was influential. Stephen King's book *On Writing* came out while I was still in high school and it made a dramatic difference in my appreciation for the craft of writing and my approach to the task. I believe it is the finest book on writing that I've ever read, and cannot recommend it highly enough.'

True to his own 'noir' style, the noir mystery, Koryta loves the atmospheric detective films of the 1940s and 1950s. 'I grew up watching old crime movies, because my dad was a fan of the genre, from Humphrey Bogart and that type of noir to Alfred Hitchcock suspense.' But Koryta, a master of the sombre and suspenseful, also knows how to laugh. His favourite television series include not only *The Sopranos* but also *Seinfeld*, 'the best sitcom that ever aired,' he says.

What does he think about what other people think about his fiction? 'I try not to worry too much about the things people say about my writing, whether they be praise or criticism. Reading is subjective, everyone has their own tastes, and the minute you get too down about a jab from one critic or too cocky over the praise of another is the minute you begin to lose focus on the task at hand. The comments that have meant the most to me, by far, are the comments from other writers, particularly those whose work I've been reading and admiring for a long time.'

'Reading is subjective . . . the minute you get too down about a jab from one critic or too cocky over the praise of another, is the minute you begin to lose focus on the task at hand.'

Unlike many writers, Koryta doesn't find it helpful to start work early in the day. 'I know some writers love to work in the early part of the morning, around dawn, but for me that's never been an option. I'm just not enough of a morning person in terms of mood or creative energy to pull that off. I don't write in long sessions, either, but in fairly short, intense bursts. I almost always have headphones on and music playing while I write.' And the workspace? 'A desk with a computer on it,' he says. 'There's a window above it, but I don't notice that when the writing is going well.'

And does he miss the creative work when it's done? 'I find that the time spent writing is always enjoyable, and the time away from the book is when the negative emotions begin to creep into my head. When I am not writing, I tend to worry about plot direction, character development, and so on. When I am writing, all of that fades away and it's just me and the characters.'

For the
Love of Julie
Ann Ming

'My daughter Julie was beautiful from the day she was born. She had a dry sense of humour and an infectious giggle. She liked dancing, gymnastics, and doing people's hair. She was a fantastic mother to her little boy Kevin . . . She was full of life and fun to to be with. She was my little girl and I adored her.'

Words spoken by Ann Ming, remembering Julie, her daughter, who disappeared from her Teesside home in November 1989.

This is Ann's remarkable story . . .

Chapter One
Julie's Arrival

In Middlesborough in the late 1960s it was the custom for mothers who had had one straightforward birth in hospital to deliver their babies at home after that, which is a daunting prospect for anyone, even for someone like me who prides herself on being a down-to-earth Yorkshirewoman. What if something goes wrong? What if the baby comes early, or gets stuck? When a newborn baby's life could be at stake it is very comforting to know you have all the technology and expertise of a well-equipped hospital at your disposal, rather than one midwife, a panicking husband and a pan full of boiling water. That option, however, was not on offer to us.

My mind was buzzing with fears of imagined disasters and imminent emergency ambulance rides as the pain started to build up. My mam took my two-year-old son Gary off for a walk in his pushchair to keep him out of the way. The midwife had popped in when the contractions started in the morning but then she disappeared off, breezily saying she would be back at lunch time. No doubt she had plenty of other patients to tend to; for her it was just another day's work, even if it meant a lot more to us.

By eleven o'clock I had to go upstairs and lie down; memories of just how painful the whole childbirth business is were coming rushing back with every spasm. How is it that we women manage to forget all that agony almost the moment it is over? I could hear Charlie making frantic phone calls downstairs as I concentrated on the pain upstairs, wanting it all to be over but not wanting the baby to come before the midwife got back.

The girl answering the phone at the doctor's surgery must have asked Charlie if I was starting to push.

'Are yer starting to push?' he shouted up.

'No,' I yelled back.

'Well, if the baby's born,' the girl told him, 'just wrap it in a blanket, wipe its eyes and put it on the side. Don't try to cut the cord.'

'This is good,' I heard him grumbling as he put the phone down. 'I pay me National Health stamps and there's nobody here when you need them!'

The doctor sauntered in at about twelve to take a look and immediately saw that I was ready to deliver, whether the midwife was there or not.

'I'd better go and wash my hands,' he said, but just then the midwife bustled in and he decided to go downstairs to keep Charlie company instead.

'I'll wait around in case you need stitches afterwards,' he said.

I dare say the two men were brewing up for a cup of tea as we women got down to work in the bedroom.

The birth itself was blissful and peaceful. 'She's arrived like an angel!' exclaimed the midwife, as Julie emerged into the world with her arms folded beatifically across her chest. 'My goodness,' she marvelled, 'I've never seen a baby with so much hair.'

She was right: a thick mop of blue-black hair stretched down the back of the new baby's neck, a clear sign of her Chinese ancestry.

'She'll probably lose it all over the next few weeks,' she said, 'before she grows it back in again.'

But she didn't lose it. Julie's hair just grew thicker and darker and more lustrous with every passing week. After a month we had to push a hair-slide into the side to keep it out of her eyes at an age when most babies have no more than a few tufts of fluff. She was beautiful from the day she was born, with a slight oriental look from her dad's side of the family.

I needed a few stitches after the delivery so Charlie was sent back to the kitchen to boil some needles for the doctor in a pan of water that he'd been preparing to cook some vegetables in for our lunch.

It was a Wednesday, February 22, 1967. 'Wednesday's child is full of woe,' as the saying goes, which is what we used to say to Julie later whenever she was moaning about something or other. We could never have imagined how prophetic that silly little saying would turn out to be. As I lay in bed that afternoon, holding her in my arms for the first time, I never for a second would have believed that this tiny, helpless baby would die before I did, or that she would die in one of the most terrible ways possible. Such a thought would have been simply unbearable.

When your children are small you keep an eye on them most of the time, although even then accidents can happen or terrible luck can befall them. But once they have grown up and left the nest you can do nothing but have faith that they will be all right, that they will not take too many risks or make too many bad judgments. And be there for them if things go wrong. But no matter how grown-up and capable they become, I don't think a mother ever loses the instinct to guard her babies and fight for their safety and their rights against the rest of the world. Thankfully, not many have to do it in the horrific circumstances that I would have to.

Chapter Two
Meeting Charlie Ming

I first spotted Charlie Ming in 1962, sitting with a group of other men in a Chinese restaurant in Middlesborough called The Red Sun. I was just sixteen but had been out of school for a year and was more than ready for a bit of life. It was an exciting place for a young girl to be because there weren't many Chinese restaurants around in those days and people didn't have the money to eat out much at all.

Everything going on around me seemed exotic and foreign, including the men at the nearby table and especially Charlie. I couldn't tell how old he was, but it certainly wouldn't have occurred to me that he was twenty years older than me. I'm not sure I gave the question any thought at all. I'd never met a Chinese man before—and in our area they were still viewed by most people with considerable suspicion. These were the days before race relations acts and political correctness; people still clung to their comforting prejudices and spoke their minds to the point of rudeness.

It all seems a bit like ancient history now, even though it was only forty-six years ago. This was the year when a young Nelson Mandela was imprisoned in South Africa and when Marilyn Monroe was found dead in suspicious circumstances in Hollywood. It had also just become the Chinese Year of the Tiger, traditionally said to be a year of massive change. It certainly was for me!

I'd been invited to the restaurant that night because a friend of mine was going out with one of the waiters and wanted me to go along with her for moral support. I'd been keen to accept the invitation, wanting to have a look at him. Boyfriends were still a very new experience for both of us, objects of considerable mystery and curiosity.

The group of Chinese men who had caught my eye were sitting at a table near ours. To my young, inexperienced eyes they all looked the same, except for Charlie. Something about him kept drawing my attention to him. Apart from anything else, he was very good-looking.

'Who's that?' I asked my friend's boyfriend as he hovered round the table, bringing us food and flirting a little nervously at the same time.

'That's Charlie. His mother's English and his father's Chinese.'

'Not a bad result when you mix them,' I said cheerfully, and probably quite loudly, assuming that none of the men would be able to speak English.

'Oh, thanks very much,' Charlie piped up in a thick Yorkshire accent, bringing the blood rushing to my face.

'You speak English?' I asked, shocked.

'I should hope so.' He grinned at my discomfort.

From that moment I was hooked, fascinated by someone who looked so mysterious and oriental but sounded so down-to-earth. As I got to know him and we told one another about our families, I found out his father had been the first Chinese man to come to the Middlesborough area, having travelled over from China to Birkenhead as a ship's steward. It sounded like something from the movies, suggesting worlds beyond anything that my friends or I had ever experienced, or could even imagine. None of us had ever travelled outside our own home towns, let alone gone abroad.

When he came ashore, Charlie's dad met an English girl, married her and decided to stay. He set up his own Chinese laundry, something that Chinese immigrants were doing all over the world in the first part of the twentieth century. It must have been a good business to be in then, in the days before washing machines or launderettes had been invented.

Charlie had had a difficult upbringing. He didn't really belong to either nationality—English or Chinese—so he was always the outsider, watching and smiling patiently, learning to be philosophical about life. Charlie never expected life to be easy and he knew that you had to stick up for yourself or other people would walk all over you.

There was an immediate spark between us that night and he asked me out on a date. Unlike boys of my own age he had a car, and on that first date he drove me over to Whitby for a day out. After I'd been out with him a couple of times I didn't think any more about his Chinese origins than I did about the age gap between us. He was just Charlie, the man for me. But other people didn't adapt quite so quickly and we got our fair share of racial abuse when we were out together.

I'd been born and brought up in Billingham, which was then not much more than a village on the outskirts of Middlesborough. Nothing much happened in Billingham apart from the giant ICI chemical works, where my dad worked as a research chemist. The factory covered several hundred acres at the side of the town and provided employment for thousands of locals. It's hard to imagine when you look at the wastelands around Billingham now just what a huge factory complex it once was, dominating the landscape for miles around with its gleaming towers and chimneys, belching smoke and steam, all part of the 'white heat of technology' that politicians liked to talk about in the 1960s.

My dad died very suddenly at the age of sixty-two after having a massive brain haemorrhage. I was only fifteen at the time and I was completely devastated. It was such a shock because he hadn't been ill at all; it came right out of the blue. Dad had always pampered me and I idolised him. I was an only child and he and Mam had adopted me as a baby, but neither of them ever let me feel for a moment that I wasn't their daughter. I couldn't even boil an egg by the time he died because he would insist on doing everything for me. We never argued about anything. Maybe that was why I was attracted to an older man like Charlie—especially one who was happy to do all the cooking.

Dad had looked after Mam well, too. She had never had a job outside the house that I could remember, had never written a cheque or paid a bill herself; he took care of everything like that. I think most men of that generation did in those days.

Once he'd gone I automatically took on the role of doing all these practical things for her, which meant I had to grow up a lot quicker than I would have done otherwise. That part of it didn't worry me. I just got on with things, but I still missed him terribly.

I didn't tell my mother about Charlie for a while, knowing that she was going to find it a bit difficult to get used to. It wasn't until a few months after I first went out with him that we were spotted together in Middlesborough by a friend of the family, who gleefully reported the news to Mam. She went mad at me when I got home.

'You've been seen in Middlesborough with a Chinaman,' she announced the moment I walked through the door. 'Your father would turn in his grave. You know what's going to happen to you, don't you? He'll get you on a slow boat to China and he'll fill you full of opium. I'll tell you something else: they breed like rabbits and they're full of TB!'

There'd been an outbreak of tuberculosis in Hong Kong a few years before, and this added to all the myths and prejudices that surrounded the Chinese in those days. The fact that Charlie had never been outside Yorkshire in his life didn't seem to make any difference to Mam's fears about disease-carrying foreigners whom she imagined pouring off the boats like rats.

Although I got on well with Mam and Dad, I had become a bit of a rebel in my teens, and I knew my own mind right from the start. When it came to choosing the man I wanted to be with I certainly wasn't going to take any notice of anyone else's prejudices. By the time Mam found out about us I already knew Charlie was a good catch and I wasn't going to give him up just to please her and a few neighbours who might disapprove of a mixed marriage. I didn't argue with her all that much; I just took no notice of her tales of doom and gloom and carried on with my life.

'Well, you might as well bring him home then,' she huffed eventually, once she realised I wasn't going to change my mind about the danger I was putting myself in by consorting with a 'foreign devil'.

Of course, the moment she met him Charlie worked the same gruff, twinkly charm on her that he had on me and a year later we got married, by which time she couldn't praise him highly enough. He was always happy to do any odd jobs she needed doing, he'd include her without being asked when we were going on holiday or for a day out, and I'd sometimes arrive at her house to find he'd popped in for a coffee and a chat with her.

'I couldn't wish for a better son-in-law,' she would always tell her friends, cutting off their prejudices before they could leave their lips.

If I ever grumbled to her about anything Charlie had said or done she would immediately jump to his defence, making it clear she believed I was lucky to have landed such a good man. Although it sometimes felt as though they were ganging up on me, I was relieved we all got on well; if you can't keep your immediate family together around you, what hope do you have of leading a happy life? I've always believed that family is the most important thing for anyone. Perhaps knowing that I was adopted and feeling lucky at being taken in by two such loving parents made me more appreciative than others, who might take such things for granted.

It was Charlie who wanted to get married and start a family quickly because he was already in his late thirties. He wanted to have children while he was still young enough to enjoy them and I was quite happy to go along with him, thinking there would be plenty of time for me to work and have a life of my own once the children were at school. We had only about twelve people at the wedding, which made it feel more like the Last Supper, because none of my other relatives were speaking to me, even though they knew Mam was now happy about the match. I wasn't too bothered. If they felt like that I didn't want anything to do with them anyway.

It wasn't just the family who didn't like the idea of a mixed marriage. When we bought our first house in Acklam, a nice area outside Middlesborough, the next-door neighbour almost immediately got together a petition to persuade us to move straight back out again. The first I knew of it was when she turned up on the doorstep with a letter that she had persuaded five of the other neighbours to sign. It was a shock because I'd thought we were all getting on very well whenever we talked face to face.

'We don't mind you,' she said, 'but it's when your husband's friends come to visit that it lowers the tone of the area.'

Shocked, since I had always found Charlie's friends very pleasant, I told Charlie I thought we should move after that, not wanting to live somewhere we weren't wanted. But he wasn't having any of it.

'No.' He was adamant. 'We're staying here.'

When I thought about it I realised he was right. Who was to say the next set of neighbours wouldn't be even more hostile? We couldn't allow them to bully us like that so we took the petition to a solicitor and asked his advice. He wrote to all the neighbours who had signed it, pointing out the error of their ways. I guess they hadn't had their hearts in it—maybe they had just done it to please the woman next door—because they all apologised after that, even her. Perhaps they assumed we would just pack up and scurry off into the night, and anyway, ordinary people were still intimidated by official-looking letters from lawyers then. Like all potential bullies, their resolve crumbled as soon as they saw we were going to fight back. Everything settled down after that. It was really just a question of sticking up for ourselves, something we would become very good at over the years.

We had our first child, Gary, in 1965, a couple of years after we married, by which time I'd just turned nineteen. Julie came along in 1967 and then Angela made her appearance in 1969. With three small children running around, the house was soon too small for us all and we put it up for sale. The woman who had organised the petition when we first moved in asked me how much we were asking for it.

'That depends,' I replied.

'Depends on what?'

'Depends on the colour of the buyer's skin,' I said. 'The darker they are, the cheaper they can have the house.'

Although I was only joking we did end up selling to a man who had a half-African wife, so that probably confirmed the neighbours' worst fears about how the neighbourhood had now gone completely to pot. Times were changing in so many different ways.

Gary was always the mischief-maker among the three children, while Angela took after me, brimming with confidence and always having plenty to say for herself. Julie was the quietest, shyest one of the bunch. She didn't make friends quite as easily as the others, but once someone had become her friend she tended to keep them in her life for a long time.

As she grew up she looked a lot like the few pictures we had of Charlie's English mam, although her pretty, almond-shaped eyes gave a hint of the oriental blood that flowed in her veins, showing she was definitely a member of the 'Ming dynasty'.

While the children were young we lived in a house round the corner from our first home in Acklam. Charlie worked for Shell as a 'heavy goods fitter', which is another way of saying he was a mechanic working on their lorries. He worked hard and was a good provider, but bringing up three children was never going to be cheap. From soon after Julie was born, I worked on Friday and Saturday nights at the cash desk of a Chinese restaurant in Billingham. The restaurant was owned by one of Charlie's friends and they used to get quite a few actors and performers coming in from the nearby theatre after the shows finished. (We didn't call them celebrities then, although I guess they were because they were usually off the telly.) I'd intended to help out at the restaurant for a week and ended up staying fifteen years, mainly because I enjoyed the buzz of the place.

Once Angela started school I found I had a bit of time on my hands so I got myself a job at the local hospital as an auxiliary nurse to earn us a bit of extra money. I was lucky that my mam could look after the kids while

I did my shifts—usually twelve till nine—and Charlie took over when he got in. I had always liked the idea of being a nurse, even when I was a little girl. Meeting Charlie and starting a family had only temporarily distracted me from doing something about it.

Soon I was working in the operating theatre, doing a bit of everything. Despite having always thought that I wanted to be out on the wards, chatting to the patients, I loved the work and I quickly got used to dealing with the temperamental surgeons, men whom everyone treated as if they were gods. Hospital life was still very formal in those days with a strict hierarchy. The surgeons shouted a lot and none of us ever dared to answer them back; we were too busy running around doing their bidding.

Julie was never any trouble to us or to her teachers at school. She took up gymnastics and soon proved able to fold herself in two and make her body do all sorts of things that seemed impossible to me. She was a good dancer as well, being small and slightly built.

Of all our children she was the one who could always wrap Charlie round her little finger the easiest. If the others wanted anything they would tell her to go and ask him for it, knowing he could never refuse her anything. It was a bit like my relationship had been with my dad, I suppose. She was a proper daddy's girl and I think maybe he saw a bit of his mam in her.

We led a very normal, contented family life, with all the usual ups and downs, petty rows and reconciliations, family treats and family chores. Every year when the kids were young we used to go down to Devon or Cornwall for our holidays, always taking my mam with us. For seven or eight years in a row we hired a big caravan in Looe. On our final trip there, with Charlie's brother and his wife, we had fourteen days of solid rain and decided that next time we would go to Majorca for some guaranteed sun. Julie was eighteen by then and the highlight of the holiday for her was buying herself a white leather suit that she wore almost constantly once we got back. It looked terrific on her.

We used to go out as a family in the summer afternoons too, once Charlie had finished his shifts and the kids were home from school. I would ring Mam up and she would catch a bus over and join us for a run over the moors. All of us would pile into our old blue and white van, Mam sitting in state in the front with Charlie, and the rest of us rattling around in the back with no seats. We even had the pram in with us when we still needed it.

When the kids were in their teens, Charlie and I took the opportunity to travel to China with a couple of friends, leaving the kids with my mam. We spent a month in Hong Kong and then a week in Canton, where Charlie's dad had originally come from. In Hong Kong we stayed with Charlie's aunt in a village in the New Territories called Fan Ling, where I was the only European face to be seen and no one spoke any English. The streets bristled with life as people went about their daily business on bicycles and carts, and mah jong was being played on every corner.

Then we travelled to a village called Sha Tau Kok on the border with China, where a friend of ours lived. I stood out even more there and I got used to feeling like the Pied Piper of Hamelin, followed by a trail of curious kids wherever I went, everyone wanting to touch my blonde hair.

My mother was living in a council bungalow in Billingham at that time and the rent kept going up every year, leaving her very short of cash.

'Why don't we buy the house as an investment?' Charlie suggested. 'Then your mam can live there rent-free.'

At first the council refused to sell to us because they said the bungalow was supposed to be for old people, but I'd known the area a long time and knew that wasn't true, so I wrote to the Secretary of State in Westminster and got the council overruled. I've never been willing just to accept what people tell me simply because they're in a position of authority, but I had no idea then how far my stubbornness would one day be tested.

We eventually bought the bungalow in the April of 1980 but Mam had a stroke a couple of months later, which turned all our carefully laid plans upside down. She was still able to shuffle about on her feet once she'd recovered, but we soon realised there was no way she was going to be able to look after herself for much longer, so we sold our house in Acklam, had the bungalow extended and moved the whole family in there together. It was an easier option than trying to uproot her from her own house.

If I had known how difficult looking after Mam was going to be I don't know if I would have had the courage to take on the job for those last few years. By the end she was incontinent and away with the fairies most of the time. The kids were always good at helping out with her; we couldn't have done it without their support. We developed a routine of caring. I had Mam during the week and went to work at the hospital at weekends, when Charlie and the girls would take over. Charlie never complained. In fact, it was him who insisted that she stay with us and not be put in a home. She had done too much for us over the years for us to think of abandoning her to the mercy of strangers. So we soldiered on until she died five years later in 1985.

With Mam gone and the children growing up, Charlie and I thought that perhaps now life would get a bit easier for us. We had some money in the bank and a chance to stand back and think about what we wanted to do with the next part of our lives together. Charlie decided to take early retirement from Shell and invest some of his money in buying a catering trailer, which he set up in a lay-by on the A66 to Darlington.

We worked hard and we were proud of how we had brought up the kids. Now we felt we could relax a bit and enjoy ourselves. How wrong could we have been?

Chapter Three
Our Julie Grows Up

When Julie was sixteen, just after leaving school, she met a Billingham boy called Andrew at a local youth club. She was the same age as I had been when I met Charlie but somehow she seemed much less mature than I had imagined I was at that age. Maybe we all kid ourselves that we are more grown-up than we are when we first start to spread our wings.

Although she was never outgoing in a crowd, Julie was a bit of a rebel in the way she dressed. She always liked to wear weird clothes, and at that time she was going through her Boy George phase, dressing like him and doing her hair the same way. She would get Angela to tie rags in it and then put a black hat on the top of the whole thing. She would pinch Charlie's white shirts and cut the collars off and wear black gloves and lots of eyeliner to go out in the evenings. Once she was out on the dance floor all her usual inhibitions seemed to vanish. It's strange how some people can be shy and introverted in some ways and extroverted in others; when she was dancing she really seemed to come into herself.

She liked to wear really high heels to try to make herself look taller, fed up that she was so much smaller than Gary and Angela. As a result she didn't always choose the most practical shoes for everyday life, but that never worried her. I went into Middlesborough with her once when she had on these bright-orange high heels.

'My feet are killing me,' she grumbled after we'd been walking round the shops for a bit. 'Will you swap, just for ten minutes, Mam?'

'Only ten minutes,' I said firmly.

What is it about being a mother that makes you willing to put yourself through agony rather than see one of your children in pain, even when they have inflicted it on themselves in the first place? A mixture of natural instincts and motherly love, I suppose. I was still wobbling along in these ridiculous bright-orange stilettos when we bumped into someone from my work and I had to do some fast explaining.

Julie started training as a hairdresser when she left school. She had always been interested in messing around with her own hair, dying it shocking pinks and blues long before this was generally accepted, so it seemed like a good choice of career for her. Her hair was still incredibly thick, just as it had been when she was a baby, and when she permed it, it became even more spectacular. Big curly perms were all the fashion in the 1980s, and Julie's was the biggest and curliest. When she came home with blue hair after my mother had had her third stroke, Mam was convinced it was a hat.

'What a lovely hat,' she kept saying. 'What a lovely colour.'

'It's not a hat, Mam,' I told her, 'it's her damned hair!'

Charlie and I liked Andrew from the first time Julie brought him home. He was very relaxed about life and good at gently humouring her if she was in one of her moods. He was a couple of years older than her and working as a painter and decorator. Having been married for nearly twenty years to Charlie, who was a strong and sometimes controlling character, I could appreciate the attraction of a man who was a bit more easy-come, easy-go. Andrew just fitted into our family as if he had always been there.

In 1985, the year Mam died, Julie and Andrew got married and moved into a council house five minutes' drive from us at 27 Grange Avenue.

I was very happy for them. I'd been born and brought up in the area myself and knew it well, so it felt as though Julie was staying close to her roots. It was a lovely wedding and when I watched Julie and Andrew dancing to her favourite song, 'Ave Maria', at the reception I felt like the complete proud mum, happy to have brought up such a pretty girl and to be able to see her settling down with a nice man. She looked so beautiful and so joyful as they whirled round the dance floor that it didn't seem possible they wouldn't have a wonderful happy life together.

Even though Julie was now a married woman it often felt as though she hadn't left home at all. Gary had moved out and started work as a bricklayer and, although Angela was still living with us, she was very independent and had just starting her training as a dental nurse. But our Julie wouldn't let go of the apron strings.

'Are you in, our Mam?' she would ring and ask at least once a day. 'I'll pop round then.'

Sometimes she would come round for her tea, then go home and ring half an hour later, even though she didn't have anything new to say. Although I would get exasperated with her sometimes if I was trying to get on with doing something else, I wouldn't have had it any other way; I loved having her around.

Even when I was at work she would be ringing all the time and the others in the operating theatre often used to tease me about it. They were used to her ways, though, having known her since she was little. She came into the hospital to see me one day when she was about seven months pregnant, the year after she and Andrew were married. It was the weekend and there were just three of us on duty. Nothing much was happening so we were able to pay her some attention.

'Get up on the table,' one of the other nurses told her. 'We'll get the stethoscope and see if we can hear the baby's heart beating.'

She was up on the table with her belly exposed when one of the surgeons, Mr Clark, suddenly burst into the room.

'What the bloody hell is going on in here?' he wanted to know.

'Our Julie's pregnant and we're trying to find the heartbeat,' I explained nervously.

'Oh, get out of the way,' he barked. 'I'll find it.'

Julie went bright red as he took over and found the heartbeat almost immediately. This same surgeon had been very generous when Julie was married, passing on a load of furniture that he and his wife didn't want, to go in her new home. Everyone around the hospital was good to us like that, treating us like family.

When she was close to her due date both she and Andrew came to live with us for two weeks because she wanted to be at the heart of the family at such an important time. I guess maybe she still didn't feel ready to leave the nest, even though she was soon to be a mother herself, and Andrew was always happy to go along with whatever Julie wanted.

The birth went smoothly and Julie instantly took to motherhood. A few weeks after little Kevin had arrived she and I popped out to the off-licence to buy some chocolate, leaving the baby with Andrew and Charlie.

'I feel really strange,' she said once we were away from the house. 'This is the first time I've come out without Kevin since I had him.'

'I feel like that with you,' I told her, 'even though you're married now. I don't think a mother ever feels complete without her children around her.'

'Ah, Mam,' she teased, 'but I'm a woman now.'

'Yeah, I know, but I still feel the same about you.'

When the time came to take Kevin to the mother-and-toddler group, Julie wanted me to go too. 'Ah, come on, our Mam,' she wheedled when I said I didn't think any of the other girls would be taking their mothers. 'I don't want to go on my own.'

Charlie and I were always very happy with Andrew as a son-in-law and to start with the marriage appeared to go well, especially once they had Kevin. They were both so proud of him and so anxious to do the right things. But becoming a mother seemed to bring Julie a bit more out of her shell and after a couple of years things began to go wrong between them. I think it was mostly down to them both being so young and immature—she was just eighteen and he was only twenty when they married. It's hard to sustain a marriage when neither of you knows anything about life. I think they both thought it was all going to be a bed of roses, which it never is once you've got a small child. I was young too when I married but at least Charlie was older and more experienced.

Andrew liked to go out playing football and snooker, like any young lad. That would make our Julie get all possessive and grumpy and they would end up arguing about stupid things. They were each just as bad as the other. There was one time when Andrew was obsessed with getting his car mended. Julie and I had been out shopping at Asda and when we got back we found he'd swapped their microwave for a particular engine part that he needed. She was furious, but she could be just as daft herself sometimes. She'd bought a lemon and grey striped pushchair for Kevin and one time she said she wasn't able to come out with me because his matching lemon suit wasn't dry from the wash and his others wouldn't have matched the pushchair's upholstery! They were both still just a couple of kids really.

Andrew had been doing some work at a pizza place in Station Road in Billingham. Bizarrely, the shop, which was called 'Mr Macaroni', was owned by an Iranian family. Some time around 1987, Julie started working there as well, driving a pizza delivery van in the evenings to earn some extra money. Looking back, I suppose she and Andrew had less time together then and they started drifting apart.

Things must have been worse between them than Charlie and I realised because in 1989, when he got the chance of a job down in London with his uncle, Andrew decided to take it. They both seemed to see it as the first step in a separation. Charlie and I were very sad about it, but at least we were close by to help Julie with Kevin and we never felt that Andrew was to blame for the breakup any more than she was. It was just one of those things that happens in families and you have to adjust and move on.

Julie coped quite well on her own, with us in the background to help her. On the nights she was working late she would leave Kevin to sleep over with us. It was a good arrangement for all of us because Charlie and I liked having a child around the house and we liked feeling we were helping her. She enjoyed working with the Iranians, and they obviously must have valued her as an employee.

Charlie and I had been thinking about what we should do about the bungalow now that the children were growing up. Once Gary and Julie had moved out, and Angela was getting close to leaving, we decided we didn't need such a big house so we put it up for sale. It sold before we'd found anything else to buy, so we moved into a rented property while we worked out where we would like to go next.

As the autumn of 1989 arrived I fancied a break. I've always liked going to Blackpool for holidays but Charlie doesn't much like the place, so I asked Julie if she would like to come with me for a few days away. We always had a laugh when we were together. Andrew said he would mind Kevin (he hadn't left for London by then) and we set off for some mother and daughter time. We hadn't even booked anything—you didn't have to at that time of year; we just turned up and found ourselves a bed and breakfast before setting out to enjoy the sights. Julie had always liked the fairgrounds, riding on the big dippers and all the rest, and I was happy to watch her, just as I had when they were all small children.

'I think I'll have me fortune told,' she said as we walked past a gypsy's stall in a shopping arcade. 'Do you want to come?'

'Oh, I'm not wasting my money,' I said. 'You go ahead.'

I wandered off, leaving her to it. She reappeared a few minutes later.

'That cost me five pounds,' she complained. 'She said I have a son who's going to be musical, but we all know Kevin's tone-deaf, and after that she said she couldn't tell me anything else. It was like I didn't have any future.'

That Blackpool clairvoyant will never know how right she was with her predictions that day.

Chapter Four
Our Julie Goes Missing

On Thursday, November 16, 1989, two months after our trip to Blackpool and about a month after Andrew had gone down to London to work, Julie was due to go to court in nearby Stockton to apply for a legal separation.

'Andrew and me are not going to get back together,' she told me when I asked if she was absolutely sure this was the route she wanted to follow. 'I've been to see a solicitor and he says it's best we make it official.'

Realising she had made up her mind I said I'd go with her because I thought she might need a bit of moral support.

On the 15th, the afternoon before we were due to go to the court, I went down to her house to pick up Kevin just as I normally did when she was working late, making deliveries in the pizza van. She was double-checking all the arrangements as usual. She always got anxious about things like that.

'You won't forget to call me in the morning, will you, our Mam?' she said as we were leaving the house. 'I have to be in court at ten, so we'll need to set out around nine. Ring me about half seven to make sure I'm awake.'

'Why don't you come and stay at home tonight?' I suggested. 'Then you can take your time in the morning.'

'No, I want to stay in my own house,' she said casually. 'Just don't forget to call me at seven thirty.'

'Don't worry,' I said. 'I will, and I'll be down to get you about half eight.'

How many thousands of times have I wished that I had kept on nagging her to come and stay with us that night? I'm sure I could have made her if I'd kept on at her for long enough, but it didn't seem worth arguing about at the time. After all, it was perfectly reasonable that she would want to sleep in her own bed after a long evening's work.

I'd just got back to our house with Kevin when the phone rang and I knew it would be her again, because it nearly always was.

'It's just me again, Mam,' she said. 'You won't forget to ring me in the morning, early, will you?'

'Stop worrying,' I grumbled. 'I'll be ringing you.'

That was the last time I heard her voice. There are so many things I wish I'd said in that call, but why would I have thought to say any of them since I expected to see her again in a little over twelve hours' time? I wish I could just have told her how much I loved her. I wish I could have said goodbye properly, but you can't go through life treating every phone call and every conversation as if it is going to be your last.

That night I didn't sleep well. I woke at ten past three with a horrible feeling of foreboding churning around inside my stomach. It was as if something bad was happening somewhere else, giving me premonitions. I told myself not to be stupid, that I must just have been having a bad dream or something, but still the feeling wouldn't go away and wouldn't allow me to get back to sleep. Small worries can grow like weeds in the darkest hours of the night and I hate lying in bed once I'm awake, so I got up and tip-toed downstairs, being careful not to disturb Charlie, and made myself a cup of tea. If it had been an hour earlier I would have rung Julie to check she had got in all right from work, but I assumed she would be in bed by then and asleep, so I didn't call. Eventually the feeling of dread eased a little and I went back to bed for a few hours' fitful sleep until the alarm went off.

The next morning, I got Kevin up to give him his breakfast, and dead on seven thirty I rang Julie's number. When I got no reply I assumed she must be too deeply asleep after her late shift for the phone to penetrate her dreams. Muttering irritably to myself, I strapped Kevin into the car and drove to Grange Avenue to wake his mam up and hurry her along.

As I parked and got out of the car I could see all the curtains were tightly closed upstairs and downstairs so I was pretty sure she was still fast asleep. Not expecting to be more than a couple of minutes, I left Kevin in the car and bustled up the front path, mildly exasperated with her for putting me to all this extra trouble. I knocked on the door but it had no more effect than the phone call had. I tried calling through the letterbox.

'Julie! Julie! Wake up. It's yer mam.'

I pressed my ear to the door to see if I could hear any sign of her stirring, but everything inside remained deathly silent. I didn't want the whole street to know our business if I could help it so I went round to the back of the house to see if I would have better luck attracting her attention from there. I peered in through the kitchen window, knocked on the back door and called her name again a few times. I was puzzled. Julie wasn't that deep a sleeper normally.

None of us had mobile phones in those days, so I decided to drive down to the main road where there was a phone box. Watching Kevin sitting patiently in the car, I dialled Julie's number, not sure what I would do next if she didn't pick up. The phone rang and rang. Still no answer.

Maybe, I thought, she had gone to stay with a friend at the last minute. She was, after all, a grown woman and might have met someone during the evening and decided to go home with them, although it was very out of character. But why wouldn't she have rung to tell me where she would be? She had been so insistent about me ringing to wake her at seven thirty, surely she wouldn't have forgotten so easily? Perhaps she had fallen asleep somewhere else and just didn't realise the time. All these possibilities were going through my head, but none of them seemed very likely. I drove back down to the house, with Kevin still chattering happily in his car seat. As I tried knocking and shouting through the letterbox a few more times I noticed a man over the road watching me from his window. I went across to talk to him. 'Have you seen our Julie?' I asked.

'No,' he said. 'I normally hear her coming in around one thirty when she's working. I don't remember hearing anything last night.'

You can't usually keep much secret in a small street like Grange Avenue, where night-time noises travel easily up to people's bedrooms.

Trying not to panic, I drove back down to the phone box once again and called a couple of her friends in case she had gone round to one of their houses unexpectedly for some reason. None of them had seen her or had any suggestion as to where she might be. They were as puzzled as I was. I wanted to ring the Iranians at the pizza shop to find out whether they could tell me if she had gone home after her shift, but I knew the shop wouldn't be open for hours yet so there would be no point.

I went back again to bang on the door some more, unable to think of anything else to do. Kath, the woman who lived next door, came out to see what was going on. 'I can't raise our Julie,' I told her. 'Have you heard anything in the night?'

'I never heard anything at all,' Kath said.

By this time there was a feeling growing in my guts that something was seriously wrong, but I had to keep calm because I didn't want to alarm Kevin. There just didn't seem to be any logical reason as to why Julie wouldn't be in the house. I wanted to share my worries with someone else in the family, hoping they would tell me I was being stupid and that there was an obvious explanation.

I knew Gary was working as a brickie on a job nearby in Billingham, so I drove to the site. He was obviously surprised to see me. 'What's up, our Mam?' he asked.

'I don't know where our Julie is,' I blurted as soon as I saw him.

'She phoned last night asking me over,' he said, 'but it was too late by then. I haven't heard from her since.'

His boss could see how worried I was and told Gary to go with me and sort it out. We drove back to Julie's house together. The curtains were still tightly drawn, no sign of life anywhere. We went round to the back once more and I took Kevin with me this time, not wanting to leave him in the car on his own now that the street was waking up and there were people around. We knocked and shouted, but there was still no answer.

'I need to get in,' Gary said, now obviously sharing my anxiety. 'We'll have to break something.'

There was a narrow panel of glass beside the back door, which Gary smashed and climbed through.

'Go round the front,' he told me, 'and I'll find the keys and let you in.'

I hurried back to the front door, clutching Kevin and trying to answer his stream of questions about why his uncle had just smashed his way into his mam's house. Nothing happened for what seemed to me like an age.

'What's going on, Gary?' I shouted, no longer caring who I might wake up. 'Open the door!'

A few moments later he pulled back the curtains in the front room and opened the window to talk to me. 'There's no keys in here, Mam,' he said. 'I'm just going to look upstairs.'

I stood at the window, my heart thumping as he searched the rest of the house. He was back a few minutes later, although it seemed like hours.

'There's something wrong in here, Mam,' he said, his face serious. 'Everywhere's tidy. The bed's all made and the kitchen's been cleared, everything's been put away neatly. There's no sign of our Julie anywhere.'

Julie had always been untidy and when she got out of bed in the morning she would throw the duvet back and leave it like that until she was ready to get back into it again at night. Why would she do anything different today? When she washed up in the kitchen she would always leave the stuff to drain on a rack; she never dried things up and put them away. Leaving the house like this wasn't like her.

'What about the keys?' I asked Gary through the window, the feeling of foreboding inside me making my voice croak uncomfortably in my throat.

'Can't find them anywhere,' he said.

Kevin, sensing our worry, was starting to cry. 'Where's me mammy?' he wanted to know, in his little toddler voice.

'Pass the phone out to me,' I told Gary, cuddling Kevin at the same time and trying to comfort him. 'I'm calling the police to see if there's been any accidents in the night that she could have been involved in.'

That was the only explanation I could think of, that she had been in a crash in the pizza van and was lying unconscious in a hospital somewhere with no means of identification on her. I got straight through to the station and explained that my daughter had disappeared during the night and asked if they knew of any reported accidents.

'There's been no incidents that we know about,' the duty officer said, 'and it's too soon to report someone missing. I suggest you make the house safe and go home and wait for her to phone you from wherever she is.'

I had wanted to hear something more proactive than that, but I could see it was all I was going to get for the moment. To make the house safe we were going to have to do something about the window Gary had broken. I went back to the man across the road and told him what was going on. He brought over some wood and Gary climbed back out through the window and between them they boarded it up. I was feeling so agitated, so desperate to do something positive to sort the situation out, that I could hardly stand still. I went over to talk to Kath next door, asking her to keep an eye on the house for me. If Julie came back, she was to get her to ring me straight away. I could see her son sitting in the kitchen with one of his friends. She promised to call me immediately if she saw anything at all.

Next I drove down to find Charlie at his catering van, and I was fighting to keep my panic under control. He was already open for business, serving customers through the hatch, and he looked surprised to see me hurrying over.

'Our Julie's missing,' I blurted out the moment I got to the hatch, hoping he would have some logical explanation.

'What do you mean?' He looked totally puzzled.

'I've been to the house and she's not there. I've no idea where she is.'

'I'll close up and come home,' he said, starting to pack up. Seeing him take it so seriously I knew I wasn't overreacting and my worry increased.

Once we were back at home I rang everyone I could think of to ask if they'd seen her. I made the calls as quick as possible, nervous that if I wasn't careful I would be on the phone at the moment Julie tried to ring and I would miss the call. No one I spoke to had any idea where she could be. After an hour or so I went down to the pizza shop to see if there was any sign of life yet, but the premises were still all closed up and as silent and deserted as her house.

The hours were ticking past. Julie's appointed time at the court came and went and still there was no call. It didn't seem likely now that she had just overslept somewhere, but what other explanation could there be? Charlie wasn't saying much but I could tell he was as puzzled and worried as I was. We both knew this wasn't like her, but neither of us wanted to voice the fears that were beginning to grow inside us.

In the afternoon we left Kevin with Angela and went back down to the pizza shop again. To my relief the lights were on now and we could see people moving around at the back, preparing for the evening's orders.

'Our Julie's disappeared,' I told them the moment we were in through the door. 'Which of you took her home last night?'

We must have been sounding frantic by then, and maybe they felt we were accusing them of something, because they seemed to become evasive, shrugging their shoulders and avoiding our eyes, talking among themselves in their language, which only made us even more angry and panicked. We just wanted a simple answer to the question of who had dropped Julie off at the house and when, to give us some clue as to what her movements might have been after she finished work.

'Why won't you just tell me who dropped her off last night? What's your problem?'

I couldn't understand it; every way we turned we seemed to bang into a brick wall. The police wouldn't accept she was a missing person yet and these people weren't telling us what they knew about her movements the previous night. The neighbours knew no more than we did and nor did her friends. It was as if she had been abducted by aliens and everyone was frightened to tell us the truth.

Gary and Charlie were both getting heated and frustrated by the Iranians' defensiveness and I could see there was going to be a fight, so I went out onto the pavement to get out of the way and leave them all to it. There was some angry shouting and one of the Iranians came out of the kitchen brandishing a knife sharpener, wanting to chase Charlie and Gary out of the shop. He lunged at them and there were some blows exchanged. Someone must have called the police because the next thing I knew there was a patrol car screeching to a halt outside the shop.

I tried to explain the situation, but the Iranians complained that Charlie and Gary had attacked them. After some more shouting and gesticulating, Charlie and Gary were carted off to the police station, leaving me in shock on the pavement outside. Everything had become a thousand times worse and I was frantic now.

Charlie and Gary were kept in the cells overnight. The police wouldn't tell me what was going on or whether they were going to charge them with anything. Angela and I spent the evening alone and desperate, trying to keep things normal for Kevin. Our whole world had suddenly been turned upside-down. Every hour of that night felt like an eternity.

Friday dawned and nothing had changed. Julie was still gone. We hadn't heard from her since Wednesday. The police let Charlie and Gary go and when they got home Charlie told me he had hardly slept during the night because it had been so cold and they hadn't given him a blanket. They wouldn't even let him stop off at home on the way to the station to get the blood-pressure tablets that he needed to take every day. It was all adding to my feeling that the entire world had turned against us.

Charlie and Gary were sent home without any apology or explanation. It was only later, when we made a point of asking, that the police told us that charges against them had been dropped. I probably would have had a lot more to say about the matter if I hadn't been so beside myself with worry about Julie, and desperate to get the police to help us.

Once they realised they weren't in any sort of trouble, one of the Iranians admitted that he had dropped Julie home at about one thirty in the morning, and that he had seen her put her key in the door before he had driven away. At last we had a piece of the jigsaw, which we could use to start building a picture of what might have happened during the night. But the information didn't make the overall picture any clearer; if anything, it made it even more confusing. If Julie had been in the house at one thirty, how could she just have been spirited away between then and seven thirty?

The feeling of foreboding in my stomach was a hundred times worse than it had been the day before. Something had definitely gone very badly wrong and it was time to insist that the police became involved in the search, whether they wanted to or not. We drove to Billingham police station and found a woman sergeant on the desk.

'Our daughter's disappeared,' I told her, fighting to hold myself together.

'Disappeared?' she asked, one eyebrow arched sceptically, her jaw methodically chewing on a piece of gum.

'Yes,' I said. 'I want to report her missing.'

'When did she go missing?'

'I last saw her the day before yesterday, in the afternoon.'

'It's too soon to report her missing,' she said, still chewing. 'There's probably a logical explanation.'

'Like what?' I asked.

'She probably came home from work and decided to go to a nightclub.' She shrugged. 'Maybe she got drunk and she's sleeping it off somewhere.'

'For a day and a half? She wouldn't do that,' I protested. 'She's got a young child. She was due to appear in court yesterday morning.'

'Listen,' Charlie interrupted and I could hear from the gruffness of his voice that he was getting annoyed again. 'Our daughter's disappeared mysteriously and we want to know what's happened to her. If you won't take our statement we'll go to the main police station in Stockton.'

Other officers were appearing from behind the scenes to help the desk sergeant with what must by then have seemed like a pair of difficult customers. To pacify us, they promised they would send someone round to take a statement from us the next morning.

I hardly slept at all that night either. My mind was whirring over all the terrible possibilities, picturing unimaginable scenes as the hours ticked past. I knew for sure that something really bad must have happened but I felt totally helpless; half of me wanted to get out and scour every street in the area and the other half didn't want to move from the phone in case she called.

Kevin was crying most of the time, wanting to know where his mammy was, sensing the tension among the grown-ups. We were finding it really hard to come up with cheerful answers to his questions or to think of anything to say that might placate him. Distracting a small child when you are already distracted yourself is almost impossible, but we did our best.

We rang Andrew's mum and dad and asked them to get in touch with Andrew down in London because we didn't have a contact number for him. There was just a chance Julie could have turned up there. Perhaps she had changed her mind about the whole separation thing; but if that was the case, why hadn't she rung to tell me?

They rang back after speaking to him to tell us Andrew knew no more about where Julie could be than we did. It didn't surprise me but it meant one more avenue of hope had been closed off.

The next morning, Saturday, a policeman and woman arrived at the house to take our statements. The young man, PC Newman, may have thought he was trying to put our minds at rest but to us it seemed that he was being totally unsympathetic and offhand. 'She's a perfect case of someone who would be likely just to take off,' he said.

'What do you mean?' I asked, my hackles rising at being told about my own daughter by a complete stranger.

'I've been in community relations for several years,' he said, as if he knew everything about everything. 'She's a typical case; she had marriage problems; she was due to go to court. She's probably come in from work to a cold, dark, empty house and decided to make a fresh start. Knowing the boy was safely looked after by you, she's probably walked down to the A19 and hitched a ride to London.'

'You must be joking,' Charlie exploded. 'It's totally out of character.'

'Listen,' I chipped in, 'I'm telling you that she has not just taken off to London. Something has happened to her, I know it has. I can feel it in my gut.'

It was becoming obvious to us that the police weren't going to do anything, not until Julie had been gone at least a few days. But how could we sit around for even a moment longer without doing something about the situation? It was the opposite of any parental instincts we might have; it was pure torture. Suppose she was trapped somewhere and needed our help? I considered the idea that she might have gone to London. Apart from Andrew, she knew only one person there—an old school friend called Margaret who worked with Down's Syndrome kids. Julie had visited her the year before, the only time I can remember her travelling anywhere on her own. It had been a big adventure for her, which was one of the reasons why I had known she would never just disappear off to London without saying anything. I didn't have a contact number for Margaret but I told the police about her and they tracked her down. She rang me after that to say she hadn't heard anything from Julie.

On Sunday, after another sleepless night, our brains stretched to breaking point by a mixture of worry and exhaustion, we went back down to Grange Avenue to see if any of the neighbours had managed to remember anything at all that might shed some light on what had happened.

When you are desperate to know what is going on you tend to grasp any straw that is offered to you, however flimsy it might be. When Kath from the house next door said that a police friend of her son Mark had rung him to say they'd had an anonymous tip-off, we immediately took it seriously. The tip-off had come from a woman caller who reported that she had seen a drunk woman being bundled into a car by three men behind the pizza shop in the middle of the night that Julie had disappeared. When I rang the police about it, they were shocked that I knew anything about the call.

'That information should be confidential,' I was told.

In the end the lead came to nothing as no one else ever came forward to back up the story. This left me feeling angry with the police yet again; I thought that they had acted unprofessionally by gossiping about Julie with the neighbours when they had nothing to follow up with.

Despite this setback we still talked and talked to anyone who would give us the time, but no one knew anything. There was not even a single lead.

Later on that Sunday, I drove down to Stockton police station, determined to keep on pestering them until I found someone who would take us seriously. There's a saying that it's the wheel which squeaks the loudest that gets the oil first. I intended to keep on making as loud a noise as I could till they did something that would shut me up.

There was a long queue at the counter when I walked into the police station and my stomach was churning with tension by the time I came to the front. My brain was fuddled with a mixture of anxiety and exhaustion, so when I looked up and saw the Iranians from the 'Mr Macaroni' pizza shop being led down the stairs, something snapped in my head. I started screaming hysterically at them, 'What have you done with my daughter?'

I assumed they must have been brought in for questioning. They had behaved strangely when we went to see them and now I jumped straight to the worst conclusions. I probably would have attacked them physically if there hadn't been police around to hold me back. The sergeant who had been handling the desk quickly steered me into a side office where he introduced me to a detective called Inspector Geoff Lee. I certainly had their attention now, even if it was only because the police thought I was a madwoman who was likely to attack innocent people in their station.

'I'm telling you as a mother,' I ranted on, 'something has happened to my daughter. This is totally out of character for her; she wouldn't disappear off to London. She wouldn't even go into town on her own; she always liked company wherever she went. This is a girl I see every day; go and check with the neighbours, they'll tell you she's always round at my house.'

'We are taking you seriously,' Inspector Lee assured me. 'We are making enquiries. We're going to send a team of forensic officers into the house tomorrow.'

Part of me was relieved that they were finally listening to me and believing that I might be right, but another part of me felt a terrible foreboding at the thought of what they might find once they started searching. I would have given anything to get a call from Julie now to say she was down in London. I don't doubt I would have given her an earful for all the worry she had caused us, but how wonderful it would have felt to be able to do that. Suppose I was never going to be able to talk to her again? The thought was unbearable.

Chapter Five
The Search

The following morning, Monday, November 20, five forensic officers went into the little three-bedroom house in Grange Avenue. Five men, I thought, should be more than enough to comb the place from top to bottom in search of evidence; after all, how many hiding places could there be in such a small house? We were naturally pleased they were being so thorough, but at the same time worried that they must be expecting to find something bad.

If anything had happened to Julie in that house during the previous Wednesday night, they would now discover what it was, using all their scientific knowledge and policing experience. I'd seen lots of crime programmes on television, both documentaries and dramas, and it seemed that forensic teams pretty much always got their man.

Every minute of each day we seemed to be waiting for something to happen; waiting for Julie to ring or for the police to call and tell us they had found something in the house. When you are waiting without knowing what you are waiting for, every hour seems to last for ever. Most of the time is filled with talking over and over the same things, asking one another the same questions over endless cups of tea.

I suppose I had thought they would come up with something almost the moment they crossed the threshold, but there was only a terrible silence from the house as they went about their business behind closed doors.

On the Wednesday, a week after I had last seen Julie, Inspector Lee finally rang. 'Will you and your younger daughter go to the house,' he asked, 'to see if any of Julie's clothing is missing? We'll send a policewoman to fetch you.'

Of course we agreed instantly, glad to have something positive to do.

We waited nervously for the policewoman to come for us but the hours passed and we were becoming more and more worried. Eventually I rang Julie's number to speak to the police in the house, hoping to find out what was going on. One of the forensic team picked up the phone.

'It's Julie's mum here,' I said. 'The policewoman hasn't come for us.'

'She should be there in about half an hour,' he promised.

'Have you found anything?' I asked, unable to contain my curiosity for a second longer.

'There's no dead bodies in here,' he replied, 'if that's what you mean.'

I felt as though I'd been punched in the stomach. He had spoken out loud the words that had been circling round and round in my head ever since Gary first broke into the house and found it silent and deserted.

'Do you think I needed to hear that?' I snapped. 'I know my daughter's dead and I don't need you to tell me.'

I slammed the phone down, furious at his insensitivity, and shocked to hear my own words. I felt dizzy. It was the first time I had actually voiced the fear that I had felt almost from the start. I rang Inspector Lee and told him about the detective's tactlessness.

'Leave it with me,' he said, obviously aware of just how upset I was becoming. 'The policewoman will be with you very shortly.'

When the policewoman arrived and took us down to the house the detective I'd spoken to was waiting outside for us.

'Mrs Ming,' he said, 'I just wanted to apologise for what I said. I didn't mean to upset you.'

I let him know exactly what I thought of him, which he took manfully, and then we went into the house. I was in a daze, trying to be as helpful as possible but finding it hard to keep my emotions in check. I could remember that on the last afternoon I'd seen her, Julie had been wearing a black skirt and a peach-coloured blouse. They were the only clothes that Angela and I couldn't find in the wardrobe. I told the police.

'I don't see any shoes missing either,' I added. 'If she'd gone down to London she would have taken shoes, wouldn't she?'

The policeman nodded his acceptance of what I was saying but said nothing himself. We went through into the bathroom and looked around.

'Look at this,' I told them, pointing to a bag on the side. 'Are you suggesting she has taken off to London and left her make-up bag? Our Julie wouldn't have stepped outside the house without putting her make-up on.'

I could see from the way the head of the forensic team was looking at me that he thought I was a neurotic mother, too emotionally involved to be thinking clearly. But I knew that however untidy Julie might have kept the house, she was always neat with her own appearance. There was no way she would have walked out without taking these things with her; someone else must have forced her out of the house against her will, or worse.

Time continued to drag past and on the Friday, when the investigations were finally complete, Inspector Lee came to see us to tell us their results.

'I can't guarantee you that Julie hasn't come to grief somewhere in the country,' he said as we all sat awkwardly in our front room. 'But I *can* guarantee you that nothing untoward happened to her inside that house.'

In other words they had found nothing. Not a single clue. They were still as mystified as Gary and I had been when we first discovered the neat, empty house. I jumped out of my chair, agitated.

'If you are certain that nothing happened to her in that house,' I said, 'then I'm telling you she can't have been in there. But I know something has happened to her, and we are pretty sure she went into that house after being dropped off.'

Inspector Lee stared at me as if I was daft. As far as he was concerned his team had done their best. They had responded to my request for help, but had found nothing. Perhaps he thought that this would help to put my mind at rest, but it actually did the opposite because it raised even more new questions without answering any of the existing ones. It didn't seem possible, or bearable, that we were still no further on and yet the investigation was over.

The police believed they had done all they could for the moment. The house was locked up again, as dark and silent and empty as it had been on the morning when I first went round to find her. Because Julie's keys were still missing, the police had changed the lock on the back door so they could get in and out while they were investigating.

'We've also put an alarm in the house,' Inspector Lee explained, 'which doesn't sound on the premises but will ring in the police station if anyone tries to get in with Julie's keys.'

The following morning, he called to tell us that the house had been broken into during the night. The alarm had malfunctioned, he said, and the intruder had got away with the video.

'How did they get in?' Charlie wanted to know.

'Through one of the front windows,' he said.

Once the police were off the phone we drove down to have a look but there was no sign of forced entry. Charlie phoned the inspector and told him that we couldn't understand what they were saying had happened.

'Did you look in the loft properly while you were there?' Charlie asked while he was on the phone. It was something that had been worrying us, since we couldn't think of any other hiding places in the house.

'Do you think we're thirteen-year-old school kids?' the inspector retorted angrily. 'We're professional police officers.'

We knew we were getting on their nerves with our refusal to accept what they were certain was the truth—that Julie had just walked out of our lives. But we were her parents and we were so frantic with worry we wanted to be sure that every possibility had been addressed.

Every day was another nightmare, with Kevin continually asking us where his mammy was and us not able to think of anything convincing to say. There were too many people coming and going for him not to be aware that something was badly wrong, that his family were all deeply unhappy. We just kept telling him that we were sure she wouldn't be away for long, having no idea at what stage we would have to tell him something different. How could we tell him that his mammy might be dead if there was still even a remote possibility that she could walk back through the door? Andrew came back from London to help look after him, but none of us went near the house in Grange Avenue. We didn't have keys for the new locks anyway.

The police were treating it as a normal missing persons case, and they asked us to do an appeal in the local paper. We were happy to go along with it. But was Julie likely to see it if she was down in London, as the police kept suggesting? They assured us this would be the best thing to do; I suppose it was their standard procedure in such cases.

Our solicitor, with whom we were spending a lot of time by then, suggested we go on Tyne Tees Television as well, to try to reach her that way. We were happy to agree; we were willing to try anything. If Julie was alive we just wanted her to let us know she was OK; we wanted her to know that we all loved her and that we were desperate with worry. I was sure that if she realised that, then she would also realise she had to make contact to put our minds at rest. It was impossible for me to hold back the tears as I talked to the cameras with Kevin on my knee. If she saw Kevin's little face she wouldn't be able to stay away from him another day.

As long as the police hadn't found a body we still had hope, and however faint it might be it was just enough to keep us going from one agonising day to the next, from one hour to the next. Making the appeals gave us something to think about, something to distract us from the pain of the anxiety and fear.

Christmas was approaching and every happy, smiling face or cheerful Christmas carol was a reminder of just how empty and fearful our lives had become. We wrapped presents for Julie and put them under the tree, all ready for her to return, and we did yet another appeal in the newspaper.

Inspector Lee was in touch with us most days and he tried to find positive things to say to keep us going. His attitude was that 'no news is good news'. As long as we didn't find a body, he said, there was still a chance that Julie was alive somewhere.

'Julie's description is in the main police computer now,' he explained, 'so if anything is found anywhere in the country it will be traced back to Stockton.'

'Why don't you do a national appeal if you're so sure she's in London?' I wanted to know.

'No, we don't need to do that,' he insisted. 'We'll keep it local.'

Did that mean they didn't really believe she was in London any more than I did? Were they just saying they did in order to give me some hope? It was announced in the local papers that they were sending out divers to search the pond and dogs onto the wastelands surrounding Billingham, but were they just going through the motions to humour us? There was no way of telling.

It was my birthday on December 22, and Inspector Lee told us that if there was one day that Julie was most likely to get in touch, that would be it. He suggested we warn all our friends and family not to ring, so that the line would be clear. All day we sat beside the phone, never moving from the house for fear of missing the call, hardly daring even to go to the bathroom. Every minute was an agonising silence as we stared at the silent instrument, desperately willing it to ring. By ten o'clock that night we knew she wasn't going to call. If she didn't phone me on my birthday, what hope was there that she would do it any other day?

Inspector Lee called the next day to see if there was any news, but we had nothing to tell him. Although he hadn't been able to find our Julie for us, he had always shown a personal interest, as if he really cared about what we were going through. We appreciated that.

'Maybe she'll phone over Christmas,' he said, desperately trying to find something encouraging to say. But she didn't and neither did she call to wish us a happy new year. On New Year's Eve I watched the cheerful, smiling crowds in Trafalgar Square on the television, wondering if Julie was anywhere among them, lost to us in the streets of London.

January dragged past, cold and grey and miserable, with none of us knowing if we would ever see Julie again. Frustrated with the reluctance of the police to go national with their appeals, I contacted the *People* newspaper, because they run a book of missing people. They told me there was a queue of families waiting to get their loved ones onto the list and they would let me know when Julie's details reached the front of the queue. The thought that there were so many missing people all over the country just made it all seem even more hopeless. For each of the names on the list there was a family somewhere, just like us, going out of their minds with worry, unable to get on with their own lives until they found out what had happened to their loved one. Yet we had to keep on going for Julie, for Kevin and for our own sanity.

Chapter Six
Finding Julie

At the end of January the police said there was no more they could do at Grange Avenue and they gave Andrew the keys to the new locks they had installed. He had been staying at a friend's house ever since coming back from London, and Kevin had been sleeping with us at night, seeing his dad during the days if Andrew wasn't working. Now they needed a place to live, so Andrew decided he would move back into

Grange Avenue with Kevin and try to rebuild their lives together from there. Charlie and I were grateful to think that our grandson had a good father who loved him and wanted to look after him.

I went down to the house with Andrew to collect and take away all Julie's clothes. I didn't want Kevin coming across his mam's possessions, making him wonder and ask more questions about where she was and why she had left us. It was important that he just got used to life without her, in case she never came back.

It had been shut up for nearly three months of the winter so the house was freezing cold as we stepped into it, and messy. It had been left neglected and unloved for too long, making me shiver from more than just the cold. At least, I told myself, we knew that nothing bad had happened to Julie there, because the police had told us so. I wouldn't have wanted Kevin to go back to live there if I thought something had happened to his mam on the premises.

The first day of February, Andrew went back to Grange Avenue again to start clearing up. The police had left a lot of mess with all the fingerprint dust and it was going to take him several days to clean it thoroughly. The first thing he did was switch on the gas heating to get rid of the chill. The radiators creaked and cracked into life and warmth slowly spread through the rooms, forcing out the chill.

He phoned me up at tea time to let me know how he was getting on.

'There's a horrible smell in the bathroom,' he told me.

'That'll be the toilet after all these weeks,' I said. 'Put some bleach down and don't use it for a while.'

That day the *People* rang to say Julie's details would be in the paper the following Sunday. It was a small shred of hope, but I clung to it anyway. Maybe this time she would see it and get in touch, or perhaps someone who knew her in her new life would spot it and ring to let us know where she was. Or if she was wandering around somewhere with a lost memory, perhaps someone would recognise her and bring her home. All these remote possibilities were constantly flitting in and out of my mind.

When I woke on the Sunday morning I noticed I had some scratches on the back on my hand. It reminded me of Julie and the way she used to threaten to scratch her brother and sister when they annoyed her. I showed Angela while we were having breakfast.

'This reminds me of Julie,' I told her. 'Maybe she's trying to communicate with us from the other side.'

'Oh, shut up, our Mam,' Angela said, shuddering. 'Stop being so spooky.'

I knew I was probably being silly but I just had a funny feeling, which I couldn't explain. I didn't say any more. That afternoon I was in the car on my own and I started talking out loud to Julie, just as I would have done if she'd been sat beside me.

'If I just knew whether you were dead or alive,' I told her. 'Only I can't carry on any longer like this, not knowing.'

I felt close to my breaking point, as if soon I wouldn't be able to cope on a day-to-day basis—not even for Kevin's sake.

On the following day I knew Andrew would be going back to Grange Avenue to finish the cleaning. I was due to take Kevin to his playgroup at one thirty so I thought we would drop in on the way to see how Andrew was getting on, and to remind him to pick Kevin up again at three o'clock.

I knocked on the front door and Andrew opened it. 'Have you got rid of that smell?' I asked as we went through into the kitchen.

'No,' he said, 'it's getting worse.'

'Oh, get out of the way,' I said. 'I'll go and see for myself.'

I left Kevin chatting happily with his dad in the kitchen and marched upstairs to investigate, wondering why men are always so useless at these sorts of practical things. Halfway up the stairs the stench reached my nostrils. I'd been working for twenty years in an operating theatre by then and deep inside I knew what it was.

It was as if I was outside my own body, watching myself on a CCTV screen, going up those stairs and into the bathroom. I'm told it's called 'psychic numbing', a condition caused by intense shock. There couldn't be anything that bad in the house, I was telling myself, because the police hadn't found anything. Five forensic officers had been there for five days and had found nothing. *There's no dead bodies in here, if that's what you mean*, the detective had said. There had to be another explanation.

The bathroom looked just the same as it had the day I'd been in there with the police. I looked behind the toilet and behind the basin, but found nothing that could be causing the problem. Before going to London, Andrew had stripped off the wall tiles, intending to replace them, but hadn't yet got round to doing it. I wondered if it might be the fixative on the walls that was making the smell. Please God, let that be what it was.

I leaned across the bath to sniff, my knees pressing against the flimsy hardboard panel on the side. The wall smelled of nothing, but the panel was loose and a gap sprang open under the pressure from my leg. The smell suddenly grew much stronger, becoming almost overwhelming.

Whatever was causing the smell was under the bath. Part of my brain told me that I was going to find Julie there, but how was that possible? The police would obviously have found her body if it was there. I was being melodramatic even to consider the possibility. So what was it? Maybe a rat had died in there. I had to look and see, to put my mind at rest, and didn't consider what effect it would have on me if I did find Julie under there. I knelt down and pulled at the panel so that I could peer behind it.

Even though it was wrapped in a blanket I knew that what I was seeing was a body. The stench billowed out, filling my lungs and making me retch. I let go of the panel, allowing it to spring back into place, and scrambled onto my feet and out of the room, stumbling down the stairs, screaming hysterically for Andrew, the smell filling my lungs and my head, unable to control myself, not even enough to protect Kevin.

'She's under the bath!' I screamed as I half-ran and half-fell into the kitchen. 'She's under the bath!'

Andrew stared at me blank-faced. Later he told me that at that moment he thought I had cracked up, finally caved in under the pressure of the previous three months. How could she be there after all this time? After so many policemen had been in there? It didn't seem possible, but I knew what I had seen and what I had smelled and I couldn't get a grip on myself. I too thought I might be about to lose my mind.

Kevin was standing beside me, open-mouthed, staring up at the horror of his hysterical grandmother. I grabbed Andrew's arm.

'Please, tell me it isn't her,' I begged. 'Please.'

'I'll get a screwdriver,' he said, as calmly as he could, 'and take the panel off; see what's there.'

I couldn't stop weeping and shaking, even though poor little Kevin started crying as his dad went upstairs. I hugged him tight, trying to comfort him although I couldn't manage to quieten my own sobbing. There was a terrible few seconds of nothing as Andrew must have been undoing the screws, a few moments when it was still possible I had imagined it all, but then I heard his shout and I knew it was all too real.

'Oh, Jesus Christ, no!' he exclaimed as he thundered down the stairs. 'What do I do? What do I do?'

'Dial 999!' I yelled.

I put Kevin down and ran out of the house, desperate to get away, frantic to get help. I just wanted it all not to be true. I couldn't think straight, couldn't work out what to do. I was still screaming like a madwoman as I burst into Kath's house next door.

'She's under the bath!' I shrieked. 'She's under the bath!'

I just wanted someone to make the nightmare end. How could life possibly go on after this? How could I go on living with those few moments imprinted on my memory for ever?

'She can't be,' Kath shouted back, trying to shock me out my hysterical state. 'She can't be! You've got it wrong. It must be something else. The police have been in.'

'No, I've just seen her,' I insisted. 'She's there.'

Within minutes the street was full of police cars and vans, wailing sirens, shouting voices and hurrying feet. I ran back out, like everyone else in the street. I saw Inspector Lee getting out of one of the cars and I charged straight at him. I moved so fast no one had time to stop me and I grabbed him and pinned him against the fence, punching him and screaming at him. He was the one person in the police force we had been able to relate to during the previous three months of hell, and I now felt that he had let us down as well. He had promised me she wasn't in there! He had promised!

'I told you she wouldn't have taken off to London but you wouldn't listen,' I screamed.

'We don't know what you've found yet,' he said, attempting to hold me back and retain at least some of his dignity.

'Come on then,' I shouted, challenging him, trying to force him to face what Andrew and I had had to face. 'Come and see!'

This was the man who had sworn to me that nothing had happened to Julie in Grange Avenue. He had absolutely guaranteed it. He was the man I had trusted.

By the time I got back to the door the police had cordoned off the house with their blue-striped tape, and they wouldn't let me back in again. There was total confusion everywhere; so many people, so many uniforms. I was still hysterical as they led me away, gently putting me into my car with poor little Kevin, who was crying his eyes out. He didn't know what was wrong, but all the adults being so upset must have been very frightening for him. A policewoman was told to drive us home.

I knew I had to get Kevin away from the house, but part of me felt I should have been with Julie, my baby, not handing her over to the care of strangers, strangers who had done nothing up till now but let her down. At the same time I didn't think I could bear to see her again in the state she was in now. And I knew it didn't matter where I went because I would never escape the pictures now imprinted in my head and the smell in my nostrils. At least Julie had escaped to the other side; I was still trapped here in a hell that was getting worse with every passing moment.

The police went to fetch Charlie and Angela and brought them both home so that we could all be together. Two policemen were sent to Gary's home in Middlesborough. When he opened the door to their knock they greeted him with the words, 'We've found your sister.'

'Where was she?' he asked. 'In London?'

'No,' they said, 'under the bath.'

It wasn't until he arrived at our house with the police that he discovered it was me who had found Julie, not them. It seemed as though they were embarrassed to admit what had actually happened, that they were hoping to gloss over the fact that their search of the house had failed to find her.

There were so many people coming and going from our house in the following hours, so much confusion, that I didn't even notice Andrew had gone missing. The police had taken him straight in for questioning. Never for a moment, not even a single second, did it occur to any of us in the family that he could have had anything to do with Julie's death, but the police knew his relationship with Julie had been going wrong, so I can understand why he was at the top of their suspect list.

When Inspector Lee arrived at our house later with another policeman I still wasn't able to control my rage towards him for what he had allowed us to go through, and for the way the police had treated us all, and for letting Julie down. Before anyone could stop me I had run at him again, knocking him off his feet and pinning him over the chest freezer in the kitchen, punching him and screaming at him with renewed strength. In the end Charlie had to drag me off before I did him some serious injury. I was so angry I wanted someone else to suffer for what I now knew Julie must have suffered.

I couldn't imagine how the pain I was feeling at that moment would ever go away. I couldn't imagine how I was going to be able to face the coming hours and days and years.

Chapter Seven
The Aftermath

Inspector Lee stayed with us for a while, bravely facing up to my tirades of abuse. There was little he could do or say in the face of my hysterics and my anger. He just bowed his head and accepted responsibility for everything that had gone wrong.

'I don't know how it happened,' he said, 'but there will be an investigation to find out.'

Eventually, when I had quietened down a bit, he made his excuses and left. A few hours later a copy of the local evening paper plopped through the front door onto the mat, fresh from the printing presses. The front page was covered in a story about a skin specialist in Middlesborough who had been murdered, but there was a flash at the bottom of the page, which said: *Detectives have found a body at 27 Grange Avenue.*

I couldn't believe they'd had the nerve to claim in public that it was they who had found the body, as if dogged police work had triumphed in the end. I immediately phoned the reporter who had helped us with all the appeals over the previous three months.

'I just wondered who gave you that information?' I asked.

'It was the police press office,' he said.

'Well, you can get it retracted,' I snapped. 'Because it was me who found my daughter, not them.'

I slammed the phone down without another word. The anger inside me hadn't abated; in fact, it was still building and I needed someone else to vent it on. I snatched the phone up again and called police headquarters, my fingers trembling as I dialled. I got a duty sergeant on the line and told him, in as calm a voice as I could manage, that I wanted to make a complaint. He asked if I wanted to make an appointment.

'I want to see the Chief Constable,' I said.

'I'm afraid you can't do that,' he told me, sounding as if he thought I was mad even to suggest such impertinence.

'Don't tell me what I can and can't do,' I snapped. 'I want to know why I found our daughter's decomposing body when your so-called forensic officers didn't.'

It went very quiet at the other end of the line.

'Is that Mrs Ming?' he asked.

'Yes, it is.'

'Can I ring you back?'

He rang back a few minutes later to say an appointment had been made for me with the Deputy Chief Constable for eleven o'clock the following morning. It seemed that now they had a murder inquiry on their hands they were going to be paying a bit more attention to us.

I was in such a hysterical state I hadn't even noticed that Charlie had slipped out of the house until he came back with our doctor, Dr Geoghegan, who gave me an injection to calm me down. Dr Geoghegan had been really supportive over the past months. He had known our family a long time and he had been giving me tranquillisers to help me get through the long days and nights of anxiety. I was grateful to him for coming that day, even if I didn't show it at the time.

The sedative injection didn't seem to make any difference; I couldn't stop smelling Julie's body, as if I was still in the room with it, and I kept seeing the panel coming away from the bath and then her lying behind it, wrapped in a soiled blanket. It was as if I was continually being transported back in time to that one terrible place and moment, trapped on a repeating loop, like a trailer for a real version of some gruesome horror movie.

'Don't hesitate to come for me at any time,' the doctor told Charlie as he left, 'even if it's the middle of the night.'

To my dazed, shocked and now medicated brain, our house seemed to be full of people coming and going, with nothing making much sense. When something so shocking and horrifying happens, it is hard to discern between reality and the nightmares that come with sleep. I was constantly asking myself if I really had seen what I thought I saw or if I was going mad. The surge of adrenaline I had experienced at the discovery was still coursing through my veins and there was no way I was going to be sleeping that night, whatever medication the doctor might give me. My thoughts were rushing everywhere at once and I knew I needed to keep myself busy.

I sat up all night that night, writing out a list of complaints I had against the police, from the moment we tried to report Julie missing to the moment I found her body. I brought up every single thing that had angered me, from the leaking of anonymous information by a policeman to Kath's son Mark, to the way Charlie was treated when he was arrested at the pizza shop and carted off to the cells for the night without his blood-pressure tablets. Venting my anger against the police gave me something to focus on, something to distract me from the knowledge that Julie really was dead and would never be coming back, and to keep myself from imagining what could have happened to her in the hours before she ended up under the bath. Not yet having a culprit at whom I could aim my hatred and anger, I was left fuming at police incompetence.

If I had dwelled too long on the thought of her lying there on her own in that cold house for three months, I would have been tipped over into complete madness. So I just kept scribbling furiously away, pouring my anger and thoughts and feelings onto sheets and sheets of paper. I wanted to shout my grievances from the rooftops. I wanted to get justice for Julie and for the rest of the family.

All this activity was just to cover up what I really wanted, of course. What I really wanted was for Julie not to be dead and for things to be the same as they had been three months earlier. It's hard to accept that the one thing you want more than anything is the one thing that is totally impossible to achieve.

Charlie was also in a state of shock that night and was finding it increasingly difficult to cope with my hyperactivity. He was exhausted and just wanted to rest for a bit, so Laurence, his brother, said he would come with me for my appointment with the police the next day.

'Oh, look,' Laurence said as we drew up outside the police station. 'There's a television crew here. I wonder what's going on?'

I looked over to where he was pointing and saw a Tyne Tees outside-broadcast lorry parked up. It didn't occur to me for a second that its presence might have anything to do with me. If I had known the police were holding a press conference about Julie's death in that building that morning, I would have marched straight into it and given them a piece of my mind—and given the press a good story at the same time.

The Deputy Chief Constable, Jack Ord, was waiting for us in the entrance hall, as if we were visiting dignitaries. He led us courteously into his office.

'May I,' he said, once we were settled, 'on behalf of Cleveland Constabulary, offer our condolences?'

'I don't want your condolences,' I snapped, not being in the mood for any of this flannel. I was like a madwoman. 'I want answers to these questions.'

I flung the piece of paper I'd been working on through the night down onto the desk in front of him.

'You haven't given us time to put things right, Mrs Ming,' Ord said. 'You're putting in a complaint in less than twenty-four hours.'

'Put things right?' I yelled. 'What the hell are you going to put right?'

He told me that another high-ranking officer from Northumbria Police was on his way to start an investigation into Cleveland Police and their handling of our case. No wonder they were all suddenly being so polite and attentive—they were under investigation themselves.

'I'm going to introduce you to a detective called Sandra in a minute,' he went on. 'She is going to be acting as your liaison officer.'

I was having trouble taking in what was being said to me. I knew that nothing was going to bring our Julie back, but I had to do whatever I could to find out what had gone wrong. I had to do that for Julie's sake, but I had no idea how.

At the end of the meeting, Sandra, the liaison officer, followed us back home in her car. Once we got there she came in with us, sat us down and explained that the missing persons team had now been taken off the case and been replaced by the murder squad. As I calmed down, Charlie said he thought I should ring Inspector Lee and apologise for the way I'd attacked him the day before. I decided he was right. Inspector Lee had been the one who had been kindest to us throughout the three months; it wasn't really his fault that his team had messed up. But when I tried to ring the station to speak to him they wouldn't put me through, telling me that he was now off the case. It seemed that he had gone from being our main point of contact to being completely out of our lives.

That afternoon Andrew rang from Stockton police station asking us to go and pick him up. It was only then that we realised he'd been gone all that time. I suppose I had assumed he was at home with his mum and dad, trying to recover from the shock of what he'd been through in some peace and quiet, but in fact he had been held overnight.

After questioning him for about thirty hours the police had decided that Andrew really didn't know anything more than he was telling them and they let him go. They didn't even offer him a lift home. The poor man broke down and cried as soon as we had him in the car. Like me, he was still in a state of shock, but he had the added pressure of having been under intense interrogation for twenty-four hours.

'They told me you were in the next room,' he explained when he could get the words out, 'and that you'd told them I'd phoned you from the house and asked you to come and take the panel off the bath.'

'There's no way I told them anything like that,' I protested.

'I know. They were just trying to get me to admit I'd put her there and that I wanted you to find her to avert suspicion from myself.'

As if failing to find her body under the bath wasn't bad enough, when the murder squad searched Grange Avenue they found Julie's diary, cash card and watch in the loft. Yet when Charlie had asked Inspector Lee if he was sure the forensic team had searched the loft thoroughly, the inspector had accused Charlie of treating his officers like thirteen-year-olds. It seemed to us that even thirteen-year-olds would have found those pieces of evidence.

Later we discovered that a total of twenty-nine different police officers had been through that house in the course of those three months, and none of them had spotted any of the clues, let alone the body.

Sandra, our liaison officer, turned out to be a very nice woman, but by the end of the first week of the investigation she was so traumatised by what she was hearing that she had to go off sick. I believe she ended up leaving the police force altogether, unable to take the strain. The senior investigating officer on the murder squad, Derrick Dobson, didn't bother to make contact with us. We did, however, get to see him talking on the television evening news, calling himself 'the Hunter'.

'I will hunt down this killer,' he assured the viewing public. 'Julie's killer will be found.'

It was as if our own lives were drifting away from us, becoming public property. Often we learned what was happening in Julie's case only from the television or the newspapers. Charlie, Gary and Angela cried the whole time, but I kept looking for things to do, to keep myself occupied. Among other things, I started a scrapbook of press cuttings and pasted in any articles I found about the case.

After a couple of weeks we were assigned a new liaison officer called Mark Braithwaite. He was a tall, good-looking, very nice man, who was a detective sergeant at the time and number three on the murder team. He was to become a close friend over the following years, sharing our many trials and tribulations, our hopes and our disappointments. He has since gone on to become a Detective Chief Superintendent and Head of Crime for Cleveland Police.

During the coming months our house always seemed to be full of police officers. We also had Kevin there, and Andrew had decided he didn't want the boy to be told that his mother had been murdered, so we constantly had to be aware of what he might be overhearing. All this was after the three months of torture that we had already endured when we didn't know if Julie was dead or alive.

Our doctor said that we really should tell Kevin the truth about what had happened, but Andrew was so adamant that we just went along with his wishes. We concocted a story between us that Julie had slipped in the bath because there was no bath mat, hit her head and died. When we told Kevin she had gone to heaven he seemed to accept it, and didn't ask what had happened during the three months that she was missing. Because he was only three, he didn't question any of it.

On clear nights he would say, 'Come and look for me mam,' and we would stand together by the window of his bedroom, looking up at the sky, searching for the brightest star.

Now that I knew Julie was dead I wanted, more than anything else, to know who had killed my daughter and left my grandson without a mother to kiss him good night and tuck him in. I wanted justice to be done.

Chapter Eight
Introducing Billy Dunlop

On February 14, 1990, less than two weeks after I had found her body, the police arrested and charged a man called Billy Dunlop for our Julie's murder. When I first heard his name, I had trouble remembering who he was, but then I realised he was a man I had met at Julie's house a couple of times. He was one of the lads that Andrew used to play football with, but I couldn't say I knew anything about him. That situation would soon be remedied dramatically as the police, and everyone else we met who knew anything about him, filled us in with stories about his past. Those tales painted an ugly picture of a side of local life previously unknown to me. I certainly hadn't realised that Andrew and Julie mixed with these sorts of men.

I could recall having a conversation with Billy Dunlop in Julie's kitchen once about the Chinese restaurant in Billingham where I used to work on the cash desk. I remembered him as a stocky man with dark hair and a moustache, who told me he'd been to the restaurant to eat. We chatted about it for a bit, but that was the only memory I had of him. He struck me then as a quietly spoken man, not at all aggressive or violent. In fact, he didn't make much impact on me at all. It seemed that I had talked to the devil himself without even realising what I was doing.

Later I found out that he'd been brought up in the house next to the one I'd lived in all through my childhood. It's shocking how everyone ends up being connected to everyone else in a town like Billingham if you delve deep enough. It is also shocking how evil can so easily reside at the heart of a seemingly normal life. None of us ever knows what dark thoughts lurk in the hearts of our neighbours, or what black deeds lie in their pasts.

Billy's best friend was a young man called Mark Ward. Mark lived next door to 27 Grange Avenue with his mum, Kath, who was the woman I'd run to for help on finding the body. Mark was also the one who had received the call from the police about the anonymous tip-off. As I learned more and more of these facts, I struggled to piece them together to try to make sense of what had happened that night. But there were too many pieces of the jigsaw missing, too many pieces of misinformation.

Billy, I was told, had been living with his girlfriend, Jayne, but they'd had a row a few months before and so at the time Julie was killed he'd been lodging with a mate of his called Don, in the next road to Grange Avenue. Billy and Jayne had since made up and he was now back living with her.

The day that Julie first disappeared, when I went next door to ask Kath if she had seen or heard anything, Billy was actually sitting in the kitchen with Mark. I didn't really take him in at the time, being too distracted and worried, but when I thought about it later it struck me as strange that if he was the murderer, why was he sitting there, cool as a cucumber, the next morning? I certainly don't think he said anything while I was in there or showed much interest in what I was saying. I was later told that this type of behaviour is typical of psychopaths—they often return to the scene of their crime.

Gradually we learned more and more from the police about what had happened on the night of the murder. Billy had been to a stag night at the local rugby club with half a dozen mates. They apparently had a reputation for starting trouble wherever they went and were known locally as 'the Crazy Gang'. The police knew all about them, as did anyone in Billingham who frequented the same pubs and clubs and had witnessed their rowdy behaviour.

Billy had convictions for violent assault going back to 1975, when he was just a young lad. There were many stories circulating about things he had done, but it was hard to know how many of them were true and how many were myths. It was said he was shockingly violent, particularly when he was drunk, which was often. If you went into any of the pubs in old Billingham and mentioned his name, people would readily tell you stories about him. He was the leader of the pack and had been since he was a kid.

One story that was widely told concerned the time he was trying to escape from some institution he'd been sent to when he was about sixteen. The police went looking for him and let a dog off the leash to track him down. People said that when the dog found him Billy turned round and cut the animal's head off with a knife. The tale had been told so many times it was impossible to know if it was true or not but it added to the aura of violence and fear that surrounded Billy wherever he went.

Andrew had been to school with him and said that even back then all the other kids were frightened of his bullying ways. Whether all the stories about Billy Dunlop were accurate or not, everyone in the area wanted to see him safely behind bars, but most were too intimidated to speak up and the police never seemed to be able to pin anything on him and make it stick.

This group of men, 'the Crazy Gang', often hired strippers for their rugby club stag dos and sometimes, I'm told, the girls were willing to perform sex acts with the men on stage and that sort of thing. During the course of the evening at the club, while Julie was still delivering pizzas, the story goes that Billy, fuelled by a cocktail of drink, had dropped his trousers and exposed himself while trying to get up onto the stage with the stripper. Egged on by his cronies, who were just as drunk as he was, he frightened the girl half to death.

Drunk and dangerously sexually aroused, he got into a fight with another man and he started to cause so much trouble that the doormen intervened and threw him out into the street. On the way out he headbutted the door in his rage and cut his eyebrow badly. By the time he got outside, his face streaked with his own blood, he was lathered up into such a fury that he attacked the man again, knocking him to the ground and punching him until the doormen dragged him off.

Once he had calmed down enough to realise he was covered in his own blood, Billy got someone to give him a lift to the local hospital to have his eyebrow stitched. I guess the doctors in casualty departments are used to seeing the results of pub brawls in the small hours and just get on with patching up the wounded and sending them on their way to sleep it off. I doubt they bother to ask many questions.

At about one thirty in the morning, Billy lurched back out of the hospital onto the streets, his cut stitched up but his frustration at having his evening of drunken fun interrupted still fermenting inside his head.

When the police arrived on the doorstep of the house where he was lodging during the earlier missing person enquiry, Don told them that Dunlop had returned home from the hospital at two o'clock in the morning, which wouldn't have left him with much time to get up to any serious mischief regarding Julie. If Don was telling the truth, then Billy must have walked straight back home from the hospital. The police asked Don how he knew the time so precisely and he said his video clock was lit up beside the bed and he looked at it when Billy woke him up by coming in. In response to further questioning, Don told them that he'd heard Billy going straight to bed once he got in. That had been a good enough alibi for the police to move on to the next house on their list.

Once I found Julie's body and it became a murder enquiry, the police went to see Don again, to check what he had told them. This time, realising things were a lot more serious than he had first imagined, Don changed his story, knowing that if he was caught lying in order to cover up for a murderer he could end up inside himself. Even Billy couldn't intimidate him to that degree. He admitted that Dunlop hadn't returned to the house at two o'clock, as he had claimed before, and that he was in fact unaware of what time Billy had arrived back at his lodgings. That left Billy potentially with several hours of the night unaccounted for between leaving the hospital and arriving home, easily enough time to kill Julie and clean the house up after him. If they had had their suspicions about Billy before, the police were now sure they were on the trail of their prime suspect.

They took out search warrants for Don's house and under the kitchen floorboards they found Julie's missing house keys. Dunlop's fingerprints were on the distinctive Playboy key fob, which Julie had brought back from her trip to London the previous year. But that wasn't the only evidence they were able to put together. The night that Julie was murdered, Billy had been wearing a Billingham Rugby Club shirt, and fibres from a shirt of that type had been found on the blanket that her body was wrapped in. There was also semen on the blanket that DNA testing showed could be his, along with human hairs.

'We haven't just got 100 per cent evidence that he's the guilty one,' the police assured us, 'we feel we have a 110 per cent-strong prosecution case.'

It seemed that they had redeemed themselves a little by conducting a fast and thorough murder investigation and catching the culprit almost immediately. There was some comfort for us in knowing the man responsible for taking our Julie from us would almost certainly be paying a just price for his crime. It didn't alleviate any of the pain of losing her, but it helped in the struggle to hold onto our sanity.

We would have felt a great deal better, of course, if Billy Dunlop had come clean and admitted everything, but when he was arrested he denied the allegation, saying he had no idea how the keys got under Don's floorboards. He suggested that maybe someone was trying to frame him, even going to the trouble of planting his fingerprints on the brass fob. But such a ridiculous claim didn't rock the confidence of the police. They were sure they had their man and were relieved to think they were going to be able to get someone as dangerous as Billy Dunlop off the streets for a significant time.

Our liaison officer, Mark Braithwaite, was keeping Charlie and me updated on relevant developments as they happened, probably because the police were desperate to ensure they didn't let us down again as they had at the beginning of the investigation. We really couldn't have faulted the murder squad for the meticulously considerate way they treated us during that stage of the investigation.

My biggest fear at that time was that Julie might still have been alive when Dunlop pushed her under the bath, and that he had left her there to die. The thought of her regaining consciousness and finding herself imprisoned behind a bath panel in an empty house kept going round and round in my head. But eventually the police were able to tell me categorically that she had been dead before he put her there. It's strange the things you can find scraps of comfort in when everything is so bleak.

The pathologist's report made it clear that there would have been a lot more evidence to tell us how she had died if the police had found Julie's body when they first went into the house to search.

'The autopsy findings in this case,' the pathologist wrote, 'have been to a large extent obscured by quite advanced post-mortem changes.'

He concluded his report by saying it was not possible to state exactly what the cause of death had been. 'There was certainly no evidence of any natural disease to cause or accelerate death,' he wrote, 'and the circumstances and the presence of a violent sexual injury indicate that death must have been from other than natural causes. There was no evidence of a violent beating up and no broken bones. Given the negative findings and the general nature of the case it is likely that death has been due to some form of asphyxia, say strangulation or suffocation, and of course the subtle signs of these would easily be obscured by putrefactive change.'

Earlier in the report he had written in detail about the damage that had been done to Julie's vagina by whoever her killer was. To read and hear such things about your own child is unbearably painful, but I found my need to know the truth about what had happened to my baby was stronger than the revulsion I felt as more and more gruesome details came to light. I could hardly bear to think about it, but I still wanted to know everything.

'There was present,' the pathologist wrote, 'about the body only a single unequivocal injury. This consisted of a huge vertically running laceration running the whole length of the vagina posteriorly and on the left. The lesion could not have been caused by normal sexual intercourse and must be taken to be the result of a deliberate act of violence, perhaps even violation or defilement.' He thought it likely that the injury had occurred after death.

Any mother stopping for a moment to think how they would feel to read such things about their daughter will know how I felt at that moment, but I was not going to allow my own horror to defeat me. I had to be able to cope with the information if I was going to make sure that Julie received justice for what had happened to her.

Mark Braithwaite explained that now the pathologists had finished with Julie's body, the coroner would hold an inquest and then release the body for the funeral. I expect he thought it would be a relief to us to think that we would be moving forward, but it actually worried me.

'Have you got all the test results back?' I asked.

'We're just waiting for two more to come through,' he admitted.

I didn't feel too happy about that. What if we had Julie's remains cremated and the police then discovered that something had gone wrong with one of the tests? It would be too late by that time to do anything about it. I was paranoid about allowing anything to go wrong in the process of getting a guilty verdict for Billy Dunlop. Charlie and I made an appointment to go and see the coroner with Mark and we told them both about our reservations.

'But the pathologists have finished with the body,' Mark protested.

'Listen, you,' I said, as firmly as I could manage. 'Your lot have cocked enough up. She's been dead since November and it's now April. A couple more weeks is going to make no difference to us or to Julie. I would prefer to wait until all the test results are back.'

The coroner looked at me over his glasses for a moment, and then turned to Mark. 'Mrs Ming isn't very happy about me opening the inquest,' he said, 'and neither am I. We will wait until all the results are back.'

Eventually all the tests came back and the inquest could safely be held. We went along to listen to what they had to say. Even though I knew it would be painful, I felt that Julie needed to have a representative everywhere that her death was being discussed. Besides, I still found that the only way to cope with my raw grief was by channelling it into action, so if there was anything at all I could usefully do, then I would do it.

The pathologist stood up and talked about his findings. As his words flowed round me, describing the most intimate details of Julie's corpse, I started to feel bad and then I suddenly found myself back in her bathroom. I couldn't see anything except a massive bath and Julie underneath it. I tried to blink the pictures away but they just became more vivid, the putrid smells filling my nostrils, making me gag.

Terrified at having to relive the whole thing yet again I stood up and ran out of the room, but there was nowhere I could run to that would actually allow me to escape. Wherever I went, the thoughts and pictures went with me inside my head and I knew they always would. But I couldn't let them frighten me off, any more than I could let Billy Dunlop's reputation for violence intimidate me. Julie needed us to stay on his trail and that was what we were going to do.

Chapter Nine
The Funeral

Once the test results were in there was no need for the authorities to keep hold of Julie's poor battered body any longer. She could finally be allowed some peace and dignity and we would have to face up to saying goodbye to her once and for all. Charlie and I went over to a funeral parlour in Middlesborough where Gary and Angela were going to meet us.

The funeral directors respectfully showed us into the room where they had laid the coffin. I found it hard to breathe as my grief hit me full-strength at the sight of it. It was yet another confirmation that she was gone, that we would never be able to speak to her again, never be able to say goodbye properly or tell her how much we loved her. The lid of the coffin was closed and I laid our flowers gently on the top. It felt a bit as though we were reclaiming her for the family after all the months she had spent away, being manhandled by strangers.

'I hope you're all right now, Julie,' I whispered, wondering whether she might be able to hear me somewhere. 'I hope it's OK where you are.'

It was the first time the whole family was together in the same room since Julie had disappeared and none of us wanted the moment to end, because we knew that once it was over we would never be together like that again; there would always be a part of us missing. All I had ever wanted was to have my family around me.

Eventually I forced myself to walk outside on wobbly legs to see the woman running the funeral parlour, moving as if I was in a trance. Following my lead, Angela offered to give Gary a lift back home, leaving Charlie in the room on his own with Julie. Only later did he tell me that once we had all gone he moved the flowers to one side and stretched himself over the lid in order to be close to her one last time.

'I promise you, Julie,' he whispered through the thick wood, 'that before I die I'll make sure I get the bastard who killed you.'

The funeral was booked for April 20 at St Mary's Church in Acklam. I went to see Dr Geoghegan the day before, hoping he could help me find a way to get through the ordeal.

'Do you know that song?' I asked him.

'What song?'

'The one that says "Make the world go away".'

'Yes,' he said, ' I know it.'

'Please can you give me some tablets to make tomorrow go away?'

'I wish I could,' he said, and I knew he meant it.

We had decided to hold the service back in Acklam, even though we didn't live there anymore, because it was where Julie had been born and brought up. It was where she had been to school and church and had joined the Brownies and the Guides. Most of her good friends had come from there and most of the memories that we had of her were from the years we had spent there as a family. I wanted her school friends to be able to attend the service because it would have meant a lot to her to know they cared. It wasn't that long, after all, since they had all been school-children together.

Charlie, Gary, Angela, Andrew and I were picked up in a big black funeral car. As we drove past our old house we turned to look out the windows and I voiced the thought that was going through all our heads.

'I wish we'd never moved from there,' I sighed. 'Maybe if we hadn't, then she would still be alive.'

I immediately wished I hadn't said that because it made Andrew feel that we blamed it all on her meeting and marrying him, which wasn't true.

The church was already packed with friends and family as Charlie and I and the rest of the family walked slowly down the road towards it, following the coffin. I could see photographers from the papers standing around the bushes on the way through the churchyard, discreetly taking pictures, trying their best not to intrude. I didn't mind; I was in a different world anyway. They were nothing to do with what was going on inside my head.

I looked up at the coffin resting on the men's shoulders in front of us and pictured Julie's little body lying inside. It suddenly seemed all wrong. It should have been me in that box, not our Julie. Parents are supposed to die before their children. I wasn't sure I could take another step because every step I took was carrying me closer to the moment when I would have to say goodbye to her for ever.

A powerful wave of emotion that my subconscious must have been keeping a tight rein on for weeks rose up inside me, rushing up through my chest and into my head, cutting out all the sounds around me and bringing tears to my eyes. I was panicking at the thought of losing my child and being helpless to do anything about it. It's hard for any mother to endure the feeling of not being able to help their children when they need help. I started to scream, unable to hold the grief in, unable to maintain my composure a second longer.

'Nobody would listen,' I sobbed. 'I told them she hadn't gone to London but nobody would listen.'

Charlie put his arm round me but there was nothing he could say. He was struggling to hold himself together and didn't have any strength left to help me. Somehow I kept walking, just planting one foot in front of the other, wailing as I went and hanging on to Charlie and his niece for support. Gary and Angela were behind us, with their partners.

As we drew closer to the church and to the moment when I would have to walk down the aisle through the crowd inside, I couldn't bear to go on. I was terrified of being trapped inside the church with all those eyes on me as I battled to hold myself together. I had asked for 'Ave Maria' to be played while the church was filling up and as I heard the beautiful sounds floating out of the building I could see in my mind a picture of our Julie and Andrew swirling round the dance floor at their wedding, so innocent and young and happy, with their whole lives ahead of them. But in front of me were the men carrying the box that contained the reality of what had happened to their dreams.

As the church doors loomed up before us I knew that once we were through them there would be no going back; Julie would finally be dead and gone and I was going to have to accept that I would never see her again in this life. All my hopes had gone.

'I don't want to go in,' I told Charlie and his niece. 'I can't do it.'

His niece took a firm hold of my arms and looked into my eyes. 'You've got to go in,' she said firmly. 'You've got to.'

She almost had to push me through the door. One of my work colleagues told me a long time later how they had all been sitting in church, with the music playing around them, many of them remembering the wedding, and all of a sudden they heard a terrible noise at the entrance.

'It sounded like a child crying,' she told me. 'For a moment I thought you had brought Kevin with you. Then we realised it wasn't him crying, it was you. There was this deathly silence. It was electrifying. The next moment you were in the church among us.'

Standing in those pews, with Julie lying in the coffin a few feet away,

I just wanted to hold her in my arms and never let her go. I felt as though my heart had finally broken and I didn't know how I would ever be able to cope with the pain.

After the service we went to the crematorium, where I'd asked them to play Harry Secombe's 'I'll walk with God' on a continuous loop. I was adamant that I didn't want any lulls in the music, no uncomfortable silences. I wanted his voice ringing out all the time as Julie's body made its final journey through the curtains and out of sight. If she had had her way in the planning of the day we would probably have been listening to Boy George's 'Karma Chameleon'. People do that sort of thing these days but not back then, when they expected to hear 'suitable' music at funerals.

Finally it was all over. The coffin had vanished and Julie was no more. All that remained of her now was in our memories.

We had booked the Bluebell Hotel for tea and everyone went back there once we'd finished at the crematorium. The room was packed with dozens of familiar faces from Julie's past and as I looked around all I could think was that the only person who was missing was Julie herself. The rest of the day passed by in a blur of tears as well-meaning people tried their best to find the right words to say to me. It was a hopeless task because there were no right words. Nothing could comfort me at that moment.

The newspapers printed their pictures the following day under headlines like 'Family Farewell to Tragic Julie', and all I could think of when I looked at them was, what in God's name did Charlie's hair look like? He still had the curly perm that Julie had given him, but over the previous few months it had turned nearly white with grief. The wind outside the church had lifted it almost vertical and he looked like Don King, the boxing promoter, in his heyday.

'If Julie's looking down on us now,' Angela said when I showed her the pictures, 'she'd be saying "What on earth's happened to our Dad's hair?"'

Charlie just gave a thin smile and said nothing. Whatever was happening on the top of his head was the least of his problems.

Now, finally, I could start the grieving process. We bought a bench in Julie's name for the garden of remembrance where her ashes were scattered, and set about the task of fulfilling Charlie's final promise to her to make sure we got the man who had taken her young life so brutally. We had no idea what we were about to get ourselves into.

Chapter Ten
Learning to Cope

I worked for a health authority so my bosses were very understanding about how hard it would be to return to 'normal' life after everything we had been through. But they also understood that it might help me to get back into the routine of it as soon as I could, in order to have some structure in my life.

Two days after I had found Julie's body, my nurse manager suggested that I should go to see a staff psychologist who had recently been taken on. At first I wasn't sure that I felt ready to bare my soul to a complete stranger, but she was insistent.

'I've booked you an appointment to see Martin Bamber,' she told me. 'If you don't turn up I'll be coming to get you myself.'

I didn't know if that was the route I wanted to follow, but I knew I was going to have to do something if I wasn't going to go insane. I was constantly suffering from the most vivid and realistic flashbacks, unable to get the smell of Julie's body out of my nostrils. I couldn't shut my eyes to sleep because I would immediately see her under the bath and I was in danger of collapsing from the mixture of stress and exhaustion.

I was shocked by how young Martin Bamber looked when I walked into his office for our first appointment. He seemed like an academic type with mousy hair and little round frameless glasses. I soon discovered he was still only in his twenties and I wasn't sure that I was going to be able to talk frankly to a man so much younger than myself, but I knew I had to try.

'I only know a bit about the case,' he told me as we settled down, 'because I've just moved to the area, so if you'd like to tell me what happened in your own words that would be very helpful.'

I didn't want to be rude since he'd been kind enough to give up his time for me, so I took a deep breath and started talking. Three hours later I was still talking. He was the easiest person in the world to communicate with and I went on seeing him for three or four years after that. He was absolutely brilliant at helping me to analyse everything that was going on inside my head. Martin was able to explain so much to me about why I felt the way I did, why I acted the way I did and what I needed to do in order to be able to overcome the pain and live as normal a life as possible.

The nights were always the worst times. Unable to sleep, with thoughts of what might have happened to Julie during her last hours swirling round and round in my head, I wouldn't be able to lie in bed for long. I often got up and started doing housework to try to distract myself. I just had to keep my mind busy so that it couldn't dwell on the many questions that still had no answers.

Although Julie had finally been laid to rest and we had said our last goodbyes, we still had Dunlop's trial to go through, so there was no chance of being able to forget what had happened for even a few minutes at a time.

Lack of sleep was making things worse, stretching my nerves like brittle elastic, and I was dangerously close to breaking point. My behaviour was damaging my relationship with Charlie as well. He was dealing with his grief differently from me, blocking the memories, forcing them to the back of his mind. I couldn't understand how he was able to do that, any more than he could understand why I couldn't. It was then that Martin introduced me to the term 'psychic numbing', and explained that this was what was making me feel emotionally detached from other people. He told me that was why my relationship with Charlie was deteriorating. I've been told that as many as nine out of ten couples end up apart after losing a child to murder and I can quite believe it. If all your energy is going into holding on to your own sanity, it is hard to pay attention to repairing a damaged relationship.

Over the years Charlie and I have been to a lot of conferences about bereavement together, searching for any crumbs of comfort we can find and hoping that by sharing our experiences we can help others. It is always comforting to be with people who understand exactly how you feel and what you have endured.

At one event there was a vicar and his wife whose daughter had hung herself. The wife spoke about how she thought her husband was cold and believed he was not grieving for their daughter whereas she was having friends over, talking about it and crying openly. One day, she told us, she came home early from shopping and found her husband sitting in their daughter's bedroom with her ballet music blaring from the sound system. He was holding a picture of the girl and crying. That, she discovered, had been his weekly routine ever since their daughter had died. It was his way of coping with the grief, like an emergency valve regularly letting out the steam that was constantly building up inside him. I heard many stories after that of how men would cry in private, in the shower or sitting in their cars with the music on, and I have been moved to understand how deeply fathers love their children, even if they are often unable to show it in the same way as the women.

Gary and Angela both reacted more like Charlie than like me, neither of them wanting to talk about how they felt, keen to block out the pain as quickly as possible. I think in some ways it brought them a bit closer to each other; perhaps they talked about things together that they didn't share with me in case they upset me more.

When I was about to sort through Julie's clothes one day, Angela stopped me, whipping them all away.

'You don't need to have bags of old clothes to remember Julie,' she said firmly. 'You're just getting morbid.' And she was right. I wouldn't have been able to throw them away myself.

However quiet they were on the outside, I knew Angela and Gary were both hurting inside. Gary did tell me that he blamed himself because he hadn't gone round to her house that night. If he'd been there, it wouldn't have happened. I think he struggled with his guilt about that for a while— but we all had something we regretted not doing. If only I had talked her into coming back to stay at my place that night, it wouldn't have happened either. We each dealt with our feelings separately, in different ways.

One unexpected beneficial side effect to come from the shock of finding Julie's body was that it seemed to cure my asthma attacks. I had always had to carry an inhaler around with me, but I never needed it after that day. According to the chest specialist at the hospital, the shock could have made the asthma worse; it could have gone either way.

Eventually the stresses of living together with our grief became too much for Charlie and me. We both needed to be on our own for at least a few hours each day, so he stayed in the house and I rented another place while we both tried to sort out our feelings and find a way of coping.

By then Martin had explained to me that I was suffering from post-traumatic stress disorder (PTSD) while Charlie was suffering from severe depression, and it was just too much for us to be together under the same roof. I would come in from a hard day's work in the hospital and Charlie would be going on and on about Dunlop until I thought my head was going to explode. Meanwhile, I would want to talk about Julie and about how I felt but he was unable to listen to me. No one who hasn't experienced it can imagine how much damage a bereavement like ours does to a family.

Underneath it all our marriage must have been very strong, because even though we didn't live together for a year, we would still see each other every day. We had been together for so long it was hard to be apart, almost like losing another part of ourselves. I felt as though I couldn't live with Charlie, but at the same time I couldn't live without him.

I felt furious that Dunlop had been able to do so much harm to my family beyond the obvious damage he did to Julie herself. I saw no solution to our problems, nothing that could bring things back to how they were when we were all together as a family. And the flashbacks would never leave me alone.

'I want you to go back physically to that bathroom in Grange Avenue,' Martin told me a few months after I started seeing him. 'I think confronting your fears will really help you to move on.'

Go back? But in my head I was going back there all the time; that was exactly the problem I was trying to cure. I knew he had been right about other things before and he deserved my trust, so I agreed to do as he asked.

'All right,' I said. 'I'll do it.'

Mark Braithwaite, the police liaison officer, realised how frightened I was at the thought of revisiting the scene of all my worst nightmares and agreed to come with me. The council hadn't allocated the house to anyone else yet and we still had the keys. I was quite calm as we drove into Grange Avenue and pulled up outside, but when we walked through the door and I saw the stairs stretching up in front of me I felt a terrible shudder of fear pass through me. Was this really going to help? Or would it just tip me over the edge into insanity once and for all?

'Can I hold your hand?' I asked Mark.

'Of course,' he replied, kindly.

Holding on tightly like a little girl on her way to her first day at school, I climbed the stairs with him, then paused outside the bathroom door.

'Do you want me to come in with you?' he asked.

'No,' I said, 'just leave me. You go down. I'll be all right.'

I waited till he had disappeared from sight before stepping into the empty room. The police had stripped the bath and the panel out and sent them off for tests, so it looked more like a building site than Julie's home. My knees wobbled and refused to support me. I sank down onto the floor, leaned back against the wall, and felt as though my heart was breaking. I waited for my breathing to steady itself and then looked around, taking in every detail, trying to force out the old pictures and replace them with new ones from the empty, harmless room in front of me.

In the corner of the floor was a stain where Julie's bodily fluids had seeped into the floorboards and the only thing I could think about was all the long days and nights she had lain there without us knowing. I pictured all the policemen coming and going while she lay there, twisted and still, the last of her life's juices ebbing out of her. I remembered standing there with Angela, talking to the police about her, looking through her make-up bag, when all the time she was lying just inches away.

When I felt calm enough, I pulled myself back onto my feet and left the room. Although it was a painful experience, the next time I had a nightmare I saw Julie actually walking away with a bath panel under her arm.

'You've moved on in leaps and bounds,' Martin said when I told him, 'because you're not stuck under the bath any more.'

While Dunlop was in Durham Prison on remand, Gary found out that another lad he knew was in there too, so he and Charlie cooked up a prison visit. Charlie says he wanted Dunlop to see him, wanted him to know that we were not just going to leave it all up to the police, that we wouldn't rest until he was behind bars for what he had done to our child. It was part of the promise Charlie had made to our Julie when she was lying in her coffin.

When they got back home from the visit they told me they'd seen Dunlop across the visiting room and they knew he had seen them. We later heard that the sight of Charlie sitting there, staring at him, had rattled Dunlop badly. I dare say it reminded him of stories he would have heard as a boy about the powers of the inscrutable Chinamen with their knives and their opium and their 'slow boats to China'.

There had always been a lot of local media interest in the story of Julie's death and at one stage Billy Dunlop's dad agreed to talk about his son for a television documentary. He maintained that he didn't believe Billy had killed our Julie because, as he told the cameras, strangling 'wasn't Billy's style'. His dad said that if Billy ever killed someone he would do it by 'battering them to death', as if somehow that made his son out to be a better person than everyone was saying.

He openly admitted that he had always brought up his children to stand up for themselves in fights, but that even as a boy Billy had never known where to draw the line when it came to fighting back. Most people, he suggested, would just knock their opponent down and consider they'd won the fight, but once his opponents were on the floor Billy would keep on kicking and beating them until his temper was spent. That certainly bore out eyewitness reports of what had happened to the man Billy had attacked outside the rugby club. Maybe something similar had happened to Julie, even if there hadn't been any evidence of a beating.

The more we learned about Billy Dunlop the more we believed he was a danger to society and the more determined we became to have him convicted and imprisoned. We planned to follow Billy Dunlop's case every inch of the way until he was convicted. We wanted to do everything we could to ensure that he was given a sentence that befitted his crime.

At least now we had a focus for our lives, something proactive we could do for our child.

Chapter Eleven
The Police Complaints Authority

We launched an official complaint against the police force while the internal investigation into the Cleveland force was still underway. It was based on the list of grievances I wrote out the night after I found Julie, when I was still in the initial stages of shock and anger.

The investigation took a few months and then Deputy Chief Constable Jack Ord had to write a report to the Police Complaints Authority in London, giving the reasons why they had failed to find Julie. When I read a copy of the report I couldn't believe my eyes. It seemed to me to be an absolute whitewash. The following are extracts from the letter that we received from G. V. Marsh of the Police Complaints Authority on September 17, 1990:

Dear Mr and Mrs Ming,

I am writing on behalf of the Police Complaints Authority about the complaints you made on February 6, 1990. Before discussing those complaints, however, I want you to know how sorry we are

about the tragic death of your daughter and the way in which
subsequent circumstances added to your grief . . .

Clearly, your greatest concern is that the police failed to find
Julie's body. The investigation into your complaints has found that
her disappearance was in fact taken extremely seriously from the
outset and a large number of officers were involved at one time or
another. You have complained about the attitude of some of them. For
instance, you believed that the woman constable, to whom you first
reported that Julie could not be found, showed little interest—an
attitude underlined by the fact that she continued to chew gum.
She admits that she chews dental gum occasionally but the records
show that she dealt with the matter meticulously and diligently.
Accordingly, the complaint about her cannot be substantiated. As to
the officer who you alleged made a distasteful remark, he insists that
he did not intend to offend and he thinks it possible that you took his
comment out of context. We note that he apologised to you later for
inadvertently causing you distress and we believe the matter should
rest there. We take the same view about your complaint about the
officer from the Community Relations Department. He has been
interviewed and regrets that his attempts to reassure you were
construed as implying that he did not recognise and believe
your concern. He says that in fact he was disturbed by Julie's
disappearance but, despite his own reservations, tried to give you
some hope that the matter would be happily resolved.

Your complaint that information was improperly disclosed to Mark
Ward could not be investigated fully, owing to the reluctance of the
witness to assist. However, the limited investigation that was carried
out revealed no evidence to substantiate this allegation.

Your arrest, Mr Ming, and that of your son were justified on the
evidence available at the time but the investigation has shown that the
period you both spent in custody was excessive. Your complaint in
this respect is substantiated as is your complaint that the inquiries
into the alleged assault were not satisfactorily concluded and
communicated. However, the investigation of your complaint that
you were left in a cold cell with no blanket has found no evidence
that the heating system was malfunctioning during the time of your
detention and your custody log indicates that in fact you slept well.

But to return to the police's failure to find your daughter's body, the investigation into your complaint found that the endeavours of many officers to find her came to naught because of a basic failure of communication between those concerned. They, and the Force in general, are well aware that the result both showed the Force in a poor light and added considerably to your distress. The Deputy Chief Constable has told the Authority that valuable lessons have been learned and that, while he does not consider that the officers concerned were guilty of neglect, he is disappointed with their performance. He does not think that formal disciplinary charges should be brought . . .

The official line, therefore, was that the reason why they had failed to find Julie's body was 'lack of communication' between the forensic officers inside the house. Hard as it was to understand how five grown men could fail to communicate effectively in such a small space, it seemed to us he was saying that each of the officers in the team thought someone else had searched the bathroom and the loft properly, so didn't bother to do it themselves. Having worked out that, in their opinion, that was all that had gone wrong, it was then decided that no one was going to be sacked. All that was going to happen was the officers concerned would be given 'strong advice'—whatever that meant. Inspector Lee, who had been in charge of the investigation, actually went on to be promoted, eventually becoming the Commander of Stockton police force.

If I had been angry with them before reading the report, I was even more furious afterwards. In fact I was so angry I asked our solicitor to write to the Deputy Chief Constable and request a meeting. I wanted to hear the forensic officers explain to me personally what the hell they had been doing in that house for five days. Had they just been humouring me all that time? Were they so certain that Julie had disappeared off down to London, leaving her child behind, that they all sat round the kitchen table playing cards for five days? (Apart from one man sticking his head through the loft hatch, of course.) I wanted to hear some straight, honest answers, not read some official report designed to cover everyone's backs.

Our solicitor received a formal reply from the Deputy Chief Constable saying that he could not agree to meet with us. As the matter was dealt with by the Police Complaints Authority, it would not be appropriate for him to discuss these issues.

Incensed, I told a local journalist who had kept in regular touch from the beginning that we were thinking of suing Cleveland Police. He must have passed that comment on—maybe he asked the police for their reaction—because the same day the police commander rang and asked to come and see us. It seemed that journalists could get action from public officials that the rest of us could only dream of.

'I'd rather have talked to the organ grinder,' I replied grumpily, 'but since they're only sending the monkey, you'd better come.'

Despite this put-down, the poor chap still turned up and he must have been expecting the worst. Looking back, I feel sorry for that commander, but at the time I was so stressed out and medicated I wasn't in a mood to show any of them any mercy. He had walked straight into the lions' den.

'Nobody would ever say you weren't entitled to compensation for what you have suffered,' he assured us.

'But compensation isn't going to bring our daughter back,' I reminded him, 'is it?'

'We've been made to look very foolish in this case,' he admitted.

'You've been made to look complete idiots,' I agreed. 'I didn't even speak to the press initially; it was you who made the big headlines about how you were sending out divers to the pond and dogs onto the wastelands around Billingham.'

After a while Charlie started giving me a look that suggested I should shut up now but I was on a roll, and kept on going.

Shortly after this meeting, Cleveland Police offered us £5,000 compensation, which sounded to me like a bit of an insult. Our solicitor was keen for us to take it, saying that it was very rare for the police even to admit they were in the wrong, let alone offer compensation, but I still refused. After all, they could hardly deny they had been in the wrong, considering the evidence—we actually had a dead body to prove just how wrong they had been. The next offer was £10,000 and although it still didn't seem enough to compensate us for everything they had put us through I was too stressed to carry on with the fight. I wanted it all to end, so I gave in and accepted.

We also got some money from the Criminal Injuries Compensation Authority—£15,000, which was supposed to compensate me for having post-traumatic stress disorder and Charlie for having severe depression. There was no satisfaction in any of this, though. What we really wanted was to watch Billy Dunlop being found guilty of Julie's murder. Only then would it feel as though we could start to move on and rebuild our lives.

Chapter Twelve
The Trial

The trial of Billy Dunlop started in May 1991, eighteen months after Julie was killed. It felt as though we had been waiting for that day to come for ever. As we walked up the steps to the court we came face to face with Derrick Dobson, the senior investigating officer in the case.

'At last,' I said, 'we get to meet "the Hunter".' I couldn't resist reminding him of the way in which he had styled himself on the television. Since he had managed to find and charge Billy within two weeks of knowing Julie had been murdered, I couldn't claim that he hadn't done his job properly.

Although I was nervous about standing up in front of a packed courtroom as a witness, and terrified about having to listen to every detail of what had happened to Julie that night, I was also relieved to think that we might finally be approaching some sort of closure. Once it was over and Billy had been convicted, I thought, I would feel that we had succeeded in getting some justice for Julie and we could all concentrate on trying to get on with repairing our own lives.

The trial was being held before a judge called Swinton Thomas, at Moot Hall in Newcastle, a famous old courthouse down by the river. The case went on for three weeks and was the most gruelling experience imaginable. When Dunlop was brought into the courtroom on the first day, I felt physically sick. Did he have any idea of the trauma he had put my whole family through? Did he ever think about that? There was no sign of it. He sat in the dock with a fixed expression that never changed throughout the trial, not an ounce of emotion visible.

Giving evidence and having to relive those early terrible months was like a waking nightmare. The defence barrister kept asking me for more and more detail, making me search further and further into my memory, digging up facts I had chosen to bury deep.

'When you went into the bathroom, Mrs Ming,' he would ask, 'and you put your hand behind the bath panel, was it your left hand or your right hand?'

As I struggled to answer correctly I was transported back in flashbacks so lifelike that the smell of Julie's body filled my nostrils all over again. The pictures were so vivid I couldn't see the courtroom at all; reality had disappeared from in front of my eyes, leaving me in some dreadful, dark, haunted corner of my own memory. I forced myself to stay put, listening to the questions, trying to answer them without crying or fainting.

When I was back in the gallery, listening to other people talking about Julie, it was just as painful. It's hard to hear someone you love being discussed in a courtroom. She was our baby, our Julie, so how come these people knew things about her that we didn't? The facts sounded so cold, the descriptions so matter of fact. I remembered Julie as the pretty little girl who liked to dance and do gymnastics and dress up in strange clothes. But these men were discussing the sexual habits and morals of a grown woman, making assumptions about her, judging her, making it sound as if she was the criminal on trial, rather than the innocent victim.

I didn't recognise the woman the lawyers and witnesses were describing. Even though I used to see Julie every day and we talked about everything under the sun, I hadn't realised that she had started seeing other boys since her relationship with Andrew had begun to fail. But now I was being forced to sit there and listen to every liaison in clinical detail, as if they were crimes she had committed, proof that she deserved to be killed.

It wasn't just that I didn't like having to listen to details about Julie's private life; I also hated the thought that other people were hearing them and would be making judgments about her, people who knew nothing about her beyond what they had heard in court.

I had to admit it sounded as though she had been careless and foolish with her affections, but having it spelled out to me was yet another shock to my already battered system. The biggest shock was to find that Julie had actually slept with Dunlop once, some time before. The court was told that Dunlop had gone back to see her on a later occasion, about ten days before she died. After that meeting a friend claimed that it was almost as if Julie had changed personality overnight, as if she was absolutely terrified of something. What could he have said to her or done to her on that visit to make her so frightened? Why hadn't she confided in me? It was as if they were describing the life of someone I didn't know at all.

The following three weeks in the courtroom passed almost as though they were happening to someone else. I watched the proceedings from the public gallery through a fog of shock, noticing strange little details like the three jurors who appeared to sleep through virtually the whole trial. It worried me that they didn't seem to be paying attention but, I told myself, the case was so cut-and-dried maybe they had all made up their minds that he was guilty and didn't need to hear any more. Still, it seemed disrespectful to Julie that they couldn't be bothered to stay awake.

Jayne, the girlfriend whom Billy had moved back in with after Julie's death, arrived in court looking threatening and tough, as if she had deliberately got herself up to look like a hard man's moll. Her hair was all spiked up aggressively and her ears were full of piercings. I'd heard about her from people who'd been at school in her year and they all said she hadn't been like that till she met Dunlop, that she'd changed to please him.

After all the medical evidence had been heard I felt sick and had to go outside for some air, leaving Charlie to follow what was happening for both of us. I was sitting alone in the corridor, trying to regain my composure, when the door to the courtroom opened and I saw that Jayne had followed me out. I averted my eyes, not wanting to provoke a confrontation.

'You must hate me,' she said, and I knew she was talking to me.

'Why would I hate you?' I asked, too weary to fight with anyone else. 'I don't even know you. But I hate the man you live with.'

She sat down next to me uninvited.

'I've got two children to him,' she said, 'and they keep asking me when their daddy's coming home.'

'At least he's going to be coming home one day,' I reminded her. 'My daughter is never coming home.'

'I didn't want to believe he'd done this,' she went on, as if she hadn't heard me. 'But it sounds from all the evidence like he did.'

'He's an absolute psychopath,' I said. 'What's he gained by doing this?'

She shrugged, obviously having no more understanding of him than I did. I began to realise she was as much his victim as the rest of us.

'Didn't you notice anything different in his behaviour during the three months before I found Julie's body?' I asked.

'I've tried to think about that time,' she said. 'The only thing I remember is that because of Julie I scanned the local paper every night for news. If there was anything in it I would read it out to him, but he never once made any comment. I thought nothing of it at the time, but when he was charged I started thinking about it.'

At that moment our victim-support woman walked by and Jayne didn't say any more.

It was only once the case came to court that we found out more about the police investigation. When the officer who said he had checked the loft was called to the witness stand he admitted all he had actually done was stand on the banister, push his head through the hatch, strike a match and look around. Satisfied there was no body up there he closed the hatch, jumped down off the banister and left it at that.

'Are you still employed by the Cleveland Constabulary?' the examining lawyer enquired, obviously having trouble believing what he was hearing.

'Oh, yes,' the policeman replied innocently, as if such gross negligence was just another normal occurrence in his working day.

We also discovered that the alarm the police had installed when they left the house hadn't malfunctioned at all. It had actually rung in the police station when the intruder got in the day after the police had gone. Two officers had reached the house within four minutes of the alarm going off. When they got there the back window was wide open. The television was on the draining board in the kitchen and the video had been stolen.

They'd radioed for a police dog handler to come to the house. The dog came up with nothing downstairs but as the handler started to go up the stairs the dog had become highly agitated and dragged its handler into the bathroom where it became even more excited. It still didn't bark, so he decided to pull it out of the bathroom and take it into the garden to search for intruders there. The dog was trained to bark only when it smelled a live person, not a dead body.

I couldn't believe what I was hearing and it was all I could do to stop myself shouting, 'You bloody idiot!' If his dog was agitated in the bathroom, why didn't he try to find out what had caused it?

One of Billy's claims was that he had got so drunk at the rugby club he hadn't any idea what he was doing after that. Wandering around the town drunk gave him a sort of alibi for the lost six hours, I suppose.

However, when the doctor who had stitched up his eyebrow was called to the witness stand he said that, although Billy had obviously had a few drinks by the time he got to Casualty, he wasn't out of control in any way and would have been perfectly capable of remembering what he was doing after leaving the hospital. He said he could be sure of that because he had given Billy some anaesthetic for the stitches and he would have judged how much to give him by how much alcohol Billy had in his blood at the time.

'If he had been blind drunk,' he explained, 'I wouldn't have administered any anaesthetic.'

As I listened to the evidence, more pieces of the story fell into place. I realised that Billy had been sitting on the other side of the wall in the house next door with his friend Mark Ward for much of the time that the forensic team were supposedly pulling Julie's home to pieces in their search for clues. He must have been expecting any minute to hear shouting and sirens and see a flurry of activity in the street outside as soon as the police realised they were dealing with a murder case. As every day passed without incident he was probably beginning to distrust his own memory, wondering if he had dreamed the whole thing, wondering if he was going mad.

The police believe it likely that once Dunlop knew the forensic team had left the house he went back in, using Julie's keys, to see if her body was still where he'd put it. That could explain the mysterious burglary, when the video disappeared and the television was found in the kitchen by the open window. By doing that he made it look as though it was a simple break-in, in case anyone saw him coming or going. If the police had got there as quickly as they said they had, he certainly wouldn't have had time to move the body somewhere safer, even if he had wanted to.

Every hour of the day and night my brain was churning over all the new facts and theories that were being produced in the courtroom, trying to make sense of them, trying to understand what had happened. It seemed that the night that he killed Julie, Dunlop must have stayed around afterwards to tidy the house and cover his tracks. It's possible that he might even have still been inside the house the next morning when I first came round to wake Julie up at seven thirty, since he didn't get back to his lodgings with Don till after that time (according to the evidence presented in court). 'It's lucky you didn't have a key to let yourself in,' one policeman told me, 'because if he was still there he would probably have killed you and Kevin as well, to eliminate you as potential witnesses.'

It was terrifying to think how close I could have been to catching Billy red-handed that morning. Was he really still cowering behind closed curtains as I banged on the doors and shouted through the letterbox? Was he sitting in there as impassively as he was now sitting in the dock, knowing that I didn't have a key? Or was he standing behind the door, waiting to pounce the moment I came in? Would he have strangled us too, or beaten us to death as his dad thought was more his style? Would he really have been able to murder a small innocent child? And why did he come back a couple of hours later to sit in Mark Ward's kitchen? I wonder how many times a day any of us are that close to danger without ever realising it.

The police also wondered if the original reason he took Julie's keys with him when he left was because he intended to return to dispose of the body. Maybe, they suggested, he was planning to dissolve it in acid just as soon as he was able to get it out of the house. Or maybe he would have gone back and done it in Julie's bathroom. If he had succeeded, we might never have found out what happened to her, and been left in the same state of limbo that we suffered for the first three months after her disappearance.

For so much of the trial Charlie and I were just sitting in the gallery staring down at Dunlop, willing him to speak up and tell the truth. On the whole he seemed remarkably composed for a man who was on trial for murder, but we noticed he kept taking his slip-on shoes off, turning them round and trying to force his feet into them back to front. It was a strange nervous tic suggesting that behind his immobile, hostile façade something was going on. Maybe a psychologist could explain that one.

His defence lawyer was good at his job, able to talk to the jury as though he was just holding a normal conversation with friends. He was much more convincing than the prosecuting counsel, who didn't seem to have much idea how to talk to ordinary people. We noticed that when the defence counsel was talking to the jury they stopped dozing and hung on his every word, nodding along to the points he was making. We convinced ourselves it wouldn't matter in the long run because the evidence against Dunlop was so overwhelming. He could give no plausible explanation as to why the keys were under his floorboards or why his semen was found on the blanket. He couldn't account for his movements during those hours between leaving the hospital and arriving home. He had a history of violence, particularly against women. So we assumed it didn't matter that a quarter of the jury was asleep and the defence lawyer was sounding so plausible; they were bound to find him guilty once the final question was asked, weren't they?

Towards the end of the three weeks Dunlop himself was put in the witness box and Charlie and I watched his every move like hawks, trying to work out what was going on behind his expressionless face. He would shut his eyes, as if thinking deeply, before answering each question from the prosecuting barrister. It made him seem strangely believable, even though the things he was saying, like the fantasy about someone trying to frame him by putting his fingerprints on the key fob, made no sense at all. It was as if he was honestly puzzled by how the whole misunderstanding could have come about.

'Somebody's trying to frame me for this,' he said again, his voice even and convincing. 'I didn't do it. I wouldn't. She was a lovely girl.'

It sounded so sincere we almost felt like believing him ourselves at times. All through the trial he stuck to his story that he knew nothing about what had happened that night, insisting that someone was trying to frame him. He was in the witness box for almost a whole day as the prosecution lawyer kept battering away at him, trying to break him. The strain did seem to be getting to him and by the end of the afternoon he was shaking so violently that even his hair seemed to be trembling.

'You're losing your bottle, Mr Dunlop,' the prosecutor said, pressing his advantage, 'because you did kill this girl.'

Charlie and I were on the edges of our seats, certain that he was about to crack and confess. 'You're shaking,' the lawyer kept on at him.

'No, I'm not,' Dunlop grunted. 'I didn't kill her.'

The shaking was getting worse and it looked as if he was about to give in and confess when the judge glanced up at the clock.

'It's quarter to four,' he said. 'We'll recess until tomorrow.'

I was bitterly disappointed as I watched Billy being escorted from the court, sure that if the prosecutor had been given another ten or fifteen minutes he would have been able to finish the job off. We had been so close and now we had to wait yet another day.

By the next day Billy had recovered his composure. The shaking had passed and he was back to sitting as still as a statue. But I still felt confident we were going to get a conviction. The representatives of the Crown Prosecution Service I spoke to were equally confident. We felt we were nearly at the end of our long and arduous journey.

The trial came to an end and the jury was out for a whole day, deliberating on what their verdict should be. Charlie and I sat waiting for news, barely daring to go to the toilet in case something happened. They were unable to come to a conclusion that day so they stayed in a hotel overnight and kept going the following day, during which they sent some pointless questions into the court via the usher. This puzzled everyone, even the judge.

'I don't understand this jury,' he said at one point. 'Their questions don't seem to be about anything relevant to this trial.'

By the time they came back into the courtroom I could hardly breathe with the tension. What if something went wrong at this stage? What if they decided he wasn't guilty, that there was 'reasonable doubt'? He would immediately be back out on the streets and none of us would be safe.

'Can your foreman please stand?' Words I had heard hundreds of time in courtroom dramas were suddenly being spoken right in front of me.

At that moment there was a flurry of confusion as the jury realised they didn't have a foreman. No one had thought to elect one. A buzz went round the room as everyone wondered what this meant. How was it possible that they had gone the whole three weeks without realising they needed a foreman? Why hadn't an official made sure they knew what to do? What had they been talking about in that hotel room for the past two days? What was going to happen now? We soon found out.

Not only had they given no thought to electing a foreman, but it seemed that they had also been unable to reach a verdict, even on a majority basis. The judge ruled that he would have to discharge them from their duties and order a retrial. He was obviously exasperated at the three weeks they had wasted, but his feelings didn't come close to the horror that we were feeling. This meant we were going to have to go through the whole nightmare again, and I truly didn't know if I would have the strength to endure it. Every ounce of energy I possessed had been used to get me through this first trial. How would I survive another?

Chapter Thirteen
Reliving the Nightmare

The retrial of Billy Dunlop didn't take place until October 1991, so we had to endure six more months of living in limbo, not knowing what the future held for us. After the fiasco of the first trial my confidence had been shaken. The police told us that they were just as certain of a conviction this time as they had been before the initial trial. But now I realised that however strong the evidence, you couldn't be sure of anything when it came to the legal system. If the jury simply didn't understand what was being said, or they allowed Billy's confident lies or the defence barrister's easy eloquence to convince them, then all the police's certainties were worth nothing. It was like being with Lewis Carroll's Alice in Wonderland, in a place where good sense and logic didn't necessarily mean a thing, and where anything might happen, however mad, impossible or contradictory it may seem.

I had learned the hard way that there are no certainties in life and nothing can be taken for granted. After the trial I bumped into Jayne, the mother of Dunlop's two boys, coming out of the health centre.

'How are you doing?' she asked when she spotted me. It sounded as though she genuinely cared and wanted to know the answer.

'I'm all right,' I replied cautiously, not wanting to open up too much, still not quite sure what to expect from her.

'I hope they get him next time,' she said, 'because if they don't it'll be me he'll kill next.'

Her words shocked me, reminding me just how important it was to other people that Dunlop was convicted, not just us. The police had told me how dangerous they believed he was, and now I was hearing the same from the woman who probably knew him better than anyone. Sometimes I worried that I was becoming obsessed with keeping him off the streets only because I wanted revenge for Julie's death. But when I heard Jayne saying she feared for her own life I knew for certain that our cause was just. Dunlop couldn't be allowed to get away with this murder and come back out to terrorise and kill again.

This time the case was being heard by Judge Harry Ognall, who had presided over many high-profile murder trials before, including that of the notorious Peter Sutcliffe, known in the media as 'the Yorkshire Ripper'. That news was encouraging as I felt we were in safe, experienced hands.

Charlie and I then had the nightmare of having to sit through the entire trial again, all the medical details gathered from Julie's poor abandoned body, all the details of her sexual flings in the last few months of her short life. As the days passed and the voices below us droned on, I spent a lot of hours staring at the jury, desperately trying to convince myself that things were going to turn out all right this time. At night, when I had finally calmed down enough to climb into bed, all the arguments and facts and worries would go round and round in my wakeful head as I waited for the moment when I would have to get up and start another day's ordeal.

Once more the judge sent the jury out to deliberate on everything they had heard and to decide if Billy Dunlop was guilty of the crime he was accused of. We hadn't heard a single new piece of evidence that had changed our minds in the slightest as to Dunlop's guilt. All we had to do, surely, was wait for the jury to announce the obvious conclusion.

The police allowed Charlie and me to come down from the public gallery into the courtroom and there we waited, one agonising hour after another.

'It's not looking too promising,' one of the detectives, Detective Inspector Dave Scott, told us quietly. For a moment I thought I must have heard him wrong.

'What do you mean?' I was shocked. How could they be talking like this now when they had been so confident of a conviction at the beginning of the first trial?

'If this jury are unable to reach a verdict, it's possible that the judge will acquit Dunlop,' he said.

'But what about all the evidence against him?' I asked, aghast.

He shrugged his shoulders. 'That's what could happen.'

I couldn't make his words sink in. The thought that Dunlop might walk free was too terrible even to contemplate.

A few minutes later, after five hours of waiting, Judge Ognall called the jurors back into the court.

'Have you reached a unanimous verdict?' he asked.

'No,' came the reply.

He asked if they could agree on a majority verdict. The answer was still no. So the judge acquitted Billy Dunlop, just as the police had feared he would. He would walk from the court a free man.

It took a few moments for his words to sink in and then I leaped to my feet. I felt a wave of hysteria rising up inside me, threatening to sweep away what was left of my sanity. I couldn't stop myself from screaming out at the top of my voice all the thoughts that were crowding into my brain.

'He killed our daughter and he's walking free!' I yelled. 'What's going to happen now?'

As I grappled with what had gone wrong I remembered that the reason the pathologist had been unable to confirm whether Julie had been strangled or asphyxiated was the condition of her body. If the police had found her earlier we might have had a very different outcome.

'The police should have found her!' I screamed.

All my anger and my fears and my grief poured out, the rush of emotion too much for my legs to cope with as they buckled beneath me and I found myself on the floor of the courtroom, still screaming and thrashing helplessly around, unable to believe that after a year of suffering our nightmare had just become even worse. Mark Braithwaite had to lift me up off the floor and help me from the courtroom, trying to console me as we went, because Charlie was caught up in his own state of acute shock. I remember I was punching Mark as he pulled me from the room.

'What happens now?' I kept crying. 'What happens now?'

I felt as though I was the one who had been given the life sentence; a sentence that I would be serving in purgatory. We would now have to go home knowing that Billy Dunlop was living up the road, as free to come knocking on our door as we were to knock on his.

I was so confused. None of it made sense. No one involved in the case could understand why the jury could have been left in any doubt that Billy had killed Julie that night, nor could they understand why the judge was willing to allow Billy back out onto the street after listening to all the evidence of how evil and violent he was.

The only thing that the jury didn't have was a confirmed cause of death. Somehow the prosecution barrister had failed to paint in the final detail of the actual moment of death vividly enough for the jury, leaving an element of doubt hovering in the air. And while that doubt hovered they couldn't bring themselves to convict him.

But what did it matter whether Julie was strangled or asphyxiated? They had a dead girl who had come to a violent end, and they had the man who had done it to her. It was the simplest thing in the world to piece together, wasn't it?

Eventually the police managed to coax me into a car and I was driven home, sobbing uncontrollably. I was unable to imagine how I was going to cope with the years that now stretched ahead of us with no Julie, no justice and no way of feeling that anything had ended. By the time we were sitting indoors I was drained of strength and we all just sat in a devastated silence as we tried to get our heads round what had happened.

The next day there were big pictures in the papers showing him back with Jayne and his boys, and she was saying she would stand by him and that she had always known he was innocent. I suppose she had to say that for fear of what he would do to her if she didn't, but at the time I felt she had betrayed me too. I felt we had been entirely defeated and Julie's life had been shown to be worth nothing to anyone but us.

The following afternoon Billy gave an interview on Tyne Tees Television in which he complained that he had been wrongfully locked up for twenty months and now he wanted the police to reopen the case in order to point the finger at the right man. He also said he thought he should receive compensation for what the police had put him through as an innocent man. He sounded strangely convincing but we still didn't believe a single bit of it.

Billy Dunlop had gone from being a murder suspect facing a sentence of at least twelve years, to a free man who could claim he had been wrongfully accused and imprisoned. If he had a reputation in the area for being frightening before the trial, he had even more power to intimidate and bully now, because he was the man who had proved he could kill and walk away, scot-free. He had shown that he was above the law and that no one could touch him.

Once I had recovered from the shock of his acquittal, I decided I was never going to give up hope of getting him back in front of another judge. He might be feeling cocky today, I thought, but he reckoned without the determination of two parents who were intent on getting justice for their child.

The police must have realised how strongly we felt. When Billy Dunlop was first released they came to see us and warned Charlie and Gary to stay away from him, fearing that if they did anything to Dunlop they might get hurt themselves, and it could spoil the police's chances of getting him for something else later. They were pretty sure he'd step out of line again before too long and hoped to be able to put him safely behind bars when that happened.

I know how much Charlie and Gary must have wanted to do something to avenge Julie's death, because I felt the same way. I would actually drive around in the car sometimes, hoping I would see him crossing the road so that I could run him over. I didn't care what happened to me as long as I got some justice for Julie. I'm told that is typical of someone suffering from post-traumatic stress disorder. I have no idea if I would actually have done it had the opportunity arisen but I certainly wanted to.

I was terrified to go into Billingham town centre, even in the middle of the day when it would be crowded with shoppers, for fear of bumping into him. I didn't want to risk losing control in front of him. Martin, my therapist, said that I had to force myself to start going into town in order to get over my fears, just as I had forced myself to go back into that bathroom.

'Begin by going round the perimeter of the town first,' he said, 'then go quickly in and out, staying a little longer each time.'

I did everything he advised me to do because I did want to get over my fears. I didn't want Dunlop dictating where I could and couldn't go for the rest of my life. But all the time I was in town I was looking around, trying to spot him, not wanting to come across him unexpectedly.

Some while later, I got a phone call from a friend of mine who lived near Billy to say that she'd seen him drinking in a pub in town.

'Ann, you're not going to believe this but he was a bit drunk and I heard him boasting to anyone who would listen about how he had got away with killing Julie; how he had pulled off the perfect murder.'

I felt a rush of shock and sheer rage so fierce that I nearly collapsed. 'If I tell the police, will you testify to this?' I asked, and my friend said she would. I hung up and rang Mark Braithwaite straight away to let him know.

'I think you'd better come and see me,' he said.

A few more friends I spoke to corroborated the story that Billy was gloating about getting away with murder. It made me even angrier and even more afraid of what he might do to us if he got a chance. But at the same time I felt a chink of hope; if he was openly boasting about what he had done, surely that was a confession, wasn't it?

When we went to discuss this with Mark Braithwaite, it turned out that he had also heard the rumours of Dunlop's alleged boasting. 'But there's nothing we can do about it because of the law on double jeopardy.'

'What does that mean?' I asked.

'Because he's been acquitted formally by a judge he can't be tried again for murder. That's the law. It's been that way for hundreds of years.' Apparently in the eighteenth century a juror described the law as meaning 'no man shall be brought into jeopardy of his life and limb more than once for the same offence,' and this had been the situation for as long as there had been widespread law and order in England.

I couldn't believe what I was hearing. I was Alice in Wonderland again, thrown into a world where nothing made sense and everything was the opposite of how it should be. How could it be possible that this man was openly admitting he'd killed Julie but he couldn't be arrested for it because of some ancient law?

It had been suggested to us previously that we could consider taking out a private prosecution against Billy Dunlop. In civil cases the burden of proof is not as great as that in criminal trials. But even if found guilty in a civil court he couldn't be jailed as a result, so it wouldn't achieve the one thing we wanted, which was to get Dunlop behind bars. Also, we wouldn't get legal aid to pursue a private prosecution and though I would have considered our money well spent if it got him a life sentence, it meant only that we could claim compensation from him for damages. And no money could ever compensate us for what he'd done.

Well-meaning people kept telling me that I just had to accept what had happened and hope that Billy would be caught for something else later on. I could see that in many ways they were right. But how could I give up on my fight for justice for Julie? And how would I feel if I turned a blind eye and he killed someone else's daughter? There had to be something we could do, if I could just work out what it was.

That evening as Charlie and I sat at home together, he began to feel very unwell. His face was pale and he complained of tightness in his chest. I called an ambulance and he was taken to hospital where they told us he had suffered a minor heart attack. It was yet one more way in which Dunlop had injured my family. After that, we decided that Charlie should stop running his catering trailer and take things easier. I'd lost one person I loved with all my heart and there was no way I was going to risk losing another.

Chapter Fourteen
Whispers and Rumours

Once I'd had time to find out more about the law of double jeopardy, I still didn't see how it could apply to our situation. Its defenders claimed it provided an essential limit on the power of the state. They said there was a danger that if a court came to an unpopular decision when they acquitted someone, the police could force them to keep trying and retrying the same person for something that they had been acquitted of fairly and squarely. But I couldn't see how that could apply to someone who was openly boasting about a murder he had committed. I was aware, of course, that it could seem that I thought that way only because I was personally involved. But when your daughter has been murdered everything becomes personal; that doesn't make your point of view any less valid.

I decided that there were now two possible options open to me: one was to campaign to get the law changed, and the other was to hope the police would arrest Dunlop for another crime that attracted a life sentence. The former would be the most satisfactory outcome, but the latter might be the easier result to achieve. Rather than wait for Billy to commit another crime, we decided it would be better to try to get him tried for something he had already done. There were plenty of rumours circulating about other crimes that Billy Dunlop was believed to be responsible for—in fact we were quite spoiled for choice. Often he didn't even seem to try very hard to cover his tracks, almost as if he felt himself to be above the law.

I was constantly nagging the police to get Dunlop arrested and taken off the streets again before he had time to kill anyone else. I didn't want any other family to have to go through what we had all been through. Aware that I had no real influence over the police beyond my ability to be a permanent nuisance to them, I needed to find other people who would be willing to campaign on our behalf to get Dunlop behind bars. I went to visit our MP, Frank Cook, to ask if there was anything he could do.

To be honest, I'd never had much of an opinion of politicians up till then, thinking they were all talk and no action, but Frank Cook was brilliant from the start. He understood exactly what I was trying to achieve and why it was important, and agreed to give us his support in any way possible.

Good as his word, he started by getting in touch with the new Deputy Chief Constable and asking him to talk to us. The man agreed immediately and arranged to come to my house with another high-ranking officer— maybe they'd heard about my reputation for attacking officers and felt safer travelling in pairs. It's amazing what a different result you get when it's an MP asking for something to happen rather than just a normal member of the public like me. The other officer even rang up before they arrived to check that we didn't mind his boss turning up in his uniform.

'I don't care if he comes in the Full Monty,' I said, 'as long as he comes.'

The Deputy Chief Constable tried to explain to us how the police were doing their best to take Dunlop off the streets. I had to admire him for having the bottle to come and see us in person, away from the safety of his own office—something his predecessor had never done—but I wasn't convinced they were anywhere close to succeeding in their aim.

Over successive years I noticed that things improved a great deal in the way the police force dealt with the public in general and with victims' families in particular. The notorious Stephen Lawrence case definitely had an influence on this. Stephen Lawrence was a young black lad who was murdered at a bus stop in South London in 1993 by a violent gang of white racist thugs. The police made such a mess of the investigation that the perpetrators got away with it, despite reports that they were swaggering around and boasting that they had done it. After an official investigation it was admitted that there was 'institutional racism' within the police force that had contributed to things going so badly wrong for the prosecution. The Macpherson Report into the case made a number of recommendations about the ways in which murder cases should be handled differently in future. It was as if the police realised they couldn't patronise the general public any more, that they had to acknowledge we were intelligent, feeling human beings like themselves, and that they needed to communicate with us accordingly.

The new Chief Constable for our area actually started holding 'police meetings' in local halls, where a few high-ranking officers listened to any issues or questions raised. Charlie and I went to one and sat ourselves down in the front row, right beneath the podium. We stayed quiet until everyone had asked their questions. When one of the officers began to wind up the proceedings, I raised my hand in the air.

'I have a question for the Chief Constable,' I said. 'There's a murderer walking the streets of Billingham. I just wondered when you are going to get him off the streets before he murders someone else?'

A deathly silence fell over the room.

'Can I first say how much I admire your courage for coming?' the same officer said, almost seeming to choke on his own words.

'I don't wish to appear rude,' I persevered, 'but I have directed my question at the Chief Constable, if you wouldn't mind letting him speak.'

'I don't know the case you are referring to,' the Chief Constable said, realising his colleague wasn't going to be able to get him off the hook, 'because I wasn't in the job then.'

'No,' I said, 'I understand that. And I admire your courage for coming here too, but I would like an answer to my question.'

'I think,' he said, 'on that note we'll close the meeting.'

That was the end of that interaction with the public, and someone from lower down the ranks was sent out to talk to us again a few days later. It seemed there was a limit to how open and communicative they were willing to be with the public, whatever impression their public relations division wanted to give. I realised the police must be getting fed up with hearing from me by then, but I didn't care. I wasn't going to stop making a nuisance of myself until Billy Dunlop was convicted of Julie's murder.

After he was acquitted there were people who started to wonder whether he was the culprit after all, whether in our grief we might be persecuting an innocent man. If you hadn't actually been in the courtroom and heard all the evidence for yourself, you could have been forgiven for assuming that the jury got it right and that the wrong man had been fingered for the crime. But as a family, having followed every twist and turn of the case, we never wavered for even a moment in our belief that we had the right man in our sights. Nor did any of the police we were in touch with.

Our campaign (which I dare say seemed more like a vendetta from Billy Dunlop's side of the fence) probably helped to keep me sane during the next few years. I needed something to focus on, something to take my mind off the flashbacks and the anger seething inside me. I couldn't just accept that it was all over and kept on thinking about how I could find another way to get Dunlop convicted. It gave me a positive channel for everything bad that had occurred since that November night in 1989. If we could succeed in taking Billy Dunlop off the streets then Julie's death would not have been completely meaningless; some good would have come from it.

Chapter Fifteen
Living with the Consequences

After a year of living separately, Charlie and I decided that we should try to be together again. I wanted to take care of him if I could, especially after he had his heart attack. We still had the money from selling the bungalow in Billingham just before Julie died, so we bought ourselves another bungalow in Norton, a village a few miles away, and tried to find a way to get through the long days and nights together as we continued to wait for an opportunity to get back on Dunlop's trail.

Living in the bungalow was harder than we had imagined. As long as Billy Dunlop was on the loose we felt in danger of being attacked by him. It is hard to get to sleep in your bed at night when you know there is someone out there who is capable of doing such terrible things, who doesn't seem to care who he hurts or kills, and who knows where you live. I was determined not to allow my nervousness to stop me from pursuing my campaign to have Billy Dunlop imprisoned for Julie's murder, but that didn't make the fears any the less. Eventually we moved into a flat in a big block in Norton, feeling we would be more secure there.

At the same time as I was learning more and more about the murky underworld that men like Billy Dunlop inhabited, I was also learning more about what was going on in the darkness inside my head. My counsellor, Martin, was a huge help in making me understand how the symptoms of post-traumatic stress disorder (PTSD) manifested themselves, but after three years the pain and the unhappiness hadn't really got any better, and I decided to stop going to see him, as I felt ready to try fighting my demons on my own.

In 1994, I watched a documentary on television about a hospital in East Sussex called Ticehurst and I realised that I was by no means the only person to suffer from PTSD. The documentary featured Gordon Turnbull, a consultant psychiatrist who had been in the RAF and had become a specialist in PTSD. Several Middle-Eastern hostages went to Ticehurst after their release for help in sorting out their emotions, in order to readjust to normal life. As I watched the stories of four different patients, I realised that their symptoms were very similar to mine. One of them was a girl who had found her parents' murdered bodies. Just like me, she was suffering from intrusive thoughts and an inability to concentrate, and Gordon Turnbull seemed to know exactly how to help her.

At the end of the programme I sat down and wrote to him, telling him what had happened to me. He wrote back a lovely letter, saying he thought he could help me. I went for an assessment and my GP helped me to get funding to go to Ticehurst as an inpatient. It was a turning point for me.

I was part of a group of five patients with similar symptoms and we all went together into an intense, deep therapy. Gordon Turnbull was wonderful. One of the other patients was a very arrogant and bombastic police officer. Initially I thought he was the last person I needed to be exposed to given my hostility towards the police, but actually he and I were really good for each other; everything had been very black and white in my world ever since the day Julie vanished but this encounter helped me to appreciate that there might be some shades of grey in between, that there are two sides to every story.

Ticehurst is a beautiful, big old house set in its own tranquil grounds. Just to be away from the area surrounding Billingham was a relief, a chance to breathe different air and get some perspective on where our lives were going. It was hard to move forward when everything I did or saw reminded me of Julie. In East Sussex I was free of those reminders.

I was an inpatient at Ticehurst for two weeks. One day I saw a video designed to help patients deal with their flashbacks, and this rang a lot of bells for me. A year or so earlier I had been in a bathroom showroom with Charlie and I came across a bath where they had taken the side off in order to show all the workings underneath. One look and I was running from the shop as hysterically as I had run down the stairs at Grange Avenue after finding Julie, frantically trying to escape all over again from the phantom smells invading my nostrils and the sights I was seeing in my head.

Being in Ticehurst helped me to accept that these flashbacks were a normal reaction to an abnormal situation. Until then I had been terrified of them, just as I might have been of a terrible physical pain. I told the staff there things I have never told anyone else in my life. You're frightened that if you talk about some things you'll transfer your pain to someone else. But with the Ticehurst staff and the group therapy sessions I was able to talk about my intrusive thoughts, and I learned that they are normal. Before going there, there had been times when I thought I was actually going mad, but they taught me I wasn't. I was a sane human being in horrific circumstances, just getting by as best I could.

Chapter Sixteen
Billy Runs Amok

We had heard from other people that Billy was still acting violently towards his girlfriend, Jayne, and that one day she'd finally plucked up the courage to go to the police. She told them that he had threatened to kill her. Knowing what Billy was capable of the police took her fears seriously. At this time Jayne moved to a safe house near Manchester, but Billy tracked her down. He had come across a phone number on the phone of a friend of Jayne's and sat going through phone directories in the library until he could put an address to it. Then he went to look for her.

So confident was he of his untouchability, he even went into a police station to ask for directions to the address where she was hiding out. It was almost as though he was daring them to try to stop him, showing them that he could go wherever he wanted and do whatever he chose. The police were already onto him after the threats he had made, and he was recognised at the station. He was arrested and charged with threatening to kill Jayne, and in January 1997 he received a short custodial sentence of a few months. Charlie and I watched from the public gallery as he was convicted.

It was nice to have him behind bars for a bit, but as soon as he was released from jail he returned to Billingham and took up with a girl called Donna, who lived in a block of flats near to his. I don't know what happened between them but I guess there was some sort of row because it wasn't long before he badly assaulted her and a friend of hers called Shaun Fairweather. He broke several bones in Fairweather's face and knocked him unconscious in the process. Next he turned on Donna and stabbed her with an oven fork, puncturing her lung. Had her brother and friends not arrived at that moment Dunlop would almost certainly have kept on beating and stabbing them without so much as a thought for the consequences.

On this occasion his violent assaults had taken place in front of witnesses and both his victims were still alive to explain what had happened. Dunlop was arrested and charged with attempted murder.

This all happened over a bank-holiday weekend when Charlie and I had taken Kevin to Scarborough for a break. I got home on the Monday because I had work the next day. Charlie and Kevin stayed on for the rest of the week. I let myself in through the front door and picked up the Saturday evening newspaper lying on the mat. Immediately I noticed the headline: *Billingham man charged with attempted murder of two people.*

Just as I sat down to read the article, the phone rang.

'Where have you been?' Mark Braithwaite wanted to know the moment I picked the phone up. 'I thought you might be interested to know that Billy Dunlop has been arrested and charged with the attempted murder of two people over the weekend.'

I realised he was talking about the story that I had just started reading.

The 'Billingham man' was Billy Dunlop and I felt a rush of different emotions all at once; there was horror for the two victims, anger that Dunlop had been free to ruin yet more lives, and a mixture of excitement and relief that he must finally have pushed his luck too far.

A few days later, once the swelling on his face had subsided, Shaun Fairweather went in for surgery. Despite everything I had seen over the years I was still shocked to see the extent of the damage that Billy had caused in those few frenzied minutes; Shaun's face was completely pulverised. I was there as they wheeled him in on a trolley, and I shuddered to think that the legal system had allowed a man who was capable of doing this out onto the streets when it had had the chance to lock him up. It was like letting a savage dog loose in a children's playground.

We went to Billy's court appearance, just as we'd been to all the others, haunting his every step, wanting to know every detail in case something came up that would give us a chance to pin Julie's murder on him. Sometimes on these occasions Charlie and I would be the only ones sitting in the public gallery, like a couple of tireless avenging angels.

One day during the trial the police had trouble getting Dunlop to come out of his cell and into the courtroom and he told the detective in charge that he was frightened of Charlie. Maybe he'd watched too many late-night martial arts and Triad gangster films in his time—who knows? Seeing Charlie's impassive face across the visiting room in Durham Prison back in 1990, and then in every courtroom he had ever appeared in since then, must have been getting to him; he must have wondered if we would ever give up. We could have told him the answer to that question—never!

To start with he was charged with the attempted murder of both victims, but he offered pleas of guilty to two counts of wounding with intent to cause grievous bodily harm. The court accepted his pleas even though the judge knew Billy's history. Despite almost killing two people in front of witnesses he was sentenced to just seven years in prison.

Donna, the girl he had stabbed, was watching from the public gallery just near us and the two of them started shouting up and down to one another. He asked her to come and visit him inside, and she agreed.

'Are you stupid?' Charlie asked her bluntly.

'He's already killed our daughter and he's tried to kill you,' I said, 'and you intend to go visiting him?'

She went quiet after that; maybe she was just too frightened of him to refuse anything he asked for, in the same way that Jayne had been too frightened not to take him back after he was acquitted.

While it was a relief to know that he was finally off the streets, seven years did not seem an adequate punishment for what he had done to Shaun and Donna, let alone what he had done to Julie. The chances were that he would be out again before the end of his sentence anyway, and then he would be back in Billingham to mock the system again.

Even once he was inside he still seemed to believe he was invincible. It is my understanding that he sent a threatening letter to Donna, describing what he would do to her when he was released.

Terrified, Donna took the letter to the police. They added it to the file of evidence they were building up against him, though he still couldn't be retried for Julie's murder while the law of double jeopardy remained the same.

What I didn't know, however, was that while in prison, Dunlop had befriended a woman prison officer. The two would talk casually together for hours when they met around the prison and the police saw another opportunity to tempt him to incriminate himself. With the support of the prison service authorities, they wired up the officer to record all their conversations.

After weeks of patient work, the prison officer had recorded a staggering sixty hours of tape, during which Dunlop openly talked about killing Julie, crowing about how there was nothing anyone could do about it now because of the law relating to double jeopardy. With the tapes in their possession, the police would be ready if they ever managed to get him back into court. The tapes were filed along with the threatening letter to Donna as they prepared to spring their trap.

Once they were ready to pounce, two officers, Peter Wilson and Dave Duffy, came to tell us what their new plan was. They explained that although Dunlop couldn't be retried for the murder, now they had his confession on tape they could charge him with perjury. Perjury means lying when you are under oath in court and it is a serious charge, for which the maximum sentence is seven years.

'Surely to goodness,' I said to Charlie once the police had gone, 'they'll give him the maximum. If he serves seven years for each of the times he lied in court that will make fourteen years in all. That would be a good result for us because if he'd been convicted for killing Julie in 1991 the tariff for murder then was only twelve years, so at least he'll be behind bars for a decent length of time, even if it's not for murdering our Julie.'

I imagine Dunlop was pretty angry with himself when he found out he was going to be charged with perjury. It was a stupid mistake to make just to give himself the chance to brag and act like a hard man around the prison. When he realised the police had everything on tape, Billy agreed to give them a formal confession. Maybe he thought they would go easier on him if he finally cooperated.

In his confession he told the police that after coming out of the hospital on the night of the rugby club strip show, he had gone to look for Mark Ward at Kath's house in Grange Avenue to tell him what had happened. According to Billy, Mark had already gone to bed when he reached the house, but Billy noticed that Julie's lights were still on next door, having just been dropped back from her pizza delivery round. He said he'd decided to knock on her door and that she'd let him in and made him a cup of tea. They sat chatting for a while and he claimed that she had laughed at him, telling him he looked funny with his stitched eyebrow and black eye. According to him, she kept saying that the other guy must have got the better of him in the fight and then she giggled.

Our Julie did have a bit of a nervous laugh so that sounded quite plausible, although I'm sure she wouldn't have meant it maliciously. I doubt if she would have risked making him angry if she knew even half of his reputation for violence, which we were pretty sure she did. He claimed he lost his temper at being mocked, jumped up and strangled her right there in the sitting room.

'I just lost it,' he kept saying.

So much for his dad's belief that he would never do such a thing. The only part of the crime that he never confessed to was how his semen might have got onto the blanket she was wrapped in, or how the injury to her vagina occurred. Perhaps he thought that if he made it sound like a murder committed in a moment of blind temper it would go better for him than if there was a sexual motive.

Most of the people involved with prosecuting the case didn't believe his story. They thought it was more likely that he had attacked her in a sexual frenzy, having got himself worked up at the strip show. It seemed probable that he had gone round to Julie's hoping she would sleep with him and when she refused he attacked her and killed her and then defiled her.

He said that when he realised she was dead he went upstairs and got a blanket off the bed, then he took off all his clothes, and all Julie's, wrapped her naked body in the blanket so he wouldn't leave any DNA, and carried her upstairs on his shoulder. He thought about putting her up in the loft, but when he couldn't lift her through the hatch he hit on the idea of unscrewing the bath panel and hiding her behind the bath. He gave a graphic description of how hard it had been to force her body into the confined space, how he had pushed at her with his feet.

It was presumably because he planned to return for her that he took her keys. He never explained what he'd done with the clothes Julie had been wearing that night, or with her wedding ring, but the binmen came the next day so perhaps he just put them in the bin. By the time the police started searching, the bins had been emptied and the evidence destroyed.

'We're going to get him for you, Julie,' I whispered in my head when I'd heard the confession. I felt sick to my stomach that he had ever laid a finger on my beautiful daughter, that he'd taken off her clothes and touched her lovely skin, that he'd wrapped her in a blanket and carted her round the house like an old piece of furniture. 'If it's the last thing I ever do, I'll get him.'

Chapter Seventeen
Rolling out the Publicity

No matter how long I spent working with the police and others in authority, I still continued to be surprised by how little they seemed to take into account the feelings and needs of the relatives of murder victims. But there were efforts to try to improve things.

During this period the police introduced a pilot scheme in various parts of the country for something they called 'victims' impact statements'. What they wanted was for people like us to write statements that could be given to the judges before passing sentence, to let them know the effect the crimes had had on our families. It seemed like a good idea, a way of humanising the legal process a little.

The police asked us to write one of these statements for Billy's perjury trial, which I was keen to do if it would help to get him the maximum sentence. To be honest, it was just nice to be asked, making it seem as if someone actually cared about us.

Sitting down to write yet again about those traumatic days brought terrible flashbacks, but I was determined not to let them defeat me. I kept going, focusing all my energy into my pen, pouring everything I felt about Julie's murder and its effect on my family out onto paper.

Once the statement was finished Charlie and I took it to the head of the Crown Prosecution Service in our area to make sure it got directly into the judge's hands before he passed sentence. 'I will personally make sure this gets to the judge in time,' he assured us.

Dunlop confessing had knocked me back in a way I would never have anticipated. It was as if I had been banging my head against a closed door and suddenly it had sprung open and I had fallen through without having any idea where I would land. I tried to keep going as normal but turning up at work at the hospital each day was finally becoming too much of a strain, and in 2000 I retired on medical grounds, after thirty years of doing the job.

In April of that year Billy Dunlop appeared at the New Court in Middlesborough and brazenly confessed to Julie's murder, confirming everything he had said on the prison tapes and in his confession to the police. It was a staggering thing to do. He must have felt so totally safe hiding behind the double jeopardy law that he believed nothing else could touch him once he had served his time for perjury.

He was sitting behind glass at the back of the courtroom, like a prize exhibit in the Chamber of Horrors.

'This man has made British legal history,' his barrister trumpeted, as if it was something to be proud of. 'No one has ever confessed in a court of law before, after being acquitted for a killing. This man has confessed because he is full of remorse, especially for Julie's family and her son.'

When the prosecuting counsel replied, he quite rightly dismissed that claim as a load of rubbish. He said he thought that all that had happened was that Dunlop had taken legal advice and knew that there had been a recommendation to look at the double jeopardy law after the Macpherson Report into the Stephen Lawrence case.

'He thinks that if he gets his confession in now he will be charged only with perjury and that will be the end of it for him. If or when the change of law comes in, he's assuming it won't be applied retrospectively.'

I didn't believe for a moment that Billy Dunlop felt any remorse for what he had done. If he had felt remorse after the killing, why did he go to so much trouble to hide Julie under the bath? If he had felt any pity for us at all during those three months when we were waiting for her to come home, he would have put in an anonymous phone call to the police, telling them where to find the body. He did none of that—he just waited to see what he could get away with. Nothing I had heard during any of his court appearances had ever made me feel even the tiniest tremor of sympathy for him. To me, Billy Dunlop was simply evil.

As I sat listening to the fatuous arguments being put forward in his defence it suddenly seemed like the most important thing in the world that he be given a full fourteen years for the perjury charges because then at least I would feel he was serving a decent sentence.

When the judge announced that he was going to sentence Billy to only six years for the perjury charge I felt all my hopes crumbling away. How could a man so evil and dangerous be treated with such leniency when he showed no leniency at all towards any of his victims?

As the judge's words rang in my ears a terrible uncontrollable rage swept over me. I leaped to my feet and ran full tilt towards the dock, with no idea what I'd do when I got there. Charlie tried to grab me but I was away like a rocket, leaving him with his arms flailing in the air. If I'd had a gun in my hand I would have shot Dunlop at that moment, protective glass or not.

'Six years?' I yelled at him. 'I'll see you rot in hell. You weren't full of remorse when you were sat in the house next door watching all the comings and goings. You murdering bastard!'

I was absolutely out of control, and lucky that the judge didn't hold me in contempt of court. The police and court officials finally managed to get a grip on me and calm me down, but as I walked out of the building with Charlie my mind was still whirling.

'If that's all he's going to get for perjury,' I said, 'then this change in the double jeopardy law needs to be looked at. I'm going to do something about this law.'

'You're wasting your time,' Charlie sighed, exhausted by the whole thing.

'I don't care.' I was adamant. 'I am going to do something about it.'

Fed up with being continually knocked back, I was now determined to take my cause to the very top. My first step was to go back to our MP, Frank Cook, who had been so helpful in getting the police to talk to us.

'If I write a letter to Jack Straw, the Home Secretary, about our case,' I asked him the moment I had sat down in front of him, 'will you be able to get me in to see him?'

'I certainly will,' he said. 'You just bring me the letter.'

Encouraged by his positive attitude, I went straight home and wrote out the details of the case yet again, glad to have something to focus my mind on. One way or another I was going to get justice for our Julie.

The thing that had surprised me the most about the perjury trial was that the victims' impact statement that I had written for the judge hadn't had more of an effect on the sentence he handed out. No longer willing to accept anything without question, I wrote to him expressing my surprise. I received a response by return of post saying that he had never seen the statement. The Chief Crown Prosecutor had assured us he would pass it on and we felt let down yet again. What was the point of asking for these statements if they weren't going to use them? Over and over again I felt that our suffering wasn't important enough for anyone to put themselves out.

But now I had a new campaign to focus on and the injustice of the double jeopardy law was constantly on my mind. I was always on the lookout for allies, and if they were establishment figures so much the better. Lord Mackenzie, the former president of the Police Superintendents' Association and a former Chief Superintendent of Police in Durham, came on the television saying that whenever there's been a miscarriage of justice, whether it's a wrongful conviction or a wrongful acquittal, the case should be looked at again. So I got in touch with him too.

This was my new habit; whenever I heard anyone speaking out either for or against the idea of changing the law of double jeopardy, I immediately fired off a letter to them. It didn't matter how important or famous or grand they were; I knew they were mostly fathers and mothers just like us and I was banking on them being able to understand a heartfelt plea from another parent.

Although it was painful to have to talk about Julie's death, I was keen to do any television or radio interviews or documentaries that came my way. I went on 'Tricia' and 'Woman's Hour' and all sorts of other programmes. Most ordinary people knew nothing about the double jeopardy law, unless they were involved in a case like ours. Anyone I explained it to was just as shocked and scandalised as I had been when I first learned about it.

By now I was so used to telling our story I could usually do it without becoming too upset, like an actress reciting a script. In a way I felt that by talking about the case I was keeping the memory of Julie alive. People who would never have met her or heard about her had she lived got to know her name and to hear of the great injustice that had been done to her. I didn't expect anyone to call it 'Julie's Law' or anything like that, but if I could get it changed it would still be a legacy for her.

The producers of one documentary wanted to do a reconstruction of the morning when I went round to try to wake Julie up, and another of me pulling the panel off in the bathroom on that fateful day three months later. They talked about getting an actress to do it but I thought it would be just as hard for me to explain everything to another person as to get on and do it myself. I was quite frightened about the flashbacks it would cause, but I remembered how much better I had been after forcing myself into the bathroom on Martin's advice, so maybe this exercise would help to exorcise them.

'It's OK,' I told the television people. 'I can do it myself.'

We didn't use the actual house because the woman who lived there by then had a little boy and we didn't think that would be nice for him, so we used the one next door from Mark's mum, Kath, for some scenes.

The bathroom scene was filmed in the producer's house where there was a room big enough to fit a whole camera crew as well as me. They'd hired an actress to play Julie under the bath, but she'd put some weight on since the producer had last seen her and there was no way they were going to be able to cram her in there. They had to use the producer's thirteen-year-old son instead and get him to put a wig on.

It seemed almost unreal that I could be laughing about something that had so devastated my life, but I think perhaps that is all part of the healing process—learning how to live with what has happened and see it in perspective. I know Julie herself would have been giggling away if she'd been watching. The final result was very effective when we saw it on screen.

A German television company wanted to do a debate on double jeopardy as well, and wanted me to appear in a short film to open the programme. Mark Braithwaite, with whom I was still in regular contact, advised me to do it because if our campaign to change the law failed in the UK and we had to go to the European Court of Human Rights it might be helpful to try to influence public opinion over there too.

A lot of people in the legal profession opposed the idea of changing the double jeopardy law and I had to try to lobby every one of them and explain why I thought they were wrong. One of them, surprisingly, was the lawyer who had worked on the Stephen Lawrence case, Imran Khan. I was asked to discuss the issue with him on camera for a television programme. His main argument was that changing the law would lead to sloppy police work because the police would know that if they made mistakes they could keep on bringing suspects back for retrial. But I had already read the proposals that were being put forward and I knew there were going to be safeguards built in to stop that kind of thing.

I also knew he had a daughter, because he'd mentioned it earlier, so I went for the personal angle.

'Do you have any family?' I asked as the cameras rolled.

'Yes, I do,' he admitted.

'If your daughter had been murdered,' I said, 'and a man had confessed in a court of law to the killing, would you be happy with a perjury sentence? I don't mean as a lawyer, I mean as a father.'

He started to waffle again.

'Just answer the question—yes or no,' I insisted. I'd spent so much time sitting listening to lawyers in courtrooms that I was even starting to talk like them. 'As a father, would you be happy?'

'No,' he said, 'of course I wouldn't.'

'Then you can stop the cameras,' I said, 'because that answers it all. As a lawyer he's opposing changes but as a father he wouldn't be happy with a perjury sentence. We are willing to go to the European Court of Human Rights if necessary to get justice for our daughter.'

I was getting quite good at this campaigning business, surprising even myself sometimes. It's amazing what you can do when you have to.

Around 2001, I joined a support group called Support After Murder and Manslaughter (SAMM) and at one of their meetings, I got talking to a police officer who asked if I would be interested in addressing police officers as part of their family liaison training. By hearing what it is like on our side of the fence, it was hoped officers would gain greater insight.

On one occasion I went out with a senior investigating officer to visit a bereaved family and we got talking on the way.

'You won't remember me,' the officer said on the way there, 'but the day you found your Julie I was a young constable and I'd just been transferred to Billingham. It was my first shift and the first call I got was to come to 27 Grange Avenue. All I remember was you out in the street, hysterical.'

'The day when I punched Inspector Lee, you mean?' I chuckled.

'It really upset me,' he went on, ignoring my flippant interruption, 'because I had a family and I could imagine exactly how you must be feeling. I went home that night and I said to my wife, "It was terrible; this poor woman was hysterical from finding her daughter." It was awful.' His words caught in his throat at the recollection.

I could see then that Julie's death and everything that happened after it had changed a lot of people's lives, not just ours. But I wanted it to change a lot more than that. I wanted it to change the way justice was dispensed in Britain. I was no longer doing it just to see Billy Dunlop fairly sentenced for what he had done. I wanted to achieve something bigger than that, something that would potentially help everyone.

Chapter Eighteen
Telling Kevin

Journalists and headline-writers like to label murders with catchy phrases that will remind readers for ever more about that specific tragic event. Whenever Dunlop was back in the news the local press would print headlines like 'Body behind the bath murder' or they would talk about the 'Pizza delivery girl killing'. I didn't like to see Julie's whole life reduced to such clichés, but I soon realised that when you are the victim of a gruesome murder you somehow become public property.

Whenever another of these stories appeared, kids at Kevin's school would start talking about it, passing around snippets of information that they must have got from their parents or maybe overheard in a shop or on the street somewhere. Ten years after his mother's murder, we had still not told Kevin anything other than the story that she had slipped and died in the bath.

He used to live with Andrew during the week but he spent virtually every weekend and holiday with us. Andrew had met a new partner quite soon after parting from Julie and Kevin now had two half-brothers. Everyone got on well with one another, even though there was always this secret hanging in the air when Kevin was in the room, and at times it was a strain.

In 1999, when Kevin was thirteen, the case was back in the papers again because of the approaching perjury trial. I told Andrew I really thought he should talk to him about it, but he still wasn't keen. I suppose he didn't want to have to rake up so many painful memories for himself as well as giving Kevin things to think about that he might not be able to cope with.

'Unless he asks,' Andrew said, 'I'm not going to tell him.'

One afternoon the school welfare officer came round unexpectedly and asked if she could talk to us. Alarmed, we invited her in and she told us that Kevin had been to see her at school that day.

'He said that other children have been telling him that his mum didn't slip in the bath,' she said. 'They told him that she'd been murdered. Now he says he's going to find out the truth for himself.'

'I'm going to the library,' he told her, 'and I'm going to look in the archives of the paper and see what I can find out.'

Aware of how Andrew felt about Kevin being told, she hadn't said anything to him but she had come straight round to see us so that we would be forewarned. I realised then that we couldn't lie to the lad any more. I rang Andrew and he came round to talk to the welfare officer himself.

'I don't want to tell him unless he asks,' he still insisted.

'But he isn't going to ask,' she explained. 'He told me he didn't want to ask any of you in case he upsets anybody. But he wants to know the truth.'

I could see that Andrew was wavering. Eventually he realised she was right and he went home to find Kevin and ask him straight out what it was he wanted to know.

'Was me mam murdered?' Kevin asked.

'Yes, she was,' Andrew replied. 'By a man called Billy Dunlop.'

'Why did he murder her?'

'Who knows why somebody murders another person?' Andrew said. 'I don't know why.'

'I want to go back to my nana's,' Kevin said.

Over the years I had been building up a scrapbook of newspaper cuttings, which I had always thought I would give Kevin one day. When he came round I gave it to him and he sat reading for a while. I could see his heart was broken and I just wanted to hug him and make the pain all go away. I knew exactly what he felt like because I had been experiencing the same thoughts and feelings myself for ten years.

'Nana,' he said, 'I never wanted to ask in case talking about it upset you, but now I know the truth I feel like a weight has been lifted from me shoulders. Is the man who did it in prison?'

'Yes, he is,' I said.

'Is he in prison for what he did to me mam?'

'No,' I said, 'he isn't, but we hope to change that.'

For a while he went quiet and I didn't know where to start with telling him everything that had gone on behind the newspaper stories. I still wasn't sure how much he needed to know and how much he would prefer not to think or talk about yet. I decided I needed some professional help, so I got in touch with a London-based organisation called Mothers Against Murder and they told me about a specialised counselling service in Sunderland. Kevin got on well with them there and went back every week for over a year, seeming to find it helpful.

Looking back now, I believe it is always better to tell children the basic truth from the start in traumatic situations like murder, however hard that might be at the time.

We found out only recently that, after hearing the truth, Kevin went back on his own to the house where it happened and knocked on the door, asking the new people there if he could come in and try to remember his mam. They very kindly let him in and he looked round the house, even though it must have changed a lot. He told us later that he still couldn't remember Julie at all. I know he finds that very hard.

Once he knew the truth, Kevin became an active part of our campaign team, often travelling with us to see people who we thought might be able to help the cause. It helped the emotional argument for people to be able to hear directly from a boy who had been left motherless when he was only three years old.

Month by month and year by year I felt we were building up more and more support for the cause, but we were still a long way from our goal. I knew that as a family we had to keep up the pressure right until the day we heard a judge pronounce Billy Dunlop guilty of murder and sentence him to life, however exhausted and dispirited we might sometimes feel along the way.

Chapter Nineteen
Making Friends in High Places

Just as he promised, Frank Cook arranged a meeting for us with Jack Straw at the Home Office in London. I took with me a picture of Julie and a picture of Dunlop. What's that saying—'A picture's worth a thousand words'? Just looking at her pretty young face and his glowering, evil stare would bring the whole story instantly to life for anyone.

I didn't have mountains of notes; this was going to be an appeal to the Home Secretary's emotions as a father, not his intellect as a politician or a barrister. As we headed up to the top floor in the lift, Frank suggested that I let him do all the talking. He probably expected me to be nervous and tongue-tied in front of such a famous and powerful man. I didn't say anything but I had no intention of sitting there in silence.

Jack Straw greeted us and led us into his office. Before Frank could open his mouth I placed the two pictures on the desk in front of the Home Secretary. His eyes went straight to them and I knew I had his full attention.

'That's our daughter, Julie,' I said, 'and that's the man who murdered her. He's confessed to it in a court of law and I want to know what's going to be done about this double jeopardy law. He's making a complete mockery of the British justice system.'

'Well,' he said, reaching for a big thick law book, 'you know, retrospective law is a very grey area.'

'Don't bother to touch that book,' I warned, 'because there is no case in that book like ours. Am I right?'

'Well, yes, you are . . .'

'His defence lawyer admitted in court that Dunlop's made British legal history,' I ploughed on. 'So this law needs to be looked at.'

Frank had given up and sat back by this time, realising there was nothing he could do to stop me having my say.

'The Home Affairs Select Committee has already held a debate,' Straw purred, 'and they are recommending it be changed, and they've also suggested it would apply to retrospective cases but there's a long way to go.'

I could see he was doubtful about being able to change the double jeopardy law to apply to retrospective cases such as ours.

'What's the next step?' I wanted to know.

'It goes to the Law Commission.'

'Right,' I said, gathering up my photographs. 'I'll have the name of whoever's dealing with it in the Law Commission.'

'My secretary will sort that out for you,' he assured me, probably quite keen to get me out of his office by that stage.

That was pretty much the end of the interview, but it had got me what I wanted. I now knew that there were some very important people thinking about changing the double jeopardy law. All I had to do now was make sure they hurried up and came to the right conclusion, and they made it retrospective, otherwise we would never be able to get the justice Julie deserved. As we left Straw's office his secretary told us the name I needed was that of a judge on the panel called Alan Wilkie.

'I'm going to write to this Law Commission,' I told Charlie once we were back home on the sofa, having a cup of tea and thinking what to do next.

'You're wasting your time,' Charlie halfheartedly protested yet again. The poor man just wanted a bit of a rest.

'I'm doing it,' I said. 'I don't care what anybody says.'

I sat back down at the dining table that evening and outlined the whole case yet again, and sent it all off to Judge Alan Wilkie.

A few days later I received a lovely letter back, bringing with it the first definite glimmer of hope. He told me my letter had arrived at a crucial time, just as the members of the Law Commission were getting their thoughts together to recommend changes to the double jeopardy law. He said ours was the most compelling case in the country. He asked if we would like to meet him. That was an invitation I wasn't likely to pass up.

In the meantime, back down in the real world of police, courts, solicitors and prisons, Dunlop had been given the right to appeal against his six-year sentence. By this time, 'victims' impact statements' had become the law and the police asked us to write another one. Although I was still seething that the last one I'd written had never even been sent to the judge, I was willing to have another try, so I wrote the whole thing out again, and the police came to the house to collect it.

Having been let down so often before, however, I didn't trust them to pass it on to the right people, so I phoned the clerk of the court and asked for the name of the man looking after the Dunlop file. When I got through

I asked him if he would mind looking to see if my impact statement was in there. He promised to call me back as soon as he had looked.

'There is no impact statement in this file,' he told me when he phoned back later.

I immediately rang the head of the Crown Prosecution Service, my blood boiling, spoiling for a fight.

'He's in a meeting,' they told me when I got through.

'Then you can go into that meeting and tell him I am going to be down there in half an hour to pick up my impact statement,' I told them. 'You let me down when Dunlop was first charged with perjury and now you've done the same again for the Court of Appeal.'

Ten minutes later I got a call from the clerk at the Court of Appeal.

'I don't know who you've spoken to or what you've done,' my contact said, 'but we've just had your impact statement faxed to us.'

Twice the authorities had failed to pass on our impact statements—now called 'victims' personal statements'—which suggests they don't understand how important they are to the families of murder victims. They might not make any difference to the sentence that a judge eventually hands out to a murderer, but still it makes us feel better to know that our words have at least been considered. If the people at the CPS had appreciated this, I'm sure that they would never have been so careless.

The appeal was to be heard in London, so Alan Wilkie suggested that we have a meeting with him at the Law Commission offices in Holborn the day before.

When we arrived at the Commission's offices I assumed we were just going to meet Judge Wilkie, but as we entered the room we found ourselves being seated before the full panel, including a man called Jacques Perry, who was the head of the inquiry. We all sat round a big table, drinking tea, and they were absolutely charming.

'Off the record,' Alan Wilkie told us, 'there wasn't a dry eye on this panel when we got your letter, because we're all fathers. We all know how we would feel if it was our son or daughter who had been murdered.'

'I just want to bring the human side of things into the debate,' I said.

'Can we use your letter to take to the government?' he asked.

'Never mind me letter,' I said, 'you can use me. This law needs to be changed. We've met a number of other families in a similar position to us and there are about thirty-five cases around the country where people are desperate for this law to change so that justice can be done. When there's been a proven wrongful conviction the person is immediately set free, so surely the same should apply with a proven wrongful acquittal?'

At the end of the meeting they told us to leave everything with them and I refocused my mind on preparing myself to go to the Court of Appeal the next day. I was terrified something would go wrong and Dunlop would be allowed back onto the streets of Billingham again.

When we got to the court in the morning we found that Jacques Perry, the head of the Law Commission, was also there. He came straight over and gave me a cuddle as though we were the oldest friends in the world.

'I didn't expect you to come today,' I confessed.

'Oh yes,' he said. 'We're very interested in Mr Dunlop's case.'

The three judges presiding over the court were not impressed by the appeal and to our relief it was dismissed in just a few minutes. They also mentioned our impact statement and it made me feel better to know that they had actually read it. Billy was expressionless as always but we hoped he knew just how hard we were working to keep him behind bars.

'So what happens next?' I asked Jacques Perry once we were back outside the court.

'We'll do our consultation paper,' he explained. 'That will go to Lord Justice Auld for his consideration.'

I got on the train back home that evening feeling that maybe we were finally making some progress. The wheels were certainly moving slowly, but Dunlop was still safely behind bars, which gave us the time we needed to go through all these different layers of the legal system.

The Law Commission published its paper in January 2001, and then the judiciary and legislators thought about it—for two and a half years.

We were back to living in a state of limbo, with no idea which way things were likely to go, but I never rested and never became complacent. We had been disappointed and let down too many times before to believe that anything concerning the law was certain. The fight for justice occupied my thoughts from the moment I woke in the morning to the moment I finally went to sleep. I just wanted to do everything I could to keep the ball rolling and gather support wherever I could find it.

So many years were passing that contacts we had made at the beginning of the campaign moved on and were replaced by new people, meaning we had to start all over again. Jack Straw left the Home Office in 2001 and was replaced by David Blunkett, so I prepared a letter for the new Home Secretary to make sure that he knew all about the case. I found a blind lady in Middlesborough who translated my letter into Braille. It was worth going to that extra little bit of trouble because Blunkett wrote back to say that he was committed to carrying on with the Law Commission's recommendations. We breathed a huge sigh of relief; we were still in business.

Finally, after two and a half years, Lord Justice Auld announced that not only was the law to be changed but that it might apply retrospectively in particular cases. The bill went through the Houses of Parliament and was put into a White Paper released in July 2002, entitled 'Justice for All'. (A White Paper is a document that lays out a new policy and signifies the government's intention to introduce it as legislation.) David Blunkett arranged for us to collect our copy of the White Paper on the day it was published. When we arrived at the Home Office we found that the press officer had very kindly stuck a post-it note on the front that read: *Double jeopardy will be retrospective.* I burst into tears as I read it. The press were all waiting outside and I ran out shouting the news at the top of my voice.

The bill was then dragged through many more debates; some people were in favour of the changes and others vehemently opposed them. I was constantly searching for new people in influential positions who I could win round to our point of view, by explaining the human side of the story.

The Criminal Justice Bill finally passed through the House of Commons in May 2003, but then we had to get it past the House of Lords. This was going to be the really tough one I was told. The first debate in the Lords went OK but we still weren't home and dry.

All this time Charlie and I had been busy on every possible front. We'd made another documentary, met what felt like a thousand new people, and every year we went to a conference in South Shields for the North East of England Victims' Association. That year, one of the guest speakers was Tony Blair's friend Lord Falconer, the Lord Chancellor.

At one stage during the lunch break he got up and walked past our table towards the door. I had been coiled like a spring for some time, waiting to pounce. As soon as he was within reach I jumped up and grabbed his arm, dragging the startled man into a seat beside me and explaining who I was as quickly as I could before he had a chance to get up and run for his life.

'Lord Falconer, can you help me?' I begged. 'We're desperate for the double jeopardy law to be changed. I know it's got to go through a second debate, so can I come to the House of Lords and speak to the people who are going to be debating it?'

'Would you do that?' he asked, obviously surprised that anyone would want to volunteer themselves for such an ordeal.

'I will if you can organise it.'

'All right,' he nodded, smiling. 'I'll be in touch.'

Within a week I got a call from Frank Cook saying I had an appointment to go to the House of Lords. It often surprised me how people right at the top of the Establishment tree were good at doing what they promised, while those lower down the ladder were constantly letting us down.

We were so nearly within reach of our goal now; we couldn't afford to let this opportunity slip through our fingers. After all these years of waiting, the thought of falling at the last fence was unbearable. I wanted to ensure I was completely prepared.

I sat down at the dining-room table once again and wrote out a five-page outline that would be my statement to this final bunch of grandees, giving all the reasons why I thought the law should change and why it should be made retrospective. I was going to be appealing unashamedly to their hearts as well as their heads. By the time I'd finished I was pleased with what I'd done—Lord knows I'd had enough practice by then.

On July 9, 2003, Frank Cook met us in the lobby of the Houses of Parliament and introduced us to Lord Goldsmith, the Attorney General, who was going to be chairing the meeting.

'Do you have any notes with you?' he asked, eyeing my slim statement suspiciously.

'No,' I said, tapping my head. 'It's all stored in my grey matter.'

'Will you be all right?' He seemed concerned.

'I'll be perfectly all right,' I assured him.

He led the way into a room where there was a table that was practically the size of our whole flat set up for our meeting, and he showed us to our seats. As the lords started filing in I felt a tremor of anxiety. There were walking sticks and Zimmer frames and hearing aids all over the place and I couldn't help thinking that these people didn't look as though they were going to like the idea of retrospective law changes in the least. An elderly baroness plonked herself down on the chair next to me.

'I do hope you are going to speak up, my dear,' she said loudly.

'I'll do my best,' I promised. 'I'll talk to your good ear.'

'I don't have a good ear,' she said.

'Then I'll shout.'

I knew this was my last chance to put the message across effectively. If we didn't get the bill past the Lords we would end up having to go to the European Court in Brussels, which would make everything a hundred times more complicated and frustrating.

As I talked to these learned and distinguished people about our Julie and about Billy Dunlop I became so passionate that I did go off at a bit of a tangent at times, but it must have gone OK because at the end of the meeting the Chief Whip asked if I would mind if she gave a copy of my statement to everybody in the House of Lords.

Lord Goldsmith thanked me for coming and explained that they would now be looking at all the safeguards they were going to need to insert into the law once double jeopardy had been removed in order to make it really sound. There would be a couple of small debates before the second big one. He promised to send me copies of all of them.

'You've forgotten one little word, Lord Goldsmith,' I said.

'One little word?'

'Yes: "retrospective".'

They all laughed because by then they had got the message as to just how desperate I was that the changes allow for cases from the past to be retried. True to his word, Lord Goldsmith sent me copies of all the debates from then on and it felt strange to read about these senior law lords saying things like 'and I quote Ann Ming', with chunks of my statement then reproduced as if I was one of them. It was like reading about someone else.

Soon after, I bumped into one of the surgeons I used to work with and he asked how I was getting on with my campaign. I gave him a brief outline and told him about the trip to the House of Lords.

'How did you find the courage to go down there and speak to those people?' he asked.

'After working with you,' I laughed, 'the lords were pussy cats.'

Immediately after the second debate had finished, Frank Cook rang us. 'It's my birthday today,' he said, 'and it's the best one I've ever had. The changes are through and they are going to apply to retrospective cases.'

I couldn't believe I was hearing him right. After waiting and fighting for so long, was it really going to happen just like that? Were we actually going to see a change in the law which would mean we could start to demand that

Dunlop be retried for killing our Julie? It was hard to take in his words and, after so many years of trying to hold in the tears in order to get my message across, I wasn't able to stem them any longer.

A while later I spotted Lord Falconer at another conference. He was talking to the press and I went over to thank him for all he'd done to help.

'Well done you,' he boomed when he saw me. 'What an achievement!'

'And well done you,' I replied as he enveloped me in a great big cuddle, 'for getting me the appointment.'

I did feel proud of what we had achieved, but at the same time I wondered why, in a free country, I'd had to fight so hard every inch of the way just to get basic justice for Julie.

At the next opening of parliament the Queen talked about changing the double jeopardy law and Tyne Tees Television took Charlie and me down to London to film us listening to her.

'At the heart of my Government's legislative programme,' she was saying in her familiar voice, 'is a commitment to reform and rebalance the criminal justice system to deliver justice for all and to safeguard the interests of victims, witnesses and communities.' Her words were going past me as if in a dream. 'The bill will also allow retrials for those acquitted of serious offences where new and compelling evidence emerges.'

I was surprised how moving I found it. After waiting for so many years to hear the words that she was now speaking so matter-of-factly, it was bringing tears to my eyes. I could allow myself to dream once again about hearing Billy Dunlop sentenced to life for murder, when I had begun to fear I would not live long enough to see it made possible.

Chapter Twenty
The Final Verdict

On April 4, 2006, the law actually changed and became enforceable retrospectively. On April 5, the local Chief Crown Prosecutor rang us and asked if we would like to go in for a meeting with him.

'There's still a long way to go,' he warned when we arrived. 'But hopefully within a couple of months we will get all the paperwork polished off and down to the head of the Department of Public Prosecutions.'

He explained that he would have to get Dunlop's original acquittal quashed before another trial could begin, and that because it was a landmark ruling case there would be five High Court judges in attendance.

'They probably won't make a final decision the same day,' he warned. 'Once they've heard the case they'll most likely ask you to come back again in two weeks or so, once they've had time to think about it.'

In May, Charlie, Kevin and I went down to London to attend the hearing about quashing the acquittal. It had been six years since we had seen Dunlop in the flesh and when we walked into the courtroom and saw him sitting in a big glass case we were shocked by how much weight he'd put on in prison. His thinning, greying hair was greasy and pulled back in a ponytail. His bloated face was even more immobile than before, if that was possible. The dangerous, bullying, self-styled hard man of a few years before had degenerated into a fat, middle-aged slob of a jailbird.

Although we were sitting only a few yards away from him he didn't look in our direction once throughout the proceedings. He must have expected Charlie and me to be there, but this time we were accompanied by Kevin, the boy he had deprived of a mother. His last memory of us would have been me flying across the courtroom towards him at the end of the perjury trial, shouting abuse and having to be restrained. I was calmer now, praying that I was about to see him brought to justice at last.

They had escorted him down for the hearing from Rampton Prison, a high-security psychiatric hospital that housed a number of dangerous and violent psychopaths. There were seven wardens standing around the glass case, ensuring that nothing could go wrong at this final stage. It was like a scene from a Hannibal Lecter film. Maybe they were protecting him from me as much as the other way round after the last time I flew at him.

The five distinguished law lords listened as the defending lawyer pleaded that had Dunlop known the law was going to change he would never have confessed, and that he had been encouraged to come clean by his barrister. My heart was in my mouth the whole time for fear that he would say something that would influence the judges the wrong way. I tried to read from their expressions what they were thinking but it was impossible; their wise-looking faces were just as inscrutable as Dunlop's or Charlie's.

The prosecuting barrister said a few things in response after a short lunch break and then the judges all stood up and walked sedately out of the court, shutting the door firmly behind them. I assumed we were now going to be told to come back in a fortnight to hear the decision, and I prepared myself mentally for yet another delay. I was used to waiting; I could handle a couple more weeks as long as I got the result I wanted.

It seemed as though the judges couldn't have done more than stand outside and count to ten before the door opened again and they trooped solemnly back in, sat down and instantly quashed the acquittal. A stunned silence fell on the room at the announcement, everyone looking around at one another in disbelief. Even I was silenced. How could it have been so easy after such a long and hard struggle? Now Billy Dunlop could be tried once more for a murder he had already confessed to. Surely this time nothing else could go wrong? I watched as he was led out of the court by the guards but he didn't once look back at me.

The safeguards that had been put into place in the new law included an embargo on publicity during the retrial and the stipulation that it had to be held at a different end of the country from the original trial. I suppose the thinking was that if there was a press outcry it could prejudice the case and the whole thing would then be deemed a mistrial again. So the general public knew nothing about what was going on as we waited to be given a date for a retrial at the Old Bailey in London.

When Ken Macdonald, the Director of Public Prosecutions, asked to meet us we returned to London with our hearts in our mouths, certain that something must have gone wrong, that a new obstacle to us obtaining justice must have arisen.

'We've had massive interest from abroad,' he told us once we were sitting down in his office. 'From Australia, New Zealand, America, the Caribbean, all the places that follow British law. Have you thought about writing a book?'

'Oh aye,' I said. 'It's in hand.' It was an idea I'd been considering on and off over the years but I'd decided I couldn't start writing until my story had an ending, until I had some kind of closure.

We headed home feeling deeply relieved that our fears had been raised for nothing. We were still on course for victory as long as nothing else went wrong at the last moment.

At his first appearance in the Old Bailey, Dunlop pleaded 'not guilty', and my heart sank at the thought of having to sit through the whole trial for a third time. I couldn't understand how he could be allowed to do that after he had already confessed in court, but our barrister explained that when he came back to court the next time he would probably plead guilty.

'It's just a delaying tactic,' he said.

Sure enough, on the second appearance Dunlop changed his plea to 'guilty'.

I had waited so long to hear him actually saying that word as an admission rather than a boast that it was hard to believe my ears. Now we didn't have to go through another trial, we could go straight to the sentencing.

By the time Dunlop returned to the Old Bailey for sentencing it was October 2006, just a month short of seventeen years since Julie was killed. Jayne, his ex-girlfriend and the mother of his three children, came down to London at the request of the prosecutors because she was a potential character witness. I can only imagine how fearful she must have been that he would ever be released back into society, free to come knocking on her door, demanding to see his kids.

'Jayne wants to have a chat with you,' the police told me.

I couldn't see any harm in it. I certainly had nothing against her and in many ways we had a lot in common. I followed them into a little room where we could have a cup of tea and found her already sitting there. I was shocked by how much she had changed since I'd last seen her and it reminded me just how many years of the lives of all of us had been eaten up by the fight to bring Billy Dunlop to justice. 'In the end I had to leave him because he tried to strangle me,' she said once we were talking. 'As he was doing it he told me he would do the same to me that he'd done to Julie.'

She explained how she had eventually managed to get away from him, but only after years of horrendous abuse. She talked about the daughter she'd had with him and said that her boys were grown up now and that they hated their dad as much as she did for what he had done to Julie. As we were talking her phone rang and it was one of her lads. He asked her to pass the phone over to me. I took it from her, not quite sure what to expect.

'I just want to apologise to you for what my father did to your daughter,' he said.

'You don't need to apologise,' I told him.

'He might be my father,' he said, 'but he's an animal.'

Jayne and I went on talking together for a while.

'I've been considering going to visit him in prison,' I told her. The idea had been growing in my head, but I knew Charlie was strongly opposed to it so I hadn't done anything. 'Do you suppose he'd agree to see me?'

'I think he might, yes,' she said after a moment's thought. 'I'll tell you something; you're the only woman who's ever stood up to him in his life. Everyone else has always been scared stiff of him.'

She obviously didn't realise how scared I had been all those years when he had been out on the streets and I had lain awake in bed imagining him turning up at the front door drunk and armed with God knows what.

When they told us it was time, we filed through into Court Number One and took our seats. This was it, the moment we had been fighting for. The judge came in and I tried to read from his face what he was likely to be saying, but it was expressionless. Would he think that Billy had served enough years in prison and didn't need any more added to his sentence? Or would he decide to make an example of him, to show that no one was above the law? It was impossible to guess which way he would go.

Billy Dunlop sat silently in the dock as the judge announced that he was to receive a life sentence, with a seventeen-year tariff before he could apply for parole. I knew this was a long tariff. The judge was showing that he agreed with us that Billy should be made to pay the full price for what he did to our daughter, even if it had happened seventeen years before.

At last we had got justice for Julie. After all the waiting and all the fighting and all the heartbreak I had finally heard a judge pronounce the word 'life' on Billy Dunlop for what he did to all of us that night in 1989. I stared hard at him but he didn't look surprised or upset. He didn't turn to look at any of us watching; he was as emotionless as always.

It took a while for the full impact of what had happened to sink in. The first man in Britain to be retried for a crime in 800 years had been found guilty and sentenced. History had been made. I was in a daze, not sure if I was going to laugh or cry as we were led from the courtroom. I thanked the barrister, Andrew Robertson QC.

'You don't need to thank me,' he said kindly. 'It's the whole of the Establishment who need to thank you for your campaign.'

When we emerged from the gates of the Old Bailey it looked as though the whole of the world's press was waiting for us outside. It seemed that Ken Macdonald had been right, and the law of double jeopardy was of interest to a lot of other countries that modelled their legal systems on the British one. I wished I'd been given a few minutes' warning so I could have composed myself before I was brought out into this barrage of noise and cameras at a moment when I was feeling so many emotions at once.

'How do you feel?' I heard someone ask from among the explosion of questions and shouting voices coming at us from every direction.

I actually felt like jumping up in the air and shouting 'Justice for Julie, at last!' I felt that after all the fighting and all the stress and all the knock-backs, my little girl, who had arrived into the world like an angel, could now rest in peace knowing that her killer was behind bars for what he did to her that night. We had created a lasting legacy for her, and Charlie had carried out the promise he made to her that day in the funeral parlour when he lay across her coffin to talk to her for the last time.

Once it was all over the police asked us if we would like to hear the tape of Dunlop's confession. I don't know why we agreed to do it—maybe because we thought it would give us some closure, or maybe because we were in a bit of a daze and did whatever anyone suggested. I think with hindsight that the police wanted us to hear it privately before excerpts of it were broadcast to the rest of the world.

It felt strange to hear his voice actually talking about what he had done, making real all the images that had been travelling around in my imagination for so long. In his version of the story he told them that he had killed her about an hour after arriving at the house, which would have made it around ten past three, the moment that I woke up at home with a terrible feeling inside me and thought about calling Julie. The thought sent a shudder through me.

Now that it is all over I do feel I might be able to visit Dunlop in prison and actually ask him to explain why he did what he did. Of course, he might not answer my questions. He might be unhelpful and sullen or even threatening. But hearing the story in his own words might help me, I think.

Charlie still doesn't agree with the idea of going to see him because he says we wouldn't be able to believe anything Dunlop said anyway, and I can see what he means. I don't know if I would believe him or not.

I had a dream a couple of years ago where I found myself in Blackpool Tower Ballroom. I was in a disco, watching a crowd of people dancing under one of those big silver balls that reflect all the lights. The music was loud and the dance floor was packed. In the middle of the crowd I could see Julie, dancing like she used to, wearing a bright turquoise dress. She was always such a good dancer. I felt relieved to see she hadn't been murdered at all, that she was there in front of me. I pushed my way through, parting the gyrating crowd as I went.

'You've never been murdered,' I said when I got to her. 'You're all right.'

'Been murdered?' she said, not stopping her dancing. 'What do you mean, been murdered?'

I grabbed hold of her skinny arm and I could feel every bone in her and I knew for sure she was alive.

When I woke up my first thought was that the scene on the dance floor had been the reality and that she was all right, but then the truth all came rushing back and the sadness returned. I guess having a dream like that must mean I've travelled on a long way from the years when my mind was trapped under that bath, just as Julie's body was. But Julie will never travel on anywhere now. While Charlie and I have grown old and her brother and sister have become middle-aged, she is still that 22-year-old girl, whirling around the dance floor in a turquoise dress without a care in the world. I sometimes wonder if she will still look like that if we are allowed to meet in the afterlife.

People often ask me if I have ever 'seen' Julie since her death, knowing that I believe strongly in that sort of thing, but I have to tell them I haven't. Charlie believes he has, and I know she is still there inside both our heads somewhere, but I would love to see her again, even if it was only as a visitor from the spirit world.

I was giving a talk to a group of trainee bereavement counsellors once and an Indian woman in the audience was waiting to speak to me as I came out.

'I hope you don't mind me saying,' she said, 'but all the time you were doing your talk your daughter was stood beside you. She's really proud of what you've achieved. She said, "Just say to our Mam that I'm holding a bunch of pink carnations."'

Pink carnations were our Julie's favourite flower so that was a very moving moment.

Like Julie, I like dancing and recently I've taken up line dancing. It takes me out of myself and gives me a chance to meet people who know nothing about murder cases or double jeopardy laws. For the two hours we are dancing I don't have to think about anything except the steps and the music. I still need to keep myself busy, even now, to keep my mind distracted.

If I'm sitting on my own doing nothing I tend to find myself getting out all the sympathy cards and letters we've received over the years and I read through them and have a really good cry, just like that vicar we heard about with the picture of his daughter and the ballet music on the stereo system. Then after a while I feel better and put them back in their drawer.

I have a blouse that belonged to Julie, the only piece of clothing that I kept when Angela cleared all the rest out. I keep it rolled up in a drawer, and every so often I take it out and press my face into the material, breathing in the scent. It doesn't smell of Julie herself anymore but it still brings back the memories. From what I can understand, all bereaved mothers do something like that.

The Chief Constable wrote recently to tell me I had won a 'good citizen award'. He wrote: 'Your actions following the death of your daughter, your determination in helping to secure the successful conviction of William Dunlop for murder, have been remarkable. This investigation has literally changed the course of British legal history.' It seems a long way from the days when men in his position wouldn't even come to talk to us.

At about the same time I got a letter from the Cabinet Secretary at 10 Downing Street, telling me I was going to be awarded an MBE. I thought it was a joke at first but it wasn't. In October 2007 I went to Buckingham Palace and received my award from Prince Charles. He was very compassionate and said to me that I'd done a 'splendid job', adding that hopefully I would get some form of closure now.

When the case was all over and I was sitting at home being interviewed for another documentary, the producer asked me what I thought Julie would say if she was watching from the other side. I thought for a second.

'I think,' I told him, 'she'd say, "Well done, our Mam."'

Epilogue

Whenever we walk around Billingham town centre, even today, people still come up and tell me they support us and congratulate us on what we have achieved. Sometimes we end up with quite a crowd round us.

It's nice to have succeeded in what we set out to do, but I'm still angry. I can't pretend I'm not. I'm angry with Billy Dunlop for what he did to Julie and angry with the police for making such a mess of everything in the beginning, causing us so many years of extra agony and struggle when we should have been recovering from the pain of losing our daughter.

Having said all that, if the police had found her body within those first few days Dunlop would almost certainly have been convicted and the maximum sentence then for murder was twelve years. In that case he would have been back on the streets years ago. I would also never have heard of the law of double jeopardy, and who knows if it would have been changed yet without the extra pressure of Julie's case? So maybe everything really does happen for a reason.

Because of all that went wrong we got a chance to make a little bit of history, but that still doesn't bring our Julie back. Nothing will.

Kevin has left home now and is living with his partner, Amber. His mum would be so proud of him. I see and speak to him all the time, just as I used to see Julie. He's in and out of the house for cups of tea and chats, and he's a really good support to Charlie and me.

Gary is married with a family and Angela has a boy and a girl. Her daughter Emily is twelve now and physically she could be a reincarnation of Julie. She's not quite as dark but she has a certain look about her that's like my beautiful daughter all over again. She was stir-frying something in the kitchen the other day and turned to me and I almost jumped with shock at the strong resemblance.

You can't ever turn the clock back, but at last I can look towards the future again after all those years fighting for justice. I can move forward and help my grandchildren to make happy lives for themselves, and I can look after Charlie as we both get older. I'll keep doing my talks to the police, because it's good to feel I can make a bit of a difference, but I doubt I'll be taking on any more campaigns again. I'm all campaigned out now!

ANN MING

Home: Billingham, near Middlesborough
Claim to fame: campaigned for 17 years to end the 800-year-old double jeopardy law

When Ann Ming received the letter saying she had been awarded an MBE, her first reaction was that it was a joke. Unassuming as she is, she little realised how much she'd achieved and, even today, three years after Dunlop's sentencing, she still seems amazed by the size of the challenge she took on, and that she pursued it almost single-handedly. 'I mean, when you think about it, I took on the government, to change a law that had been in place for eight hundred years!' she says with feeling. The things that kept her going, above all, were her love for her daughter, a determination to see justice done, and a belief that 'common sense had to prevail'.

Ann's life does now contain a measure of peace, although she's had to come to terms with yet one more sadness. Her husband, Charlie, was diagnosed with Parkinson's disease six years ago and is now in a nursing home, suffering from dementia and often tormented by blurred memories of what happened to Julie.

Not one to let life get her down, however, Ann now helps others through the Teesside branch of SAMM (Support After Murder and

Ann Ming is presented with the MBE by HRH the Prince of Wales on October 26, 2007, in recognition of her services to the Criminal Justice System.

Manslaughter), a charity that offers emotional support to those whose lives have been turned upside-down by such horrific crimes, as hers once was. 'Because there was no one there for us, that's why I want things to be right for other people,' she states firmly.

Another positive outcome is that Julie's son, Kevin, who is now twenty, is currently involved in founding a group within SAMM to help siblings of murder victims. 'Kevin's fine now, and I'm so glad he's doing that,' Ann comments of her grandson.

Ann Ming beside her husband, Charlie, outside Buckingham Palace after the awards ceremony.

In early 2009, Teesside members of SAMM and other mourners in the community gathered for a day of reflection, marked by a memorial service at St Mary's Roman Catholic Cathedral in Coulby Newham for 'anyone who has lost loved ones in tragic circumstances', and Ann wrote a special poem for the occasion. 'The funny thing was, when we went to book the cathedral, the only date the Monsignor could do in February was the 22nd—Julie's birthday. It was quite sad, but also very poignant.'

Listening to Ann, it's clear that she will continue to provide help and support to others—even though, apart from her local MP's help, she herself had little of it—and that she'll go on fighting for justice. Asked what advice she would give to others struggling as she did, she says, 'Try to keep focused. Keep positive. One person *can* make a difference. That's how I feel, anyway. A strong sense of purpose kept me going.'

Ann's eyes are now on America and other countries where the double jeopardy law is still in place, and she dreams of furthering her campaign through a film dramatisation of her book. 'Julie Walters would be perfect to play me,' Ann says, with a laugh.

Dream it may be, but apparently the two women have already exchanged letters . . .